Praise for *Palinuro of Mexico*

"*Palinuro of Mexico* is an immense book in scope, length and beauty . . . pages of romantic lyricism, heady erudition, unbridled eroticism."
—*L'Express*

"This tour de force is *the* novel of modern Mexico and its sprawling capital. . . . warm and very funny . . . Elisabeth Plaister's translation is brilliant." —*Sunday Telegraph* (London)

"Truculent and epic, *Palinuro of Mexico* follows in the great tradition of those universal masterpieces by Homer, Rabelais, Virgil, even Joyce. A fascinating book." —*Humanité Dimanche*

"Gargantuan, not to say Dantean and Ulyssean . . . [it] exudes the art and craft of loving care and infinite labor." —*Manchester Guardian*

"At its deepest level, the narrative of *Palinuro of Mexico* embodies a totalizing ambition, reminiscent of Joyce, to investigate the conditions of culture and knowledge, to explore the relationship between myth and history, and to demonstrate the potential of literary language to revolutionize our ways of seeing the world." —*Times Literary Supplement*

"A vast encyclopedia of sensuality and farce." —*L'Evénement du Jeudi*

"A firework display of culture and jest." —*Le Canard Enchaîné*

"Joycean and surreal." —*Libération*

"This is lush, jewelled and confectionary writing." —*Books* (London)

"An excessive novel and an encyclopedic compilation of data on the human body. This is what makes the book unique: nowhere in literature can we find a book anything like it, a book into which such vast knowledge, organized by language, has been poured in an overweening aspiration to totality. . . . *Palinuro of Mexico* viewed from the perspective of future years will be perceived as a milestone in Mexican narrative for having achieved 'passage' through cultural barriers to what lay beyond, to universal discourse." —*Review: Latin American Literature and Arts*

"A novel that, more than fifteen years after its original appearance, remains a puzzle, an enchanting homage to confusion, and, in my judgment, a perfect embodiment of Calvino's hypernovel. . . . His work is about Mexico's difficult history and arduous present, about the ambitions of an all-encompassing knowledge, about freedom of body and mind, and about the demons of possibility." —Ilan Stavans, editor, *The Oxford Book of Latin American Essays*

"Grotesque, macabre and Dionysiac . . . del Paso is a great and unorthodox writer." —*Le Monde*

"Read it: it is a breath of fresh air, it has a universal voice rarely heard . . . it runs the gamut from laughter to tears, from the crude to the tender, with an incredible virtuosity." —*Madame Figaro*

Fernando del Paso

PALINURO
OF
MEXICO

Translated by Elisabeth Plaister

Dalkey Archive Press

First American Edition 1996

Originally published as *Palinuro de México*.
© 1977 by Fernando del Paso.
English translation first published by Quartet Books (London), 1989.
Translation © 1989 by Quartet Books Limited.
(Errors in that edition have been corrected for this edition.)

Library of Congress Cataloguing-in-Publication Data

Paso, Fernando del, 1935-
[Palinuro de México. English]
Palinuro of Mexico / Fernando del Paso :
translated by Elisabeth Plaister. — 1st American ed.
p.   cm.
I. Plaister, Elisabeth. II. Title.
PQ7298.26.A76P313   1996   863—dc20   95-53205
ISBN 1-56478-095-3

Publication of this book was made possible in part by grants from the Illinois
Arts Council, the National Endowments for the Arts, and from the
Universidad de Guadalajara, Dirección General de Extensión Universitaria,
Departamento de Estudios Literarios. The Publisher also gratefully acknowl-
edges the invaluable assistance of Ilan Stavans with this project.

Dalkey Archive Press
Illinois State University
Campus Box 4241
Normal, IL 61790-4241

Typeset by AKM Associates (UK) Ltd, Southall, London.
Printed on permanent/durable acid-free paper and bound in the
United States of America.

ACKNOWLEDGEMENTS

The subtitle of Chapter 18, 'This House of the Sick' ('Esta Casa de Enfermos'), was taken from *Pregón de los Hospitales* by the Colombian poet Alvaro Mutis. One poem quoted is by the Mexican Octavio Paz. 'The bones of Palinuro pray to the Pole Star . . .' is taken from the title of a poem by the American poet W.S. Merwin. The chapter entitled 'A Bullet Very Close to the Heart' was inspired by a story written by the American writer and journalist Ambrose Bierce and what may have happened to him during the last hours of his life. This book, of course, contains numerous and obvious allusions to other poets and writers. For instance, the chapter 'Palinuro on the Stairs' contains several references to José Gorostiza's *Muerte sin Fin*.

Part of this book was written with the sponsorship of the International Writing Program of the University of Iowa and with a grant from the John Simon Guggenheim Memorial Foundation.

This is a work of fiction.
If certain characters resemble people in real life, it is because certain people in real life resemble characters from a novel.
Nobody, therefore, is entitled to feel included in this book.
Nobody, by the same token, to feel excluded.

CONTENTS

PART ONE

1

The Grand Illusion

The science of medicine was a spirit which haunted Palinuro's heart throughout his life. Sometimes it was a sad spirit, drawing along the hospital corridors of this earth a train of floating kidneys and iron camisoles. At others, it was a wise spirit which came to him in dreams to offer to him, as Athene to Ascelpius, two phials filled with blood : the first serving to resuscitate his dear departed and the second to destroy them, and himself, both.

Uncle Esteban was among the dear departed, or would be one day, when in his chest ceased to be heard the infinitesimal crepitations which choked him, dark and barely perceptible as the wing beat of butterflies – yet another of the beings beloved or admired by Palinuro and who, like himself, had always been held in the thrall of medicine. In effect, Uncle Esteban, who had long white hands which could trace master operations in the air and, with two arabesques, link the iliac artery of John Abernethy, the English surgeon who a hundred years previously had invented this very operation to the awe of posterity; this Uncle Esteban, as we were saying, had also dreamed of one day becoming a doctor.

The bells of Leopoldstadt Cathedral were pealing when Uncle Esteban was born, on the left bank of the Danube, within the empire extending from Transylvania to the frozen peaks of Tirol. His father, a surgeon and also chamber musician on Sundays and public holidays, raised him up between his hands and dedicated him to all the gods of medicine he knew: Apollo, Dhanvantari, Eshmoun the Phoenician and Khors the Slav. However, in 1916, when Uncle Esteban was sixteen years old, his birthday having coincided with that of the century in which von Hofmannsthal's prophecy was to be realized and Austria, together with the entire Kakania, was to fall – his father already dead and far removed from the surgical instruments and the medical books he had inherited – Uncle Esteban, studying in Berlin at the time, found himself suddenly conscripted into the ranks of the German army.

And thus was his fate sealed, and Estefania's and my own. In July of that same year, Uncle Esteban took part in the Battle of the Somme and, a bullet failing through a defection of scant millimetres to perforate his aorta, he was saved from becoming one of the 400,000 soldiers of the

German army who never left the battlefield and whose blood mingled with the sap of French sugar beet while the vultures bore away in their beaks the pages of the Star of Alliance. That was the first time Uncle Esteban escaped death.

During the initial months spent in hospital – if indeed that series of dirty and evil-smelling tents where he met the Polish nurse could be called a hospital – Uncle Esteban had the opportunity to read several books on surgery and medicine and, yet again, confirm his vocation. He vowed that when the war was over he would begin his university studies and, in time, become a surgeon of note in his beloved Budapest. It would have been true to say that Uncle Esteban had a difficult time of it, one complication succeeding another, relapsing fever followed by dysentery, infection by delirium. And, to make matters worse, he had several times to be moved, along with the hospital and all the wounded and the dying. Uncle Esteban never knew, for instance, if he only dreamed it or if, in fact, at one point they took him up the Alps in a stretcher hung from a ski lift. The fact of the matter was however that, absorbed as he was in his twin loves of medicine and the Polish nurse, Uncle Esteban spent in that hospital some of the happiest days of his youth.

Between one convalescence and the next, he became the Polish nurse's assistant and learned to bandage patients : the ordinary capeline bandage, the Velpeau bandage and the figure-of-eight gauntlet bandage. Later, when their supplies of cotton bandages were exhausted, he was taught to improvise dressings with sphagnous mosses. After a few short weeks, Uncle Esteban could insert a gastric catheter and give intravenous injections of salvarsan to syphilitic comrades-in-arms and, during the same few weeks, he learned to diagnose correctly cases of sepsis, to prescribe a venesection for a victim of toxic gases, to interpret the sombre prognosis of temperature charts featuring the oscillations of a pendulum swing and to apply solutions of physiological salt and water to wounds to stimulate the production of pus. But Uncle Esteban also took it upon himself to carry out certain more humble tasks which later proved to be the best example he could have given Estefania, such as merely cleaning the gums of the wounded or washing their bodies with ointment of zinc and castor oil when they soiled themselves in bed or picking lice from their heads with infinite patience.

'One thing we were never short of during the Great War was lice,' Uncle Esteban told his daughter Estefania. 'There were more lice than Germans, Russians and Brits added together and multiplied by a thousand.' Whenever Uncle Esteban and the Polish nurse made love, whether in the old, horsedrawn, South African-style ambulances or in the mobile bacteriological laboratory, either afterwards or during lulls, they would always remove each other's lice. Then they would go to sleep or make love again

4

after tying around their heads woollen bandages soaked in mercury and beeswax. But not for this did they love each other less : she a nurse and he a future doctor and living as they did surrounded by what were coming to be considered the horrors of the war, Uncle Esteban and the Polish nurse lost their disgust for life. Uncle Esteban was quite equal to whistling a Brandenburg concerto while he incinerated the excrement from the latrines. Uncle Esteban – and with him his Hungarian friends, the Polish nurse and the other nurses – continued to eat and laugh as they worked in the tents among the rotting limbs of patients suffering from gaseous gangrene and they talked of books and of their families, of the spring and of going to dine in restaurants and dancing the night away when the war was over, after going to the cinema to see Mary Pickford in *The Paris Hat*.

And the filth accumulated and the lice multiplied and Uncle Esteban developed trench foot and the Polish nurse was smitten with itch mite and the teeth of both became encrusted with tartar and still they continued to love each other. Although, if the truth be known, they did once – or perhaps twice, or five times – frolic with their friends in a huge wooden barrel full of water, reminding them of the barrels in which grapes are pressed and they dreamed that they were bathing in Tokay wine.

From then onwards, Uncle imagined himself in the future as an ophthalmologist, married to the Polish nurse; it was her eyes which made him decide on this specialization. However, his own plans for the future were one thing, while the orders they gave him and the fate awaiting him were another. He was refused permission to continue working at the hospital and was sent back to the front. Uncle Esteban and the Polish nurse made desperate love throughout several nights and the intervening days: sometimes in the filth of the trenches, sometimes under the tarpaulin of a lorry loaded with thousands of doses of anti-tetanus serum and once again, and for the last time, in the mobile laboratory. Afterwards, Uncle Esteban trapped a louse and, observing it under his microscope, told the Polish nurse that he had discovered that her lice were in fact female because they all had a pair of black tits. They laughed so much that the Polish nurse's tears bathed the swastika hanging around her neck which, she had explained to him, was a symbol of good luck and represented the source of life and sacred fire. Our uncle believed her, since neither he nor she – they were both Jewish – knew at that time what the swastika would come to signify. In fact, she never had time to find out because she died, her body riddled with shrapnel, just a few months after Uncle Esteban marched off to the eastern front to join the Austro-Hungarian army. And, for the time being, he had little leisure to mourn her death; when the Russian offensive was launched by the general who, according to Uncle Esteban, bore a name more suited to a vaccine – the Brusilov vaccine – than to a military man, it was Uncle Esteban's lot to become one of the thousands of Hungarians taken prisoner in the Carpathian Mountains. And that was how he escaped death for the second time. But, before he was finally captured, he flung down his rifle and ran, ran for all he was worth while, thousands of miles away in Mexico, the land he was eventually to adopt, Grandfather Francisco fled from the punitive raid led by John J. Pershing. Grandfather Francisco, later to become Uncle Esteban's father-in-law, was a revolutionary and initiate of a rite dating back to the Son of Hiram and the Living Caltzontzi, who rode as always beside General Villa.

But in Siberia, that Siberia of legend, below the tundra carpeted with moss and lichen, that Siberia which was after all not as inhospitable and as far removed from the world as he had been told, Uncle Esteban had days, weeks and years to spare for mourning the Polish nurse. More than enough time when the snow thawed each spring, when the corpses hidden throughout the winter began to emerge, here and there a hand, a foot, an elbow, to picture her likewise, pale and frozen, beneath the snow. Thus he imagined her whenever the whiteness was blemished by a black and liquid hollow from which protruded a lock of silken blonde hair. So profound was his grief that, when he was released, he knew that he had forgotten her. Such was his grief also for his homeland that, although the House of Austria had failed to fulfil its proud, bilingual five-worded motto: *Austria est imperare orbi universo – Alles Erdreich ist Oesterreich unterthan –* and Hungary was therefore free, Uncle Esteban no longer desired to return to the land of his birth. To him, Europe was rotten. And so it was that he came to escape death for a third time, failing to become one of the 20 million Europeans who died between 1918 and 1919 in the influenza epidemic.

With four languages and a World War behind him, Uncle Esteban headed for Vladivostok. He made part of the journey on foot, bidding farewell to the passengers travelling on the Trans-Siberian Railway. Another part he completed on the Trans-Siberian, bidding farewell to those walking across the countryside. From Vladivostok he went to Hong Kong, from Hong Kong to San Francisco. There, in America, while he worked as dishwasher in Chinatown, as downhill tram driver, as crab cleaner on the quay and as doorman of a whorehouse in Haight-Ashbury, Uncle Esteban continued to dream of becoming a doctor and of plumbing the mysteries of *sal reverberatum*, described by Paracelsus, which purifies the whole of Nature, of contemplating through the eye of a microscope the sinister black spirilla of gallic disease and of identifying the cause of death of a sailor who succumbed to an embolism with his heart full of foam. He visited museums at weekends, bought second-hand books and magazines and collected old instruments: Dr Wirtz ophthalmic electrodes, Gibson spoons for giving medicine to children and lunatics, along with anatomical illustrations, sets of homoeopathic instruments and golden microscopes.

At night he devoured the books and memorized everything, quite without method: ancient and modern knowledge, prescriptions written in verse by doctors of the Salerno School and anecdotes of the life of Liston, who used to walk through the hospitals of Edinburgh in his wellington boots proclaiming the supremacy of Scotland in the medical world of his day. And so the years passed for him and when he was over thirty years of age, never having attempted to sit an entrance exam for any school of medicine, Uncle Esteban packed up his treasures and, with these and a group of gypsies, he set off to travel right across the United States until he reached New Orleans. This particular city was also visited, two or three times a year, by Grandfather Francisco – at that time at the peak of his political career – to listen to jazz, practise his English on the Irish prostitutes and eat mackerel in white wine on Bourbon Street. Yet Uncle Esteban, who was destined not only to become his son-in-law but also to make him a true grandfather for the first time, did not meet Grandfather Francisco in that city. They may, perhaps, have crossed in the street without knowing it. Grandfather Francisco may have passed a tall, pale young man with hair blacker that the grapes of Corinth, and Uncle Esteban – who at that time was nobody's uncle – may have passed a very fat man with immense whiskers – which were not yet white – sporting a walking stick with a mother-of-pearl knob and a sterling silver railwayman's watch. Perhaps. But there were so many such very strange people in New Orleans in those days and such a number of extraordinary events occurring which nobody even noticed; you could meet Louis Armstrong in the street and not know it or attend the funeral of a musician and doff your hat as the carriage of coloured windows passed, drawn by black-plumed horses whose eyes had been rubbed with onion to make them weep throughout the burial while behind them the jazz widows mourned to a blues rhythm.

But, though they may not have met in New Orleans, there was no doubt that Uncle Esteban was fast approaching his destiny and he took pains to do it in style: it was there that he not only learned to drink milk with salt like certain Cubans – something which always greatly amused Grandfather Francisco – but, more important still, he became well-versed in the swaggering arts of poker, the favourite game of the mayor of the San Angel district of Mexico City.

One day a Mexican boat, *El Tabasco*, anchored in New Orleans, arriving as usual with a cargo of bananas and plantains, before returning by way of Tampico to the fair city of Veracruz – the other two cities often visited by Grandfather – stuffed full of contraband: whiskies, cognacs, cashmeres, French perfumes and Florentine cameos. The ship's captain, by pure coincidence a distant cousin of Grandfather Francisco's, won twenty dollars and a Ricord vaginal speculum from Uncle Esteban in a poker game and then invited him to travel to Mexico. And so Uncle Esteban became part of *El Tabasco*'s contraband and entered Mexico riding the crest of a puff of trade wind, at the very port of arrival, twenty-six years previously, of Jean Paul, the French botanist whom Aunt Luisa, only sister of Grandfather Francisco, had never married. When they said goodbye, the captain returned the speculum and gave Uncle Esteban the address of his cousin in Mexico City who he said was a senator and might suddenly, when least expected, rise to the dizzy heights of state governor.

But Uncle Esteban was not to witness the golden era of Grandfather Francisco who did, effectively, become state governor, but only for a few months as his nomination was merely of an interim nature. And those few months were reduced to a few weeks when Grandfather had an unfortunate accident which forced him to retire permanently from politics and the good life: he was in a bar in Tampico, gossiping about Obregón's assassination in La Bombilla, when a lorry crashed through the wall and came to rest against the counter. Grandfather just managed to leap aside and throw himself to the floor, as though expecting a bomb to explode. But a huge cash register toppled over and crushed his leg, the same leg which had previously caused him suffering when it had caught a bullet during the revolution, and which they had since, more than once, been on the point of amputating. The contents of the till showered all over him and, when the ambulance arrived, Grandfather – who never lost his sense of humour – threw notes and gold coins into the air shouting: 'I'm rich, I'm rich.' But, from then onwards, subject to a consistently ironic destiny, Grandfather Francisco's fortunes began to wane and finally he sank in a sudden and spectacular manner – as ships and liners sink, as the *Titanic* and the *Lusitania* sank – and his final glories coincided, give or take a few years, with the apocalyptic blowout of the Meriwether and Morrison oilwells which had at one time or, more specifically, on account of the First War, made Tampico the greatest oil emporium of this orb.

His wife, Grandmother Altagracia, who loved her garden above all else in this world, got up one day determined to resolve her financial straits without having to sell the house. 'You haven't burned the dry leaves,' she said to Ricardo the gardener the moment she emerged from her room. 'No ma'am,' replied Ricardo. 'You haven't burned the dry leaves,' she said again when she returned from mass. 'No ma'am.' 'You haven't burned the dry leaves,' she repeated after breakfast until, finally, Ricardo the gardener raked the dry leaves into a pile in the yard and consummated the funeral rite of autumn. Ricardo the gardener breathed a sigh of relief and, in the kitchen, Grandmother Altagracia contentedly sniffed the scent of short circuits and expiatory caterpillars. It was then that the notion struck her – actually bearing no relation to the dry leaves – and that very night she painted a sign and hung it on the front of the house. And thus it was that when Uncle Esteban, sporting a stetson hat of beaver fur and socks of

8

Egyptian yarn, made an appearance to pay his respects to the governor, almost two years after disembarking in Veracruz, he came to be confronted with a sign saying : 'Rooms to Rent' and concluded that he must have come to the wrong address. But no, Grandmother had simply transformed the Porfirian mansion into a guest house. And the house was of such dimensions – dimensions on a par with the governor's political career – that there was room in it not only for the traffic police commander, a retired cabaret artist, don Prospero the encyclopaedia salesman, the mother of the Under-Secretary of State for the Mexican Navy and several other guests, besides Francisco and Altagracia themselves, their daughters and sons-in-law and of course Aunt Luisa, but also for Uncle Esteban who after conversing with the ex-governor and meeting Aunt Lucrecia (who gazed at him from beneath her Marlene eyebrows and rainshower lashes with two moist green eyes closely resembling the fish of her birth sign), that very same day and without a second thought, rented the Provençal bedroom.

And it was in this house of trellised arbours and lilac walkways and shadowy portals, that first Aunt Lucrecia and Uncle Esteban – later Papa Eduardo and Mamma Clementina – beneath a diamond cloak of virtues, swore, back to back, an enigmatic love and, standing, kissed in the region of the Adam's apple. And it was thus, in these caresses, that Palinuro and Estefania started to be born and in this same house, of perfumed corridors and blue attics, where they finished being born and where they lived their first years, as cousins, as brother and sister, marvelling at the Japanese lodgers and the luminous grubs of the garden, at the huge bath tub and the kaleidoscope chandelier in the dining room. There, in their grandparents' house, Palinuro and Estefania would sit of an afternoon, with their Aunt Luisa, discovering faces in the chiaroscuro of the forget-me-nots. And some were faces they had never seen before, white and of stone with startled moss on their lips, and others were the faces which looked down on them from the tapestries and from the walls of the room belonging to Grandmother Altagracia, who not only knew the secret of grooming her hair with soft brushes soaked in salt water to make it shiny, but also managed to fill her life with portraits, silhouettes, photographs and miniatures of all her relatives, living and dead, who nightly rescued her from hell through the vicissitudes of their chequered fortunes.

Then, Palinuro and Estefania would sit beside Uncle Esteban to hear him talk of medicine. Uncle Esteban had waited many years for my cousin and me, that is Estefania and Palinuro, to reach an age to become his listeners. Sometimes our cousin Walter, who was a few years older than ourselves, also appeared. Formerly, Uncle Esteban had no sooner mentioned poultices, bubonic plague or tuberculin eye drops, than Aunt Luisa, or the lodgers, or Grandmother, would exclaim: 'How ghastly, how

9

ghastly!' Uncle Esteban was eventually obliged to accept that nobody derived any amusement from his conversations about the marvels and horrors of the art and history of Hippocrates and Avicenna. And this was not because Grandfather Francisco and the others were uneducated people. Even don Prospero who, when Uncle Esteban arrived, had already reached the letter D in the encyclopaedia, already knew who wrote *The Decameron*, who Daedalus was and where the Delaware River was situated. Even Grandmother Altagracia, who played 'Clair de Lune' on the piano and knew how to lower her lashes in gatherings to hide her spiritual myopia, read the *Reader's Digest Selections* and remembered having once seen a Titian original. The fact of the matter was, quite simply, that their interest in medicine went no further than pills, injections, syrups, enemas and paregoric tinctures to cure or relieve their constipation, angina or lumbago. Moreover, not everybody had the stomach or courage to hear of mutilations and amputations, even adorned as they were by Uncle Esteban with egg yolks and rose oil which were the ingredients of the poultices prepared by Ambrose Paré, surgeon to Francis II, to apply to truncated stumps. Not everyone was equal, either, to imagining John Hunter dissecting foetuses in his Covent Garden home, however alluringly Uncle Esteban portrayed the Elysian spectacle of the square with its vegetable and flower ladies calling the day's wares of extroverted artichokes and cauliflowers while, close at hand, in the opera house, Parsifal slew the swan with his arrows and Ariadne lamented the loneliness of Naxos. Only Aunt Clementina, Palinuro's mother, was moved by such references to the opera. Otherwise, nobody – with the previously referred exception of Palinuro, Estefania and Cousin Walter – could understand the delicate metaphors – based on the same humble fruits and flowers of Covent Garden – evoked by Uncle Esteban to attenuate the decay and delitescence of corpses and their metamorphosis into sugar animals, maintaining that the figures in Madame Tussaud's Wax Museum could, from one day to the next, be converted by a madman's pyromania – after melting in the darkness like Medardo Rosso sculptures – into the apples, plums and peaches, also of wax, which Grandmother Altagracia placed every Sunday in the centre of the dining-room table.

It goes without saying that Uncle Esteban never actually studied medicine. What is more, he never set foot inside a school of medicine: he was never seen in Budapest University, because he never returned to Hungary. Neither did he visit the Mexico City University School of Medicine, although he always said that one Saturday he would go there and take photographs of the Fernando Ocaranza Laboratory and of the coiled serpents and onyx globes adorning the stairways of the former Palace of the Inquisition. But he didn't need to: from hospital orderly he graduated, in Mexico, to errand boy in a laboratory belonging to

10

Czechoslovakian immigrants who were later to begin producing sulfonamides and other miraculous drugs and, by the time he arrived at our grandparents' house, Uncle Esteban already spoke Spanish and had become one of the laboratory's best-paid salesmen, as well as writing articles for the *History of Medicine* quarterly.

To become the star salesman of the laboratories, Uncle Esteban was obliged to understand and retain an infinite knowledge of bacteriology, physiology and biochemistry. Infinite were the mysteries and wonders of the body revealed to him: the dance of the arteries in the neck, writhing like serpents from aortic insufficiency; the five hundred functions of the liver in the human metabolism; the journey of the sperm, travelling like silver salmon against the current in search of the egg which had existed since the woman's birth, lying in the darkness for twenty years, or perhaps forty, waiting to be fertilized; the fresh eyes of the dead submerged in citrated water in Lariboisière's eye bank in anticipation of the opportunity to open in another body, to look on other landscapes. Infinite also the histories and biographies of researchers and doctors which he had to read in order to write his articles on the history of medicine – the triumphant life of Pasteur and the dark life of Mendel, the tragic life of Servet and the legendary life of Albucassis – and infinite the illustrations and plates that passed through his hands, from the macabre dances of Holbein of Basel which inspired Saint-Saëns and Glazunov, to the Pesthouse at Jaffa by Baron Gros, by way of all Bosch's cripples, van Ostade's dentists, van Noort's possessed, Teniers' barber-surgeons, Breughel's blind and Giovanni della Robbia's ragamuffins, and not only did Uncle Esteban never feel frustrated, he even came to think and act as a true physician and believed that he had by some art of metempsychosis – or metemsomatosis – lived the life of those men he admired or, at least, of their closest colleagues.

Uncle Esteban repeatedly demonstrated his knowledge of twentieth-century medicine, executing the not least important or spectacular of his feats when the gynaecologist detected that Aunt Lucrecia's baby – none other than Estefania – was the wrong way round: within three minutes, never before having attempted such an exploit but without hurting Aunt Lucrecia or my embryonic cousin in any way, Uncle Esteban turned Estefania right round inside her mother's womb, so delivering her from the danger and embarrassment of entering the world bottom-first. Estefania was born one year and one month after the marriage of Uncle Esteban and Aunt Lucrecia. Palinuro, only twenty days after Estefania.

And we, my cousin and I, always believed that Uncle Esteban had in fact, in another life, been a Doctor Wertt of Hamburg who was burned alive, skirts and all, for having attended a delivery disguised as a woman; and, in yet another life, Alphonse Ferri the inventor of famous *alfonsin* or forceps for extracting bullets – such as the one in Grandfather Francisco's leg – or even Doctor Harvey himself. He would tell Estefania and me how the master, wielding a baton of whalebone with an engraved silver handle, would point out the viscera of the corpse and, to ensure that the students and gawkers did not get bored, he would talk to them about a thousand things at once. He spoke not only on the subject of the actual viscera, such as the lesser curvature of the stomach and the left colon angle, but also of many other totally unrelated things, such as the iron regiments of Oliver Cromwell or the arrival in St James's Park of a pair of Brazilian toucans with orange beaks which drank the dew cupped in the hearts of the flowers and which Charles I was never to see. And, of course, more than once Uncle Esteban was Andreas Vesalius himself – or, at least, one of the assistants who helped him to frighten off the vultures and the rats from Montfaucon's scaffold so he could collect the bones he needed to reconstruct a skeleton.

'How revolting!' said Estefania in horror, thus becoming the first of Uncle Esteban's assiduous and loyal listeners to display any sign of displeasure at his stories. And that was not all; Estefania had to run to the bathroom to vomit when Uncle Esteban added that, of course, when the illustrious sage arrived home with his sack of bones he had to finish stripping them with the bone scraper to remove clinging ligaments and tendons and then leave them for months on end in a bath full of lye soda, alum and wood ash. And only then, said Uncle Esteban, only when the two hundred and six bones of the human skeleton were clean, without trace of blood or marrow, of agonistic muscles or nacreous tendons, clean indeed and as white as in Testut illustrations or the Quiroz *Anatomy*, as those sold by Charon, the aged porter of the School of Medicine, only then did the bones recover their innocence and cease to be the bones of a beggar or wrongdoer – or even the bones of a murderer such as Helen Torrence or Jane Waldie who spent their time strangling babies in order to sell the corpses to surgeons – and become no more, though also no less, than the bones of *Man*, Man who is the measure of all things, as described by Pythagoras; man beyond Good and Evil who has ceased to be Marcus Aurelius, master of the slave Epictetus; Man, microcosmos of creation, in the words of Scotus Erigena; Man who is the image rather than the vestige of God; Man, finally, of the cosmic fall related by Jakob Boehme, who is torn from the Creator by a centrifugal force but will, promises Schelling, one day be restored to His bosom: in short, *Homo sapiens*. 'But what if they are a woman's bones,' said Estefania, wide-eyed. 'Is it then Woman *sapiens*?' 'Well,' answered Uncle Esteban, 'in such cases, when the bones are clean and white, men and women are closer to the celestial man spoken of by St Gregory the Thaumaturge than to earthly man and, therefore, have no sex.' 'And what does sex mean?' asked my cousin.

12

Many years before Estefania truly learned the meaning of sex, before they ever dreamed, she and Palinuro, that they would discover it together, one afternoon, on the sands of Mocambo beach and would carry on discovering it, throughout thousands of afternoons and nights, in the room in Holy Sunday Square, Estefania was obliged to take one of the most important decisions of her life. She went and sat in the garden, to think it through. At that time, it was the magic garden of our grandparents' house that furnished us with all solutions. The garden was in the centre of the house and in it proliferated woodlice which rolled into balls when we touched them and worms which multiplied by the act and grace of a penknife and would perhaps, like the long-memoried planarians, forever recall our cruelty. At first light, invisible stalactites roved among the rose bushes, sharpening their fangs on the morning breeze and preparing to petrify the roses in a single bite. At that time of day, on Saturdays and Sundays, Palinuro and Estefania were already in the garden and the smell of their own skins and the scent of the soap with which the pillow slips were laundered were overwhelmed by the fragrance of citron blossom. Crouching, they searched for beetles encased in drops of water. Very soon the rugged orange tree would succumb to the morning sun. Then would come the blue, spreading from branch to branch: a squally blue, frothy as cake frosting which, when it dissolved into the red of the roses, produced a gentian violet to which Aunt Luisa helped herself to daub our throats and stain our tonsils in their juice of staphylococci. Grandmother would call 'breakfast's ready' and Estefania and I would leave in the grass the rose thorn rings we had made and run to wash our hands for breakfast. And if by chance we had been pricked by a rose, the peroxide they dabbed on would mix with the blood to form a cluster of red bubbles. This in itself presented no problem; the problem was not the blood, but the word *blood*, which could not be mentioned in front of Estefania when she was having breakfast – or when she was having lunch, which amounted to the same thing. And, whether she was eating or not, any mention of saliva, faecal matter or cephalorrachidian liquids made her nauseous. This happened for the first time when Uncle Esteban told the story of how they cleaned the bones and, since it happened again on several occasions, Uncle Esteban gave up and promised her that he would never again speak of medicine – or of anything remotely related to it – in her presence. And Estefania wept and asked why Uncle Esteban was punishing her, saying that she wished to become a doctor and that when she was grown up she would no longer feel sick. Uncle Esteban was not fully convinced but, on that morning on which she went to sit in the garden, my cousin Estefania resolved to control this nausea once and for all. And she succeeded in doing so for many years. That is to say, she was able to hide the terrible disgust that the words produced in her. Because, the things in themselves – not the things in themselves in the sense used by Kant whom she had not yet encountered – but simply the things in isolation, without the names that went with them – be it blood or the greeny-blue urine of cholera sufferers or the ghastly Kaposi's sarcomata – never caused this disgust and she was always able to deal with them, to see and even touch and smell them, without ill effect.

And the strangest thing of all – a result of the second major decision of her life – was that Estefania never became a doctor, but a nurse. In other words, this contact with the most horrifying and wretched aspects of the human condition became the daily routine of her existence. Only when she was in the hospital with her patients and her cultures, in her white uniform and coif, could she forget nausea and apprehension. For the same reason, she discovered that she could study her nursing books only in the hospital wards, surrounded by her patients and their detritus, their mucopurulent sputum and breath of newly mown hay. And finally, after several years of heroic effort, Estefania qualified as a nurse, tall and slim and blue-eyed, immaculate and white, stern and compassionate as the nurses of her dreams: the deaconesses of the *Diakonissenanstalt*, the hieronymites of Rome, Florence Nightingale in Scutari, Edith Cavell shot by the Germans, the Augustine sisters of the Hôtel Dieu de Paris who, during the great epidemics, laid the living and the dead in the same beds. Even so, the minute her shift ended and she changed out of her white uniform into a flowered dress, she forgot the wretchedness of hospitals and no illness could be mentioned in her presence: neither by syndrome nor cause, neither by prognosis nor treatment and, much less, very much less, by name.

It was, above all, her enduring love of animals that led Estefania to study nursing rather than medicine. Her favourite saint was St Anthony of Padua because, according to legend, he preached to animals, and fish came to the surface to hear him. She knew by heart the ten animals entitled to enter Paradise, among them Balkis' dove, Ishmael's sheep, the Queen of Sheba's ass and Jonah's whale. She collected stamps for the Larin chocolate zoological album. She held a markedly Jainistic attitude towards the animal kingdom and respected the existence of tarantulas and anacondas. She would ask Grandmother to play Chopin's waltz of the dog and waltz of the cat. When still a child, my cousin had been distraught when her cat was giving birth to a seemingly infinite number of kittens, believing that her pet was going to die because all her lives were coming out of her. Once, Uncle Esteban gave her a collection of postage stamps from Guinea and other countries depicting all kinds of animals: tigers, pelicans, monkeys with multicoloured iridescent behinds; Estefania loved Uncle Esteban more than ever for this gift. However, she was not sure she could continue to love him – or love and respect him – when she later discovered in his library a plate from Jean Pecquet's *De Nova Anatomica* showing a dog split open from top to bottom which revealed to her, for the first time, that medicine had advanced through endless experiments on animals by innumerable researchers.

'But of course, child,' said Uncle Esteban, 'you wouldn't expect them to experiment on human beings now, would you? Experiments on animals go back to Galen, the father of medicine, who spent his life vivisecting monkeys, cows, mules, asses, lions and lynxes and, it is said, at least one elephant, though it hasn't been definitely proved. It is a fact, however,' he added, 'that Astley Cooper made an agreement with a menagerie near the Tower of London to send him corpses of rare animals and he certainly did dissect an elephant, in the open air in the forecourt of St Mary Axe. Empedocles, Alcmaeon and Democritus also dissected animals.'

Estefania continued to love and respect Uncle Esteban. But she never forgave Galen or Astley Cooper. Neither did she forgive Alexander Read for chopping off a dog's leg, nor Malpighi for cutting up silk worms, nor Edward Tyron for dissecting porpoises and rattlesnakes, nor Lister for spying on the does in the Royal Park of Windsor to note when they mated and then opening them up a few weeks later to study the embryos. Neither did she forgive Lavoisier – some hope! – for suffocating sparrows in a glass bell to demonstrate that animal respiration is analogous with chemical combustion. Nor could she forgive Claude Perrault for devoting his life to the murder of doves and eagles, particularly as he was the brother of the man who wrote *Mother Goose Tales*, who had led her by the hand through the lands of marine fairies with moon skin, of footmen holding aloft agate fires and of castles with proud towers greenly inundated every four hours. 'It was not for nothing,' thought Estefania, 'it was not for nothing that God punished him and, like Paracelsus who was castrated by a pig, so Perrault died of a fatal injury after dissecting a dromedary . . .'

But it was for Flourens that she reserved her greatest hatred. For Pierre Jean Louis Flourens, the French physiologist who removed the cerebrum and cerebellum of doves to pin-point the organs governing balance and transmission of motor impulses. Removing the cerebellum, the doves had no sense of direction and balance: they got lost in the nave of Notre Dame, among the bridges of the Seine and in the Porte de Lilas and crashed into the stained glass and rose windows. With the cerebrum removed, their flight was in no way impaired when Flourens released them but they never rested of their own accord, flying ever onward as though blindly crossing an infinite sea to convey a message of love or scorn to an unattainable lover. When at last they fell to the ground in exhaustion, their hearts almost bursting in their chests, they remained prostrate, indifferent to food, to the blue flames of the bunsen burners, to ether explosions and other such efforts by Flourens to provoke a reaction, even when he threatened to wring their necks or melt their feathers with sulphuric acid. Estefania was never able to understand why these macabre experiments should be essential to the advance of medical science, as Uncle Esteban so often assured her: 'Physiology would not be where it is today if Claude Bernard had not cut the left sympathetic nerve of a rabbit to demonstrate that the left side of the head would become red and hot as a result. Nor would we at this stage know anything whatsoever about the velocity of tears or the functions of the risorius muscle. In fact, we wouldn't even know why we cry or why we laugh. And sailors would still be dying of scurvy . . .'

'I don't care,' replied Estefania, who knew quite well why and for whom she cried.

'And if Richard Lower had not linked the carotid artery of one dog to another's jugular vein with a goose feather, the process of blood transfusion would never have been discovered. Can you imagine how many children would have died on the operating table, how many men in war? Can you imagine a world without people of compatible blood?'

'I don't care,' replied Estefania.

'And if Pasteur (and this is something you will be better able to appreciate) had not inoculated rabbits with rabies in order to study fragments of the spinal marrow, Joseph Meister would have died. And you too, Estefania . . .' And here Uncle Esteban stopped short, because he was loath to allude to the past, future or possible death of any of his loved ones.

'Yes, I know: I too would have died,' admitted Estefania, thinking of the time she had been bitten by a rabid dog. 'Even so, I don't care.'

And the list of the poor animals that had contributed to the advance of science, and of those that would do so in the future, was endless. Avenzoar removed the bronchial tubes from goats. Galen himself left animals speechless by cutting the recurrent nerve. Pliny dissected chameleons. Rufus of Ephesus carved up monkeys in order to study their anatomy, Behring burned rabbits with trichloride of iodine. And, while Pavlov drove dogs neurotic by playing tricks with their most sacred reflexes and confusing them with lights and bells, Bard and Mountcastle deprived cats of their rhinencephalic structures, causing them to turn savage, and exposed the trembling brain of a living dog. Block opened up rabbits, deliberately damaged their hearts, operated on them and then sewed them up again and returned them to life. Klüver and Bucy removed monkeys' hypothalami to prove that they lost all sense of fear and anger, became libidinous and engaged in oral sex. Papez also undertook experiments on monkeys and Harlow bamboozled baby monkeys into accepting rag figures as their mothers and Kitasato inoculated the tails of rats with tetanus bacilli. 'And in all the hospitals of the world, in all the laboratories and schools of medicine: in Rochester, in the Children's Hospital, in Guadalajara University, in Vienna, Moscow and Houston, in the Lewisham Hospital, by the way of the Albany School of Medicine laboratory which Carpenter crammed full of every imaginable type of rabbit and including all the names of famous doctors and researchers from Cardan to Koch, from Bell to Ochoterena, you will encounter in these hospitals and in the biographies of these individuals, rearers of white mice and guinea pigs injected with sputum, squirrels with sarcomata, marmots with colds, chimpanzees with trichinosis and dogs and canaries sacrificed to the cause of progressively reducing human illness and death from such diseases as gout, angina pectoris, rickets, poliomyelitis, cancer, leprosy and lumbago.'

All this Estefania was told by Uncle Esteban, over and over again, and he never knew that at night my poor cousin had ghastly dreams in which were equally represented the horrors and the marvels, the hopes and the fears, which these and other conversations had sown in her fertile child's imagination, fed by her reading of children's books and by other dreams, both her own and those of other people. And my cousin's anguish was greater still when she awoke the next day because, just as she always believed the fairy tales of Perrault, Andersen and Grimm, and stories of horror and crime – she believed them all: lock, stock and barrel, from the silver ear to the prince of Arabia Felix, from the victim set upon with dagger thrusts to the red steps following the road to the aquariums – so Estefania always believed her dreams to be true.

2

Estefania in Wonderland

It is difficult to know who was more important to me, whether Palinuro or Estefania. What is more, there are times when I would be unable to say which came first, which of them I had always known, which first established themselves in my life with their words and gestures and trapped my foot in the door to keep me from running away, that I might relate, to the one who came afterwards, the events, signs and luminous loves of the history of the one who came first.

This is, of course, a manner of speaking because, in truth, one of the first things they showed me when I was born was Estefania, then my cousin-sister and later to become my cousin-friend and cousin-lover and who was already twenty days old, having been born not only in the same city of Mexico – a city which at that time revelled in the glories of spring – but also in the same Porfirian mansion belonging to our grandparents and, what is more, in the same room where twice within less than a month the same white sheets spread forth their brabant tentacles in honour of the occasion, the same servants carried silver bowls of boiling water and the same Doctor Latorre arrived to frighten off the stork with the Biiip! Biiip! of his hundred-horse-power, yellow and white Hispano Suiza complete with ebony steering wheel. There was however one difference: when I was born, the stork flew off towards the left, the sinister side, which is none other than the side of vague, foggy stopgaps and of etchings drugged by the onward march of failure. But when Estefania was born, her stork – which came from Alsace – took wing towards the right, in other words, towards the bandstands where musicians unfailingly spring up on Sundays to offer us virtuous concert airs. All this is to say that, though Estefania and I did not share the same smiling fortune – forget the green fortune of green clover, we didn't even share the same tangerine fortune nor the cold fortune promised by the orange, sky-blue clover – we did none the less share certain uncles and aunts and the same pair of maternal grandparents, Francisco and Altagracia, with the corresponding four great-grandparents, sixteen great-great-grandparents and thirty-two thousand etcetera-grandparents. Other things we had in common were, of course, certain famous vases and the wines blushing in the dining-room decanters beside the docile cheeses. Also the treasured streets of the neighbourhood where we were born, which knew themselves by heart – Jalapa, Orizaba, Rio de Janeiro – and a large proportion of that childhood and that life which passed by irretrievably in chewing pencils and nails and accompanied by the camphor-scented roars of stuffed lions and butterflies of silver foil perching humbly on the sugar bowl and on Grandfather Francisco's tins of Prince Albert tobacco: this was the world shared by Estefania and myself since birth. We did, however, have different parents: my cousin was the child of Uncle Esteban and Aunt Lucrecia. I myself, of a sister of Aunt Lucrecia's, Clementina by name, who I will henceforth call 'Mamma Clementina', who was married to Eduardo. That is to say, 'Papa Eduardo'.

Palinuro, on the other hand, I met much later and the memories we share have very little to do with the story which goes: 'once upon a time there was a very poor girl who lived in a house where the gardener who tended the roses and the purslane was also very poor, the cook who prepared the squid in its ink was very poor and the maids who swept the Louis XV bedrooms were very poor', a story which came true when the governor went bankrupt overnight and Altagracia decided to keep the furniture, the garden, the menu and the servants for the use of her lodgers. None the less, these memories – Palinuro's and mine – *are* related to other sensations. For example, the memory of jumping puddles of blue vitriol over and over again, outside the school laboratories, which at night were shut up, dark, deserted and smelling of creosote while in the depths of the water courses emerged the damp ring of the Atayde Circus. And neither can I forget our adolescence: the spiralling amphitheatre of the School of Medicine, the local chemists, the twisted stills and incorrigible theorems; how often did Palinuro and I not declare our passion for the first girl to cross the path of our youth, her skirt minisweet, her ankle socks torn and fantastic; so often did we talk together, get drunk together and together invent Laënnec's stethoscope and Hutchinson's syringes and so often, again together, did we discuss the desirability of bathing hands in melted wax to cure arthritis and recite Virchow's pathology and memorize the burning regions outlined by acupuncture, in that room of sloping ceilings and celestial spheres which might so readily be extirpated if the electricity bill was not paid, that often I quite simply thought that I was he and he was me, to the extent that often I adopted his name and lent him mine. And, as might be expected, Palinuro and I also had several mutual friends, among then Fabricio – not Fabricius ab Aquapendente – but another Fabricio, tall and pale as an ear of Byzantine corn, and Molkas, who was to us as a brother, suckled at the same breast.

Hence Estefania's confusion. And the confusion also of Palinuro himself, born of the shadows of this platonic feast in which each of them was both: and so often did he – Palinuro – and she – Estefania – ask me to tell how I had met the other, how much I admired him and adored her,

19

what amphibian ardour I felt when I touched her – or saw him – at a tea dance or on an excursion to Las Dinamos Park or which suit of what colour and cheeks of what art had I worn to say to her: 'Good afternoon, Estefania,' or: 'How are you, Palinuro?', that I realized that each was consumed with jealousy of the other. And I, mustering my full reserve of malevolence and scant sense of fair play left to me with the passing of the years, decided to confuse them even further. But there was nobody to warn me that, in playing with those tears which bathed the face of thirsty Tantalus but never wet his lips, I would also be permanently plagued by a thirst to know more about you, Palinuro, and also about you, Estefania, and I myself would be confused, knowing not who was first: whether you, Estefania, or I, Palinuro.

The source of this confusion may possibly lie in the children's habit of speaking of themselves in the third person: 'Palinuro is sleepy.' 'Palinuro wants sugar on his bread and butter.' And here Palinuro was no exception: he spoke of himself as though it were I, or any other person, talking about him: 'Palinuro this, Palinuro that, Palinuro the other.' Or even: 'Palinuro the otherest otherest.'

And this he did, not because he was as yet unaware of his personal reality or had not yet confirmed the concept of his own ego – of his *I*, Palinuro sleep drifting on my mother's plaits; *I*, Palinuro wake up with her at night under the lee of her hair and *I*, Palinuro stand with her at the window as we gaze at ourselves in the retort of the moon – but for exactly the opposite reason: at that time Palinuro loved nobody more than Palinuro. And in this, as in other things, Palinuro was like Caesar although, of course, one would have to render unto Caesar what is Caesar's and unto Palinuro what is Palinuro's. For example, Palinuro's was the power to reinvent life and family cosmogonies and crystallize them into a world held up, here and there, with pins: here to the remembrance of a Dutch still-life which memory had forgotten in a pantry; there, to the perpetuation of a coded phrase fertilized by the fortuitous presence of an aster plant, on one of the many occasions he went with Estefania to Walter's house in Cuernavaca. Palinuro never forgot the sight of those flowers, clustered in candyfloss corymbs of magenta, against a backdrop of stars which seemed to make up for the distance between the name of the plant and its objective: Aldebaran, the Pleiades, Sagittarius. Neither did he ever forget that he had to describe to his cousin the roundness and the itinerary of the stars because Estefania was short-sighted and the twinkling orbs were drowned in the vitreous humours of her eyes before reaching her own shining spheres. Palinuro's was also the privilege of embracing in memory the joint existence within a single square centimetre of a river about to freeze and estival grass, of the falling of a dove's wing in the orange marmalade forgotten on the porch and a pyramid of Christmas-tree decorations on the point of collapsing. That minuscule space also contained the fifty-two Sundays of the year, when Grandfather and all his sons-in-law organized family gatherings where the refractive index was marked by a fistful of blood: Uncle Esteban's assertions to the effect that he had buried his shotgun many years previously were of no avail in changing the subject of conversation because any excuse, be it the mention of a cold or the picture of a Magyar seated upon a waggon with a multi-coloured hood – the idealized image of Uncle Esteban himself travelling across the yellow plains towards New Orleans – any excuse served to stoke the flames and speak of wars and revolutions; if it was not Grandfather who drew Pancho Villa and his *dorados* out of the hat – so to speak – or from under the table or out of Venustiano Carranza's beard, then it was Uncle Austin who plunged into a monologue on the defects of the one-hundred-millimetre Skoda cannon or on the shortcomings of the *Sturmtruppen* or, without ceremony, traced the ellipse of two tots of whisky and three decades of time and jumped from the naval battle of Jutland to the occupation of Rhenania and Rudolf Hess's parachute jump into Britain. The best that Uncle Esteban could do when thus confronted with the immutability of someone who believed for a start, as did General von Bernhardi, that war is a biological necessity, was to find a means of introducing the subject of medicine without however ceasing to talk of war: perhaps gas-masks or the giant magnets used to extract grenade fragments from the eye or the Royal Pavilion in Brighton which was used as a hospital for the Indian troops. This was the only way in which he could more or less mollify Uncle Austin, who was not only his brother-in-law, being married to Enriqueta, another of Grandfather Francisco's daughters, but also drank enough to float a ship in spite of the ipecacuanha and other nauseous substances Aunt Enriqueta forced him to swallow in efforts to put him off alcohol. But, while he may not have had many, Uncle Austin did have at least two good reasons not to stop drinking: one was that, of every five bottles of whisky smuggled into Mexico aboard *El Tabasco* – he maintained – four had been filled in Gelaion's Phrygian fountain, the waters of which brought laughter to any who drank them, and only the one remaining in Claion's fountain, the waters of which were reputed to bring tears. And the other good reason, according to Uncle Austin, was the force and honour of habit acquired during his years of sailing before the mast of the British Royal Navy. Uncle Austin, who had left the navy to work in the Foreign Service, had never become a high-ranking official but he had, on the other hand, attained ninety-six on the Gay–Lussac scale; at four o'clock in the morning, when the only other of the house's inhabitants awake was Aunt Luisa, when birds rolled into blue balls still shivered on the pentagram of the telephone wires, Uncle Austin sat drinking a tea of aromatic Earl Grey spiked with pure alcohol. At eight o'clock, he breakfasted on eggs and beer

- his favourite was the toasted malt Saturno beer - and by ten in the morning he already had at least five whiskies inside him. 'You drink too much,' Aunt Enriqueta would reproach him. 'Me? What can you mean? I drink so little,' he always answered. And Aunt Enriqueta held her tongue but, ten minutes later, she would say: 'You're getting old, Austin, you get drunk in no time at all. You used to hold your drink much better.' 'What nonsense you do talk, Enriqueta, I've drunk a vast amount today and I'm still as sober as a judge.' 'Ah, you see, didn't I tell you!' said Aunt Enriqueta triumphantly, 'I told you you drink too much.' And Uncle Austin, faced with an alternative of confessing that he had had a lot to drink or sacrificing his prestige as a hardened drinker, accepted the first and poured himself another whisky to reinforce the second. By four in the afternoon, Uncle Austin had succumbed to the periplus and taken to his bed, although he always woke when Aunt Enriqueta joined him. Then Uncle would mount her, tickle her peninsulas and sow a storm of vibrations between her thighs. On Sundays - although he drank more than ever: brandy given to him by the senator, gin given to him by Uncle Esteban without tonic for fear of another attack of tertian fever, tequila given to him by Papa Eduardo - Uncle Austin made a tremendous effort to survive a few hours longer, in order to talk and argue about war, forgetting the peace of the lands in which he lived his childhood: Surrey, Kent, Sussex and the Elizabethan houses, barns exploding in *ennui*, girls slim as ears of corn carrying garlands of lilies in their hands, golden pastures where apples slept the siesta preceding putrefaction and cows stood so still they seemed to expect to be transformed at any moment into milk princesses and, when the subjects of the First and the Second World War, of the last one and the one before, of the past and of the future, had succeeded in rousing his anger, Uncle Austin would run to his room to fetch his pistol with which he proceeded to shoot blanks in the yard to relieve his frustration. At the far end of the yard, next to the green and orange striped canvas curtain of the garage, he would line up all the pint and one-and-a-half-pint bottles which he had drunk during the week and bring out the pistol. 'I bet you, governor,' he would say to Grandfather Francisco, 'that with every shot I can break a bottle.' And so it was, every time, despite the uncontrollable trembling of his hands. His secret was very simple: he always aimed at one bottle and hit another. 'That is the best definition of luck that I could ever have imagined,' Grandfather thought philosophically, although he wasn't quite sure that it was so; Uncle Austin was still a good shot, despite the alcohol and the passing of the years and the best proof of this was that one afternoon he suddenly shouted: 'I'm going to shoot the balls off the autumn,' and, instead of aiming at the bottles, he fired into the garden and with two shots he hit two oranges. Grandmother Altagracia, though she doted on her garden, said nothing, she greatly admired the English -

believing them to be born aristocrats – and it was more painful to her to discover an Englishman of good name and fair-skinned prestige who did not respect plants than to watch the juice of the shattered oranges trickle along the branches and seep into the earth towards the belly-button of the seeds, bitter and amber, like rancour by another name.

Estefania was always fascinated by the name of our grandmother: Altagracia, because this name – said my cousin – conveyed so much of what my grandmother would have liked to be: of what the bird Aeropos, eternally fluttering its wings in the purple solitude of its entrails, whispered daily to her that she should have been: a marchioness, who would step out on Saturdays at five to fan her titles beneath the ahuehuete trees of the park; a lady, slender and coveted as a column entwined Corinthian-like in exuberant ivy, versed in the arts of displaying her grace and swirling her magnificent gowns resplendent as rushing waters among the *crème de la crème* of social gatherings. But Altagracia was neither the daughter of a duke nor did she marry a marquis: the only thing possessed by Grandfather that could be said to resemble the roar of heraldic dragons or synoples, the only thing appearing to cement the polysyllables of an empire was, likewise, his name. Though not his first name by itself, but the first and second name his parents had given him and which made Uncle Esteban think with distaste of the Emperor of Austria and King of Hungary, Francis Joseph. However, Uncle Esteban's mind was put at rest when Grandfather spoke of the republican and liberal stock from which he was descended and swore his hatred of all monarchs and emperors of the world, from Sardanapalus to Emperor Norton of the United States. What he omitted to mention on such occasions was that one particular emperor, none other than the younger brother of Francis Joseph – the similarly blond Maximilian of Hapsburg who had, in honour of his beloved, set the Borda Gardens alight with flame trees – did evoke a certain sympathy in Grandfather; perhaps because Maximilian had been a liberal or perhaps because, like himself, Maximilian loved the bougainvillaea which freshened Sunday afternoons with hollows of darkest blue shade or, again, because the story of Maximilian and Carlota reminded Grandfather of another story, also of love and madness, which had caused the unhappiness of his only and dearly loved sister, Aunt Luisa.

On the subject of Grandmother Altagracia and the magic of names – 'What's in a name?' quoted Cousin Walter – Estefania received one of the most agreeable surprises of her childhood and Grandmother Altagracia a great disappointment when don Prospero reached the letter 'E' in the encyclopaedia and Estefania learned that nobody in the house had a name of such importance, with such diverse and pretty derivatives. And this coincided with my cousin's dawning awareness of her own beauty, though her western-pointing breasts were yet but a budding promise as tiny fruits patiently moulded by the wind; not only in her face and in her eyes, twin turquoise gems, but also in the rest of her body: in her thighs, in the foreshortened wings of her shoulder blades and her swan's neck arching in interrogation over the pillow, intimation of that beauty already shone forth with the uncontainable force of a fountain of roses shortly to well from every pore of her skin. And also, woe is me, also in her hair, which had begun to curl like hyacinth stems and which she adorned with iridescent ribbons twirling and fluttering like the ribbons of Moebius, laying siege to my heart with their fulminating equations.

But, to return to Grandfather Francisco – always, when all was said and done, we returned to him – as far as Estefania and Palinuro were concerned, and also Cousin Walter who sometimes came from Europe or from his home in the country to spend the weekend with his cousins, Grandfather Francisco was indeed a king, quite apart from his sonorous name and quite apart from the fact that he had been born, as he maintained, in Baghdad: also because he was so fat and so magnificent with so many kilos and bacchanalias to his credit and with canvas sails and plantations of tobacco following him along the paths of history behind the wheelchair he used to go from the Revolution to the Senate and from New Orleans to the Revolution's Tragic Ten Days or simply to go from the table where he had breakfast to the desk where he wrote his letters and from the desk where he wrote letters to the table where he played poker and from the table where he played poker to the secretaire where he wrote his memoirs and from the secretaire where he wrote his memoirs to the desk where he told us stories; the stories which peopled our world with caliphs drowning in *aljibes* as green as yawns, with bridges of pure brightness between two lands sunk in insoluble blacknesses and ships of which the entire crew died of a miraculous plague and which sailed over the sea and through legend like slow cemeteries. All this was necessary to make him the greatest and most memorable of grandfathers, only later exploring the bounds of his realms, searching the carpets of his room to discover the eagle of a lost coin and opening the drawer of his bureau to find tablets to cure hiccups. And later still, many years later, approaching the mirror of the wardrobe, the huge and sinuous mirror in the depths of which a child might be lost: Palinuro himself at that age when he first became curious about the erotic digressions of his parents, on which he might have spied through the skylight or pictured in the depths of a less luminous but no less transparent awareness which eventually yielded to the slow learning of fabrication and the language of inversions: the prince who was turned into a fish, the pebble turned meteor. This was the age, also, when a porcelain angel hung above his bed and acted as his pilot through hells and paradises which were like boxes of surprises, and the age in which he began to draw and discovered that the lines of a compass rose or the silhouette of a silk

24

cotton tree could put the seal on the magnificence of his Cousin Estefania's days. She, who sat beside him, who marvelled at his skill and thanked him for being her cousin, for being with her, who spoke to him in that language of slow emanations capable of making a lily of an imagined outline, of incorporating herself, Estefania, into the world of chiaroscuro. 'Very good, very good,' said Grandfather Francisco when Palinuro showed him the portrait of Estefania beneath a tree. 'What are you going to be when you're big? An artist? A painter?' Palinuro answered his grandfather yes and asked him what he was going to be when he was little. 'Ahhhh . . . mmmm . . . when I'm little,' answered Grandfather Francisco, 'let me see . . . When I'm little, yes, of course, that's it! When I'm little I'm going to be a boy like you, your age, with your eyes and the fun you have.' 'And when you are even littler?' 'Ah, when I'm even littler, I'm going to be the age you were when you were born.' 'How old was I when I was born, Grandfather?' 'Well, not years. You were less than a year old. Less than a month even, less than a week, less than a day. How can I explain that you were not even an hour old or a minute, or even a second . . . But as soon as you were born . . . Goodness me, as soon as you're born time starts to catch up with you and never leaves you in peace for a minute of the day.' 'And how old will you be when you die, Grandfather?' 'Well, I don't know exactly, but I'm sure I'll be quite old, because I'm quite old already now. And I sometimes think I'm even older than I am, even though my father always told me that I lost a few years. And anyway, as I told you before, when I die, I will also be several months and several weeks and several days old. So if I don't die on my birthday, or even if I do die on my birthday, I'll still be several minutes and several seconds and several milliseconds and several millionths of a second old and so on for ever because I promised your Grandmother Altagracia that my death, even if it runs faster than Achilles, will never catch up with me while I'm alive: this was taught to me by an old gringo you will meet later.' 'And what do you keep in your wardrobe, Grandfather?' 'My wardrobe? Ah, there are lots of things in my wardrobe. For example, my binoculars which are up at the top, in the most impregnable part of the wardrobe, from where they look out over the Revolution. But I put them back-to-front, so that they see everything in miniature because it's so far away. And in my wardrobe there are other things too, which I'll tell you about if you promise not to tell anybody else. Come here, sit down by me and listen: in my wardrobe there are three soldiers who have been hidden there since the time of the Revolution, since before Venustiano Carranza was assassinated in Tlaxcalantongo. One is a very young captain, barely more than a youth. He has an olive-green uniform with a tear in the leg of the trousers and on his shoulder the golden epaulettes which he won in the Pact of the Ciudadela. The other is a major who found a star on the orange flanks of El Rellano and stuck it in the

25

band of his cap with the permission of General Villa. The third is a colonel, quite old and very thin, who kept his Rexer rifle as a souvenir and afterwards retired from the army to devote himself exclusively to politics. At night, when everybody is asleep, I open the door of the wardrobe to let them out. We have a few drinks to give their uniforms time to become a little less creased and then we take a walk in the garden so that they can stretch their legs. Afterwards they shave, particularly if I've forgotten them for a few days; remember that their beards grow twenty-odd metres a day. And by that I don't mean to say that when they come out of the wardrobe their beards get tangled up around their legs and their swords and the rose bushes and the trams, no: twenty-odd metres is the sum total of their combined length, as we calculated the other day when we were very tired of all the thousands and thousands of hairs which grow from their three chins. Then they rub on some eau-de-Cologne to get rid of the smell of mothballs and we sit down to chat. What do we chat about? About everything, because the one who was not a cadet in the military academy and visited West Point like the captain, was a libertine like the major, or a mason like the colonel; and so our discussions, like me between one table and another, go back and forth, like a swing, from the battles they fought to the girls of the tropics who smoke violet-coloured cigarettes in gold holders, then return to the battles and back again to the girls and again to the battles. Or, sometimes, we simply kidnap the girls and take them with us to the battles and we tie the swing to a tree, as though it were a horse, to use in emergencies. But also, at other times, the captain and the major and the colonel go to visit the Great Architect and return by train to Somora, there to put a torch to a mighty camp while the snow falls. Then we start playing poker at the table for playing poker. The captain likes the "swords" of the Spanish pack best: what can you expect? he is very young, he has just read von Clausewitz and only yesterday he took part in the charge of the six thousand dragoons in Paredón. The major prefers "cups": now that the revolution is over, you have to relax and follow the example of Uncle Austin, or the major: take the ship *Siboney* to New Orleans, drink to the flowing rhythm of the blue tides and play in the casinos which spring up in mid-ocean like the Sporades Islands. Ah, every time I hear that a famous traveller loses the shirt off his back and jumps overboard at night to become a printed squid, I remember those gaming rooms where I fatted my golden fleeces; what wouldn't I give to live those times over again, with those girls, their hair tied back with silk lace or in black plaits, to love Patty O'Hara, the Irish girl who, when she met me, also took me for a fortune-teller, as you sometimes do, and asked me if I could read her future in the palm of her hand. And I showed her my hands of a Mexican railway worker, council chairman, captain and major, smelling of gun powder and carbon paper, and I told her that her destiny lay not in her hands but in

mine. And then . . . Ah, but that's another story. But now, let's get back to
our game: the colonel, of course, kept his "gold" in the sleeves of his
uniform and not only because he was a little old and mean but also because
he had to finance his campaign to become governor of the state and he
wanted to buy a desk in which to keep his memoirs, a house in which to
keep his desk and a garden in which to keep his house. And, of course, I
have lost interest in swords, I have no gold left, I don't feel well when I'm
in my cups and the clubs I keep to beat everybody with. But, before we start
to play, we pull down the blinds, we draw the curtains and we close the
shutters outside and inside, in case dawn should catch us unawares: they
have not been outside for so many years that if the sunlight were to shine
on them they would turn to dust and it would be a lot of work to sweep
them away, just imagine, we would have to invite our friends to come and
help us sweep: don Prospero, the lottery-ticket vendor, the general with the
glass eye and then, how would we know which dust belonged to which of
them? Senator, the captain says to me every night, I have three horses of the
sword suit. And I reply, well then, my three kings of clubs are going to ride
on your three horses. Do I always win, you ask me? Look, the major beats
the captain, that's an order. The colonel beats the major, that's another
order. And then I come along and I beat them all. But don't think that
therefore I'm rich. It's been a long time since I won all their money from
them and then they started to bet other things in order to continue playing
rather than bore each other with their stories. The colonel, who had
become very fat since he was promoted to major, bet me all the kilos he had
gained at political lunches held in the Prendes Restaurant and the
breakfasts in the Waldorf Hotel in New York, during the course of which
he ate at least half a dozen eggs and a hot cake raised by the power of three
and that's why you see me now with this paunch like an elastic barrel and
in which I always keep my reserves of laughter. And that is also why I need
a very big tub in which to take my bath, as I do every Saturday without
fail, unless Saturday happens to fall on 23 July, which is the anniversary of
the death of one of my sons who fell in the tub and drowned when he was
four years old and then I don't take a bath, as I said, because every 23 July
your grandmother Altagracia fills the tub with flowers. In the major's
case, it was his treasured love letters that he lost, one by one. He gradually
lost all those from Patty O'Hara and once, with a pair of aces, I myself
won from the major a love letter written on blue paper and scented with
myrurguia perfume in which Francine, a French girl as her name would
suggest, threatened the major that she would embed a crystal tear in her
cheek if the major did not return to Tampico. One Saturday night, against
four queens of clubs, the major lost a letter still in its envelope in which
your grandmother Altagracia swore eternal love to the captain. For this
letter originally belonged to the captain, who lost it to the major. Ah, the

poor captain; eventually he had nothing left to bet with but his memories, which he also lost one by one. He became increasingly quiet and sad because he no longer had grandparents or dogs or girlfriends or battles about which to reminisce; it transpired that the major, as well as being a captain, had taken the captain's first communion and that the colonel was the only son of the captain's mother and that I bore on my leg the scar of the bullet wound sustained by the captain. Finding this excessively sad, we sought to return some of his bets to him, but he didn't remember them and said that they did not belong to him. It seems to me that the best thing would be for him to invent another childhood, another military academy and other friends; he no longer remembers even his friends, he no longer remembers anything and sometimes I am afraid that he will no longer remember that he is alive and that he will die. Now I am going to show you something. But first, draw the curtains . . .' And Grandfather Francisco put 'The Blue Danube,' on the gramophone, wheeled his chair over towards the wardrobe, turned the key, knocked three times on the floor with his cane, like an usher, and the doors started to open; slowly they opened, like the gates of a besieged and conquered city, like the gates of Troy, like the gates of Carthage, like the gates of Celaya opening before Villa's *dorados* and there, inside Grandfather's wardrobe, were the uniforms and the bundles of faded letters and the colonel's rifle and the captain's memoirs. 'Look,' said Grandfather. 'See, children: that was how the captain looked when he was fifteen years old, like Dick Sand. And that is what he looked like when he was three years old with long hair: they still dressed him like a little girl because that was the custom then. And this photograph is of the captain's mother and she is surrounded by a garland of camellias, her favourite flowers. She was tall and had blue eyes like you, Estefania, or like the sky of Castile, her homeland. From her, your mother Clementina inherited the gift of whistling the arias of Don Juan and Pasha Selim like an angel. What am I saying, like an angel: like Amelia Leovalli, like Deanna Durbin, like Al Jolson. Not even whalebone stays could stifle the blackbird nestling in her breast since she was a child, no bigger than her mother's patience . . . Ah . . . and this, this is the first sword given to the captain in the academy. And here he is with his sweetheart in La Piedad Park; as you can see, his sweetheart would be identical to your grandmother Altagracia, if she weren't so different . . . So many years have passed! And these are the Jules Verne books the captain read. As soon as you learn to read they will be yours and you will travel with Hector Servadac in a comet and by night you will accompany the musicians who play on the streets of Propeller Island.' Grandfather Francisco lit a cigar, spitting the tip into the spittoon of gleaming brass. 'I think,' he said, 'that the captain is the dearest of my friends.' 'And are you going to tell me about the bullet in his leg, Grandfather?' asked Palinuro. 'Yes indeed, on the day you least expect it.'

28

'And are you also going to tell me about the day I was born, Grandfather?'
'Yes of course, also on the day you least expect it.'

And so it was; at night the grey-green frogs amused themselves, lending a hollow resonance to the silence and a black breeze slid along the corridor between the majolica flower pots which looked like elephants' feet crowned with plumes of fern, tacking down in long-memoried backstitch the snores of Grandfather Francisco and Grandmother Altagracia, the whistling of Uncle Esteban and Aunt Lucrecia, the gurgling of Uncle Austin and Aunt Enriqueta and the sighs of Mamma Clementina, of Papa Eduardo, of don Próspero and all the other inhabitants of the house, accompanied by the tick-tock of the clocks which marked the different hours according to whether their hands pointed towards the window dazzled by the poplars or towards the wardrobe in which hung Mamma Clementina's coat, abandoned and dusty as the ghost of an old tree, next to the cotton, darn-infested smocks and Papa Eduardo's trousers, hanging themselves with his red braces. And Mamma Clementina – Mamma who read *Bruges the Dead City* by Rodenbach and Clementina who made Palinuro promise that he would visit Bruges for her – dreamed, wearing that very coat and head scarf gnawed by silk worms, that she a widow wearing the crepes and cashmeres of mourning, went walking on the Day of the Dead on the arm of the Duchess of Guermantes along the green way on a golden afternoon fulsome as the wine of Tours while, on the watery breath of mirrors, swans expelled from the escutcheon of a murdered nobleman lamented their exile above the whiteness of the water lilies. Two bedrooms down and forty years on, in the withered intimacy of her inner self, beneath her patchwork quilt of family reminiscences, was Aunt Luisa, a moment before waking, dreaming as usual of Paris. And, believing Paris to be as old and ailing as she was herself, she dreamed that she wrote letters to Paris asking how the Seine was getting on, whether they had finally operated on her Place de l'Opéra and given her Arc de Triomphe spectacles and whether the Bois de Bologne had sprouted grey hairs.

Ten years previously and in a bedroom one floor down, Grandfather Francisco, after sounding the curfew with his formidable farts, was dreaming that he was parading from the desk for remembering the Revolution, to the window for looking out over the street to watch the girls with calves as thick as zeppelins passing by, to the safe to count the blue bank notes bearing historic gargoyles, to the table for dictating orders: and then he ordered that a life-size monument of the ahuehuete tree of the Noche Triste be erected before the real one disintegrated, like the old waterman from where it takes its name, on the road to Popotla, and he ordered that the remains of Iturbide be removed from the metropolitan cathedral and buried at sea that they might continue their course between the devil and the deep blue sea, as had been the emperor's wont in life, and he ordered that he be sent a wheel-aeroplane to carry him from the table for dictating orders to the chair for reading the Sunday newspaper, to the bed for having breakfast in bed, to the photograph for looking, from above and among the living, at Grandmother Altagracia's bedroom. Because, three months below Grandfather Francisco's years, twenty centimetres to the right of the living and another twenty to the left of the dead, two metres below the ceiling and four above the geysers of hell, with a stucco smile and a black-hot conscience, Grandmother Altagracia fell asleep, after begging providence for a syncope as she did every night, and dreamed of all her existing live relatives and of all her future deceased ones. The living, such as Estefania and myself and our parents and Uncle Felipe and Aunt Luisa and so many others, hung in frames on the left side of the bed, while the dead portrayed in silhouettes, in pencil and chalk portraits, caricatures, first-communion photographs and newspaper cuttings, covered the right half of the wall. Here hung Great-grandfather Uwe, who had deserted during the Franco-Prussian war. Great-grandmother was beside him, complete with diamond ear-rings and Valencian fan. Here hung also a cousin of ours who had been suddenly struck down by an attack of peritonitis during her fifteenth-birthday dance and had died with a posy of orchids on her breast as the ambulance was passing beneath the golden birches of the park. And there were other distant uncles and aunts and cousins and great-grandparents that Estefania and I had never known. Only Uncle Alejandro, who had gone to Germany with his whole family and was never heard of again after the first bombings of Berlin, hung alone for several years in the middle of the wall, beneath the crucifix, neither dead nor alive. Until Altagracia awoke one morning with sufficient courage to dress in mourning, weep a little, receive condolences and say nine rosaries before moving Uncle Alejandro's portrait to the side of the dead. And Grandmother Altagracia, who loved her garden and, like Grandfather, missed the snow of the north, dreamed that she gave the rose bushes, lemon trees and bunches of violets a touch of snowy dignity. She dreamed that she left her room at midnight, seated herself on a very high ostrich-leg bench, unrolled a document and read out to Ricardo the gardener instructions for spring cleaning the garden with talcum powder: you begin at night, walking on tip-toe, with the chaste mimosa trees. When this has been done, you proceed to sprinkle talcum powder on irises or roses, it is immaterial which, are you listening to me, Ricardo? Special care must be taken with the heliotropes which at these hours are asleep and need several days or thirteen years to return to earth. The camellias and narcissi would appreciate a sprinkling but since ours are white anyway the purpose is defeated, are you listening to me Ricardo? And the hortensias and fuchsias should be sprinkled from a certain distance and the forget-me-nots and delphiniums left till last. Next day, you understand, Ricardo, the whole garden will be covered in snow, to the astonishment of the colonel, the major, the captain, the lodgers and the police.

And three and four rooms respectively to the right, and sixty years previously and sixty years and twenty days previously, also respectively, at a distance of ten metres from each other in space, but only a few millimetres, several grains of sand and the time to bathe in the same sea and in the same dreams, Estefania and Palinuro slept and dreamed. Palinuro slept, Estefania dreamed. Estefania slept, Palinuro dreamed.

Palinuro had never known a place like it. It was like a huge zoo, like Noah's Ark on the knees of Hurtali. There were snakes, seals, duck-billed platypi, giraffes, cows whose milk overflowed on to the peaks of prehistoric stones, guinea pigs, lizards and centipedes, geese tamed with vast quantities of bread crumbs and saliva, opossums, zebras, herons with equinoctial feathers, dung beetles, hippopotamuses and countless seabirds of which the mere names were in themselves a guarantee of foam and marine phosphorescences: the pelican, the cormorant, the albatross which cleaves the waves with wings sharp as Bristol paper. There were also does, the favourites of Lister, the prince of surgeons, enveloped in an aura of carbolic acid and English glory, and Lister invited Palinuro to accompany him to the Royal Park of Windsor and together, as they discussed the ovariotomy performed by McDowell in Kentucky, they spied on the mating deer. When it was over, when the bucks and does had finished their love dance beneath the amber leaves of the maples and the dark foliage of the scarlet oaks, treading the red madder of the meadows and the witches' rings of mushrooms, Palinuro and his teacher decided to open up a doe. They incised the belly of the first with a scalpel, half an hour after coitus. The second they opened up two days later. And yet another – they promised themselves – they would open up when three weeks had passed. From the first they removed the womb and uterus, which was like a blue pear, and beneath the microscope they observed the floating ovules bathed in immaculate sperm and there, wonder of wonders, there were the new deer, so tiny, so very tiny, that it could not be sworn that they were indeed they. Delighted, Palinuro and his teacher drank a toast in ginger wine. 'Incredible, Mr Lister,' said Palinuro. 'I'm not Lister, dear friend: I am Dr Harvey,' said Mr Harvey-Lister, showing Palinuro his hands, and Palinuro saw that his fingers never ended, that the fingers of one hand turned into blue and red veins and arteries which extended to the tips of the fingers of the other hand, where they again became fingers. 'Excuse me, Dr Harvey, I was mistaken,' Palinuro begged Lister-Harvey and when both individuals had forgiven him he was happy again, because he knew he was capable of doing, achieving and conquering what so many other geniuses had done, achieved and conquered: geniuses who knew the value of human life and were strong virtuous breakwaters and, here and there, in the west tower of the University of Glasgow, in the Salpêtrière in Paris or in the red-roofed houses on the banks of the Potomac, had burned their midnight lives, drop by drop, in the cause of science. And while Palinuro One conversed with Mr Listervey and Palinuro Two discussed with Mr Harlister the potential progress of medicine through raping a mare with half a litre of cough syrup, it happened that Metchnikoff walked down the street with a tankard of beer in his hand. There were few things that Palinuro – and even Estefania – enjoyed as much as looking at themselves with the star-spangled beard of Metchnikoff, the Russian scholar, planning the course of his suicides, the first, second and third, whether in Heligoland, Odessa or Tenerife, discussing histology with the iguanas and rhinoceroses, and belching black landscapes and silver sickles. So he accepted this second invitation to walk down to the beach while the children of Sèvres ran after him shouting 'Père Noël! Père Noël!' and he threw them china toffees in the shape of piglets and shells. Palinuro took his leave of Messrs H. and L. who waved him goodbye with seagulls in their hands and he went with Mr Metchnikoff. They reached the shore where the infinite sea bathed in the sun and they hunted for starfish because they intended to find out how these animals digested the light of the moon and its clots of semi-heavy milk. They caught five or six stars, injected them with carmine distilled from Mamma Clementina's lipsticks and as they were transparent it was possible to observe how certain prodigious cells devoured the foreign particles. They cut off the legs of the stars and threw them into the sea so that each would grow a new star with a fresh memory. And who should emerge from between the humps of the waves, covered in seaweed and starfish legs, antlers of white coral and mermaid scales, but Robert Koch, who had just caught an eel of two kilowatts and three gold fish which he was going to inject with tuberculosis bacillus. Palinuro found a book on the beach and asked Koch if it was his. Somebody was whistling a tune and the wind turned the pages. Palinuro was going to ask Metchnikoff the same question but the latter decided to follow the example of the German scholar and plunged into the sea, to return a moment later with a perch in his hand. When Palinuro blinked, there was nobody left on the beach, not even himself. The truth, of course, was that it was not Palinuro who was dreaming this dream, but Estefania who was dreaming that she was Palinuro. Anyway, the fact was that, according to the moon clock, it was between eight and a summer morning, an afternoon on which eternity flew over the cities beneath nimbi of dead suns, and nobody was on the beach except Estefania, sitting on the sand surrounded by books of fairy tales and love stories and wearing her new dress of sea foam. But it was an uncomfortable dress, growing very long when the tide went out which caused her to trip over and scatter bubbles, and then rolling up to her neck and almost drowning her when the tide came in bearing thirsty sea snails which clung to her skin. Somebody continued to whistle a tune and the breeze turned the pages of the novels and the fairy tales into pink birds which flew away. Metchnikoff re-emerged from the sea. The water had dyed his beard to the greeny-blue of tourmaline and the perch had turned into a golden key. 'Take this, child, keep this key, but don't open the door,' he said to Estefania, pointing out a door which led somewhere and giving her the key. But Estefania played the innocent, she put on a diadem of bees which buzzed around her honey locks and with her own little hand, toasted at the touch of the cindered fishes, opened the door. After tumbling into the depths of her memory, she met a white rabbit who was in a great hurry and half of whose head was red and hot. 'Where are you going?' Estefania asked him. 'To Dr Bernard's funeral, nosey little girl,' he answered. 'Are you cross?' Estefania-Alice asked him. 'Only half-cross,' the rabbit answered. 'Before he died, Dr Bernard cut my left sympathetic nerve.' 'What a half-nasty individual,' thought Estefania as the rabbit scampered off. By this time it had stopped raining and umbrellas blushed at being caught open when the sun came out. In the next room, Estefania saw herself asleep in a wood, beneath a glass dome in which thought became rarefied and, with blond curls and purple breath smelling of formaldehyde, Prince Lister approached, raised the dome and kissed her on the lips. Estefania awoke very frightened because she thought that she had conceived a stag and that Lister was going to cut open her womb with a knife. But Lister reassured her, saying that he was only going to perform an autopsy, that he was merely going to open her heart and clean out the clots and that it would be taken in a Petri dish to Stepmother Queen Estefania. In the next room, Estefania met two dogs who insisted on signing a blood pact. 'But what should we write with?' said one who was very thin because his pancreatic duct had been rerouted to the outside of his body. 'That's the least of our problems,' said Mother Goose, pulling out a feather from beneath her wing. The dog took the feather and pricked a vein. 'Why is your blood so red?' Estefania asked him. 'All the better to die with,' the dog answered her, and these were his second-to-last words. His last words were, in fact, a series of bubbles which came from his mouth, each containing a miniature replica of one of his organs: a cancerous lung, a cirrhotic liver, a scarlet-fever tongue. Finally, from the glass tube attached to the end of his pancreatic duct, emerged a last bubble, transparent and bright as a paperweight and which contained, also in miniature, the islets of Langerhans. Estefania opened the door to another room and discovered the entire funeral cortège of Claude Bernard. Never had Estefania seen such a long and, particularly, such a sad procession of sick and maimed animals, with crutches and canes and sticks, with open wounds and festering sores, with tumours and deformities, with leukaemia and limping, undergoing transfusions and struck dumb. A bull frog came past in a wheelchair, accusing Abbot Spallanzani of ripping off his legs at the moment of coitus, to prove that not even this would induce him to release the female. A cart went by full of hibernated dogs whose hearts were exposed, embedded in shaved ice. Skinner's pigeons appeared, playing Ping-Pong. Also a cartload of immensely fat rats with needles stuck in their hypothalami. The seven dwarf wood harts came past suffering from thyroid disorder. Also a pair of newlywed white mice who showed their tails pumped full of tetanus bacillus. Then passed a fatherless canine solicitor who respectfully removed his hat, revealing his exposed brain, palpitating and serous: 'Just look at the state Dr Roux has left me in,' he said to her, 'and, as a result, in winter I can't think, because my thoughts freeze solid, and in the summer all my illusions trickle down my face and neck.' Next to come by were three geese, two goats and a cat, with signs hanging around their necks explaining that they were dumb because Dr Galen had cut their vocal cords. And many, many other animals came past, to the infinite sadness of Estefania, including ten of Pavlov's neurotic dogs, fifty smoking rabbits and a horse who complained that day and night he saw, floating in the air and in his dreams, enormous golden worms and this was all the fault of Dr McKinley of Alabama University who had injected agar-agar and streptococci into his eyes. And bringing up the rear of the cortège were two dogs, that is to say, one dog; well, no, actually, two dogs. Anyway, the fact is that there appeared one dog with two heads – or two heads with one dog, Estefania could never be sure which – and they complained bitterly: 'I was a whole dog,' she was told by Tweedledum, as he was called, 'until Dr Guthrie of Chicago came along and cut off my head and grafted it on to Tweedledee's body. And now I am only a head without a dog.' 'I also used to be a whole dog,' complained Tweedledee, 'until Dr Guthrie of Chicago came along and grafted Tweedledum's head on to my body. And now I am a super-whole dog, with two heads.' 'That's not true,' protested Tweedledum, 'my head is not your head.' 'Grrrrr,' growled Tweedledee, 'if you continue to insist that your head is not one of my two heads I'm going to refuse to have my stomach digest your food and my feet take you walking and my heart carry you clean blood.' 'Calm down, for goodness sake!' begged Estefania, offering them a piece of bread but immediately thinking better of it and offering them, instead, two pieces of bread. 'No thank you,' said Tweedledum, 'I'd sooner die of hunger than feed a body that is not my own.' 'No thank you,' said Tweedledee, 'I'd sooner die than feed a head that is not my own.' Estefania sat very pensive until eventually a silk worm came along complaining that Mr Malpighi had split him open from end to end. Estefania put her hands into the silk worm's stomach, pulled out the end of a silk thread, and pulled and pulled and it seemed that it was endless. And the silk stockings of all the ladies of the world unravelled. And a Mandarin who was eating lychees with jasmine tea lost

34

the gown he was wearing, embroidered with the entire history of the Ming dynasty, from the victory won by Chu Yüän-chang and the occupation of Karakorum to the reign of Kin Khan. And some Madison Avenue executives, who were in the Twenty-One Restaurant in New York, wining and dining clients from Lux soap, lost their striped silk ties, as did nine out of every ten Hollywood stars. And in the last of the rooms was Estefania, alone and mad. It was an immense chamber, with walls, ceilings and floors covered in immaculate white mosaics. Flourens' doves, deprived of their cerebella, flew headlong into the mosaics and fell into the jars of methyl orange and cut their throats as, in their clumsy flight, they broke test tubes of Bohemian glass and flasks of Jena glass. Drops of red blood and orange methyl dripped into agate mortars and white sinks corroded by nitric acid, as Estefania's tears trickled down the long glass pipettes, leaving a drop of transparency here and there, filtering through a silk sieve, leaving a drop of blue here and there, and overflowed from chrome crucibles. Only much later, when Estefania forgot about Flourens' doves and all her animals killed and tortured in the name of science, not till then did her tears evaporate and each turn into a tiny, violet, butterfly-shaped flame, the colour of a flame of potassium and hydrogen.

3

My first encounter with Palinuro

'Dr Palinuro, goodness me, what are you doing?' 'None of your business.
Give a copy of the key to this young man and take your gossiping
elsewhere! Don't let me catch you here again! Wait! Come here! Hold out
your hand! Aha! Open your eyes wide! Wider! Wider! Mmmmm . . . . .
Looks like foetal erythroblastosis. Have you been subject to dyspnea
lately? Or enuresis?' 'Oh, Dr Palinuro, am I going to die?' 'We all die
sooner or later. And you will certainly die if you don't take these
hydrochloride of chlortetracycline pills.' 'Thank you, thank you, Dr
Palinuro. How much do I owe you?' 'Nothing, the consultation and the
medicine are free if you promise not to bother me again, ever again, about
paying the rent. Take half a tablet once a month and come back when you
finish them. And you,' Palinuro said to me, 'don't be surprised to see me
like this. Your tender years prevent you from accepting the fact that the
labyrinthine rejuvenation of the species sometimes runs into trifles such as
these which are so difficult to uproot.'

I sat down on the edge of the bed and, for a supreme instant, Estefania, I
thought that I would never be able to share a room with someone like
Palinuro who received me in such inauspicious circumstances.

'Do you study or work?' he asked me. 'I study. I've just enrolled in the
School of Medicine.' 'Doctor! Doctor! You're going to be a doctor, man,
like me! Congratulations. Never in your whole life or, at least, let's say,
since the fourth week of your intra-uterine existence when your heart
measured barely a quarter of an inch, until this moment when your heart is
big enough, I am sure, to accommodate all the blessings of this world and
its horrors and even a cathedral of books and your future friend Palinuro,
never, do you hear? never have you taken a wiser or more important
decision. Let's have a cigarette. They're over there, on the book shelf.
Could you light it for me, please? My hands are dripping vinegar. Thank
you . . .' Palinuro took a puff of his cigarette and continued: 'Of course,
times have changed a lot, doctors no longer cauterize wounds with red-hot
sea shells nor teach the art of letting blood through lotus stems. Romance
is no more in this age of ours: surgeons sew up their patients with
Minnesota Manufacturing Company cat gut and not, as they used to, with
harp strings which allowed the doctor to play a *glissando* while examining

a patient. Nowadays, things are very different. How can they be romantic when frozen placentas by the thousands are transported by air and sold like Findus hot cakes to the Merieux Institute so that we can all have our ration of gamma globulin? Nevertheless, there is no doubt that to be a doctor is the best profession in the world,' he said, then blew a couple of smoke rings before continuing, 'because, to be a physician, my friend, is to be everything. The physician is an architect, a lawyer, a cook, a magician, a policeman, anything you like: the physician is all things. But please, could you pass me that patchwork waistcoat, I'm freezing to death . . .'

Of the forty-five times that Palinuro appeared in my life, it is this, the first, that I will best remember. The clockwork of winter, accurate to the instant in its whiteness, clung to the first sepia step of the colonial mansion in Holy Sunday Square. You must remember it well, Estefania, because, just as you and I were born in the same room in the same house in the same city, so Palinuro came into the world – that is to say, he came into *my* world – in the very building, and none other in the whole of Mexico City, where you and I lived and dreamed of each other and, what is more, the room in which Palinuro lived on the fifth floor was the very room and none other in that building, in the whole of Holy Sunday Square and in the entire universe, where you and I, Estefania, tirelessly and amazingly made love, on the bed, on the floor and in space, naked, clothed, awake and half-asleep, to the envy of our friends, of our relatives and of the Farmers' Almanac. In the very room where we fought with words and with objects and made up with them. In short, in the very room which we had had made to the measure of our desires and of our memories and to which you would return in the early mornings after your night shifts at the hospital, tired from shaving the pubes of patients going to the operating theatre and of pre-warming bed pans and washing the sores of patients in perpetual coma, and to which I would return after passing through the advertising agencies and other imaginary islands, tired from creating campaigns and advertisements for Canada Dry, slogans for Palmolive and jingles for Campbell's Soup and firm in my intention to enrol once again in the School of Medicine and never more forsake it. The concierge walked ahead of me up the stairs where you and I were one night to come across Palinuro crawling on all fours in pursuit of glory, there on the second floor, do you remember? Outside the postman's door, the concierge explained to me that I was going to share and adorn my room with a rancid medical student and my happiness knew no bounds. A cluster of diverging clover leaves entwined their hesperidiae, a sturgeon of ice slid down a thread of silver and loosed its eggs into the air and that splendid caviare turned into a flying fruit shop. 'He always has his record player on that loud, you'll get used to it,' the concierge said to me, unstinting in her belches. From corner to corner, on the snowflakes carried in the white crows' beaks, the chipped cups dusted themselves with Nescafé and through the circle of the skylight, lean and earnest, the light scattered over the concierge's Medusa locks. 'And, to make matters worse, he's only got one record. Perhaps you can persuade him to buy a new one.' And so we reached the fourth floor, do you remember, Estefania? where the drunken doctor lived and his mad lady neighbour and, now and again, you could hear the spores of a gelatinous conversation, and I continued to climb the endless stairs of that old colonial building of red foam, submerged in the darkness of a brew of seaweed, between greenish and opaline, with hints of apple camphor and rotten egg yolks, towards the immense organ of burning wind composed of the glass flasks, test tubes and retorts of the alchemic cathedral belonging to Palinuro, whom I was about to meet, as the concierge told me, around the corner of a cornice or in the drainpipe of shadow which acquired, suddenly, a tempestuous translucency. And so it was; I swear I will never forget it: beneath that light of oily cellophane, in the middle of the room and some way from the window which looked out over the street and the afternoon, was Palinuro, naked from the waist down and from the waist up, prescribing for himself a sit-down bath in an aluminium tub full of vinegar. The pandemonium as we entered was such and so often was that sweetest swaying of Vivaldi's 'Winter' repeated, leaving a creeper of lithe notes hanging in the air, that I had to walk over to the record player and turn it off.

Palinuro stood up, dripping vinegar, put on his patchwork waistcoat, raised an arm in heroic pose, and said: 'Before we go any further, brother, allow me to salute you: Salve! Welcome to this decadent reincarnation of the best-known personalities of the medico-literary species. Welcome, and resign yourself to the idea that you and I will found in our country two unforgettable dynasties of men dedicated to the noble science of medicine, like the Norcini and the Preciani of Norcia and Preci, and thus will our names be linked for ever, like those of our illustrious colleagues and predecessors, St Cosmas and St Damian. And now I suppose I'm going to have to give you an abracadabradizing explanation of why you find me thus, twiddling my dicotyledoneae and taking a bum bath in this purest of vinegar. Do you know something? I got the most tremendous shock when I saw you come in; I thought I was seeing a mirror image of myself. We are identical you know, like a pair of univitelline twins. Or perhaps it would be more accurate to say that you are as I will be and that I am as you were . . .'

He walked over to the table and showed me a skull.

'In fact, exactly what I wrote on the forehead of this brachycephalic "as I see you now, so was I, as you see me so will you be". How ridiculous! Can anybody see themselves when they're dead? Well, she's responsible . . . not the skull, but that girl in the photograph. You see, my friend, the fact is

38

that I'm covered in crab lice, the fatal fleas of the pubes. There are of course cases of lice in the moustache. But I don't let my moustache grow because I'm superstitious: I have thirteen hairs on each side. And you, have you ever suffered from these wretched anoplura of the groin? Have you ever felt them burying themselves in the pores of your private parts and giving you the most damnable itch?'

'Are they a venereal disease?' I asked him.

'Well, not exactly a disease, no. And not exactly venereal, either. When did you ever see a disease with legs? But the fact is, you only get them through sexual relations. You've never had them?'

'Estefania never had anything like that.'

'Who is Estefania?'

'My cousin.'

'But another friend, another cousin . . .'

'Estefania is the only woman I've ever slept with.'

'What's this! This very day you shall enter with me the kingdom of brothels. I've just decided, this very second, to become the hierophant, the mystagogue who will initiate you in the mysteries not only of Medicine, but also of the world of prostitutes. I swear it by Apollo the Healer, by Asclepius, by Hygeia and Panacea!' he shouted, pointing to the oath of Hippocrates hanging on the wall and taking my hand. 'I will lead you through the houses of the sick and through the hospitals overseas. I will teach you the secrets not only of venereal diseases but also of all calamities unforeseen on urinal walls. I will make you learn by heart the four cardinal points of inflammation of Celsus' quadrilateral: redness, swelling, heat and pain. I will initiate you in the art of asideration, brutal death through immersion in freezing water, so that you can kill your creditors with a bucket full of cold water and the crime will never be discovered. I suppose it can also be done with vinegar. Look, touch it. It's freezing, isn't it? And then, to establish gradual links, we will go night-clubbing like the Hyperboreans, from the peak of this night to the oasis of a very distant noon, beyond the frontiers of vice. I should warn you that my *Booziculum Vitae* is most impressive so, after returning nostalgia to sender by regular mail, we will go and drink ourselves into a stupor in Pepe's cantina, where I can not only sign the walls with urine but also certain IOUs which I pay when I get the urge and the money. And then we could go to a seedy nightclub frequented by all our down-and-outs and which we call El Tijuana because there, like the gringo tourist, you can get cheap drinks, a cheap whore and a cheap dose of the clap. Or, if you prefer, we'll go to a brothel which I have named Elysian, or Delysian, Fields, because there the soul and the body receive their just desserts: houris of saffron promised by Mohammed, odalisques with hair long and blue as the Nile. And anyway, I'm good friends with the madame, Doña Amabile. This itching is driving

me crazy, damn it! What do you think of the plan? Any objections?'
'My only objection is that I'm hungry.'
'So am I, you'd better believe it,' said Palinuro and he took off his
waistcoat and put on a shirt and then the patchwork waistcoat on top.
'Look, I told you that this is the friend that I got mixed up with and the
reason I tell you is so that you may learn not to trust your girlfriends and
especially not if they're the type of prostitute who parade around at dawn
on the fringes of the law and of your awareness. You won't believe this,
but during the daytime she was a Cinderella, a cook, who loved me so
much that every time she peeled a carrot she thought of me and when she
diced it she felt the pain herself. Ever since I discovered the lice, a mighty
anger has avariciously seized this viscus, diagonal to Arantius' ligament.
It's easy enough to get rid of the lice, you just spray on DDT powder and
they all fly away, so to speak. But it's the eggs, called nits, which stick to
the hairs and there's no way you can get rid of them. And then, of course,
the baby lice are born and no sooner do they open their eyes than they start
to suck your blood, and so it goes on in a vicious circle. They recommended
that I bathe in vinegar, but it's done no good, the nits continue regardless.
And the worst of all is that for the last three days everything has tasted like
Sanborn's salad: my white coffee, my cornflakes, my rum. And even my
sweat smells of vinegar, my urine smells of vinegar, my saliva smells of
vinegar. I've wept in desperation and of course my eyes burned like hell
because I wept vinegar.' Palinuro doused his cigarette in the bath and then
threw the end out of the window. He grabbed the hand mirror. He looked
at his sad face. Then he looked at his happy face and, filled with joy, he
exclaimed: 'The physician is an actor *par excellence*! Because, if you don't
know how to dissimulate, you'll never be able to put on a happy face
before a patient who is dying of gastric cancer and say to him, 'Of course
you'll recover, you have a very good colour today: yesterday you were
yellow but today you're green! and green is the colour of hope.' Well,
anyway, time to get dressed! Then it'll be your turn to talk about yourself,
to tell me about your life and Estefania's, OK? We'll talk and shine
alternately, like Castor and Pollux. And for that, when the time comes I'll
lend you my waistcoat which has magic properties: when you put it on,
you are invested with eloquence and learning, you become a ventriloquist
of the heart and all your points of view change, as does your outlook on life
and even the way you walk and talk. And don't worry about being hungry:
in Pepe's cantina they will give us some wonderful snacks and some
incredible onions pickled in vinegar. In vinegar? I must be mad!'
'Well, are we never going to leave?'
'I'm going to get dressed this very minute,' he answered and he put on a
sock. 'Yes, indeed, I'm infinitely pleased that you are going to study
medicine because, I repeat, there has never been such a rich and noble

profession as that of the physician. The physician, and the surgeon in particular, combines all professions of the Universe. Although, of course, all physicians are surgeons and vice versa, as Lanfranc said: *Omnis practicus est theoricus, atqui omnis chirurgus est practicus, ergo omnis chirurgus est theoricus.* Crystal clear . . .'

'I didn't understand a word. I don't speak Latin.'

Palinuro threw Lanfranc's book on the floor and sat on the bed.

'You don't have to speak Latin to know *some* things in Latin, or even to make them up. For example: have you heard of the expression *fiat experimentum in corpore vili?*'

'Let the experiment be carried out on something worthless.'

'Very good, very good! But what you haven't heard is a variation that occurred to me: vile bodies experiment in a Fiat (usually in the back seat). Pretty good, huh?' Palinuro walked over to the window and gestured towards the roof tops, the bell tower of the Santa Expiración Church, the silver-crested sky-scrapers. 'Aren't all these buildings and houses magnificent? Could you ever imagine an old School of Medicine with architecture that can be invented at your discretion and adorned with voluptuous obscenities and beskated Atlantes holding aloft the dim lecture halls? Well, that's nothing: the physician, my friend, is the architect of the body who repairs fractures and sprains and creates cupulae and femurs of platinum.'

Palinuro put on his other sock and walked over to a huge trunk standing in one corner, opened it and took out a chequered cap and a pipe. 'Forget Grandfather Francisco's wardrobe. My chest contains treasures which would leave you with your oral sphincter gaping and mumbling medical oaths like "systoles and diastoles!" ' and he put on his cap, jammed his pipe between his teeth and started crawling around the floor. 'The physician, my friend, is the detective . . . the investigator who follows the trail of *rigor mortis*, the inspector who interrogates the cerebral convolutions . . . how dirty this floor is! We must sweep it tomorrow without fail or next week at the latest. Here, I'll also lend you my cap so that you can develop your faculties of observation as did the famous Dr Joseph Bell who served as inspiration to Conan Doyle in creating Sherlock Holmes. I have old books and magazines here: no less than thirty-four issues of the *Lancet*, the *I Ching* and a chamber pot of Aunt Luisa's which still smells of Roger et Gallet.' Palinuro raised his arm and pretended to perfume his armpit. 'Some other day I'll show you everything I keep in here. For now, remind me when we leave that I must take my electromusigrams with me because I want to show them to you as we walk. And also my dirty clothes, to disinfect them in the hospital sterilizer. Here's a pair of underpants that has been here for three months. And socks . . . well, these might just as well go straight into the rubbish: they've got more holes in them than Emmenthal cheese!'

'You must mean Gruyère cheese,' I said to him.

Palinuro snatched his cap off my head, put it on his own, wrinkled his nose and said: 'Emmenthal, my dear Watson . . . and now, on to pastures new: today, book covers are skipping like goats at the smell of fresh grass! You'll never be able to read the whole of this copy of *Malleus Maleficarum* because, look, I hollowed out the centre of all the pages, to keep another little gift from Walter: cannabis from the greenest of all valleys. In other words, marijuana, as its name indicates. But we'll keep that for when we get back. Ah, here are my suits. I only have two actually, but I can always lend them to you whenever you like. This one which, as you see, is of a very nice French blue, I use for weddings and christenings. And the other, black, which I've never worn: I'm keeping it for my funeral which I plan to attend incognito to see how much my friends weep for me.'

'Why talk so much of death?'

'It is death which speaks through my lips; as a medical student, you'll get used to death of the common or garden variety. As Claude Bernard said: *La vie, c'est la mort*. Personally, however, I prefer the attitude of the Divine Marquis who considered death to be one of the most precious laws of nature. Look,' said Palinuro, showing me a toy boat, 'this was the first boat, and the last, that my father built for me. Which leads me on to the thought that the surgeon, my friend, in the operating theatre surrounded by a team of nurses dressed in green and white, is the captain of a ship sailing through a sea of blood and lymph, through cystotomies and trepanations, between Scylla and Charybdis, his face bronzed by the lamps of the operating theatre! To port . . .'

'There's an anaesthetist, doctor . . .'

'To starboard . . .'

'There's a lymphosarcoma, doctor!'

'Very good, *bravo*, you're getting the hang of it! Here, take this,' he said, handing me a roll of papers. 'This is what we're going to take with us. Also a few medical samples which come in useful. By the way, if there's ever anything wrong with you, in this trunk you'll find the medical *Larousse*, the *Larousse Médical de Guerre* which belonged to Uncle Esteban, an old edition of the *Merck Manual* as well as hundreds of medical samples I've collected over the years. One of these days, we can give a banquet and organize a whole week of meditrinals, for our friends and neighbours. Or, if you prefer, we can keep them and then, if ever you have any symptoms: splenomegalia, vascular spiders, itching of the occiput, boutonneuse fever or a cephalalgia, just consult the *Manual* and choose your medicine. I've got all sorts of things here, including amphetamines which act on your diencephalic centres to make you intelligent and capable of great feats of memory. Amphetamines, of course, though pink and heart-shaped, may prevent you from getting an erection . . . but in this trunk you will also find for emergencies, a little yohimbine . . . have you ever tried it?'

'No, what is it . . .?'

'It's an aphrodisiac. Be honest, you don't know anything about anything, do you?'

'Not a lot.'

'Well, all I know is that I haven't eaten yet so let's make a move. And, speaking of anatomy: did you buy the Quiroz book?'

'Yes, it's in my suitcase.'

'You shouldn't have, I already have a copy. Although it does occur to me that we could pawn yours and buy food with the proceeds. It would be an act of symbolic anthropophagy, don't you agree? It would be like eating breaded ears, pituitary-gland tacos and grilled prostates! And, while we're on the subject, well, not exactly the same subject, but never mind: bear in mind that the physician is also the Demiurge who, in the wink of a scissor snip,' Palinuro formed a victory V with his fingers and made as though to snip off his member, 'can change your sex and fashion from your own intestine a velvety and palpitating vagina.' Then, raising his hands to his chest, 'By the same token, the physician is the artist who sculpts breasts and models stomachs. Forget Michelangelo, Canova or Tolsá; like Tagliacozzi, the father of plastic surgery,' and here Palinuro pinched and touched successive parts of his own body as he spoke, 'the physician is a magician who draws forth a lip from your chest, a chest from your elbow, an elbow from your stomach, a stomach from your bum and a bum from your nose . . . no, excuse me, it's the other way round: a nose from your bum. That's quite clear, I take it . . .'

'Yes, yes that's quite clear, thank you.'

Palinuro put on a pair of flowered underpants and held out a book to me. 'While I comb my hair and clean my teeth, I'll leave you this book on post-mortems so you don't get bored.

'I'll also tell you about my first autopsy, which was, of course, on a young and very beautiful girl,' craning his head round the door of the bathroom with his mouth full of froth. 'While you leaf through the book, remember that the physician before the corpse is not only a detective but also an archaeologist of the body . . . the scholar who, in the ruins of your human frame, in the triumphal arch of your pelvis and in the inscriptions of your brain, unearths your entire clinical history and prehistory. Incidentally . . .'

Palinuro walked over to the trunk, took out a photograph and held it up to the light to examine it.

'Speaking of hieroglyphics, I think that the doctor, before an X-ray, is the latter-day Champollion who deciphers the pink stones of the vesicle. Look, what you see here in the photograph is *not*, of course, a vesicle even

43

though it *is* bright yellow. It is my friend Fabricio who is, in fact, very white; the yellowness is due to the developing. Fabricio, who in secret reads the books of Havelock Ellis and the novels of Vargas Vila, has, as you see, the typical appearance of the asthenic: narrow thorax, long legs, prominent nose. And this other object is *not* an arsehole, but my friend Molkas who, in contrast, is a pyknic, the bastard: squat, square, short-necked. He was born during the month of March, the symbol of which, according to the Greeks, is a glass of milk. And so Molkas' fate is linked to milk, as you will find out soon enough. We'll invite both of them to come and get drunk with us.'

At that moment, Estefania, a dove came to rest on the windowsill.

'And this is Palinuro's dove,' said the Palinuro in question. 'For the last few months she has visited me every day and appears to the people I want her to. Through her I send messages of love to my girlfriends, and messages of hate to the concierge. Go along, little dove, fly to Pepe's cantina and tell the general with the glass eye, the lottery-ticket vendor, don Prospero and all our friends that Palinuro is on his way and is going to introduce them to a sensational new friend. A future doctor!'

The dove flew off and disappeared into the distant sky. Palinuro leapt up and then fell to his knees beside me.

'A physician, my brother, is nothing less than the priest bound to honour the secrets of the confessional, to whom you may confess all your unnameable ailments; I confess, doctor, that I had sex with a whore and a white chancre has appeared.' Palinuro smote his breast, '*Mea culpa! Mea culpa!* I confess, doctor, that my period is late, that I have oxyuridae, that I have cysts on my penis, that I am not a virgin, that I have lice . . . Oh my god! I'd forgotten: I have lice . . .! Where are you going?'

'Out, I told you that I'm ravenous and I've had enough of your speeches.'

'Wait for me. Just one more minute, I promise. For the time being, to keep our spirits up, we'll drink what's left of this bottle of VSOP brandy, the initials of which mean, as you know . . . you do know, right?'

'Right.'

'Good, well, in that case, let's keep the secret. Cheers, cheers, kindred spirit!'

'Cheers!' I shouted, hugely happy to have met Palinuro.

Palinuro also got to know you that afternoon, Estefania. Or rather, he started to get to know you. Because you can't imagine what a drinking session we had! We walked along arm-in-arm like school children, swearing like troopers, our heads brimming with orange thoughts. We were so callow then, so fundamentally innocent and Palinuro so very mad! Just imagine, Estefania; he would suddenly stop at a corner and shout at the top of his voice: 'Do you know what chiropompholyx means? Have you seen the *Endomyces albicans* lately? Eh? Answer me! You know damn all, right? And you're the one who wants to be a doctor? Well, you're going to have to start from the letter A of the alphabet!' And I, taking no notice of him whatever, carried on talking to him about you all the way; I revealed to him your eyes, your way of speaking love and the luminous gifts I was to offer you when you came back one day. We passed beneath the windows of the National Press Library which reflected several scenes, including the golden splinters of a poster of the Society of Ornithologists. And we walked along San Ildefonso, and along Justo Sierra and we continued to walk along the streets of the old quarter, determined to discover a sharp-edged mystery in every beggar or in the Relox y Perpetua shoe shop where we chose several pairs of shoes for some future time, including one pair of very modern vintage. Our walk that afternoon was so long, Estefania, so full of the streets and landscapes, that there was no iridescent mosaic or column, cupola or patio inundated with yellow flowers, through which we did not pass. In El Extasis y La Esperanza book shop, we reviewed the ranks of an entire catalogue of celebrities and bought a picture postcard of Nietzsche, another of Girolamo Fracastoro, another of the famous anatomist Guillaume Rondelet, yet another of Ruelas with the huge mosquito burying the barb of its sting into his frontal bone, 'like a nail, like a nail nailed in the forehead', said Palinuro, quoting Efren Rebolledo, and finally a postcard of Fabricius ab Aquapendente to whom the other Fabricio owed something more than just his name. We also bought a 78 record of the voice of Marlene emanating from a eucalyptic tube, we had a look at a few young atlases which demonstrated the greenness of the earth and we walked beneath the sticks of rock of the barbers' shops where the barbers bleached their victims and fixed their hair and their problems with fleet razor strokes. We also bought several prints of Avicenna's deformed skeletons and started to plan, almost reluctantly, without prior agreement, a kidnapping comparable perhaps only to that of Europa but, in this case, instead of 'the renowned robber', said Palinuro, *he*, Palinuro, and me and Fabricio and Molkas would be the perpetrators. 'A twenty-year-old girl?' asked Palinuro, and answered his own question: 'No, she'll have to be younger, young and pure as a selfish lineage, so that we can practise on her all imaginable splints and bandagings, and test all kinds of supernatural germs . . . and very beautiful, like that cousin of yours you were talking about . . . what did you say she was called?' And I continued to talk to him about you, Estefania, I told him that you were a wonderful nurse, an expert in first aid, in second aid and in third. I told him that you had one eye of one colour and the other of the same colour and both were blue as though by prior agreement. I spoke to him of your body, of your thighs. I told him of your nipples coupled with the twin stars of the Dioscuri by threads of invisible saliva and that, when you bathed, I

45

told him, they attained all the prestige and splendour of sailing grapes. And when it suddenly occurred to me that Palinuro might never really meet you, I made the most of the opportunity to pull long-eared hyperboles from my hat and I decided to confront Palinuro with the unknown, with the conductor wire of a catechism which would reveal his inner skin when he removed his mask. What a piss-up that was, Estefania and, in some ways, what a waste of your immanent potential! Because Palinuro wasn't listening to me, although he occasionally knit his brows, took a sip and looked at me as much as to say: 'Don't worry, I'm with you.' Only when I mentioned your eye did I see a fleeting reflection in his own. But when I told him of my vocation for you, when I related my affection for your corners and your methodical fortresses, when I told him that for your sake I was capable of shutting myself up like a compass, in the vault of a mine, in order to shower you in a fountain of ferns and powdered gold, of palm trees and lumps of sugar which would cover you as only my love – my love between the crossbars and the aerostats, between the mobs and the markets – could cover you, I'm sure that he did not hear me; he was mad. 'I've just read Semmelweis' biography by Céline,' he said to me, 'and I'll lend it to you, but first I'm going to act out a few of its scenes for you.' And then, Estefania, as we walked along Cinco de Mayo, he went up to a pair of young lovers and – just imagine! – he begged them, when they had children, to urge the doctor to wash his hands and to remember the story of - Professor Kolletschka whose autopsy, he shouted at them, revealed suppuration and inflammation of the lymph glands, of the pleura, of the pericardium, etc., to such an extent that it seemed that the poor professor was filled with custard. And the same applies, he added, to the tragic death of the bacteriologist Suraisne in *Bodies and Souls* and so we see, said Palinuro to the couple, that not only is literature infected by literature, but infections are also infected by infections; this is what happened to Professor Suraisne when the rotting breast of an old lady with cancer burst in his hands. Beware of lumps in the breast, please, beware . . . and you, young man, if you find that your girlfriend has a lump, take her to see my friend Molkas GPRSVP who is an excellent breastologist. And now, I'm going to show you my electromusigrams, based on a theory of Joseph Struthius, the King of Poland's physician, who studied the pulse and interpreted its rhythm in accordance with the laws of music, based also on Baglioni's *Physico-Psychological Foundation of Musical Aesthetics*,' said Palinuro to the terrorized couple, and unrolled the first electrocardiogram. 'This graph, for example, showing the linked beats caused by digitalis poisoning, has been turned into a romanza for piano. This other one . . .'

Palinuro had scarcely taken the second roll from his pocket, Estefania, when two policemen approached, eyeing us with surgical precision, and we had to take to our heels and run for it and, fortunately, we were able to scramble aboard a moving bus. What a piss-up that was, Estefania, and what a tragedy, because Palinuro dropped several of his electromusigrams on the way!

'My God!' he exclaimed, 'I lost a Tachycardia in D minor and a Thrombosis for percussion in C major! What an irreparable loss!'

We got off two streets further on and Palinuro wanted to go back. I had to hang on to him by the lapel of his jacket.

'Forget it. We'd just be looking for trouble.'

'But don't you realize? How am I going to just let so much work be lost? I've been collecting these electrocardiograms for years and I've been studying them every night to turn them into music! Look, for example . . .'

'Come on, walk faster!'

Palinuro unrolled another electrocardiogram.

'Hang on a minute! How can I show you if you don't stop to look?'

'They're coming, I tell you, walk faster!'

'OK, OK, but just look at them at least,' he begged me and with his index finger he followed the ups and downs of the graph.

'You couldn't get music more modern than this. Schönberg and Stockhausen wouldn't mind getting their hands on this for special occasions. And each person can interpret it as they like, as long as they just follow . . . slow down will you! . . . as long as they just follow the rhythm! I have things that you wouldn't imagine: mitral whispers for wind instruments, pizzicato ventricular fibrillations . . . and this one, for example, is the electrocardiogram of a dead patient and represents a minute of silence, the music of silence of which Maeterlinck and Cage dreamed! And I also have . . .'

'Hey, aren't those the policemen who were following us?'

'Who cares? I have stops for organ and trumpets . . .'

'Run for it, they're the same ones!'

'And anginas in high C from the chest and this is my masterpiece, look . . . wait for me! Oh hell, I've lost my masterpiece! I dropped my requiem Opus One Number 1 which I composed in honour of Mamma Clementina! Hey, get a move on or those bastards'll get us!'

'Into the shopping arcade, quick! Watch the cars!'

'The first movement . . .' shouted my friend, but I couldn't catch the rest.

'The fourth movement, oh, oh, I can't breathe,' he puffed, when we were safely inside a shop, 'is an *allegro molto fortissimo* which is pretty much what I'm feeling just now: oh, oh, a paroxysmal tachycardia! My heart's about to burst! What am I going to do, now that I've lost my Opus Magnum?' he continued in great distress, but presently his eyes lit up, 'a miracle, a miracle, this is a miracle!'

'What . . . you've found it?'

'No, listen, are they still following us?'

'They walked past.'

'When I said it was a miracle I was talking about something else. Do you realize where we are? In a musical-instrument shop. This is kismet, brother, our moira. In other words, fate. Isn't that the damnedest coincidence?'

And so it was, Estefania; we were surrounded by guitars, horns, oboes, trumpets and dulcimers, music books and music stands. Palinuro applauded, wound up a metronome, opened 'Buds and Blossoms' by Gurlitt on a music stand, climbed up on a bench, took a pencil from his breast pocket and, after blowing kisses to the barefoot violas and the newly milked bagpipes, to the bassoons carried away by Weber's adagios, to the winged harps and the designer-clad pianos waiting to be invited to waltz, he said: 'The surgeon, ladies and gentlemen, tac-tac-tac, with his scalpel of steel, swift and slender as Sir Henry Wood's baton, tac-tac, is also the conductor who modulates the cadences of the heart and the alpha rhythm of the brain . . . *ancora più forte*, ladies and gentlemen, *ancora più forte!*'

'Did you want something?' the saleslady asked us.

Palinuro climbed down from the bench, placed a handkerchief between his chin and his shoulder and pretended to play a few notes on an invisible violin, using the pencil as a bow. Then he wiped the sweat from his brow and bowed respectfully: 'Madam, the only thing I want is to inform you that the art of playing the violin is a question purely of guts. Good afternoon,' he said and we walked slowly out of the shop, in true gentlemanly style.

'Did you notice how pretty the saleslady was?' Palinuro asked me, 'I'd love to do a PM on her.' 'A what?' 'Don't you know what PM means?' 'Post meridian?' 'How dumb can you be? . . . PM means *post mortem*, necroscopy, autopsy, to go to Morgagni's house. I should warn you that anyone initiated in the Eleusinian mysteries had to wait at least one year, but not more than five, before being admitted to an Autopsy, in other words, the contemplation of truth. This goddamned itching! And the trouble with biting your nails is that you can't scratch properly. Only then was the novice, crowned with myrtle and after washing his hands and listening to the lectures and laws of Ceres, admitted to the place of shadows which was imminently to be rent by the blinding light of revelation, serving also to illuminate monstrous figures. But, if you're a good boy, I'll initiate you early. Perhaps in a fortnight's time. And then, afterwards, you can learn the ins and outs of the job. Suffice to know, for the time being, that a litre of formol has to be poured into the stomach of the corpse. Samples taken from the left lung are cut in squares; from the right, in triangles. You have to obtain the closest relative's permission if, for some reason, you want to keep the fingers. Finally, you have to stuff the penis with cotton wool and stitch up the foreskin. But that won't be necessary the first time because I will make sure that you get a young and beautiful woman, as did Manuel Acuña, José Asunción Silva and Palinuro. Although I can't promise that she'll be a virgin. The pupils of my eyes, my spoilt darlings, are the only virgins that I know of within a lap around my belly button.'

And we continued on our way, Estefania, and in the pawn shop, among the blue garters of widowed brides and watches and clocks marking the various hours of diuturnity, among the Chippendale chairs and bangles and manila shawls covering the old pianolas with their smell of mangos and crocodiles, we left my Quiroz *Anatomy*, though not without first promising that we would redeem it within two weeks or two centuries. And afterwards we wandered among the crystal fishmongers and greeted the frosted poppies sprouting between the oysters and the crabs splitting their sides with laughter and the iridescent octopuses rotting in the sun and the mamey-pink sweeping machines collecting up the fermenting scales and skeletons. So many streets, Estefania, so many shops did I see that day! There were streets of ostentatious mien where the canopies bowed deep as we passed; streets with silk shops and embankments of captive carpets and cornucopiae spilling over the pavement in showers of naphthalene and waterproofed zephyr! And there were also streets lined with stalls of fruits and vegetables with a life of their own and where the stall-keepers' wives, with breasts the size of time bombs, engaged in bulbous battles, hurling missiles of tired-looking tomatoes, rabbit artichokes and gaping-sugared apples. And then there were the shops which reverberated with spasms of rice and the coalition of corn; shops with cycloramas of luminous liquors; opticians staring out at us with their hundreds of dispersed eyes; ironmongers where wire hatched barbed plots and shops selling bathroom tiles and others selling sportswear and travel agencies lost in Alpine digressions. And again there were streets spreading like fans to the ebb and flow of cars lighting up the atmosphere with their chronological fumes and empty streets dark as soot-stained foreboding, streets and alleys chained to the last century, having forgotten even their own names; streets inundated with streams of foaming ice, streets astounding in the nostalgia with which they bathed our childhood shoes in copper; streets with throngs of dogs which licked the wounds of the trees, and streets and alleys with proclamations raffled off to posterity to win a place of honour in the annals of architecture. And in the Americana gun shop, where a bullet of gigantic calibre kept its forecasts to itself, we spat on the heads of the bison hunted by the Arkansas trappers and, in full view of the stuffed stags' heads entwined in honeysuckle and of a rifle stretching infinitely into legend, Palinuro exclaimed: 'The physician, brother, is not only the hunter of Paul de Kruif's microbes, he is also a soldier of life, Great Knight of the Small Sword, Cobalt-60 bomber pilot bum bum! archer of the antirabies bow and laser gunner rraaatttatarrrat!' And, hearts filled with Vivaldi's 'Winter', that music eternally recommencing, over and over ascending the stairs of the building in Holy Sunday Square to fling itself from the windows and drown in the city's smog, we visited the French chapel and wandered through the suburbs of mirrors and greeted the dancers motionless beneath their domes of glass and the saints dead on their feet. And there were streets which disguised their financial wrinkles with paving stones and pompous hides; terminal streets exuding fly-ridden odours and rubbish bins spilling over with wasted dreams. And, by then, it was not only Palinuro who was mad: I was too, Estefania, with happiness to see that every time we drew back the veil concealing a street, we would find that another followed, and yet another, and so on to infinity, linked by a geographic rhythm which tortured the blood, but unrelated in either merchandise or fable. One might be República de Argentina Street where the women sunned slips and vests on their balconies from Monday to Friday and at weekends hung out their mats to welcome Sunday. Another was República de Guatemala Street with old buildings of hewn volcanic rock, different in that here summer exploded on the pavements and only the odd drunk horizontally blotted the landscape. And as we walked by the bookshops selling law volumes, Palinuro pointed to the windows and exclaimed: 'Look, look at those tomes where the worms shit on the law! Never forget that the physician is the lawyer who saves you from the death sentence for a few years or a few days; therefore, he is also the judge who can prolong your suffering by forcing you to live shut up, indefinitely, in the prison of your own body! . . . *Complete Works* of Lombroso! . . . and that gives me the notion that the physician is also . . . but, ahhhh . . . don't tell anybody this: the physician is also the criminal. Let's go, let's creep out of here on tiptoe, cover your face, so that they don't see us . . . the physician, brother, is also the thief and the assailant. Do you know what dichotomy is?'

'In botany, dichotomy is . . .'

'No, no, no! Dichotomy, in medical jargon, is when you, the general practitioner, refer to a surgeon friend of yours, a patient you have told will have to be operated on for an appendicitis or for an anal fistula, whether it is true or not, that's neither here nor there, telling the patient that physician Z is the best surgeon in the world in that specialist branch. Patient X is operated and survives, or doesn't survive – that's also neither here nor there – and surgeon Z divides the fee with you: that is dichotomy.'

And, as at that particular moment we came abreast of a plumber, Palinuro stopped, asked him the time, asked to borrow his blowtorch and threatened him with it: 'What right have you to call yourself a plumber? The true plumber is the physician, who unstops the drainpipes of the body! With the bone scraper he removes the cottonwool residues from the

50

arteries; with the scalpel, he opens the aorta and removes clots of up to twelve centimetres in length, as you may read in Ody's *Testament of a Surgeon*, if you know how to read anything other than comic strips.'

And in every one of them, in every street: in Capuchinas, in Plateros, in San Ildefonso, in el Carmen, ghost horsemen had been galloping since the times of the Viceroy and ash-strewn rivers flowed beneath the fever of the asphalt and in each house suddenly arose an unexpected castle. And thus we saw streets where the humours of dawn were revealed and fountains of crystal yielded to us the empress's jewels; streets where Dutchmen in blue caps distributed their five-o'clock ice-cream to the beggars; streets got up in their Sunday best; pitiless streets; streets where we learned the arithmetic of the distilleries and the loquacious fluorescence of the public clerks; streets crowded with salubrious civil servants and red magistrates; streets where highly illustrious plots were hatched; streets which flung in our faces the texture of linen shops and the thirst for cards; streets with electromagnets rotting in the mud; and houses, buildings with battle-mented parabolas and windows through which peered prostitutes with eyes dressed with piranha powders; and temples, churches with fortuitous niches and bejewelled chapels, fountains of lofty sparkle, lacerated obelisks and foaming arcades. And shops and more shops, stores, snack bars, grocers, haberdashers, herb shops, butchers stacking their purples right at the mouth of the sewers, and furriers, shops selling ex-votos and paraffins, off-licences, restaurants, taverns, police stations and post offices; what a drinking session that was, Estefania! And suddenly, just like that, we found ourselves at Pepe's cantina.

Palinuro placed his hand on my shoulder. 'One moment. I have to tell you something very important: first and above all else, the physician, take note, is the satrap, the dictator *par excellence*: Stick out your tongue! Undress! Close your eyes! Say Ah! Nobody in this world dares to disobey such orders. Not even the pope can refuse a prostate examination! And now, brother, to drink!'

'Cheers, cheers, gentlemen,' exclaimed the general with the glass eye.

'To beer or not to beer!' replied Palinuro, raising a tankard of beer in the Statue of Liberty stance.

What a piss-up that was, Estefania, that afternoon on which I walked through the boiling springs of mythology in the warmth of an alcoholic rite consummated with Palinuro, the general with the glass eye, don Prospero and so many other friends! Palinuro was quite right: Pepe's cantina was as a temple where the glasses, flung into a vacuum, could circumnavigate the world a millimetre above the salt of the sea and come straight back, brimming with the clinking of suns and tongues peeking over the glass edges, red with premonitions. Exaggeration, which knew no bounds, flashed momentarily from bottle-necks and spilled on to the table-cloths while I tried to take them all by the hand and lead them to the very entrance of your luminous triangles. And so successful were my efforts to outdo myself in cosmographing your favours and your hair, your way of making love and of removing your bra and panties that our friends, fully convinced, fell over each other in expressing their admiration. But it was useless: Palinuro refused to lend me his patchwork waistcoat and everybody was so drunk . . . suffice it to say that every time the general came back from the bathroom he would ask: 'May I attach myself to your group, gentlemen?' and Palinuro would answer: 'Of course, we appoint you our military attaché!' and the general would laugh until he cried and had to remove his glass eye and rub it dry on the golden braid of his sleeve. And just once, when he was tired of talking of revolutions, rifles, the lottery and the student movement and seeing me so quiet and alone, the general asked me: 'And tell me, this beautiful girl you say is called Estefania, how old is she?' and when I was about to say 'Twenty, general,' Palinuro got in ahead of me: 'As old as you please, general,' and when, half an hour later, the lottery-ticket vendor, out of politeness, asked me what your skin was like, Estefania, and I was about to answer: 'Soft and tanned by the sun,' Palinuro exclaimed: 'Like the skin of a female elephant in the eyes of the male elephant,' Estefania, and his audacious rhetoric moved every flashing fibre of the assembled company. And when, many hours later, don Prospero asked me: 'And what colour are Estefania's eyes?' and I was going to say 'Blue,' Palinuro, who hadn't listened to a single word of all I had told him about you, expressed the opinion: 'I think they are brown,' and a wave of protest arose on which we tossed for a long while, splashed by the foam of the beer. 'They're blue,' I shouted. 'They're doe blue.' 'I've never seen a blue doe,' the lottery-ticket vendor ventured to remark, taken aback. 'Neither have I. What I mean is that if does were blue, they would be exactly that blue and no other.' 'Gentlemen!' exclaimed the general, 'this calls for a bottle of cider!' and so it was, Estefania, the cider arrived, we poured it into glasses and the bubbles rose through the opal-coloured sky and they raffled some roast chickens and we won them because we bought all the tickets, and several of the locals joined us and among them an organ grinder and a little old lady who sold cloth dolls to fathers with bad consciences and the general bought one for each of us and called them all Estefania: Estefania I, Estefania II, Estefania III, Estefania the Mad and Estefania the Prognathous. The time came for the cantina to close, Pepe offered us several rounds on the house and Palinuro started to distribute symptoms and medication to all and sundry. The lottery-ticket vendor got an allergy and an antithistamine. The waiter, genital herpes and a jar of camphorated oil. Don Prospero, a migraine halfway across his skull corresponding to the sad half of his body and some codeine citrate tablets. And, as for the general with the glass eye, my friend pointed to him and said: 'Artificial organs also become diseased! Surely you have heard of the termite which reduces wooden legs to dust?' and to him he allocated smallpox of the windscreen and a solution of boric acid in which to soak his glass eye overnight. When everybody asked Palinuro how much they owed him, my friend predictably answered: 'Nothing! The consultation and the medication are free. But, if it makes you feel better, you can pay our bill!' for which he won a round of applause. And when at last everybody was hanging on my lips, when at last the kindled air swept every nook of your body and everybody clamoured to know what you were like, Estefania, I was so tired and so drunk that I could no longer tell them about you. But I swore that I would return to the cantina ('Within a week,' insisted the general) to relate to them your life and your miracles ('Specially the miracles,' the lottery-ticket vendor begged me). And, meanwhile, I resolved to read and re-read every book of art and philosophy that I could get my hands on: the *Complete Works* of Hrabanus Maurus and Hegel's *Philosophy of Art*. To go over the *Works of Love* by Kierkegaard. To work through the *History of the Carolingian Renaissance* and the same with Croce's *Aesthetics as Science of Expression*. To buy Ruskin's *Seven Lamps of Architecture* and Arnold's *Literature and Dogma* and to borrow from Walter the works of Eric de Auxerre, Bentham, Hobbes and Clement of Alexandria, that I might describe you, my beloved and wondrous cousin, in a way that nobody on this earth would ever forget. At last the cider swept the cantina like a storm. Don Prospero said: 'By your leave, gentlemen,' and we gave him leave. The old lady selling the rag dolls tumbled down an unexpected slope and disappeared into the depths of a cauliflower. And the rest of us left the cantina, in a group, our shoulders thick with the flaky residue of a night of carousing. The scents of the street were uncorked with a roar of war and a dawn of bitter lemons settled lightly on the shoulders of the statues and on the amber of the tramlines and on the tall spires of the churches and on the telephone wires crusted with droppings over which was seeping the superfluous vapour of dawn in which we were rapidly becoming dissolved. We left the lottery-ticket vendor happily engaged in making boats of paper to launch in the gutters which, in brief seconds, swallowed a fortune in yachts and safaris. A newly declared astronomer remained behind at the junction of República del Brazil and Justo Sierra, studying the configurations of the sky. The organ-grinder took his leave of us beside some blocks of dry ice conglomerating their dancing spirits on the pavement. The general accompanied us for a good distance, drank in great draughts of morning, insulted the gargoyles which spat dribbling hailstones at him and finally came to a halt before a non-existent object. 'Estefania, Estefania, at last I have the immense pleasure of meeting you,' he said, removing his cap and then, as he bowed, he fell flat on his face. His glass eye stared up at him from the grass. 'Get up, general,' we said to him, 'remember West Point and your flight over Africa when, through a spyglass, you tracked the movements of the Desert Fox!' But this proved counter-productive because he immediately surmised that he was among the cembals and clarions of a battle and started to wriggle along the ground, squashing the beetles in his path. At the corner, he decorated himself with dung. We left him, after picking up his eye and pocketing it for safe-keeping, fully persuaded that we were students of the House of Troy wandering the streets of Salamanca and Santiago de Compostela, wrapped in our gowns and, top hats in hand, we fanned the air and bade him farewell: 'Long live literature! Long live Galicia! Down with the French Revolution!' Only Palinuro and I were left, and you, Estefania, walking before us, invisible among the dogs with spotted sickness and the dispossessed latrines, to the old house in Holy Sunday Square.

'Shhhh! Don't make any noise, the concierge will come out and kick up a fuss. She doesn't get up until half-past six, the lazy old slug. Turn on the light, it's too dark to see properly yet! The concierge is the physician. Sorry, no, the physician is the concierge. The concierge of the body! The bulb's gone again. Or rather, it's *still* gone. Don't trip. There are sixteen steps per floor. The doctor bars the way to butter and tobacco and lets proteins and vitamin pills in! Hey, are we having an earthquake or am I dizzy? On this floor lives a mean bureaucrat. The physician is the bureaucrat. Come on, come on! These stairs seem to get longer every time. Why don't we move down to the second floor, next door to the postman? Of course, I've always said the physician is the postman who brings us good news and bad, who tells us, hic! that we're going to have a baby, careful, shhhh! I told you not to make any noise! or who tells us: Mr Palinuro, you have very little blood in your alcohol stream. Come on, don't sit down on the stairs, give me your hand. But, I'd never move to the third floor, because a policeman lives there and I get the distinct impression that he doesn't care for me. Courage, there's only thirty-two steps to go! Shall we go up two at a time? Basically, he's jealous because he knows that the physician is the policeman of the body: he guards it, curtails its freedom, shuts it up and tortures it, hic! It is a well-known fact that no torture, ancient or modern, from the rack to electric shocks to the testicles, shit! and kicks in the shins, look where you're going will you! can be compared to the torment and physical abuse inflicted (inflincted?) by the physician with his electric shocks, his curved needles, scalpels, purges, amputations, saws, enemas and mandrins. The torture scenes painted by Bouts and Lochner, by Tempesta and Pomarancio, are nothing compared to the amputations performed by Lloyd, Liston and Farabeuf. The doctor is a drunk . . . I'm talking about the one who lives here on the fourth floor. Come on, keep up with me, only ten more steps. Lend me your key. Forget it, here's mine. So, hic! to be a physician, as I've always maintained, is better than being an engineer, public accountant, communication-science graduate, operator of the mechanical hares at the greyhound track or better even than being an expert on coprolites . . .'

'Coprolites?'

'Don't you know what a coprolite is? It's . . . well, it's fossilized excreta, like what the concierge's cat did next to the front door a week ago . . .! Turn on the light. No, on second thoughts, turn it off, I want to see the sky. But it's daylight already! Hic! Promise me that if I don't get rid of the hiccups you won't let them do a bilateral phrenecotomy on me. Swear? Close the door and come over here . . .' Palinuro went over to the window and threw it wide open: 'You and I will go out into the world . . . into the world, listen well, curing and alleviating the suffering of men with illnesses resulting precisely from their jobs or professions: cancer of the scrotum of chimney sweeps, snow blindness of mountain guides . . . Please can you get my old gastroscope out of my trunk,' said Palinuro and he raised his hands to his throat and continued: 'carbon sulphide poisoning of rubber-factory workers and lead poisoning of typesetters!'

'Aniline poisoning of dye-factory workers,' I said, bending double and clutching my stomach.

'Just look how beautiful, the morning star! No, that's not it, it's a long tube, like a telescope,' Palinuro instructed me and he dropped his hands to his chest, 'athletes' heart of football players!'

'Is this it?'

'Yes that's it, thank you, give it to me.'

'Silicosis of miners . . .' I said and started coughing.

'Knife grinders' phthisis,' added Palinuro and we coughed in chorus. Then he gazed at the sky through his gastroscope.

'I never imagined that there were so many illnesses,' I said to him.

'Neither did I,' he admitted. 'You sure we're not making them up? Listen . . . do you know what's going through my mind at this particular moment? That the physician is the astronomer of the body! He's the wise man who observes the nebulae of the bronchial tubes and the spots on the solar plexus! The physician, can you believe? is the discoverer of the black holes of the blind intestine and the Milky Ways flowing from the breasts of women who have recently given birth . . .'

Palinuro sat on the edge of the bed, holding his head in his hands.

'I'm sorry, I could carry on all night with these wonderful comparisons but I'm very drunk and I can't keep my eyes open a moment longer . . . good-night,' said my friend as he lay down and closed his eyes.

'Don't you want to get undressed?' I asked him, but got no reply.

I walked over and took off his shoes and his socks.

'A physician, when he works as an anaesthetist,' I said to him, putting a sock over his face, 'is the Virgil who leads you through the waters of Lethe . . .'

And Palinuro, Estefania, descended into the nether regions.

4

A *few words about Estefania*

Pure, innocent, fearless, as though there had never been anything between us, as though we had never done all those things that would have made our grandparents turn in their graves had they known and which, in fact, caused them to turn fifty-two times in a year: not in the grave, but on the wall when Estefania, one Saturday, turned their pictures so that they would never again see us making love at weekends. My cousin was like that.

And beautiful too, and angelic, and pale.

And as though that were not enough, or nothing. As though her huge eyes, open wide as if in perpetual amazement at her own beauty, were not enough.

As though her cheeks, flushing eternally in shame at having always, since infancy, carried a skull within them, were not enough.

Nothing her two hands, born to caress me.

And not enough her five senses, her twenty years, her thirty-three vertebrae, her hundred thousand hairs, her million cells and her trillion atoms.

Or, in a word, her body.

That body which I loved and knew so well that today I could sculpt it, from memory and with my tongue, in a block of salt.

As though all this were nothing, my cousin Estefania, my cousin consummate and sleek, my cousin pure and shining, the bitch, would sit motionless by the window beneath her portrait, contradictory as a petrified hurricane, as though gelatine of stone flowed through her veins.

Then again, pure and chaste, immaculate as a rice-paper promise, blameless as a whirlpool of white owls.

And still, too, distant but distinct, as though she had been buried alive in a prism of mist.

Thus was my cousin, thus beside the window, her gaze sometimes following the course of the sun throughout a whole afternoon, as though her eyes were filled with heliotropes, the slut.

And, particularly, as though nothing had ever happened, as though we hadn't made love, as though we didn't even know each other, as though I were a poor lowly mortal and an outcast, a slave, a wretch, half a man, and she, my cousin, a goddess. And, above all else, faultless, inimitable and without stain, like the God of St Anselm, of Leibniz and of Spinoza, like the God of Scotus Erigena who it was better to love than to know, like an infant creature whose elemental qualities included that of a necessary and perfect existence.

So much so, gentlemen, I said to the general with the glass eye, the lottery-ticket vendor, don Prospero and all the other friends when I returned to the cantina to fulfil my promise, so much so, that I could speak of Estefania as Clement of Alexandria, Dionysius the Pseudo-Areopagite and Maimonides spoke of God, and, in the interests of shortening my description of her, I could use the Negative way to relate to you, on the road to essential darkness, all that she never was, over and above being classic, admirable and unique.

Estefania, gentlemen, never had black eyes, orange skin or a golden belly.

Estefania never measured one metre seventy-five centimetres in height, forty-three sacred beetles in width or twenty emeralds in depth.

Estefania was not a telephone, an acrostic or a marzipan mute. Estefania never got fat from the waist down like an hourglass through which trickle half the cereals, appetites and days.

In other words, among this race of bandits and wooden fruits in the midst of which her childhood unfurled like a river of paper streamers, Estefania was never a southern Sargasso, the sound of spray or an unravelled suspicion.

Estefania, of course, was my cousin. Estefania's age, at least for most of her life, was seven thousand days, which revolved around her like the chipped white horses and swans of a merry-go-round. Estefania went to an English school in Mexico City and Estefania, although she held a privileged place in the caparison of flowers and had received, as an advance gift for all the Christmases of her life, a whole range of innumerable beauties which I am about to enumerate to you, of which her laughter-curled lashes and her tongue of sharp red lacquer were not the least; none the less, Estefania was a human being with her full share of human limitations and never had either more or less than the full complement of organs, viscera and members belonging to any whole, normal, pale, pure and virginal woman.

For this reason, I cannot tell you of my cousin's ten sow's teats or of Estefania's half eyelash.

Of her two hundred shark teeth or of her two thousand tree navels.

And neither can I describe to you her single buttock, her luminous buttock, her buttock-moon delight of one hundred poets, her buttock rounded and white as half a crystal ball to tell the fortune of the coldest half of the night.

Likewise, for this reason, and throughout my whole description of Estefania, you will tire – I myself never tire – of hearing of the identical number of arms, breasts, clitorises and bellies belonging to Estefania, with the identical names they always had – hair, hair; ribs, ribs; lips, unpolluted and sweet-winged beings floating among the white cirrus-cloud lips. Because while it is true that I did once place myself inside a year, between two mad Februaries, and kiss the moist nipple of her right forgetfulness and see myself reflected in her blue triumphs, it was possible only because, just once, her breasts were called forgetfulnesses, her thighs Februaries, and her eyes triumphs. For the rest, the names I gave to the various parts of her body changed many times; so many, in fact, that I rarely remember, for example, the true name of her sex. And since they themselves interchanged their old and new names, who knows, who will ever know, gentlemen, whether my not remembering isn't actually a triumph, or whether to remember would be to forget; the fact of the matter, finally, is that the name of her sex, in brackets, was always on the tip of my tongue.

But if anybody should be put in brackets – in a house of glass, in a fish bowl of snake eyes, in a drop of dried sperm – it is Estefania herself, so that you, gentlemen, might dwell upon the essential substance of my cousin's beauty. And, for this purpose, she must be set apart from the world, apart from all that which never was, because my cousin, apart from being sublime and deserving admiration and, above all, unattainable and stainless, delicately wrought and tranquil, trollop that she was, apart from having a star between one eyebrow and the other and apart from the tamed galaxies which dogged her steps and licked her heels, Estefania was never of the night, she did not rain on the harvests of bread and was never a market woman with the radiance of a sprig of parsley between her teeth. And, while it is true that within her body – whether for instance, her mouth or her nipples – might always be found a cherry-coloured alternative or a scarlet exception; and while it is true that in the nape of her neck on which I had showered my blessings and in every rounded centimetre of her skin and in her obsessive seeking of discord between her second teeth and her milk teeth and in her way of pointing to the birds as if, half-wit that she was, she knew that they would eventually come and perch on her index finger, and in her way of casting dice on the green baize of Las Vegas as if, day-dreamer that she was, she expected their corners to be worn away to become snowballs of citron blossom; while it is true that in this and in all else Estefania was unique and marvellous, adorable and above all spotless, hypocrite that she was and, while I must admit that Estefania's eyes, in generosity as in pretence, bore a certain musical resemblance to a marine scene in which the beaches, the steamships and the seafronts bathed in mouthfuls of saliva gaze upon a captain standing high on the bridge of a ship and tearing a calendar leaf from leaf.

You will think, then, that Estefania was perhaps an ancient crone, a fruit map or a surprising obligation: and you should know that, in spite of certain distractions of wine and of blood which plotted to draw towards evening in her lips; in spite of her distant travels under and over the months, by way of Venice and of my arms, which transfixed her in mirrors of silk and surrounded her with green amnesias; in spite of everything, I repeat, she was never the chaste death of a flag, the defenceless mask of a tree or one of those cork and goldleaf landscapes with the captain flinging himself into the sea and duly featuring snow-covered islands, pirate attacks, the captain's winged head and the illusion of pale tropical nights.

Moreover, among other things and like the nymph Eucharis with whom Telemachus fell in love, and like Anaxarete, the most beautiful and insensitive maiden transformed by Venus into a block of stone, Estefania was indeed a woman of overwhelming beauty, a being removed beyond any geometric hierarchy, beyond all mortal splendour, all vitreous tongues but, none the less, this side of the stars. In short, always tall and thin, with love disarmed and clasped to her breasts as in a painting by Watteau, beautiful as *Heresy* described by Winckelmann or as Wiertz's *Belle Rosine* naked and gazing at a hanging skeleton, mysterious as Berenice and Ligeia, and with her name, Estefania, written on her forehead and her gown amethyst among the amaryllis, Estefania was a being in whom it was possible always to see yourself as a whole, as cousin and friend, as admirer and lover, and rekindle yourself daily from a flame of omen.

Apart from the fact, of course, that her perfection never had anything to do with what she was in reality, in this world, in Holy Sunday Square and in our room, because, close up and viewed in the light of her death and of her will, sitting by the window with a story of the *Illustrious Navigators* on her knees, its pages open to the wind, billowing white as a ship's sails, Estefania was full of imperfections:

She sometimes squinted a little and had athlete's foot.

She never read a poem through to the end.

On Mondays she awoke with bad breath.

And on Sundays, like Vishnu in the sea of chaos, like the woman in Anacreon's poem, my lust would leave her body swollen and her eyes gummed with sleep.

And, as though that were not enough, I have to confess that my cousin was also full of blinding and magical asymmetries. We won't even bother to go into those that are common to all mortals:

The rose-hued right bronchial was shorter, broader and straighter than the left one.

The light-blue, left kidney was longer and narrower.

And the right, translucent, luke-warm renal artery was longer than the left.

Meanwhile, the spongy, airy, right lung was larger than the left lung and, at the same time, two or three centimetres shorter.

This is no small thing.

And neither were other minor imperfections common to us all: a more muscled calf, a slightly shorter leg, an infinitesimally drooping eyelid. No. The worst of the matter was that the asymmetries of my cousin transcended her body to include the whole of her, because her days were never the same: she had good Thursdays and bad Thursdays, widowed days as did Apollinaire and Fridays as bloody and slow as funeral processions. She had Septembers bursting with glittering talismans and Septembers rainy and horrible. She had, at times, a look which was more intelligent than the same look five minutes previously.

She was sleepy and cold and flu-ridden.

She had a more sweetly perfumed ear, a more caressing hand, a more thoughtless arm and a sweeter clitoris.

Finally, one of her thighs was always warmer and more thickly coated with saliva than the other.

Of her two nipples, the other was always rounder and harder.

And of her two buttocks, both were always colder.

But, even so, my cousin, my admirable and stainless and celestial cousin, was perfect; perfect because she was an angel without trace of limitation other than her mere substance; perfect because her ideas – her long and shining ideas which she allowed to grow apace with her blonde hair – were as her divine essence; perfect because she was the first, the only, the ultimate representative of the species of Estefanids and, particularly, because she was the finest and brightest, the most delicate and alphic of its representatives.

And this may be attributed, principally, to the simple reason that my cousin was identical only to herself, faithful to her mirror of everyday: so much so, so eternally identical to herself, that one day I got up at seven o'clock and sat down in the winged chair, picked up the newspaper and made a hole in it to spy on Estefania and, while she thought I was immersed in other worlds – in the mud and misery of the slums of Netzahualcoyotl or in Vietnam bearing the brunt of gelatinous crimes – I watched my cousin in the middle of the carpet patterned with squares of orange and magenta, magenta and reds, reds and blues, as she thought, wrote, chewed the eraser on the pencil, screwed sheets of paper into balls, innocent as always, innocent and tranquil and docile, kneeling on the rug, submissive and almost without petulance, as though acknowledging her own contours and the fragility of her atmospheres. I didn't want to interrupt her; I folded the newspaper down the middle of the Angel of Independence logo, tip-toed over to the wardrobe, dressed soundlessly and returned to my seat and, while I smoked and blew Saturn rings which circled her nipples, she, who always strove vainly to write poems and on occasion was wont to scribble them on menus, on tram tickets, in the margins of clinical records of dyspneas, on newspapers across Khrushchev's bald pate – just as the amanuenses of the Prophet took down the Koran on the scapulae of camels, the bark of trees, the wings of birds and the thighs of odalisques – then, at that moment, my cousin bethought herself of the necessary plagiarisms recommended by Eliot and said to me – as she dislodged with her brush a shower of golden isotopes clinging to her hair – that the visions and angels appearing to Rilke and Desnos sometimes led her to conceive of immaculate passages: 'Winter is a salamander, morning rose like a heron,' she exclaimed by way of example, with the undeserved naturalness of Aunt Luisa pronouncing French as though she wanted to learn it. Again I said nothing and left the house. I found her in the park at about eleven o'clock and I saw that, in effect, she was identical to herself, identical to her portrait beneath a tree, seated as she was, beneath a shaggy ahuehuete tree, rising, scratching her nose with the nail of her little finger, tearing the pages into tiny, peck-sized scraps which she put in the beaks of the thrushes and the tanagers who came all the way from Peru to pay her a visit. In the distance could be heard the tinkling of an ice-cream vendor. I pretended to be a gentleman dressed in black, with an umbrella and the beard of an archimandrite, so as not to disturb her. I saw her again in the afternoon, in the advertising agency, transformed from four to five o'clock into the queen of the Max Factor Festival: Red Romance for going to the ice rink with friends, Frosted Pink for going to the drive-in cinema to neck and eat hot-dogs and Sonatas in Purple, variations for resplendent frenzies embracing all shades of red, crimson, scarlet and granate and which usually ended up in bed. From five to six, Estefania, dressed as a white cowgirl, posed in the middle of the salt desert of Arizona and declared her love for a Standard Oil petrol pump with an excessively long rubber penis and the promise of a burnished, green-blooded tiger. I left there and, to kill time, went to the Alameda Hotel bar and had several Tom Collinses and fifteen minutes later I felt two hours and six cherries younger and when I returned home, as was to be expected, I found Estefania on the same carpet and in the same position, as if she hadn't moved all day, surrounded by medical books illustrating some of the more florid aspects of life. Estefania took hold of my penis and greeted it: 'How do you do, sir,' but my penis did not deign to show the courtesy that Estefania expected and, the fact is, she was always like that: ever faithful and unchanging for the tanagers, the false-hearted, for the advertisements, the hypocrite, for love and books, the bitch, in spite, as I have said, of her defects.

In spite, for example, of the fact that I had never seen anybody with so many moles and marks on their lily-white, satin-smooth skin at any one time.

Not just an inoculation scar on her arm, the size of a cameo.

A beauty spot on her thigh in the shape of a reliquary surrounding a demonstration of blonde hairs.

On her stomach, a souvenir of a burst appendix and the traces of rabies shots.

And on her head the birthmark of unknown colour growing beneath her hair, hidden like the face of a virgin in the depths of a patera and which only Uncle Esteban, Aunt Lucrecia and Estefania's hairdresser had ever seen, or suspected, and possibly don Prospero, who, when he reached the letter C in the encyclopaedia, had discovered craniology and discovered also, on my cousin's head, the protuberance of ideality.

But, on her nose and cheeks, my cousin also had archipelagos of freckles which might have been caused by the impact of bubbles of champagne and which, maintained Uncle Esteban – because he adored them and because he adored Estefania and drank her tears from a thimble of ivory – added sparkle to her fizziognomy. And also on her shoulders, those shoulders like blue dunes, caressed by scorching Levantine winds, and from which grew, like scattered vegetation from desert sand, single golden hairs tasting of apricot. And when my cousin sunbathed, whether in Acupulco, in the YMCA or in Walter's house in Cuernavaca where she lay naked on the lawn framed in passion flowers and plumbago, her freckles appeared to emigrate from her shoulders and congregate on her back, forming adventitious continents like shadows of butterflies hovering with out-spread wings a few centimetres from her skin.

The skin of that back of hers, aflame, which forgot its name, its morals and its good intentions as soon as it started to mount distracted and interminably over her buttocks.

The skin of that back of hers, traversed in all its length and all its sweetness by a mountain range of shivers which might be read with a single finger like the Braille alphabet until it reached the puritanical springboard of the coccyx from whence it could take a dip in search of greater misdemeanours, dark plankton and tiny peristaltic stars.

And this is not just talk for talk's sake, since the love that Estefania and I had for each other, and not only because we loved each other but because we loved our love, led us into all possible encounters: naked, sweating, with blood open to the breath of wings and, during the minutes passing between a trip to the cinema and the hours at a time that Estefania spent adorning her breasts, while on high the moon swelled up in envy like a Dutch sponge, we explored all the orifices born of heaven, both to Estefania and to her cousin, the moon.

Once I ejaculated between my cousin's legs and smeared my sperm on her thighs, her knees and her frothy pubes.

With my tongue I managed to spread the last drops right to the brim of her belly button full of fluff and spinning remorse.

Fifteen minutes later, I came on her back and with my semen anointed the nape of her neck, her goose-flesh armpits, her shoulders and the warm foothills of her breasts and, two hours later – and an eternity of kisses, caresses and sexual machinations later – Estefania masturbated me with her feet and, after salving with my semen the rough and the smooth of the soles of her feet, the impressions of all her walks through the city and the unshod future of roses, I rubbed my sperm between her crooked toes, over her solid calves and into the hollow behind her knees furrowed by winged shadows and invisible wrinkles.

Soon there was not a single centimetre of Estefania's skin left.

A single hairless valley.

A single glandular junction.

Protuberance or hollow, heel or avid brow that I have not smeared with my sperm.

As though my sperm were the milk of an Egyptian ass, onyx pomade, mother-of-pearl tincture or a whale-gland beauty cream which would penetrate and fertilize all Estefania's skin.

And so my cousin remained, taut and white as a fibreglass angel, as starched and niveous as if she had just emerged from a hospital laundry.

And as though pregnant, poor girl, a million times at once: once for each of her pores, once for each of my spermatozoa.

But this illusion of having an infinity of children did not last long because on her neck and on her stomach, there began to appear a purple rash which, like her freckles formerly, started to gather into consortia of rubies and, when the itching and the rash spread over her face and arms, I had no alternative but to don a top hat of ebony brilliance, crown my cousin with a diadem of orange blossom and carry her in my arms to the bath tub, as the grooms of old carried their brides, to give her a *bain-marie* which was to leave her, by dint of steam and delirium, rinses and colophonies, not ineffable, not pure, not innocent, but purely and simply and marvellously smooth and precise.

Because, not for a single instant, a single ten thousandth of an instant or a single ten millionth of an angel did she cease to be innocent, pure and ineffable as may be testified by the mirrors of her soul: her eyes, those blue eyes composed of an infinity of particles which, Mr General, Mr Lottery Ticket Vendor, just as the homoiomeriae of Anaxagoras contained the seeds of all existing things, so her eyes held the semen of all my future poems and writings.

The poems I wrote about her in the hospitals, in her coif and mallow-coloured uniform, like the nurses at St Thomas's Hospital.

The novels I swore to write about her, while I squandered my most

64

precious life in the Advertising Agency, tightrope-walking a Dacron thread and gargling with ginger ale.

And also the tragedies that came to mind, about Palinuro on the stairs, the masked balls with Scaramouch and Colombine.

All was preordained in those numberless particles which imbued every glance of hers with the vital energy of Restif de la Bretonne's intellectual magnetic fluid, of Teilhard de Chardin's noösphere.

All was destined and written in the millions of monads, blue as Reich's indium, palpitating in my cousin's eyes like windows open on the world, each reflecting the universe from its own finite point of view and each aware of how infinite its reflection.

And when I say that my cousin's eyes – those eyes which were created to perceive and to be perceived, sometimes by me, perhaps by you and always by God – contained the semen of my poems and writings – I speak, of course, ladies and gentlemen, in allegory, because the only semen that her eyes ever really contained – and that only once – was on an afternoon when she asked me to come in one of her nostrils, one of those divine and inimitable orifices, dark tunnels leading out into the opaline light of her olfactory stars.

I chose the left nostril, the one with which Estefania was best able to inhale the foetor of toilets and the aroma of roses.

I remember how, when I finished, a cloudy liquid cloaked her eyes for a few seconds, dense and translucent, as though the eyelids of a surreptitious snake had grown beneath my cousin's own prodigious eyelids.

Within five minutes, my poor cousin, my perverse cousin, started to complain of irritation in her lachrymal caruncles and weep thick, white tears which solidified halfway down her cheeks, while snot dribbled non-stop from her right nostril, nacreous as bird's-nest soup or glue of emeralds.

That night she dreamt that I had fertilized an unknown gland in her brain and that, like Jupiter, a child was growing in her head, to which she would have to give birth with a toothache beyond all imagination: the child was Pallas Athene, she of eyes which were white, but not so bright, certainly not so blue, as the eyes of my cousin when she visited her patients in the hospital or when her clients visited her in the Imaginary Islands.

Ah, you should have seen her then, in the ad agencies, bathed in slogans like the beast of poetic fame, cheeks flushed by Eastern's aeroplanes and languishing under an excess of cocoa. Ah, you should have seen Estefania through the eyes of her patients in the hospital where my cousin was holier than Bernadette, the nurse of the Franco-Prussian war. It is easy for me to say that Estefania was as beautiful as Mahamaya, mother of Buddha, or as Psyche who captivated love itself. But which of you even knew Kali, she who was beauty *par antonomasie*? Who ever saw Iris Chrysopterus

65

swabbing the throats of diphtheria patients in the General Hospital? Or Gerd, daughter of the giant Gymir, or Princess Draupadi, whose hand was sought by a thousand kings, who ever saw them squeezing their patients' boils with bare hands to remove the root as Sister Angela and Estefania did? Which of all these goddesses was like Estefania the nurse: tall and slim, sublime and bright, and expert in draining pus and puncturing excrescences of the ilium.

Her patients, who knew nothing of Jean Lorrain's *Princesses of Snow and Ivory*, who had never heard of Clorinda, of Zephyr, of Madame Baudelaire beautiful as a dream of stone, adored Estefania in all simplicity when each morning she would come to their beds to wish them good morning and take their temperature, empty their bedpans and their accumulations of phlegm and, if she had the time and the inclination – Estefania always made sure she had both – she would read aloud the sports and crime pages of the newspapers to the patients who could not read, in the bright, clipped tones of a Radio Moscow broadcaster and, for the patients who could not write, she would pen, in a hand as tall, luminous and slim as Estefania herself and with spelling so faultless it seemed false, their letters, their *adieux* to life or to the trees and, often, declarations of love to herself and poems describing or writing about a cousin such as she, an Estefania who was born, like a written page, full of rounded paragraphs and sentences scented with sandalwood and menstruation; full of asterisks, in her eyes, proudly referring to her sex, and of hyphens which divided our love into two complete chapters: afternoon and morning, morning and night, night and bells, bells and clouds, clouds and swords.

Hence, it would be pointless for me to tell them that Estefania's legs were longer than Rita Hayworth's and that her lips were more sensual than Sophia Loren's. Or even that my cousin, no longer in the hospital where she was so radiant and neat, so extraordinary and yet so classic, but Estefania in slippers in the kitchen, severing the interstices of a ham and surrounded by dirty dishes, devastated plums and pheasant peels, was more beautiful than Greta Garbo in *Camille*, or Marlene Dietrich in *The Blue Angel*.

First, because Estefania hated such comparisons which she knew to be a betrayal of herself, in that she always sought to be the only owner of her body including her arms, her hair, the apogee between her legs and other grey splendours, although, or perhaps not although but precisely because, like any other human being, she knew that she was insignificant and limited, and that, when all was said and done, all her hair would barely suffice to make a wig for Marilyn Monroe and her pubes a blonde moustache for Emiliano Zapata; that the skin of her body would scarcely be sufficient to cover a statue of Brigitte Bardot and the skin of her breasts to make me a pair of gloves; that of her belly perhaps to cover my death mask.

She also knew that if her body were to be reduced by magic to its primary elements, it would become water or less than water: wind and dust or less than wind and dust:

Little piles of carbon, a few grains of potassium scattered here and there.

Perhaps a pinch of phosphorus that might burn for ten seconds.

Perhaps fifty litres, if that, of oxygen escaping through the window towards the castles of mint, but insufficient to inflate a blue dinghy to save her life.

But certainly less than wind and water, less than ashes of flour, less also than dust, and the dust not even in love.

And second, because only Estefania, and nobody but Estefania, was the adored nurse who daily passed through the wards dressed in white, pushing a healing retinue of shining instruments and tinkling jars full of iridescent liquids and capsules like aquamarines or garnets, between the disciplined ranks of carnations and Montezuma roses, whose water Estefania changed every morning, like a faithful cistophore, while behind her followed the trainee nurses, to whom she, Estefania, explained which poultices should be applied, and why Cheadle's forceps should be kept in a jar of dysol and how to remove stitch clamps, how to make dressings of iodoform gauze to contain uterine haemorrhages and how to use the Vilbiss atomizer, while the doctors and residents waited for her in the corridors, quoted her in the operating theatres, trapped her in the lifts and waylaid her in the amphitheatres to declare their love for her beneath the yellow skylights, swear fidelity on the antiseptic-smelling operating table, kiss her between the fourth and fifth floor or between Pathology and Maternity, between Infectious Diseases and X-rays or rape her among the icy breaths and green delitescences of refrigerated corpses.

'How beautiful she is,' a surgeon suddenly said halfway through a trepanation and stood rapt, drill in hand, thinking that Estefania was indeed exquisite and so wise, when she cleaned patients' nostrils with a warm borated solution or rubbed petroleum jelly on their anal sphincter to dilate it. And similarly: 'How humble she is,' thought an intern as he walked the hospital grounds fiddling with his stethoscope but listening to the heartbeat of the trees. And yes, without doubt, how dextrous and quick and delicate was Estefania in introducing analgesic suppositories with the aid of cocoa butter; how careful in washing patients' ears with a Higginson's pear; how capable in lubricating nasal catheters with butter. 'How disagreeable, how proud, how shameless she is,' muttered the other nurses among themselves, dying of anger and envy, green and with hair of snakes and masks of powder like Beardsley's embryos, though they did

67

admit that Estefania was an angel, but of the race of beautiful devils like Fata Morgana.

Of the cruel angels, like Azrael and Abaddon.

Or even of grotesque angels like Melezimuth of the twenty hands:

Because they could not tolerate that my cousin Estefania should reveal only one side of the coin, only one of its two faces and that, like another St Vincent de Paul, another St Louis with the lepers and another St Elizabeth of Hungary painted by Holbein the Elder, she should pass through the hospital like an endless blessing with her head held high and her eyes illuminated by the living flame, uncreated and uncreatable, of Meister Eckehart.

'How beautiful are the angels,' said a young man, when he came to after swallowing twenty-seven nembutals in a suicide attempt to forget a girl and an unlucky star, awaking in hospital to find himself with Estefania and with an angel, the two in one person, with my cousin Estefania, the nurse, who with her own hands so often covered with eczema produced by her allergy to antibiotics, cooled the duodenal catheter with shaved ice and placed the youth in the Trendelenburg position to pump his stomach and force his organism to expel the barbiturates, along with the remains of his last supper and a solitary moribund tapeworm, so restoring him to life and to a new disappointment when the young man, like so many others, declared his love for her and she took his temperature rectally, his blood pressure and his pulse, examined his tongue, checked his reflexes with a hammer and turned him down, declared him fit, said goodbye, gave him his clothes and ordered him never, alive or dead, to set foot again in the hospital unless, of course, he was sick: unless the degree of his love for her caused his heart to grow huge like those who suffer from bucardia or bull's heart; unless, of course, the extent of his desire for her was such that he entered a state of continuous and painful erection proving immune to any cure by douches of lemon or baths of alcohol or fountains of saliva.

And so it was that, in the eyes of so many people, Estefania was an angel, although she never had the wings in the winged sense of the word nor the face in the classical sense of the term, nor the eyes in the adverse sense of luck, though she did have the sex in the upside-down sense, with prop roots which Uncle Esteban stole from transparent Hungary, as you yourselves may corroborate, don Prospero, General, Barman, whenever you wish, when you one day discover, perhaps if God wills and particularly if Estefania wills, all the surprises my cousin harbours in the curve of her breast, in the hollow of her neck and the roundness of her buttocks.

But life is full of coincidences and while the absence of wings in Estefania was not so much a negation as a privation – like, for instance, the blindness of the Greek poet – none the less, at least once in her existence, my cousin truly did have wings, when she was pretending to be an angel; at

68

her school, like so many other girls made famous in novels and in cinema, she was an angel in an end-of-term play and it goes without saying that, when it was known that she had been chosen to be her own guardian angel, the whole household was aflutter, particularly with wings:

Transparent wings, black wings, butterfly wings, cherub wings, stowaway wings, budding wings and wings of Altazor the parachutist. Wings, also, red as the wings of the Virgin painted by Fouquet, as don Prospero suggested.

Wings, tricolour like the wings of the angels holding aloft the Virgin of Guadalupe's half moon, as Grandfather Francisco requested.

Drab wings with peacock-feather eyes like the angels painted by Filippo Lippi and armour-plated wings like the wings of Perugino's angels, as Cousin Walter desired.

Golden wings like the wings of the Archangel Gabriel painted by Masolino da Panicale and exploding wings like Tintoretto's angels, of which Aunt Luisa bethought herself.

Grey wings like the wings of the angels painted by El Greco, as Grandmother Altagracia remembered.

And wings, finally, like those designed by Uncle Esteban for Estefania, in an effort to please everybody, which actually bore a marked resemblance to the wings of the angels of *The Annunciation* by Monaco and to Memling's musical angels, fringed in yellows, purples, whites, mauves, reds, greens, pinks and blues, as though upholstered in technicolor zebra skin.

The next step was to make love to her in the right ear. This was the ear with which Estefania was best able to hear the frothing of a head of beer, Brahms' concertos, the lashing of the wind, the songs of Bilitis and my rag-and-bone-man's cry insisting on exchanging her caresses, her kisses and her thighs for soulless lamps and other intangible and almost invisible objects such as a flask filled with dreams to drink on sleepless nights, liquid turquoises to fill her eyes, a clock with arms of stalactites to tell the time of eternity, an umbrella of bats' wings to shelter from a possible shower of glow-worms, a racket of ice to play tennis with balls of snow and countless other things which never interested her, because Estefania was tired already of the eulogies which all poets alive, dead or imaginary always heaped on her; the fact of the matter was that poor Estefania could not even laugh without Cousin Walter, Ricardo the gardener, or any other of our friends or relatives, composing a maritime ode to her teeth or an elementary ode to her armpits and she could not even sit down to read a story or a novel on even the most diverse subjects, such as the October Revolution or the conquest of the Matterhorn but that, sooner or later, some poetic character would materialize to wreck the plot and escape from the book, sliding down the bookmark ribbon to extol the scent of her thighs and the bitter-sweet code observed by her eyes; and, moreover, since she knew that the selfsame relationship existing between the poets of today and their lovers of yesterday existed also, pure, precise, clean, between her and me and, in the same way that I have always felt myself to be master of others' poems, as though I had written them with my own hand and soul (to the extent that on several occasions I have, quite seriously, considered adopting certain anonymous poems) so, for just such a reason, my cousin Estefania was unable to hear, read or remember a poem without feeling morally implicated: hers was the stabbed host tongue of André Breton's woman, hers the coat the colour of milk and insolence belonging to Isabelle, friend of Louis Aragon, hers and nobody else's the hot-water hands of Efraín Huerta's intoxicated girl. And the ear described by Alfonsina Storni, pink cavity of iridescent hollows, was hers too. It was there that, one afternoon, I made love to her; but, although I barely and with utmost caution nudged the newly washed, smooth bell of her ear with my silken glans penis, although I deposited in the recondite shell only the first pearl of semen while the remaining jets of sperm trickled down her neck like a thread of light-grey blood, nevertheless, I repeat, Estefania lost her sense of balance, of days and holidays, she complained of a ringing in her ear and had more nightmares; she dreamt that a huge penis, deep pulsing purple, entered one ear and came out of the other, entangled with lymph nodes and Easter eggs. I insisted that it was all in the mind, that she was full of bourgeois prejudices; that I wouldn't be a bit surprised if on a Sunday least expected she would find dogs sniffing at her heels as she went to mass; that if she carried on like this she would be sure to encounter a ventriloquist priest who would make her confess non-existent sins and abominations deserving punishment over a slow fire in the bilges of hell; that this, that the other, that her belly-button, that her legs, that her eyes. But Estefania did not heed me, perhaps because my sperm really had blocked her ear and left her deaf for a few hours or, perhaps, simply because she didn't feel like paying any attention to me; the fact is that Estefania, who always had very sensitive hearing, who since childhood had been able to hear the dark nocturnal dialogues of her parents three bedrooms away, almost in the other wing of the castle, could hear slugs slithering over the marble gravestones and, seated beneath a slippery elm, listen to the blue grass of Kentucky growing, did not, on this occasion, hear my words; moreover, she didn't even hear the crashing fall of evening and the diagonal plunge of the sun which shattered the coloured panes, raising clouds of golden dust.

And, as may be imagined, she wanted nothing to do with love-making, for a few hours anyway, and suggested we take a walk around the neighbourhood. You should have seen her: calm, innocent, entrancing and pure as ever, aware of her talent and her crystal anniversaries and, particularly, of that grace which magnifies all powers and attracted to her lips the most beautiful phrases which floated, helpless, in the air: those most borne on wings, those which kindle a tickle at funerals, those which cause you to awake from the rottenness of night slim as a dinosaur. For example, that time we were wandering at random away from the church, with no expectation of meeting Palinuro or anybody else of importance, given the congenital magnitude of the city, and having no particular plan other than to walk together, as we often did, like two children, detached from the universe which invented us, simply walking to the end of the street, to raise a cathedral of white horses in front of La Bombi, to lie down on the flagstones paving Cinco de Mayo Street to square our love and kiss roundly, between one lamp post and the next, to scatter the passers-by on Mesones Street in a *coup de grâce*, little suspecting that our glances intersected in a voltaic arc. And she, my cousin Estefania, paused beneath a one-eyed traffic light, left off eating a sausage which she declared to have no phallic intent whatsoever and pointed to the grove of trees which used to multiply during the night. A fat old man sat reading a magazine in the shade of the living, trembling bridges of branches and, when she noticed him, my cousin pronounced a sentence concerning our grandfather, as was to be expected by anonymous association of chairs and bald pates, and the sentence, no sooner out of her mouth, steered its own course along the phenomenal muck channels running through the city, took a dip in a moving fountain and returned clean and perfumed, simple and virgin as Estefania herself: 'Doesn't that old man look just like Grandfather Francisco?' said my cousin and, from that moment onwards, we knew that everything was – and always had been – possible, that we could invoke a poem by Eluard or decipher the name of immortelle flowers in the green language of Linnaeus, knowing that we were unlikely to lapse into poetry. Then, because she hated the contagious order of the calendar and it frustrated her horribly to know, for example, that after a Tuesday on which we stayed in bed and sent the office and the Salem cigarettes complete with their sequoia forests to hell, there followed a Wednesday laden with Alka-Seltzers and an impeccable and military Thursday, we decided that, that day at least, it was the end of a weekend and we walked through the city, from the silence of the lake one Sunday night when swans arch their necks and workers return home dead with exhaustion and candyfloss, to the Plaza Mayor one Saturday morning, when the pealing of bells was drowned by the roaring of cars and buses and of tanks marauding though the presidential palace, because the time had come: the time of students, the time of demonstrations and of skulls cracked by rifle butts, the time, in short, when Palinuro, like Aeneas' pilot, would no longer be able to distinguish night from day.

How I penetrated my cousin's mouth and how, also, her vagina, is

71

something I will relate another time, along with further admirable and exquisite aberrations. Suffice it for now to say, on the subject of my cousin's anus, that it was more familiar to me than the palm of my tongue and over a hundred times – I fear to exaggerate by saying over a thousand – I penetrated her rectum with all my prolongations and especially with my penis. I particularly remember one occasion when Estefania dressed up as an effeminate cabin boy with her hair caught up in a fair-weather sailor's cap and she lay face downwards on the bed, removed her flared trousers and offered me her buttocks, and I, after putting on a ginger-coloured false beard which I found in the supermarket, eased through my fly a member tattooed with souvenirs of Constantinople, covered it with Richard Hudmut cucumber crème and, grasping her two buttocks in my two hands, my cousin's immensely round and fruit-like buttocks resembling the two polar halves of a globe accomplished in contracting to the rhythm of childhood's solitary pleasures, I inserted into her anus the entire lenth of my member and clasped her firmly by the hips to rock her to the rhythm of my spasms, until in ecstasy and fury she ripped to shreds the embroidery of the pillow-cases, until from her mouth flowed threads of red and burning silk and shuddering she gasped: 'O Captain! my Captain!' and when, at last, I launched my stream of sperm into the golden depths of her intestine and withdrew my cock, limply diminished and its tattoos shrivelled, she herself wiped it with a Kleenex because, although in her innocence she had used an enema of rosewater to rinse her rectum of faeces, my poor *Mutinus Tutunus* was smeared with a sticky yellowish mixture resembling shit and pineapple jam.

Ah, my cousin, my cousin luminous as a sweet amethyst or a winking ash tree!

My cousin, tall as an order and beautiful as going to the zoo on a Sunday of crystalline eyes!

My cousin, my clean and well-licked Estefania who, though never an eagle of salt nor a horoscope of silver, was as beautiful as eternity embroidered with forget-me-nots and surprising as samples of coloured ribbons entangled in the propellers of legend!

You should have seen her, bright and fresh as oranges after a fast, splendid as four o'clock on the dot in springtime or an aniseed policy, slipping through the halls and wards of the hospital, through the corridors, the clinics and the dispensaries, the eyebanks and the bloodbanks, the lunatic asylums and the leper colonies!

You should have seen her surrounded by her nurses, who followed her like a swarm of bees in natural flight or a chatter of white confetti daring not to touch her!

You should have seen how her patients adored her, cirrhosis sufferers forgot their Medusan stomachs and tuberculosis sufferers their violet

72

sarcoids when my cousin walked by, beautiful and mysterious as flying through a starry night on the back of a question mark of steam!

You should have seen how the heartrate of patients suffering from palpitations reached two hundred beats per minute and how Parkinson's disease patients stretched out their trembling hands when my cousin passed through the wards!

How her green radiance permeated the eyelids of diabetics in coma and porphyria sufferers smiled at her with elongated, pink, vampire teeth!

Ah, my cousin, my chaste, my ineffable, my diabolical cousin who – while she had never been the bark of a year or the roundness of midday, the clamour of mirrors or the yolk of the wind, nor even a splinter of cloud, the flip-side of a dream or the peal of a rainbow, though her brush with the world, with sand, with lotteries and with the froufrou of crows caused some light and some spite to adhere to her soul and some sweetness and some intelligence, some good humour, to infect her manner and her conversations with the sea and with miracles – was sublime and celestial and absurd, absurd as Celan's black milk or Gongora's red snow, absurd as a marshmallow devil or an angel of coal, a bridge of air or a white-hot darkness, a foam-rubber vulture or a lily of excrement!

And particularly so after making love, seated by the window beneath her portrait, pure, meek, motionless and lascivious, forbidding me to touch even a hair of her head or the button of her breasts, tranquil and, thus, innocent and ageing ten years per hour, tamed and dreamless and white and modest and clean and newly purified by the eucharist, like all my future granddaughters, and enclosed intact in a bubble of saliva, in a glass parenthesis, in a cellophane drum, weeping tears of celery jelly and with her head encased in the translucent, deaf-and-dumb enigma of a diver's helmet, my cousin thus was a contradiction of flesh and blood: fragile and impetuous, admirable woman that she was, at once brittle and unbreakable, treacherous woman that she was from the day and the night I smeared my sperm all over her body; lacking substance, yes, almost ethereal, but at the same time solid and dense as a virgin of snow wrapped in iron celluloid, the whore, or as a statue of pollen covered with vitreous milk, the sweet innocent.

5

The Universal Eye

Since sleep was completely beyond me, I set about emptying Palinuro's trunk which was full of surprises and strange objects. Among the things I found was a phial of glass which gave off vapours to preserve dried butterflies, a hundred sheets of paper with a watermark depicting Mercury's staff, some scissors used by Palinuro to cut the hair of the dogs (as we called the first-year students), five different-coloured devil masks from Michoacán and two old pharmacist jars. One was labelled INF. CALUMB Conc., in which my friend kept his used condoms. The second, LIQ: MORPH: HYD, containing a little box with all the nails that he had bitten during the last five years and a bottle holding the sperm of our friend Molkas' masturbations during the same period, for which reason it was marked 'Semetery'. I also found a tame set of dentures belonging originally to Grandmother Altagracia, a Flemish medical cabinet with little drawers full of herbs and lumps of benzoin, a phial with a colour scale printed on its label for measuring the alkali or acid content of urine and two of the three huge volumes of *Mexico Through the Centuries* which, as Palinuro explained to me, had carminative properties or, in other words, might be used to relieve flatulence: for this purpose, you had only to lie on your back and put the volumes on your stomach: instantly – he said – you started to produce the most almighty farts.

And while I was busy unearthing these and a thousand other wonders, my friend Palinuro, the sock still covering his face and very quietly – as though he were talking to himself, almost as though he did not wish me to hear him – told me that soon after leaving school and before starting classes at the School of Medicine, Cousin Walter had invited him to a series of conferences. Palinuro, full of high hopes, had just bought his uniform and his white shoes, his medical bag, his stethoscope and frontal mirror. As usual, the neighbourhood with its old buildings gaunt with moss and winding alleys hinting of death and the Holy Spirit, heightened the spell which held his imagination in thrall. As he walked along Los Santos Sepulcros Street he could readily picture himself arriving at the school dressed in white, carrying his books and his instruments, greeting his new friends and Charon – aged and wise porter in charge of the dissecting room – mounting the stairs beneath the portrait of St Luke and entering the dissecting room. It was huge, with circular tiers of carved oak, ushers carrying flaming torches of perfumed resins and boys who, in other happier times when dissections were open to the public, distributed orange blossom to the ladies that they might not be offended by the odour of corruption. They were the brides of death, thought Palinuro, as he imagined them seated next to the dwarfs, the street vendors and the coachmen. But, on this occasion, there was a redolence of apples, tar and vanilla: the scents of a street and a market at eleven in the morning, full of sun and cars, among which Palinuro walked, lost in dreams of the first body he would contemplate on the dissecting slab. Palinuro agreed with Balzac that a man cannot marry before studying anatomy and dissecting at least one woman and, when he read Torquato Tasso, he gained an inkling of the relationship linking beauty and death. Palinuro shared with Villon a fascination for dead women and with Edgar Allan Poe the belief that the death of a beautiful woman is the most poetic event imaginable. Hence, for just such reasons, his first corpse would have to be that of a beautiful young girl, of rust plaits and skin so white and sheer that the blue viscera could almost be seen through it and 'her heart, a snowflake' as a sad and trite poet had once said. One Sunday, some time later, he found a suction pump and a gastroscope in La Lagunilla fleamarket: both old and rusted, but he intended to restore them to mint condition. And he stood enraptured for hours before a display in the window of a shop selling surgical instruments and medical equipment in Brasil Street, which not only reflected his own full-length image but also re-created an ideal surgery with its scales, examination table, sheets of letters for testing eyesight, filing cabinets, saliva dish, couch for carrying out gynaecological examinations and two cupboards: one full of medicines and books and the other of gleaming instruments.

During the opening lecture they were shown a colour film of the removal of a kidney. This was the first time that Palinuro made the transition from a diagram in a book to reality – or at least a faithful approximation of reality. When the surgeon made the first incision of the skin and then of the panniculus adiposus, Palinuro felt a hollow in his stomach but thought that it would soon pass and tried to concentrate on the marvels that were to follow. But a few moments sufficed to realize that the so-called marvels that followed were marvellous strictly in the world of words and illustrations: the ligature of the intercostal artery made him feel nauseous and his first glimpse of the uncontrolled spasms of muscles and organs filled him with alarm. As the surgeon cut the fibrous tissue of a visceral peritoneum and then the renal vessel, Palinuro felt a shiver run down his spine, his eyes clouded and he knew that he was about to faint. When the kidney appeared, Palinuro rushed stumbling from the room. Back home, Cousin Walter assured him that he had nothing to worry about, that the same happened to a lot of students at first, but that they later learned to control their revulsion and eventually such sights ceased to bother them at all. Palinuro thanked him for his encouragement and tried to convince himself that Cousin Walter was doubtless right. At that time, he was far from believing that the painful process that would distance him from medicine had scarcely begun. During the same holiday prior to the first university term, Palinuro also visited several hospitals and discovered that his reactions were exactly opposite to those of Estefania. She couldn't bear to hear disagreeable things mentioned but she was quite capable of coming daily into direct contact with them. He, on the other hand, could speak about anything: blood and excrement, tumours, urine with the fishy smell characteristic of certain *coli* bacteria infections, massive lipomatosis and whatever other revolting or monstrous ailment came into his head, even over meals, with no qualms whatsoever. But when he was obliged to come face to face with them; when he breathed the real, infinitely bitter-sweet and hopeless smell of the operating theatres in the General Hospital and the Women's Hospital and when, in Red Cross emergencies, he saw a man with a metre of intestine hanging from his anus; when he smelled the nauseating fumes of gangrene; when in the leprosy hospital he saw patients whose boils burst open under the pressure of thick yellow pus and in the pathology laboratory they showed him two cancerous tumours of the lung, small, green and pearly as a pair of peas, Palinuro was forced to admit that there was a distinct possibility that he would never succeed in dominating the atavistic nausea, the cosmic horror instilled in him by all such human wretchedness.

Medicine was all very well – Palinuro said to me that night, quietly, as though talking to himself – when, with Cousin Walter's help, you venture forth and discover the origin of the word *bistoury* in the name of the Italian city Pistoria. Medicine was the promise of a cabalistic world when you gaze in shop windows at anaesthesia instruments with their four gauges half full of different-coloured liquids which rise and fall like organs playing the coloured music invented by Rimington and Burnett. Medicine was a fairytale when you leafed through a book on bandaging and discovered the beauty and elegance of the spica, the capeline and the spiral reverse, bringing to mind the swathing of Egyptian mummies, the sandals of gladiators who gave their lives for Rome or the turbans of caliphs who sallied out at night, disguised, to walk the streets of Baghdad. Medicine was also something to dream of when Palinuro and his friends met in bars to talk of catheterization of the heart and pictured themselves yet again dressed in spotless white, viewing on a fluorescent screen the rubber tube inserted in the vein at the right elbow and its passage through the innominate vein, the superior vena cava, the right auricle and the right ventricle, to emerge in the pulmonary artery. Medicine, of course, was a wonder when on a night of revelry, having eaten little but drunk a lot, the three friends planned to save money and between them buy a microscope to discover for themselves the seething, hotchpotch world of micro-organisms. Palinuro bought himself a second-hand book on bacteriology and continued to dream. But, between the mythology of the word *bistoury* and a stomach resection – he told me – there was a world of difference. A world as vast and unspannable as that existing between the colours of the anaesthesia gauges and the white suffocation accompanied by instant death that could occur at any moment during the course of an operation; or between that same multitudinous Lilliput world of micro-organisms and the ravages they wrought in the human body: ulcers and scabs, suppurations, diphtheritic membranes, septicaemia. And, in the final instance death.

Death, as represented in treatises on sarcology and angiology, was very different also to true death, and the techniques described in books were aimed not to emphasize the pitifulness of a lifeless body but, rather, to dignify it, purify it, transform it – through diagrams and unsuspected colours – into a sculpture of alabaster. The first operation, Palinuro told me, was called *hydrotomy*. An incision is made in the corpse's primary carotid – and in his dreams the corpse was yet again that of a beautiful lily-white, young girl like those found by Berlioz on the streets of Florence – into which is inserted a pipe connected to the water tap. Next the jugular is severed. Or rather – the book stated – the thorax is opened along its upper central line, the heart is left exposed while the right ventricle is perforated and a glass tube inserted into the orifice. The water is left running. And from the tube begins to emerge a jet of murky, red-tinted water. Then the water turns pink and carries clots and bloody detritus. Finally, it is left for hours – or days, if necessary – after making small incisions in the skin in order to let the excess water drain out. The corpse is then ready for the second operation. For purposes of conservation, certain substances can be injected into it: white sugar and grey salt, carbolic acid and glycerine. And, in order to reveal the secrets of veins and arteries, it is necessary to employ a system invented many years ago: Sylvius, during the eighteenth century, was able to give the first ever description of the brain by injecting boiling wax of different colours into the arteries. Palinuro conjured up in his imagination the snow-white body of the girl with the veins and arteries beginning to appear, spread and multiply like a river, like a thousand rivers. The veins would have to remain red and therefore Scarlet Carmine or Ultramarine Scarlet Red could be used. The arteries, blue, and for them Prussian Blue or Methylene Blue, and thus reality would concord with the colours of text diagrams. Palinuro thought a thousand times of the body criss-crossed with the red and blue rivers of veins and arteries with their endless meanderings and tributaries, and his imagination ranged further still and he considered, why not? experimenting with waxes dyed other colours. Martius Yellow could perhaps be used to highlight the veins of the lungs and Janus Black, the arteries of the brain. With Hofmann Violet the liver would be entwined in a web of mauve veins. Naphthol Green would enclose the eyes in a net of olive-coloured arteries. After that, other magic procedures requiring a detailed knowledge of optics could be employed – for instance, the refractive index of muscles, glands and liquids – to render transparent a section of the body in which the veins and arteries had previously been injected with coloured substances. Such a process, called diaphanization, would make it possible to transform the statue of alabaster into a body of glass revealing the clockwork mechanism of the human organism, the mysteries of this wondrous machine composed of fifty billion cells, capable of breathing three thousand, three hundred gallons of air in a single day and of processing forty tons of food in a lifetime.

The first corpse with which he was confronted, Palinuro admitted to me, was not that of a young girl. And the job in hand was not a hydrotomy but an autopsy. And again it was Cousin Walter who invited him. The corpse, by a strange coincidence, was that of a youth of Palinuro's age and build and who, in life, must have harboured the same illusions as Palinuro. The coincidence went further still: Palinuro discovered that the colouring of the youth's skin, eyes and hair were similar to his own and, although there was little likeness in the nose, forehead or mouth, there were none the less other undoubted resemblances: between the youth's heart, intestines, bones, tongue and bladder, and the heart, intestines, bones, tongue and bladder of Palinuro there was little appreciable difference. Apart from that, it was an unidentified youth, with blood in his nose and mouth, with Cushing facies, swollen lymph glands, purple patches on his arms and legs, distended testicles and oedema on his feet and whose blood had already started to discolour even while he was alive, before shooting him full of water, for the simple reason that he had died of leukaemia. He was an unidentified youth. But his hands were like Palinuro's. And so was his brain, his spinal cord and his aorta. Palinuro held out for only a few minutes. He got as far as seeing how the professor, with a single sweep of the knife, cut the skin down to the ribs from the left to the right shoulders. He saw how the abdominal incision was made and how, also in a single movement, the professor cut the costal cartilage and separated the soft tissue of the thorax. Palinuro left the dissecting room and ran to the bathroom to vomit. He didn't make it to the toilet: in the urinal he left a mess of curdled milk and half-digested lumps of meat and vegetables. The pungent odour of his own vomit made him throw up over and over again until his stomach ached. Then he went out to walk, he knew not where nor why. But his mind could not tear itself away from the horror. He also knew by heart everything that was to follow. As he walked down San Ildefonso, in the shadow of those huge ash trees which seemed to hold all the birds of the world, he saw the gloved hand of the doctor sliding over the lungs in search of adhesions and he felt himself suffocating, as though an iron hand were constricting his chest. As he walked past the photography shops and the photocopying businesses, the ammonia smells that wafted out made him feel unbearably nauseous. He saw the doctor snipping the pericardial cavity with scissors. He saw him pull out the small intestine and place it in a kidney bowl. And he couldn't stop himself imagining that the youth's body was his own. When a smell of chips and beer assailed his nostrils he vomited again on the corner, beside a lamp post. He aimlessly wandered all the streets which he and I had walked together, trying to stop thinking about the autopsy and he almost succeeded. But, when he had reached the flower market, he saw the doctor removing the anal tract, removing the oesophagus and the cervical structures. He threw up yet again and the acid stench of his vomit polluted the fragrance of the roses and gardenias, the lilies and the daffodils. As he left the market, he saw as clearly as if he were witnessing it in the flesh, how the professor severed the dome of the cranium with an electric saw and prised the two halves apart with a hammer and chisel. A new and ghastly mixture of odours assaulted his nostrils: on the one hand, the reek from the fishmonger's where hake, squid and oysters rained down like manna on to the ice; on the other, the smell of Reina Victoria, Caprichos and Alfonso XIII cigarettes manufactured by El Buen Tono: smells of Virginia, Burley and Turkish tobaccos, aromas noble and sun-dried, light and dark, which wrapped Palinuro's adolescence in all the fragrances of the Garden of Allah. Two images came to his mind: the words of Flaubert when he spoke of the repugnant mixture of smells produced by citrus fruits and the plague victims of Jaffa and a story told to him by a friend about a plane which crashed in the mountains with two men on board and a load of contraband perfumes, lotions and eau-de-Cologne. Several days later, the rescue team located the remains by the wind-wafted scent of these fragrances combined with a stench of decomposing corpses. Down the mountainside they transported the bodies on the backs of mules and one of the corpses, swollen up like a balloon, omitted ear-shattering gases throughout the journey which also mingled the nauseous fumes of corruption and faecal matter with the sweet, fresh scent of lavender. Palinuro then saw how the surgeon emptied the cranial cavity by pulling out the brain with his own hand. Next, the doctor slit through the arachnoid membrane with scissors to expose the middle cerebral artery. And Palinuro vomited what was left in his guts: an endless, burning, grey slime like melted lead.

Palinuro told me all this when we reached the room at dawn.

I was left with a question in my mind, which I asked him five hours later when we woke up: 'So, what year are you in?'

'What year? I haven't a clue! It's like this: when I look back and see that the '50 to '55 generation of doctors was the last to have studied in the old School of Medicine here in Holy Sunday Square which we visited today, that venerable building which was nothing less – and nothing more fitting – than the Palace of the Inquisition built by Pedro de Arrieta and declared a National Monument in 1963 and which is full of commemorative plaques to Rafael Llucio and the poet Manuel Acuña who allowed himself the luxury of committing suicide in that very building . . . when I look back and see myself begging an autograph from Roberto Ortiz, who was something like the Babe Ruth of the poor who hit his baseballs all the way to the French Graveyard . . . or I see myself writing letters to another monument, María Félix. When I see myself with my mates going to the Tivoli to watch Don Tongolele, or to the Cineac to watch *Objective Burma*, or to the Novelty to see *How Women Bathe*, I feel that I am living far in the past and that you and I, at this very moment, need only cross Holy Sunday Square to reach the school. But when I look the other way and think that the University Campus, so far removed not only from Holy Sunday Square but also from my life, as José Tablada would say . . . when I see the students going out into the streets to demand an end to poverty, ignorance and hunger . . . are you going with me to the demonstration? When I see, as I was saying, so much injustice, when I think of Vietnam, Jaramillo, the Ché, I feel that I am living in a future far beyond anything I had ever imagined and in regard to which I feel virtually impotent but also responsible. So, depending on which way I look, I live in one year or another, very different and very far apart . . . but perhaps this confusion is due more than anything to my obsessive habit of going to the Press Library to read old newspapers. Newspapers from the year I was born, can you imagine? I'll take you with me to the Press Library one of these days, OK? . . . God, I'm even more hungover than I should be! If you don't go and buy some drinkables we'll die of alcoholic insufficiency. And perhaps we could do with something solid, what do you think? All we have in the larder is two hard rolls produced by spontaneous generation . . . go on, I know you're a good spirochete. I'll make you a list.'

'I was talking about the university year,' I explained. 'What year of your course?'

'What year? No year.'

'So you're not studying any more? The concierge told me that you're at the School of Medicine.'

'I go to the school, every day. I wander about dressed in white with my medical bag and my gastroscope, I flirt with the girls, I put dead men's

80

fingers in their pockets and I sometimes attend dissections . . .'

'But . . . didn't you say you couldn't stop yourself from spewing up?'

'Ah, but now it's different. I attend dissections, not as a medical student, but as an artist. I'm illustrating a book on anatomy. Later I'll show you what I'm doing; my latest masterpiece is a drawing in India ink of the rounded protuberantia occipitalis, with the pathetic nerve and the whiskers of the calamus in canary yellow.'

'I don't see the difference,' I confessed.

'I don't either. I suppose I must effectively be learning to control my revulsion, as the infallible Walter said I would.'

'I thought for a moment that we were going to be classmates . . .'

Palinuro leapt out of bed and landed on his feet on the floor: 'But of course we are! I told you yesterday, you and I will walk together beneath the mask of Algos, and Apollo will be our God, *Apollo Fatidicus, Apollo Paean*, since, as you know, it was Apollo who invented medicine; Ovid says so in the *Metamorphoses*. It's quite true that I lost my faith in part, but not entirely: I reckon that I still have at least fifty-three point eighty-six per cent left . . . anyway, did I not solemnly promise you that your first corpse would be that of a young and beautiful woman? I could not fulfil my dream, but you will, I swear it, and in this very room, even if we have to steal a corpse from the School of Medicine or lure a girl here and kill her!'

'So you're going to go on studying? You're going to graduate as a doctor?'

'You bet. And just as in ancient times there was a Rufus of Ephesus and a Xenocrates of Aphrodisias, I will one day also become so famous that future generations will link my name with my country of origin and call me *Palinuro of Mexico*.'

'Are you sure?' I asked him.

'Well, I'll be surer after drinking and eating something. Come on, be a good boy scout and go and buy the stuff for the beanfeast. I'll make you a list of what we need while I put on a bit of Wagner. The concierge is a lying toad: *The Seasons* is *not* the only record I own . . .'

I revelled in the fact of having met Palinuro, on that afternoon bedecked in extraneous laces on which I could see how our friendship glowed in the wings of flies and the streets creaked beneath my steps. I crossed the square in the shade of the trees submerged in a trance of greenness, I greeted the buses filled with passengers, the glowing sun encircled by a garland of clouds, the paper boats which sailed, Estefania, at the water's whim and I reached the market clutching my list in which Palinuro, in his broad and learned hand, had written: sea salt, vinegar, bread to frizzle in the oven, tomato sauce to murder a hamburger, vinegar, Jamaican pepper for a hypothetical ham, sugar, a gallon of vinegar, etc., etc. (and also vinegar);

and when I returned, when, keeping abreast of the boat of Tristan and Iseult sailing towards the lands of King Mark, I ran two at a time up the stairs to the fifth floor and opened the door, Estefania, my surprise was this time greater yet and I felt like Donatello who, on returning to the house of his friend Filippo Brunelleschi, found the Christ. I dropped the oranges, the pomegranates which had recently sprung from the blood of Dionysus, the salt, the vinegar, the eggs, a dozen pygmy peaches and four penguin onions: everything, in short (and also the vinegar) leaving the carpet strewn like a still-life model.

There, in the centre of the room, stood Palinuro, naked and white as a statue, his pubic hair lathered in foam and a barber's razor in his hand. 'Since you told me that your sweat, your saliva and your tears reek of vinegar, I bought different kinds so that at least you'll smell different every day,' I said to him. 'I brought you a litre of apple vinegar, another of pineapple vinegar and another of wine and tarragon vinegar.' 'Thank you. But it's no use; life does not smile on me . . . it roars with laughter,' complained my friend Palinuro and he raised one foot on to a stool which he had placed beside him, as though he were going to climb on to a pedestal. But he stopped short and therefore will I always remember him thus: half human, half sculpture, half stranger and half hero, half Palinuro who got snarled up in the abbreviations of life and half Palinuro who triumphed over public opinion and crepuscular inclinations. 'Therefore,' he continued, 'I have taken the heroic decision to shave myself and I am going to ask you a favour with a capital F: would you do it?' 'Do what?' I asked him. Palinuro raised his hands to his head and exclaimed: 'But what have you done? What's all this mess?' Palinuro sometimes reacted like that, he sank himself deep in his own thoughts, walked streets with the *demoiselles* of Avignon, revised in his mind the twelve pairs of cranial nerves, applying the old mnemonic technique of the Twelve Peers of France, then suddenly came back to earth, eyes shining more brightly, to take stock of the tragedy. 'Let's get on with it,' he said, half climbing down from the stool, 'and meanwhile I'll explain what you have to do. Over there, under the bed, are two oranges.' 'Here under the bureau, is an unbroken egg,' I answered him. 'Since you are going to be a doctor anyway, I am sure you won't mind. Here's a nut, inside your shoe, did you buy nuts?' he asked me, squatting down on the carpet. I was searching under the piano and answered on hearsay: 'No, those are nuts from a past age.'

Palinuro picked up the nut and examined it as though he expected it at any moment to become transparent. 'As I was saying, when you become a doctor, you're going to have to face up to hairy backsides sooner or later. All kinds of backsides, of all colours, shapes and sizes: from black assonant ones to pink bumptious ones. There are two oranges over there, under the red chair. Following a pure association of ideas, I will continue: did you know that sometimes doctors have to remove all kinds of strange objects which people insert into their rectums and then can't get out again?' 'Two oranges?' I asked him. 'I wouldn't go quite that far,' he said, throwing away the nut from a previous era, 'but, as you might expect, bananas, candles, Chrismas lights. Flaubert's father, who was a doctor, relates how he had to remove a long solid object, which was not precisely the neck of an albatross, from the arsehole of an old sailor,' said Palinuro, as he got down on his hands and knees on the carpet. He sniffed it. 'Hmmmm, smells like salt.' He tasted it. 'Hmmmm, tastes like salt.' 'It is salt,' I told him. 'Hmmmm,' he answered me.

'So, what's this favour you're going to ask me?' I asked him, while thinking, among other things, that salt has no smell. 'To shave my bum,' he answered and stuck his head under the bed. 'Here are two peaches and another egg, also intact. As I said before, since you're to be a doctor, you won't mind at all. I'm sorry that I can't do it myself, but the last time it was a disaster. Here's a cigarette end.' 'Here's the ketchup . . . what makes you say it was a disaster?' 'I'll tell you frankly, look at me.' I peered out from beneath the chair. Palinuro picked up the razor and squatted. 'This is the second time it's happened to me. As I said yesterday, lice die with DDT, but the nits don't. Well, that first time, like now, the vinegar baths were useless and so I finally decided, in utter desperation, to shave my pubes and their immediate vicinity. I lathered myself in soap, took the razor and placed on the floor a mirror round and beautiful as a Venice moon with my glands drifting across it and began the arduous task. The mirror is important because you can't leave a single little hair with a single nit or you'll end up covered in lice again.'

He pointed with the razor to a corner of the room. 'Over there are four peaches and a can of beer. Well, you can imagine what happened: there came the moment when I lost my balance, tumbled over backwards and broke the mirror. The seven years of bad luck began immediately: I got hundreds of splinters stuck in my backside, started bleeding and had to run to the nearest doctor who, as always happens, was a specialist in venereal diseases . . .'

'Here's a nut,' I said to him.

'It's the same nut,' he answered. 'Are you listening to me?'

'Yes.'

'Just a second, I'll help you,' he said and began crawling around on all fours again.

'The embarrassment of it,' he continued. '. . . here's a shoe. Did you buy shoes?'

'Here's the other shoe,' I said.

'The embarrassment of it,' repeated Palinuro. 'You try swearing to the doctor that what you were doing was not asking the mirror: "mirror, mirror on the wall, whose is the fairest arse of all?" . . . here's a carpet. Did you buy a carpet?' 'Here's the missing egg,' I answered. 'Here's a chair.' 'Here's the dissection manual I lost three months ago.' 'Here are two tram tickets.' 'Here's your address book.' 'Ah, give me that, I have to call a friend.' 'Here's a corner.' 'Here's the wall. Did you buy walls?' 'Here's you, is that you?' 'Yes it's me, and I'll thank you to keep your hands to yourself. And if we carry on like this we'll go completely crazy. Are you ever going to shave me? Here's my arse.'

Let me tell you, Estefania, before I started shaving Palinuro, he reminded me that since ancient times, since the times of Lanfranc, the father of French surgery, and Thomas Vicary, sergeant-surgeon of King Henry VIII and, of course, before William Pott rode his horse through the snow of Kent Road and shortly after Rhazes beat his brains over the book which spoke of the philosopher's stone and was condemned for not having been able to turn lead into gold, barbers were extremely proud to be surgeons and vice versa. Palinuro quoted from *Il Barbiere di Siviglia*:

> Rasori, e pettini
> Lancette, e forbici,
> Al mio comando
> Tutlo quì stà!

We discussed also the frustration that must have been felt by the surgeons of that time who had to start out wearing short robes and were not permitted to perform surgery until examined by the gentlemen in long robes. 'Neither could they sit on a jury,' said Palinuro. 'And,' I added, 'among their other duties, they were responsible for brothels.'

'Well. That's not so bad. That's how venereology advanced,' stated Palinuro.

We talked of *Florarium Bartholomei* and touched again on *The Barber of Seville*, the opera in which the protagonist expresses his pride in his double profession, '*Io son barbiere, chirurgo!*' and then we bemoaned the fact that we didn't have the records which would have served as background music for the operation, but Palinuro undertook to sing some more excerpts. We then discussed the best position: whether the lithotomic or the prostatic. Palinuro suggested the position for urogenital operations invented by Aecius, Justinian's physician, namely: thighs pulled up against the abdomen, knees apart, the left wrist firmly secured by a rope passing beneath the respective knee, around the neck of the patient, beneath the other knee then to secure the right hand. But he changed his mind immediately since this position left him totally at my mercy.

'You never know,' he said. 'The flesh is the flesh.'

We decided on the prostatic position.

I left the room, closed the door and rapped with my knuckles: rap, rap, rap.

'Who is it?' asked Palinuro.

'The barber from the corner!'

'The barber from the corner? What do you want?'

'*Vengo a farvi la barba!*'

'You've come to shave me? I don't feel like it today!'

'Well, do you or do you not want me to come and shave you!' I said, very sternly. I opened the door, went to the bathroom and entered the room again. Basin in hand, I whisked the soap until the foam overflowed and in my best Buck Mulligan accent, exclaimed: '*Introibo ad altare Dei.*' And I went on to say: 'And please control your wind.'

'Don't worry,' he answered:

> '*Una voce poco fà*
> *Qui nel cor mi risuonò!*'

Palinuro assumed the prostatic position and I started to smooth out the skin after observing, at the manual's advice, the lie of the body hair and noting the dextrogyral conformation of the creases.

'Remember that the first duty of the physician,' my friend said, 'is not to harm the patient: *Primum, non nocere.*'

'Do I shave you all over?' I asked.

'Of course, everywhere . . .

> *Figaro sù, Figaro giù,*
> *Figaro qùa, Figaro la!*'

And when I brought the razor closer and with my fingers separated the borders of his anus, Estefania, my astonishment knew no bounds. My first thought was that Palinuro mistrusted me and had decided to spy on me; you won't believe this, Estefania, but there, in his anus, Palinuro had an eye.

'It's an optical illusion,' he said.

'No sir, it's an eye,' I answered.

'What colour?'

'Blue.'

'It's the Universal Eye.'

'That's a metaphor,' I said to him. 'And what you have in your arse is no metaphor, but a real eye.'

'Are you crazy?'

'No, I'm not crazy. The general's glass eye, which you must have swallowed last night in your drunken stupor.'

'No way. His eye fell on the grass and that's where it stayed.'

'Yes, it fell on the grass, but we looked for it. I remember that we took off our shoes so as not to crush it and walked on tip toe as though we were in the Tuileries Gardens and they were mined. I found it, picked it up and put it in my pocket.'

'But why didn't you give it to the general?'

'The general had already gone. And then, when we got home, you asked me for it, you stuck it on your forehead with Plasticine and carried on drinking and pretending you had a Third Eye. After that, I didn't see it again. It must have fallen into your glass and you must have swallowed it without realizing.'

'I don't remember swallowing it,' said Palinuro. 'That's ridiculous!'

'Then something else must have happened,' I said and started to shave him.

'*Piano, pianissimo!*' he begged me.

'*Basta! Basta! Non parlate!*'

I ran the razor over the upper edge of the gluteal crease.

'What else could have happened then, if I didn't swallow it?' Palinuro asked me.

'Nothing, nothing, forget it.'

'Tell me.'

'All right, all right, if you insist. I wouldn't be a bit surprised if, after taking out the eye, I don't find some Christmas lights, a blow torch . . .'

'*Ah, canaglia!*'

'. . . a governor's identity card, the orange we can't find . . . Cleopatra's needle, the Dead Sea Scrolls and other such goodies . . .'

Palinuro started and pointed at the ceiling: '*La calunnia è un venticello . . .!* Think what you like, but I have no taste for such goings-on! You're not thinking of taking the eye out, are you?'

'Just as soon as I finish shaving you,' I answered him, noticing an uncharacteristic blinking of Palinuro's eye.

'Your eye has a nervous tic,' I said to him.

'It's the result of an anal fixation,' he explained.

And I patiently continued to smooth out the creases and shave hair by hair and, I swear to you, Estefania, that Palinuro's single eye took on an ever more grateful expression and I couldn't resist the temptation to mimic a scene from a famous film, passing the blade of the razor before Palinuro's blue eye . . . then I recalled the whole of the *Histoire de l'Oeil* and the transformations of the eye into an egg, a sun, a bull's testicle, protohistory, panspermia, desoxyribonuclease acid and then I thought of Polyphemus and wondered who might be the Galatea ('when in the sky an eye was seen') to whom Palinuro offered hippogriffs, unicorns, Condillac's vegetable statues and other monsters produced by his miserable imagination. And then I remembered the symbol ℞ by which all medical prescriptions are introduced and which represents the eye of Horus. Finally, I remembered Ulysses in Sicily and, before Ulysses, Estefania, I felt I was nobody, less than nothing.

'I have . . . *un non sò che nell'occhio*,' said Palinuro, quoting the *Barber of Seville* for the umpteenth time.

'What's that?'

'I have an I-don't-know-what in my eye,' he translated.

'It's the soap that's stinging. Close your eye and shut up!'

'And what if nobody can take my eye out, whatever will I do, for God's sake?'

'You will, like Quevedo, write a story entitled *Fortune and Misfortunes of the Arse's Eye*,' I predicted.

'But can you imagine what's going to happen if I can't go to the toilet? I'll burst and shower shit all over the Valley of Mexico,' he lamented.

'You'll be given an artificial anus, young man.'

'Will you perform the operation, professor?'

'Personally, and if you don't keep still I'll also clout you one.'

But Palinuro continued to bemoan his fate . . .

'Somebody must have cast the evil eye on me. Imagine the difficulties: from today onwards I will have to crawl on all fours, with a hole in my trousers to see through. Think how ridiculous it will be to say to Estefania, for example, "Happy the eye that beholds you, Estefania" . . .'

'Eyes are needed even within eyes themselves, said Baltasar Gracián. You can spend your life in contemplation of Duchamp's constructions, the ones that can be seen with one eye only and that closed,' I said to comfort him.

'My God! My God! If my third eye is as short-sighted as the other two, just imagine! I'll have to buy a monocle for it and I'll never again be able to sit down!'

'It doesn't matter: you can always use a contact arse. And I already warned you, shut up, because your eye reminds me . . .' I said to him, the razor raised.

'Reminds you of what?'

'It reminds me of Sir John Taylor who called the eye: Proteus of the Passions. It reminds me also of the fearful eye of the Caliph Vathek, Commander of the Faithful, who struck down anyone who came within his sight when he was angry. And the flaming eye in Ixora's forehead, with which she reduced Canteven to ashes, when he dared to deceive her with his wife Paramasceri . . .'

'I don't understand the comparison. My eye is not the kind that reduces people to ashes . . .'

'But your eye, Palinuro, shits on any who dares to look at it, which is pretty much the same thing . . .'

'What am I to do, what am I to do,' wept Palinuro (above), winked at me (below), burped (above), sighed (below) and begged me (above) to hurry up and finish shaving him (below).

But I insisted on continuing with my comparisons, so impressed was I with the greatness of Palinuro's eye, comparable only to the Ace of the Spanish gold suit, the Eye of the Trinity Triangle, the motionless Eye in the wall imagined by St Bonaventure to observe the movements of all people and things, or the single unblinking and eternally open eye of the Macroposopos, or Great Countenance of the Zohar. I swear to you, Estefania, that the ruby representing the Penine Eye never shone with such intensity, never was the terrible third eye of Shurem so hallucinatory or so frightful the eye in the neck of the giant Argus or that in the back of the child-monster Cuchulinn's head, or so beautiful the hundred eyes which other mythologists say that the same Argus had before he became a peacock, and never so fine Devandiren's spots which were, conversely, changed into eyes when Guadamen pardoned him. Likewise, Estefania, the Eye of Night which gazed on Virgil as he lay dying in the street of Misery and the eye of Jupiter Trioptalmus encountered in the war of Troy, were never so omnipotent or oracular. Nor so beautiful the eye which Odin exchanged for a drink from the well of Mimir which contained the water of knowledge and out of which rose the moon. Nor so luminous the eye of that other Scandinavian giant, Junner, from which rose the sun. And when I ran out of comparisons, I went over to the bookshelf, opened a history of art and found Salvador Dali's eye/clock and eye/painter; the eye of stealer of women by Sirio Musso; the eye in the spoon of the painter of eyes by Clerici; the eye-sun-dial by Trevisan; the destructive eye of Man Ray which destroys space, and so many other eyes, not forgetting those painted by Magritte and Max Ernst and the heavenly eye of Odilon Redon. Palinuro himself recalled Cabañes' *Curiosities of Medicine*, in which the author quotes the case of children born with a single eye in the forehead. I, in turn, pointed out that St Augustine in *The City of God* and Montaigne in his *Essays* also mention monsters such as these. Herodotus, in his *Histories*, mentions the similarly one-eyed Arimaspis, I told my friend, and went on to show him *Lo Inganno degli Occhi* by Accolti and *Le Symbolisme de l'Oeil* by Waldemar Deonna. We spoke of the Simenon character in *La Nuit du Carrefour* who, like the general, had a glass eye. Deonna reminded us of the immense tiger eye gazing down over infinity in *La Fin de Satan* by Victor Hugo, the prophylactic eyes inscribed by the Egyptians on their tombs, the sceptres, carried by justices of the peace bearing an eye on the pommel and the eye in the open palm symbolizing justice. And none of them, not a single one of these eyes, seemed to me as portentous or original as the unique eye of Palinuro.

I noticed then that in a momentary lapse of concentration I had nicked Palinuro and the eye shed a tear of blood. ' "Thou hast no eyes, no thoughts, but for gain, for innocent men's undoing,' " I said to him, 'Jeremiah, chapter 22, verse 17.'

'Do you know the Bible by heart?' he asked me.

'Two thirds of it: "therefore if thy right eye is the occasion for thy falling into sin, pluck it out and cast it away from thee": St. Matthew, 5: 29. And St Mark, 9:47, adds: "better for thee to enter blind into the Kingdom of God, than to have two eyes when thou art cast into the fire of hell". And then St Luke, our illustrious patron, states, fifty pages on: "the body has the eye for its lamp; and if thy eye is clear, the whole of your body will be lit up". And Job . . .'

But Palinuro had grown impatient: 'What's going on? Have you finished yet?'

'By a hair,' I answered him and effectively, I severed it with the razor, on the bias and at the root.

'Ready!'

'Are you sure? There's not a single hair left?'

'Not one!'

'Take care!' he said. 'There's much truth in the proverb that a nit in the hand is worth two in the bush . . .' I merely cleaned the razor and put it away in its case.

Then I sprinkled Palinuro with a little talcum powder and warned him: 'I'm very sorry, my friend, but to take out the eye I'm going to have to insert my fingers . . .'

'An eye for an eye, a finger for a finger,' Palinuro answered me.

Next, Estefania, I pulled a rubber finger glove on to my left middle finger, covered it with petroleum jelly and performed a simple operation, which I will describe in Latin for fear of offending your sensibilities: *digitum in* arsehole *eius imposui* and removed it, pronouncing but a single word:

'*Touché!*'

'What do you mean by that?' Palinuro asked me, considerably piqued.

'I've removed your eye.'

'What? But I hardly felt anything.'

'That's because I have physician's hands as I've already told you and, besides being warm, they're very dextrous! Astley Cooper would have been dead jealous, up there in Edinburgh.'

Then I showed him the glass eye which I took from my trouser pocket, as though it hadn't been there all the time.

'It's a bit yellow,' I said to him.

Palinuro diagnosed: 'Infectious hepatitis. Poor general, to think that he is ill and doesn't even know it.'

'Poor general,' I agreed and then asked, 'What are we to do with it?'

'I want it alive,' answered Palinuro. 'I never want it to forget the Battle of Santa Rosa, when the general fought shoulder to shoulder with General Obregón, nor the students he tortured in Tres Culturas Square. I want him always to remember that, when he was a revolutionary captain, he made the sign of the cross when he killed his first Christian of the day and that, when he was an old general, he cleaned his rifle with the gusto of a wanker. So put the eye in a glass of alcohol.'

'We don't have any alcohol.'

'OK then, put it in a glass of tequila.'

This I did, and the eye stared at us in considerable fright, Estefania, because it thought it was going to drown. Palinuro went to the kitchen to prepare something to eat. When he returned he looked and found that the eye was watching us.

'I swear it has changed expression,' he said to me. 'It's gazing at us in infinite pity. Do you know why?'

'I've no idea.'

'Quite simply, because it's blind drunk.'

6

Sponsalia Plantarum and the room in Holy Sunday Square

Aunt Luisa, in part because she had been born in Paris in the heart of the Faubourg Saint-Honoré, lived her whole life by French time. At midnight Mexico time, when in Paris dawn was breaking and birds in scarlet livery announced the beginning of the world on Boulevard Sébastopol, Aunt Luisa would open her eyes – almost always a few seconds before the alarm clock sounded to remind her that she was alive – put on her dressing gown and slippers and say her morning prayers. The dance of the hours continued at one in the morning when Aunt Luisa tiptoed through the house to the kitchen, where she would breakfast on coffee and milk and croissants. And, of course, at seven in the morning Mexico time, one in the afternoon Paris summer time when the temperature blossomed and the incandescence beneath the Alexandre III Bridge became unbearable, Aunt Luisa would dine in style with Burgundy wines and floor-length tablecloths. At three in the afternoon, time of the Paseo de la Reforma, Plaza de la Constitución and the Casa de los Azulejos, Aunt Luisa would sup alone in her room while on the other side of the Atlantic, six meridians over, night was falling, beggars gathered the day's newspapers and the Montmartre nightclubs lit up, like another century, to the beat of condemned men and red-columned bodices. A few hours later, Aunt Luisa would retire to her room, draw the thick black curtains over her windows, perform her bedtime devotions in a voice unsteady as the candle's flame and go to sleep at, give or take a minute or two, five p.m. Mexico time: eleven p.m. Paris time, when the bohemian population commenced their revelling and butterflies left their windowsill perches to frolic with their shadows in the night life of the Seine.

In the year 1900, Aunt Luisa's father had been appointed to administer the Mexican Pavilion at the International Exposition in Paris: a neo-Grecian construction situated on the left bank of the Seine, a few steps from the Pont de l'Alma and next to the House of Serbia, boasting nine arches and eighteen alcoves – equal to the number of Aunt Luisa's years – in which were exhibited the tobaccos, fabrics and precious metals of Mexico. And, as a birthday gift, Great-grandfather decided to take Aunt Luisa to see the city of her birth which she had left at three months of age and of which she had so often dreamt: Paris without rainfall. Paris baptized in laughter and urine. Paris of the stereoscopic plates and chimneys which read Eugène Sue. 'Paris of four hundred cheeses,' Walter would have said.

'Paris,' said Great-grandfather, 'of four hundred cheeses and of widowed champagnes.'

Great-grandfather, much occupied with figures and correspondence, used his few moments of leisure to apply the Cartesian principle of methodic doubt to the proud existence of the two phenomena of the exhibition which most fascinated him: one, the Eiffel Tower and, the other, the Giant Hugo which, though it did not have the green feet or fulminating eyes of the basilisk, appeared to Great-grandfather to be an incarnation of Armilus the Antichrist rather than a representation of Gargantua in the reconstruction of Le Vieux Paris. Great-grandfather never was able to choose between the Giant Hugo, which measured two metres and twenty-five centimetres and whose index finger would cover a five-franc coin, and the Eiffel Tower which was three hundred metres high and painted in deep orange at the base merging to pale yellow at the apex and blazed at night with the light of nine thousand lamps. For the rest, he was unimpressed by the Palace of Civil Genius, or the Pavilion of Hunting and Fishing and refused point blank to visit the Japanese Garden when he learned that Japanese gardeners had succeeded, through centuries of patience, in cultivating miniature firs and willows. Nothing bothered Great-grandfather as much as hearing speak of such experiments which reminded him of the degenerative alpinization of plants.

Thus, Aunt Luisa was left alone freely to roam Paris and the exhibition. And, in effect, she was seen to let down her hair in the Luxemburg Gardens the better to immerse herself in the ceramics and in the realms of the roses. Strolling from café to café and from rhyme to rhyme along the boulevards of Saint-Germain des Prés. Going to the Champs de Mars to visit the Party Salon and alighting from a car, in Trocadero, to see the Castle of Water and the Congo Panorama. Or doing a thousand other things like buying on impulse a dozen melba pears in Rue Mouffetard or wandering for hours together around the Maison Aristide Boucicaut in Rue du Bac and she concluded, at the sight of the stained-glass windows in the Sainte Chapelle and the sunlight decomposing into the seven colours of the spectrum beneath the dome of the Optical Palace, that she, Luisa, must indeed have been born under a propitious confluence of the stars to have been privileged to contemplate this fierce inventory of lights and surprises and, leaning out of her window on the Champs Elysées, to admire the rolling sighs, the rivers of canopies and sun shades, the long-breaded French and the tourists of tulle and spices who never tired of parading, day and night, be it Mexico time, or the time of the Café de la Paix, the time of the Pavilion of Bosnia-Herzegovina or the time to go to bed and sleep in order to get up

92

early next day to visit the Jardin des Plantes. And since, at that time, Aunt Luisa's skin bore some resemblance to animated porcelain and her waist, it so happened, was as French as might be desired, she left in her passage through Montparnasse, Place Vendôme and the Rue des Ecoles, a trail of lovelorn admirers robbed of sleep or repose for four days at least after meeting her. But first they followed her through the Court of Miracles, through the Ponsin Luminous Palace and the Rue du Caire where Arabs sold damascened swords and mother-of-pearl-inlaid furniture, they found out the name of her hotel, the number of her room, the comet of her name and sent her love letters which Aunt Luisa never understood because she spoke only a few halting words of French.

Nobody knows why Aunt Luisa, familiar as she was with the mysteries of Paris and having yet several weeks to learn its further secrets, should take it into her head one Saturday to follow the route recommended by the *Bon Marché Illustrated Guide* for seeing the city in three days, '*a vol d'oiseau*', in other words, a bird's eye view. But the fact remains that so it was and explains how she came to be in the Jardin des Plantes after visiting the Place de la Concorde – Jardin des Tuileries – Rue Royale – La Madeleine – La Bastille from where she took the Bastille-Alma streetcar, at the junction of Boulevard Henri IV and Pont Sully, exactly ten minutes after Jean Paul had entered the tropical plant house. In other words, all that stood between them were the houses of aquatic plants, edible and industrial plants, medicinal plants, annual plants and ornamental perennial plants, on all of which Aunt Luisa bestowed a bird's eye view, as recommended by the *Bon Marché*.

Jean Paul was a French botanist who spoke Spanish and, by strange coincidence, specialized in opuncia and other cacti of the high desertic plains of Mexico, having a particular weakness for the whip flower with its hanging stems and for the scarlet satin blooms of the prickly pear. Perhaps it was not such a coincidence, in that Aunt Luisa went to Paris to feel homesick for Mexico and returned to Mexico to feel homesick for Paris and the same was true, to a certain extent, of Jean Paul who went to America not only to follow Aunt Luisa but also with the intention of tracking down the plants and trees which owed their names, or their discovery, to French and other European botanists and adventurers. According to his information, these included the bougainvillaea, thus named – like one of the Solomon Islands – in honour of the French seafarer Louis-Antoine de Bougainville, and the flame tree named 'poinciana' by Tourneforte in honour of M. de Poinci, patron of botany and governor of the Antilles. Although, if the truth be told, Jean Paul was also interested in seeing the Mexican Gardens which Bernal Díaz del Castillo compared to the wonders described in Amadis of Gaul and in studying the aristolochiales with their pelican faces and nauseous smell, antidote for tropical snake

93

bites, and in admiring the humble flowers of the *cacahuanantli* casting their scented shade over the cocoa plants. However, some say that Aunt Luisa fell in love with Jean Paul under the spell of the language and knowledge of the young botanist. Never before had she met anybody who spoke of marine vegetation, multiplication by schizogenesis and the rising sap making for the head of plants with the naturalness of someone talking about the weather, the play they saw last Sunday or the most recent outbreak of Asiatic flu. Never had she imagined that anybody could call rose thorns emergences, or an inflorescence an *anthesis* or give the name wings to the membranes attached to the fruit of maple trees. With Jean Paul, Aunt Luisa learned of the existence of the Flora Calendar, she learned that certain trees have Dutch diseases and that an exsiccatum is dried and processed vegetable matter, accompanied by a label stating its family, order and common name, together with the place and date found and the name of the finder. Jean Paul gave Aunt Luisa a bunch of exsiccata of the most modest flower, the violet – or *viola odorata*, as Jean Paul said it was called in scientific language – composed of the most beautiful violets that he had collected over the years: one from the Haute Loire, another from Normandy, yet another fom the estuary of the Rhone and so forth.

The third theory is that Aunt Luisa fell for Jean Paul for another, very simple reason: among her other obsessions, she had always been terrified of old age and she had merely to see a hint in the transparent face of her suitor of the old man into which he would sooner or later be transformed, through wrinkles and libidinous thoughts, to refuse to see him ever again. And this insurance sought by Aunt Luisa against old age, against deforming arthritis and the temptation to paint cheeks green, could only be found in a man destined to die young: Jean Paul. But Grandfather Francisco, who was an assiduous reader of Cicero and had closely followed the steps of Alexandrinism and of Cousin's school of philosophy during the reign of Louis-Philippe, was always of the opinion that harmonious coexistence could only be achieved through eclectic solutions: Aunt Luisa, he said, fell in love with Jean Paul for three reasons: because he was a French botanist who spoke Spanish and loved Mexican plants, because he dazzled Aunt Luisa with his language and knowledge and because he was a man destined to die young. Moreover, had he not always said that you can fall in love with a person for many reasons? 'Never marry for money, marry for love,' he told his daughters. 'But fall in love with a rich man and you will be happier.'

But nobody, at that time, guessed the deepest and most powerful reason for which Aunt Luisa fell in love with Jean Paul which was, quite simply, that she confused her feelings for him with her love of Paris.

A year before he died, Jean Paul fell in love with Aunt Luisa and declared his passion among the tropical foliage, under the eyes of spying

94

customs officials who visited the hothouse in order to copy the exposed prop roots of the mangrove trees, while outside, in Paris, it might be hot or cold, it made no difference, even if snow fell like in Zola's novels on savage Paris, the Grand Guignol, the Hôtel-Dieu and the exhibition's Siberian Palace which was also called, on account of its ramparts, the Ephemeral Kremlin. Aunt Luisa rejected his suit. Two days later, in the sculpture exhibition of the Grand Palais, fearing that Rodin's *Gates of Hell*, before which she was standing, would open on the day of her death to receive her, Aunt Luisa repeated her refusal. A week later and eleven months and two weeks before he died, when they were inside the huge Celestial Globe, contemplating the movement of the stars and listening to the music of the spheres conducted by Monsieur Saint-Saëns, Jean Paul pointed out the seven stars composing the Coma Berenices, compared them to the constellation beneath the brim of Aunt Luisa's hat and then, in a veiled allusion to all the different men into which he could transform himself if Aunt Luisa would but accept him, Jean Paul spoke to her of the Roman god Vertumnus who, to court Pomona, the nymph of the gardens, changed himself into a peasant, a soldier, a fish and an old woman. He spoke of Jupiter. Jupiter who assumed the guise of a cuckoo to love Hera, a bull to love Ceres, a swan to love Leda, a pigeon to love Phthia and a dolphin to love Melantho. The same Jupiter who became a satyr to love Antiope, who wrapped himself in a flame to visit the nymph Aegina and who descended upon Danae as a shower of gold. Aunt Luisa refused him.

Twenty days later, one afternoon of the year '79 of the Christian era, that is, one thousand eight hundred and twenty-two years before his death, when they visited Vesuvius in Paris, Jean Paul, dressed in a Roman toga and surrounded by slaves with shaved heads, declared his love to Aunt Luisa at the moment when the volcano began to roar and spew out the burning ashes which buried the town of Pompeii, and Aunt Luisa, terrified, refused him. Jean Paul repeated his declaration by telephone and by telegraph in the Palace of Electricity, as his Twentieth-Century self. And, between Venice and Constantinople, when they were sailing on the Paris Mareorama, she in the guise of a young traveller seeing the sea for the first time and he as an old salt who knew all islands of the past and of the future: the Celebes, the Hebrides, the Falklands and Nearer-Land Island, Jean Paul declared his love to Aunt Luisa and then, yet again, at the top of his voice in the Acclimatization Gardens of the Bois de Bologne as he travelled disguised as a Scottish explorer on the back of a dromedary behind the elephant on which Aunt Luisa rode dressed as an English huntress. And Aunt Luisa refused, smiling, when they left the House of Laughter where Jean Paul, in an effort to win her, became before a mirror the world's fattest Spanish-speaking French botanist.

One day they visited La Tour du Merveilleux which was, much to Aunt

Luisa's surprise, an upside-down house: they went in through the attic, then climbed to the third floor, then the second, then the first, so reaching the ground floor and the cellar. The carpets and furniture were nailed to the ceilings, the lamps rose in the middle of the floor like crystal fountains and through the windows, by an ingenious arrangement of mirrors and panes, they saw the whole of Paris upside down. In the attic, Aunt Luisa refused Jean Paul. On the third floor, she said she'd consider it. On the second, she said perhaps. On the first, Jean Paul jumped in the air and picked a *narcissus poeticus* which hung from the roof in an upside-down flower vase and on the ground floor he gave it to Aunt Luisa, who thanked him wordlessly. In the cellar, Aunt Luisa realized that not only had Paris and the world been turned upside down by the exhibition but she herself too, and her heart, by Jean Paul, and she finally gave him an unequivocal yes. And so, hand in hand, they ran down to the attic and flew out into the sky through the chimney.

Eight months before his death, when the old man's beard was still flowering in Mexico, Jean Paul began his preparations for a long voyage, during which he would once and for all solve the riddle of the wind and gauge the density of seascapes. Six months later and two before he died, when both in Mexico and in Paris the crimson Christmas roses were still in bloom, accompanied by three trunks full of clothes and manuscripts, letters of introduction and his Raunkjaer stick for measuring the frequency of botanical species, as well as books and yet more books including the works of Baron von Humboldt, the *Biologia Centrali Americana* by W.B. Helmsley and Lamarck's *Natural History of Invertebrates*, Jean Paul crossed the Atlantic Ocean and saw for himself, among other things, not only that the sea is eternal, but also that the nocturnal phosphorescence of the waters, produced by millions of microscopic organisms, was of the same chartreuse green as Aunt Luisa's eyes. The streets of Veracruz welcomed Jean Paul in April with a yellow budding of the golden mimosa, a month and a half before his death, minus the six hours he had lost in crossing the ocean and which he would never recover. Two days later and two weeks before asking for Aunt Luisa's hand, the jacarandas of Mexico City carpeted the parks with violet flowers in honour of Jean Paul and Luisa. Three weeks later, Great-grandfather and Great-grandmother gave a banquet to announce the engagement, the entire menu consisting of a series of delicacies prepared with flowers; the guests ate, among other things, pumpkin-flower soup, nasturtium-flower salad, cactus-flower stew, Alexandrian or temple-flower dessert with crystallized roses and the health of the betrothed couple was drunk in hibiscus-flower juice. Nineteen days later and six months prior to the date fixed for the wedding, Jean Paul travelled to the city of Guadalajara to study the flora of its gardens and arrived there two days before his death, when the city was decked in poinciana blossoms. One and a half days later and eight hours before he died, Jean Paul explored the streets of Guadalajara, consulted Dr Hernández' *Historia Plantarum Novae* in the library, purchased some shirts and returned to his hotel to write, in tournefortia-red ink, a letter to Aunt Luisa and another to his mother in France.

Two hours later, when the night had already fallen, he went out for a walk and made for the park which he reached an hour and a half after leaving the hotel and fifteen minutes before he died. Five minutes previously, a man had entered the same park. Ten minutes later, Jean Paul sat down on a bench, beneath a poinciana tree, and fell to dreaming of the honeymoon which he would have with Aunt Luisa six months later and during which they were going to follow a floral itinerary through the Mexican Republic, to see the carnation bushes growing in the cemeteries of Alpuyeca, the tiger flower appearing along the roadsides of Guerrero, the bird's-foot flowering in the shade of the Tajín pyramids. And he mused also on their children and the house they would have in a few years' time. Four minutes later, Jean Paul had already reached the age of forty and was a botanist as famous as were, in their time, Lobelius, Mutis and Valivov. Two minutes later he was an old man rich in diplomas, memories and greenhouses in which grew orchids and convolvulus. One minute and thirty seconds before he died, Jean Paul was on his death bed, attended by Aunt Luisa and a priest, a halo of glory about his head and surrounded by his children, his grandchildren and his friends who had come from afar: from the Botanical Garden of Buenos Aires, from the Arnold Arboretum of Boston, to be with him during his last moments. Ten seconds later, the man cut his throat. One minute and twenty seconds later, sixty years before dying in his bed and twenty-eight before the manuscript of the Indian peasant Juan Badiano was discovered, six weeks after arriving in Mexico and twenty-three years after arriving in the world, Jean Paul died from loss of blood, five hours after a cerebral haemorrhage, two days before his funeral, eighty-three years after arriving in the world and sixty after his death, at the hands of a murderer, in a Guadalajara park.

And it was this Aunt Luisa – and none other of the world's Aunt Luisas – who was responsible for taking the first photograph of Estefania beneath a tree. That was in Veracruz, when my cousin and I happened to be there at the same time as Aunt Luisa who made a yearly trip to visit Jean Paul's grave, whose body for one reason and another neither remained in Mexico City nor ever reached Paris. From then onwards, Estefania's destiny – like the wood nymphs' – was linked to that of a tree. Or rather, hundreds of trees. On returning to Mexico City, my cousin wanted Uncle Esteban to photograph her beneath an orange tree. When she went to Berlin, many years later, she was photographed beneath the lindens. In Oaxaca, beneath the ancient Santa Maria del Tule cypress. Then, beneath a birch in Russia, a Bengal fig tree in Palm Beach and the tree of the Noche Triste in Popotla. She dreamed then of someday visiting the tree in Woolsthorpe in the shade of which Newton discovered the law of universal gravity, the Ilissos palm which shaded Plato's teachings and the rhododendron beneath which Buddha died. In a mythological dictionary my cousin discovered the Persian Heom which sprouted from the body of the first man and the cypress from which Helen, wife of Menelaus, hung herself. The pages of the Bible revealed to her the sacred cedar crowning the peak of Mount Lebanon and those furnishing the wood to construct the columns of Solomon's temple and the thorn tree of Christ's crucifixion. And she made me swear that one day I would take a picture of her, or at least draw her, beneath these and all the other famous trees of history and literature, including the sacred tree of *The Golden Bough* and the *Little Prince*'s baobabs.

Of all these pictures and drawings of Estefania, my favourite was a photograph which my cousin had sent me from the United States when she was seventeen years old, seated beneath an American oak which brought on a case of allergic fever which reoccurred at the same time each year thereafter. This photograph was the first object that we took to our room in Holy Sunday Square, after having an indigo-coloured surround cut for it and a frame of gold leaf made. Afterwards, and always with the photograph in mind, we went on to acquire and instal in our room all the objects which, without conscious thought, matched it: the ashtrays, the bedspreads – in fact, only one: the patchwork quilt given to us by Aunt Luisa and which inspired Walter's famous patchwork waistcoat – the books – which included *Letters from a Portuguese Nun, Homage to Sextus Propertius* and *The Adventures of Tyl Ulenspiegel* – Estefania's skirts and stockings, my socks and underwear, letters from our friends, a shell from Verde Island, a glass egg laid specially for us by Brancusi and a thousand things more.

In time, we had a special wall built on which to hang the photograph and, later, when we had saved up enough, we had a further three walls built. The wall opposite, with a window so that each morning the autumn sun might light up the golden leaves of the trees and the spring sun their green leaves. And to this window, also daily, came Palinuro's dove which more than once appeared when my cousin was mourning her ancestors. The fact was that, since she discovered the portraits of her dead relatives in Grandmother Altagracia's room, Estefania had started to weep for the Hungarian grandparents she had never met, her Mexican great-grandparents who had died many years before she was born, a distant aunt she did not remember and so many other relatives and almost-relatives like the unfortunate Jean Paul, until finally I one day explained to her with facts and figures that we might well have anything up to 64,000 ancestors, or even more, and that it was not just for her to weep for some and not for the rest of them and that her entire life would not be long enough to mourn them all. From then onwards, she wept for no one.

The wall on the left-hand side of our room we designed with two doors, so that Estefania's portrait would have a bathroom and a kitchen matching her blouse and her eyes. And on the right-hand wall we opened up another door so that our friends could come in and look at the photograph, for which reason we had a stairway made after ordering a made-to-measure building, taking care that all internal and external details – in other words: windows, electrical fittings and drains, corridors, cornices, attic and archways – matched Estefania's portrait. Moreover, it seemed to us that the best thing for the photograph would be to have four floors beneath our room and above it only the sky which shone through a skylight that we had specially made so that the birds, cats, pilots and particularly the poor man who cleaned the skylight, would have an opportunity to admire the photograph. We did not forget the inhabitants of the building: we had made a concierge and some neighbours – among them the doctor, the policeman, the mad lady and the bureaucrat – and, on the pretext of spying on us when we were making love or asking to borrow an onion or half a cup of flour, they went into ecstasies over Estefania's portrait. We loved them to spy on us, but the concierge started to neglect her duties to the point that one day, in order to scare her off, we asked the general to lend us his glass eye, which we stuck to the inside of the keyhole. We found out later that the concierge had complained to the policeman that we spied on her when she was spying on us.

We also had made several neighbours who were indifferent to our lives and even to the portrait, who were but a few of those other millions and millions of people – as many or more than all our ancestors and probable descendants put together – which we had made later on and who we considered should be unaware of our existence, so that the photograph would not feel overcome by the curiosity of so many admirers and begin to question its own worth. Their number, of course, changed second by second as thousands of unknown people died or were born, and minute by minute and week by week, as my cousin walked the streets of the city making new friends and taking new lovers.

As is only natural, we had a city made around our building and we decided that it should be Mexico City for the pure and simple reason that we ourselves were born there. Then we had a country made about the city, a world about the country, a universe about the world, and a theory about the universe, taking care not to omit any detail: churches, squares, shops, streets and fire stations of Mexico City and of all the tentacular cities cursed by Verhaeren, and also Grandmother Altagracia's bad temper, the Boer War and Uncle Austin's deliria regarding *potu nimio* and *potu suspenso* and the Lisbon earthquake, as well as Hernani's first night, the birth of psychoanalysis, Mayerling's tragedy and Pentecost Sunday, ensuring always as I said that all these details matched or contrasted with Estefania's portrait. In other words, we had to have made, also to measure, time *before* the portrait and time *after*. Estefania was not the least interested in the fact that the dawn of creation went back millions and millions of years and that man had gone through 650,000 years of living, suffering and dying on earth. In other words, she was indifferent to the age of the Universe, provided that it had had a beginning. Thus, she agreed with *Dr Seraphicus* (St Bonaventure) in that at least time *before* was not infinite, because, if an infinite number of days had to pass before the appearance of the portrait, the day of its appearance would never have come and therefore there would never have been a time *before* and a time *after*. This would have obliged us to have recourse to a different concept of time and eternity and, therefore, to *Dr Angelicus* (Thomas Aquinas), towards whom Estefania's portrait never felt, shall we say, overly affectionate.

Next, within time before and time after, we had made – to our specifications – a series of cosmogonic, historical, literary and political events with retroactive delivery dates which, from time inmemorial up to one August morning of nineteen hundred and something, coincided to bring about the inevitable creation of Estefania's portrait. And we proposed also to have made – as we needed them – another series of social, linguistic, psychological and electronic events which combined to bring about its – equally inevitable – disappearance and passage into oblivion.

The former included the shifting of Ice Age glaciers and the appearance of the seed from which grew the mulberry tree which provided the leaves which fed the silk worm which produced the thread which made the fabric of which was made the dress worn by my cousin on the afternoon the photograph was taken. We also ordered the invention of the anti-rabies serum which saved Estefania's life several years prior to her journey and a Canadian photographer measuring one metre and eighty centimetres above sea level who travelled through the United States on foot reciting aloud whole chapters from Thoreau's *Walden*. Events in the second category included – apart from an imminent nuclear holocaust – our laziness which caused us to delay having a glass made-to-measure for the portrait and the absence of which, with the passing of time, caused the photograph to become covered in dust, the face of my cousin in fly specks and the tree trunk in entwined hearts.

But when we realized that time, the time which would make its disappearance possible, was irreversible, we ordered the Theory of Relativity and turned our room into a space vehicle which travelled, immobile, at the speed of light in the eternal present. The other photographs which we had hung in our room beside Estefania's portrait, of Uncle Esteban, of our grandparents Francisco and Altagracia, of Mamma Clementina and Papa Eduardo and dozens more of our friends and relatives quick and dead, all mixed up to the extent that we forgot which one of them had been alive and which were going to die, served to substantiate the illusion that we had at our fingertips the different stages of our lives and had only to look around us to live the future and transform it into the past, or to remember the past and to live it for the first time in the present; once again Estefania and I were in our grandparents' garden, picking green mint leaves to chew so that Grandmother Altagracia would not notice the smell of tobacco on our breaths. Again the sunflowers of September were in bloom and Uncle Esteban placed his gold American Waltham watch, covered in seaweed, in a jar of petrol in order to keep it alive until the year 2000. Again, in that far-away place, in the kitchen, Flavia was placing a cooked eggwhite in the steaming coffee to conserve its aroma and flavour and enacted the dry law on Uncle Felipe's shirts. Then Flavia would go and ask Grandmother Altagracia for money to buy bread, but Grandmother had recently hit upon a new and obsessive idea: to eliminate the possible causes of problems which worried her, thereby eliminating at a stroke the cause, the problem and the worry. 'Bread has gone up two centavos ma'am,' Flavia would say to her. 'It can't have gone up. The bakers earn enough and the Government hasn't authorized a price increase.' 'The Government's just authorized it, ma'am.' 'It can't possibly have authorized it. The Government is there to protect people,' answered Grandmother Altagracia and persisted in giving Flavia the same amount of money. Then Estefania and I would ask Grandfather to tell us stories. And he would take us to his room and bring out a box of sandalwood which contained his collection of old coins and he would put a silver Napoleon of nineteen reals in one ear and tell us that the Emperor was relating his victories in Marengo and Austerlitz. Then he would place in his other ear a one-peso coin bearing the bust of Victoriano Huerta and he would tell us that the traitor was revealing, in confidence, details of the plots he had hatched with Ambassador Wilson. Then he would put one coin in each ear and tell us that Napoleon and Huerta were speaking together and that they got on very well because all tyrants speak the same language. Oh but it was hot, on those afternoons when Estefania and I sat in the garden where the lizards attained immortality in the pots of geraniums and we would ask St Isidore the Schoolmaster please to send us rain. But, with any luck, while Aunt Luisa continued to embroider Mallorcan patterns on the envelopes of her letters to Paris and Ricardo the gardener taught us the art of creating labyrinths with walls of clover and Grandmother Altagracia baked almond biscuits, with any luck, yes, at any moment, Mamma Clementina might appear with a jug of iced lemonade which would split the summer heat into two polar caps.

It was in this room – or *atelier*, as we sometimes like to call it – in Holy Sunday Square that I set aside my medical books and devoted myself to painting. Estefania, who flashed through the days like an exquisite shooting star dazzling the city inhabitants and her colleagues at work, would come home tired in the afternoons when I had painted at least five different versions of our room: in one, the curtains were white with a sunflower motif, as Van Gogh might perhaps have painted them; in another, the curtains were red, wrinkled and foetid as Soutine's carcass of beef; in another, the curtains, and with them the entire room, reverberated with Escher's optical illusions. At four in the morning, when I could barely stand, the room filled with Bosch's elves and demons. And the fact is that the real room, our room, was unattainable. In vain did we stroke the walls and kiss the floor. In vain did we one night plan to lick every square centimetre of the walls. We ended up in the early hours of the morning with dry tongues covered in flakes of lime and cobwebs and, in that time, the room had changed who knows how often in colour, dimension and light and had evaded us once again. Some nights we would go out to walk and occasionally, in the lighted window of a miserable tenement or in the illuminated eyes of a palace, we would discover our room. We knew that it was our room, that it was calling us, that if we had responded to its call we would have entered another dimension of our lives; but we were too lazy to change our name and appearance, to become old all of a sudden, learn by heart another's memories and gladly receive old friends we had never seen before. On such nights, we always ended up in the parks after endlessly walking along a river of ash, very slowly, like birds stripped to the back. We would pause by a bridge over a dark lake, watching how the trees sought their sadness and the breeze adrift on green fountains was reduced to oblivion. Then we would lie on the grass while the lake froze over from its heart outwards and return home very late, very tired, at the hour when whores offer their love potions and the multitudes adjust their periscopes; the hour when dreams hang heavy on the eyelids and children undress in the fog and drown in memory. And I, like a sailor returning from affront, sightlessly sailed Estefania, I sailed her through the salty spaces of our room and, at six in the morning, it returned to us once more as it was and as it had always been.

Then, as day began for the world, for us began an endless night, a journey through the constellations and the orange stars and through the black velvet tides of Venus and hazy waves and showers of meteors and six-tailed comets. A journey during which we conversed with Russell's rational virus, Lauri's thinking atoms and Van Vogt's tetra-dimensional cloud. At such times, shirt collars alighted in cups. Fried eggs detached themselves from the frying-pan and sailed through the air like exploding stars. The image of Uncle Esteban stepped from his portrait and came between us as we were about to kiss. We laughed and the caviare escaped from our mouths like black bubbles. When I sought to enter Estefania again and she parted her legs to receive me, my sperm issued forth from her vagina and sketched pornographic arabesques in the air. Gravity was reduced to a point where the stripes on the tiger skin hanging on the wall lifted from the hide and wound around our bodies and bound us. Then all the fruit motifs floated off the dinner service and so we made love among bunches of tiny grapes and mounds of Lilliput apples. Then the flowers that Estefania had embroidered on the pillowcases floated away, as did the mark embedded in her cheek by the embroidery every time she slept. Then the white moons detached themselves from my blue tie and we made love surrounded by tiny silk-flavoured moons. Then all the coloured dots from a Seurat painting detached themselves and showered us in confetti. Then the headlines and the articles from the newspapers and the words from books detached themselves and mingled and then we made love between the death of Che Guevara in Vietnam and Madame Bovary crossing the Atlantic in the *Spirit of St Louis*. Then the meaning of words and sentences became detached and we made love in a wash of senseless mumblings and syllables. Then all the fingerprints that we had left on the door, on the glasses and on the curtains detached themselves and caressed our bodies. Then the skin of our tongues became detached and licked our backs. Then the darkness escaped through the window of our room and we made love in full sunlight. Then all the colours of the world detached themselves from objects and with them the colour of our skin, of our eyes, of our veins and of our bones and then we made love invisibly, immersed in all the colours of paradise. Then wakefulness detached itself from our bodies and we made love asleep. Then sleep detached itself from our eyes and we made love awake. And so we continued, making love, for over two hundred years and when we finished, five hours later, we realized that our building had been knocked down three months previously and that our room had become a space ship of flesh and bone.

Nothing more natural: we loved our room so much that we considered it to be a living being, we celebrated its birthday and told it stories at bedtime. One day we gave it a carpet for its floor and another day we bought it a table for its carpet, a cloth for its table, a vase for its cloth and flowers for its vase. Or we told it the story it liked best, saying it was the Ugly Duckling, because it was always imagined that some day it would become a beautiful room with windows looking over the gardens of Versailles. We promised it that one day we would buy it a mirror the size of its floor and another the size of its ceiling and four mirrors the size of its four walls so that it could see itself full length and discover itself full of the flying carpets and floating tapestries of *Gaspard de la Nuit*.

To give you a better idea of our room, I can let you have all its measurements. I will always remember, because Estefania and I measured it over and over again to find out how much it had grown. Our room measured four metres and twenty-five centimetres across. In length, almost five metres. Three metres in height and as much again in depth. That gave us twenty-one square metres of floor and over sixty cubic metres of space. My desk measured one metre and twenty centimetres by eighty centimetres. Our bed, one and a half metres by two and the distance between the bed and the table was sometimes one metre thirty centimetres and at others, when I didn't feel like drawing or writing, it was immeasurable. Between one cup and the next, lined up two by two at the back of the cupboard, was a space of almost always two centimetres and between Estefania's portrait beneath the American oak and all the other portraits of Estefania beneath other trees in our photo album, there was a distance of two metres fifteen centimetres and several months and years. Between the ashtray and a book which I was reading, three inches. Between the children's shoes in which I had learned to walk and my white medical student's shoes were many illusions and feet of different sizes. Between an invitation to a black-tie do which I kept in a drawer and the shop which hired out dinner jackets, there was a distance of some two hundred pesos. Between eating squid in its ink and walking through the woods one bright afternoon was an intervening Sunday and several periods of solitude. Between chewing a muscle in Estefania's neck determining the longitude of a marble-like expression and a swan shattered by the foam there was but a shade of difference. Moreover, our room could not have been better situated: it was only three hundred metres from the National Palace, two leagues from Chapultepec Park, two hundred and fifty miles from Acapulco, and a hundred and ninety-two light years from Betelgeuse, sixty yards from the corner shop and six hundred and sixty-six thousand kilometres from the infinite number of points in space lying six hundred and sixty-six thousand kilometres from our room.

As for the distances which separated us and united us, I can only say that they also were impossible to measure. There were times when we both woke up to find ourselves lying face to face and then between my nose and my cousin's there was a distance of some twenty centimetres which first dropped the nought to become two and then dropped the two to become naught. However, at other times, when we argued and turned our backs on each other, the distance between my nose and hers was some forty thousand kilometres, measurable from the tip of my nose and following a straight line around the curve of the Earth's surface across the mountains, the valleys, the pencil factories and ships' funnels, to reach the tip of Estefania's nose. At other times, I measured the seven centimetres of my index finger and inserted six and a half into my cousin. She then would kiss thirty of my forty millimetres of lips. I would lick a round centimetre of nipple. She would take into her mouth two cylindrical inches of my penis. I counted ten tongue lengths from her tongue to her thighs. She swallowed two cubic centimetres of my sperm. I bit a spherical inch of buttock. She calculated twenty kisses from my navel to my right knee. I savoured three lineal fingers of saliva. She promised me four ounces of tears when I died. I pledged her a litre of blood should she ever have an accident.

7

In the name of science

Ten minutes after being relieved of the Universal Eye, Palinuro heaved a sigh of relief (above) and said: 'Ah, at last I can shit! By the way,' he added, as he opened the bathroom door, 'in the bathroom I have all imaginable kinds of literature, from *Penthesilea* to magazines you read with only one hand like *Playboy*. But please, don't touch a novel by Nicholas Blake that I'm busy with, called *The Worm of Death*. Every day I read three pages while I'm shitting and afterwards I rip them out to use them for purposes of personal hygiene. Please, as I say, don't touch it. I once lived with a friend who got it into his head to use the same book and we came to a bad end. As I'm sure you'll understand, you can't read pages 76, 77 and 78 of a detective story and then not read 79, 80 and 81 and then read 82, 83 and 84 and so on. Our friendship came to an end on the day that he got a phenomenal attack of diarrhoea and fifty whole pages disappeared, from 26 to 75.'

'I suppose you never found out who the murderer was,' I ventured to remark.

'Worse than that: I never found out who was murdered. However, I forgave my friend because I realized that he was very sick and he lost so much diarrhoea, but so much, that he had to be given a shit transfusion.'

From the toilet, through the closed door, Palinuro shouted: 'As you must know, the anal passage is protected by an internal sphincter muscle and an external sphincter muscle which normally maintain a state of tetanic contraction, is that not so?'

'It is indeed,' I answered.

'In that case,' he went on, 'mine are now in an abnormal state and, as if that were not enough . . .'

A thunderous report. And another.

'As if that were not enough,' he continued, 'my diaphragm has descended and my colon is in a state of vigorous peristalsis!'

Much alarmed, I did not know whether to look up all these words, at that time incomprehensible to me, in the *Dictionary of Medical Terms*, or ask my friend: 'Palinuro . . . are you OK?'

'I think not,' he answered, his voice betraying an alarm greater even than my own. 'At this moment I am having a haemorrhage of a horrible substance composed of water, bits of undigested food, metallic elements and bile pigments . . .'

'Shit!' I exclaimed.

'The flow, which has now become a veritable flood, also contains cholesterol, purines and inorganic salts of sodium, calcium, magnesium and iron . . .'

'Palinuro!' I shouted. 'Open the door!'

'God help me, God help me! I do believe that all sorts of micro-organisms are coming out of my anus, products of bacterial decomposition like indole, skatole and mucus and epithelial cells . . .'

'Palinuro!' I repeated. 'Open the door!'

But my friend continued regardless: 'In other words or, more precisely, in a word: shit! Shit, man, Freudian gold, the first gift of a baby to the world and its loved ones! Pure gold distilled by the intricate coil of my intestine!'

'Are you sure it's shit?' I asked him.

'Yes. I'm never wrong,' he answered me, speaking *ex cathedra* (from the seat) and added: 'And why do you want me to open the door, if I may ask?'

'Because I need to go too,' I answered.

'I would suggest,' my friend said, finally opening the bathroom door, 'that you wait for it to air or else burn a stick of incense. Do you know something?' he added, pointing to the toilet.

'What?'

'I produced green shit.'

'And why do you think that might be?' I asked him.

'Chance, of course. If I had set out to do it, I would never have managed it . . . and now, how about if I show you my drawings?'

One afternoon, when the study of anatomy had palled on Palinuro more than usual, when endless repetition of the names of utriculi, lobes and ligaments had made them meaningless, my friend took up his palette and started to sketch and paint the section of the face which he was studying. In garnet red and chrome yellow he painted the fibres and fascicles of the digastric muscle. The facial vein in Antwerp blue. In crimson, the lingual artery. When he had completed that section, Palinuro took a lead pencil and drew in the rest of the face. The pencil followed a trajectory unforeseen in any of the marvels familiar to us: just as the embroideries of Lisandra, his paternal grandmother, followed the route of oceanic days to the Azores, the pencil allowed itself to be borne along the Florentine path of the Uffizi gallery and drew the lips, nose and forehead of a head sculpted by Donatello for the pleasure and landscapes of Cosimo Medici. The skin, milky as Rilke's alabasters; the lines – perfect as the equation of a shoreline

– suggested the same profusion of warm and noble strokes. In the absence of museums, Palinuro went to the libraries and devoured illustrations of works by Raphael and Paul Delvaux, Piero della Francesca and Lucas Cranach, by Vermeer and Georges Latour. Back in his room and armed with his sable and camel-hair brushes, black oil of Giorgione's invention and pencils mimicking the earth tones and colours Palinuro loved so much: Naples yellow, the bone black used by Diego Rivera, Cremnitz white, the Seville earth used by Velazquez in *The Royal Family* and Veronese green for shading flesh tones, my friend drew from memory – or copied from a postcard or from one of the second-hand dictionaries and histories of art that he had bought – faces or hands, legs, thorax or full figures, but always departing from a section of an anatomical plate. Thus, Moreau's *Salomé*, Petrus Christus' *Nativity*, Rodin's lovers in *The Kiss* and Gauguin's orange women all displayed in some part of the body a perforation or gaping wound where the skin parted to reveal the world of the viscera; Michelangelo's *David* had a horrible wound in his chest which revealed the coronary arteries, the diaphragm, the descending aorta and the heart purified by love for Bathsheba. *The Hands of Judas*, by Goltzius, exhibited the flexor muscles of the fingers and the blood-covered metacarpi. Sandro Botticelli's *Venus*, with her stomach slit open as though slashed by a blade of mother-of-pearl, showed the peritoneal fold with trimmings and arborescences of yellow fat to which clung jellyfish and seaweed, and a section of the blind intestine hanging from the wound, bristling with mermaid's scales and lumps of white coral, rose-tinted by the sun, irritated by the sea salt, pecked by seagulls and cormorants. The examples were endless: the *Medusa's Head* which fascinated Shelley; Van Eyck's portrait of Arnolfini and his wife or Léger's builders; none was spared from revealing, through the magic of a shivering pencil line or brush stroke, a fortuitous cranny harbouring boils or tumours, a heap of ganglia and cyanosities or a mob of arteries. Likewise, Courbet's lesbians or Isabelle Vigée Lebrun's self-portrait; no sculpture or figure in painting known to Palinuro, including Fortuny's *Little Count*, Tintoretto's *Massacre of the Innocents*, whose blood flows over the floors of porphyry and serpentine, or even the figures in Rembrandt's *Anatomy Lesson*; all were branded in some part of their body, the chaste, white triumph of marble or canvas sundered – on the arm, the breast, the thigh, the virtuous plateau of the stomach or wherever the skin might erupt – by some opening or wound, archway or excavation revealing the inappetent and fermented luxuriance of the bronchials, the liver covered in honey and mother-of-pearl or the rusted cortex of the lungs drowning a herd of transparent snores. Palinuro soon realized that by merely drawing an anatomical section he could imagine the rest; all roads led to Florence, to the Prado, to the infinite museums of the world; if he drew the sartorius muscle, he would sooner or later arrive at Rubens' *Three Graces*. Again in the absence of museums, Palinuro scoured the parks and avenues of Mexico City and copied Neptune, the Tritons and the *Malgré Tout* in the Alameda Park, the sculpted group of the Danaids and the lansquenets each holding aloft a globe of glass; then, in the Paseo de la Reforma, the statue of Charles IV, the Angel of Independence bathed in molten gold with Law and Justice at her feet and, further on, Christopher Columbus and the monks of La Rábida, Diana the Huntress, Ariel and the caryatids weeping tears of hail in the fountains of Polanco. Palinuro felt sorry for the hopeless fate of statues and figures in paintings for, beneath their skin of oil-paint and canvas, of granite, watercolour or numismatic gold, they must be filled with air and space, roses and electric liquors, sunflowers, cinnamon and wild marjoram essence or, at least, with all the materials employed in their creation: the translucent marbles of Paros and the pearly marbles of Carrara, malachite or mahogany, rosewood, bronze or lacquer, oils of opium and orpiment, gum arabic and plaster of Paris but, none the less, in their misery containing the same quantity of lymph, blood, of unhealthy kiosks, muscular putrefaction and sebaceous choler as the men, women and children they portrayed. That was the motive – my friend explained to me – behind the strange drawings he began to produce; first, when he realized that he wasn't made for medicine and, second, when he found out that painting was not made for him. That was why – he insisted – in the neck of Modigliani's student (in some cases Palinuro liked nothing more than to state the obvious) he had drawn two horizontal incisions and a vertical slit so that, folding back the two resulting flaps of skin, it was possible to see among other things the trachea, the yellow and sulphurous thyroid gland and the internal jugular vein. This was the reason also that the Mona Lisa, older than the rocks among which she sits and dead many times, exhibited to the world her teeth and tongue, previously unknown, the superior coronary arteries and the risorius muscle endowing her with her enigmatic and bisexual smile.

Palinuro went on to explain to me that he saw nothing wrong in these drawings. That however faithful they might appear – and must indeed be – the artists who executed them belonged to the heuristic category since their art was not restricted to merely producing the visible appearance of the corporeal world but, on the contrary, revealed that which lay beyond surface appearances; that Clerici painted anatomical plates for a living; that Leonardo himself made over six hundred preparatory sketches which Ruskin mocked as belonging to 'the science of the sepulchre'; that the famous English surgeon James Paget created veritable masterpieces from the models of his own dissections: to wit, the time a widow bought from him the marvellous drawing he had made of a section of her husband's ulcerated intestine. That there was nothing more beautiful and dignified than Hogarth's autopsy engravings, or Vesalius' skeletons in *De Humani Corporis Fabrica* which dazzled Baudelaire by the wondrous, abstract beauty of the ribcages, or Sir Henry Tonks' watercolours executed during the First World War which showed all the facial wounds of the past and of the future, and so many other drawings, plates and illustrations – the examples of these were also infinite, he told me – in which great artists or, at least, great scientists had demonstrated their profound interest in the human body – which Schlegel had stated to be the greatest of hieroglyphics – and of which one of the most beautiful and fascinating was that appearing on the frontispiece of William Cheselden's *Osteography or Anatomy of the Bones*, in which Galen was to be seen meditating beside the skeleton of a dead brigand and, behind him, the skeleton of a crocodile from the River Nile and, in the background, a pyramid and the skeleton of a heron carrying in its beak the skeleton of a fish and, on the other side, the arched skeleton of a cat recoiling before the threatening skeleton of a dog; this illustration always reminded Palinuro, so he told me, of what he and his friends called 'Charon's Cave', and which he promised to take me to see.

'Corpses,' he assured me, 'have become as scarce today as they were three hundred years ago. In fact, I have even heard it said that an international traffic in corpses has been established, to the benefit of our poverty-stricken Third World which has an abundance of this raw material: yes, you heard right, the dead now travel as much as the living. They sail across the Indian Ocean, are smuggled through the Suez and the Panama Canals and disembark on the frozen beaches of Atlantic City to appear three days, or three weeks, later in the Faculty of Medicine of some college in New Jersey. *Die now, travel later.* I'm telling you all this because skeletons are becoming increasingly expensive and there are very few students who can indulge themselves in the luxury of owning a set of bones, apart from their own, which are no good to them for purposes of study. In the United States, or so Walter told me, universities already have bone libraries – their osoteques you might say, which lend out bones to osoteque card-holders and even paint them different colours according to which osoteque they belong to, so as to be able to identify them later. If you are lucky, you might get the pink skull of a Tupamaro freedom fighter, the golden cage of an African guerrilla's yellow-painted ribs or the blue shinbone of a Vietnamese. Elsewhere, of course, they already produce plastic bones using moulds cast from real ones. They are perfect. A plastic femur, for example, exactly produces the cavity for the round ligament, the lesser trochanter, the crist of the minor adducter muscle, whatever! But I'm not keen on the idea, not at all; I want to study *homo sapiens* and I'm not in the least interested in *homo plasticans*. And to do so, my friend, you have only to avail yourself of Charon. Nowhere, but nowhere, can a student obtain authentic bones, bones of flesh and bone, as cheaply as we do . . .'

Palinuro heaved an enormous sigh, consulted his wrist (he had never worn a watch but looked at his wrist in order to guess the time) and added: 'On the subject of Charon, it is now time for you to meet my soul mates: Molkas and Fabricio. At this precise moment, Molkas is about to finish his biochemistry class and Fabricio will be eating strawberries and cream in La Bombi, as he does every Thursday at this time. Shall we go?' And Palinuro explained that my addition would bring the Three Musketeers (in fact four) up to complement. I would be Athos – temporarily absent – since he would never relinquish the role of D'Artagnan.

For a start, Molkas admitted that he masturbated daily and at all hours. The first conclusion drawn by Palinuro and Fabricio was that their friend was prey to primary narcissism and an autoplastic temperament, causing his impulses to become symptoms, and that he had translated a hovering anxiety without ideological content into a compulsive ritual, the result of a self-punishing combination of viscerogenic and psychogenic needs of a focal, diffuse, proactive nature.

'Bullshit,' said Molkas. 'I masturbate in the name of science.'

'It may not however be your fault, since, as Leonardo [Leonardo again] said, the male member has a will of its own: *anima e intelleto separato dall'uomo*.'

'Bullshit,' insisted Molkas. 'I masturbate in the name of science.'

Fabricio started, causing his glasses to slide down to the end of his nose. 'In the name of what did you say? Of science?'

'I can't believe my ears,' retorted Palinuro, scratching his right ear.

But young Molkas, undaunted, first reminded his friends that since Paracelsus had identified the difference between semen and sperm (though it was in fact the other way around) and then took an orange from his jacket pocket, polished it on his shirt sleeve, asked for a knife to peel it and, when he was given one, started to peel the orange in a spiral and, while Palinuro drew the curtains and turned on the table lamp with the light directed into Molkas' face, the latter said that his original intention – for which purpose he had brought a second-hand silver microscope and a set of dyes – had been to discover whether or not he suffered from azoospermia, in other words, the total absence of spermatozoa in the semen or, failing that, from any other related complaint: asthenospermia, oligospermia or etceterospermia and, after Palinuro had told him off for dropping the orange peel on the floor and Molkas had picked it up and without further ado thrown it out of the window, assured them that one of the greatest satisfactions of his life had occurred on the morning on which he had placed on the platelet of the microscope and examined a drop of his five cubic centimetres of ejaculation, sharing the excitement, incredulity and surprise which only one other man in history could ever have felt – he meant Leeuwenhoek – the millions and millions of flagellum-endowed little creatures wagging their tails in lively fashion, surrounded in their seminal halo of green with a magenta sheen (because he had used FD and C No. 2 dye with safrosin) and forging ahead at a pace of half an inch per minute, the little innocents, newly ejected from the testicular ducts . . .

'Which testicle?' asked Fabricio.

And Molkas, chewing a segment of orange and spitting out the seeds on the floor, had to admit that he wasn't sure and that on several occasions he had masturbated with the sole intention of proving the accuracy of Hippocrates' theory to the effect that girls are engendered by spermatozoa from the left testicle and boys by those from the right, but he never noticed any difference, despite L.B. Shettles' assertions that there were feminine spermatozoa and masculine spermatozoa: no, he had never seen any with long curling lashes, moustaches, mammary glands or deep voices but, he said, he had with considerable alarm noticed certain sperm which gave the distinct impression by the way they moved their hips that they might be a touch gay, the deviants!

'Which hand do you masturbate with?' Palinuro asked Molkas. Fabricio told him off for spitting seeds on the floor.

Molkas placed another segment in his mouth, left the orange on the table, picked up the seeds and this time, instead of throwing them out of the window, put them in the flowerpot on the sill, expressing the hope that one day an orange tree would grow there so that the upstairs neighbours might never want for their morning orange juice, sat down and stared at the palm of each of his hands alternately, moving his head from side to side as though watching a game of tennis and, after making several comments on the shortness of his life line, the breaks in his love line and the length of his masturbation line, replied that sometimes with the right, sometimes with the left, sometimes without hands and sometimes with both and when Palinuro accused him of being ambidextrous, he protested he was actually ambisinistrous which was more or less the same thing, but not quite, and went back to peeling his second orange, turning a deaf ear to Fabricio's warning that he heed the recommendation made in the Talmud to the effect that you should never curse with both hands so as always to have one with which to forgive and bless.

Fabricio removed his spectacles and squinted at the lenses against the light, convinced anew that cobwebs had grown over the glass but, yet again, he found that the lenses were scratched and so he forgot all about it and started to twirl his glasses in the air as he paced the room with giant strides. Palinuro lit a cigarette and suddenly Molkas in very Spanish fashion (it should be remembered, of course, that he was the son of an

112

immigrant Spanish greengrocer) shouted: 'Oh shit . . . God damn it!'
'What's the matter?' asked Palinuro.
'I've cut myself,' explained Molkas, sucking the thumb of his right hand.
'It is God's punishment,' said Fabricio.
'For masturbating?'
'No. He punished you because you said: God damn it! He knew you were going to say it.'

That gave them the cue to open a discussion on determinism and the freedom of man; on the necessity – or possibility – of reconciling free will with divine omnipotence; on whether God knew that Molkas was going to masturbate and could prevent it; on whether God knew and gave a damn; on whether Molkas either knew or could prevent it; on whether the Milky Way was the product of an act of masturbation by God and on other related questions which were more or less fresh in their minds because they had only recently graduated from secondary school, although this conversation was conducted principally between Palinuro and Fabricio, because the drop of blood which gleamed on the tip of Molkas' thumb served him as an excuse – without interrupting consumption of his orange – to relate how he had one weekend masturbated ten times, fifteen, who knows how many, in an unending *tour de force* intended to confirm the theory of Dino del Garbo, the fourteenth-century physician who maintained that semen originated in the heart and how, though he discovered no trace of ventricles, coronary arteries or Arancius' nodules in his semen, he did eventually manage an almost transparent ejaculation containing a drop of blood; a drop of blood that must have come directly from the heart to judge by the subsequent palpitations and, moreover, since it was arterial blood as brilliant and scarlet as the blood on the tip of his finger, he was sure that it came from the left side of the heart. Palinuro and Fabricio, bogged down in a philosophical morass, paid him scant attention, one contending that, as the great French philosopher Helvetius said, self-interest is the basis of all human action, the other maintaining that although Rousseau had rated the work of his compatriot to be despicable, he none the less maintained that the arts and sciences are born of our vices, the first adding that Spinoza held that emotions can be transformed into instruments of fulfilment, the second being in agreement with this, while the third – when Kant was mentioned – raised his hand to speak.

'The accused wishes to go to the bathroom,' said Palinuro understandingly.

'Tie him down, he's going to masturbate, the pig!' shouted Fabricio.

But Molkas said that he had no intention of going to the bathroom but that, apropos of Kant, what he wanted to say was that he, Molkas, masturbated precisely in response to a categorical imperative, and he offered them several segments of orange. His friends, however, not only rejected the bribe but pointed out that they were digressing and that the sexual digressions of young Molkas were quite sufficient unto the day and they asked him therefore to cast further light on his statement to the effect that he masturbated in the name of science. Molkas told them about Pythagoras: that Pythagoras believed that semen originated in the brain and, for this reason, Molkas had begun one day to masturbate in a cold and cerebral manner in an endeavour to substantiate the theory. Dozens of attempts yielded not a drop of cephalorrachidian liquid nor the merest fragment of Reil ribbon nor even any meninges cells, in short: 'not a dicky bird'. On the other hand, his brain was so enfeebled that he could no longer remember why he was masturbating, a fact which in a way confirmed the scholar's theory. Molkas examined his injured thumb and mused that it was truly amazing that, in the whole world, no two thumb prints were identical. This prompted Palinuro to blow a cloud of smoke in his face and ask whether he had ever found what might be called 'sperm prints'. Molkas was baffled and so Fabricio explained to him that, according to certain contemporary research, a man's spermatozoa display particular unique characteristics or sperm prints which are as distinctive as fingerprints and are therefore equally useful for purposes of criminal identification. Molkas stuffed the last five segments of orange into his mouth, causing juice to dribble down his chin and, after telling Palinuro off for throwing his cigarette end on the floor, they discussed how inconvenient it would be to have to masturbate every time you were taken to the police station or needed a new passport. Molkas assured them that on his own penis (the *corpus delicti*) might be found thousands of his own fingerprints, while Palinuro apologized and dismembered the cigarette in the flower pot, saying that this would help the orange tree to grow up more healthy and robust, since tobacco was a good fertilizer. Eventually Fabricio tabled a motion that the meeting be brought to order. 'I really can't tempt you?' insisted Molkas, taking another orange from his pocket and protesting when Fabricio suggested that Molkas had doubtless stopped masturbating after his first sexual contact since it would no longer have been necessary, to which Molkas replied that masturbation had never been *necessary* and that, in all events and from a scientific point of view, it had been pragmatic and, to a certain extent, empirical and even propaedeutic. Of course he hadn't stopped masturbating and, what was more, the first thing he had done after his first experience of sexual intercourse, with a prostitute on Las Vizcaínas Street, was to masturbate – he explained, starting to peel his third orange – terrified of discovering in his sperm the sinister spirillum producing syphilis.

'The *treponena pallidum*!' exclaimed Palinuro and Fabricio together, entranced at the idea of having a friend who like Baudelaire, Nietzsche, Maupassant, Strindberg and so many other cursed poets and famous individuals, became covered in garlands of Venus, developed chancres the size of rupias, contracted vasculitis, the brain rotting away, suffering from progressive dementia, the optic nerve deteriorating, succumbing to pleiades of ganglia and paranoiac and grandiose notions with inflamed meninges and losing hair and eyelashes, moustache and eyebrows, nails and eyes.

Finally Molkas resorted to an ancient process which his infinite learning and wisdom told him could not fail: he made a culture from his sperm mixed with agaragar and a small piece of rabbit's kidney, employing the Lipp Colouring method which recommends the use of 4 R Victoria Blue, and that night . . .

'What happened that night?' breathed Palinuro.

That night, and by association of ideas, Molkas had a horrible nightmare: he dreamt that he was floating submerged in a sea of sperm and that suddenly Queen Victoria appeared before him, very pale and dressed in blue, surrounded by ghastly bacteria, viruses and protozoa magnified thousands and thousands of times and he had had to fight bare-handed with the *staphylococcus pyogenes*, with the *vibrio cholerae*, with the *pasteurella pestis*, with the *mycobacterium leprae*, with the *entamoeba histolytica*, with the *brucella abortus* . . .

Until Fabricio interrupted: 'Enough, this isn't a bacteriology class . . . what happened next?'

Molkas said that he had awoken terrified and with a fever but that, although he had taken a blood sample to the laboratory to have the Wassermann reaction done, in a parabolic condenser, it had not been possible, to the untold loss of literature, to discover in his organism the terrible agent of the French plague, of the Italian pox which contains all the rest of the world's diseases, of the *morbus gallicus* contracted by the young shepherd Syphilis in Fracastoro's poem, of the disease, in short, for which the Spaniards blamed the American Indians, the Russians blamed the Portuguese, the Italians blamed the Germans, the Rumanians blamed the Barbarians and Baudelaire's biographers blamed the Negress he screwed every night though, unfortunately, there did afterwards appear in a drop of pus which issued from Molkas' member a number of seemingly inoffensive little creatures, round as muscatel grapes and clinging together in bunches, which were none other than the agents of gonorrhoea and, of course, the fact that their friend did not suffer from the disease which had for centuries been the scourge of 'Western Syphilization', as Palinuro said, and on the contrary had nothing more exotic than a dose of the clap, was a great disappointment to his friends, although Fabricio had the civility to write in his notebook: 'To summarize, masturbation is more hygienic than fornication . . .'

'It's more agreeable too,' Molkas ventured to comment, rising to his feet and quoting the bard:

> 'Pleasures practised by Onan
> Unbeknown to don Juan!'

After which, he ate the rest of his orange.

'Ah ha! now the truth is coming out! You finally admit that you masturbate for pleasure! Is that not so?' exclaimed Palinuro, triumphantly.

But Molkas was not prepared to put up with any more:

They were bastards and perverts, imbeciles and morons. He forgot his orange, his thumb, his friendship, and assured them that they would never understand the terrible anguish of spending nights in wakefulness, driven by an irresistible *élan vital*, trying to solve once and for all the long-standing dispute between the ovists and the animalculists, endeavouring vainly day after day and through the intervening nights to discover Paracelsus' cagastric and iliastric semen, Hippolytus' Panspermia and St Augustine's seminal rations. No, during his long nights of eternal insomnia he had seen none of these and, as God was his witness, for all the times he had masturbated, so many that he could not count them on the fingers of his hands even by resorting to the base tricks of Erik Satie (who had once counted over two thousand fingers) neither could he discover the plastic origin of semen which St Thomas Aquinas believed to produce resemblance with parents: the famous *principium corporis formativum*. Oh no, how would they know, ignorant fools unversed in the works of Naudin, Mendel and Morgan, unacquainted with the latest advances in genetics! And if he, poverty-stricken Molkas, could one day indulge himself to the extent of purchasing an electron microscope which would magnify his spermatozoa twenty-five thousand or a hundred thousand times, what wonders would he not discover! The mere thought of such a possibility caused the dorsal vein of his penis to become compressed and the spongy tissue to fill with blood: in other words, he got a hard on! When you read *The Microbe Hunters*, he told them, when you learn of the suffering endured by Robert Koch destroying his hands with corrosive sublimate to discover blood serum gelatine and the process of staining; when you picture Yersin burning the midnight oil to discover the bubonic plague bacillus and Ronald Ross braving the infernal summer of India to dissect cockroaches and flying fish in order to look upon the spears and half moons of malaria: then, and only then, could they comprehend poor Molkas, devoting his life and his youth to science, stooping over his worktable night and day like a Florentine scribe, suffering headaches, vomiting and reflex pains, seeing stars and luminous constellations, threatened by the horror of the post-orgasmic void, one hand grasping the column of the microscope and the other his penis, masturbating like one possessed, observing like one possessed, yes, to the point of often no longer knowing whether he stopped masturbating his member to masturbate the microscope and wrest from it its enigmas and milk its secrets, or removed his eye from the microscope to squint down the length of his member to discover there, in the depths of the orange-coloured tube of his urethra and in the ovoid spheres of his testicles, the minuscule figure shown by Plantades and Rondelet to inhabit each spermatazoon!

And Molkas buried his face in his hands and wept.

'All right, all right, it's not as bad as all that . . .' said Palinuro, handing him a Kleenex.

'In fact, virtually everybody has masturbated at some time in their lives,' said Fabricio, passing him a handkerchief.

'I've done it twice,' confessed Palinuro.

'It's not as though we even have anything against masturbation.'

'Besides, it has been shown that Voltaire exaggerated: masturbation causes neither blindness nor sterility.'

'In our own day and age, it is generally considered that as long as it is done in private and does not impinge upon public susceptibilities . . .'

'Men of science as formidable as Freud, Erb and Fürbringer gave the phenomenon serious study.'

'Agathias Scholasticus wrote a defence of masturbation,' Fabricio reminded them, scratching his head.

'And Dali [Dali again] accorded a very special place to the Great Masturbator,' stated Palinuro.

'In *The Age of Gold*, Buñuel attributed a particular significance to auto-sexuality, also called autism, auto-eroticism and palmistry, which many Mannerists [it had to be Mannerists] held to be a very distinguished, anti-barbaric and anti-animal vice,' expounded Fabricio.

'Although certain animals do masturbate,' Palinuro reminded them and went on to recite:

> *A monkey given to narcissism*
> *Devoted his time to onanism*
> *With such dedication did he jerk*
> *Society considered him a pervert*
> *Moral:*
> *Though opium is indeed perverse*
> *Self-love is certainly much worse.*

117

'The no less famous Tissot was another great scholar of masturbation,' continued Palinuro.

'I wonder if he had anything to do with the watches?' Molkas mused aloud. 'I have a Tissot watch which I never have to wind because it is powered by the natural movement of the wrist . . .'

'So I am sure it'll keep going till kingdom come,' said Fabricio.

'We just feel that you are concentrating on practice at the expense of theory,' said Palinuro, patting Molkas on the back.

'We recommend that you purchase *Onanism and Homosexuality* by Stekel,' said Fabricio, pinching his chin.

'I am going to lend you a paper presented by Mark Twain to the Club Estomac of Paris, under the title "The Science of Onanism",' promised Palinuro.

'And be sure to read a little novel by Apollinaire in which the young protagonist discovers sex through masturbation,' advised Palinuro.

At once they were embroiled in debate, Palinuro pointing out the need to broaden the field of scientific research by trying masturbation in different and unusual circumstances. Molkas maintained that he had masturbated in the bathroom. Palinuro in the kitchen. Molkas in the car. Palinuro with butter. Molkas in histology class. Palinuro in the sea. Molkas in a spiritualist session without letting go of his companions' hands. Palinuro on a bicycle without touching the handlebars.

Molkas in a procession. Cousin Walter flying in the Pan Am helicopter. Palinuro without undoing his fly. Molkas when he wasn't doing anything. Palinuro in a park. Molkas in a wake. Palinuro in a minute. Molkas in thirty seconds. Palinuro dressed in a tuxedo with a red carnation in his button-hole. Molkas without a carnation and without undressing. And what about Fabricio? Palinuro when he was eight years old. Molkas when he's eighty. Cousin Walter, in the bath. Palinuro, with his eyes. Molkas, with a smile. Palinuro with a banana skin. Gagarin in space. Molkas with the same banana skin. Palinuro thinking of Raquel Welch. Molkas, thinking of Vesuvius. And what about Fabricio? Palinuro with shaving cream. Molkas with McCormick mayonnaise. Karl Marx in the British Museum. Cousin Walter also in the British Museum, thinking of Karl Marx. Palinuro in slow motion. Molkas on the wheel of fortune. Palinuro in a lift. Walter in the Paris metro. Molkas with Colgate toothpaste. Palinuro with Estefania. Molkas never. Palinuro standing. Molkas kneeling. And what about Fabricio? Palinuro in the Statue of Independence. Count von Zeppelin in his dirigible balloon. Molkas with his father's gloves. Palinuro with Mamma Clementina's handcream. Adam in Paradise. And what about John Milton? After all that, and although Molkas had told the truth, but not the whole truth and not nothing but the truth, they decided not only to find him innocent but also (in their own words) 'to vindicate him in the eyes of society'.

'None the less, dear Molkas,' Palinuro said, 'we insist that you pace your experiments: science needs you alive and well. We advise you to take cold baths, bromides, valerian, etc., etc.'

Immediately and unanimously (three ayes and no nays) Molkas was awarded the Order of the Radish, consisting of a red ribbon tied around his penis which would, moreover, serve to remind him not to masturbate more often than strictly (and scientifically) necessary.

And Fabricio, yes, Fabricio the country bumpkin, had set out from his village, leaving behind mosquito nets flapping in the ash and honey of evening, against the advice of his mother who wished him to be a farmer, and headed for the great city in a truck full of goats and chickens, taking as luggage several white shirts which billowed on the clothes lines and a sackful of illusions which he recited every night, evangelically. When the ebb and flow of blood in his mother's carotid arteries plunged into a dance inspired by aortic insufficiency, Fabricio returned to his village, but only for a few days. Afterwards, he forsook for good the bucolic summer of his birthplace and the western sky bejewelled with stars which disappeared from view in the loveless morass of the great city. Instead, he slipped around the profile of the clocks and gave himself up to the fascination of that dissonant region. But, no sooner did he lay eyes upon the foetid furrows of the city and the ocean of recurrent loneliness and as, incredulous, he walked the flagless and desolate space, his face raised towards distant Sirius, his sixteen years cast upon the world like a bottle of chrysalides adrift upon the sea, his brow yet entwined with effervescent vines, knowing that every nodule of his gut contained an illusion and with an aching itch in his brain which was the certainty that the time remaining to him to live was but a tree, lamp post, the next traffic light or the name of a street, than he had the presentiment – without confessing to a majestic ignorance of the future and without the least desire to strengthen the bitter sap rotting in his chest – that his fate, which had at some point fixed the hour of sidereal succession in accordance with the fortune read in his hand by the village witch, was to burst forth in a blaze of fireworks and that, like so many other defenceless yokels unprepared for the sluice-gates of transition which open in a nightclub with the glory of a premature death and close with the mirror of a bloody dawn, a tickle dialysis would sweep him down the rivers of the city and leave him dumbfounded before shop windows and markets; and, just as Palinuro was to be seduced by the bookshops in which the multifaceted Universe lies revealed, Fabricio was to dream of plunging his adolescent heat into the sweet courts of the whorehouses and, his anxieties and his ambitions on ice to await the spell which would disperse them into thin air, he would dedicate himself furiously to reading medical dictionaries revealing how the buds of gangrene blossom blackly on the skin and how the white waterlilies of tuberculosis proliferate in the lungs of dazzling adolescents. He, Fabricio, was also a dazzling adolescent. At least, in his dreams. At least, when he dreamed he was beautiful as Apollo and, like him, enemy of shadow and crime, little suspecting that he would also be as unlucky in love as that god who loved so many women and nymphs: Cassandra, Cyrene, Coronis and Clytie, who never reciprocated his passion. Short-sighted and sickly, far removed from the world and from reality, Fabricio's failure lay in the solitary sexual habits he developed during puberty. As a young boy, like all young boys, by trial and error, he learned to do and to repeat in his life and with his body what he enjoyed, and not to do and not repeat what caused him anguish or pain. Bilious, hyper-emotional, vulnerable, he made his pillow his enemy. Or, all his enemies in one. He fought them every night, he fought the bully of his class who sent him to buy cigarettes and the boy from flat five who had bloodied his nose and the cousin who had better marks and more money. And he beat them, he forced them back on to the bed and the floor, he obliged them to beg forgiveness with tears in their eyes which were his own: tears of frustration, of loneliness, of fear. One night, after Fabricio met a schoolgirl with tatty exercise books, white ankle socks and a rosy smile, who had bent down in Avenida de los Pensadores to pick up a golden apple which she thought he had lost and, at the moment when Fabricio sank his teeth into the neck of his enemy, the pillow became the schoolgirl and the bite turned into kisses beneath the shaggy trees beside the lake carpeted with duckweed. From then onwards, he wrestled every night with his friend and forced her to lower her back to the ground and yield to his desires, to his teeth and his saliva and the liquid streaming from his member in warm spurts. Then he grew. Not agnostic, as his friends proved; but apathetic as his biochemistry teacher maintained. And a weakling and gangling and thin, but not slim, and fearing hell, the hell described by a rabid priest who foamed at the mouth and ranted in nasal tones; and this fear lead him to immerse himself in a solitude in which the pornographic postcards given to him by his friends became ever more scarce, as did certain unnamable verses tossed on the seas of memory. He promised the priest, the Virgin, God and Fabricio (particularly Fabricio) that he was going to mend his ways from that night onwards, from the next week onwards, the next year and that never again would he commit the mortal sin which had caused him a humiliation and ten Our Fathers in Rosario Church; and so, in order to refrain from committing the sin, he remained without hands, forsaken, submerged in the terrors brought by the night with its garrulous intersecting of planets and ancient curses, which forced him awake a second before the flood burst, his member swollen with iron ants, bathed in sweat and remorse between the sheets, burning from his dream that his body was aflame. But the instinct –

not a sick mind, nor the devil either – but the need, his nature and nothing but his nature, proved stronger and one day he started to masturbate alone, alone in a world without priests, without enemies, without God, without remorse, in honour of that schoolgirl and of all the schoolgirls in the neighbourhood. The error was not in the fact that while he masturbated – contrary to Palinuro – Fabricio would think of those possible lovers, the sight of which made him imagine the female anatomy as a potential luxury which he would meet at the school gates, in the Wong Café or in *thés dansants* at the Riviera, or how attached he would become to their breasts, their armpits perfumed with lavender water and their round and shapely thighs. No. The problem – as my friend Palinuro explained to him – lay in the method. Instead of beginning each session by imagining himself and her naked, after entering her and she having been entered, Fabricio started to fondle his member as soon as he touched her hand in the Avenida de los Pensadores, as they whispered the strength of their love and the conspiracy of their shortcomings. A logic of inexperience had caused him to believe that the act of penetration was, among all forbidden things, the most forbidden, and should therefore correspond to the supreme pleasure. And thus, with his hand and in his thoughts, he timed his ejaculation to coincide with the imagined penetration, believing that what he felt at the moment of entering her, she would feel at the moment she was entered by him. This girlfriend, born to make love with Fabricio, was called Celia, she was called Carmen, Carla and Catalina, though she was always the same: a faceless woman but, none the less, with large eyes prodigiously peopled with spasms, a girl without a body though her sex was neither dark nor bitter, nor did it have blue pastures which turned into spiders' knots. And thus, at the express desire of Fabricio, the girlfriend chosen for these interminable nights was passive and fictitious and almost white, like a clipper just waiting, waiting for him, while Fabricio fondled his penis with the right hand and with the other, with the pirate's hand, he removed her clothing item by item, undressed her like a bird, prepared to triple her flesh, the deepest and most legitimate, until she was stretched naked on the bed and in his life, that he could enter and inundate her. Fabricio thus developed a reflex which conditioned him to ejaculate at the very moment his member entered a woman, or ten women. This was not his fault: he was unable to imagine how to make love before making it, and then he didn't know how to make love after imagining it. And therefore was he little loved.

8

The death of our mirror

Something we were never able to measure was our love, for it was infinite. Just as when Palinuro used to ask his grandfather how much he loved him. 'Very much, very much, indeed,' Grandfather Francisco would answer. 'But how much, how much Grandfather? From here to the corner?' 'More, much more.' 'From here to Ajusco Park?' 'More, much more: from here to the sky and back, going the longest way of all and coming back an even longer way. And that after making several detours, getting lost on purpose, having a coffee in the Pluto café, going around all Saturn's rings on a scooter and sleeping for twenty years, like Rip Van Winkle, on one of those planets where the nights are twenty-one years long; because I like to get up early, at least a year before dawn.'

And the best proof that our love was infinite was our room, faithfully reflecting our love. And the best proof that our room was infinite was a crystal egg we had on the windowsill which faithfully reflected our room. This egg was colourless and transparent, as big as an ostrich egg and spent its time, every morning, reproducing the view upside down: mountains hung from the ceiling, the ceiling was a lake and when the sun rose in the world outside, in our little crystal world the evening set: the sun sank over the horizon, round, luminous and orange as a giant yolk sinking into a sea of collyrium. And in the afternoon the opposite happened: when the sun descended in the sky outside and the stars sprinkled the boats' masts, in our sky the dawn was breaking. And so it was that, like the chocolate emperor who spoke in German to his horses, we could say that over our kingdom, over our little room in Holy Sunday Square, in which our bed was America, our kitchen Europe and the bath-tub Oceania, the sun never set. It was the golden egg floating in the primordial waters in which Brahma was born: the egg in the shape of Father Mersenne's Great Lyre of the Universe; the egg hanging over the head of Piero della Francesco's *Madonna dell'uovo*. This was the egg that if you shut one eye and placed it in front of the other, you contemplated the universe and its surroundings as Borges contemplated the world in *El Aleph* or as Faust and Vasco da Gama, from the peak of Paradise, contemplated the Ptolemaic orb.

And of course, apart from Estefania's portrait, the crystal egg and the shell from Verde Island, we had many other objects in our room, some as good as impossible, such as a miniature mountain of gold and a little statue of the present king of France and other very particular objects which we could touch, which had names and makes. Or titles, like a book by the author of *Waverley*. And also Grandfather Francisco's Dunhill pipe, our Osterizer liquidizer, Uncle Esteban's American Waltham watch. Likewise, an Ockham razor and an Oldenburg typewriter which melted under my fingers every time I sat down to write a novel. In the larder, there was never any shortage of tins of Campbell soup autographed by Andy Warhol. And we also had – or my cousin had – a bikini which she had seen advertised in Evergreen and ordered by mail and which, one fetishist afternoon, it occurred to me to murder: I drowned the bottoms in the washing machine, the top I hung from the shower. Besides our mirror, we inherited from Aunt Lucrecia the camphor-scented bird which turned into a Japanese fan when it fluttered its wings and Uncle Esteban also gave us a silver samovar which gleamed during the white hours of night. Our furniture included a Bruce Conner sofa and an Abraham Lincoln rocking chair of the Kenneth Koch brand. And in a heap on the corner table we would reproduce Wesselmann's still life: a packet of Lucky Strike, a Coca-Cola, a milk shake, the nuts, the pear, the plastic roses, etc. In short, we had exactly all those things which make today's homes so different, so appealing.

The reason I dwell at such length on the objects we had in our room in Holy Sunday Square is that I wish to relate to you, Mr General, Mr Lottery-Ticket Vendor, don Prospero and dear friend Palinuro, the incredible things that we experienced in connection with them.

The first thing I used to do when I returned to my room, after kissing Estefania, kissing her portrait and kissing the reflection of her portrait in the crystal egg, was to raise the Verde Island shell to my ear. Then I would listen to the sound of the sea, the lament of the waves eternally circumnavigating themselves as though they had lost their memory, and the whistle of the fish flying over them like silver arrows. I would listen also to Estefania's laugh at the age of ten, her mouth full of sand. Next came Grandfather's old pipe: I would press the bowl to my ear and listen to the sound of the wind in the tobacco fields, then I would part Estefania's legs and press my ear to her sex and hear the pure sound of Creation. Soon we would be making love, she riding with the haste of a horseman with an appointment in Damascus, until a thread of saliva trickled from her mouth and entered mine and down this thread descended luminous little spiders. This was the beginning. Then she would weep with pleasure and her tears fell into my open eyes and clouded my landscape. That was the end.

Then she suggested that I should include her in our room. Or no, perhaps that is not how it was. Perhaps I was one day painting our room for the umpteenth time and suddenly the brush followed Estefania's shoulders and encountered her eyes. I recognized her on the instant and invited her to dance. It had been so many hours since we had looked at each other face to face, that I almost planted a kiss on her cheek right there in Avenida Cuatro. I suggested that we live together; she agreed, and from then onwards we walked together, we had breakfast together, we wrote together and did so many things together, that wagging tongues said that when we made love we also did it together.

I apologize for harping on this subject but, if anything filled our room with meaning, it was this: our love for each other since childhood.

If you got up at midnight, you tripped over love.

If you lifted the corner of the carpet, you found a little pile of love.

If you opened the window, love had never just flown out of the window.

Things were so infused with love that we began to confuse them with our love:

One afternoon I caught Estefania washing the dishes.

One night she caught me reading a book.

One day it caught us both fast asleep.

Until at last the things got fed-up and decided to impose on us their will to live. I have a very clear memory of that occasion on which suddenly, in the middle of an after-dinner conversation, we stopped talking at the same moment as though an angel had passed and we discovered in the middle of the table a glass which we had never seen. By this I do not mean that it appeared miraculously. No, it had been there since morning, and before that it was in the cupboard and long before that in the shop where we bought it. But we had never *seen* it. 'Did you notice?' Estefania asked me. 'It looks like a glass.' 'Where could it have come from?' I asked her. 'What can it want from us?' she wondered.

That afternoon, Estefania cleared the table, except the glass which remained there, untouched. She wanted to write a posthumous letter to Uncle Esteban but she couldn't concentrate. I started to paint the room and she was in the room, unable to concentrate on writing her letter to Uncle Esteban, and I was in it trying to decide which blue to use to paint her eyes: whether it should be Antwerp blue or Thénard blue – which is cobalt blue – or the blue of Rimbaud's O, the blue of the third movement of Bliss's *Colour Symphony* or the blue of the Gamma star of the Andromeda constellation, when suddenly, on the table which I was painting, the glass appeared. The surprise was such that, for the first and only time ever, I forgot the unsolved problem of finding the exact tone of blue to reproduce the blue of Estefania's eyes, which was so unique and so pristine that Flavia, the maid, was convinced that my cousin saw everything in blue: that for her the houses, the trees, the dogs, the films and the lamp posts were blue. In other words, everything under heaven and on Earth, including rivers and seas: from the Blue Danube at its greyest

124

moments, to the Red Sea in its greenest instants.

We decided then to take a walk in order to forget the glass but knew, however, that the glass would remain there. Then we went to the cinema, but we were unable to concentrate on the happy ending and we were left with the impression that we had watched a tragedy. We returned home and, of course, the glass hadn't moved a millimetre. We went to bed before supper – we had bought some hamburgers which we ate in bed – and all the while we were aware of the glass, thinking of it, feeling ourselves thinking of it. At one in the morning, happy as a child who just found its lost fountain pen, I said to Estefania: '*Sind wir vielleicht hier, um zu sagen: Haus, Brücken, Brunnen, Tor, Krug, Obstbaum, Fenster, höchstens: Säule, Turm?*'

'I didn't understand a word of that,' she answered me and I had to translate:

'Have we come here only to say: house, bridge, fountain, door, jug, olive tree, window or, at the most: pillar, tower?'

Estefania fell fast asleep and then at half-past one in the morning she asked: 'Who said that?'

In revenge, I didn't answer until two in the morning: 'Rilke.'

'No, no good.'

We fell silent once more. Fifteen minutes later she asked me: 'Are you awake?'

I didn't answer her so that she wouldn't think that I was suffering from insomnia and worry about my health.

Five minutes later I asked her: 'Are you asleep?'

And she, being in fact asleep, didn't answer me so that I wouldn't think that she was talking in her sleep and worry about her health.

Then I too fell asleep.

I dreamt first that I asked her if she was asleep.

She dreamt that she replied that she was.

I dreamt that I had just met Palinuro and that again I dropped my shopping on the floor and that I then went after a floating egg. Christopher Columbus was crouching on a table with his right hand outstretched, palm upwards, to see if it was raining and there was the egg, in his hand, as though a passing bird had just laid it there. I poked my head out from under the table and said to him: 'Excuse me, Mr Columbus, but that egg is mine: it's the one from our room,' and Christopher Columbus squeezed the egg with his fingers and shot the yolk into my heart. Then I was crawling after an orange which was rolling over a blue carpet and came to a standstill beside a pair of silk-stockinged legs which turned out to belong to Edward III who held a butterfly net and said to me, furious: *honi soit qui mal y pense, merde!*, and then he caught me in his net and I was the head of Marie Antoinette in the net and I was vomiting nuts and little balls of grey hair. 'Your problem is that you have illusions of grandeur!' the French teacher with Papa Eduardo's face shouted and he pointed at me with his index finger which turned into a little green worm crawling towards a green glass while the teacher shouted at me: 'Repeat, repeat the tongue-twister!' Later on I dreamt that I was drowning in a glass of water. I dreamt of Roquentin and I dreamt of Lenin. Then, that I was walking naked down República de Argentina Street.

Meanwhile, Estefania was dreaming that she sat two blocks along, in Holy Sunday Square.

I dreamt that I was arriving at the square.

She dreamt that she entered our building and climbed the stairs.

I dreamt that I climbed after her.

She dreamt that she entered the room and got into bed.

I dreamt that I lay down beside her.

She dreamt that she fell asleep.

I dreamt that we woke within the same dream.

'Are we awake or dreaming?' she asked me, somewhat alarmed.

'I have no idea,' I answered her. 'But they say that if you pinch yourself and it hurts, it means that you are awake.'

'I don't believe that, you can dream that it hurts.'

'Well, anyway, let's try,' I said to her and squeezed one of her nipples. She pinched my belly-button.

'You didn't hurt me,' she said.

'You didn't me either,' I admitted.

'Does that mean that we are dreaming?'

'No, it means that we love each other.'

'What are we going to do with the glass?'

'God damn it!' I shouted. 'Why the hell did you remind me of the fucking glass? I don't bloody know what we are going to do with the goddamned glass!'

Estefania took exception to my language and said no more. An hour later, she gave a start of happiness and exclaimed: 'Intellijence: give me the exact name of things.'

'Who said that?' I asked her.

'Juan Ramón. Haven't you noticed Juan Ramón writes intelligence with a j?'

I took a good five minutes to analyse the verses and reached the conclusion that they were in fact of use to us. We got up. We exchanged kisses and bad breath. Estefania made breakfast. We sat down at the table and half way through a fried egg I said to her, pointing to the glass: 'Estefania, pass me the knife please.'

And Estefania picked up the glass and passed me the knife.

And so we solved the problem: with intellijence.

126

Finally, she said to me: 'I didn't know you spoke German.'

'I didn't either, it was a sudden revelation.'

'Let's see, say something in German.'

'I've forgotten it all,' I answered her, 'I haven't spoken it for years.'

We thought that from then onwards our life would be simpler, since we would be able to cut an illusion with the edge of a glove, read a throw of the dice or put on a pair of new plates and walk along the stoves, towards the litanies of the sun, with the green suspicion that we would never return. And so it was: one Saturday, the glass – or rather the knife – became the paragraph of a book – at least in name – and all other things in our room also started to change. But not all at once: one morning, the carpet was a landscape for two or three hours before recovering its original identity. At midday, the wall-clock became a stationary comet which in turn disintegrated into a little pile of red ashes. But later, at five in the afternoon and as though nothing had happened, the cuckoo poked its head out and gave time five pecks. From that day onwards, the surprises were infinite and amazing: we opened a drawer of the sideboard and found it full of silk Coca-Colas decorated with lace of syrup. But when we opened the oven we found Estefania's nightdresses inside, half-cooked and seasoned with parsley sprigs and powdered nylon. We looked out of the window and it became apparent that we lived in the North Pole and that some workers were building an underground submarine and when they came up to the surface they carried in their hands sponges of aluminium and octopuses of noodles and from their backs rose little bubbles of yellow incense. Things reached a point where, instead of towels, we would find mirrors hanging to dry in the bathroom and every time Estefania sat down on the toilet she produced a huge quantity of flowers: magnolia, poppies, violets, heliotropes and a shower of microscopic yellow roses which filled the bathroom with an unbearable stench. We went to the market and bought rounded clouds which turned into tears when we arrived home. The silver samovar was a samovar at 11:22 and at 11:23 it was a Roman centurion's helmet. And then, in the time it takes to reach for a glass, it changed names ten times. Then a thousand. Then a million. And they never stopped; objects we held in our hands continued to reverberate and, finally, not only our room but the entire universe was flooded with winged words: tympans, gnomes, solstices, gamesters, romances, flaming spurs that tamely changed into oblong pigs, and anchors, septicaemia, chocolate soldiers and afternoons clothed in firedamp and velvet ripped to shreds by the green fangs of the lawn.

There followed a period of unhappiness. We became suspicious of everybody and everything. Whenever the concierge said good morning to us we spent the whole day wondering what she had meant . . . *what she had said to us*. 'Do you think it meant that we are behind with the rent?' asked

Estefania. 'No, it seems to me that what she wanted to say was that it was cloudy today.' 'You are stupid. That's what she said when we came in. She pointed to the sky and said: "It's cloudy today." ' 'You're the stupid one, Estefania. When she said that it's cloudy today, she meant something else, *she said* something else.' 'What?' 'How the hell should I know? *That* is precisely the problem: we will never know what people mean when they speak to us.' 'But isn't it just possible that when people say that it's cloudy today they mean exactly that?' 'One chance in a thousand, perhaps.' 'And how do we know?' 'I don't know. And perhaps it isn't enough that you love somebody and that person loves you. Of course, if the day really is cloudy there is a chance that they may be telling the truth.' Estefania got up, walked over to the window, and said to me: 'It's cloudy today and I want to make love to you.' We rarely spoke of love when we were making it. We simply started doing it, like putting on a record and sitting down to listen to it without having to say beforehand: 'Let's listen to the quintet in A major for clarinet and strings, K. 581, by Wolfgang Amadeus Mozart.' The first movement was calm, like walking through a field of roses, with a *cantabile* which Estefania adored. There followed a *larghetto* performed with deliberation and nobility. In the third movement, as the critic has commented, the clarinet became anew the rustic instrument to be found in Bavaria and other Alpine provinces. At last, the finale, full of amusing variations, caprices, impromptus, obbligatos and ritornelles. The applause was overwhelming. That is why, on occasion, I not only believed Estefania but also believed in her. 'Love is cloudy,' I said to her, 'and I want to make the day to you.' This stupid inversion made her laugh until she recovered her innocence.

This presented us with further perplexity. We discovered that just as a person may say one thing, for example: 'Good morning', but mean to say, and in fact be saying, a thousand different things, so the contrary may also apply: a person may say a thousand different things when in fact they are trying to say and indeed are saying but one thing. Pursuing this same example, I will relate that one afternoon I said to Estefania: 'Would you like to go to the cinema?' and she, with that intuition which dangles from the beaks of birds, perceived that what I was really saying was: 'I love you.' And we did go to the cinema, to see *Yellow Submarine*, and I asked her: 'Would you like some popcorn,' when what I was really saying was 'I love you.' After the cinema we waited for our tram and when it arrived I said: 'This is ours.' And Estefania understood what I meant by that. For a while, this was very pleasant and in a way flattered Estefania since, when we were with our friends or in the hospital or in the advertising agency, I could declare my love for her at all hours of the day unbeknown to anybody else. And so remarks as straightforward as: 'We have to do an advertisement for a new deodorant' or 'The patient in bed eight needs a venoclysis' or

'Pass me the salt' all meant, of course, 'I love you.' As you may well imagine, the whole thing became obsessive and one time when I said to Estefania 'Don't expect me for lunch,' she became furious and beat my chest with her clenched fists and shouted 'Don't keep saying that you love me, just prove it!' Since the worst thing that I could say at that particular moment was 'Estefania, I love you with all my soul' (because she wouldn't have believed the half of it), I thought it would be better to keep quiet and stop talking to her for a few days.

We had to make love in silence and we restricted ourselves to communicating only in the tongue of our tears, our kisses and caresses, our belches and our gestures, speaking not a single word either in Spanish or any other language. None the less, to demonstrate to my cousin that I did actually speak more than one living language and one dead language, I kissed her one day in French. She merely yawned in Swedish. I hated her a little in English and made a rude gesture at her in Italian. She stormed into the bathroom and slammed the door in Russian. When she came out, I winked at her in Chinese and she stuck out her tongue at me in Sanskrit. We ended up making love in Esperanto.

I don't remember when we started speaking again, just as nobody remembers starting to speak as a child; and the fact was that, every time we quarrelled and made up, my cousin and I were reborn. What I do know is that, when we broke the silence and the silence shattered and we started to marshal our mumbling and our senseless syllables, our monemes and phonemes and signs, to form words and sentences and thoughts, we reached the conclusion that we could not continue to live like that: we accepted that the objects we owned, being a part of our lives, were themselves alive and, after rejecting a series of possibilities inspired by the murder of the bikini – possibilities as gruesome as refusing to break the ice between us and our refrigerator, sending our stove to the gas chamber, electrocuting our iron or suffocating our pillows – we decided to learn to live with them.

We also decided, after reading a pamphlet on Shintoism, never again to allow our intelligence to be jinxed by language. And thus our recon- ciliation with objects was immaculate and absolute, as though they were of marshmallow and we enjoyed lighting bonfires in the middle of the woods. We refused to accord them their value as symbols – they themselves and the words which named them – although this was effectively to return to the very infancy of the human species and not just to our own childhood, when we believed that umbrellas could fold their wings, spoons could mourn the death of the sugar bowl or books read other books or stand in front of the mirror and read themselves back-to-front. We accepted them, therefore, as animated and necessary beings to the extent that, once they had existed, they could no longer never have existed and we were grateful for their testimonies and the generosity that they wove into our days.

Later, we got used to their moods and their fits of insanity.

Later, we grew fond of them.

And how could we not, I ask myself now in this place so far removed from our room, remembering the tireless glitter of the porcelain cups we inherited from Aunt Luisa and the red of the curtains which accentuated their movements with diadems of astrakhan: how could it be otherwise?

At first, the relationship was civil although, even at the best of times, Estefania had an inclination for Grecian profiles and occasionally looked down her nose at others. But our policy was to maintain a certain distance and we began by merely greeting them: 'Good morning, calendar; goodnight lamp,' and so on, little caring in truth that the days were nibbled away and the nights were orphaned and fulminating. Then we became closer friends, just like you and me, or you and the general, or the general and Estefania herself; we invited the cups to partake of tea and cakes, we invited the glasses to drink a Châteauneuf du Pape which I brought specially from Paris to celebrate our crystal wedding anniversary and on one particular occasion – which I will paint for you in silver and blue – we invited the whole dinner service to dine: soup plates, sauce boat and soup tureen, tea cups and coffee cups, welcoming even a couple of distant cousins who dropped in from Delft. All our objects – I can say this with the perspective lent by the passage of years and improvisations – behaved in a reasonably helpful manner. The stove prepared our breakfast, the clock told us the time whenever we asked, the taps presented us every day with a bath of plentiful hot water and the books told us wonderful stories.

Later, with the passing of time, as grey hairs started to appear on my chest and the calendar reached a path strewn with dead leaves and undergrowth, the relationship became more intimate; Estefania and her polaroid glasses went out to gaze at shops and eclipses every afternoon and returned a little more intelligent and tired from the sight of so many respectable illusions adorning the shop windows disguised as felt hats and crocodile handbags. My underwear, which included some boxer shorts accustomed to the leisure of silk, learned of certain secret illnesses which decorated my penis with a Gothic stigma. As though that were not enough, Estefania was wont to get into bed in her nightdress at the most unlikely hours of the day and in the most provocative positions. Finally, my typewriter and I together wrote novels without end, without beginning and without mercy.

This relationship certainly had its drawbacks, since such excessive intimacy caused not only my cousin and myself but also our objects occasionally to take advantage of each other, to the extent of playing crude jokes on each other, like the day we filled my fountain pen with whisky so

130

that it could write double, or the night we placed four candles around our bed to make it think it had died.

Unfortunately, happiness is not eternal. That was made apparent by Aunt Lucrecia who smoked with an amber cigarette holder as long as her fear of dying of cancer. And you see it with tunnels, absorbed in contemplation of their profound stylization of space. And you saw it in Grandfather Francisco who was like a welcoming lion, a friendly whale, like an asthmatic dragon and he also died on us, because he was so fat, because of the kilos and victories he carried with him and particularly because he talked about himself so much. This I discovered on a fresh and luminous day, after one of those nights of revelry when you forget your name and the colour of your smile. I got up to see what kind of mood the bathroom mirror had awoken in. I returned to bed very sad and cuddled up to Estefania. I covered my face with the sheet and dedicated a few tears to our initials (Estefania's and my own, which my cousin painstakingly unpicked every week from the sheets, the pillowcases, the face flannels and the towels, and embroidered over again, intertwined in different positions).

'What's the matter?' she asked me.

'Our mirror is not very well. Today for the first time I realized just how old he is.'

Estefania went to see for herself.

'You're quite right, the poor thing. Do you think she's dying?' she called from the bathroom, giving her voice a resonance of snow and angels.

'I don't know,' I answered. 'We'll have to call in the mirrorologist to take a look at him.'

'Oh, but what can we do for her in the meantime? Is there anything you can think of?'

'Yes, make funny faces to amuse him,' I said to her and I started counting the money left over from the night before.

'It's no good,' she shouted. 'I stuck my tongue out at her and it looked horrible.'

'Why don't you get dressed,' I suggested. 'He'll certainly cheer up when he sees you looking as beautiful as that magnificent creature Clara Dea.'

And Estefania, who when she put her mind to it, could unleash the gold of her hair in two minutes, sprinkle her cheeks with red surprises in another three and curl her false eyelashes in four less, said to me at the eleventh hour: 'She looks better, but I think she is going to die anyway, the poor thing.'

'He's going to die,' I corrected her: because, of course, our mirror changed sex depending on whether Estefania or I was looking at him/her.

We then decided that his/her last hours of life would be the happiest and we took her/him out to see the modern world. Out on the street, his/her face shone with colour and movement. We took her/him to the

131

museum and to a market and his/her face filled with Tula giants, wheels of fortune and rifle ranges, cherries and water melons. She/he was so fascinated and showed such widely differing faces of amazement and surprise, that friends to whom we introduced him/her and the strangers we passed on our way confused her/him successively with a policeman, a greengrocer, a general with a glass eye, a schoolgirl, Cousin Walter, a pastry vendor, a film star and the waiter at Bottoms Up, the bar where we ended up at eleven that night and where we got phenomenally drunk.

We left Bottoms Up at four in the morning and went to sit in Ariel Park, laying our mirror on the grass. And, since the night was dark and cloudy, starless and moonless, we realized that our mirror was dead and should be buried.

If you ever have witnessed the death of a friend who has seen you grow to your most diaphanous height, a companion who has listened to you in silence and mocked you and pitied you, a buddy who has been witness from Monday through to Sunday of how the love between you and Estefania is condensed in formerly uninhabited seeds, you will understand the enormous grief we felt at the death of our mirror. Enormous to an extent that Estefania, fearing that all the memories of us which she took to the tomb would be devoured by unknown worms, wrung her hands and begged me to agree to leave her in the open for the birds to eat. 'But do you realize what you are asking? They'll shatter him,' I said to her, thinking of the silence and of our mirror, which were so similar. 'And it would be as though we, we and our memories, we and our loved ones, we and that which we have been, were also shattered,' I added, remembering that the mirror had belonged to Grandfather Francisco after the death of Great-grandfather José Antonio and to Grandmother Altagracia after the death of Grandfather Francisco and to Aunt Lucrecia after the death of Grandmother Altagracia and to my cousin Estefania, not after Aunt Lucrecia's death but when she was still alive and she gave the mirror to my cousin and she took him to our room in Holy Sunday Square. Perhaps I didn't mind so much that he might carry away memories which were not my own, such as Great-grandfather's waxed whiskers, or memories I didn't like, like the smallpox scars on Grandmother Altagracia's face which she daily tried to diminish by anointing them with mother-of-pearl ground in lemon juice. But other things: my cousin's very face, her adored body of a precipitous bride whose presence I sensed behind the curtain of papyrus and flowers of already extinct species, her sex, fragrant and tight as an explosion of African roses, her belly where water eels sought the hole in the sand in which to lay their spawn of little bubbles; these and other memories of the countless times we made love in front of our mirror, I couldn't just from one moment to the next resign myself to losing them for ever. And there was another thing, another memory which came back to me unexpectedly: the mirror used to hang in Aunt Lucrecia's bedroom and one afternoon, several days after my cousin and I returned from our trip to Veracruz, Estefania removed her blouse and looked at her back in the mirror. 'I'm peeling,' she said. I asked if I could pull off a little bit of skin and took between my fingers a hanging tatter on her left shoulder over which had passed oceans of foam and salt and pulled downwards, detaching a strip as fine and near-transparent as the skin of a lily stem. I left the strip hanging and caught hold of another peeling fragment visible beneath the right shoulder blade and peeled it back to reveal my cousin's new epidermis, that infant epidermis which was like a shell of infinite tenderness, like a fiery red cashmere susceptible to golden infections and salves of cognac. I remember how at the height of the fourth vertebra below the neck I caught hold of another little fragment and this time the strip followed the undulation of her spine all the way down her back and came away when it reached her coccyx. And thus, time after time, I continued to peel off ribbons of skin, fine and soft and translucent as the tunics of onions and lilies and finding, here and there, the odd grain of sand, microscopic fragments of coral, tongues of sea urchins and the traces of a bonfire. And, every time I detached a bit of skin, a cascade of amperes flooded down Estefania's back and my cousin fainted for a ten-millionth of a second. Until, at last, the flush of Estefania's skin was exposed on its very surface and her back was like a shirtless autumn bedecked in flags and posters, streamers and tattered banners scattered throughout the city, though a few particles, minute as bees' feathers, had been whisked away by our sighs and our laughter. I mentioned this to Estefania. I reminded her that afterwards she had pulled similar ribbons of skin from my back and that we had pressed them in our books. She put hers between the pages of *Heidi*. I put mine in *Oliver Twist*. She in *Snow White*. I in *Tom Sawyer*. She between the pages of *Little Women*. I between the pages of *Niels Lyhne*. I remembered that, many years later, when we had grown up, we put our strips of skin together, between the pages of *Paul and Virginia*, of *Daphnis and Chloe*, of *Beauty and the Beast*.

But Estefania would not be swayed.

'That is exactly what I want,' she said. 'I want them to shatter our mirror and our memories, let all the birds come: goldfinches, greenfinches, crows, bats . . .'

'Bats aren't birds.'

'That doesn't matter: let all the birds come and all the fowl of the world: swallows, wagtails, hawks, cardinals, robins, blue tits, canaries . . .'

'Enough. You don't need to make a list of *all* birds,' I said.

'Of course I do; if we want them to come, we have to call them. How do you think they are going to come if I don't call them by name?'

'All right, let me know when you've finished,' I said and I went off to smoke a cigarette on a bench next to a wall where, that particular night, a blue blossoming of bored trumpets was occurring. I was so ravenous that I could have devoured live daisies. Which, in fact, I did: it was my habit, like all faint-hearted lovers, to pull the petals from daisies to find out whether Estefania loved me or loved me not. But my way of pulling petals from daisies had always been much smarter than simply leaving the outcome to chance: with each succeeding petal that I pulled off and put in my mouth, Estefania loved me a lot, she loved me more, she loved me a lot more. Meanwhile, thinking of the plurality of worlds foreseen by Bernard le Bovier and Origen, the existence though not the possibility of which have been denied by Nicole Oresme, I wondered whether the world which had fallen to the lot of Estefania and myself could be juster or more beautiful, or more stupid and paler, or more evil and less liquid. I also wondered whether our universe might be left-handed or right-, which led me to think of my cousin's eyes and then I wondered why everybody said they were so sweet and if this meant that her eyes were made of sugar and whether in this case her right eye might be of ordinary sugar, polarizing light towards the right, and her left eye of levulose, polarizing light towards the left and by the time I got to the last daisy petal and my mouth was full of them and dawn was already breaking and Estefania's love was almost as great as Grandfather Francisco's love raised to the power of a polyhedron, Estefania came over to me and said that she had finished naming all the birds. The hem of her iridescent dress brushed the grass, raising a dust of almost invisible violets.

'So, you are sure now what you want?' I asked her.

'Yes. This is exactly what I want. I want each of them to carry off a piece of you or of me. May an eagle come and carry away your eyes . . .'

I felt a certain resentment at this notion and retorted: 'And may a cockatoo come and carry away your tongue.'

'And may a bat come and carry away your blood.'

'May a hummingbird come and carry away your clitoris.'

'May a vulture come and carry away your cock.'

'May a bird of paradise come and carry away your soul,' I said to her and then we fell silent.

'Why don't we place flowers on the mirror?' she asked me, a time and half a time and half a half a time later.

'Good idea,' I answered. 'I'll pick some roses: one for you and one for me.'

'There's no need,' she answered. She plucked a splendid rose and placed it on the mirror.

'You see? There are two roses.'

We fell silent again. Suddenly, Estefania's face lit up.

'Look!' she said. 'She's gone to heaven.'

'Who?'

'The mirror.'

And so it was: in the place where the mirror had previously lain, there was nothing to be seen but a patch of blue sky and white clouds.

We returned home by way of a castle surrounded by green and defenceless gardens, where no desert was likely and muck was drowned at the bottom of a lake which piously rocked reflections of any princess that might be living imprisoned in the ivory wing of the castle, and I wondered then – thinking of the roses in the mirror – whether it might not be possible that, by some genetic error of creation, a Siamese universe had been born and, if this was so, I wondered where we ourselves were, on which side of the mirror, but Estefania interrupted me to say that she had never before considered the existence of a heaven for objects. And I, hoping to cheer her up a little, told her that certainly, that's where all things went when they died: ashtrays, bedspreads, rubber cheques . . . 'And vases too?' she asked me, 'turbans, mosaics?' 'Everything,' I answered, 'dental pliers, newspaper headlines, television antennae, the corners of houses and law degrees: they all go to heaven.' 'And what do they do there?' 'They don't do anything. On the contrary, they go to heaven to not-do. Or, if anything, to do very different things. Don't you see that by the time they get there, they're sick to death of doing the same thing all their lives? In the heaven of objects, it is forbidden to hang coats on coat hangers or to look through windows. There, wine bottles are always empty and compasses always point South or West, although that is a little difficult to ascertain because West and South are not, as on earth, always in the same place but turn up where they are least expected: one day you go out walking and suddenly you find West lying in the street and, because it is so brilliant, so viscous and perfumed, it appears to be anything but a cardinal point. Anyway, as you may imagine, in that place ice is not cold and sugar is not sweet. And not only is it forbidden to read books, but the pages of books are unblemished white, just as it is not only forbidden to go upstairs but also stairs don't go anywhere, in the same way that windows don't look out over anything. Although, of course, to say that books have white pages is not absolutely accurate, in the first place because there books don't have pages and nor do stairs have steps nor do windows have panes and, in the second place, because there white does not have the same function as on earth: blue or green, or not even a colour at all but some other thing: a boat or a tree; bearing in mind, of course, that boats and trees can be anything other that boats and trees.'

'And tell me,' Estefania urged me, 'what do coffins go there to do?'

'Ah, let me think . . . yes, of course: there, in the heaven of objects, coffins put on skirts, trousers and coloured dresses and all carry a live person inside them.'

'Such confusion!' my cousin remarked.

And she was happy again for a few moments: Estefania always had a photogenic soul in which could be encapsulated streams and parties, and her heart was attentive to the poor in spirit, such as Grandmother Altagracia – and sometimes even Palinuro – who were incapable of appreciating the valour of a king of spades sacrificing itself in two for love of a queen of hearts. In other words, Estefania was as much a child of the schoolroom as the pupils of her eyes, of sterling equality and a sense of fairness open to the stumbling of the wind.

Once again, happiness was transitory. The death of our mirror was but the first of a series of calamities which started, and seemed never to end, one Sunday in May when Estefania wanted to iron a shirt and discovered that we had to operate on Juana, our iron, for a short circuit in the stomach. Not three days had passed when our salt cellar started to suffer from water retention and Admiral, our television, succumbed to an attack of colour blindness and started to get colours mixed up. 'Good God, what are we going to do?' Estefania asked me, leaning her elbows on our only table which had, by that time, fallen lame. 'I have no idea,' I answered her, 'among other reasons because I am not God.' And so it was: I neither knew how to solve the problem nor had I any idea of the number of household disasters that were to occur, one after the other, virtually every day: on Friday, our lamp went blind and the keys of my typewriter jammed and developed a stutter. A fortnight later, we discovered that our pipes had arteriosclerosis and that Pancha, our door, had developed acute rheumatism of the hinges. After that, not a week went by without our carpet, Alicia, losing a tuft and Rodrigo, our comb, losing two or three teeth. One afternoon, in the middle of a radio play, our wireless, Philco, lost his voice under the strain. And the last straw was when my wristwatch, Alfonso, develped a nervous tic, lost his memory and forgot to remind me when it was time to go to the cinema. But none of our objects – or I should say perhaps *nobody* among our objects – gave us such a fright as Gleem, our toothpaste, and Pedro, our toilet. Gleem had but recently been brought home from the supermarket, when she was still a young and virgin toothpaste with a smile on her lips, when a horrible thick, white suppuration appeared. And, while it is true that Pedro was already very old and suffered from a throat complaint, sufficiently serious to require a daily gargle with detergent and unblocking liquids, we never thought that one morning he would decline so far as to start to vomit faecal matter. There came a time when my cousin and I were the only healthy ones left in the house. This reassured us to a certain extent but our happiness ended when Filipe, our thermometer, suffered an internal haemorrhage followed by an extremely high fever and, in his delirious state, hallucinated that we had contracted all manner of imaginary diseases.

'We have to do something for them, while they're still alive,' said Estefania, who always felt guilty for not having shown Uncle Esteban the love that she felt for him while he played cards, slept the siesta or drank dry Martini, spearing the olive on a pin which served to metallize the virtues of the gin: in other words, while Uncle Esteban was alive and kicking, his nostrils plunged in the ancient smells of Transylvania. 'Why did I never write his autobiography?' mused Estefania aloud, 'why did I never tell him that I loved him more than I hated him?' Then she thought of Matthias Stomer's picture *Roman Charity* which had impressed her greatly when she saw it in the Prado museum because it illustrated the legend of an old man who was sentenced to starve to death in a prison and whose daughter kept him alive by giving him to drink of the milk of her breasts. 'Why did I never suckle Papa Esteban,' she said, 'when he was imprisoned in Siberia?' 'Impossible,' I cried jealously, on the point of warning her of the possible dimensions of anger. 'You hadn't been born and Uncle Esteban did not die of hunger in Siberia.' But then she realized that, for the time being, I was still alive and, though it was three in the afternoon and as yet no milk circulated in her breasts, she insisted on suckling me, on bringing me my slippers, on telling me stories and turning out my bedside light. And, protest as I might, it was hopeless to try to reach the conclave of her ears; if anything, only the spotless white ermine found a soft and resplendent echo; other than that, each word that entered her ears was lost in the violet labyrinth of her brain from where it had called for help in a little voice reminiscent of the tinkling of the atmosphere. The fact is that, when we realized that we were alive, as were our objects, we decided to save each other the least exertion. Estefania combed my hair in the mornings and I undid her plaits, Estefania shaved my chin and I shaved her armpits. We even went so far as to bite each other's nails. And I smoked her cigarettes and she smoked mine. I defined her thoughts and spoke for her. She invented my ambitions and fought to realize them. I dreamt her nightmares and she studied my books. I fed her and she gave me to drink. Finally, I saved her the trouble of caressing herself and caressed her from head to toe. And she saved me the trouble of hating myself and hated me all day long.

As for our objects, it occurred to us that we could provide them with a foretaste of the happiness they would find in heaven, either by letting them do nothing or by allowing them to do things that were very different from what they usually did. So, for some considerable time, we peed in the handbasin, cleaned our shoes with mayonnaise, ate soup with forks, slept underneath the bed and stopped answering the telephone.

9

The happy half, the sad half, the fragile half of the world

'Con qué nobleza se revuelven
Todos juntos estos muchachos
Y claman por una justicia
Perturbando, vociferando . . .

with what nobility they seethe, these youths one and all,
clamouring for justice, disrupting, vociferating . . .'

said Cousin Walter, sitting with Palinuro in La Española cantina eating
snails à la vizcaína and drinking beer when, effectively disrupting and
vociferating, entered seven, ten, fifteen, who knows how many youths, one
and all talking, laughing, telling jokes and making speeches, handing out
pamphlets, and then, as suddenly, they left, happy, noisy, disrupting.
'Why don't they forget politics and get down to a bit of studying?' Walter
mused aloud but he said what he did – not his reference to politics and
studying but the quote from Jorge Guillén's poem – not so much because he
was moved by the students or cared about their problems and illusions but
merely to demonstrate to Palinuro – or to himself – that the recondite area
of his brain corresponding to what might be called auditive or literary
memory – or what don Prospero might perhaps have called the
protuberance of poetic memoracity – was functioning splendidly on that
particular night and that, like every other night, it was the child of chaos
and the mother of dreams and death and delirium and the two cousins were
prepared yet again to drink and talk about it until the cocks with goitres
full of coal heralded the day and butchers began to cleave the fat from their
carcasses with the lightning stroke of vertigo: Oh! night, begetter of
deceptions! Walter might have exclaimed, the oh! being an addition from
the crop of ohs, ooos and ahs growing in lyrical state in his own orchard, if
Palinuro had not insisted that his cousin explain the meaning of auditive
memory and the nature of musical memory and tactile memory, in short,
all the memories Walter had mentioned to him, since – he added jestingly –
Walter obviously had a good memory or, at least, heaps of good
specialized memories. And then Walter, Walter the Elegant, Walter of the

patchwork waistcoat, Walter who had lived in London, Walter who like Dante Gabriel Rossetti had a penchant for the sad and the cruel, Walter who had read everything, Walter who knew of the four thousand four hundred and forty-eight illnesses described by the Indian sages of old, who knew why the substratum of a disease was called peccant matter and was the only one in the house who had heard of Caradrio, the fabled bird whose mere gaze cured jaundice; in short, the same Walter who had foretold that just as in Bologna there was a statue of Tagliacozzo holding a nose in his hand, so there would one day be in the town of Molkas' birth a sculpture of their mutual friend holding a breast in his right hand (not his own but a woman's), Walter started to explain to Palinuro, between gulps, with the object of opening his cousin's eyes to the poverty and fragility of human life, how our brains, like our bodies, are but a tiny collection of organs: one for smelling, another for defecating, another for feeling hunger or remembering a poem and so on, although of course this was a very superficial explanation and, he added, the matter was really much more complex, though not for this reason more encouraging – quite the contrary – and, of course, when we slice a brain (as you told me you yourself did and saw being done) you don't find inside a tiny nose or miniature eyes or a toy stomach and, much less, fortunately, an illusion in the shape and mustard colour of a university pullover or a thought with little orange wings; you don't actually find anything, except on those rare and surprising occasions on which you have the privilege of opening a brain and discovering inside one of those ovoid and pearly tumours which look like mother-of-pearl and are formed by cholesterin and calcium carbonates bringing to mind a chicken's egg inside an ostrich egg which might suddenly crack open to give birth to a fresh, new, recently-varnished brain the size of a dove's egg containing, in condensed form, all the knowledge of the world. This explanation by his cousin in La Española might never have taken place if Palinuro, after a second, huge and almost superhuman effort to overcome his revulsion and after his journey through painting, advertising and the Imaginary Islands, had not returned to the School of Medicine and attended a second autopsy which, by pure coincidence, was also that of a youth of more or less his own age. Impossible (said Cousin Walter), corpses of twenty-year-old youths don't grow on trees, and he started again to speak of the dissection of corpses undertaken in other ages when the surgeon's assistants placed a carpet on the floor (would it be a red carpet to camouflage the blood?) so that, like the Shah of Persia, Emperor Montezuma and the Magistrates of the English Courts, their feet would not come into contact with the impure ground. And the fact that Palinuro did eventually pluck up the courage to return was due to Walter's repeated insistance that with time anybody can master revulsion simply by deciding to do so and that he hoped that Palinuro would one day graduate as a doctor and surgeon *magna cum laude* with all necessary honours (and horrors) in the beloved School of Medicine, in the ineffable Alma Mater, so that he, Walter, could receive him as John Hunter received his brother William in his London home (it had to be London) with open arms, not necessarily his own arms but certainly arms because, like the breast that Molkas would have in his hand, the arms would not be Johnny's own but those of a corpse and Johnny gave them to Bill to dissect and which he did, said Walter, in admirable style. And he would have liked to continue talking about Graham's *History of Surgery* which he had just finished reading and of the dissections performed in Bologna, for example, where only one body was dissected per year, just before Christmas, since as Woodall said: 'It is no small presumption to dismember the image of God', and about the young criminals who were strangled with a great dexterity and mercy and promised indulgences if they bequeathed their corpses to science, and about the Mexican Academy of Surgery, the symbol of which Palinuro would be able to reproduce in three dimensions and for real on the day he got a corpse (he meant a corpse all to himself) since it consisted of a right hand with the Eye of Wisdom in its palm and whether the hand belonged to Wisdom or whether the Eye belonged to the hand was an unsolvable mystery, but the fact was that both stood out against a scarlet background of the blood of the world and, what is more, Walter might have added, to say that corpses were becoming scarcer was an exaggeration and the fact of the matter was that there were too many students (live ones, of course) and that in his time it was worse because there were fewer universities in the provinces and the students looked like vultures around the corpses and that now, in contrast, if Palinuro didn't get a corpse within the first year, a corpse which he could get to know millimetre by millimetre and ventricle by ventricle (although unfortunately it would become increasingly rubbery) and of which he would eventually become extremely fond to the point of making up his life history and his past and of speaking to him and of begging his pardon for poking out his tongue (he meant, of course, the corpse's tongue, not Palinuro's) and, failing that and as a last resort, he could always visit Charon, the old caretaker of the dissecting room who was nothing to do with the old gravedigger of the county, although he was long-haired like Mandrake, and ask to be allowed to work with a fresh corpse for a few hours, under the protection of the dark wings of night, because corpses – he said, or might have said – no longer cost two guineas as they did a couple of centuries ago but just a bottle of tequila, that being the price set by Charon who wasn't of course called Charon but, for obvious reasons, had been given the nickname in honour of the Hades boatman responsible for ferrying the dead and rejecting the souls of the unburied and neither, obviously, was it any longer necessary – he told him – for a William Burke and his lover to go around murdering drunks to sell their bodies to Dr Knox, although it was now increasingly unlikely that Dick Turpin or some other famous criminal would turn up on your dissecting slab since corpses were now of anonymous old men and derelicts, prostitutes and why not? perhaps also students who disrupt and vociferate. Clamouring for justice, murmured Palinuro without realizing what he was saying, his intention merely to complete the quatrain. But Palinuro wished to hear no more of imaginary dissections and autopsies or of dissections advertised with great ado in the *Daily Advertiser* or the *London Evening Post* but wished, as he explained to Walter, to discuss a single dissection or, to be more precise, a single concrete and real dissection: that of the second youth, which he had endured to the end, until the professor had taken his brain in his hand (not his own, of course, but that of the youth) and started to slice it into sixteen parts and it was this that he wished to talk about with Walter and to hear Walter talking about: about the moment when the professor, after removing the tongue, the oesophagus, the eyeballs and the brain, proceeded to cut the liver transversally with a long sharp knife and open the kidney and the testicles and the arm and then started to slice the brain, and the silence in the dissecting room (Palinuro told him) was absolute and, though the screeching of a tram, the rumble of cars or the odd shout reached them from the street, they heard no sound that could be taken for God, just as within the room there was no sound that could be taken for a groan when the professor removed the vocal cords, and no sound that could be taken for an exclamation when the professor cut the lung tissue and the only noise remotely similar to those made by a living organism were those to be heard when the professor's assistant, in a room beside the dissecting room, emptied the contents of the stomach into a bowl and squeezed the intestine to expel the faeces and, of course (why of course? asked Walter), neither was there, when the professor started to cut the brain, any spark of pure awareness nor a last posthumous firework betokening a miracle: the brain was simply an organ which could be held in one hand, an organ which, as Walter said, was effectively egg-shaped and covered in a grey substance and was white inside and had fissures, furrows and mounds and which could be sliced in exactly the same way as a ham or Emmenthal cheese. And Walter, Walter who knew so many things, Walter who was familiar with the most ancient and exotic histories of medicine relating the art of healing from the times in which Soranus called ovaries testicles and it was said that scorpions came from the land of Gog and Magog; Walter who, at the drop of a hat, would relate how Aristotle refuted Alcmaeon's theory that goats breathed through their ears; Walter, in short, suggested to Palinuro that perhaps the last comparison was the most fitting and reminded him of the process of porosis of the brain whereby the post-mortem action of the microbes of putrefaction riddle this organ with tiny, regularly-shaped cavities which are very similar, so it is said, to the holes in Emmenthal cheese. And, of course, nobody had ever found, inside a brain, Schopenhauer's Fourfold Root of the Principle of Sufficient Reason nor Van't Hoff and Le Bel's Hypothesis of the Asymmetric Carbon Atom or even, as demonstrated by the second youth, the multiplication tables and the alphabet – or the call to strike and chaos, if he was indeed a vociferating student – and a girlfriend's letters: none of these was to be found either in one or all of the sixteen sections of the brain and not just because this student had never studied philosophy or because he had never been interested in music or chemistry and not just because he might have been a youth who had not learned to read and do sums – and was therefore never a student – and who was never interested in football or had a girlfriend to love and torment; not just for all these reasons but simply because nobody, Walter told him, neither Galen nor Albucasis nor Avenzoar nor Asclepius nor the first physician among the gods when, for the first time, they held in their hands the brain of a dead man, had ever found anything inside the cerebral hemispheres. Although to say that they had not found *anything* is, of course, going too far because, after Silvius injected the veins of the brain with molten waxes and as the architectural study of the cortex of the brain advanced and after Stilling invented the process of cutting the cerebral tissue into successive sections and Golgi developed a method of dyeing the tissue with silver nitrate to reveal the structure of the brain as a network of nerve cells or a system of inter-related networks and after the invention of the microscope, then naturally – Walter told him – researchers had discovered in the brain certain tissues, infinitesimal cells and other wonders until they reached the very heart of the nerve cells. And, moreover, after Max Dad and Broca had situated the speech centre at the base of the frontal gyrus of the left hemisphere (the fact that this was later refuted by Henry Head was totally irrelevant to their discussion which activated the requisite gyri, whichever they might be) and after Helmholtz had demonstrated that the nervous impulse travels on a return ticket, and Fritsch and Hitzig proved that an electric stimulus to the cerebral cortex produces an involuntary movement of the eyes, after all this (and also before, because Walter pointed out that he was quoting names and experiments in total chronological disorder) researchers had discovered wonders in that small organ which Palinuro had seen sliced into sixteen sections; or, to be more precise, not only in the brain alone but in all the organs and aggregates therefore which, in conjunction with the two cerebral hemispheres, form the encephalon. And Walter would have continued speaking and discoursing and convoluting had Palinuro not, after ordering more snails and beer, redirected the conversation; not this time to the autopsy room but to the very cantina in which they were sitting, La Española, and where he, Palinuro, and a group of friends and

142

fellow medical students had been a few days previously, also vociferating and disrupting, happy and thirsty, but for other very different reasons: after the autopsy (he told Walter) when somebody pointed out that the sixteen slices of brain laid side by side would form a strip of almost two metres in length and when the professor revealed that the right lung of the youth weighed four hundred and fifty grammes and that his mitral valve measured ten centimetres or, in other words, after the youth and all that he had been – his memory, his recollections and his experiences and, with them, his childhood and his friends – came to be scattered throughout the world, decanted in jars and rubbish bins, in Petri dishes, in test tubes, on glass slides and in microscopic preparations, on platelets and in sinks and toilets, Palinuro and his friends decided to go and have a few drinks in La Española where, besides snails *à la vizcaína,* you could order marinated oysters, beef tartar sandwiches, barbecued onions and other delectable delicacies; right there, in that very place which Palinuro and Walter had at that moment (or rather at another moment) entered, were voiced more statistics and more measurements of the human body and more jokes; it was revealed, for example, that all the youth's capillaries – and, for that matter, those of any one of their group – would together form a pipe of twenty metres in diameter, that is, a pipe far larger than any ever built to remove Mexico City's waste water and, speaking of water – not waste water but just aitchtwooh, water plain and simple, sister water (Walter would have said, quoting Amado Nervo), water which is water and steam and snow and frost and cloud and waterfall, but is also brain and tongue – if you were to drink in one go the forty-odd litres of water contained in the body, said one of Palinuro's classmates, you would of course drop down dead with an instant attack of hydropsy. In the same vein: if you were to breathe, started to say one of the students before being interrupted by Molkas who always distinguished himself with his sterling vulgarity and now came to the conclusion that, if a normal penis in an erect state measured about fifteen centimetres in length and a rectum including the anal tract measured the same number of centimetres, it would be his pleasure to touch with the head of his cock the very tip of the sigmoid colon of any of his friends prepared to have their intestinal flora starched by their loving and obedient servant (Molkas). On the above subject, continued the other student (who was actually one of those very much involved in the strike and demonstrations) and without taking it particularly personally said clearly: 'I can't stand being interrupted when I'm speaking', nobody could breathe in all at once the entire twelve thousand litres of air, 'just imagine! . . . twelve thousand litres of air!' which pass through the lungs daily: you would quite simply explode or shoot like a satellite into Earth orbit, covering an incredible, unspecified, sudden and winding distance like an inflated balloon when the air is released, just like that: prrrrt! And, speaking of gases, said Molkas, but it might be easier, said Fabricio, to drink in one go the litre of saliva produced daily by the organism although, of course, you would vomit in sheer revulsion. On the other hand – Walter would have said if he had been there because he never lost the opportunity to remind everybody that he had lived in London – on the other hand, said Walter – since he was in fact there in La Española, when Palinuro was telling him about the time he was there with his mates – on the other hand, if the English were to drink the pint of bile they produced daily like any other normal human being, they would in a year save the tidy sum of pounds sterling (at least fifty) which they spend on Youngs extra bitter beer, he said, and raised his glass to drink Palinuro's health. And, speaking of gases, said Molkas, remembering that beer produces gas and despite the fact that Walter wasn't with them at that particular time, though Molkas was, likewise drinking beer in the same cantina and, by pure coincidence, in the same chair in which Walter was to sit – talking of gases (he repeated after making it clear that 'I can't stand people speaking when I'm interrupting'), the one thousand three hundred cubic centimetres normally contained in our organism, that is, over a litre, are more than enough to allow you to keep your farts in a can like this one (he said, toasting with a Tecate beer) and start a business or at least send them to friends and relatives who really love you very much and don't take such a gift as an insult. At which point Fabricio, on a more poetic note, reminded them that the human embryo grows from a single cell to two thousand million cells in the course of nine months and if you were to grow at the same rate from the time of birth to the age of twenty, you would be almost one million kilometres tall, taller than the giant Micromegas, you could tell the moon to kiss your arse, he added, threatening to do a moony there and then. This allusion to the astral spaces spurred the imagination of all present and, while nobody was able to calculate the surface area of the planet that might be covered by the ashes of their own bones scattered by a hurricane – somebody blew into the ashtray to provide a scaled-down demonstration – nor was it practicable to calculate the number of light years corresponding to a line composed of all the electrons of the body placed one behind the other in single file, it was however known, within a reasonable margin of error – though it serve only to emphasize anew man's earth-bound condition and his inability to embrace the heavens – that the ten metres of the human intestine would stretch two and a half times around the globe in the office of their secondary school headmaster, but not once, not even once, around the star-spangled dome of the Zacatenco Planetarium.

And Cousin Walter, after commending himself to Fortuna, daughter of Ocean, and to the god Farno presiding over erudition, after quoting Thomas Aquinas to the effect that it was more worthwhile to study man

144

than to study the stars, and Severinus who maintained that stars suffer the same ills as human beings (and that, in fact, each star is a man), after agreeing with Campanella that in a sense all knowledge is knowledge of ourselves and after downing his glass of beer in two draughts and entreating his titular ancestral spirits to arrange things so that each time he collapsed from alcoholic excess during the course of the night he might, like Antaeus, be filled with new strength when he touched the ground, he went on to state that the wretchedness of man and, together with his wretchedness, his fragility, is to be found (he had found, you will find) not in those intestines which are not long enough to encompass the galaxies, but in other concentrations of stars, in those grey and ultra-microscopic nerve cells, the protoplasm of which may stretch a metre or more (no shooting star ever had such a long tail, he assured Palinuro) in those cells, the neurons, which are as abundant within each head as the stars in the heavenly vault and as irreplaceable as each of those same stars but certainly don't live for the millions of years that a star may live and certainly don't die in the spectacular manner of a supernova and which, when we are born, he said, are virgin and almost empty but from the very moment we open our eyes they start to feed on light and sound and, later, to fatten on words and recollections, on memory, on life: when you gain a superficial notion of how the neurons work, Walter said, and thus how our nervous system works; when you learn that a tumour or a blow or a toxic substance can kill or cause millions of these neurons to go mad; when you know that a clot in a certain part of the brain can give a person an insatiable sexual appetite; when you learn that injury to a person's reticular matter can cause them to lose for ever the ability to wake up; when you are aware of this, and awake of course; when you know that the most brilliant intentions of being a good lad in life, calm and amiable to one's neighbours and fellow man, can disappear into thin air in the blink of an eye when the neurons grouped in the kernels controlling the anger centre become deranged, Cousin Walter told Palinuro after ordering another round of beers from the balding waiter sporting green mica visor, red and white striped shirt and enormous, *fin de siècle* moustache and sideburns, only then do you begin to realize, sadly to realize, what we are. And what are we? asked Palinuro. Yes, what are we? Walter the know-it-all asked himself, with such seriousness and expression of such perplexity, that the two cousins burst out laughing, ridiculing solemnity, repudiating the telluric, though Walter could not resist dredging up certain of John Donne's better poems and quotes from Shakespeare's characters in which the former and the latter cry aloud into the void and the darkness their anguished pleas for enlightenment on the origin, the fate and the role of man in this world of tribulation and, for a time, the conversation went off on a tangent to Hamlet. But no, it was not a tangent. In fact, they continued to pursue the same, or virtually the same, subject: Hamlet holding Yorick's skull from which used to hang the lips which he had kissed he knew not how oft and asking him what had become of his gibes, his gambols and his flashes of merriment, asking him if he had not one to mock his own grinning; then they passed on to Mathilde with the adored head of her beloved and never-to-be-forgotten Julian and to the skeleton of Jan van Calcar with the palm of one hand, or rather the bones which had at one point supported the palm of one hand, resting on the round, smooth skull of another skeleton, in a thoughtful attitude, but thinking of what? How can you think without a brain? said Walter, going on to add how he would like, how he would love, skull in hand or, better still, a live and pulsating brain, to discover what nobody, no surgeon, not even Frugardi in Palermo, da Saliceto in Verona, Guy de Chauliac in Avignon, Paré in Flanders or Dupuytren in Paris had ever been able to discover in the whitish, ovoid mass or in any of its parts, adjuncts or addenda, neither in the medulla oblongata nor the protuberance nor the thalamus nor the hypothalamus, neither before the microscope was invented nor after Leeuwenhoek and Janssen had discovered it so that man could peep at an effervescent microcosmos infested with rainbows and chromatic aberrations, because none had ever succeeded in spotting a two-legged thought, a naked illusion, even a word or the vestige of an idea. And Walter started telling Palinuro about the experiments that Hess, Hediger, Penfield and other researchers had performed on animals, and of which Estefania fortunately never learned because they were so horrible that, compared with these scientists, Flourens was as a white dove; so perverse, maintained Walter, they consisted of removing the lid of the brains of living animals to insert electrodes in certain parts of their encephalon which would be stimulated when the animal awoke, with the purpose either of destroying the sleep centre situated in the frontal region of the hypothalamus or altering the functions of the olfactory centre so that the poor animals: dogs, cats, monkeys or whatever, either spent the rest of their lives frantically and compulsively smelling all the objects in the universe whether edible or otherwise: chairs, trees, cage bars and clouds and tram tickets, or lost for ever the ability and the desire to sleep and died with their eyes open, ever-more open and ever-more amazed by the unending reality of the world, Walter told him, exalted, and Palinuro meanwhile thought that the most extraordinary, if not the most false, of the relationships which any of his acquaintances had or had had had with medicine, was undoubtedly that of Cousin Walter who, by an irony of fate, was always the one who had most money, most books and most opportunities at his disposal, who was the only one among Palinuro, Estefania, Uncle Esteban, Molkas, Fabricio and so many other friends, to have been in a position to view Scotland from the top of the West Tower of the University of Glasgow, as

146

Lister used to every morning, and had also had the opportunity to admire the diaphanized and iridescent foetuses, the child with two skulls and other preserved wonders in the Hunterian Museum as well as the ivory and glass nipple shields and the obstetric doll used by the professors of Pistoria University in the eighteenth century, on display in the Wellcome Museum of the History of Medicine, and, finally, the only one who had been to La Salpêtrière in Paris and the Museum of Science and Industry in Chicago, but none the less he preferred always to maintain this pseudo-erudite and pseudo-literary relationship with medicine and its history, an ambiguous relationship smacking of dilettantism, consisting of disordered and frequently impressive fragments of knowledge which always, sooner or later, irritated his listeners. Palinuro, emboldened by beer, said as much to Walter who heard him out in silence, only to return immediately to the original thread of the conversation, telling Palinuro how, through experiments and the passing of time, scientists had discovered the biochemistry of jealousy and the visceral content of the various emotions: how Charles Darwin in his day had studied the physiology of laughter and stimulated it artificially by manipulating the zygomatic muscles; how Sechenov insisted that intelligence was a function of the cortex reflexes and, finally, how other researchers had initiated similar experiments even earlier: at the beginning of the last century Aldini stimulated one of the cerebral hemispheres of a recently-beheaded man causing movement of the facial muscles on the opposite side of the face and, during the nineteenth century, but towards its end, Bartholow succeeded in inserting electrodes into the heads of two patients, largely by virtue of the fact that these poor creatures' skulls had been rotted and softened by abscesses, and had thus produced movements of members on the side of the body opposite to the cerebral hemisphere stimulated because, as Palinuro must surely know (everybody must surely know), it is the right-hand cerebral hemisphere which controls the movements of the left side of the body, and vice versa, so that left-handed people (like Molkas) are, in reality, in their most intimate and cerebral reality, right-handed, in that the cerebral hemisphere of the right side is far more developed, so to speak, than the left; and that was no mean feat: Penfield himself had penetrated the brain of living patients, of lunatics, psychopaths and mental retards, who had submitted passively to his experiments in implanting electrodes in certain regions of the brain which, when stimulated, caused the patients to remember entire episodes of their lives with an admirable and almost cinematographic sharpness, clarity and exactitude, memories of the past which would otherwise have remained buried for ever or, at least, fragmented and deformed, the best proof of this being that, when the stimulation ceased, the patients automatically stopped remembering; it is as though you, Palinuro, Walter said to him, were suddenly given an electric shock in the

147

brain and who should appear before you, not in the middle of La Española
cantina, of course, but in the middle of your life and of the street, but Papa
Eduardo himself climbing down from his favourite yellow tram, at half-
past six of an afternoon, complete with his straw boater and cane, greeting
the Holy Family with his boater and pointing to the roses in Rio de Janeiro
Square with his cane, accusing them of red and fragrant misdemeanours,
and then discovering Mamma Clementina's whereabouts by the mere
splashing of the fountains and the diamonds cascading, kissing her and
returning home arm-in-arm and climbing into a photograph to become
newly-weds and have a son and so on infinitely and, if that is what we are,
added Walter, it is quite frankly rather sad and, as I said to you before, not
terribly encouraging: although neither Penfield, nor Cannon, nor
Brodmann, nor anybody else that he knew of or could imagine, either
when the microscope was invented or years, decades later, centuries, when
Köhler's experiments and Huygens' luminous theories and Koch's findings
and the advent of fluorescent microscopy and ultraviolet microscopy and
electronic microscopy and stereoscopic microscopy had made it possible to
study the nerve cells and their tentacles so avid for memories and
knowledge and their chromophiles so thirsty for pigment, nobody had
ever, either in a live and trembling brain, still swollen and warm with the
arteries carrying scarlet life to the protuberance, to the nucleus olivaris, to
the white commissure and to the callosum, or in a dead and hardened
brain, dry and cold the venous sinuses which had swept towards the heart
the blue waste and suffocated blood from the pineal body, the corona
radiata and the tree of life, nobody, but nobody, not even somebody other
than a physician or surgeon: philosopher, alchemist, witch or saint: St
Damian in Sicily or Malebranche in Paris or Freud in Vienna or Roentgen
in Würzburg or Cagliostro in Naples, none of them had ever discovered a
single thought which could be touched, touched or seen through a
microscope, seen through a microscope or I don't know what else, smelt or
tasted, a thought firm as a stone, an idea crystallized like an icosahedric
virus, an obsession with bad breath and elephant's ears, or a memory like a
soap bubble bristling with prickles; nothing at all, no thought or thoughts,
be they infinitely small or as huge and uncontainable as those of Nietzsche
and other geniuses who ended up mad because the magnitude of their
lucidity and their thoughts – stated Walter – exceeded the capacity of their
poor skulls and their skulls burst – in a manner of speaking, of course,
because skulls only burst, he said, when you fill them up with chickpeas,
one of the oldest and best methods for separating the bones of the skull in
order to study them (I am referring, as you can imagine, to a previously
debrained skull) being to stuff it full of damp chickpeas and allow them to
swell until you can see with your own eyes how the bones begin to separate,
how the sacred bregma where once there was a palpitating fontanelle,

148

creaks and dilates and splits to allow you to so contemplate . . . contemplate what? some mystery? the avalanche of the sixty thousand Balakhilya genii which came from the head of Brahma? no, merely to contemplate the chickpeas with which everybody's head is filled (although I hope that my own is filled with cockpeas) that is, when they are not full of shit, since Hippocrates was quite accurate when he said that excrement originates in the head and it is not without reason, said Walter the cultured, Walter the knowledgeable, that strange links exist between the highest and the lowest, the heavens and the earth, like lysozyne which is an enzyme present in tears and in excrement and it is a fact that when your eyes are compressed the albumin in your urine increases; and perhaps the most ancient physicians of Europe were also right – or approximately right – when they stated that the brain is composed of pure snot, the very same that dribbles from the nose (and even today, Walter told him, there are people who say that every time you sneeze you expel thousands of irreplaceable neurons) and this, quite apart from the dexterity of the Egyptian embalmers who, so as not to touch the head or the face of the corpse, managed to remove the entire brain with long hooks introduced through the nose, brrrrr! And, do you know? I might never have become interested, or more correctly, it might have taken me a lot longer to become interested, in the fact that the hypothalamus governs the metabolism, sweat, appetite, urination and hundreds of other things, nor have become interested in the phenomena of epilepsy, in Dostoyevsky, in the incredible fact that olfactory, gustatory, visual and auditive hallucinations preceding or following epileptic attacks come about (it is supposed, anyway) when the corresponding neurons spontaneously become active and, I repeat, I would have remained completely ignorant of all this if it had not been for don Prospero, do you remember him? said Walter gazing at himself in one of the bevelled mirrors of La Española which reflected, besides the images of Walter and Palinuro, the smiling faces of a number of satyrs peeping over festoons of fruit; anyway, continued Cousin Walter, you no doubt remember only a don Prospero who was half sad and half happy, but I still remember when the two halves of don Prospero were happy which was, of course, before he suffered the hemiplaegia which paralysed the right half of his face in a permanently sad expression; what an incredible guy, that don Prospero, who spent half his life (the happy half of his life) reading the encyclopaedia, do you remember? Do you remember that when he reached the letter E and he told Estefania that nobody in the house, not Grandfather Francisco nor Uncle Esteban, nor Grandmother Altagracia, nor Papa Eduardo, had a name and derivatives thereof so numerous, so different and so pretty or, in other words, that nobody else was remotely connected with stephanoberycidae, stephanidaes or stephanians, because their names could not be linked in any way with beryciformes,

149

hymenopteras or carboniferous rocks? Do you remember? Anyway, the fact that I remember so much is not thanks only to my own memory but also to Estefania's: she never forgot what don Prospero told her and repeated it to all and sundry until everybody was sick to death of hearing that none of the family's names was hidden beneath the ground with the name of silver antimony sulphide or could be used for measuring halos, rainbows or aurora boreales, since they were not remotely similar to stephanite and stephanome, until everybody was not only fed up but also a little envious to know that nobody had the name which had inspired Lope de Vega, *El Fénix de los Ingenios,* to write *La Desdichada Estefania* and nobody – but for one exception – had a name which had the immense honour of belonging to an asteroid; yes, because among the seven hundred-odd asteroids discovered to date, dear cousin, Estefania and Clementina have their namesakes and, if you promise not to accuse me of having a protuberance in the area of symbolitivity, I will say that it could not be otherwise because those two, of all your memories and all your loved ones, are the most celestial and the most unattainable and, if the beer were not so chilled and the snails not so delicious, I would invite you to walk the streets until the morning star appears and, perhaps, with a little luck, and on the subject of stephanomes, we might be lucky enough to see one of those wonderful lunar halos which, according to St Albertus Magnus, appear every fifty years and also, up there in the far distance, the luminous trace, the incandescent trail of Mamma Clementina and Cousin Estefania quitting our memories at the speed of light; but no, perhaps we would see them better without a moon, without even neon signs and tetragonal lamps evoking the dead, that the night without may become one with the night within, with *the dark night of the soul* as St John of the Cross would say and that we be guided only by the astral light, the light which sweeps the forgotten of God towards death and sin; and anyway, I was talking to you about don Prospero who started selling encyclopaedias ten years before he turned up at our grandparents' house, about don Prospero who, just imagine, must all through half of his sad life have been absorbing an imperceptible education which never let him suspect that the explosions of human knowledge encompass only the minutest expression of nostalgia since, as you well know, Palinuro, forgetfulness is not a forest that can be encompassed in dreams, did you like that sentence? and he therefore believed that encyclopaedias contained the world, the seven seas and the latter-day truths and every morning before the mirror rehearsed the sales pitch which was to hook his potential clients, combining this with gymnastic exercises – or that's what don Prospero told us anyway – so that his praise of the Spanish binding, glossy paper, the Bodoni typography and the colour plates of the League of Nations flags and the plumage of hummingbirds flowed effortlessly, innocently, don Prospero unaware of

what he was saying, between muscle flexes and stretches which prepared
him for the long day ahead and, well, the first revelation which changed
the course of his life – as don Prospero himself also told us – occurred one
morning when as usual he got up early, breakfasted on a couple of boiled
eggs, put on his black suit – stoically-dazzling patches on elbows and
backside – and his inevitable navy-blue tie and, when he was ready to do
his exercises (he always did them fully dressed), he realized that his
spectacles had not greeted the day on the bedside cabinet as they did every
morning, so first he looked for them under the cabinet, should they have
fallen, then under the bed and on top of the dressing-table, then under the
carpet depicting the king's dromedaries (should the naughty pixie have put
them there), then he emptied the pockets of his overcoat and of his suit
from which he drew the conclusion of a dirty handkerchief, a ten-peso
note, some loose change, a pencil sharpener, a pencil and a leaflet headed
Men Only, then he examined every one of the objects on the bedside
cabinet: the lamp, the blotting paper, a ballpoint pen, an ashtray and a
crochet mat, but he had to accept that none of these objects even remotely
resembled his spectacles and it was only then that his guardian angel –
who, in his case, was a bald, short-sighted angel who was happy however
you looked at it – gave him the idea of looking for his spectacles in the
encyclopaedia, leading him to open the volume corresponding to the letter
O on page 3621 and, with some difficulty, read the relevant article and, of
course, he found there all sorts of optical instruments such as Metius'
eyeglass and Galileo's theodolites and tachymeters and spectroscopes and
Kepler's theory of optics, Benjamin Franklin's spectacles and the
parallactic eyeglass and even a plant called St Lucy's spectacles but,
needless to say, he didn't find his own spectacles nor, in a broader sense,
any of those featured in the encyclopaedia so, that very day, don Prospero
went to the optician's and ordered a new pair of spectacles and started to
devour the volumes because, in order to know which things *were not* in the
encyclopaedia, as he explained to us, it was necessary to know which
things *were* or, at least, which things people thought were and, though the
written word initially gave him the satisfaction of discovering that not
only his spectacles but also his toothbrush, his bedspread, the curtains of
his bedroom, his boiled eggs and his navy-blue tie failed to feature in the
encyclopaedia, as was true also of the first person or thing that he
encountered on leaving his room, whether Ricardo the gardener or Uncle
Esteban's yellow, dew-filmed Oldsmobile; none the less, as his poor brain
was progressively peopled with luxuriant proverbs, sharp waterfalls and
twisted empires; as, in short, he started to climb avocado trees, to
penetrate ever-deeper into the Aleutian Islands, following Ariadne's
thread and losing himself in Andromeda's spirals, don Prospero came to
mistrust simple things like white coffee and postcards and to wonder how

151

people could spend their lives talking about the weather, the children's school, servants and prices when, but a step away, there awaited the Defenestrations of Prague and the War of the Cakes and even how people dared to say good afternoon without being familiar with Maimonides' *Guide of the Perplexed* and then, faced with the impossibility of persuading everybody of the benefits of erudition, don Prospero, another beer? decided to employ Olendorf's language-teaching technique by means of which he proposed to educate those around him, this method being pretty harmless and unlikely to incur major didactic consequences in that it consisted of answering any question with a totally irrelevant reply: *Have you been to New York? No, but I have got red socks*, and so, when his landlady (that was before he went to live in our grandparents' house) would ask him: How are you feeling today, don Prospero? the reply came, concise and unhesitating, Köchel 221 by Mozart, madam, or when grandfather (years later) asked him if he wanted to play poker, don Prospero would answer: Ovid's *Metamorphoses*. But, for the rest, he was a well-mannered gentleman, not above afterwards adding Very well thank you, or, I never learned to play cards, or some such thing which caused him to grin in embarrassment with both halves of his face and, by that time, other real-life objects had begun to appear in the encyclopaedia: the tram map which he used to mark his place, egg stains, razor blades and, once, when he stayed up reading all night, Flavia the maid even found don Prospero's head resting on the map of Charente, but the beatitude of his expression (reminiscent of that of St John the Baptist) and the snores which ruffled the vineyards of Cognac lead Flavia to conclude that the time had not yet come for don Prospero's heart to stop for good, and I mention Flavia (said Walter) because, by that time, don Prospero was living in our grandparents' house, where he had arrived one unforgettable afternoon and asked Grandfather if he wanted to buy an encyclopaedia, in response to which Grandmother Altagracia had stuck her oar in and said that she would seriously consider the possibility if don Prospero rented a room in the house and don Prospero had answered: 'The Winged Victory of Samothrace, madam, it's a deal,' and, well, from Cognac to Cranoscopy, added Walter, there is but the odd city and a few more-or-less famous people but, more important, but a few pages, so that not three days passed before don Prospero received the second great revelation of his life on discovering the science founded by Franz Joseph Gall, Cra-what? asked Aunt Luisa and don Prospero explained that the human brain is a collection of organs, each of which corresponds to a different activity, function or intellectual faculty, which are developed to a greater or lesser extent in each individual and that, as Gall discovered (he was, of course, expelled from Catholic Austria for his revolutionary theories, expounded Walter), this development, or lack of same, is reflected in the shape of the head and so the examination of a person's skull, of its depressions and protuberances, allows an assessment to be made of their character, inclinations and capacities since, as Professor Cubi y Soler stated, the skull moulds itself to the brain, exclaimed don Prospero triumphantly and, after speaking of Juan Bautista Bascolpo's trip to the moon where the inhabitants are hairless and the distinguishing cranial protuberance of each individual is painted a different colour, be it on the forehead, the temple or the occiput, like a globe painted all in white with a single country or mountain superimposed in red or yellow and, barely pausing for breath, don Prospero went on to tell Aunt Luisa all the original and comic names given by the cranologists – later phrenologists – to the thirty-odd protuberances of the skull, such as the protuberance of mirthfulness, the protuberance of auditiveness and the protuberance of giftedness and, when Aunt Luisa confessed that she hadn't understood a word, don Prospero asked her to take a good look at the bumps on his forehead, corresponding to the area of deductiveness no less, which meant that he, don Prospero, possessed a very highly developed level of that great intellectual capacity called deduction, to which Aunt Luisa replied: I don't believe it, and don Prospero, in all respect, said to her: Madam, if you don't believe it, it's because you no doubt have a cerebral depression in the area of creditiveness. But from there, said Walter, from the theories of Gall and Spurzheim, which soon degenerated into quackery and went from failure to failure, which, as you may imagine, was inevitable when you think that when Sade died and phrenologists seized his skull in search of the protuberances of malignity and lasciviousness, they found only a small, well-formed head, polished and smooth as that of an innocent youth; so, between that and knowing that stimulation of the septal region produces a sensation of joy and euphoria – by which may be achieved the artificial happiness of someone who is dying of cancer or is to be a shot at dawn – between that, as I was saying, and discovering that behind the speech centre is located the area of typographical memory and knowledge, between that and the conclusion that although the various parts of the brain are each specialized in a different function, none the less not all can function independently and there are even the so-called commissures, said Walter, serving as bridges of communication between the two cerebral hemispheres of which the more important is the corpus callosum; well, between that, between all those theories of the little philosopher of Tiefenbrunn and modern discoveries, decades had intervened, centuries, and not just the three thousand-odd pages which don Prospero still had to read to reach the letter N of Neurology from the letter C of Cranoscopy although, as he had said before (repeated Cousin Walter, drumming his fingers on the table) never had anybody anywhere ever seen or even glimpsed thought, which consoled him to a degree, making him think, yes, *think* that after all we are not merely matter, but something more, a viscous teleplasma, or something less, something apart from spirit and matter, something more – he said – than Descartes' old dualism but which goes beyond the dissolution of dualism proposed by Ryle, something, yes, like the *ombra* which Sisyphus sweated by the bucket-full and which permitted Hercules to travel to the depths of the underworld for, as you will know, the Greek hero didn't travel to Hades in body and soul, but in *ombra* and, by the way, about what you were saying before (slow off the mark in taking up the challenge, thought Palinuro to himself), yes, I confess, I who on the least pretext quote from memory a paragraph from *De Re Medica*, I who had the opportunity in the British Museum to leaf through Vesalius's book from which the bone of light and Adam's rib had disappeared and who held in my hands the original of *Select Observations on English Bodies* by Hall (son-in-law of the Swan of Avon) I, in truth, will never be able to operate on cancer of the rectum as did von Volkmann or cut a trigeminal nerve as did Krause, although I know by heart the exact date on which these two surgeons performed these operations for the first time; I, such an elegant young man-about-town, as you say, not only lack the least ability to empty an armpit cavity or take out tonsils but, what is more, I actually believe that I was not born for tasks as vulgar as performing a circumcision or introducing a pessary into a vagina to lend support to a prolapsed uterus because true gentlemen, said Walter, showing Palinuro his manicured fingernails, do not work with their hands; this may be left to labourers and, anyway, I am quite incapable of stitching a wound without getting it infected or of giving an injection in the buttock without injuring the sciatic nerve, although I do know (and you don't) the name of the exact point where it should be administered, namely the Galliot point; but my attitude to medicine, my attitude to life and death, I should say, is far more profound, or attempts to be, than your own, or Uncle Esteban's and Estefania's combined and therefore, my dear cousin, I will not take your criticism to heart, nor will I answer you as Aunt Luisa answered don Prospero: brandishing her brolly and warning him that if he continued to offend her, she would stick it in his protuberance of insultiveness. But don Prospero didn't take Aunt Luisa seriously and so was quite happy, at least for a time, at least until he suffered the hemiplaegia which paralysed the right half of his face, causing him to become half-unhappy for the rest of his life, turning him into a walking representation of tragedy and comedy with an eternal smile on the left side and a miserable moue on the right and, not only that, but the embolism (or whatever caused the hemiplaegia) must also have affected part of the left cerebral hemisphere which, as I told you, governs movement of the right side of the body – because don Prospero was from then onwards somewhat incoherent, a little forgetful, I don't know, a bit odd and, what is most

154

curious, said Walter, I now realize that don Prospero's happy half corresponded to the half of his brain which still understood the world, the half still capable of being astonished by its oriental birds, its cloud factories and its patched-up heroes, while his sad half reflected the side of the brain which could no longer comprehend it since, as I said before, although a link does exist between the hemispheres through the commissures and the corpus callosum, none the less each hemisphere is responsible for learning certain things, of which only superficial notions are transmitted to the other hemisphere, as though to be held in reserve. In fact, the brain is rather like the cosmic egg of the Hindus: one half of silver corresponding to the Earth and one half of gold corresponding to the Heavens, the first half containing but a reflection, a feeble copy, of that contained in the other. Hence, there are certain specific functions which are carried out only by one hemisphere or the other or by the remaining aggregates forming the encephalon, how about another beer? insisted Walter, craning to peer between the excrescence-laden necks of the satyrs and then the fresh beers arrived together with the snails *à la vizcaína* and pickled Cambray onions and the two cousins drank, ate and smoked and Walter told Palinuro that, though it doubtless went without saying, he did want to clarify that in his own case, naturally, and in contrast to don Prospero, it was with the eyes of the sad half of his persona that he looked upon the world and its mysteries and with the happy half that he became befuddled in order to forget the world and its absurdities and he told Palinuro that other researchers had gone even further, severing the corpus callosum of monkeys and cats and so isolating and cutting communication between the two cerebral hemispheres and then, after covering the left eye of the cat or the monkey, they had placed before its right eye certain things which it therefore learned with its left hemisphere and which it was unable to transmit in turn to the right hemisphere and then they uncovered the cat's left eye and covered its right eye and taught it the opposite through the left eye and so its right hemisphere learned very different things and which it could not communicate to the left hemisphere; in other words, let's say, for instance, that the cat learned with its right eye that if it touched a red tube it would get an electric shock and if it touched the blue tube it would get food and then with its left eye it learned the opposite: that if it touched the blue tube it would receive an electric shock and if it touched the red tube it would receive food, or let's say that it learned to fear a dog with its right eye and learned with the left eye to attack it and if on successive days of the week its eyes were alternately covered and uncovered, the cat – or the monkey – would behave in one way on Mondays, Wednesdays and Fridays and in another on Tuesdays, Thursdays and Saturdays. And what happened on Sunday, the seventh day? Well, they uncovered both eyes and the cat went mad; or perhaps we should say that both cats went mad, or should we say the two half-cats? Horrible notion, isn't it? Makes you think of a future surpassing all the horrors conceived in the utopias of Huxley and Orwell, where the corpus callosum of slaves will be cut so they may learn to be faithful to one master with half of their brain and faithful to another master with the other half. Makes you think of the possibility of having half your soul embrace the nocturnal vision of the world spoken of by Fechner and the other the diurnal vision of the universe. Or of the possibility of believing in God with the left wing of your heart and being an atheist with the right wing; of fleeing with your left leg and setting to flight a lion with your right; of being loyal to the students and to your people, to your race, with the left eye and betraying them with your right, just as you caressed and fed Papa Eduardo with your right hand and with your left raised the oar that shattered him without however touching a hair on his head and without frightening off the phosphorescent fish nesting between his ribs? And what will you do, Palinuro, when you open both your eyes and the two wings of your heart? But it is some consolation to know that, though we are not one – Walter continued – neither are we two, but ten, or a thousand, who knows how many, and between the lot of us we do not make that one which we are *not* and, in fact, what we know of ourselves is less than what we do not know, although not to the extent, of course, of those poor devils who, due to a little tumour or a clot or an injury in the left hemisphere of the brain, become paralysed on the right side, as happened to don Prospero, but they are worse off because they not only lose the neurons responsible for movement of the right arm and leg but also neurons containing awareness of the existence of those members and so these invalids do not recognize their own arm or leg and don't know who they belong to or why they have them attached to their one and true side and when they are in bed they feel that someone (or half of someone) is lying beside them and try with their left arm and leg to kick out of bed the arm and leg which is no longer their own right leg or arm and is nothing to do with them, is totally alien to their being. And then the opposite might happen to the general with the glass eye or to the one-handed lottery-ticket vendor (or Grandfather Francisco if they had finally cut off his leg) and happens to many who lose a member: they know that they have lost it, that it has been amputated, but sometimes the neurons refuse to acknowledge it, giving rise to the phenomenon of the ghost member; they cut off your right leg and then, one day, all of a sudden, months or years later, the corresponding neurons activate the sensation of itching in the big toe of the right foot and the itch becomes desperate because the big toe no longer exists or, at such moments, exists only to you and to nobody else and not only in your mind but in physical sensation also and the mere thought, of course, sends shivers (or itches) down your spine and this is why people are terrified of epileptics and visionaries and miracles; that is why, cousin, they repudiate opium, marijuana, acid; because they not only produce a big toe which doesn't exist but more than that: a particular conception of the world or even a conception of the world exclusive to the epileptic, the lunatic or the drug-taker, to the chosen one or the poet and to no one else, but it is as real as any other world for the simple reason that the relationship existing between the auditive, gustative and tactile neurons bursting suddenly into spontaneous activity and the hallucinatory world they produce and the relationship between neurons which behave themselves and the real world which surrounds us and which we believe to be pretty much common to us all, is one and the same; centuries ago, just imagine, in the Middle Ages when nothing was known of neurology, Ockham already had some intuition of this when he said that God could produce in a human being all the physical and psychic conditions involved in the act of seeing an object though this object might not exist in exterior reality and, knowing nothing of the speed of light, the same Ockham said that, even if God had already destroyed the stars, it would still be possible to produce in us the act of seeing what had ceased to be. And tell me . . . are the stars that we see today not the same as those that, even as Tycho and Rudolf II gazed at them from the belvedere of the Hradschin, had already been dead for thousands or millions of years? But this, your creating an exclusive world, is not to be pardoned with the excuse that you don't understand or that you fear to understand, because perhaps the majority of people continue to think, like Schiller, that the true is useful and the false is useless; of what use is a unique and personal world, Palinuro, when it is to be supposed that we were born to share our lives and together graze our dreams, when it is supposed that we are here not only to share snails and beer, but also our laughter, our wars in technicolor and our hollow philosophies? It is not to be pardoned precisely because it is too close to the most terrible and, at the same time, the simplest and most obvious truth of all and the fact is that a universe is born and dies with each of us, others have said it before me, even Grandmother Altagracia (high priestess of platitudes) said so when she stated that every head is a world unto itself, a complete universe with all its planets, its stars, its millions of people and ideas, its students and its strikes. Well, she didn't put it quite like that, in such detail, but it boils down to the same thing. And our fragility is such, such our wretchedness, that it is not only for profound philosophical reasons that we can never *be* but are always *being* and only with death can wholly *be*, but also for other less highfalutin and more mundane reasons: our glands, our hormones, our food. When I eat this snail, for example, I am perhaps ingesting an unknown alkaloid, a mysterious drug, a slow poison which will insidiously change, shall we say not just the course of this night, but my whole life. And it is not because man is the measure of all things, Palinuro, that this smell of disinfectant which wafts to us from the toilets is unpleasant to you and to myself, but simply because the neurons of our olfactory centres are awake and functioning well because, as you must know, there are brain lesions which make the smell of a daffodil unbearable, even painful. And when it is seen that the scent of flowers can cause suffering, why not then that of the red roses to which Papa Eduardo pointed with his cane in Rio de Janeiro Park, in the sense that you find it painful to have lost for ever all that which their scent recalls to your memory? Therefore, my friend, considering that the precuna of the occipital lobe is held to be the area connected with sexual stimulus, is it not? I would suggest, Palinuro – or son of Jason, as Virgil also calls you – in honour of the strange beings that we are, so strange that we think with the left side of our brain but sing with the right, I would suggest that at this hour of Oypris, the hour of food and pleasures, we take to the street and head for the whorehouse to partake of the generous dew of Gunleuda from which springs all poetry and beauty; I would suggest that we wander through our old haunts and heed the oracles whispered through the bars of the drain covers by the head of Orpheus and the feathered tongue of Quetzalcoatl; that we render homage to Hecate, goddess of alleyways heaped with copper coal; that we allow the Valkyries to bathe us in beer and maguey juice and ambrosia of gonococcus and let us remember that, while night is the mother of sleep and of death, so it is also of friendship and old age; I would suggest, then, that we gorge ourselves on lotus flowers to forget our human wretchedness, but just a little, just enough to kill the pain, as for nerve resections, but not to the point of killing the idea of pain; and that we drink, yes, that we drink until we quench the fire of our sign, until all our aggression and our fury disappears as though by magic or by lobotomy and, with it, fire, the fire which inflamed so many illustrious Arians like Goya, Van Gogh and León Gambetta. Let us drink, indeed, until we quench the fire, but not the idea of fire. And my dear cousin, my beloved cousin, Palinuro, my never sufficiently prudent child: my dearest wish, as Grandmother used to say, is that the blue sky of your existence never be shadowed by the least cloud; forget about strikes and demonstrations: the day that a protuberance appears on your head in the area of politicity, a member of the constabulary or of the riot police will sooner or later materialize before you, all set to smash your head with a baton and, at that moment, you will realize that the alternative between seeing and understanding the world in don Prospero's terms (with his happy side) or understanding it as I do with my sad side, ceases to be of any consequence because at that instant, I repeat, you will understand that the right hemisphere of the general with the glass eye's brain alone had learned to see the world as it is: a world, of course, where all is of glass and crystal in which people and your loved ones, the trees, the clouds and the earth itself,

are of crystal, but a breath suffices – a pin-prick, just as they say a pin-prick
to the medulla oblongata suffices to produce instant death – to bring the
world, the whole universe, crashing down and reduce it to dust in total
silence and darkness in an infinitesimal and endless fraction of time,
because each and every one of us is Shiva, the god whose eyes have only to
be covered by Parvati and the sun is quenched and the lamp post on the
corner is doused and Boötes goes blind and the Swan is drowned and the
Great Bear closes his eyes and makes ready to sleep through an eternal
winter. But this fragility of ours and of the world – said Walter, pausing
for breath and sighing hugely – is not necessarily good or evil, glad or sad.
It depends on your mood on waking, on which side you get out of bed.
Today, for example, tonight – perhaps on account of the beer, perhaps on
account of the snails, perhaps on account of your company – shit, I've
stained my jacket, perhaps on account of your being here, I was saying –
don't take it too much to heart, I might think differently tomorrow –
when all is said and done, I believe that the world, being of crystal, being as
it is full of luminosity and transparency, of brightness and the flashing of
water and glass, is not evil; and not for nothing does my Catholic
education (which I gainsay repeatedly) lead me to ponder the superiority of
what they call the spirit; I mean, matter pure and simple we are not, but
neither was the deluded Coleridge right in believing in the corporeality of
thought and neither were Cabanis and Karl Vogt when they said that the
brain secretes thought as the liver secretes bile. And do you know why?
Because we are made of words and so are things; because we are but
memory, and things exist and are real when they allow themselves tamely
to be clothed in the world of words, in the iridescent and trembling aura of
volts and watts and protons and neurons with which the positivists
masked the shriek of lightning; but this does not make them ours, this will
never reveal to us what lies behind them; though they swear to us that the
memories of the Alhambra are composed of organic formulae of sugar and
architectural amphibology, my dear cousin, it will not prevent the essence
of its arabesques and lattice-work from disintegrating before our eyes like
Mediterranean foam. My saying *behind* is, of course, just a manner of
speaking: it is not that the essence of things lies behind them or anywhere
else: neither below, nor within, nor around. All these words are of no use
for designating something which exists neither in space nor in time,
because space and time are also words. And who ever saw a round word?
Who ever saw a pink syllable? Who ever saw a sentence running down the
street yelling at the top of its voice? Who ever saw a paragraph, sleekly fat
and smelling of Prince Albert tobacco, sit down on a park bench to read the
newspaper? Who ever saw an illusion dressed in purple lace or a poem
bursting like a sneeze in the solar plexis and shooting blood to the heavens?
Neurology may have succeeded, my dear cousin, in circumscribing the

murky and virtually impenetrable region of total and organized and eternal memory, memory in its highest and most profound and most heart-rending human manifestation, absurd memory capable of recalling word for word throughout an entire life a poem about students or even the complete works of a man who endowed the heavens with art by way of a macabre ray and a new shiver or can even, just think how absurd! can even learn the entire telephone directory of Mexico City, name by name and number by number, or the contents of Ford technical manuals, but which is capable, none the less, of such baseness and treachery as for ever to forget, instant by instant, the scented and fragrant roses of childhood, the voices, the damp and golden haunts of a dauntless and triumphal adolescence: but never has anybody found in that egg which you beheld, in that brain composed of white and varnished and compressed intestines, in that labyrinth of discordant concord surrounded and guarded by compressed white snakes, never, Palinuro, has anybody ever discovered or even glimpsed the trace of a memory, the romantic imprint of an illusion, the absinthe-coloured mirage of a sophism, or the sign, the imperial explosion, of a classical idea, the furrows and the blisters, the scars veiled by rainbow cobwebs of the vestiges and shadows which should be left in the wake of the words learned there and of the reasoning conceived there and of sensorial images of the world and of its things: of the round world and of the scent of flowers and beer; of the sweet earth and the coldness of ice and the ardour of sphinxes; of the dark homeland, the softness of felt and the pealing of bells; of youth (of our youth, Palinuro) of agony and of the sound of turbines, of the shape and colour of houses and clouds and women and of the barbaric brilliance of the sun; never, ever, even in a thousand years.

'Tomorrow, of course, is another day. Tomorrow we will have lived, but we will not live to tell the tale. Tomorrow I will forget everything I have told you or, worse, I will wake up and deny everything . . . and now, do me a favour, would you? Just stop thinking that the brain you saw sliced into sixteen equal sections was that of a young man. In the first place, you have to set aside your sentimentality and remember that Uncle Esteban used to say: that the body and the organs you study are always those of "Man", just that, with a capital letter and in quotation marks: *Homo Sapiens*. Secondly, you should know that, in order to slice a brain, you have to let it harden for several days in Kaiserling solution. And thirdly, even if it was the brain of a young man – and a student, at that, which is most unlikely because students were incinerated in the Campo Marte army barracks to wipe them out once and for all – in any case, that brain could not be *his* brain. Do you understand?'

160

'No, I don't understand,' said Palinuro.

'Remind me to send my waistcoat to the dry cleaners,' instructed Walter. 'I'll explain some other time.'

10

The Olendorf method and the general with a hundred glass eyes

If the truth be told, Estefania and I were never rich or even remotely so. If there was anything of note about our room in Holy Sunday Square in Mexico City, it was that it was a well-oriented room, with egg-shell walls like the houses of those pygmies who had a deadly enmity for cranes, but nothing more. And we never even had friends of the type which, when you arrive home, erupt from nowhere with caviare and champagne. And, talking of champagne, only once, that I remember, did we open a bottle and it was Cousin Walter who brought it one afternoon, having recently returned from one of his trips to Europe. 'I've brought this bottle to celebrate,' he told me. 'To celebrate what?' asked my cousin with that naïveté which overcame her at her most lucid moments, causing the hooks of her bra to spring undone. 'To celebrate being able to buy it,' answered Walter and he promised that one day he would surprise us with a monster five-hundred-and-twenty-liquid-ounce bottle of Nebuchadnezzar. But he never did. We, on the other hand, with great effort and several months' savings, once bought twenty-one bottles of cider to bring in the New Year with twenty-one cannon reports, appointing it general-in-chief of the 365 days which would likely follow, through the crushing winters of Iowa City, the eternal springs of the Valley of Mexico, the summers of the living desert and the autumns of Paris which celebrate themselves by tossing golden leaves by the thousand into the air.

I may have told you that we went to Paris or had just arrived back from London but, the fact is, we liked to play this game and speak like that when we went to the street named Paris or arrived home by way of London Street. And I may have told you that we visited the Prado, the Louvre or the Orangerie, but it is just that we borrowed books on these museums and other galleries from the library – we didn't have the wherewithal to buy them – and we liked to pretend afterwards that we had been to this place or that place. And the only one of us, as I have said before, to have gone to Europe, not once but many times, was our cousin Walter, who lived for several years in London for the sole purpose of writing us endless, mad letters: about how the queues of black taxis driving up the Strand daily buried their prestige; about how he had met a pair of old-age pensioners who were selling chunks of English park and deer with whisky-sprinkled antlers; how, every Sunday, he rounded a corner to find the renewed Thames dragging the weekly culture in its wake, amazing him, as it did the good Pound, with its occidental tossing.

Nevertheless, contradictory though it may seem, everything we had in our room and in our lives was of incalculable worth. And don't think, don Prospero, Mr Lottery-Ticket Vendor, don't think, Palinuro, that I'm talking about the sentimental value they held for us: that goes without saying. No, I'm talking about their real value, their economic value, the value which has sweetened business through all the ages. Because, although we didn't possess Wedgwood cups or Madame Récamier sofas or the jade mask which immunized an Aztec baron's soul, we were none the less surrounded by objects which had, by the law of supply and demand, attained astronomical prices.

This we discovered one day when we were poorer than usual, when our debts were on the point of excommunicating us and our savings on the verge of suicide, and Estefania had the incredible idea of organizing a series of auctions to sell off our possessions to the highest bidder. By her calculations, we could with a little luck realize some three thousand pesos. Of these, two thousand would go on making the first payment on all the objects we might sell, so that we could replace them, but brand new. We could perhaps survive a few more weeks on the other thousand pesos. So we invited the milkman, the general with the glass eye, the postman, our mad neighbour, the concierge and we invited you, don Prospero, and Cousin Walter.

Everything went without a hitch, despite Walter's absence. The first object to go under the hammer was our Osterizer liquidizer. The general with the glass eye bid thirty-five pesos. Don Prospero immediately said: 'Forty.'

'Forty what?' asked the general.

'Forty pesos, of course,' answered don Prospero.

'Of course nothing: it could have been forty horses or forty cannon. There can be forty of a lot of things.'

'Forty pesos, who bids more?' said Estefania, contentedly, rapping the table lightly with her hammer.

And suddenly, without knowing why, I stood up and said: 'Five thousand dollars.'

Those present stared at me somewhat startled, somewhat sad, and I, of course, ended up with the liquidizer. In the explanation that I gave them, which I made up as I went along, I discovered the reasons for my attitude. I told them of the many times that you, Estefania, in your dressing-gown and with sleep in your eyes, or in a white apron and chef's hat, had, the morning after, prepared for me a strawberry milkshake to help me get over a drinking-bout the night before, or a cream and nut dessert for a birthday dinner. And I asked you, Estefania, to place yourself in the stance of the Statue of Liberty, liquidizer jug held on high, so that all could behold the decomposition of light in the luminous spectrum of carrots, tomatoes, beetroot and Brussels sprouts which had so often saved us from starving to death. And I pointed out to them that, in the liquidizer (better than in any other object in our room) they might perceive the truth of Karl Marx's statement to the effect that the value of an article is labour substantivized; and then I spoke to them of the origination of private property, linked by Engels with the change-over from matriarchy to patriarchy, but which occurred in our case when we freed ourselves respectively from the one and the other: I, from the matriarchy of Mamma Clementina and Estefania from the patriarchy of Uncle Esteban, when we left home and set up our apartment with our own belongings. Mamma Clementina and Uncle Esteban had always assured Estefania and me that everything in the house belonged to the whole family and so to us but, when we broke something or borrowed money, it turned out that the lamp belonged to Mamma Clementina or the pesos to Uncle Esteban and, in fact, were not *ours* at all. Using arguments of this type, speaking to them of love, of the black oranges which appear in pentagrams, of Estefania's legs and, particularly, of Adam Smith and of the workers in the Bimbo bread factory who are obliged to take a bath every day before making their bread, and of Social Security and Christmas bonuses and surplus value and Fanon, I went ahead and that same night bought our Simmons mattress for seven thousand five hundred pesos, Uncle Esteban's portrait for five hundred pounds sterling and four Gillette razor blades (belonging to Estefania) for nine hundred million lira. The milkman, don Prospero, the postman and the general with the glass eye made every effort to be understanding but, at the end of the auction, finding themselves empty-handed and gazing at my riches, jealousy oozed out between the rocky outcrops of their souls and they swore that they would never again attend an auction. I then bought from Estefania three bottles of wine at fifty thousand pesos each and a fried chicken *à la Kentucky* for two hundred and fifty-three dollars and we invited them to supper. By the second bottle of wine, everyone had forgotten the affront and agreed to return next day.

It goes without saying that, when we went for a stroll that night through the Zona Rosa, I felt for the first time what rich people feel and I walked and talked and yawned in a different way and even looked down my nose in a different way.

We had a coffee in Paris and a pizza in Genoa, we looked at the shop windows in Hamburg and entered a bookshop in Nice where my cousin asked them to put aside Ortega y Gasset's *Complete Works* and Fuentes' *Where the Air is Clear*. When we returned to our room, without the books

164

and without a cent to our name, we realized that I had not been fair and at this rate Estefania was going to end up destitute, swimming in the millions of pesos I owed her. So I promised her that next day I would sell off my things and she would sit with the bidders.

And so it was: Estefania bought my toothbrush, my poster of *Hedda Gabler* at the Aldwych Theatre, my Bruno spelling and reading primer, as well as my ties, my two old suitcases and all my cufflinks, paying huge sums which filled our guests with fear and trembling. But I was never as grateful to Estefania as when she bid five hundred thousand dollars for the manuscript of a novel on which I had been working for many years, by which Estefania wished to show me that unknown authors can be famous without anybody knowing it. This time nobody accepted our invitation to supper. They all had a different excuse for leaving halfway through the auction, except the general, who said that he had forty.

'Forty what?' Estefania asked him. 'Forty excuses?'

The general didn't answer; he put on his cap and his decorations, glared at us with an eye full of fury and marched out, slamming the door, to become lost in the dimensionless night in which the stars, the neon signs and the cars were all situated on the same plane, as from a bird's eye perspective.

The second person to leave was our mad neighbour who, finding no better excuse, said that she had to leave because she was expecting a letter. Next the postman said he was going because he had to deliver the letter. The concierge leapt at the opportunity to say that she had to go and open the door to let the postman in to deliver the letter. And don Prospero told us that he had to go and offer condolences with the sad half of his face and then go to a party with the happy half.

'And why don't you come back after the party?' Estefania asked him.

'Ah, because I have to write the letter.'

My cousin and I postponed the auction until after the TV film.

This time it was again my turn to join the bidders. But there was nobody to bid against me when Estefania opened her jewel box to display the brooch with four real pearls that she had inherited from Aunt Luisa and Uncle Esteban's ring and so, taking advantage of the situation, I gave her thirty cents for the brooch and two shillings for the ring. Estefania said not a word, but next day she bought my stereophonic Garrard record player and my Blaupunkt radio as one lot for two Argentinian pesos. Then she bought my stethoscope and my bistouries, my *Biochemistry* and the complete collection of Surgeon's *Quarters* from Fort Winnebego, Illinois for half a franc. Not satisfied with this, she proceeded that afternoon to acquire all my Charlie Parker records for six US cents and a whole opera for three pence.

When we had finished buying and selling each other all the tangible and external objects belonging to us, including the walls of our room, the foundation of our apartment building and the colours of our flag, we bought and sold everything imaginable, such as the organs of our bodies and their functions, our joys and our sorrows.

I bought from Estefania her entire circulatory system, including her celiac trunk and its branches.

She bought my metabolism.

I bought her grief when Uncle Esteban died and she bought my happiness when I saw her free of pain, which was so great that I gradually bought all her deceased.

But we were obliged, eventually, to face up to two problems. First, that we continued to be poverty-stricken because we spent our time mutually granting each other credit and increasingly long-term IOUs. Second, I couldn't spend my whole life asking my cousin to lend me her breath to fill my lungs, her stairs to go down to the street and her city to walk through my gardens and neither could she spend her whole life asking me to lend her my heart to harbour her thoughts, my window to look out and see her sky and my rain to break in the umbrella that she had just bought from me.

And, above all, as though Estefania didn't already have enough pedestrians, viaducts and parking meters to her credit and I wasn't already burdened with so many problems, countries and undeserved monuments, the cynical bitch accused me of withering her forests with my winter.

Therefore, we decided to return all our things to each other and so liquidate our debts, and to buy *El Universal* newspaper to go through the small ads and find a job.

'Walter Thompson, Young and Rubicam, McCann Erickson all need talented individuals,' said Estefania. 'Why don't we work for an ad agency?'

Estefania's question seemed so stupid to me that I was lost for words. On other occasions, I had got a kick from the surrealistic game of definitions similar to the Olendorf method in the absurdity of completely unrelated questions and answers but, on this particular occasion, I couldn't forgive my cousin for taking things so lightly when, before our very eyes, our life was taking a desperate turn.

'And what is a desperate turn?' Estefania asked me and her question, which perched on her lips with the innocence of a hummingbird, shook me from a tattered dream going to the very end of the line.

'A chance to rape you,' I answered, falling into the trap. I sat down on the bed and shook the sheets to arouse them from their slumber: five innocent bed bugs unanimously turned into five flying drops of blood.

'What is a chance to rape me?'

I put on a green sock on the side closest to spring and answered: 'A starling in the jungle.'

166

'And what is a starling in the jungle?'

I did a hand stand, walked on my finger tips to the cupboard, looked at myself stomach-length in the mirror and realized that I was a success in life.

'The word of an officer,' I answered her, wondering at the same time what would be more suitable for the occasion: whether I should use a long wig with tails or a bow-shaped moustache.

'And what is the word of an officer?' she asked me, stretching and showing her armpits, in which good intentions normally nested.

'A dispossessed advertisement,' I answered her as I selected the shirt with red stripes and wing collar. Estefania gambolled on the bed like an angora kitten and remained silent for thirty seconds and fifteen buses.

'And what is a dispossessed advertisement?'

'Aunt Luisa's memory.'

'And what is Aunt Luisa's memory?'

I contrived a surgeon's knot in my tie as in the heyday of Lord Baden Powell and put on my left shoe of crocodile skin with golden blisters and answered her: 'Summer's drunkenness.

'And what is summer's drunkenness?'

'Estefania beneath a tree.'

'And what is Estefania beneath a tree?' she asked me, wrapping herself in a blanket and wandering about the room like a confused ghost.

'The curse of mirrors,' I answered her and I put in my best set of false teeth and put on my left shoe of crepe paper with a violin buckle and candy laces and the left leg of my grey trousers with red stripes.

'And what is the curse of mirrors?' Estefania asked me, as she glimpsed herself in profile in the Bacardi Rum advertisement.

'A letter with no name.'

'And what is a letter with no name?' she insisted.

'An airman with nutmeg eyes,' I told her, remembering that I also had to go to the post office to post some letters, including one in which I rejected the position of Sales Manager in a perfumery, put my right stamp in the left flower of the room's most perfumed button-hole and, teat gloves in hand, I prepared to say goodbye to Estefania. But she couldn't let me off that lightly:

'And what is an airman with nutmeg eyes?' she asked me, sucking her false eyelashes.

'Let me see . . . you tell me what it is,' I challenged her.

'What is it, come on, tell me what it is?' she begged, on her knees, at the height of my belly button.

'A hat with oranges,' I told her. 'But they have to be big oranges with large pores, like the ones Palinuro bought the other day.'

She got to her feet shivering with cold. A trickle of mascara ran from her mouth, as though she had been punched in black and white.

'And what is a hat with oranges?'

'A tree in flames.'

'And what is a tree in flames?' she asked me. By that time, I was just about dressed: I only had to put on my chequered lungs, the left leg of my blue trousers with white and canary-yellow triangles, my holey flesh-coloured left sock, my designer briefcase and my coral teapot.

'The prodigious revelation of an almanac,' I answered her. She turned to gaze with almost maternal curiosity at the almanac we kept on the desk and asked me:

'And what is the prodigious revelation of an almanac?'

I put on the right sleeve of my green jacket, the red collar of my raincoat, the heel of my boots, the hem of the sheets, two new wrinkles and the ivory buttons of our Simmons mattress and said, as I inhaled a pinch of snuff:

'To have fun among the ruins. Why do you ask me so many questions?' and I placed my hands on her shoulders.

'And what is to have fun among the ruins? What is why do you ask me so many questions?'

I bit her neck until I had imprinted the scar of a perverted star and answered her: 'A congressman's aspiration.'

I went into the bathroom, took off my shirt, my binoculars, my celluloid tie and my night cap, put on my penis, peed and took out my shaving brush, my toothpaste, my shaving lotion, my hairbrush, my lighter and my sponges, the scissors and my passport.

'And what is a congressman's aspiration?'

'A woman without acoustics,' I answered her, true to the foam covering my face, after which I lathered the mirror, the bathroom curtains, the floor and my fountain pen, in order to shave them of my image, their flower design, dirt and ink.

'And what is dirt and ink?' Estefania almost asked me, but she could not guess what I was about. Instead, she peeked around the bathroom door, a crown of rollers on her head, and said: 'And what is a woman without acoustics?'

'To attack through the ivory door,' I answered, at the precise moment that I nicked myself and a drop of blood flecked the foam with blue.

'And what is to attack through the ivory door?' she asked from a long way off, from almost fifteen years back, from almost nowhere, while I tried to clean the blood from the mirror, from the curtains and from the sky.

'To stereotype one's glands,' I shouted, poking my head round the bedroom door: I saw her so very alone, in the furthest corner, full of cobwebs and dust.

'And what is to stereotype one's glands?' she insisted.

168

'A papal blessing,' I said to her as I pulled the toilet chain from left to right like in the photographs and removed my red sock and four green ribs and, undoing the zip of my hat, I stuck out my nose and answered, seriously endangering my virility:

'The cutting edge of a razor blade.'

And, no sooner said than done, I put on my Raleigh cigarettes, took off the right leg of my mauve trousers, put on an organdy-scented jacket and gave my catskin spats a cat's lick and a promise.

'And what is the cutting edge of a razor blade?'

I emerged from the bathroom like a rallying invalid and, removing my leg of orange plaster and a wound of plastic radiance, I answered her: 'The beasties born of your sex.'

'And what are the beasties born of your sex?' she asked me.

'I didn't say of my sex, I said your sex.'

'Exactly, of your sex,' she insisted.

'OK, have it your own way then: of my sex.'

'Ah, of my sex,' she said, raising her nightdress to look at her mandarin's beard. 'And what are the beasties born of my sex?'

'An enduring mania,' I answered her.

'And what is an enduring mania?'

I went over to the window, threw it wide open, took a deep breath of smoke from the boilers, urgent telegrams and autumn whims, and said: 'The journey of eventides. Isn't that beautiful? Saying such things beats getting beaten up by the police.'

She took off her nightdress, I put on my dinner-jacket, she lay down again on the bed and began to cry with her face buried in the pillow.

'And what is to get beaten up by the eventides?' she asked.

'A lawyer drowned in the marshes.'

I sat down beside her, put on a vest and comforted her with pats on the bottom.

'And what is a lawyer drowned in the marshes?' she asked me in dreams.

'A poem by Neruda,' I told her and, happy as never before, I got up, put on my raincoat and seized my cane, put on my scarf and my diplomas, put on my wallpaper, put on my knees, put on my lamps, put on the city and bade her farewell.

'And what is a poem by Neruda?' she said, leaping from the bed like an eighty-month-old child.

'The dark thoughts of spinsters,' I said and took off my underpants and traffic lights.

'And what are the dark thoughts of spinsters?' she asked me, crouching on the carpet.

'Waking up among the daisies. Speaking of which: think of me every hour of the day while I earn my daily bread doing advertisements for the protocols of Goodyear, Oxo and the prolegomena of Anderson Clayton. See you later,' I answered her as I left the room.

'Wait! Don't leave me on my own! Tell me first what is to wake up among the daisies!'

I shut the door and answered very quietly, so that she would not hear me: 'A coitus supported by the oligarchies.'

The breakfast cups, the coffee pot and my novel crashed against the door and after them followed two volumes of Fabre's *Souvenirs Entomologiques* from which fluttered two preserved butterflies and Estefania's portrait.

'And what is a coitus supported by the oligarchies?' my cousin asked me.

I knocked on the door with all the timidity of a deaf and dumb debtor and anwered her in sign language: 'Snow which turns to salt of sapphires. And don't make so much noise because it's after midday.'

She opened the door to me enveloped in a transparency of orchids and porcelain and threw her arms around my neck.

'And what is snow?'

'A congenital haemophilia,' I told her, and threw her on to the bed.

'And what is haemophilia?' she asked me, spreading her legs.

'A mere association of ideas?' I answered as I licked her salty stomach.

'And what is a mere association of ideas?' she asked, her eyes rolling whitely, bluely.

'Poets with murdered hearts,' I said and jumped out of bed, pulling off a green salad, removing my anatomy books, my wig and my buttocks, my hopes and the trees and I then quickly put on the middle finger of my yellow glove and the purple tip of my left tongue and flung my belt into the air together with my birthmark.

'And what is the poets with murdered hearts?' she asked me as I covered her with my body.

'Bureaucracies of asphalt.'

'And what is that?' she asked, but I penetrated her simultaneously with my sex and my tongue and answered with my mouth full of her kisses and her tongue:

'A colonel wearing his shoes for getting shot in.'

'And what is that?' she said. It is to spill blood in the damp crown of strawberries, I answered her, it is a well-applied tautology, it is a sleigh of aspirations, it is a spread your legs wider, it is a move over, my love, it is a come now, I said to her, and we started to move like ones possessed and to come slowly, endlessly, again and again, in bed, on the carpet, on the plates, in our mouths, in the mirrors and against the walls lit up by fireworks, boreal trout and Egyptian jellies of tattered flesh and unironed chapters, so wonderful, Estefania! mouthing spasms between magellanic foam and alternating currents fusing birds and semen and advertisements

170

and golden hours until, after making lots and lots of love and repeating it like a metaphor to the point of heart attack and to infinity, we lost ourselves in orange coincidences and we crowned ourselves with wines and exiles for love of a budding eternity, didn't we, Estefania? And my sex contracted like an accordion and turned into a little old man lost in the uterine mists of Madagascar. 'He wasn't Sanforized,' you said, you touched the tip of his nose and asked me, 'Now tell me what a budding eternity is,' and you fell asleep, calmly, on your back, with your eyes open, waiting for me without expecting the least caress or movement because you knew that I was worn out from so much making love to you. Budding eternity I answered, but never finished the sentence: I saw that it was five past three, that it was the month of November and that the sun was shining and then I took off my arms, my belly button, my right leg, my left helmet, my spectacles, my friends and my eyebrows, my surname and my legs, my hair, my ears and my crossword puzzles and felt as good as new and flung myself down to rest within your body on a glorious impulse of belated transvestism. And so we lay, asleep, the two of us made a single love. The evening entered through the open window, as did Palinuro's dove, and the names of the squares, the street lights thick with insects, Ricardo the gardener, our grandparents and the Campbell soup advertisement came in to see us.

And the general with the glass eye almost ended up coming in through the window. 'I don't want to exaggerate,' he told us, 'and say that I was knocking at the door for hours, but it was certainly for days.' I broke open a bottle of Habanero Palma and, in the warmth of the Montecristo cigars that he brought us as a gift, the general explained that he wished to beg our pardon for his behaviour on the previous day, in token of which he had brought with him, apart from the cigars, his most prized possession of which none of his friends, and much less his enemies, had ever had a glimpse or even suspected the existence: a collection of glass eyes, stored in an embossed case lined with red velvet like a Perugia chocolate box. The first eye he showed us was a shining and happy one. 'I use it on my birthday,' he explained to us, 'and to attend *vernissages*; and, though I stand before you as a general and all that, I also enjoy culture and I actually know quite a lot about it. But, when I drink one too many on such an occasion, or in the Copacabana Club, I have to exchange the happy eye for this one, which is a drunk and out-of-focus eye. And the day after, when I get up, I put in this blood-shot eye, you see?' the general with the glass eye explained, and he showed us a reddened eye with all the ciliar arteries and episcleral veins reproduced in amazing detail. 'I started using this eye when I was fifteen, the day after a phenomenal drinking spree and bacchanalia

171

which coincided with Madero's entry into Mexico City and the earthquake which occurred on the same day. It's the same one I use when I get a devilish attack of flu or when I get something in my eye.' Next the general with the glass eye showed us a very high-quality specimen of Bohemian glass: 'With an eye just like this one, my friends, I attended a concert in the Royal Albert Hall, London. Because I too lived in London,' he said, glancing at the portrait of Cousin Walter hanging on the wall, next to Big Ben, in his Prince of Wales suit which said Made in England on the seam of the trouser pocket and holding a copy of Eliot's *Four Quartets* in his right hand. And he went on: 'I was there for three months as special military attaché and I arrived there just as England started to occupy Basra. And with an eye such as this I also saw Mischa Elman in the Palace of Fine Art and Leopold Stokowsky in Tijuana. With this very eye I received the Aztec Eagle medal for services rendered in Tlaxcalantongo, where we put a swift end to the traitor Venustiano Carranza or, as my father called him, Bastardiano Fuckeranza. Although, on that particular night, obviously, I put in a killer eye; and the fact is that the Homeland comes first, which is why I have a patriotic eye for the processions on Independence Day and the Day of the Child of Heroes and a loyal eye for the President. And then I have an emotional and tear-filled eye for when the National Anthem is played, which is the same eye that I sometimes use, most reluctantly, when I am constipated.' 'Won't you have another drink, general?' Estefania asked him. 'Yes, thank you,' the general answered us and, putting in his friendly eye, he took the bottle and raised it to his lips and then showed us his eye for being in love. 'With an eye like this my father declared his love to Angela Peralta, *Angelica di voce e di nome*, as her teacher Lamperti said of her. And it's not that my father was one-eyed, as I am, but that I inherited his eye for women. That is, a roving eye for respectable ladies and a lewd eye for the chorus at the Tivoli and the tarts on 2nd of April Street. Look at this one! See what a fine specimen of the white of an eye. This was the one I sometimes used for making love in Hell Canyon where we spent almost twelve months on a diet of dried meat! But who minds that when you are getting your fill of the tender flesh of a Chihuahua Indian woman, faithful as a dog? And let me tell you,' the general effectively told us, 'I am also a well-read and written man. This, for instance, is my astigmatic eye which I use only with spectacles to watch soap operas and read Plutarch's *Parallel Lives* or *Travelling through Mexico on Foot and on Horseback*. And with this same eye I have several times read the chapter about the bullets by Martin Luis Guzmán, *Los Bandidos de Rio Frio*, *Doña Barbara*, Rousseau's *Emile* and *They Took the Cannon to Bachimba*. With this same eye I read *Don Segundo Sombra* and I learned that the heart of the gnome owl weighs the same as all the sins of the world. On the other hand, when I read *Tarzan* or *Mandrake the Magician* comics I don't need the eye

172

because, as a child, I didn't suffer from astigmatism,' said the general with a child-like eye and, after emptying the bottle in a single draught and putting in his half-happy eye, he proceeded to show us his indifferent eye which he used for playing poker with Grandfather Francisco; his irascible eye for loud students; his reverent eye which he used for visiting the Basilica of the Virgin of Guadaloupe; his admiring eye which he reserved for meeting General Freyberg who had fought beside General Villa and participated in the defence of the island of Crete; his surprised eye which he put in when he learned of the marriage between María Félix and Jorge Negrete; his prodigal son's eye which he used on Mother's Day; his clinical eye which he wore to cock fights and his incredulous eye which he opened wide when he heard that Mussolini had said that his planes could darken the sky of Italy. Then he put in his sad eye – the one that he had told us he used for funerals and at Christmas because, for him, Christmases were always sad, including Joe Christmas – and he admitted to us that he would have liked to have many more eyes, equal in number to all the shades and variations of anger, joy, contempt, happiness, jealousy, envy, resignation and boredom but, firstly, it was very difficult to carry so many eyes around from place to place and, secondly, by the time he had removed one eye and put in the other, the corresponding feeling or state of mind had frequently evaporated. 'And that is extremely dangerous,' he explained. 'As dangerous as forgetting to change eyes. For example, when I quarrelled with my wife I would often forget to remove my angry eye when I sought her forgiveness and swore to her that I loved her very much and then, of course, she didn't believe me. On another occasion which I will never forget, I was attending an Institutional Revolutionary Party Convention and someone put forward the name of one of my enemies as candidate for governor so I put in my disdainful eye and then, when he was elected on the spot, the first thing he did was to turn round and look at me with an eye of triumph and I didn't have time to put in my meek eye, for which, of course, he never forgave me and I lost even my place on the committee and was banished to the jungle of Chetumal for four whole years,' said the general, with a bitter eye, and tossed off another half bottle. Seeing how drunk he was, Estefania offered him a cup of black coffee. 'No thank you, it keeps me awake and I would have to put in my insomnia eye which is actually a bit big for me so I can't close my eyelid,' he answered and, with a proud eye, he told us that, on the other hand, he had three further eyes which were absolute marvels. The first was an eye with grey specks in the crystalline lens and the second had a convex iris revealing oedema and a touch of exudate which modified the fluidity of the aqueous humour, as the optician had explained to him. 'This eye has a cataract and this one a glaucoma, just in case,' the general told us with a worried eye, 'the flesh and bone eye should some day get one of these diseases.' And, touching wood, he took from his shirt pocket a third eye: 'This eye before you, expressionless, opaque and cold, I carry always next to my heart and I hope that some charitable soul will put it in on the day I die before they close my eyes,' said the general with a hundred glass eyes.

Estefania applauded, we broke open another bottle, we smoked all the Montecristos and the general and I reminisced about old times: the black and silver Rolls-Royce they placed at his disposal in London, which measured something like a hundred thousand pesos in length; the death of Carlos Pereyra and the invasion of Mexico City by fortune-telling witches and we sang *Mambrou s'en va-t-en guerre* and we talked about the Folies-Bergères and about Trotsky's murder and Mexico's declaration of war on the Axis powers and the *Elixir of Love* opera in the Iris Theatre and of the Colorado cannibal Alfred Packer and of the Gran Tabor Theatre with boxes of ebony brought in specially from Honduras and of *How Green was My Valley* which José Clemente Orozco had liked so much and the general, with a nostalgic eye, told us about the 'Blue Hour of Memory' broadcast by the XEW Radio station and then he started singing like Emilio Tuero and then, with closed eyes, he fell asleep. And I let him rest for a good while and spent the time polishing some verses in honour of my cousin who had that afternoon put on one of her prettiest faces and her hair was the colour of living copper like the Cardan metals. I let the cobwebs spin and, some time later, when I looked at my watch which told the exact time of Estefania's eyes, the morning of her breasts, the midday of her belly button and the midnight of her sex, I realized that it was time to awaken the general and ask him to leave. The general put in his bloodshot eye, closed his case and took his leave of us after kissing Estefania's hand. And, when we thought that he had no more eyes to show us, he took from the back pocket of his olive-green trousers a small pink package with a frayed black ribbon which he untied, then opened the package and showed us an eye which I could have sworn I had seen somewhere before.

'This eye,' he said to me, 'is a gift for you, young man, so that you may remember your general. I had this eye made in London, because I wanted to go to the Ascot Races and watch them with an English eye. I went straight to Madame Tussaud's and I told the man in charge of making glass eyes for the wax figures to make me the other eye which he would have made for Nelson's figure if the admiral had not been one-eyed. But it was no good to me because they made a mistake and gave me a woman's eye.'

'And how did you know it was a woman's eye?' Estefania asked him.

'Ah, because on the day I used it I took quite a fancy to the little blond English lad who was my chauffeur,' the general told me, regarding me first with a clinical eye and then with a tender eye.

And what do you think we got up to when the general left? What else? Don Prospero, Mr General, Palinuro, what else would I do with such a cousin who not only belonged to nature created as opposed to creating, but also fought body and soul against being known by means of Eugène de Mirecourt's *evidencia potissima* because, although her eyes could not be blue and not blue at the same time, you will have to agree that they could be simultaneously sky-coloured and not sky-coloured, depending on whether the sky was clouded or dusk was falling in her eyes? What else would I do with such a cousin, I repeat, with such an Estefania, who is discernible only, for the time being, at the lowest level of perception, if we go by Spinoza's classification: by word of mouth, gentlemen, by hearing what I tell you and guarantee to you, swear to you, by my lies and my own conclusions? What else would one do with such a cousin, with such a friend, with such an angel who belongs, as Bergson stated, to the ineffable and can thus escape concept but not image? With such a cousin who, though real and with meaning of her own like any other categorematic term, was not, I insist, part of the only reality accepted by Petrus Aureolus: that of the appearance of objects? And what to do, particularly when the general left, and my cousin's hair, followed by her clothes, fell to her knees of salt-bleached poplar and our room filled with a pervading scent of emerald shampoo? You must see that there was no alternative but to make love. And, so as not to spend my whole life talking about the same thing, I will tell you, once and for all, how my cousin and I made love.

We made love compulsively. We made love intentionally. We made love spontaneously.

But, above all, we made love daily.

Or, in other words, on Mondays, Tuesdays and Wednesdays we invariably made love.

On Thursdays, Fridays and Saturdays we also made love.

Finally, we religiously made love on Sundays.

Or we made love just for the hell of it or just in case, for its own sake and for a laugh, on the phone or on another wave length, in the first place and in the last instance, to our greater glory and to all intents and purposes, for starters and as a last resort.

We also made love by osmosis and by symbiosis: this we called making love scientifically.

But also, I made love to her and she to me: in other words, reciprocally.

And when she was half way to orgasm and I, my member shrinking to a mere flaccid muscle, could not satisfy her, then we made love hurtfully.

Which is quite apart from the times that I thought that I was not going to be able to and couldn't, and she thought that she was not going to feel and didn't, or we were so tired and so worried that neither of us reached orgasm. We decided, then, that we had made love approximately.

Or Estefania got to remembering the squirrels Uncle Esteban had brought from Wisconsin which rushed madly around their creosote-smelling cages and I, for my part, thought back to the sitting-room of our grandparents' house, with its Viennese chairs and pots of tea roses waiting for four o'clock to strike, and so we made love nostalgically, coming as we pursued old memories.

We also made love standing and singing, kneeling and praying, lying down and dreaming.

And especially, for the simple reason that I wanted to and so did she, we made love voluntarily.

We often made love *contra natura, pro natura* and in complete disregard of *natura*.

Or at night, with the light on, while the mosquitoes performed a zenithal dance around the bulb. Or during the day, with our eyes closed. Or clean of body and dirty of mind. Or vice versa. Content, happy, sorrowful, bitter. With remorse and without sense. Sleepy and cold.

And when we thought of the absurdity of life and that one day we would forget each other, we made love uselessly.

To the envy of our friends and enemies, we made a love that was limitless, masterly, the stuff of legend.

To the credit of our parents, we made love morally.

To the horror of society, we made love illegally.

To the joy of psychiatrists, we made love symptomatically.

And, above all, we made love physically.

One afternoon, I returned to our room in Holy Sunday Square with the *History of Art* which Walter had lent us and then we made love by all the rules of minimal art, op art, environment art and conceptual art.

Then we painted ourselves white and replicated Rodin's original of *The Kiss* and *The Eternal Idol* and Antonio Canova's embrace of *Cupid and Psyche*.

From then onwards, we also used to kiss before the window, like Edvard Munch's faceless lovers.

Or she would spread her legs like a large American nude by Wesselmann, or presented me a behind with the ears of a Hans Bellmer cephalopod, or lay back on the bed with her little girl curls and short dress, like one of Balthus' provocative adolescents.

Following a trip to San Francisco, Estefania wanted us to recreate the pose of Gerald Gooch's modern lovers. After a visit to the Prado Museum, we reproduced in three dimensions and over weeks on end all the madnesses of Hieronymus Bosch's *Earthly Delights*. And we embraced times without number like Leda and the Swan in Leonardo's paintings, like Hercules and Deianira in Mabuse's paintings, like Veronese's *Venus and Mars*.

Yes, I may say that we loved each other passionately like Géricault's lovers, that we were blue and sad as Chagal's lovers and we swore that, even if we grew old and snakes and frogs slithered in and out of our eyes and stomachs, we would continue to make love like Grünewald's lovers. That was what we called making love artistically.

And, meanwhile, I started very seriously to consider the possibility of applying for a job in an ad agency, as my cousin had suggested. Estefania was immediately hired as a model, writer and genius. But, for my part, I had to go to a great deal of effort to get into an agency. It was more of an effort to get out. And more, even more, not to return.

11

Palinuro's Travels among the Advertising Agencies and other Imaginary Islands

It must have been about three o'clock on the dot of a grey and soulless afternoon that Palinuro, tired of a youth squandered in neighbourhoods of rancid sweet shops colouring the cafés with geographic petulances; fed up with the shitting of all the birds in San Fernando Park who had forgotten to take themselves off south; sad, moreover, because the time was no more when every furrow of life carried a trickle of sap to lend life to good thoughts and bad; old enough, also, to know that it is not easy to change the colour of an avenue or the grammatical insignia of one's own life story. In other words: tired, fed up, sad and grown-up, he decided to take leave for the second and last time of first infancy and, for the first and also the last time, of his second adolescence and to set out on a journey through life, without paintbrushes to chew, without femoral bones to memorize, without diadems of axioms and steaming cartilages to dismember.

AND SO, LIKE LEMUEL GULLIVER he embarked on an adventure to see the fabulous islands of Lilliput and Laputa, the immortal Struldbruggs and the noble Houyhnhnms. Just as Prince Astolfo of England flew to the moon in the prophet Elijah's chariot of fire in search of the panacea for the lost reason of Orlando Furioso, just as Maelduin visited the island of the revolving wall of fire and the land beneath the waves and, finally, just as Snedgus visited the island of warriors with cats' heads and the island where the rain is of birds' blood, so also Palinuro, fortunately with his twenty itinerant years and a carnation in the button-hole of his jacket, finally decided to bid farewell to his memories: to the asthmatic flowers which wafted desires and solstices to Aunt Luisa; farewell to the crêpe paper of the white mice's grave; farewell to the limbs of Grandfather Francisco's spectacles which had grown bandy from so many years astride his nose. Farewell!
and now for a visit to the Advertising Agencies and other Imaginary Islands. Ah, the Advertising Agencies: pink with green chairs, big windows with aquariums, situated twenty floors up so you could commit suicide without leaving your body! Ah, the Agencies of thorns of rose and amethyst in which Palinuro left his best days wrapped in Celanese

cellophane, sprinkled with the kisses of his lovers! Ah, the Agencies which travelled at sixty miles per hour, gleaming and silver as a Rolls-Royce, even the clock not daring to murmur:
tick-tock . . .
tick-tock . . .!
The Agencies, the Agencies of floating soaps of ivory. The Agencies of flowing rivers of cold cream and hundreds of tiny little horses the colour of will-o'-the-wisp escaping from the boots of Ford cars to become submerged in the monopolies of shooting stars and in the currents of jam existing since time out of mind. The Agencies, the Agencies where whiskies smouldered in the icebergs which Captain Scott brought back in an album when his icebreaker snapped the spine of the twentieth century!

THE AGENCIES, like the islands, in reality as in dreams, were infinite in number. Palinuro visited but a few. But the biggest, the most important, on which depended the majority of secondary imaginary islands, was

THE ISLAND OF THE ENCHANTED AGENCY. As Bran visited the Island where it rains dragons' crystals and stones and where lies the conspicuous stone from which a hundred chords arise. Just as Hui Corra visited the Island of the liquid rainbow river and the Island of the well of all tastes. And just as Lucian travelled to the moon to see the salad-birds with feathers of lettuce, so also Palinuro, after requesting his audience's incredulity in the manner also of Lucian of Samosata, travelled to the Island of the Enchanted Agencies to make the personal acquaintance of the Colgate Fairy, the Pepsi-Cola Grandmother with her tri-colour wig and king Cadillac Brougham, little princess Kraft who menstruated mayonnaise and the spicy McCormick family who, with their gifts, enchantments and wonders, showered the earth with blessings and blossoming paradises. It seems unreal. Only yesterday Palinuro was a child, a schoolboy, a medical student. And suddenly, immediately afterwards, so immediately that Palinuro himself could not have said whether it was a matter of seconds or millionths of a second, he started work in an advertising agency and met another, a new, Estefania he had never before imagined, for all his surmising on her way of walking, of sitting down, of recreating her armpits and of talking nonsense. So, one moment he was a child playing truant to escape the complicated rigmarole which became increasingly involved, to the point of turning into three peaches, and walking along Paseo de la Reforma catching butterflies, with his ethyl acetate for killing fritillary butterflies and polyphemus moths and his white ankle socks, and the next he was a grown lad of twenty who had just renounced art and medicine but was still, however, almost an angel, almost jail-bait for a pederast and still happy, none the less, because he would never again be a poor student tormented by trigeminal nerves and lost in chemical

179

labyrinths, and then suddenly he found himself surrounded by sinister lumps of butter, by threatening tin-openers, by cats with neon paper eyes and huge Yankee females with thick, foamy thighs and pubises of Lucky Strike tobacco. Then he went up in the glass lift which deposited him in the middle of a supermarket. The supermarket was the Island. The Island was the Agency. The Agency was Palinuro's goal.

PALINURO WAS A YOUNG MAN with no experience of life. Moreover, a young man without a name. In order that he might choose one for himself, that he might select the name that would bring him fame in life, the manager of the Enchanted Agency, accompanied by Estefania (golden mother of the turtle, Hsi Wang Mu, the lady of the earthly Eden of the immortal Chinese), led Palinuro by the hands towards

THE ISLAND OF A THOUSAND AND ONE NAMES and, just as Niels Klim undertook a fantastic journey to the depths of the earth and saw the luminous nights and the walking tree and was himself turned into a satellite of the central sun; just as Teigue visited the Island of the Nine-horned Ram and the Island of the Red and Blue Bird's Eggs which caused you to sprout feathers if you ate them; just as Pantagruel and Panurge visited Ringing Island and Stealth Island and the Island of Ignoramuses, so also Palinuro reached the Island of a Thousand and One Names where, as its thousand and one names indicate, a special computer had the job of copyrighting all the possible combinations of names that could exist for the infinite number of products manufactured by the clients of the Enchanted Agency so that only they, and nobody but they, can use those names. And that is how, on those bright, sap-flowing afternoons during which he learned with Estefania to make advertisements for gin and mountains, Palinuro got to know the brilliant genealogy of Packard Automobiles, the bitter-sweet heraldry of LifeSaver pastilles, the bubbling etymology of Alka-Seltzers and the dark and magical origin of the word Kodak and of whatever other similar words existing in the possible and impossible universe, such as Zodiak, Todak, Krodak, Ikodak and Prodak which not only opened their metallic diaphragms to Palinuro upon a new and better world but also revealed to him the mysteries of the island: namely that, in order to prevent the competition from baptizing their products with the most beautiful, intelligent, suggestive, fantastic, moral, absurd, ingenuous or macabre names – the guide explained to Palinuro – on this island we have copyrighted every word in every language spoken in the world: every noun, adjective, article and adverb, so that nobody except ourselves may now or ever call a car *The Beautifully* or a mustard *The Indivisible* and we also copyrighted all turns of phrase in all dead languages and all future languages and dialects. And, in order to prevent the competition from inventing names like Kodak which don't actually mean

180

anything but somehow resemble the name of our products, in order to take advantage of their prestige, over and above their euphonic and mnemotechnical value, we copyrighted all possible combinations of two and three syllables. And then of five, ten, fifteen syllables. And then we copyrighted the unpronounceable names which our broadcasters take up to five minutes to articulate. And then we realized that such brand names did not necessarily have to be devoid of meaning and so we turned to literature and started to invent product brands consisting of whole stories, poems, novels and philosophies. And that was how a detergent was created with the brand name of the whole of *Don Quixote*, and a toothpaste whose name was composed of the whole of Bergson's *Laughter*. But, by that time, the Enchanted Agency's writers had come to scorn the computer and started to write their own novels and plays, poems and stories which became the brand name of tomato ketchup, of a tyre or of a beer. And, with the purchase of these products, we give away a copy of the book after which they are named. Or, if you wish to look at it from another point of view – the guide told Palinuro – with the purchase of each book we give away the corresponding product. All future books are also copyrighted, for which reason the book has come to be recognized as the leading mass-produced consumer item in the history of our industrial society.

AFTER WHICH PALINURO CHOSE HIS NAME which was also to be that of all his products, starting with himself and his organs, bones and dejecta and ending with all the pictures, books, operations, advertisements and inventions he might paint, write, perform and patent and that is how, led by the hand and by his guide, Palinuro reached

GIVEN NAME ISLAND where the geniuses of the Enchanted Agency obviate all the problems relating to the brand names of their clients' products through a system whereby all products, from carpets to typewriters, shirts and rolls of film, are unnamed and then, when they are purchased by a customer, a special machine prints, embosses, embroiders or engraves the customer's name on the article, so that each individual leaves the shop, the chemist or the supermarket with his Martínez ties, Martínez aspirins and Martínez cornflakes and so, while there are millions of different brand names, each client buys only one, his own. And so it dawned on Palinuro,

PALINURO BEFORE THE MIRROR, that, without leaving the Island and without leaving his house and his eyes and by means of his Palinurovision set, he could order a giant jar of Palinuscafé, a box of MacPalinuro whisky and a dozen of Palinurex condoms, to be delivered to his home and to his soul. He could also order a book, bearing his brand and name, containing the chronicle of the Islands and the chronicle of the afternoons in the Agency, afternoons of mental torments and stratified samples and instruments to gauge housewives' blinks, those afternoons, ah, afternoons when Palinuro arrived at the very moment of evocation and of cups of tea which talk to themselves, to dispense his brilliant irony, afternoons when it went without saying that toothpaste manufacturers should put a pearl in each tube, that the circus lion-tamer strip a Jaguar with whiplashes and crystal glasses murmur 'Johnny Walker' 'Johnny Walker,' as they perform a country dance on the lawn. Ah, those Agency afternoons when, among pins jinxing the globe and tropical fish jumping from American Airlines planes and descending from the sky by vinyl parachute, Palinuro and Estefania – and sometimes cousin Walter – suffocated the confused literary tapeworm in the comfort of their guts! Guts which were, certainly, young and conceited.

FROM HERE TO FAME is but a step, the guide assured Palinuro. And, just as Scipio and Chaucer set out on the flight which was to take them to the House of Fame, so also Palinuro, after sailing across a lake of boiling porridge, after crossing a sea of yoghurt culture and fizzy wheat drink and hacking his way with his teeth through a jungle of monkey wrenches and rolls of Tri X film which magnified the devil's drivel, led by the hand by the manager-guide of the Enchanted Agency, he reached what was from then onwards called, and never-to-be-forgotten,

THE HALL OF FAME. There, in the Hall of Fame, its floors covered by a red carpet several centuries thick, are to be seen the world's most famous copy-writers and publicists, captured for posterity at their moment of glory in white statues produced from plaster casts taken from life like Segal's sculptures. Aretino, the publicist, is there. Rosser Reeves, inventor of the Unique Selling Proposition, is there. Also, making love to a blonde-hooded convertible, Ernest Dichter, the man who applied the Gestalt theory to advertising. And there behind him is Vicary, discoverer of subliminal advertising. Gilbreth, inventor of the chromocyclograph, is there. And the apostles of brand image. And the discoverers of client empathy with a product. Claude Hopkins is also there, taking a steam bath in the Schlitz beer house, and John Caples flicking up his tails to seat himself at the piano to an accompaniment of audible giggles. And, behind them, the sculpture of a man pursuing a winged Coca-Cola, trying to catch it in a butterfly net: namely, the genius who decreed that Coca-Cola is it. Closer to hand, the statue of a modern magician offering the world a crystal ball containing a miniature model of a Ford automobile. Unlike the House described by Chaucer, this Hall of Fame is not built in a huge rock of ice. Unlike The House of Rumour, it is not located between the earth, sea and sky, at the juncture of the triple universe. The Hall of Fame is on the top floor of the highest skyscraper on Madison Avenue, which is higher

182

than the Empire State, higher than the Sears Roebuck building in Chicago, higher than the Ford Foundation, the Guggenheim Foundation and the Rockefeller Centre. Higher than the Nobel Prize for literature, higher than the universities of Iowa, Oxford, Leiden and Mexico City. Higher than the BBC. Higher than General Motors, Union Carbide, Sperry Rand and ITT. Higher than Kimberly-Clark, Woolworths, Du Pont, the Stanford Research Institute, the Container Corporation of America, IBM and all the world's largest companies, including Royal Dutch/Shell, Volkswagen, ICI, Hitachi, Nestlés. Higher than the Hall of Fame is but the sky, awash with Rinso Blue, and from the sky fall flakes of Lux Soap, to whiten the inhabitants of New York and of the world. From its picture-windows can be seen hundreds of the city's skyscrapers, illuminated by night with Westinghouse bulbs. Below, in the streets, like ornaments of the day, scuttle the yellow Chrysler Corporation taxis and millions of men and women travel below the earth, on United States Corporation rails. But, between the rails and through the deep intestines and arteries of the city, through the pneumatic tubes of teletex and instant home deliveries, snake strands of General Foods spaghetti and Jaffa oranges roll and salad creams, pale as lymph, flow and jams, red as blood, circulate . . .

AND, AFTER QUOTING THE FAMOUS WORDS of Aldous Huxley who said that it is easier to write ten passable sonnets than an effective advertisement which gets thousands of people to buy a product, the manager-guide of the Enchanted Agency assured Palinuro that, beyond the Hall of Fame, all fame is ephemeral and, to prove it, he took Palinuro by the hand to

THE ISLAND OF EPHEMERAL FAME where he explained that there had once been a man, whose name he could not remember, who had foretold that in the future everybody would be famous for fifteen minutes. And it was in honour of this prophet – since it was not in his memory – that the Island of Ephemeral Fame was founded, where all inhabitants without exception, and visitors also, had the right to be famous for fifteen minutes and to choose the time and the circumstances of their fame. And the guide explained to Palinuro that at first it had been thought that some circumstances would eliminate others: in other words, if at some point a man chose to be the greatest baritone in history, for example, it would not be possible for another person to aspire to the same honour, because it would be contradictory. But, in practice, we realized that this was not in fact a problem – the guide assured Palinuro – because fame only lasts for fifteen minutes, after which the fortunate individual is completely forgotten: it would only be contradictory if everybody remembered him for having been famous for fifteen minutes, as his memory would thus, effectively, be perpetuated. So, to prevent the island from filling up with people who would spend the rest of their lives swearing, from one café to the next and from one circle of friends to the next, that they had been famous for a few moments, they too forget that they have been famous. This, of course, does not prevent any of them from spending their lives swearing that one day they will be famous. The island offers the opportunity to be famous for anything you could possibly imagine: philosophers, of course, choose to be famous for their philosophy; painters for their paintings and doctors for their curative arts. Other inhabitants choose to be famous for spectacular achievements like sailing around the world or conquering the peak of the highest mountain. And it matters not at all that they have never carried out such feats because the illusion is perfect: for fifteen minutes, all former recall is substituted by the memory of books, films or discoveries of the fortunate person of the moment, or simply by the memory of a whole life of work and dedication which could only lead to well-deserved fame. But I should also mention – added the guide – that all those on the island who have no skill or vocation or particular interest are granted the right to be famous for whatever it is that they do. First, a person can be the greatest lift attendant in the world, the most important removal man in history, the most illustrious postman of all time. Moreover, it is possible to become famous for the merest trifle which, when it becomes a reason for fame, acquires the dimensions of a major achievement: you can be famous for cleaning your teeth one Monday morning, going to the cinema, walking through a park or feeding the pigeons, for simply being born or dying; for wearing a blue tie, for going to mass, for smoking a pipe, for having friends. You can even be famous for not wanting to be so: the fact is that, on the island, fame is not only an opportunity for all but also an obligation, so that even the modest and those who lack ambition and those who shun publicity and greatness are caught unawares by fame which makes them famous for their humility. Therefore, many prefer to struggle throughout a lifetime – in other words, to believe that they have struggled throughout a lifetime – in order thus to be able to choose the ideal moment and circumstances for their fame, the guide told Palinuro. And Palinuro chose to be famous for his lies. Thus, when he reached the island, he declared that he would never be famous and, since this was a lie, for fifteen minutes the wind carried his fame as a liar to the outermost confines of the island, the multitudes applauded him, his name appeared for a moment in the Universal Histories of the Future and for a few seconds Palinuro experienced the illusion of having triumphed through failure.

THE REAL TRIUMPH, HOWEVER, remained as illusive as ever and, to attain it, like any gentleman on the way to Paradise or Muslim soul heading for the peak of the Hyacinth Mountain or Hebrew spirit directing their steps to the Midrash Konen, Palinuro knew that he would first have to triumph in all the tests that Providence might set for him after answering the call to herodom and recognizing the miserable trappings of the herald of destiny who might well appear, for example, in the guise of a little frog of some synthetic material making synoptic hops as it sang: Cro-Cro, Cro-Cro-Crolan! And, to this end, he would not only have to vanquish the John Deere dragons and tractors and sail throughout a whole night aboard Cutty Sark whisky without perishing in the attempt and cross the Al Sirat bridge and word incarnate, fine and narrow as a hair and greased with Anderson Clayton cooking oil, endeavouring not to fall off the right side on to the needle-sharp television antennae nor off the left side where he was threatened by carnivorous tins of food floating in a shrieking swamp, but he would also have to pass all the other trials, tests, interrogations and exams awaiting him in life. The first thing that he put to the test, once chosen, was his name:

PALINURO. What did you say you were called?
Palinuro, like Palinurus, the pilot of Aeneas' boat.
Panuliro?
Palinuro, like the *Palinurus vulgaris* which is born in cold water under the name of common lobster and dies in hot water under the name of thermidor.
Parulino?
Palinuro, like the promontory in the Italian province of Salerno.
Paluniro?
Palinuro, the name that he himself had chosen to accompany him like a faithful mascot throughout his life.
Pariluno?
Palinuro.
Ah! How is that written?
'P' as in Pedro Pérez Palinurez, Pannuliroo, Parulino, Palinduro, Palunido, Paniduro, Pariluno, Poet, Peccadillo, Publicist, Paints Parisian Portraits Professionally, Please Pat Pigs Preciously, Produce Patent Perforated Paper, Proclaims Pink Pills Pour Personnes Pâles . . .
How was that?
I said that it is written with 'P' as in Palinuro, 'A' as in Alinuro, 'L' as in Linuro, 'I' as in Inuro, 'N' as in Nuro, 'U' as in Uro, 'R' as in Ro, 'O' as in O – he said – and, poor chap, spelt with a 'P' as in Palinuro, he also failed pnumerous ptests to which he was psubjected by the psychiatrists, including the Rorschach ptest: 'Tell me what you see here,' the examiner instructed him. 'I see ink blots.' 'Don't be funny. What do you see?' And Palinuro: 'The first one is a black blood stain in the shape of a scorpion. The second one, a black urine stain in which the scorpion is drowning. The

third, is a vampire-shaped stain drinking the black urine. The fourth one, a man who is going to eat the dog by the tail.' 'Which dog?' 'The one who's going to eat the vampire in the next stain.' 'Do you see anything else?' 'I see daggers, rapes, young girls masturbating with the middle victory finger,' said Palinuro, who did in fact see all this. And the psychiatrist, who was an amorphous blot with a vague likeness to the *Pithecanthropus erectus*, certified him mad as a hatter. But they didn't put him away. They left him free, fortunately for the Agency, for Estefania and for advertising the world over. The psychiatrist, completely schizoidmatized, broke up into a hundred different coloured pieces and Palinuro took it into his head to gather them up. Alinuro collected 75 Carta Blanca beer-bottle tops which could in turn be exchanged for more Carta Blanca beer. Linuro picked up 160 little scraps of paper flung from the Nieto building during Kennedy and Jacqueline's visit to Mexico. Inuro found 10 Paris metro tickets and 5 Primavera tram maps. Nuro saved up 87 green stamps which could be exchanged for brooms and orange plastic salad bowls. Uro stuck together 24 pieces of lottery ticket which could have won a prize of a million pesos. Ro found 104 pieces of his love letters to Estefania. And finally with the 465 pieces, O completed the Lowenfield mosaic test, using them to create a jigsaw puzzle portraying the ideal publicist.

AND THE IDEAL PUBLICIST, all set to enter the Hall of Fame, had David Uglyby's nose, Raymond Rubberham's stomach, Leo Brunette's three hairs, and Stanley Razor's dentures.

BUT IT WAS NOT AS EASY AS ALL THAT for Palinuro to enter the Hall of Fame right off after passing through the Enchanted Agency, just as it had not been that easy to enter the Enchanted Agency after undergoing all the tests and seeing reflected on the ceilings the ungraspable planispheres in which each little coloured bulb marked an agency as orange and distant as the Alpha Centauri star or the city of Panama, or an agency large and yellow as the sun or the city of New York. No, it was not easy, despite the fact that Palinuro (after registering all the variations of his name) planned his own publicity campaign and prepared several advertisements which he sent by post to the directors of McCann Erikson, J. Walter Thompson, Young & Rubicam and Doyle Dane & Bernbach:

COMING . . . (read the first announcement)

COMING, COMING . . . (read the second)

COMING, COMING, COMING . . . (read the third)

COMING, COMING, COMING, COME . . . (read the fourth)

PALINURO IS HERE! read the fifth and last, in which Palinuro, knowing that advertising is not a science because its weapon is persuasion and persuasion is an art, and using all the advertising formulas which are sometimes to be recommended and sometimes strictly not to be recommended, such as NOW! ANNOUNCING! SENSATIONAL! REMARKABLE! MAGIC! MIRACLE! OFFER! QUICK! EASY! LAST CHANCE! BARGAIN! and ADVICE TO!, emphasized his unique selling proposition and other virtues such as his economical price (Palinuro and a half for the price of one), his availability at any time and in any place, his good faith, his glorious past (almost artist and almost physician), his ability to invent pregnant fables and his love for office catechism, millenary announcements and the syntax of nausea, together with his age, address, legal status, nationality and, of course, his oft-referred name, putting himself down as guarantor of his own gifts and goodness – I drink Palinuro, I eat Palinuro, I read Palinuro – and inviting the agencies, the managers, the executives and the general public to do the same: Drink PALINURO! read PALINURO! smoke, eat, piss, shit PALINURO!

AND IT IS TRUE, it is true that Baron Münchhausen crossed the curved bridge linking Africa and Great Britain like a rainbow of stone and it is true that he travelled to the moon, where the inhabitants store their heads at home when they go on a journey. It is true that Arthur Gordon Pym travelled to the Island of Tsalal where he met the most bloodthirsty human race on earth. It is true that St Brendan visited the Island of the Rock where Judas enjoyed his Sunday rest and that Charles the Fat, a comet string tied to his thumb, travelled to the resplendent labyrinths of hellish suffering. But none of them experienced the wonders and the horrors witnessed by Palinuro in

THE ISLAND OF TESTIMONIAL ADVERTISEMENTS at the fleeting moment when, imagining the consequences that would befall those who might drink, smoke, eat, read Palinuro and admit to it, he travelled to the hell of torments suffered by all those who, in life, appeared in commercial advertisements saying I Use Such-and-Such a Product, I Prefer So-and-So, and where little pink devils spend all day boiling nine out of every ten Hollywood stars in huge pans full of Lux soap and where poets who at some time recommended Parker pens are condemned to write a thousand times a day: 'I use Parker pens' and where one-eyed baron George Wrangel is condemned to put on and take off his Hathaway shirt once every thirty seconds throughout all eternity. And there Palinuro saw how housewives who had recommended Hoover vacuum cleaners had a vacuum cleaner nozzle pushed down their throats to suck up their own words and how those who had recommended Singer sewing machines had their lips and eyelashes sewn shut and flowers and cosmoramas embroidered on their stomachs. And he saw how the devils cut off the fingers and life breath of

187

all those who had ever recommended Prestige kitchen knives and how all women who claimed to use Presto pressure cookers had their hearts and illusions pulled out and stewed in their own juice. And he saw how all those who had ever recommended some edible or drinkable product had a funnel placed in their mouths and the product poured into them until they burst. He saw how Mrs Roosevelt was stuffed with Good Luck margarine until she burst. He saw how a gentleman of distinction was burst with Lord Calvert whisky. How the taster Albert Dimes was burst with Tetley tea and Commander Edward Whitehead with Schweppes tonic water and Colonel Sanders with Kentucky fried chicken and Orson Welles with Pedro Domecq sherry and Peter Ustinov with Gallo wines.

BUT HE OPENED HIS EYES, took stock of the reality of the world, placed his feet on the ground, drew a caricature of himself, showed it freely to all and sundry and decided to try another tack: if certain famous publicists had begun by selling stoves and Bibles door to door, he would make a humble beginning selling books. So he built a sort of small boat out of soap boxes, a ship of bluish prow with roller-skate wheels, and loaded it up with the *UTEHA Encyclopaedia, The Golden Bough, The History of Madison Avenue*, the A. Porot *Dictionary of Psychiatry*, the Larousse *Medical Dictionary*, the Copleston *History of Philosophy* and countless other reference books, novels, poetry anthologies and theologies, dictionaries and thesauri. And it was supposed that every page of these books would be as a sail speeding him on his journey through life until he successfully disembarked in the Advertising Agency. And so, when the storms abated and the gentle winds kindled their call to the compass roses, Palinuro unfurled his sails and one dusk of portentous stabs of brilliance chronicled by episodes from *Sinbad the Sailor* on which a nubile languor enveloped the ports of his birth, he embarked upon the hoary sea with the intention of reaching distant lands where sows die of love on foreign beaches, to exchange his books for exotic merchandise: toothpaste, houses, travellers' cheques, automobiles, tours through Europe and jars of capers and secret formulas for making friends, making your first million dollars or turning Brazilian coffee into gold, South African diamonds into coal-black slaves, Central American bananas into the orgasms of *Playboy* bunnies and Venezuelan oil wells into a breakfast, at Tiffany's, of black pearls in their shells.

PALINURO'S GREAT FAILURE! because his boat (the same boat in which he transported all his portable and displayable culture) started to ship water, as indeed Martial's epigram so rightly says: *Minxisti currente semel, Pauline carina! Meiere vis iterum? Iam Palinurus eris.*

AND PERHAPS THE BLAME LAY, as was usually the case, with Cousin

188

Walter's unfortunate advice: 'What name would you give to a new tinned tuna?' they asked Palinuro.

'Pompilus,' he said, 'after the Ionian fisherman metamorphosed by Apollo into a tuna fish.'

'Ah . . . and what name comes to mind for a new detergent?'

'Al Borak, after the name of Muhammad's fabulous mare which carried him, through the seven heavens, from Mecca to Jerusalem in a single night. Borak means lightning, blinding whiteness.'

'Aha. And so what would you call a new syrup for hot cakes?'

'Ida, the name of a mountain in Crete, famous for its honey.'

'Ahahah. And a new aerosol insecticide?'

'Acor, like the fly-destroying god worshipped in Cyrene.'

'Ahahahah . . . leave us your address and telephone number, we'll call you when we have a vacancy in our agency.'

They never called him.

PALINURO, INSISTENTIALIST THAT HE WAS none the less (again) fell victim to the Enchanted Agency's psychiatrists who not only accused him of self-punitivism because he bit his nails and classified his psychological stance as a mixture of arrogance and shyness and attributed his sporadic stuttering to impeded left-handedness, but also submitted him to the rigours of every test and trial invented in the history of psychiatry, antipsychiatry, psychology and parapsychology, including functionalism, behaviourism and structuralism. Meanwhile, when he left the glass lift, Palinuro found himself unarmed in the middle of a field of multilateral seedbeds and obliged to fight bare-fisted against a Gorgon from whose head sprouted several dozen Goodyear hoses. And then the psychiatrist subjected him to the Morgan and Murray TAT, showing him a series of photographs which gave Palinuro a further opportunity to indulge the full extent of his morbid, pornographic and startling imagination. And, meanwhile, he had to overcome the witches of Walpurgis Night who flew around mounted on their Bendix vacuum cleaners. And then they gave Palinuro the Minnesota Multiphasic Personality Inventory test which would haunt his future like a delicious nightmare. And he also had to confront other portents, among them a mummy wrapped in Waldorf toilet paper and a ventriloquist typewriter which made him say things which he never thought he would ever dare to say.

FOR EXAMPLE: how could he, how could Walter, how could the manager, how could any of them talk of Tiffany's, of regimental ties, of the 21 Restaurant in New York and of advertising budgets of millions and millions of pesos and dollars while so many people in the world were dying of hunger? With hundreds of thousands of women and children dying of typhus and dysentery, how could poets continue to die from a blow of the full moon? But then the manager-guide took Palinuro by the hand and led him by the eyes and by the tongue, to

THE ISLAND OF PROMOTIONS, which is the planning centre of all offers designed to increase the sales of Agency clients' products. But, since the Enchanted Agency is – as the guide explained to Palinuro – a humanitarian organization, with one of its principle aims being to increase not only the prestige of product brands but also the public's feeling of responsibility towards the society in which we live, promotions are planned in such a way that the consumer, rather than the company, contributes to great causes. Thus, when a manufacturer of cocoa powder, for example, or of tinned vegetables or of any other food, wishes to do a promotion and offer its product at a discount or at two for the price of one, it is suggested to him that, rather than changing the price, they should instead include in each jar or tin a coupon for the same value in the name of a charitable organization, enclosed in a ready stamped and addressed envelope so that the only thing the consumer has to do is deposit it in the letter box. Thus, with the purchase of clothes and jewellery, we offer a small package of second-hand clothes and ask the client to give us his name and address and inform him a representative from Oxfam or Goodwill or any other similar organization will shortly call at his home to collect the package and give it to the poor. As you will appreciate, continued the guide, all these promotions have the simple and also very obvious intention of giving our consumers a clear conscience. Therefore, every bottle of gin, rum or whisky they buy includes a cheque made out to one of the various anti-alcohol organizations or to the Salvation Army; sports goods contain a postal order in the name of societies caring for spastics, dystrophics and paralytics and with the purchase of a mink coat, crocodile-skin shoes or an ivory statue are included contributions to societies protecting animals, the environment and ecological equilibrium and all those groups which fight for the preservation of species which are about to become extinct such as the vicuña of the Andes, the elephants of Kenya, the ocelot of Paraguay and the lemur of Madagascar. This, just by way of a few examples. We have not forgotten the bomb-carrying dolphins. Nor have we forgotten the people suffering hunger and disease, floods, earthquakes, droughts and hurricanes: our international airlines offer passengers on every flight small bags of soya flour and wheat flour, sugar, salt, coffee and medicines so that, when the plane flies over these tormented regions, they may throw them down from the air.

BECAUSE, AMONG OTHER THINGS, the guide told Palinuro, we are equally aware of the finite nature of human and natural resources, of the population explosion and the small dimensions of our planet, all of which are reflected in the spectre of scarcity, as you will see if you visit

THE ISLAND OF SCARCITY where Palinuro was left without a guide because on this island guides are, of course, very scarce. Moreover, Palinuro was unable to travel around the island, not only because transport is scarce, but also because distances are very scarce. Palinuro couldn't even spend one day on the island, or one night, because there the days and nights are very scarce. Also the hours and the minutes, but it is difficult to know just how scarce because calendars and watches are also becoming scarce. On this island, however, it is not possible to say that all products and all things that you can possibly imagine are becoming scarce, because imagination is also very scarce. Palinuro would have liked to write a longer and more detailed account of that island, where life and death are becoming scarce, but paper, ink, time and, especially, words had grown scarce.

HIS CONSCIENCE, AT LEAST, REMAINED CLEAR! That is, afterwards. Because before, this was not the case. And that is precisely the why and wherefore of

THE ISLANDS OF BEFORE AND AFTER in that, on the Island of Before, not only are all the ladies fat before going on Ryvita diets and all the dishes dirty before being washed by Palmolive and all the girls have yellow teeth before brushing them with Gleem, but here are also to be found all the geniuses of the Agency with dirty consciences before understanding the aims of the Enchanted Agency and accepting the role it has fallen to them to play in life. And, on the Island of After, all the ladies are thin after going on a Ryvita diet and all the dishes are clean after being washed with Palmolive and all the girls have white teeth after brushing them with Gleem and this is where you will find all the Agency geniuses who have penetrated the mysteries of motivational research and learned by heart what a status symbol is and read McLuhan and understood that the medium is the message and the massage and that all media are, moreover, active metaphors and that advertising, when all is said and done, is a boxing glove holding a posy of forget-me-nots. It would be recommendable, the guide told him, to visit the Island of Before before and that of After after because otherwise, if you visit that of After before and that of Before after, not only will the plates, and consciences, get dirty again and your flesh swell and your teeth turn yellow, but the whole of life: memory, dogs, telegraph poles, odalisques, lakes and all the islands, the chronicles and their readers will depalmolivize, degleemize and deryvitasize.

FACED WITH THE DANGER OF
DEPALINURIZING (what would most depalinurize Palinuro would be a good depalinurizer) and having decided to become a man of the big wide world, having decided to pass, on his way to the Hall of Fame, by way of

the most famous of the Madison Avenue communications-belt restaurants, like 21 itself, like the Laurent and the San Marino, Palinuro started to cover the gastronomic distance existing between a youth of twenty and

GASTRONOME ISLAND, upon which, as the guide explained to him, the horn of the goat Almatheia spilled the plenty of earthly foods. Upon it, also, fell the frost which turned into a cow from whose udders flowed the milk which suckled the giant Ymir. And this island is the home of the monsters Leviathan and Ziz, of delicious and inexhaustible flesh; here the legend of Canaan, land of milk and honey, becomes reality; it is the Utopia described by Pherecrates where roast fowl fly around the people begging to be eaten, it is the region visited by MacConglinne where the houses have doors of steak, doorsteps of bread and columns of mature cheese. The guide only showed Palinuro the poor quarters of the Island of Gastronomes, far removed from the realms of Brillat-Savarin and the Viscount of Viel-Castel but where the life cycle of the rich is repeated: the inhabitants die and their companions eat their flesh which tastes of potatoes, quiche Lorraine, lobster, saltimbocca *alla romana* and other delicacies. These inhabitants also eat their own shit because they shit live carrots and lettuces, curries, rum babas, Père Louis trout, guacamole, kebabs and soufflé au Grand Marnier. The inhabitants eat so much that they vomit but they eat and drink their own vomit because they vomit exquisite dishes cooked in their stomachs: bouillabaisse, Rockefeller oysters, Madeira sauce and bordelaise, fettucine and mushrooms in black butter. The inhabitants eat so much that they belch but they inhale their own eructations because they smell of pheasant casserole, choucroute garni, kidneys in sherry and tripe à la mode. The inhabitants eat so much that they fart but they inhale their farts because they smell of Pont l'Eveque, Irish stew and Madame Prunet omelette. The inhabitants eat so much that they weep but they drink their own tears because they weep drops of anis, of Nuits St Georges, daiquiri, Drambuie and gin and tonic. The inhabitants of this island never really die because when they burst, they start (like Erysichthon condemned by Ceres or the Kirtimukha of the Javanese temples) to eat themselves: they eat their hands, their stomach, their liver, their lungs and, when they have finally eaten their lower maxillary, they start to grow new organs of different shapes, smells and flavours.

BELCHING THEN, and not just culture (to which banquet he had come so late), Palinuro got to thinking about the vanity of vanities of human life and the manager-guide, who was capable, when in good form, of gauging the depths of the human heart, invited Palinuro to accompany him on a visit to

THE ISLAND OF LESSER HUMAN GRANDEUR which is dedicated to our least and most intimate grandeurs, in that the island is effectively a huge wax museum in which are represented all the great personages of history, but none of them in the situations or attitudes for which they are immortalized. Here, the guide told Palinuro, you will not find Giuseppe Garibaldi lighting up the Alps with his dazzling red shirts, nor Simon Bolivar swearing from the peak of the Aventine Hill to give his life for the freedom of his country. Madame Curie is not here in her laboratory writing her treatise on radioactivity nor are the Montgolfier brothers travelling through the skies of Lyon. Here, Greta Garbo is not appearing in *Ninotchka*, nor is the illustrious lawyer Cesare Beccaria denouncing the arbitrary nature of criminal justice during his time. And those who think that on this Island they are going to see Landru, Cartouche or Gilles de Rais committing the crimes that made them famous and those who think that in the museum Babe Ruth is to be seen throwing balls at the sun or Zatopac jumping vegetable stalls in Prague, are very much mistaken. On the other hand, they will find a wax sculpture of George Washington, alone and in private, picking his nose and extracting a large, green lump of snot. They will see Marie Antoinette defecating in her lofty chamber pot of porcelain and gold. Leonardo da Vinci pulling down his lover Salai's pink trousers. Sigmund Freud, adolescent and beardless, masturbating in a toilet. Hence, Bakunin, the illustrious anarchist, is not here to be seen accusing the Church and the State of being the two black beasts which enslave humanity. The famous educator Johann Pestalozzi is not here to be found inventing the Lancaster mutual education system. Errol Flynn here does not appear in *Too Much, Too Soon*, neither is Professor Max Planck explaining the quantum theory, nor is the illustrious philosopher Gustav Theodor Fechner dreaming with open eyes in the darkness of his room of the poetry of the Universe and the psychic life of plants. But they are here, yes indeed, every one of them, it's just that nobody would recognize them. For instance, nobody would recognize, in this wax reproduction of a foetus, the woman who was later to become Eleonore of Aquitaine. Nor would anybody, in this pile of bones and scraps of flesh, in this body whose sex has been swallowed by an eel, whose nipples have been devoured by sea horses, whose rib cage has been nibbled bare by goldfish and the bones of whose skull have been perforated by the tentacles of a huge red octopus like the god imagined by Victor Hennequin, re-emerging through the empty orbits of the eyes, nobody would recognize in this, the guide guaranteed, the corpse of the great pirate Francis Drake laid to rest on the bed of Portobello Bay. And, finally, the guide showed Palinuro a special section of the museum taken from the Island of What Might Have Been and for which a number of experts and computers had calculated all eventualities and possible internal and external factors, including hereditary and environmental, somatic and psychic, nutritional and climatological elements that might have affected the bodies of numerous historical figures had they lived another ten years, thirty years, fifty and, on the basis of these results, created a series of wax figures giving an idea of the likely physical aspect of these individuals. And Palinuro saw that Christ was a man of ninety years of age, stone deaf and with a sizeable nose and stomach. And he saw that Wolfgang Amadeus Mozart was sixty years old, bald and with wrinkled hands. And he saw Marilyn Monroe, who had passed the half-century mark and was immensely fat as a result of a glandular malfunction. And he saw Popeye who was in a wheelchair and Tarzan who had gone blind and Batman who had turned into an old pederast. And, finally, he saw several heaps of bone and cartilage, wrinkles and warts, tumours and varicose veins which mumbled unintelligible words, any one of which could have been the great thinker Bertrand Russell at two hundred years of age, the Cid at a thousand and one hundred years of age or Methuselah the patriarch at thirty thousand.

PALINURO WAS SUBJECTED next to test word association Jung's. In other words (better associated) to Jung's word-association test. And when Palinuro associated the needful medicant colours with the immortal rubbish displaced in the swaying luxuriance of the parks; when Palinuro associated the swelling of printing presses with rectilinear censorship and magistrates' optics with long-fanged technologies; when Palinuro, thinking of *The Three Musketeers*, spoke of damascened genuflections; thinking of the Overseas Hospitals, related his puerperal afternoons and, thinking of the psychoanalyst himself, spoke of hypothecary spirits and obedient eclipses, the psychoanalyst cleared his throat and, after swallowing several gobs of foul matter of laryngeal ilk, jotted down on a piece of paper the word 'failed', in a very particular and special hand, full of illusory cadences and flowery flourishes but, more to the point, in huge letters crossing the page diagonally from one side to the other as though he sought to cut a zig-zag slash across Palinuro's chances of ever working in an advertising agency. Although, in truth, that was unfair. Unfair that is, to the analyst, who had never in his life heard of abstract armour, painless velvets and acclimated forgetfulness, much less had he ever had occasion to attend the chance encounter between Cousin Walter's umbrella and Estefania's sewing machine on Palinuro's operating table.

AFTER WHICH, WHAT WITH ONE THING AND ANOTHER, HE WAS LEFT ULTRA-SAD and ultra-exhausted and ultra-Palinuro, wondering whether in this world, or at least in the part that he had ended up in, good things ever happened and, once more, his guardian angel, manager, guide and cicerone led him by the hand to the very threshold of

THE ISLAND OF GOOD NEWS, where the inhabitants, he explained to Palinuro, aware that the world is not all tribulation and adversity and that murders, bank robberies, shipwrecks, rapes, bombings, kidnappings and other countless tragedies and misfortunes are not necessarily the order of the day; aware that, daily, thousands of normal children, dogs and flowers are born and millions of people celebrate their silver and diamond wedding anniversaries, their five years of retirement or their ten thousand days of life and millions of others get through the morning, the afternoon and the night without having their wallets stolen, without somebody setting fire to their homes, without falling ill, without slipping on a gunpowder skin, without weeping for a death in the family, without losing their jobs, without suffering a heart attack, without quarrelling and, in short, without suffering any particularly serious misfortunes or mishap; aware that in hundreds of cities and provinces, no earthquake, flood, drought, civil war or any other kind of disaster, cataclysm or catastrophe has occurred, decided therefore to produce a newspaper and a news broadcast for every household so that the inhabitants of each house, after learning every morning that the sun had risen and after opening their eyes and learning that not only themselves but also the universe was alive, could take stock of the good that had occurred in the sitting room, the dining room and in bed, the good news of the milkman's timely appearance, the good news that the soup hadn't boiled dry and no glasses had been broken, that none of the family had felt stabs in the liver or had toothache, that the canary hadn't died and nobody had had nightmares and the iron didn't break down and nobody asked to borrow money from anybody else and auntie had a birthday and all the others had non-birthdays and two letters and three postcards arrived and the newspaper of the outside world arrived, punctually, containing a summary of the figures of all the millions of people in the world who had not suffered any fatal or unsurmountable tragedy but had effectively experienced many good or pleasant or fantastic things. Therefore, the guide told Palinuro, it's all part of the statistics and, therefore, of another less fortunate island.

PALINURO HAD NOT ACTUALLY BEEN, like St Brendan, to the Island of the Hairy Rats, the size of cats. He never entered the belly of a whale as did Lucian, neither had he ever waged battle against giant oysters and sponges, nor peeped into the mirror which reflects every city and every nation of the world, nor gone to the place where you hear every word spoken on the earth. He never went to the Hermaphrodites' Island of Artus. He had never travelled to the centre of our planet to see the Megamicres which swim in rivers of red water. He had never visited, as did Conn, the island of the house roofed with birds' wings and neither had he travelled to the Paradisiacal Island of the fifty beds. But he did, however, travel to

195

THE ISLAND OF STATISTICS
AND AVERAGES where, as the guide explained to him, the inhabitants
live for an average of sixty years. But that doesn't mean that some live for
eighty-five years and others for forty and others for fifty-five, giving an
average of sixty. No, it means simply that all the inhabitants live for
exactly sixty years, not a day less, not a day more. And it also means that
each and every one of the inhabitants of the Island sleeps for an average of
one hundred and seventy-five thousand hours of the total five hundred and
twenty-five thousand hours of their lives. On the Island of Statistics and
Averages, continued the guide, absolute order prevails: citizens of the same
generation are all born at the same time. Then they sleep, at a stretch, all
the average hours that they are meant to sleep. They all wake up at the
same time and for sixty-five thousand continuous hours they eat and then
they make love four thousand two hundred and three times consecutively
and afterwards weep for twenty days, laugh without interruption for two
and a half weeks, are bored for five years, work one hundred and fifty
thousand hours, tie their shoelaces thirty two thousand seven hundred and
eighty-four times, walk for nineteen thousand six hundred kilometres,
sneeze thirty-five thousand times without a break and wonder, for a period
of six and a half months, with all its minutes and seconds, what is the
purpose of the Island and the object of all they do and fail to do during
their lives. After that, they spend fifty-six thousand hours harbouring
illusions and three and a half years fearing death, and finally, die all at the
same moment, but for different reasons. Then, they stay dead for an
average of eternity.

RETURNING TO THE ENCHANTED AGENCY, the manager-guide
told Palinuro that it was precisely the Island of Statistics, with its
confusing accounting of the endless number of gratuitous things that all
men (and women) are obliged to do during their lives, which gave the
Enchanted Agency the idea of creating

THE ISLAND OF SALARIES which serves several ends, as the guide told
him. The most important being that of stimulating the genuine creativity
of our copy-writers and artistic directors and, therefore, nobody in this
office receives a cent for their work, but not because, as Ferenczi said,
money is dehydrated, scentless and shining filth. In our case it is, firstly,
because we consider that the talent of our geniuses is priceless. Secondly,
because it is our desire that each of our little, golden-egg-laying talents
should give of their best for love of the product and of the art of
advertising. Hence, it is essential that when one of our copy-writers writes
an advertisement for Camay soap or one of our artistic directors creates an
advertisement for Four Roses whisky, they be aware that they don't do it
for money and can therefore put all their heart and pride into their jobs.

196

The famous advertisement *Written after hours* says it all: advertising (the creative talent) is a type of work which cannot be bought with money only. Our copy-writers and draughtsmen live very well: they earn fabulous salaries, but not for their work in the Agency which couldn't be more disinterested. A long time ago, the sociology and psychology departments of the Enchanted Agency discovered that there are endless acts and activities which everybody performs every day and which can only be classed as work: jobs which nobody appreciates and which nobody has until now remunerated are, for instance, switching the light off, turning on the tap, putting on one's trousers to go to the office, catching the bus, walking, greeting acquaintances, filing one's nails, buying food and endless other things. On the basis of this study, our Agency decided to eliminate the salaries which all our executives and creative personnel received for their work and to pay them, instead, for these finicky and thankless tasks which form part of the daily routine. Hence, our draughtsmen and art directors are given a special bonus for cleaning their teeth, a monthly payment for looking at their watches several times a day, an additional sum for combing their hair and tying their shoelaces and another bonus for starting their cars and driving to the office. All activities are covered: in other words, all those which are not specifically related to the creative and public-relations activities carried out in the Agency, such as taking the children on an excursion, calling the plumber, shaving or lighting a cigarette. Of course, we know that our secretaries and our lower-echelon employees also have to do the same things every day but naturally a receptionist who does nothing but answer telephones all day cannot receive the same salary for putting on lipstick as a creative director whose ideas not only sell millions of packets of Wonder bread but, moreover, sell aspirations, illusions and ways of life. By the same token, it is not possible to pay the same for knotting a tie to a copy-writer who creates a famous jingle for Postum cereals as to an office boy who spends his time carrying messages and packages backwards and forwards. Hence the enormous differences in salary. Every Christmas we present our artistic directors and copy-writers with a generous bonus in compensation for the work involved during the course of the year in calculating how to spend their salaries and in signing the cheques with which they pay their monthly instalments on purchases and trips, life insurance, fines and bank loans, credit-card payments and mortgages.

SEVERAL DAYS LATER, or perhaps months later, several advertisements later, several forgotten incidents, pages and hams later, aware of the high cost of shoes and cars, of the expensiveness of private yachts and gold fingers, Palinuro feared that he might be offered a position in the Enchanted Agency at a huge salary and then one day lose everything in a crash on Wall Street, in a burglary, in a fire or, perhaps, in a roll of the dice on the green baize of Las Vegas. But the manager-guide explained to him that he might rest assured since nobody in the Enchanted Agency ever really needed to possess anything in life because, for this very reason, another island had been created:

THE ISLAND OF RENTALS, to travel to which Palinuro rented a means of transport, rented a road and rented a map, some suitcases, some clothes, a guide and a holiday. On this island, the guide told him, you can rent anything you like: a car, a stairway, a horse, a refrigerator, a house, a famous painting, a carpet, a designer outfit, a television. If you want a garden, we rent you a garden and we rent you the roses, the footpaths, the fountain for the garden and we rent you clippers to cut the roses, earth to fill the flowerbeds and water to overflow the garden fountains. If you wish to give a party, we rent you the hall, the waiters, the glasses and the crockery, the invitations and the guests, the jokes and the conversation. If you wish to get married, we rent you the registrar and the church, the bride and the suit, the music and the honeymoon. On this island we rent you rainy days and summer months; we rent you a happy past and glorious future. We even rent you life and death: if you wish to be born, we rent you the hospital, the doctor, the parents and the godparents, the baby's bottles and the forceps. If you wish to die, we rent you the coffin, the flowers and the obituaries, we rent you the mourners, we rent you three metres of ground. If you have no money, it doesn't matter: we rent you a fortune, we rent you wealthy patrons, we rent you a profitable business so that you can rent, on this island, anything you need or desire: a kidney, an umbrella, a language, a monument, a religious faith, a typewriter to write the chronicle of the island.

THIS REASSURED PALINURO, but only for a few hours or, perhaps, only for a minute or, perhaps, only for two McCormick mustards or for a darkening of mirrors, the time it took him to realize that the fact of not owning anything didn't protect him against losing everything – unless, of course, he rented an insurance policy for every rented object. And the guide told him that, to this end, the geniuses of the Agency had created

INSURANCE ISLAND, where we can not only insure your house, your car, your job and your television; where we not only insure you against fire, kidnapping, rape, tremor and flood, earthquake and revolution, hail, hurricane and tear gas; where we not only insure your voice if you are a famous singer, your legs if you are a football star, the steadiness of your hand if you are an illustrious surgeon or your charisma if you are a renowned dictator; where, the guide told Palinuro, we not only insure you against the loss of an eye, of two fingers, of a vertebra, of the upper vena

198

cava, the anal sphincter; where we not only insure you against strokes, against cancer, against Petruschky's symptom and against pellucid staphyloma; where we not only insure you against falls, crashes, bites and scratches, against meteorites falling from the skies and lions escaping from the zoo, against muggers, madmen and ghosts; where, finally, we not only insure every part of your body and every one of your possessions against every kind of damage or loss; in other words, not only do we insure your hair, your fountain pen, your wisdom teeth and your razor blades against loss, theft, caries and bluntness, but we also insure the chronicle you are writing of the Island: we insure it against incredulity, mockery, plagiarism, incomprehension, discontinuance and oblivion.

FINALLY THE PSYCHIATRISTS washed their hands and gave Palinuro a 'Do-it-Yourself tests' kit which included a box of matches to do your own Duncker test; a Binet-Simon scale to find out your own IQ and several instruction booklets to do your own Burt analogies and syllogisms test and the Thurstone primary mental abilities test and which, as the guide explained to Palinuro, had been brought specially from

'DO-IT-YOURSELF' ISLAND where, as the name indicates, you have to do everything yourself. It is very simple to travel to the island, because you choose the date and the point of departure yourself and yourself alone choose also the route, the length of trip, the means of transport and the storms which you yourself will invent on the way. But also, if you should so desire, you may ask yourself where the island is and how to reach it and, once you have yourself answered these and other questions, you pack your suitcase yourself and say goodbye to the friends and relatives you have yourself created. You reach the island when you recognize it for yourself, when you convince yourself that you have arrived or when, by yourself, you put it in the middle of your life. You may then invent for yourself a language for the Island and rest from your trip; shave yourself, change your clothes yourself, go out shopping. Or, in other words, you can buy a DIY kit containing razor blades, a razor, mentholated foam and a pamphlet with instructions on how to shave yourself. Or you can buy a kit of new clothes to dress yourself, with an instruction booklet on how to do up shirt buttons and get your arms into overcoat sleeves. Moreover, the number of DIY kits existing on the Island is infinite: if you want to convert the loft of your house into a room, fix the plumbing, scratch your nose or open the door yourself, you have only to acquire the corresponding DIY kit. Likewise, if you wish, for instance, to drive a car, repaint the bedrooms, put down a carpet or make a telephone call yourself, or even make a will, go duck shooting or cultivate your garden yourself. On the island, you can also buy DIY kits to make anything you want yourself: there is a DIY masturbation kit; there are others for admiring and despising yourself.

There are also DIY suicide kits and others for inventing the madness leading to suicide and the conditions leading to madness and for making the pistol, the barbituates or the rope to shoot, poison or hang yourself and, finally, there are DIY kits for printing the instruction booklets for throwing yourself from a cliff, the top of an eighty-floor skyscraper or the bridge over the Hudson River. But, when you are tired of all this, tired of living and regretting, tired of praying to God, tired of hanging up your pictures, learning English, smoking, hating, going out, reading, breathing, telling lies, sneezing and reading the chronicle of the Island, all yourself, you can always leave the island. In fact you needn't even leave, you may just disimagine it, forget that you have read the chronicle of the Island and direct your steps towards that other island where you don't have to do anything for yourself, because everything is already done.

BUT, RETURNING AGAIN
TO THE ENCHANTED AGENCY and before deciding to travel to the island where everything is already done, Palinuro – believing that at last he could fill the world with his fame; that he had already learned the meaning of the panic button and of the permanent crisis on Madison Avenue; thinking that he deserved to be decorated with a stomach ulcer; certain that he could from then onwards master the secrets of demagogy, of advertisogogy and any other existing pyrotechnical or parabolical art through the appropriate use of hyperboles, symmetries and alliterations and knowing, like Musil, that allegory is the slippery logic of the soul – begged the gods to bear him to the peak of the Helicon and, armed with a DIY advertisements kit, he took his first steps in this new science, the supreme art of the Poetic Advertisement or of the Advertising Poem, with a television commercial for which the idea came to him while he was eating Sabritas crisps and which he provisionally entitled:

COSMOCRISPAGONY, and which goes as follows: 'The woman with white hair and a little wrinkle for every day of her winter, is sitting in a rocking chair and rocking to the slow rhythm of her life. The general, for his part, is hanging on the wall, on the white surface of which the damp has traced maps of unexplored regions. The little old lady secretively opens a bag of Sabritas crisps and peeps out of the corner of her eye at the general whose crustaceous whiskers remain impassive despite the wind which is setting in motion, or should be setting in motion, the arms of the Dutch windmills embroidered in cross-stitch to be seen beside him. The little old lady raises a crisp to her mouth and takes a blissful, unhurried bite. A faint, ever so faint *crunch* is heard somewhere: it is perhaps the creaking of the lemon wood of the rocking chair, groaning as it remembers its orchard days filled with birds and sharp-tasting lemons. But no: with the second crisp that the old lady places in her mouth a slightly louder *crunch* is heard

200

and this time the general sways, from right to left and back again, as though in disapproval. Another crisp, another and another. Suddenly, the tulips in the painting shiver and the wise foam of the general's whiskers shudders. The old lady has filled her mouth with crisps – five, six, ten crisps at the same time – and rocks in time to the movement of her jaws. *Crunch! Crunch! Crunch!* reverberates from all sides and the general and the windmills start to oscillate ominously. We note the make of the crisps: Sabritas. A vase from the twenties starts to dance the charleston and the flowers in it do a striptease. The *crunches* multiply and grow louder still, so that we do not know (we will never know) if the *crunches* we are hearing come from the shattering of successive crisps as they are munched by the old lady or if they are metaphysical, telluric *crunches* caused by the San Andreas Fault, a thousand kilometres away, there where the sperm whales shoot blue fountains into the air. And the tremor intensifies, becomes an uncontrollable earthquake. The vase falls and turns into a Chinese puzzle worthy of a mandarin. The general falls, as he did many years ago in the War of el Chaco. The windmills fall, as they did under the Nazi bombs. And the walls fall, the ceiling falls, the sky falls, the solar system falls and in all of infinite space is left only our little old lady, her rocking chair and the empty bag of Sabritas crisps which, since there is no longer any force of gravity, whirl through the vacuum to join other galaxies.'

GREEN WITH ENVY, several executives, copy-writers and artistic directors told Palinuro that, while the idea was basically very good, he would have to sit down and touch it up because everything in this life has to be touched up, which doesn't necessarily mean that it has to be adorned because some things, on the contrary, have to be disadorned which, in turn, does not mean that they shouldn't be made up because everything in life, from tinned peaches to family evenings and advertisements and products – especially products – have to be dressed up, touched up, fixed up, made up, as you will see in:

MAKE-UP ISLAND where the Enchanted Agency's experts know the most intimate secrets of Messalina, the courtesan of golden nipples, and of Tristan's water formula and of the vitriol oil which dyes hair blond and the secrets of Maori tattoos and Cleopatra and Belinda's toilettes and the virtues of the crocodile gland and wolf-blood lotions used by Isabel of Bavaria and of the cosmetics created by the Macaronis and where the Max Factor, Revlon, Elizabeth Arden and Mary Quant creams, lipsticks, foundations, powders and blushers relive the past glories of Ninon de Lenclos, Madame Du Barry, Mae West and Marie Duplessis, and where, as the guide explained to Palinuro, are prepared the Enchanted Agency's products for stills and film sessions. Our experts know, for example, that beer loses its bubbles within a few seconds and that the cream on a Jell-O dessert melts in the heat from the reflectors, as do the drops of sweat on a glass of ice-cold 7-up or the fat on a joint of Parma ham. So, in order to prepare each product for the photograph which will immortalize it for eternity in the magazine by the same name or for the filmed advertisement which will be admired by hundreds of thousands of people, we put Alka-Seltzer in the beer and we replace the dessert cream with toothpaste and the drops of sweat on the glass with drops of glycerine and we varnish the Parma ham with hairspray. On Make-Up Island, the guide told Palinuro, we also comb Luxor carpets, dress tins of Del Fuerte tomato purée in their Sunday best and Players cigarettes in tuxedos, mould the breasts of Cross-My-Heart bras and paint the lips of boxes of Lipton tea in order to ensure that they smile at four o'clock on the dot. You will see how our experts excel in getting the mudguards of Mercury cars to shine until they reflect, full-length, the god of commerce and protector of thieves. We present Esso oil, on a silver tray, to be served in a Bohemian crystal glass to drink a toast to the health of its automobile's cylinders. Finally, on this island, we stick false eyelashes on Retina cameras so that every wink of its shutter produces instant and memorable love.

FROM THIS LESSON PALINURO DEDUCED that his little old lady of the crisps should be deprived of her San Andreas Fault, her orchard and birds, her sperm whales and earthquakes, effectively destroying the original idea, and the manager, the executives, the rival copy-writers and the artistic directors – in other words the *crème de la crème* of the advertising intelligentsia – filed it away in the rubbish archives.

AND, SEEING PALINURO SUNK AGAIN
IN SADNESS, the manager patted him on the back, puffed pinkly and told him that, on the one hand, there are any number of good ideas and slogans and inspired campaigns which have failed and been incinerated on the altar of good faith only to be reborn ten years later, like the Phoenix cooked in its nest of oregano and laurel, disguised as original ideas when one is a famous copy-writer in exile; and that, on the other hand, there is no advertisement or idea, the guide assured Palinuro, which does not eventually die, because all life is disposable as he would see in

DISPOSABLE OBJECTS ISLAND, where it is our duty to create the non-durable products for the non-durable needs of our throw-away society, for which reason our geniuses invented disposable beer cans, disposable Dentamatic toothbrushes, disposable Scott paper cups and plates, and disposable Kleenex handkerchiefs. It was on this island that disposable surgeons' masks and gloves and disposable syringes were born. Here, that our geniuses invented disposable cars and disposable judges' wigs and disposable jewellery. It was discovered here that illnesses, trees and water, lighters and ballpoint pens are also disposable. On this island, every moment of the day and every day of the week is disposable: we have created disposable pasts, history and memories. On this island, added the guide, we have created not only disposable diplomats, speeches, public accountants and liners but also disposable symphonies, walls and dead. The chronicle of the island and the island itself, with its mountains, its seas and its discoveries, are also disposable.

IS PALINURO, THEN, NO GOOD AT MAKING ADVERTISEMENTS? mused the guide. Palinuro can't write a book? Palinuro doesn't know how to paint a picture? Palinuro is no good at studying medicine? There is always a last resort, the manager assured him: to discover three, ten, a hundred new objectives in life and thus create the New, the Sensational . . .

MULTI-PURPOSE PALINURO! which came about after Palinuro, hand in hand with his guide, visited

NEW PURPOSE ISLAND and he learned that, on the day the international market was flooded with potato peelers, the geniuses of the Agency discovered that these could be used for peeling the skin off the Indo-Chinese, just as Frigidaire freezers can be used for the purpose of conserving children machine-gunned on the coasts of Japan and Westinghouse irons for scorching the stomachs of North Vietnamese soldiers and Pall Mall cigarettes for toasting women's nipples. It was similarly revealed that Echo kitchen knives can be put to good purpose by gangs and bands of teenagers in Detroit, Glasgow, Chicago and Mexico City, that Queen sheets can be used for the additional purpose of escaping from prisons and lunatic asylums and Cannon towels for strangling wives. But more edifying purposes also exist, the guide told Palinuro, as is the case with Simmons mattresses which can be used to keep savings with which to buy, in time, other Simmons mattresses. There are more popular purposes: all cars, from Fiats to Bentleys, can be used for making love. And there are more amusing purposes: we discovered that Betty Crocker custard tarts are ideal for Laurel and Hardy's favourite joke, and that the best plates for throwing at people's heads are the unbreakable kind from Hollywood plastic dinner services. And, finally, we discovered that anybody who doesn't like the island's chronicle may, if they so wish, use it for an alternative purpose, the guide told Palinuro.

AH, THOSE WERE THE DAYS! When Palinuro – at the very moment a mysterious chord prolonged the dahlias standing as starched in the afternoon light bordering the boulevards of Paseo de la Reforma – entered the Enchanted Agency building and met the Estefania of always, as winged, slender and diaphanous, light, delicate and volatile as a character infused by Calderón with a magic breath of life, so much so indeed that she trembled at Palinuro's least breath as did the wings of the birds suspended in her armpits which laid their Easter eggs in the newt of her belly button. How time passes! Or perhaps it would be better to ask Estefania: how have you spent your time? How have you spent every last cent of it? And, though Palinuro was far from being a vengeful knight, he suddenly appeared in armour white as ermine, prepared to perform a great feat, declaring that he was the Sun Knight who would save housewives by beating back the filth to the outer confines of the poorest neighbourhoods. On the subject of whiteness, Estefania and Palinuro liked at that time to go for picnics, because they were very good at choosing between a poisoned afternoon and an inoffensive morning and, on Sundays, after a whole week of making advertisements and visiting car factories and laboratories and plants for making matches and wallpaper and for packing meat, after visiting the tinned-food factories where olives are lubricated to plug the assholes of executives inclined to drink more than five martinis a day when they travelled from Manhattan to New Jersey and from the district of Mariano Escobedo to Coyoacán and where they beat huge saucepans full of jam to drown children who are good and manufacture mustards for the male members of hot-dogs and, finally, after visiting the carpet factory with their mounds of fibres orange as bear pelts, mounds of pile purple as volcanoes of beetroot, mountains of pile white as the itch of talcum powder, piles of pile yellow as saffron sneezes and machines weaving miracles and fairytales. And so it was on a picnic that Palinuro got the idea for an advertisement with Estefania sitting at the foot of some huge palm trees and her bottle-green dress merging into endless lawn and she lights a mentholated Salem cigarette which produces a green smoke of melting emeralds and it starts to snow and from the sky fall flakes of cold mint and it snows in the forest and in the supermarket and it snows on their publicist hearts. And Estefania felt that these ideas were so amazing that she rejoiced and hallelujahs reverberated in her eyes.

AFTER THIS MENTHOLATED PAUSE Palinuro felt that he had learned the lesson and, to save himself the bother of making his own advertisements, he decided to acquire them, ready-made, on

READY-MADE ISLAND where, as its name indicates, the guide explained to him, everything since the beginning of time is ready-made and not just the mountains and the sky, but also heroes, refrigerators, safety-pins, declarations of independence and, similarly, all imaginable past, present and future products of our consumer society, including those which cater, on the one hand, to the need to fill our leisure time and alleviate the weight of obligations which oppress so many people and, on the other, to the urgent need to adopt a generous and understanding attitude towards all inhabitants of the global village who, not without reason, wish to bring about far-reaching changes in our society. On this island, for example, nobody ever has to write a letter, because all letters are ready-written. We have a vast collection of letters for keeping in touch with friends, suicide notes for taking leave of the world, perfumed letters to girlfriends and lovers, letters to mothers, letters to cousins, business letters, diplomatic and political letters and, of each of these, the variety is as infinite as the possible number of situations and states of mind of each and every one of the inhabitants of the Island. Our computers, fed with the personal details of both the writer of the letter and of the person or institution to which it is addressed and aware of the nature of reciprocal relations and of their problems, needs and desires, take care to add to the specimen letter chosen by the client certain personal details, some endearment, when they consider it necessary, a touch of humour or of irony, a reproach or an insult. On the subject of insults, we also have a ready-made collection of anonymous messages: anonymous jibes, anonymous death threats, anonymous pornography. Similarly, on special telephone cassettes, we have ready-made anonymous slanderous calls, calls promising death, obscene calls. Another group of computers, fed by our most prominent experts in economic, political and social theory, have the task of writing weekly, daily, fortnightly or twice-monthly publications on all existing and future ideologies: Marxist, Fascist, Maoist, Christian Democrat. And each model is exclusive: the magazine acquired by yourself and your party, or chosen by yourself and your clandestine or terrorist group, is the only one of its kind existing in the entire world. We also sell pamphlets and fliers with subversive ideas and calls to revolution. Some are impeccably printed, while others are mimeographed. Some are perfectly written and others are naïve and full of spelling mistakes. There are moderate ones and there are raving, radical ones. Clients may choose their pamphlets in accordance with individual taste and the requirements of their political strategy, although we also have computers offering ready-made advice. In addition, we sell protest songs to which clients have only to add their signature: songs against capitalism, against plutocrats, against repression of intellectuals in the Soviet Union, against Zionism, against advertising, against the island itself. And, of course, we also produce exclusive posters and printed declarations which come with special adhesive to stick on walls, for or against the French Communist Pary, apartheid, the Catholic church, black power, the gay lib movement, luxury taxes, NATO, conscription, Arabs. And placards and banners for trade unions, student associations or nationalist groups, demanding wage increases, the right to strike, deportation of foreigners, freedom for political prisoners, the resignation of the rector of the University and academic autonomy, the overthrow of the government, suspension of

Rhodesia by the United Nations, increased pensions for the retired or the severing of diplomatic relations with Cuba. As with the pamphlets, some of the banners and placards are very well printed, with the letters highlighted in two colours and different type, while others are more primitive for those who wish to give the impression that they were home-made by a clumsy, honest, hasty and spontaneous hand. We also have all kinds of ready-made time bombs and booby traps; Molotov cocktails which come in red half-pint jars bearing a picture of the famous politician of that name and naturally, in deference to nostalgia for the good old days of Sacco and Vanzetti, we manufacture the classical bombs: black and rounded, with long white fuses which come ready-equipped with a Ronson automatic lighting device. As you will understand, the guide said to Palinuro, we export large quantities of ready-made articles to Do-It-Yourself Island since with a couple of Molotov cocktails, a few dozen pamphlets and two or three placards, you have a 'Do-It-Yourself Revolution' kit. Similarly, a gallon of Esso petrol, a box of Talisman matches and an instruction booklet on how to pour the petrol and set it alight, make a 'Do-It-Yourself Bonzo' kit; or even, with a few little bags of napalm and a couple of phials containing cholera vibrio cultures, you can make a kit for somebody to contaminate their own stream or defoliate their own trees or, with a few bags containing cigarette ends, empty beer cans and jars of industrial chemical waste, you have a kit for somebody who wishes, personally, to pollute the world. But there is a fundamental difference, as you will already have noticed, Palinuro, between the Island of Ready-Made Objects and Do-It-Yourself Island, in that on the first may be acquired kits containing the elements and ingredients necessary, for example, to make your own letter bombs while, on the second Island, the letter bombs are ready-made; all the client has to do is address them. And, for those who wish to send a letter bomb but don't know whom to send it to, the island offers ready-made enemies: a computer has the task of providing a name and address and all the motives and reasons clients might have – and which they do effectively have from that moment onwards – to kill them. Likewise, on Do-It-Yourself Island you will find a 'DIY graffiti' kit, whereas on the Island of Ready-Made Objects the graffiti are ready-made: the most popular are simply stickers. There are obscene and scatological graffiti: we manufacture all types of drawings of phalluses and vulvas and verses ranging from the most ingenious and refined to the vulgar and common. Words and expressions like 'Shit!' and 'Fuck off!' come in any size, colour, type of printed and handwritten letters or language you could desire. Political graffiti also come in all shades and colours: Castro red, Trotsky red, Nazi red. And there are graffiti which are ideal for public lavatories, metro walls, hoardings or walls of public and private buildings, lifts and telephone booths. Why say more? You can see for yourself that on this island nothing has to be done: houses and clouds, prayers and birds are ready-made. On this island, love is ready-made, as are all desires and all the inhabitants and the sea. Even the island's past and future, its birth and its destruction. The chronicle of your journey to the island is also ready-made.

AND, SINCE ALL THIS SEEMED A GAME to Palinuro and since he liked to take all games to their furthest extreme, the manager-guide invited him to

GAMES ISLAND, which is also called the Disneyland of the Future, and here, as he was assured, those fairs where you play at getting married and at going to prison are but an insipid foretaste of the attractions of this island which were conceived and created by our best psychologists and psychiatrists with the object of giving the man in the street the opportunity to purge his impulses and experience strong emotions more attuned to the daily life of our era. Hence, The Magic Garden, The World of Snow White and The Adventures of Peten Pan have been replaced by The House of Rape, The Bank Raid, The Kidnapping of an Executive, Urban Guerrillas and The Plane Hijack. The duration of these games depends on the price that you are prepared to pay. There are games that could go on for months or weeks. Even years. There are those who like to play for their whole lives and who leave their home, family, friends and peace of mind to come to this island and blow up buildings or start a revolution.

AS YOU CAN SEE, THIS IS NO JOKE, the guide said to Palinuro, because for jokes, jests and tricks, we have created another special island which is, not surprisingly, called

JOKE ISLAND, but it is not just a huge factory producing rubber pencils, plastic fried eggs, fake banknotes, pepper sweets and Wolfgang Paalen sponge umbrellas, not just a laboratory inventing typewriters with keys which don't correspond to the letters they print and constructing dumb pianos and publishing newspapers in non-existent languages and manufacturing stoves which freeze turkeys. And neither is Joke Island just a huge shop selling water pistols, machine guns with bullets of hail and atomic bombs of snow. And, although all kinds of bad jokes are permitted, the island is more than just an artificial paradise of Incoherent Arts, more than just a shop selling paper flowers which squirt sulphuric acid into people's eyes and bags full of lethal gases which poison with a shattering flatulence the unfortunate who sits on them and Montecristo cigars which blow the smoker's head off when they are lit. Joke Island is, first and foremost, a huge joke involving all aspects of the daily life of its inhabitants. Birth is destiny's little joke. To learn a language is also a joke because, contrary to what one might suppose, it is of no use in communicating with other people: that is, precisely, the joke. From the time of birth you don a mask which, just as a joke, is exactly the same as your own face and is later replaced by as many masks as may be necessary successively to change your appearance and lead others to believe that you are ageing with the passing of time or that you have become a powerful politician, a movie star, a beggar, a boxer, an unknown. On this island, it goes without saying, you also get sick as a joke: there is fake tuberculosis, illusory accidents, artificial heart attacks, false cancers. Then, sooner or later, death occurs and is invariably apocryphal, the mourning of family and friends is obviously a joke and the burial is likewise phoney. Just as a joke, nothing more, we sometimes remember the dead. Just as a joke, likewise, they never return. But the island is something more than just a huge factory of rubber worms, velvet tarantulas and foam-rubber catastrophes. It is sometimes said that the Island does not exist, but that's just a joke; there are chronicles, like this one, which shouldn't be taken too seriously either.

PALINURO, THUS FOREWARNED, didn't take the manager-guide too seriously when the latter, predicting that Palinuro would sooner or later end up triumphing and would eventually get to work in the Enchanted Agency, took him on an excursion to

OFFICE ISLAND where Palinuro had to blink and rub his eyes several times and refuse to believe what he was seeing or he would have had to conclude that he had taken a wrong turning and that, instead of entering Estefania's office, he had entered his much-loved room in Holy Sunday Square. On this Enchanted Agency Island, the manager-guide told Palinuro, we have outdone the Madison Avenue agencies in freedom of decorative expression. The huge black, red and yellow leather chairs of McCann-Erickson. The green carpet and furniture of Young and Rubicam: all that is past history. Just so the iron peacocks of J. Walter Thompson and his agency, where all the executives are allowed to decorate their offices in their own taste: Regency furniture, Mexican colonial furniture, Chippendale, Mies van der Rohe. In our agency, for the greater happiness of our executives, freedom of decorative expression goes much further than ever anticipated. One of our agency's vice presidents, for example, has an obsession with boats. Therefore, his office is an exact reproduction of a captain's cabin. He himself dresses in a blue uniform with a white cap and, every morning when he gets to the agency, he pins his decorations on his chest. The captain has his hammock and his navigation charts, his memories of Okinawa and his ship's log in which he records meetings with his clients, as well as his sextants, radar, gyrocompass and hydrocompass. The office is suspended on a structure which pitches and tosses constantly, simulating the motion of waves, and a tape-recorder reproduces the sound of sea and wind. Through a porthole in the end wall you can see the sky and seagulls flying by. No office boy is permitted to enter our captain's office unless he is dressed as a cabin boy. By courtesy of the agency, the captain is assigned accounts such as Bacardi rum, Beefeater gin, Calmex tuna, Del Fuerte sardines, Leica binoculars and any other products which are somehow related to the sea or to navigation. Another of our executives loves to go camping. His office, therefore, is a room of considerable size, with its ceiling disguised as the sky and the light as the sun. The floor is covered with a carpet of artificial grass. In the corner is a tent where the executive and his clients take shelter during unexpected artificial cloudbursts. But, if the day is sunny and windless, the executive and his clients discuss budgets and advertisements out of doors, so to speak. This executive is allowed to come to the office in Bermuda shorts and sports shirts. Clients are asked to dress in similar fashion and to bring a picnic lunch. This executive has been assigned accounts for portable gas stoves and petroleum lamps and camping equipment in general: caravans, collapsible tables and folding chairs, first-aid kits, rubber boots, thermos flasks and tinned foods of all kinds. We are well aware that there are many frustrated individuals among our creative staff: copy-writers who once dreamed of being great authors, artistic directors who hoped to be famous painters. To compensate their frustrations, we allow copy-writers to fill their offices with books and portraits of their favourite authors: Artaud, Drieu La Rochelle or Edward Lear. The private offices of our artistic directors are designed like painters' studios and they are permitted to have easels, painting materials and canvases and to hang reproductions of paintings by Jean Dubuffet, Caspar Friedrich or Felicien Rops, Schwitters environments, Jim Dine happenings and Le Parc light games. And, of course, advertisement posters by famous painters such as Toulouse-Lautrec, Vasarely or Paul Nash. Some of our artistic directors even have naked models for clients' delectation. As Christmas gifts to copy-writers who have been with the agency for many years and proved themselves to be faithful and reliable employees, we have famous novels and books printed – *Of Time and the River*, *Jude the Obscure* or *Papillon* – replacing the author's name with their own, for display in their offices. On the same principle, artistic directors are given perfect imitations of paintings by their favourite artist, on which their own signature has been substituted for the artist's. We also have exhibition catalogues printed, along with criticisms and essays on their work. Would-be authors and artists are assigned accounts such as the Columbia Record Club, the Time-Life Book Club and campaigns for *Encyclopaedia Britannica*, Steinway pianos and Rowney artists' materials, although they are sometimes required to contribute their talent to advertising accounts which have nothing to do with the world of art and letters. But, fortunately, this does not often happen: our agency is very big, virtually infinite, and we always find a way

209

of shuffling the accounts so as to give each person the ones they most enjoy. The extent of our organization even permits us the luxury of employing rebellion- and revolution-minded collaborators, progressive and reformist collaborators, who are permitted to dress as workers, beatniks or pseudo-hippies and hang posters in their offices of Che Guevara and Lumumba, smoke marijuana, take LSD and read Mao's *Little Red Book* and the works of Fanon, Vance Packard and Galbraith. We also allow them to read Theodor W. Adorno and C. Wright Mills. Even Marcuse, not so much to make them aware of the unnecessary necessity of doing their work every day but, more important, to make them aware that the indoctrination inherent in products is more than just advertising: it is a way of life which is not just good, but better, than ever before. These artists and writers are put in charge of publicity on sexual education, population control, environment conservation, pollution and nationalization of natural resources, as well as of advertising for subversive publishers, left-wing political campaigns and clandestine campaigns for national liberation movements. The only artistic directors who give us no problems whatsoever are those who are mad on pop art. The situation in their regard is the exact opposite in that, as connoisseurs of the aesthetic value of the Cisitalia designed by Farina, they are eager to handle all existing and future products, beauty creams, washing powders, chocolates, diesel motor oils, and immortalize them as Andy Warhol immortalized Campbell's soup and Duchamp, Stuart Davis and Wesselmann respectively immortalized Underwood, Odol and Volkswagen. But we would never get through describing all our offices, so I think a few more examples will suffice: we have other executives whose greatest passion is their own home and family life and they are allowed to decorate their office to exactly reproduce the sitting room of their house: same furniture, same carpet, same curtains, same fireplace. Toys lie scattered around the floor. The recorded shouting and laughter of the executive's own children at play drifts in through the window, behind which is reproduced the garden or street which each executive sees from the sitting room of his own home. From the other end of the office wafts the smell of good home cooking. These executives are permitted to dress in pyjamas, dressing gown and slippers and they are allocated products such as stoves, refrigerators, washing machines and dozens of others such as lawn mowers, dinner services, carpets, etc., etc. But my own situation, added the manager-guide of the Enchanted Agency, is exactly the opposite of that of the home-loving executive: my dream was always to be a great publicist and now that I have achieved it, my dream is to be an even greater publicist and so my office is a huge carpeted room, with an enormous kidney-shaped desk, bookshelves containing the complete collection of *Penrose* and *Advertising Age*, *The Hundred Best Advertisements*, *The Voice of Civilization*, Ogilvy's *Memoirs*, *The History* of Madison Avenue and Sloan Wilson's *Man in the Grey Flannel Suit*. And, of course, all kinds of files, folders, accounting books and modern technology gadgets such as computers and calculators, dictaphones, electric typewriter and electronic filing cabinet as well as a magic panel which tells me the exact position and movements of all Agency employees and a secret, closed-circuit television to spy on all of them, white video telephones directly linked with our clients and red telephones hooked into the enemy agencies. Behind my desk hangs a portrait of myself in an Uncle Sam hat and huge Lord Kitchener whiskers, pointing my index finger at anyone entering my office and saying: Advertising Needs You! And, as I have no passion or hobby in my life other than advertising, I have a room at home which exactly reproduces my office, detail for detail, where I work at night and at weekends. The illusion is so complete that sometimes I get up from my desk to go out and get something to eat and I open my door thinking that I'm at the office and it turns out that I haven't left home. The same kind of thing happens to our home-loving executives who sometimes get up from their chairs to go and make a sandwich in the kitchen and they open the door and they realize that, in fact, they haven't left the agency. There is no need to tell you that Estefania, our creative director, being an essentially home-loving woman, has an office which is an exact replica of the room in Holy Sunday Square.

SO, THE UNIVERSAL COMPREHENSION of all human foibles, demonstrated in principle in Office Island, continued the guide, attains perfection in

THE ISLAND OF NOSTALGIA AND
NATURE FREAKS, where the geniuses of the Enchanted Agency concentrate on inventing new products targeted not only at those clients who miss the good old days but also at those who distrust the bounty of modern technology: thus, on this island, they have not only discovered a Polaroid camera capable of taking photographs which have to be sent to a special laboratory to be developed and are ready two or three weeks later, but they have also invented an atomic ballpoint pen of goose-feather quill, a protonic car which attains a maximum speed of 40kph, a nuclear plane which takes sixty hours to cross the Atlantic, a hand-rotated electric liquidizer, a laser coal stove, electric candles, a cybernetic ice freezer and a 78-RPM record player with positronic memory. Similarly, in the most exposed part of the Island, products are developed for all kinds of nature freaks and non-conformists: from concentrated-lettuce contraceptives and wholewheat cigarettes, to lotions which turn hair grey and make-up to emphasize wrinkles and blemishes, from onion-perfumed deodorants and human-flesh-scented soaps to whisky-scented toothpaste.

IT WAS, HOWEVER, THE GREATEST
OF OUR ARTISTS who, confronted with our human limitations and the
inevitability of our destiny and knowing that they are impotent to alter the
course of history, founded

AESTHETICIANS ISLAND where the labour of our experts has been
directed principally, on the one hand, towards beautifying our physiological needs and, on the other, towards lending dignity to the natural and
man-induced disasters befalling the world. In other words, they not only
discovered the formula whereby each individual can regale their taste in
choosing the colour and shape of their excreta – not only, thus, may you
find on the island excrement which is silver-plated or excrement spherical
and bright as Christmas decorations, excrement transparent as a jelly or
cylindrical excrement with red and white tassels bringing to mind sticks of
rock or the poles outside barbers' shops and, on this Island, gobs of phlegm
are round as pearls and brain tumours are reminiscent of orchids and
poppies – but also, he said, the formula by which everyone on this Island
can choose the colour of the fire which might by accident consume their
house or the shade of the waters destroying their crops. There are scarlet
fires and there are navy-blue ones. There are golden floods, hail multi-
coloured as confetti, avalanches of purple snow, emerald-tinted hurricanes. On this island, continued the guide, we bestow dignity on artificial
catastrophes. The idea was inspired by Albrecht Dürer's visions and the
mushrooms of the atomic explosions in Hiroshima and Nagasaki. We
have no intention of encouraging this kind of experiment, since such
decisions depend entirely on politicians and military men. We, on this
island, have nothing to do with the danger perpetrated by the advanced
industrial society with its irrational rationality, nothing to do with
technological fetishism, nothing to do with desublimation or the conquest
of the Unhappy Awareness. Our task, since we cannot preclude disasters, is
limited to prettifying them, to rendering them more tolerable. Thus, we
have succeeded in producing an atomic mushroom with a blue peduncle
and red cap with yellow spots like the mushrooms in Scandinavian
fairytales. Other explosions produce pale green mushrooms and toadstools
with lilac hats or with thin orange stalks and spongy hats with cobalt
spots. The work of the artists on this island, since they deserve this name
rather than that of men of science, has gone yet further: each bomb carried
by the American B52 planes is equipped with a special mechanism whereby
the explosion sets off endless fireworks producing millions of stars which
bathe the foreheads of the dead in light. We are not in the habit of taking
sides in wars, added the guide, and the bombers are also equipped with a
freight of fireworks so that when the plane is blown up by an enemy rocket
or crashes into a mountain, the air is filled with castles, Catherine wheels

and waterfalls of light. The same goes for all passenger planes and automobiles. We have iridescent accidents, coloured collisions, opalescent crashes. So also for all machine guns and firearms manufactured on the island. Here tyrants, heroes and gangsters are murdered with varicoloured and luminous bullets – crimson, violet, sea green – which leave behind them a tail of sparks and produce a lightning flash on impact with the body which is never to be forgotten. On this island, the guide said to Palinuro, we are not totally amoral: each one of these inventions carries an inherent, simultaneously hidden and obvious, moral. It is not necessary to point out to the visitor to the island that all the fireworks and luminous explosions which we have described echo St John's apocalypse and that most of the mushrooms chosen to beautify atomic conflagrations resemble species like the fly agaric and the destroying angel, which are among the most poisonous. Whatever the case, ours will be the glory, should a final explosion destroy our planet, of offering the heavens a spectacle grandiose not least for its infinite duration: because the explosion of the Earth will not take place once only, but hundreds, thousands, of times: as many as may be witnessed in the future by the inhabitants of those planets lying four light years distant from our solar system, or ten thousand light years, or a hundred thousand, or a billion. It will be the privilege of the inhabitants of other galaxies – or perhaps a few earthlings able to flee the catastophe at the speed of light aboard a space ship – of contemplating, throughout every second of every minute of their lives, the wondrous spectacle of an instant of fire become an eternity.

PALINURO IN PRODUCTSVILLE. And then Palinuro, taking advantage not so much of the brilliance of the final explosion ending the world but more of the noise of the electric implosion of our age, noise having been one of the major manifestations of all ages and there having been developed during those happy days in English (and in the Enchanted Agency), for the purpose of highlighting its importance, the Universal Comic Strip of Noise in its most intimate relationship with advertising, products, consumers and agencies; a plenary session of the agency or, at least, of its geniuses having been assembled to translate the Universal Comic Strip into Spanish; the conclusion having been reached that when a dog barks in English it goes BOW! WOW! and not GUAU! GUAU! as it does in Spanish and, in addition, Palinuro having realized that this was his golden opportunity once and for all to enter the Agency and carve his future as a publicist, our friend gave a mighty leap and landed not only in the middle of the conference-room table (having slightly hurt himself as he landed *wham!*) but also in the middle of Productsville, having won the admiration of his colleagues and countrymen by demonstrating unequivocally that he was capable of being Kodakophile, Fordologue,

213

Kraftivore, Pepsi-Coladdict, Colgatist and Nabiscophage along with the best of them, for which purpose he gave them a long, very long and drawn out account of The Thousand and One Products figuring in his daily and weekly life, regardless of the fact that, right at the start, when the door first went *screech!* and then *slam!*, the manager had attempted to interrupt Palinuro and throw him out of the room and out of the Agency, also once and for all. But it was already very late. Or rather, very early, according to Palinuro, since at that particular moment his *Westclox* alarm clock had just sounded its daily 7 a.m. on the dot alarm (*Triiiing!* went the alarm) and our friend, after throwing aside his *Queen* sheets and his *Sunbeam* electric blanket, yawning (*Auuuuggh!*) and doing lesson number 13 of his *Charles Atlas* course, went to the kitchen, took an *Alka-Seltzer* (*Tssss! Tssss!*) and, burping suitably (*Erp! Erp!*) he opened the door of his *Westinghouse* fridge (*Brrrr! Brrrr!*) took out a tin of *Sunkist* orange juice, opened it with his *Ecko* tin opener (*click!*), drank it (*Gulp! Gulp!*), lit his *Acros* stove (*Flum!*), put water on to boil (*Bubble! Bubble!*), added a spoonful of *Nescafé* (*Splash!*) and a drop (*Plash*) of *Carnation* milk and two lumps of *Tate and Lyle* sugar (*Plop! Plop!*), while in his *General Electric* toaster he toasted two slices of *Wonder* bread which he spread with *Gloria* butter (*Trssss! Trrrrss!*) and *McCormick* marmalade, afterwards eating a large plate of *Kellogg's* rice krispies (*Snap! Crackle! Pop!*) and wiping his mouth on a *Scott* napkin; he went to the bathroom to clean his teeth with *Forhan's* toothpaste (like the extension of the skin of his teeth), his *Dentomatic* toothbrush making a noise something like *Buschjjjt! Brisscht! Brachjt!* as it scrubbed his incisors. It was during those moments, amid the admiring silence that surrounded him, barely disturbed by the Agency's typewriter's (*Tap! Tap! Tap!*) and the civilized ringing of telephones (*Riiiingg! Riiiingg!*) that the executidrunk, jealous of Palinuro, marched to the middle of the table and stated that our friend had stolen his idea for *Forhan's* toothpaste: an advertisement in German which could not be translated since it ran as follows: *Heil Forhans!* and he saluted clicking his heels to produce a spark of ingenuity and stood in front of the cameras of the closed-circuit television with an imaginary toothbrush in one hand and imaginary tube of toothpaste in the other; *Puten der Pasten uver as Bruschen*, he said and *Brusjchen, Brasjchen, Brischjen*, he added, scrubbing his teeth in a furiously imaginary manner, with the result that the manager shouted *Raus!*; the executives: He is a genius!; the manager: He is an imbecile!; the executives: We meant young Palinuro! the manager: So did I! And Palinuro took advantage of the reigning confusion and, miming everything he said, went on to recount that when he stepped barefoot from his *Goodrich* floor into the shower (having first removed his *Arrow* pyjamas and his *Canada* slippers) and lathered himself with his *Lux* soap and rinsed himself with his *Dolphin* sponge (because only at weekends did he treat himself to a sit-down bath with sweet-smelling *Radox* flakes) and, after washing his hair with *Alberto VO 5* shampoo and drying his body with his *Marks and Spencer's* towel and then declaring that he did not buy all these products in order to do all these things, but that he did all these things in order to be able to buy all these products, he sprinkled himself all over with *Old Spice* talcum powder (causing an executive allergic to talcum powder to cough, *Cough! Cough!* went the cough and the executidoctor recommended *Fosfocreosol* For That Cough). Palinuro applied his *Mum Roll On* deodorant (with a little magic ball for reading the future of body odour) and, after a good gargle with *Listerine* (*Gurgle! Gurgle!*), afterwards (and also beforewards) applying his *Sanborn's* eau de cologne and combing his hair with his *Pirámide* comb, after smothering his hair with *Vitalis* hair tonic and dabbing his nose (in the interests of preserving the glow of youth) with *Pond's Cold Cream*, at which the executidrug addict placed a *Flowering Cocaine*-scented handkerchief to his nose, well, Palinuro suddenly realized that he was stark naked and rapidly put on his nylon *Dupont* socks, his *Corfam* shoes, his *Aurrera* trousers, his *Fater* vest, his *Van Heusen* shirt, his *Perfect Knot* tie, his *Aquascutum* raincoat and his *Stetson* hat, immediately doffing the latter to acknowledge the applause (*Clap! Clap! Clap!* went the aplause) of his listeners.

'Don't move!' said the director-artist. 'I am going to draw you.'

'Don't move!' said the copy-writing-writer. 'I am going to write you.'

And the hurrahs and the applause continued. (*Clap, Hurrah, Hurrah, Clap!* went the applause and the hurrahs) but an even greater din greeted PALINURO'S TRIUMPHAL MORNING, produced by none other than his cat, his budgerigar, his plant, his goldfish and his dog when, after putting a few drops of *Jockey Club* lotion on his handkerchief and cleaning his shoes with *Johnson* spray (*Sprish, Sprash!* went the spray), he gave his Australian budgerigar his *Trill* bird food, and his goldfish their *French's* fish food, polished the leaves of his rubber plant with *Bioleaf-Shine*, gave his cat his *Felix* catfood (*Miauuu, Miauuuu!* went the cat) and his fox terrier painted by Frances Barraud his *Pal* dog food (*Bow! Wow!* went the dog in English and then *Guau! Guau!* in Spanish) and left him listening to his RCA His Master's Voice gramophone and after taking his (Palinuro's) daily *Plurivite* tablet and putting a few *Eyemo* drops in his eyes to protect them from the city smog and smearing *Chap Stick* on his lips to protect them from the dust and putting his *Optosun* sunglasses on his nose, he grabbed his *Latex* umbrella and his *Fleetline* briefcase and lit his cigarette manufactured by . . .

'Wonderful, wonderful!' exclaimed a rather bald, rather short and rather stupid executive who hoped one day to reach the 50,000-pesos-a-month bracket. 'Would you actually like a cigarette, my young genius?'

'Ah, *Marlboro*,' said Palinuro.

'*Where the flavour is . . .*' completed the executive.

And while Palinuro (the manager himself having lit Palinuro's cigarette with his *Flaminaire* lighter) consecrated the noses of his patrons with a smoke ring, the very same manager consulted his *Omega* wristwatch and told him not only to cut it short, that it was getting late, but also called his attention to the fact that he had that morning arrived late at the Agency, which was actually a gesture of generosity rather than of reproach, since he thereby made it understood that he considered Palinuro to be one of them.

'Don't move,' the director-artist said to Palinuro, 'I've already got to your stomach.'

'Don't move,' the copy-writing-writer said to Palinuro, 'I've already got to chapter eleven.'

'Move!' roared the manager. 'We want a dynamic image!'

And Palinuro, picking up all these tips and hints (*Tipitipitipihint*) hastened to say that he got about in a *Ford* automobile which was not only in his future but also in his present, his past, his subjunctive and his pluperfect and (which was why he had arrived a little late) after checking his *Goodyear* tyres and his *Champion* spark plugs and his *Mobil Oil* and his *Pemex* petrol and his *Gordon* tool kit and his *Eversure* jack and driven around the city greeting the *Packards, Dodges, Buicks* and *Pontiacs*, which blew their horns (*Honk! Honk!*) and the cyclists on their *Avenger* bicycles and the motor cyclists on their *Honda* motor cycles (*Prrrrrrtttt! Pratatatatarrt!*) and the traffic police who went *Priiiiiip! Priiiiiip!* on their whistles and while with the one ear he listened to all the jingles on his *Motorola* radio and kept one eye on all the advertising posters and billboards which was why he had come late (although, it was his belief, not late to advertising but, rather, late to the Enchanted Agency) having gone up to the seventh floor housing the creative geniuses in the *Otis* lift, unlocking the door of his office with his *Yale* key, sitting down at his *DM Nacional* desk and then going on to do endless things, like reading all the advertisements in the newspaper, drinking some more *Nescafé*, smoking dozens of *Delicado* and *Raleigh* cigarettes (because, in fact, all makes of cigarette were his favourite) and signing the clients' budgets with his *Eversharp* pen, answering his *Erickson* telephone, writing his private letters on *W. H. Smith & Son* writing paper on his *Olivetti* typewriter and sticking one which tore back together again with *Scotch Tape 3M* and finally, at about eleven in the morning, granting himself a refreshing break for the love of a *Coca-Cola,* prelude to a lunch in *Sanborn's* where, after buying *Newsweek*, *Vogue*, *Reader's Digest* and *Better Homes and Gardens*, he drank an aperitif of *White Horse* whisky with a splash of the sparkling bubbles of a *Canada Dry* and told the waiter to defrost a hamburger and a *Findus* salad and ordered his *Maggie* chicken consommé and after putting a

216

pinch of *Cisne* salt in his soup and *Kraft* dressing on his salad and, on his hamburger, not only *Colman's* mustard but also a little . . .

But here Palinuro was interrupted by five plump and ruddy bell-boys dressed in soutine-red-satin uniforms who held hands and sang:

> 'The five young tomatoes
> Had no reason to suppose
> That very soon a man would come
> To put an end to all their fun
> But they didn't try to run away
> They danced and sang hip hip hurray
> We are honoured and it's made our day
> To die in the cause of Del Fuerte purée.'

After which our friend said:

'That's exactly what I was leading up to: I baptized my hamburger with a little *Del Fuerte* tomato ketchup.'

This time, the applause was overwhelming (*Clap-Clap-Clap!* went the overwhelming applause).

And he would drink a *Heineken* beer with his hamburger, order a *Royal* flan, drink a *Maxwell* coffee to which he would add a few drops of *Sucaryl*, smoke a *Tampa* cigar, he would buy some *Adam's* chewing gum, ask for the bill, check the total with the aid of his *Sinclair* pocket calculator and pay either with travellers' cheques with which he was in the habit of making fifty-dollar paper aeroplanes to give to the *Pan Am* (his super favourite airline) air hostesses with a love message or else he would pay with a *First National City Bank* cheque or with his *Sanborn's* credit card, that is if he could find it among his enormously long accordion of *Diners Club–American Express–Bancomer–Access–Harrods–Bananex–Hertz–Neiman Marcus* credit cards because it should of course be explained that bank notes of the common and garden variety, like those of the one-peso denomination bearing the Statue of Independence printed by the *American Bank Note Company*, were used by our friend Palinuro only for his minor expenses, such as *Clasico* matches and *LifeSaver* pastilles.

This long journey through Productsville continued when, returning to his office, after walking through the Zona Rosa and, more specifically, through the Genova Passage to be greeted by all his colleagues in the advertising business who went to the Passage, etc. to be greeted by all their colleagues in the advertising business who went to the Passage, he dictated letters on his *Agovox* dictaphone, made notes in the margin of his documents with his *Eagle* pencil and took copies on his *Xerox* photocopier and so forth, with the result that by eight o'clock at night, utterly exhausted, there was nothing left for him to do but to take a *Bufferin* for his headache and leave the office (with all the rest of his spirit-ache) and take himself off to the University Club to drink a dry Martini made with *Beefeater* gin, *Noilly Prat* vermouth and a *Clemente Jacques* olive . . .

'That's the best idea of the afternoon!' exclaimed the executidrunk, sticking his nose out from under his tongue.

'Yes, I must admit that it is an excellent idea,' admitted the manager, cracking his knuckle joints (*Crack! Crack!* went his joints) and ordered that the magic ingredients be brought forth.

'Now you can relax,' the director-artist told Palinuro, 'I've just finished drawing your big toe.'

'Now you can relax,' the copy-writing-writer told Palinuro, 'I've just written "THE END".'

The copy-writing-writer looked at the drawing:

'What an excellent illustration for my book!' he said.

The director-artist read the book:

'What an excellent book for my illustration!' he said.

Everybody huddled together like a team of American football players to admire the masterpiece.

Brilliant! Brilliant! What are you going to call it?

> EVERYTHING YOU ALWAYS WANTED
> TO KNOW
> ABOUT
> PALINURO
>
> (BUT WERE AFRAID TO ASK . . .)

And all those who had wanted to know all about Palinuro but had never dared to ask turned to stare and point at him with their phallic fingers, with their smiles, with their phallic noses and teeth.

And Palinuro, blushing scarlet as a *Del Fuerte* tomato with shame, had to confess that he used *Boot's* hot water bottles when he had cold feet, that Estefania used tubes of *Lady Jane* dye on her hair; that he wiped himself with *Waldorf* toilet paper; that Estefania used *Tampax* for her periods; that he (ssh! he said, showing them the real thing) used *Durex* condoms (which was nothing other than the extension of his tenderest skin) for sexual intercourse with Estefania; that she in turn used *Ortho-Gynol* contraceptive gel; that he dyed his grey hairs with *Miss Clairol*; that Estefania used *Platex* girdles for her spare tyres; that he used *Sloan* ointment for rheumatism; that Estefania shaved her legs with a *Lady Remington* shaver; that he used *Solasil* ointment for his piles; that Estefania used *Cosmea* vaginal spray and, finally, that they both used *In Step* deodorant for their feet, *Dr Scholl* plasters for their bunions and *Head and Shoulders* for dandruff and *Squibb* penicillin for genital catarrh and

Ramses jelly to lubricate vaginal relations and *Acco* margarine for their anal relations but not butter, no way! Because, said the clown Palinurol, Estefanol and I an' all, know all about cholesterol.

And then into the conference room of the Enchanted Agency – which was as large as a family crypt but with air vents from which rats poked their honeyed whiskers and with no view over the street but with a view over the whole world as testified by *Thomas Cook* posters hanging on the walls with which the travelling-executive made paper boats and aeroplanes which travelled from one side to the other of the room which contained an oval table in the centre of which Merlin daily placed a box of disposable *Kleenex* handkerchiefs and pulled an advertising campaign out of his right sleeve and from his star-spangled, pointed hat produced *Ritz* cracker crumbs – came The-Gin-Queen-Estefania followed by a black bear which warmed the nape of her neck with its honeybee breath and by her pages, each of which carried a gift of a different spice: Angelica Root from Saxony, Orange from Valencia, Cinnamon from Ceylon and Juniper from the Alps and next entered Lanzarote of La Mancha who had recently had several mishaps with *Bimbo* bread windmills but who had the grace occasionally to weep in an Ugly American mood. And when all were finally gathered, executives, pages, the Gin-Queen, the court bards, the painters and the scribes, heralds sounded their trumpets round as gold-plated spittoons of tin and everybody started drinking their first dry Martini, their second dry Martini, their third dry Martini, and so on to their fourteenth and more (never the thirteenth, because they were superstitious) and, consumed with envy, after digesting the lesson taught by Palinuro, the conversation ran as follows:

'What are you doing tonight?'

'I'm going to watch Perry Mason on my *Admiral* television which is the extension of my nervous system.'

'Tomorrow I am thinking of doing a spell under my *Philips* sun lamp and going in the afternoon to my dance class at the *Arthur Murray* school!'

'I'm going on a trip with my *Aries* suitcases.'

'I'm thinking of having a cup of *Nestlé's* chocolate for breakfast and of signing all the *Hallmark* Christmas, Birthday, Get Well and Etcetera cards that I have to send to my friends and relations including Hill and Knowlton, Richard Avedon and George Gallup,' said the public relations executive.

'I'm going to play tennis with my *Yamaha* rackets and afterwards I'm going to play golf with my *Campbell* golf clubs,' said the golfer-tennis-player-executive.

'I'm going to hunt rabbits with my *Winchester* rifle,' said the huntsman-executive.

And, while the television went *Click!*, and the sun lamp went *Purrr!*, the golf clubs went *Crack!* and the gun went *Bang!*, the home-loving executive said that he would cut the hedges of his window-box with his *Wilkinson* hedge cutter, repaper his bedroom with *Vymura* wallpaper, fix his doors with his *Black & Decker* and paint the stairs with his *Fleetwood* brushes soaked in his *Marlux* paint and the executive-explorer, not wanting to be left out, said that he would go trout fishing in the country with his *Mordex* fishing rods while he listened to his portable *Sony* radio and the cultured-executive, not wanting to be left out, assured everybody that he would spend his weekend studying his *Berlitz* correspondence language course while he listened to the latest offerings of the *Columbia* record club on his *Garrard* record player with his *Wharfedale* speakers and the licentious-executive, not wanting to be left out, said that from the roof garden of his penthouse he would (with his *Optomax* binoculars) watch the girls sunbathing in their *Jansen* bikinis, smothering themselves in *Coppertone* suntan lotion and take slide pictures of them with his *Yashica* camera loaded with *Kodachrome* film which he would afterwards show to his friends on his *Agfa* projector and Estefania, determined to hold her own, stated that she would spend her time doing housework such as washing dishes with *Fairy Liquid*, slicing ham with her *Krups* meat slicer, scrubbing the bath with *Ajax*, washing clothes in her *Hotpoint* washing machine with *Persil* washing powder and drying it in her *Bendix* dryer and ironing it with her *Sunbeam* iron after sprinkling it with her *Topps* starch, spraying her house with her *Goddards* air freshener, disinfecting her *Montgomery Ward* toilet with her *Domestos* disinfectant and cleaning her *Mohawk* carpet with her *Electrolux* vacuum cleaner and then the manager of the Enchanted Agency, determined to beat everyone at their own game, declared that on Saturday and Sunday he would spend his time visiting the Universal Exhibition of the Home, Industry, Agriculture and Science, going on to list a desperate and implacable string of all the products and brands that he was going to look at during the weekend: a vast range, from *Rosedale* organs to *Ford* tractors by way of all kinds of computers, ticket punchers, freezers, astronaut suits, feed containers for chickens, cutlery, synthetic motorways, printing presses, atomic bomb shelters and dental equipment.

And while all around things went *Trish-trash! Flit-Flat! Click-Clack!* and *Krups-Kraps!*, everybody thought that Palinuro had nothing to say and nothing better to do, either during the weekend or at that very moment, than look stupid. But they were wrong, Palinuro told them, and explained that he was above all a dreamer and that, starting right away on Friday night, as soon as he got back to his house of *Portland Anahuac* cement with *Anaconda Nacional* copper pipes, after covering himself with his

220

Slumberdown blanket and laying his head on his *Dunlop* pillow he would start to dream. First, he would open the horn door and day-dream of the future that was not as distant as one might think, when he would not only have the pleasure of putting his false teeth to soak at night in a glass of *Sterident* but perhaps the great honour of numbering among his organs at least one artificial artery and a valve of *Silastic* made by the *Minnesota Manufacturing Company* and perhaps, why not? there awaited him the immense privilege of having a heart whose beats depended on an atomic *Eveready* transistor which would delay the day on which he could finally rest in a *Gayosso* coffin covered with *Interflora* garlands and wreaths. Then, he told them, he would dream half-asleep and half-awake that he lived in a world . . . the world of the future, gentlemen! where his yawns would have a registered trade mark, where his thoughts would be sold in luxury packaging, his urine in stainless steel tins, his dreams in soluble tablets and his verses in perfumed ointments . . . the world of the future, gentlemen! where there would be artists responsible for designing the logo for his sneezes, writers who would create the slogan of his tears and executives who would carry out the market research of his sighs; a world, he told them, where his smiles would go on sale at two for the price of one; where it would be possible to hire his illnesses, buy his ambitions today and pay tomorrow, offer one of his hopes free with the purchase of each disappointment and give away green stamps with each jar of his multiple varieties of shit: Evaporated Shit, gentlemen, Frozen Shit, Instant Shit Powder! Condensed Shit, Disposable Shit and washable Plastic Shit! And afterwards, he told them . . . ah, afterwards, when I turn out my *Westinghouse* bulb, I will open the ivory door and dream in sleep . . . that I am Cleopatra in my *Maidenform* bra!

And, while the executives went *Smash, Screech, Clap, Smiff, Slurp, Knock, Crack, Pum, Tap, Woo, Ehem, Erp, Cough* and *Achoo!*, Palinuro's vomit went *Splash, Gurgle, Gulp, Slurp* and *Splat!* as, there in the middle of the Enchanted Agency conference room, he spewed up all the *Oso Negro* gin that he had drunk and vomited the *Carnation* milk that Mamma Clementina had given him as a child and threw up the *Campbell's* soups that Estefania had heated for him and vomited vomigurgle and vomigulp and vomislurp and vomisplash.

PALINURO THE PUBLICIST was thus ordained once and for all. What would have become of him if he had never landed in Productsville, what would have become of him and of Estefania, what would have become of their love and of their living if he had never given up his medical studies to return to them after his long journey through the Agencies, pertains to the antepenultimate Island he visited:

THE ISLAND OF WHAT MIGHT HAVE BEEN, also called the Island of Uchronia, where the most imaginative writers and historians, the guide told him, spend their time creating an infinite number of versions of what the history of a country or the history of the world might have been if Christopher Columbus had not discovered America, for example, or if Marat had not been murdered in his bath, if Julius Caesar had died instead in the Gallic provinces. This is the island of specific truths which, as Suarez states, are known only to God, to that same God who, as St Peter Damian states, could well, if he so wished, cause the world never to have existed. And, on the Island of Uchronia, Palinuro found Delisle de Sales writing *Ma République*, and Louis Geoffroy writing *Napoleon and the Conquest of the World* and Louis Millanvoy writing *The Second Life of Napoleon* and he came across the manuscript by Roger Caillois in which it is told how Christianity would never have existed if Pontius Pilate had condemned Barabbas and protected Christ and he saw Kevin Brownlow making the film about the occupation of England by the Nazis. On this island, Palinuro also consulted the history of the United States written by Winston Churchill which relates what would have happened if General Lee had not lost the battle of Gettysburg and there, finally, he listened to all the symphonies that Mozart would have composed if he had not died at thirty-six years of age and which Maître Christophorus took it upon himself to compose instead. But our task is endless, continued the guide, because what happens is that every one of the books relating what would have happened if Marco Polo had not brought gunpowder to the West or if Hannibal had not crossed the Alps or less obvious and less well-known facts: what would have happened, for example, if Don John of Austria had married Mary Queen of Scots or if the Emperor Frederick had not had cancer or if Byron had been King of Greece, every one of these books, as he had been saying, must of necessity relate a whole series of historical, hypothetical, logical and, at the same time, imaginary facts which are then examined by others of our writers who, in turn, develop histories of what might have happened if such hypothetical facts had not occurred although, in such cases, they accept the former, in other words, those which served as the point of departure for the first history, because otherwise they would have to write the history of what would have happened if Hannibal had crossed the Alps, as in fact he did. But these narratives invalidate each other, since there are experts who have, for example, written what would have happened if Lincoln or Christ had not been born. And if Lincoln or Christ had not been born, Winston Churchill would not have written what would have happened if General Lee had not lost the battle of Gettysburg and Caillois would not have written what would have happened if Pontius

222

Pilate had saved Christ's life. Others, however, with a greater sense of self-criticism and of historical processes, know that it is not possible to write a history of what would have happened if Lincoln had not been born without first demonstrating the reasons why he might not have been born, which may also be infinite, including, for example, that his parents had never lived, that his grandparents were sterile or that his great-grandparents had been drowned off the coast of New England. And since, therefore, they would not have been his parents, grandparents or great-grandparents, the whole question becomes highly complicated, leading us to consider the need to write the history of what would have been if the world had never existed. But, since this produced an end-result of a book with blank pages, we thought it might be preferable to write the history of all that might *not* have been: had Hannibal not crossed the Alps; had Robespierre not been wounded by Merda; had Keitel, chief of the armed forces high command, not signed the surrender of Germany; had Palinuro not travelled to the Advertising Agency and other Imaginary Islands. But there is more to the Island of What Might Have Been. It is the privilege of the poet, described by Keats as chameleonic *par excellence* and who, like Beschen, the Being created by Brahma, is bird and wind and ocean, to transform everything into everything: a city into an eagle, said Thesaurus, a man into a lion. What is the ultimate enigma? as Marsilio Ficino asked himself: the ability to transform one thing into another. As in Rotrou's *Les Sosies,* where everything is everything. As in the legend of Crimissus and of Icelos. As also in Hardy's Alphaeus where people turn into rocks, fountains, trees, living dead and dead living. As in Gracian's *El Criticón* in which the monsters of the carriage drawn by his heroes ceaselessly change in height, colour, sex and being. So also in the forest of Arden, where tongues were found in trees, books in brooks, sermons in stones. So also on this island, the most exposed part of which is another island in itself and only minstrels and bards have been able to narrate its chronicle. In former days, however, before the sand-bar linking it with the main island was covered by water and detritus, it was a tongue of land stretching three miles, or a hundred, into the sea. Hence, it has come to be called the Island of the Tongue of Proteus. Although perhaps it does not lie in the sea, but rather on a heath. Or perhaps it is not an island, nor a tongue of land, nor the haunt of flocks of birds, nor a hope. Perhaps, at times, it is not even called the Island of the Tongue of Proteus and is instead called Round About Island, Pendulum Island or Mill Island. The fact of the matter is that, to travel to this island, you have first to head towards the north or towards the south-east or spin the Compass Rose and follow the direction in which it points when it comes to rest or take the opposite direction and be prepared for a journey of ten days or of a thousand years, for the simple reason that the island might have been close by, there beyond the thronging mountains and have been a fortress, but it might, alternatively, have been very far off, on the other side, many adventures beyond the Pillars of Hercules and have been a star. The island is inhabited by foxes, geese, dogs and other fantastic animals, because the island might well have been a world where these and other animals were invented by fable. But the island knows full well that other animals or beings might have been destined to inhabit it and, depending on the day of arrival on the island, the traveller may find the monerontes and sclassaberocchias imagined by Alessandri or, if he is lucky enough to arrive on the day when the island could have been Bradbury's living planet which changes in relation to the beings which visit it, the fortunate traveller will be able, by the power of thought, to change the dimensions, virtues, history and future of the island. However, the island knows that it might well never have been visited by any traveller and then, in its solitude, it wallows in bitterness and undreamed reflections, inhabited by breezes, anchors, altars, suburbs crumbling in the claws of the forests. The island also knows that it might never have been anything, ever, and then it does not exist and will never exist. But, since it could have been all things for all eternity, the traveller may not need to leave his house, or even himself, to visit it: the island is his life and his body, his eyes and his triumphs, his age and his lies. It is also the end of the world, the wings of a beetle, a broom in the corner, the bride and the bachelors, Andromeda and Byzantium. The island might, equally, have been a product of Borges' imagination. The whole island might have been a warning to travellers who, in their search for it, plunge into the unknown, ignorant of the dangers, the magic rings, the exhalations and omissions of memory that they will encounter. Because the island might also have been one great omission of memory: by its creator who omitted to remember to create it and by all those who omitted to remember to discover it, subjugate it and relate its history. There are nights, when the moon is lame, that pirates who know how to catch its smell on the wind, land on the Island of the Tongue of Proteus and bury their treasure there. But as soon as they row away from the island in their dinghies, the earth and the lids of the treasure chests open and from them escape, yet again, the superstitions, the draperies, the cyclops of jelly, the potato peelers and any other idea or thing or panic that might have a name, a word or a sign in any language of the galaxy, because the island might also have been pure language. Ultimately (or penultimately), Palinuro visited

UNIVERSALS ISLAND which is everywhere and nowhere because it is, effectively, island as universal concept inhabited by all other universal concepts: the universal horse, the universal publicist, the universal triangle, table, river, Palinuro. Since, therefore, this island is all islands and none, so all other islands, to a greater or lesser extent, share its universal qualities

224

and defects: its boldness and its shyness, its beauty and its ugliness, its wealth and its poverty, its malice and its naïveté, its sanity and its madness. And, first and foremost, all islands share in its redundancy.

AND THUS IT WAS THAT OUR HERO PALINURO, after a long and heavy sleep, finally reached the end of his journey through the Advertising Agencies and other Imaginary Islands, steeped in tempestuous Coca-Colas and mustards immemorial, in refluent psycho-dramas and slices of life, covered in crusts of ketchup, after sleeping with pale, blonde mayonnaises and vanquishing the warrior Ajax. And so our hero returned to his room in Holy Sunday Square, to his friends and to the dancing skeletons of the School of Medicine. Our friend Palinuro who did not, like Alexander the Great, discover the Island inhabited by the survivors of the Trojan War nor travel to the heavens in a machine driven by griffins nor see the land where tree roots are covered in lion and panther skins. He did not see, like Lucian, the selenites whose snot is honey and who sweat milk, nor did he travel, like him, to Lanternland lying between the Hyades and the Pleiades, and inhabited by the lanterns of all nations. Our hero Palinuro who did not, like the heroes of *Persiles*, travel to Snow Island, Fire Island and Barbaric Island nor, like Maelduin, visit the Island of the fountain which is of milk on Saturdays and of wine and beer on holidays. And he did not travel, like Psalmanazar, to the fabulous island of Formosa, nor did he descend, like Dante, though the seven circles of hell nor ascend, like him, by way of the seven circles of purgatory. Our brother Palinuro, who did not behold the wondrous land of supreme anarchy, nor Pantopantarchy, where music comes in bottles and operettas fit in a litre and songs in a glass and which was described by Count Didier de Chousy, nor did he see the wonders which the Lame Devil showed to Don Cleofas when they looked down into the roofless houses of Madrid, nor did he visit the street of mirrors and the second-hand-surnames shop. Our friend Palinuro, who did not look upon the world described by Fourier and his disciples who foresaw the transformation of the ocean into a bowl of lemonade and the advent of anti-lions, nor travel to the world of two-dimensional inhabitants described by Edwin Abbott. Who never visited, like the poet Aristeas of Proconnesus in the company of Apollo, the mythical land of the Hyperboreans. Nor shared with Baron Münchhausen the sight of the balloon which raised the College of Physicians in London into the air, nor saw the crabs and mussels which grow on trees nor the stag from whose head a cherry tree sprouted nor the horses shod with human skulls. Our friend, hero, brother and pal Palinuro who did not, like Gulliver, visit the Flying Island; the Island of books made of sugar; the land of mathematicians who talk in rhombuses, ellipses and parallelograms; the Island of Spiders which weave multi-coloured webs; the Island of

Magicians who conjure up the spirits of the dead; nor did he, like Pantagruel, visit Macreons Island inhabited by devils and heroes; Savage Island populated by chitterlings; Sneak's Island inhabited by Mardi Gras or the Sea of Frozen Words. He was a little less tired, fed up and sad than when he set out on his journey, but he certainly grew up and returned a little older, indeed, but a little wiser because, although his trip through the Enchanted Agencies and other Imaginary Islands only lasted exactly the same number of days as languages used by Panurge to address Pantagruel, namely fourteen, to Palinuro it seemed that he had spent as many years travelling through the Islands as languages heard by Pantagruel on the lips of Panurge, likewise fourteen, which is the number symbolizing eternity. Palinuro did not, at that time, know that there was still one Island left for him to visit: the largest and most desolate of all. But now that he recalls those days, those afternoons in the Agency, and vaguely feels that all will not have been in vain, he understands that, give or take a few words, give or take a few hours, Alka-Seltzers and plastic Hollywood dinner services, the experience will always be at the back of his mind like a barely beige resentment and his heart is no longer tortured by soul-searching of those depths.

12

Cousin Walter's erudition and
Tristram Shandy's apples

Cousin Walter's erudition was actually just so much ballast. Knowing that
the human eye has seven million cone cells did not appear to help him to see
better, because Cousin Walter always was a touch short-sighted. Neither,
apparently, did it help him much to know that blushing is caused by the
dilation of the peripheral facial vessels, because Walter blushed uncontrollably at the least provocation. Nor, in all truth, can it be said that
the knowledge that our nervous system consists of ten thousand million
neurons and a hundred thousand million glia cells helps anybody to be
happier in life and, if the truth be told, such scraps of information didn't
even add to Cousin Walter's actual intelligence.

Because, considered Palinuro, if you are even half-way intelligent, you
don't hurt the people you love when you are trying to do the opposite, like
the time Walter tried to console Estefania by saying that she shouldn't
worry about the experiments done on animals because they are not in fact
the innocent creatures they appear to be. And he went on to talk of Father
Bougeant's theories and of the many individuals who had mentioned the
aura corrumpens emitted by animals and the endless list of swallows, dogs,
pigs, geese and horses which through history have been judged to be
criminals and their bones and feathers cast into prison or their lives ended
by fire or the noose. There must be something in it, he added, if Lombroso
maintained that many animals are *deliquenti nati*, and Mephistopheles
appeared to Faust as the lord of rats, mice, flies and dogs . . . '*Der Herr der
Ratten, und der Mäuse, der Fliegen, Frösche*'. Estefania was reduced to
tears and Uncle Esteban had to tell yet again the stories of the St Bernard
dogs who carry cognac to helpless explorers buried in snow up to their
waists.

Or those other times – oh so frequent – when, ten minutes after
declaring his affection to Aunt Luisa and Grandmother Altagracia, Walter
irritated them by trying to show that, although these two pious ladies
spent their lives saying rosaries and prayers and not a day of the Lord went
by that they did not go to church and beat their breasts, he knew more
about religion (and apologetics) than the two of them would ever know
between them and this despite the fact that he was a non-believer: not an

atheist, he assured them, since he believed in a desiring and desired God who was beyond the comprehension of the common man and, for this very reason, he did not share Voltaire's opinion that if God did not exist it would be necessary to invent him. Walter, of course, never dared to speak to them of the heterodox gospels (such as David Friedrich Strauss's) which attributed Mary's (or Miriam's) pregnancy to a young man named Panthera. He never mentioned the theories (De Quincey's, for example) concerning Judas Iscariot's role which, if true, made him perhaps not the major victim of Christianity, but certainly the first and most indispensable. And he never quoted Rousseau who said that when Christ took communion, he had to hold his whole body in his hands and put his head in his mouth. Gymnastics of this type, of an intellectual rather than physical nature, would have been altogether too much for Grandmother Altagracia and Aunt Luisa. They could accept that the Three Kings were buried in Cologne Cathedral – as Walter maintained – while, at the same time, being alive and well in the Orion constellation – as they themselves believed – because this did not clash with the idea that all the dead are simultaneously three feet below ground and deep down in hell or way up in heaven. The apocryphal books of the Old and New Testament such as *Bel and the Dragon* and *The Saviour's Revenge*, the latitudinarian theories that any religion serves to save souls, the discovery that manna is merely a type of saccharine secreted by an insect and absorbed by the dew on the tamarind trees of the Sinai and which floats in the wind when dry, the similarity between the Our Father and the Chaldean Kodish, the possible parallels and differences between the Bible and the Shasta, the Zend-Avesta, the Koran and the Sibylline Books or other similarities between the mysteries of the mass and pagan rights and solar legends were all subjects that Walter could discuss at table, provided he trod warily and addressed himself to Uncle Esteban or Papa Eduardo or Grandfather Francisco, because the women didn't listen, or pretended not to. Although, sometimes, their indignation was such that they could not help objecting. 'That is completely ridiculous,' exclaimed Grandmother Altagracia. 'No, indeed Grandmother,' insisted Walter, 'the fact is that, according to calculations by experts, Christ was in fact born in the year 4 BC which means merely that chronology errs and we should have started our era four years earlier . . .' 'That's impossible,' insisted Grandmother, 'Christ could not have been born four years before his birth.' And Cousin Walter, with all the cunning and command that he could muster in such circumstances, stood up, wiped his mouth on his napkin and said: 'For Christ, everything is possible. Christ performed miracles, didn't he?' And, well, only once that Palinuro could recall did Grandmother Altagracia silence Walter, one Holy Friday when again everybody was gathered in the dining room very seriously discussing the death of Our Lord and, predictably, Walter had

228

suddenly exclaimed, with his mouth full: 'Speaking of which, I read in a book that Christ, according to a certain Dr Stroud, died of heart failure which caused blood to flood into the pericardium, which is borne out by the fact that, when Longinus stuck a spear into his side, spongy clots flowed from the wound, in other words, a mixture of *crassitudo* and *serum*.' Grandmother Altagracia, horrified, said: 'Our Lord could not die of what men die of, because he was the Son of God.' 'But he had to die of something if he was of flesh and blood,' argued Walter. 'If it wasn't of a heart failure, then what did he die of?' Grandmother needed only two seconds to reply: 'Of a miracle,' she said. 'His death was the last miracle he performed.'

On another occasion, Cousin Walter was left looking stupider than he had ever looked in his life. He was in the habit of taking advantage of the least opportunity to lead conversation towards the subject of his most recent reading and so, during a dinner following the christening of Aunt Enriqueta's daughter, Walter said, in reference to a coin which Uncle Felipe had flipped into the air for the children to fight over, that a fifty-cent coin falling through the air builds up a million ergs of energy and that, incidentally, Leibniz had given the name *vis viva* to the impact of objects. So, when somebody falls, he added rocking back in his chair, it no doubt produces a *vis viva*. And then – if he had done it on purpose it couldn't have been better timed – he stuck his thumbs into the breast pocket of his patchwork waistcoat, breathed deep in self-satisfaction and . . . tumbled backwards to the floor, chair and all.

Walter refused to calculate how many millions of ergs he had produced or how many microwatts had been generated by everybody's laughter. He changed the subject and abruptly started speaking, with the intention of capturing Uncle Esteban's attention, about Philippe Auguste's physician Gilles de Corbeil, who had written four works in Latin verse, one of which was entirely on the subject of urine. Grandmother said that this was not a suitable topic of after-dinner conversation, Estefania said that she was the one who was peeing, with laughter, and everybody got up from the table, leaving Cousin Walter on his own. Well, not everybody, because Uncle Esteban got the bright idea of devoting an issue of his *History of Medicine* magazine to the Urologists Congress which was to take place in a month's time and Walter suggested that he should illustrate the cover with Gerard Dou's picture *La Femme Hydropique* in which the patient is accompanied by a physician examining a glass flask of urine which he is holding up against the light and he also recommended that Uncle Esteban not neglect to mention the paragraph in *Le Roman de Renart* where the fox examines the lion's urine.

Even Grandmother's earlier retort had not caused as much hilarity as the fall in the dining room which was enjoyed not only by aunts and uncles and

229

other relations but also by Grandfather Francisco's friends (since Walter never lost an opportunity to humiliate them with his learning) and the general with the glass eye expanded the theme, saying that Cousin Walter had not only produced a *vis viva* but had also contrived to demonstrate his comic *vis*. And he went on to clarify that in West Point Academy and also, more importantly, in the school of life, he had learned certain phrases in Latin: *Dulce et decorum est pro patria mori,* he stated, fixing everyone with a famous eye. But that did not signify, by any means, that the general and Grandfather's other friends were educated. In fact Grandfather and don Prospero were the only ones who had ever taken any interest in things like philosophy, art or jazz and, on certain afternoons, they enticed their friends with their partiality to cognac and blue cheese and attempted to instil some culture into them. It was a hopeless task. A good example was that of ex-congressman Fournier who, though he loved order, progress and altruism, none the less turned stone deaf the minute Auguste Comte started holding forth on his famous Law of Three States. Nietzsche, who was wont to appear hugging a horse's head, was not well looked upon. Neither was Nerval, who was often to be seen strolling along Vielle Lanterne Street in Paris. Brueghel and his two sons – Hell Brueghel and Velvet Brueghel – were better received on account of the magic of their names. On the other hand, when Grandfather talked about Mexico, when he related that the clapper of the Dolores bell (called St Joseph's cowbell) was a hand grenade, his friends gave him a round of applause. 'Well I never,' said Grandmother Altagracia. 'Next December 15, when we repeat the independence chant, there might be an explosion!' 'There will be, there will be,' said Grandfather mysteriously, as he cut himself a chunk of Danish Blue, adding: 'Mmmm . . . something is rotten in the state of Denmark.' And that is how Saturday afternoons were spent by Grandfather Francisco and his friends; they seemed to complement each other in that the one who hadn't occupied a green seat in Congress had ridden side by side with General Obregon and the one who hadn't been venerable master of a lodge of the Rite of York was an avid encyclopaedia reader and also, of course, because Grandfather saw perfectly well with his left eye which was the one that the general with the glass eye was missing and the general heard perfectly with his right ear which was the one in which ex-congressman Fournier was deaf and ex-congressman Fournier had a whole and sound left arm which was the one which the lottery ticket vendor was missing and the ticket vendor could laugh or assume a serious expression with the right half of his face which in don Prospero's case was the paralysed half and don Prospero, finally, walked perfectly well with his right leg which was the one which was perfectly useless to Grandfather Francisco. Similarly, considerable information was stored in the collective subconscious of Grandfather and his friends, thus enabling them to excuse

Walter for knowing more than ignoramuses who, for example, had never heard of Paderewski who was not only a great pianist but had also been president of Poland, and had never had the opportunity to witness a discussion on Dvorak's fifth symphony, known as that of the New World. That Walter, in short, should know more than illiterates who were completely unaware of the existence and history of Richelieu, otherwise known as the Eminence Grise, or more even than those who had no idea that Goebbels spoke the famous words: 'When I hear the word culture I take out my revolver'; all this was praiseworthy because these were things that they themselves knew. In other words, something that don Prospero didn't know was known by Grandfather or the general or Uncle Esteban and therefore they could say that, between them, they knew it. But what was unforgivable, what they could not tolerate, when they ventured to speak of this or that or the other, were interjections from Walter to the effect that Paderewski had not been president of Poland but prime minister, that Dvorak's fifth symphony was actually his ninth, that the real author of the phrase on culture and the revolver was not in fact Goebbels – nor Goering, as the general maintained with a distant eye – but the expressionist Hanns Johst, Head of the Imperial Chamber of Writers, and that, finally, the sobriquet Eminence Grise had not been given to Cardinal Richelieu but to his assistant, Father Joseph of Paris, whose real name was François Leclerc du Tremblay.

It was nobody's fault but their own. They had started, when Walter was ten years old, by enticing him with sweets to join the band of cronies for a few minutes and amuse them with his precocity. But, like the doctors in the temple, their amusement was shortlived. By the time he had grown into a young man with the beginning of a beard, close on six feet tall, and neither the general nor Grandfather could look down at him from the lofty heights of their three decades of wisdom and he had already lived in London for a time and had stopped asking for sweets and begun accepting cigars and glasses of cognac, Walter had become a pain. The very least of it was when he started talking about things that nobody understood and about people who, as far as Grandfather's friends were concerned, had never existed and never would: Pudovkin's or Fritz Lang's films, Dilthey's hermeneutics, the works of Saussure or Lukasiewicz, Naum Gabo's sculptures or Kokoschka's paintings, the phlogiston theory or the De Quolibet disputations, Trakl's poetry or Guillaume Dufay's music: that and Bacon's Idola Fori, the so-called Sturm und Drang period, Caird's book on Hegel, the Universal Palingenesis and the difference between the poet Samuel Taylor Coleridge and the black musician Samuel Coleridge Taylor, was all double Dutch to them. And Walter was not so stupid as to fail to realize that nobody was interested (with the possible exception of don Prospero if and when the subject happened to coincide with the letter

231

of the encyclopaedia that he was reading at the time) in whether he had personally met Darii and Ferio, that he had read Sheridan Le Fanu and all the stories of vampires in Illyria or that he knew that in Egyptian mythology Buto was the designation of infinite chaos, that the German word *Weltanschauung* referred to a total conception of the world or that Madame Sosotris's clients feared the future.

And neither were any of Grandfather's friends interested in Walter's medical knowledge, but for a very few exceptions – namely, facts, with vaguely obscene connotations. Ex-congressman Fournier was surprised at the connection between the words orchid and orchitis meaning inflammation of the testicles and the general looked at Walter with an incredulous eye when he heard him talking about the links existing between the word penicillin – a wonderful new drug, he assured them – and the word penis or male member. I have always liked certain things about medicine, the general claimed. I hate to disappoint you (said Walter) but this has nothing to do with medicine; it is etymology pure and simple.

Another of Walter's obsessions was to refer to what he termed the antecedents proving that Ecclesiastes was quite right in stating that there is nothing new under the sun. Nobody paid any attention to him when he stated that the legend of Raymond Lully had a precedent in the story of Titus who was granted immortality but forgot to ask for eternal youth, nor when he said that St Augustine's *Si fallor sum* anticipated Descartes and that, without a doubt, the painter Luca Cambiaso was the father of cubism and Lyell the father of the theory of evolution, nor when he expressed the opinion that Bioy Casares must have read León Daudet's *Les Bacchantes* before writing the *La Invención de Morel* and that Oscar Wilde must have – or should have – been familiar (before writing *Lord Arthur Savile's Crime*) with the legend of Phrasius, the Cypriot seer who told King Busiris that he would have good harvests if a foreigner was sacrificed each year and he, the seer, was the first to be sacrificed.

On a particular afternoon when Grandfather quoted a verse in which the Mexican poet Enrique González Martínez orders that the neck of the swan of misleading plumage be wrung (referring, of course, to the Nicaraguan poet Rubén Darío), Walter pointed out that the concept was not the least original since Verlaine had already spoken of the desirability of wringing the neck of eloquence. And, when the general stated that the first aerial bombardment in history had been carried out by a Mexican military man (General Pesqueira, in Sinaloa, if I remember correctly, said the general), Walter could not resist contradicting that, according to his information, the Austrians had already bombed Venice in 1840 with unmanned Montgolfier balloons. The last straw was when Grandfather commented on the bad luck suffered by General Bernardo Reyes who, shortly after escaping from prison at the head of a band of rebels, no sooner entered the central Zocalo Square in Mexico City than he was killed by a bullet in the forehead; Walter said that even worse luck was that of Portheus, the first Greek to descend from the Trojan horse, who fell out head first and killed himself.

But there was a time when Walter's knowledge saved him from a second fall, as serious as the Greek's; they were discussing the Revolution when Uncle Austin stuck his oar in and accused Pancho Villa of being a savage for digging up the body of the English journalist Benton and trying, shooting and burying him all over again, which caused (as everybody well knew) a more-than-justified international rumpus. Walter, after blowing a smoke ring, pointed out that savagery of this nature was not the exclusive preserve of Mexicans and recalled the case of Pope Urban III who was already dead and buried when he was declared a Simonist and they consequently disinterred him, chopped off his right hand and threw him into the Tiber. And Walter went on to add that not only the Aztecs practised human sacrifice but also the Khonds, a Dravidian tribe of Bengal, to say nothing of the Holy Inquisition.

All, save Uncle Austin, forgave him his previous interjections (ex-pectorated learning, as the general once called it) on that occasion, despite the fact that in the wake of Pope Urban floating in the Tiber followed the heads of Orpheus and of Charles I, Actaeon devoured by his hounds, Chromius' horses, Admiral Nelson's arm, Polycrates eating his own son, several references to Titus Andronicus' daughter carrying her father's severed hand between her teeth, a quotation from Herodotus telling how Babylon was captured by a man who got into the city by cutting off his nose and ears, the remains of Adonis, Osiris and Tiranus Banderas, the genital organs of Origen and of Edward II's favourite, the Corybants' mutilations, the Turkish atrocities in Armenia, the unattached members sculpted by Rodin, Grimms' tale *Das Mädchen ohne Hande* and Pierre Quillard's poem about the girl with the severed hands (both quoted by Praz), Mark Twain's story of the maimed man, Albert-Birot's story of the man who was chopped to pieces, Holophernes' head and John the Baptist's head and Melanippus's head gnawed to bits by Tydeus, Philomela's tongue, Uranus's testicles, Tupac Amaru's remains, Prometheus's and Tityus's respective livers, Cervantes' arm, Pelops' shoulder, the eyes of Echetus's daughter, Echo the nymph torn to pieces by shepherds and the skeleton of General Levalle whose flesh was stipped from his bones on the river bank that the water might bear away the scraps. For his part, ex-congressman Fournier contributed the head of Father Hidalgo and that of Pancho Villa himself. Don Prospero, General Obregon's hand. The lottery-ticket vendor and the general, their own arm and eye respectively. And Grandfather Francisco said that perhaps, though it was certainly not what he desired (and he took a firmer grasp on his wooden cane), some day his leg might follow in the footsteps of that of General Santa Anna.

In short, Palinuro was the only one, besides Uncle Esteban, who appreciated Cousin Walter's medical knowledge and, of course, Estefania who with the passing of the years had lost her disgust for words and, provided Cousin Walter didn't talk of animals who had been martyred to further the cause of science, was prepared to listen to any horror and even allow Walter to revile the nursing profession by saying that most were like the filthy drunks Sairey Gamp and Betsey Prig described by Dickens and that Florence Nightingale, heroine of the Crimea, had been a raving lesbian and that it didn't bear imagining what had gone on in the hospital for young ladies that she had founded in Chandos Street. Uncle Esteban didn't much care for this, to put it mildly, for he had over-idealized the nursing and medical profession and declared himself against euthanasia and in favour of Asclepius's mandate ('You shall prolong nefarious lives') and disliked hearing about the experiments undertaken by Fallopius on criminals, and about the smallpox vaccine tests on children who were wards of charity in the parish of St James (authorized by Queen Caroline); in short, any atrocity perpetrated by doctors on mental patients and convicts, neglected old people, mental deficients and retarded children, with the argument that the end justified the means and which ranged from the injection of radioactive substances into the veins to research aspects of calcium metabolization to the immersion of children's feet in freezing water to measure their aortic pressure, the insertion of needles into the skull to study the protein in the cerebrospinal fluid and the deliberate inducement of strokes, all exploiting the ignorance or helplessness of patients or offering reduced sentences or discounts to the families of interned mental patients. All this, apart from the monstrous experiments undertaken on a massive scale by Professor Weltz in Dachau and so many other cases of which Uncle Esteban was at that time unaware but about which Walter, the know-it-all, would learn in the not too distant future when he read Pappworth.

Uncle Esteban was the only person – apart from Grandfather Francisco – that Walter truly respected and so he endeavoured not to mention such subjects and to speak, instead, about those which fascinated his uncle and which, in Walter's opinion, were most similar to the weekly 'believe it or not' feature in the Ripley section of the *Novedades* newspaper. Walter even suggested (and Uncle Esteban was delighted by the idea and put it into practice) that he should publish a 'believe it or not' section in the *History of Medicine* magazine: believe it or not, the fossilized skulls of Tenerife already show evidence of sincipital or Manouvrier trepanation. Believe it or not, if the DNA transmitting the genetic information of all human beings from the time of Christ were collected, it would weigh less than a gram. Believe it or not, clergymen used to excommunicate those who employed chloroform, calling it 'Satan's air'. Believe it or not, *calenture* was the name given to a raging delirium attacking sailors in the equatorial zone, causing them to throw themselves into the sea. Believe it or not, bacteriological warfare (already mentioned by the French novelist Robida, contemporary of Jules Verne) was invented by the Tartars who, when laying siege to the city of Jaffa, catapulted the rotting corpses of plague victims from their own ranks over the city battlements to fall into the streets, the houses, the trees and the cooking pots in which their enemies' stew was bubbling. Believe it or not, the Chinese physicians of antiquity always had an ivory doll on which their female patients pointed out the spot where they felt pain or discomfort, because the doctor was not permitted to touch them. Believe it or not Egyptians didn't treat all their dead equally: the corpses of the rich were rinsed out with palm wine and stuffed with myrrh; those of the poor were injected with resins which dissolved the viscera; those of the very poor were put to soak for sixty days in an alkaline solution. Believe it or not, Henry Wellcome, after whom was named the Wellcome Museum of the History of Medicine in London, submitted his most notable invention with his doctoral thesis: a number of long suppositories of pistachio, chocolate, vanilla and lemon hue.

Cousin Walter, a great science-fiction buff (he boasted that he had held in his hands a copy of *Necronomicon*, the most famous non-existent book in the world), would later see about contributing futuristic views to the newspaper on the subject of human brains placed in computerized bodies; automated electronic interpretation of medical symptoms; aseptic humans and humans psycho-chemically identical to those of the seventh century of the Ford Era; diagnosis by telephone of cardiac arrest and, finally, the process whereby, within a few decades, a surgeon would be able to operate long-distance from Hamburg on a patient in Hong Kong: tele-surgery.

It was Pope Urban III's hand, or General Obregon's hand anyway, together with the brain of the youth whose autopsy Palinuro had attended, that served as a pretext for a long talk with Cousin Walter – or, rather, a long listening session, since Walter was inclined frequently to indulge in interminable monologues – on two subjects more closely related to Palinuro's life than to medicine and which had always caused him a dark, indefinable anguish. The first was ownership of his own body.

It was in the name of art, not science, that Palinuro had made his drawings based on famous pictures showing the insides of the human body. But, deep down, very deep down, this was not true; if he had done them in the name of anything, it was of terror and repugnance and, in any case, he had not started out with a blue vein or a red muscle to work up towards the white smooth skin of statues, but had employed quite the reverse process and the main, almost unconscious, purpose behind these illustrations was perhaps to overcome that terror and repugnance that had haunted him for so many years, little knowing whether the terror had been born of the repugnance or the repugnance of the terror which possessed him when he began to understand and accept that his body was destined to be distributed among the dissecting rooms, laboratories and hospitals of the world or to turn simply to dust beneath the earth of the cemetery and some day be scattered into the vacuum. Throughout Palinuro's age of innocence, his and nobody else's, when Mamma Clementina used to sit him on her lap and tell him the story of Robinson Crusoe with his sun hat of palm leaves or of the little dwarf in the Calleja tales with a book for each letter of his name or of Heidi in the Alps, among the edelweiss and the lilies of St Bruno; throughout that age, Mamma and Papa, his grandparents, his cousins, Estefania, everybody – he himself too – were warm, soft statues of ivory which began and ended with their skins, their hands, their eyes, their hair. Outside the skin was the world and the sun, birds and fish, cars, dogs. There was Grandfather Francisco who put on his hat, and with it his political ideas, and went out into the street and, with his past of cathouses and House of Congress following in his wake, disappeared into the distance of memory and of the golden afternoon, between provinces of turf and scattered talismans exuding an atmosphere of labours lost. Outside, too, was the garden and the leaves of the fig tree which a plague of grubs had turned into handkerchiefs of green lace. And there was Grandmother in her room which smelt of the dead and the living and of paregoric drops and there was Aunt Enriqueta in her red, silk, lotus-flower dressing-gown walking along the corridor with a silver tea-pot steaming tea spirits. And this, though Palinuro was neither ignorant nor aware of it, was the world of Reimarus' divine revelation; the uncreated world of Aristotle; a world unknown to Pascal where it was not necessary to pronounce either for or against God, because there was nothing to win and nothing to lose and because that world pertained only to Palinuro's idea of it and nothing more, absolutely nothing more, just as his body pertained only to his own – and what better – idea of it: his body outside and his body inside, one and the same, without beginning or end, like the objective and subjective world, the real world and the imaginary world in which he lived. And inside, where the skin and the eyes were your own, was also a world in itself and a feeling of fulfilment, of vehement and immeasurable totality, of warmth, of pains and pleasures lying in wait, sleepiness or hunger, of wanting to laugh or to cry, while, beyond the eyes and the skin, where the skin and the eyes belong to others, was the actual reflection of Palinuro, sometimes in the guise of an image looking at itself mirrored in a pupil, and sometimes as a dimension within that other skin promising continuity and love, nameless and without description and within which, as inside himself, there might possibly dwell a cordless comet called a heart, knocking on the door of every minute of every day to gain admittance to the universe.

The main entrance to this replete interior, the door which the heart always discovered too late, was the mouth: through which entered that part of the world called water, the water of endless skin and all of which fitted inside a single drop of rounded soul and which dressed in white to disguise itself as milk and donned a glass mask to disguise itself as ice. And food entered, and strange and brilliant fruits of the earth, like green and red moons, the meats and fish and chicken invented in the markets and the mounds of grated carrot and purées and water which dressed as orange juice in the morning and the sweets which appeared in Uncle Esteban's pockets and in the jars in the sweet shops. And when these parts of the world were put into a person's mouth, they disappeared and nobody ever heard of them again and nobody worried about it. And, quite unrelated to food and just because, non-existent until the very moment of its appearance, golden excrement and water dressed in yellow simply appeared and, sometimes, multi-coloured vomit. What entered the smooth, warm, ivory statue didn't go anywhere, not even inside it. What came out of it didn't come from anywhere, not even from inside it.

But later, when the era of solar language was over, when Palinuro started to be attracted by the mysterious and the prodigious, and to feel fear and attraction and revulsion for anything that might threaten his safety, and anguish was born in him, and to the image of his own body and of his sensations and to the sound of his own name was added the continuity of his memories, words taught him then that, to have hair and a mouth and teeth ('Palinuro's teething; we must cut Palinuro's hair') and hands and tongue ('Child, wash your hands; child, show me your tongue') and nose and eyes and heart, meant that he was but a sum of different things which each had a different function and there was no possibility of these things swapping roles ('Palinuro's getting a new nose; we must cut Palinuro's hands; child, wash your heart'). And another, equally slow, learning process taught him to penetrate, fondle and worry those parts of his body which offered the possibility of contact with the interior. And that was when with his fingers he started to explore: his mouth, his ears, his nose ('Child, don't suck your thumb; child, don't scratch your ear; child take your finger out of your nose') and his anus and his penis ('Child, don't touch yourself there') and to bite his tongue and to scratch his back and to look at himself in the mirror to make sure that everything was there as it had been the day before, or three hours before, that nothing had disappeared while he slept or while he had a temperature or while he willed it. The first time he pricked himself on a rose thorn or cut himself with a piece of glass, he realized that water could dress in red to disguise itself as blood and pain; the first time he became aware that he was eating part of an animal and saw a run-over cat; the first time he saw a blind man and realized that the lottery-ticket vendor was missing an arm: these were just so many more occasions marking his dawning awareness that the unity of his body, or the unity of the body of Mamma Clementina or Papa Eduardo or Grandfather Francisco or his cousins or the people walking down the street, did not exist and could change at any moment and that some parts of his body were dispensable, in that he could live without them, and that others were essential and that without them he couldn't live or go to the cinema. But Palinuro, like anyone else, lived his childhood and adolescence without dwelling on the lack of unity of his body, without suffering on account of its fragility, or of its safety which was threatened every moment of his life. After all, hadn't a man – Christ – and a woman – Mary – ascended body and soul to heaven? Would souls not return to their respective bodies on the Day of Judgement? And Palinuro grew up and became accustomed to the interchange between his body and the world; he grew up and became accustomed to thinking in a vague, imprecise and very sporadic way of all those mysterious organs which only very occasionally made their confused and silent presence felt and which were generally so far removed from conscious thought and nearly always so distant from his life, that there was no opportunity to get to know or to explore them and therefore no chance that his mother would say, 'Child, don't scratch your liver; child, don't suck your lungs; child, don't put your thumb in your heart.' He got used also to accepting his legs, his nose and his tongue as things which belonged to him, things which belonged to him in the same way as his toys, his clothes or his parents which were his and nobody else's, without ever worrying over much about not being able to feel, in things outside himself, what he felt inside his body ('Mamma, I haven't grown a new tree; my gloves aren't tired; my mamma doesn't hurt') or not being able to use a part of his body as he did his exercise books, his shoes or his electric train ('Mamma, put my eyes away in the cupboard; Mamma, buy me some new hands; Mamma, wind up my heart').

Until Cousin Walter entered his life – also as though from nowhere – and one dawn, leaving the Española cantina, after drinking like Cossacks all night, Walter said something like: 'And anyway: even if it was the young man's brain, it couldn't have actually been his brain, if you see what I mean?' and Palinuro, though he denied it, did in fact understand – or at least sense – what his cousin meant.

'Perhaps we should start out with Locke,' mused Walter, 'to try and work out whether it is possible to own our own organs. In other words, if we can be masters of our lives, our oesophagus and our vena cava, to take but three examples. I choose Locke because it seems to me that the first thing you should do is to define where ownership of things begins and ends. I recall that in a paragraph of *Tristram Shandy,* the English writer

238

Laurence Sterne (who knew Locke by heart) wondered when the farmer's apples started to belong to him: When he plants them? When they grow? When he picks them? When he puts them on the table? When he eats them? When he digests them? When he shits them? . . . You see, cousin, I don't believe that anyone can, honestly, give a definite answer. And this, applied to a few common and garden apples (and not even the golden apples that seduced Atalanta), may also be applied not only to your body and to each of its organs and parts, but also to your own life, to your life as a whole. Do you know when your life starts to be your life? Perhaps when the shape of your nose and the colour of your hair, your height and your character are distributed among the chromosomes of one of your father's hundred thousand million spermatozoa – speaking of which, by the way, every time your father went to a whorehouse, the poor spermatozoid spent its time dodging from one testicle to the other to avoid being born a bastard – and the chromosomes of one of your mother's ovules which, if the law of probability had had its way, would never have met, but which one day – or one night, which is more common – combined to become a single being: Palinuro; Palinuro the Great or Palinuro the Small? Or, more likely: Palinuro the Mediocre? Or the five, ten, twenty different Palinuros that you are in relation to others as son, brother, lover, friend, enemy or virtual stranger, including – through Bovarism: in other words, the power given to a man to see himself as other than he really is – the different Palinuros which you successively, or sometimes simultaneously, think you are? Or perhaps I should say: the various Palinuros which the various Palinuros think they are? Tell me then, is that when your life starts to be your life? When the spermatazoon fertilizes the ovule in the pocket of the Fallopian tube? Or when you're a shapeless, eighteen-day-old embryo, more closely resembling your mother's vulva than yourself? Or when twenty days have passed since you were engendered and, seen from behind, you look, on the contrary, more like your father's reproductive organ than yourself; that is, if Ingalls' and Heuser's illustrations are anything to go by? Tell me, Palinuro, when does your life start to be your life? After twenty-three days, when your heart begins to beat or when the *septum primum* and the *septum secundum* join together, thereby shutting down communication between the right and left auricles for good? Or perhaps it is three months after your conception when you graduate from the embryonic stage to become a foetus clad in yellow? Or when you are born after 180 days, narrowly making it to the minimum viability mark prescribed by law? Or after nine months, in accordance with social norm; and when the air, the air which is life and the breath of God, fills your lungs and changes their colour? Or does your life begin to be your life when the midwife snips through your fifty centimetres of umbilical cord (which is of course twisted up in the opposite direction to that followed by the hands of a clock, just like any other child) thereby severing the sacred mother–child symbiosis and leaving you alone in the world, like a Tarzan fallen from his favourite creeper, transformed into a new and unique and dispossessed experiment of Nature? When does your life start to be your own? When they give you your first smack and you reply with your first bellow? When your mother cradles you in her arms every morning and caresses your face with a waft of foetid breath (because she's just woken up and it's only natural that her breath should be stale) and your ear with tender words and you start to perceive the world and to know that happiness and terror, the beautiful and the repulsive, may be one and the same thing? Or when you take your first step? Or when you speak your first words and you know that water is water and that you are you? Or when you start school? Or when you have your first friend? Or your first girlfriend and, with the dead cells of the epidermis of your hand, you caress the dead cells of the epidermis of her face? Tell me, Palinuro, when does your life start to be your life? When you have your first fight and your fists ache? Or when you have your first death and your life aches? Or when you reach puberty and you start to lose ten thousand never-to-be-recovered neurons a day and your gonads develop and your secondary sexual traits appear and everything around you: your mother, words, food, are tinged with sexuality and your genital tubercule – which started to grow in length from the first weeks after your conception following the fusion of your genital folds, that is the real *omphallus* which links you to your mother and to your species – continues to grow in length, confirming that you are a male and, moreover, a prepotent male? When, Palinuro? When, one afternoon blessed or cursed among all other afternoons, you leave your house at sixteen years of age to start your life and discover that, while the world is not in your home, neither is your home in the world? When you enrol at the School of Medicine? Or when you graduate? Or when you reflect on your life? Or when you get your wisdom tooth at thirty years of age and you swear fidelity to the Goddess Reason consecrated in Notre Dame and you offer your super-ego a bunch of ethical standards pressed between the pages of books, like Estefania's skin and your own? When? Tell me: when you marry and settle down and are owner of your house, your television and your car, fully qualified architect of your own destiny, convinced that you are living in a world governed by a feline justice in which, however you look at it, you have to eat and pay taxes, make love and die and where, sooner or later, everybody greets or murders their neighbours and the stars live up to sea level and you decide to beget a child with your own life? Or when you grow old and you reach the age of the Grand Climacteric: sixty-three – or sixty-four, as the Beatles would have it? Or does your life start to be your own when you begin to lose it? The moment fertilization begins in the Fallopian tube, or the moment after? Or half an hour later

240

when your mother is entitled to ask people to give up their seat on a tram because she not only has bright eyes but is also a half an hour pregnant? Or does it start to stop being your life a few days later, when the little fertilized egg finally succeeds in implanting itself in the wall of the uterus? Perhaps you think that, in truth, your life starts to stop being your life when, after birth, begins the process of chronic arteriosclerosis described by Cazalis Demange and the phagocytic struggle and poisoning by microbial intestinal toxins described by Metchnikoff and, if you're lucky, they'll be out to kill you for eighty or ninety years and you'll die of old age before they do: deaf, blind, senile, your noble tissue atrophied, your bones softened and your cartilage calcified. But perhaps, why not? your life starts to stop being your life when the cancer which will prevent you from dying of old age takes root, or when the clot which will keep you from dying of cancer and of old age starts to form, or when you take the first steps across the road on the day that you are going to be run over by a car which will save you not only from dying of an embolism, of cancer and of old age, but also from all the other deaths which will not be yours: it will save you from dying frozen in Lake Michigan, from dying impaled on an Apache's arrow a hundred years ago, from dying of lack of gravity aboard a space rocket headed for Betelgeuse in two centuries' time, from dying of a fistful of fire, from dying of betrayal, a poisoned kiss, an ambiguous passion. But perhaps you will enjoy the privilege of a prolonged death agony. Even then: when does your life start to stop being your life? At the moment when you enter coma and see the world through hazy eyes? Or when you can no longer see or speak to the world because you are in cataleptic coma but none the less you still hear it: you still hear the fizzing of cider over-flowing birthdays, and you still think it: you still think of the world and its stiffening fear, its water flags and postcards? Or does your life stop being your life when an aneurysm turns you into a vegetable statue living through the years and happy days without seeing the world, without looking upon the gross cruelty of dusks which eat flamingos and other coloured memories alive; without feeling the world, without savouring its pristine sweetmeats, without feeling the cold of its polar snows tinged with harlequin shadows and without even, like Condillac's vegetable statue, perceiving the world's smells: the bitter pine smell of Estefania's armpits, the smell of ammonia and paraffin awaiting you on the threshold of dreams, the smell of the fountains in Rio de Janeiro Park, the smell of nutmeg, the smell of blonde mayonnaise, of bread and the long-missed foetid smell of Mamma Clementina's breath which comes from beyond the tomb to cradle you and is but the smell from the cemetery's flower vases in which irises and immortelles decay? Is that when your life starts to stop being your life? When all those words which you will never again pronounce: celebrated oaths, speeches which were to move nomadic

241

multitudes, utterances couched in infinite cadences to probe your lovers' hearts and smashed to pieces by the whip of the monosyllable when you learned to mumble your tenderness, when all those words, just think, are still alive in your brain, in your pale, hortensia-coloured brain, and simmer deep down, devouring each other, flashing brilliantly here and there in phrases hidden behind barricades of roses and in mausoleums of scurvy, trapped in the turbines of your solar plexus, entangled in lymphatic spaghetti and in never-ending conundrums, slipping along the bitter-sweet diagonal of silence or on the wings of the tiger, in darkness, alone, dreaming of themselves and their flawless gymnastics? Or does your life stop being your life when you go mad and think that you are living the life of others? Or when you simply curl up your toes, in other words, give your dying gasp, that is, the right auricle of your heart which, for this reason, is called the *ultimum moriens*, stops for good and then you die completely, you die from your head to your big toe, from your liver to your spleen, from your teeth to your kidney and your cornea clouds over and your jaw sags and on your stomach settles the greenish discoloration of putrefaction and afterwards, starting with the sperm sacs (the centre of greatest sin) and spreading through the muscles of your jaw, your neck, your arms, your legs and the rest of your body, *rigor mortis* sets in, the rigidity of your corpse caused by the opaqueness of muscle fibres and from which inflexible course none has ever returned alive? Is it then that your life ceases to be your life? When they place a feather on your lips to see if you are really dead? When on the palm of your head they draw with violet ink to confirm the appearance of Terson's yellow aura which is properly the icteric aura of the dead? When they place a glass of water on your chest and a mirror against your lips? When they subject you to the Lorain test and expose a part of your skin to a naked flame to form a blister of air which loudly explodes, thereby proving that you are dead, completely dead, solemnly dead? Or when they place a piece of neutral litmus paper beneath your eyelid and the paper turns red in confirmation of the Lecha-Marzo sign? Or a little later, when you are in your coffin with combed hair, swabs of moist cottonwool on your eyelids, a little pillow beneath your jaw and a stopper in your rectum? Or when you start to turn into Hendrik de Kijeser's *Image of Delirium*, into a corpse swarming with worms and dying of not being able to die, to quote Lortigue? Only then, when you are dead, dead and in your coffin, or dead and in a hotel room, waiting for the arrival of the hosts of flies and insects described in Barbusse's *Inferno*: the green and mauve Luoila Caesar, the mites, the black dermestid beetles with pink elytra, the red-integumented carrion beetles, the great sarcophagidae and finally the tenebrio obscurus, or dead and buried and alive, or half-alive if you suffer the same fate as Mr Valdemar in Poe's story and your body starts to rot while your soul is alive and in full possession of its faculties, you are on the

242

dissecting slab (really, right there, on the slab itself!) with your stomach empty and your skin pulled back to show your innards, in other words, more closely resembling one of your own drawings or one of Anna Marandi's horrible figures than yourself. Only then, when they start to distribute your body throughout the world, because such was the dictate of destiny or because that is what you wished and we take – somebody takes – your heart away to be buried in a red box in your grandparents' garden and your brain in a white box beneath the flagstones of the School of Medicine and your lungs in two sky-blue boxes at the peak of a mountain and your testicles in two black boxes like balls of jet in the rubbish tips of the Plaza de las Tres Culturas: it is only then, generally, that people say that your life was like this or like that or like the other. People generally say: his life was happy, as a child he saw the sea dying of thirst on infinite beaches and magpies hop in its wake on the musical sands of Studland Bay, following its footprints and finding precious shellfish. His life was that of a healthy man: six million red globules can't be wrong. And he had money and he had love. And he was the greatest genius that ever lived, greater than Chaplin, than Dante and Mozart put together and raised to the power of ten and multiplied by twice the square root of Einstein plus Picasso point six and divided – painfully and jubilantly divided – by Plato and Aristotle (without realizing, incredible though it may seem, that one always dies of bad luck, that to die is an affront, a personal insult and shame, whatever the nature, hour and place of death). Or they will say that your life (and take heed, nobody can prevent it being thus; try as you might, your fate does not depend on you but on the gods: because they inconsolably mourned the death of their brother, the Hyades were turned into a constellation announcing the rains; because they inconsolably mourned the death of their brother, the Meleagrides were turned by Minerva into grouse), as I was saying, they will say that your life was sad, that because you left your toys in the garden and your socks in the kitchen, disobeying Mamma, so too when you died you left everything in the world out of place: your spurs, hanging from the wine jug; the wine, in the washbasin; the washbasin, in the sitting-room; the sitting-room, in a music box at the southernmost point of the universe, and the universe, the universe full of cybernetic concavities and hearts of helium, you left on the brink of escaping along its tangent in a quest to square the circle; and they will say that, for not heeding Mamma Clementina, for never finishing what you began: neither your dreams nor your letters, for always leaving a drawing half-way through an apple or a poem a third of the way through a lamentation, her curse came true: 'Never in your life will you finish anything,' Mamma Clementina told him and when he died – they will say of you, Palinuro – he left two books half-read, three shirts half-used and several loves and friendships half-consummated and they will say more,

243

they will say that you died half-way through a digestion and a sigh, half-way through a thought and a heart beat and that you left unfinished the description of Estefania and the room in Holy Sunday Square and, moreover, you left your life unfinished and not just because you died at the age of twenty or of thirty-five: had he lived another hundred years, they will say, he would still have left his whole life unfinished. But nobody will understand that, from the moment of your death, you will begin to fulfil all the promises you made to Mamma Clementina: you will stop biting your nails, you will stop masturbating, you will stop telling lies and you will be perfect. Or they will say, perhaps, that your life was a constant obsession with death and with words, with sex, with learning, with fame. With death, because in reality you were not so much afraid of death but of life. With words, not so much because you could not say with them what you wished to say but because they said of you what you did not wish said. With sex, because deep down you despised it. With learning, because your lack of confidence in your imagination led you to try and supplement it by amassing erudite facts and information. With fame, because you hated yourself and needed the admiration of others. And, because of this (they will say) he always failed with more commotion than was strictly necessary. He wanted to be Daedalus (they will say) but, like Icarus, he plunged headlong into the abysm of his infancy. And, finally (they will say), he was a poor, sickly devil, a puppet with sugar-water in his veins who spent his life, *your life*, between homoeopaths and proctologists, between physiotherapists and psychiatrists and who never had – you never had – either money or love but only many debts and few friends, you never went to the cinema to see *The Bluebird* or 007 and, therefore, screwed up, down on your luck, without triumphal attendants to offer you a bridge of silver or a bank account, you spent the days, *your days*, sucking telegraph wires.

244

13

Our daily bread

In the course of his life Palinuro was, among other things, a child.

To be a child was to launch yet another spiral into the air by the power of thought before closing your eyes to the blinding summer-sown swallows: a spiral flung into the vacuum which suddenly lengthened in insomnia and thus, straight and tense as the pitch of a harp, buried itself in the sea that he, Palinuro, might catch a sailing boat, open its stomach and find a shark, open its stomach and find a star, open its stomach and find a fable.

Sometimes, also, to be a child was to be ill. First, because he had a very small liver. And then, because he had very big bumps.

And always, because he had a temperature; his mother would rub his chest with antiphlogistine and wrap him up in a quilt of eiderdown lining the costume of a swooning harlequin relating his transfigurations: a series of patches and scraps lovingly composed by deft and patient hands; then, a cathedral of diamond shapes; later, with the passing of time, dampness and moths, once again a heap of rags.

But to be a child was also to have a maternal grandfather, a great gentleman, on account of his being so fat and being such a gentleman, who was at one time governor of a State of the Republic and at another was born in Baghdad: and this was the truth, the whole truth, but not nothing but the truth.

And it was to have a maternal grandmother who, when she said breakfast is ready: I said, breakfast is ready! woe betide anybody who misbehaved at table, pity on anyone who didn't know how to remove the film from the surface of the hot milk in the most practical and elegant manner, which was the way she did it: barely breathing on the surface of the liquid, barely touching the film with the tips of her thumb and index finger, she lifted it as one would lift a dead rat by the tip of its tail, at the same time informing Palinuro and his cousins that, as far as she knew, there was no specific word in English for this filmy skin because in the States they never boiled milk, so healthy and nutritious must be the precious liquid yielded by the straw-coloured Herefords and the cherry-coloured St Gertrude cows, she said, little knowing or caring whether these cows were famous for their milk or for their meat. And who would care when they had such pretty names, except perhaps Uncle Felipe during the phase when he was interested in economics?

And pity also on anyone who wasn't squeaky clean when they sat down to table. And she took it upon herself to set the example: she got up every day at the crack of dawn and, in the half-light of her room, which was pervaded by the mingled fragrance of valerian and quince jelly, with an iron full of red-hot embers, she pressed and re-pressed the starched collar and cuffs of her blouse, endowing them with the dubious prestige of celluloid. And thus she remained, immaculate, throughout breakfast and the remaining meals of the day: because never, that Palinuro could remember, did a stray bit of beetroot leave a stain of sweet and suspect blood on Grandmother's skirts and never, either, did a jumping Brussels sprout land on the silken sheen of her bosom to affix its bequest of béchamel.

And, above all, woe betide anyone who did not respect our daily bread.

Palinuro named this grandmother, the maternal one, queen of the kitchen and administrator of the bread basket.

As administrator of the bread basket, Grandmother had the privilege of counting and allocating the buns each person was entitled to eat – not one more, not one less – distributing them every night and every morning, eucharistically.

Palinuro named his grandfather who, moreover, had hands as large as turtle's flippers, commander-in-chief of good humour and bad language which caused his grandmother to wish she had a Valencian fan to hand, that she might assume the expression of a pastoral scene.

And Palinuro named Grandfather commander of his own gold-battlemented, ivory dentures and of the garden of their home where blonde-belly-buttoned daisies abounded.

But to be a child was also to have another grandmother, a paternal grandmother, who lived in another house and in another world.

So distant, so very distant; the distance between his two grandmothers was equal to that between the land and the sky.

Or perhaps between the land and the sea.

Because his maternal grandmother, who flailed her children and grandchildren with care, cold and diligent as a shower of hail stones, could never bring herself to accompany Grandfather and his friends, or Grandfather and Palinuro, along the clean, blue path of an afternoon leavened with a certain tenderness and a certain humour, for the sole purpose of creating a mystery, a well of sensations.

In contrast, his other grandmother, the paternal grandmother, to whom Palinuro gave the name Lisandra, was loud and merry indeed, there was no doubt but that iodine ran through her veins, that her eyes were of sea honey accustomed to the leisure of nets and foamy wharfs where sea urchins speared a drop of water on each spine and oysters rounded out their boredom in a pearl.

Anyone would have said that some hidden shame had led his maternal grandfather to choose a wife who personified the exact opposite of those little misses who had been his adoration, and doubtless continued to be so, just as when he was congressman and he and Grandmother were already married, he had spent twenty golden pesos on Luto De Juarez roses, almonds in brandy and Madras handkerchiefs for Grandmother, because he had a bad conscience perhaps for having spent another five hundred at the last carnival in New Orleans where he had dressed up as Haroun al-Raschid – hadn't he been born in Baghdad after all? – and spent the whole night in a whorehouse of brocatelle-upholstered chairs and walls papered with discoloured rhododendrons, surrounded by little French whores who scratched his back and bald pate with long, scarlet-painted fingernails.

In contrast, his other grandfather, the paternal one, whom Palinuro never knew because he died many years before he was born, the Customs Inspector grandfather, the grandfather who loved music but didn't want anybody else to do so, the grandfather who was puritanical and hard and inflexible; so much so that, whenever he discovered a train loaded with contraband champagne for Veracruz, he ordered that the bottles be broken one by one, smashed against the rail cars which were thus re-baptized with the curses of the loaders, the other grandfather, to whom Palinuro never gave a name because, since he never knew him, it was no longer necessary to do so, who drew his wife Lisandra from the depths of the sea, tore out the shells and coral entwined in her hair, washed away the salt with orange water and bore her, smelling of Hero de Pravia Soap, to the altar of La Enseñanza Church.

Neither of them was happy.

Or rather, none of the four of them.

And, moreover, anyone would have thought – Palinuro thought – that his paternal grandmother Lisandra should have married his maternal grandfather Francisco.

Facing each other across the breakfast table, they would have allowed everybody to eat whichever and however many buns they pleased.

Seated one at either end of the table, they would have had wars of bread pellets, they would have played Ping-Pong, they would have had competitions to see which could tell the best story and phantasmogorical tale.

Because, when they were not Grandmother Lisandra's memories (her own and those of all her ancestors) silhouetted on the horizon and long beating a retreat; when they were not these memories winning another battle against oblivion and coming to the fore once more to preside over the landscape, then it was the treasures that his maternal grandfather looted nightly from the books conquered in his battles against insomnia and from which he drew by a wing-tip the stories of General Morelos y Pavón's soldiers who ate knuckles of beef roasted on the red-hot iron of the cannon while the artillery spluttered and the band played a Technicolor march, or the legends of pirates of flaming, unbridled beards dying on the beach, their skulls become hives for bee swarms.

And his Grandmother Lisandra, at the other end of the table or at the other end of the world, could take up his maternal grandfather's story where he left off: about the pirates, for instance, then she would tell Palinuro – while Aunt Adelaida played the story of a river on the piano – how it was possible, and indeed probable, that Palinuro was descended from the pirates who terrorized the Gulf, yes, from those very buccaneers who besieged Cartagena of the Indies, and perhaps from the Black Corsair himself who, weeping, forsook the Maracaibo shores fringed with palms, although it was more likely to have been from those who, under the command of Lorencillo, disembarked in Heroic Veracruz – the birthplace of Lisandra, the city where Aunt Luisa every year visited Jean Paul's grave – kidnapping all the women of the local Jarocha aristocracy and shutting themselves up with them in the cathedral with the result that, nine months later, there appeared many children of Corsair stamp. That was just the time, of course, when my grandmother – said Lisandra – . . . who knows, who will ever know for sure.

And that was also the truth, the whole truth, but not nothing but the truth.

Because perhaps she knew that her grandmother – Palinuro's great-great-grandmother – had been in Europe when Lorencillo disembarked in Veracruz. But then again, perhaps she didn't.

But she never told Palinuro.

Just as his maternal grandfather never told him that, just as there is a town in the States called Paris, so there is another in Mexico called Baghdad, which was where he was born and which had been attacked in 1866 by a thousand black Americans under the command of Colonel Reed and General Crawford.

He never told Palinuro.

But it wasn't necessary.

Because those were times when Palinuro still spoke the language of genius and it sufficed merely to name things for them to come into existence and to materialize by the magic of their names, because the magic was made of transparencies, of invisible threads and of the slow sacrifice of saliva and the flight of vowels.

Those were the days when the world was still a round miracle bristling with secrets: when rice was put in salt cellars to prevent the salt from

248

getting lumps and when don Prospero maintained that, on the subject of salt, just as canaries should be called fringillidae, so salt, which was white and in truth almost sweet from a poetic point of view, even if only because it was born on the wings of the sea, should be given the name sodium chloride, while Flavia the maid said that, on the subject of chloride, when water tasted of chloride you should leave it to stand overnight because otherwise it spoils the taste of the coffee and hot milk and it was she, better versed than anybody in the ways of seasoning meat with sage and vegetables with dill, who said so and, on the subject of milk, said Grandmother Altagracia, who also knew how to remove calluses with sandpaper and the hair from her legs with a paste of caramel and arsenic, nothing beat the milk of Hereford cows for bleaching the keys of the piano and, on the subject of bleaching, those were the days when Ricardo, the gardener, who not only knew how to catch butterflies by spreading syrup on the tree branches but maintained that there was nothing better for bleaching dentures than ground coral and deer's antler, prompting Uncle Esteban to recommend biting on a magnet to cure toothache and Aunt Lucrecia to advise raisins and bicarbonate for gumboils and Grandfather Francisco to say, on the subject of pains, that he was not only an expert in the art of curing tobacco with apples and cognac, but also maintained that there was nothing like the snow of bicarbonate of soda for damping down the fires of acidity in the stomach and, on the subject of snow, nobody like Aunt Luisa for organizing lemon ices with saltpetre: Aunt Luisa who, besides being conversant with the art of soaking Alençon lace in a solution of gum Arabic and brandy and with the science of removing pearly warts by tying silk thread around them, she, Aunt Luisa, wrote letters to Paris in sympathetic green ink which became invisible until reconjured with the heat of a flame, just as she herself occasionally parted her lips to blow a bubble stream of invisible words which revealed their mysteries only with the passing of time and the warmth of memory.

And to be a child was to be master of this world and to raise your eyes to spot the high-flown birds and it was to know how to be cruel to the lithe wind when it was necessary to be cruel to it and to be able to temporize with the rain when the rain, for example, sang a hymn and promised the requisite wonders for breakfast: because in the middle of the garden there grew a fig tree and because Grandmother Altagracia had decided that figs should not be eaten until they are so ripe that they fall from the tree and because when Palinuro got into his soap-scented bed he set to counting the figs shaken down by the rain, perhaps five, seven, ten – the same number as would next day, in the morning, mingle their dark delight in the crystal fruit bowl with blushing apples, honey-dew melons and adventitious grapes oozing the occasional special brilliance and waxen tear. And throughout the passing night, from the depths of his sheets, Palinuro

249

immersed himself in a superstition which forbade him to interrupt the game or distrust disorder. But no disloyalty, no contradiction, could divide the ordinary from the extraordinary! And neither was it necessary, as he well knew, to struggle overmuch with imagination: it was enough merely to substitute one desire with another almost identical one for his childish eyes, accustomed to associating the whiteness of a cloud with the sponginess of moss, to light upon a new source of fascination. Or he had but to remain quiet, to ease the swarm of spells buzzing through his breast and, when the right words reached the tip of his tongue, let them go, let himself go with them to places better fitted for fantasy. Then he would shut his eyes and think that tomorrow was another day, as Grandmother Altagracia confirmed each night after adorning her headache with a ribbon of purple silk in readiness for lying with her favourite archangel. But in reality, tomorrow was never another day for her, for Grandmother Altagracia, who put on life when she was born as one puts on a worn-out dress, a worn-out long dress, long and loose, increasingly entangled in the tiredness of mirrors and regrets. Not so Aunt Luisa whose heart was a mechanism of sugar in which each cabin boy obeyed a toy intuition and wrecked the planned harmony and whose life started anew every time the sun rose, Paris time; daily she donned it as one dons a hat on a morning of flying inventions and unexampled orchids. Thus, clad in hat and skirt and clouds and garden and new Aprils, Aunt Luisa incarnated Palinuro's dream which promised to be reborn with the morning and vowed to meet his cousin again, and for the first time, as soon as he saw her seated beneath the fig tree in the garden, one with the inflorescences of the grass, radiant and tranquil in well-groomed waitfulness. Only thus was it worth living: within an eternal and ever-new present where neither the next ten minutes nor the next ten thousand years existed and where it was possible to see things through a kaleidoscope which composed a different fable every time the world revolved: yesterday, it might have been a caliph wise and fat as Grandfather; tomorrow, a maze inhabited by roc birds and red tamarisks. And in the darkness of night, when the rain stopped, Palinuro thought himself before the mirror where every morning Father shaved and combed his hair and put on his white shirt with green spots and the mirror coincided with the anticipated reflection: only a slight, contradictory iridescence gave the lie to the discoloration, as though Palinuro would at some point have to throw into the clothes-basket his fair-weather-sailor suit through which had run rivers of memories and of weed, years and, especially, so many Sundays at the fair and First Communions, in order to begin to look like his father, to begin to be as old as he was. Other contours, however, such as the lemon trees upon which the moon heaped ashes and the profile of his mother, with her skin of snowy peach, devitalized the pull of the vacuum that would have swallowed him,

250

drowned it in the possible atmospheres of his mother's eyes and forced him to confront the differences and distances existing between that which was his: his flesh, his breath, and that which also belonged to him: the flesh and breath of his mother, of Mamma Clementina which, being so close, perhaps together, maybe, and her words: then he remembered. And then he wanted to say at that time, things being as they were, under such and such a condition, on those nights or only on that single night when his mother came into his room and said Mamma wants to know if her baby washed his teeth properly and he presented his mother with his warm mint breath; Mamma wants to know if her baby washed his hair properly and she buried her face in his hair; Mamma wants to know if her baby washed his thighs properly and she buried her face in his flesh as in a mound of perfumed sand and they both fell asleep, making love in a way which yet had no name, blanketed in the monotony of silence, until the first wing-beat of day discovered him alone, staring at the ceiling, alone again, alone for the rest of his days. But it was not always like that. Palinuro did not always like to go to bed to sleep and less so when Mamma made no allowance for the fact that he was playing with his soldiers or had climbed a tree and insisted that it was time to come inside, to have tea, to go to bed: Not now, tomorrow, now climb down, now put away your soldiers, now have tea, now turn out the light, now go to sleep, now forget. And how to explain to Mamma that a high, springy branch cannot wait until tomorrow? How to tell her that you can't freeze a battle and leave the banners and the cannon immobile until morning? And would he be able tomorrow, as now, to see and tickle his face with Papa's shaving brush, smell Grandfather Francisco's Oliver typewriter, devour Mamma's soiled nightdress with kisses and feel Aunt Luisa's patchwork quilt which were all there, waiting for him, asking him to give them a name which would make them lasting in his memory? A compass was another important object: it pointed the way, always the same way. The way of the golden jungles, the hippopotamuses, the cities whose rotten roots would be turned to dust by the winds of the Pole Star. His school books, his leather satchel with its silver buckles, were closer to his flesh than theories of forgetfulness might have anticipated. Certain books, also, thick as bisons' backs: he opened them at random, smelt them to know in which river they had won their transparency, read them over and over to find the code and dare to say the words and sail again with pirates and cleave whales' spouts with his sword.

And it was the yellow star of the Whale (or perhaps the Swan's beak, perhaps the Dragon's wings) which laid down the order in which the scenes of Palinuro's life should occur. The apparent intensity and importance of each of them depended to a greater extent on that order than on his own happiness, security or insignificance. For example, it was written that at three years of age he would inaugurate a new volocipede and a new philosophy of speed. That at six, bearing on his back a quiver of coloured pencils dipped in powders of the rainbow, he would trick the grey rats out of a milk tooth and swap it for a salamander. That at seven, having already discovered the alphabet in the noodles and on the school blackboard, it was written in the same letters that one afternoon, an afternoon like an orange miracle, he would tell his father that he, Palinuro, was going to be a great man and his father, who was up to his neck in another life raffling off his own thoughts, merely smiled because he hadn't understood that the object underlying Palinuro's random words was to see if they encountered a response, because Palinuro knew intuitively that if he did indeed one day become a doctor performing wondrous operations on men's hearts – his own heart, perhaps – these words would be remembered as a premonition, like the pure awareness of a destiny and of a will, adorning his greatness; if, on the other hand, he never succeeded in becoming anything more than himself, if he was condemned to dwell in a silence too closely resembling ignorance and boast a shyness which would be taken for pride, if want or excess laid waste his life, if he achieved a beautiful death at the age of fifteen or if his talent was but a play of mirrors, mercy would turn those words to dust. Distant yet was the day he would have to test his luck for the first time; distant the moment when homework, reduced to an irritating accumulation of figures, monsoons and adverbs, would become completely meaningless as Palinuro, sitting at his desk, lost himself in contemplation of the portrait of an imaginary girlfriend and of a globe spelling out his future travels. Distant the moment when, for a time at least, for a few years, before returning to his beloved medical books, it would be necessary to open the glass door to let in the immaculate night and, back on firm ground, also imaginary, immersed anew in the camaraderie of summer, the moment he would throw the Leyden jar into the sea with a message for the eels and walk towards the aqueduct tower which stretched its shadow across the mountains to guide shepherds and wolves who had lost their way. The reason that he had walked along the aqueduct many times, with the agility and disguised fear of a tightrope walker, without looking at the arches which became higher and higher in direct relation to the increasing depth of the abyss in the bottom of which lay a hell of cactus and precious stones, and the reason that the bust of his grandfather, which Palinuro had modelled in clay with his own hands, portrayed not only the first corpse that he had ever seen but also all the corpses that he would later see in the dissecting rooms, on the pavements and in the hospitals, was because infinite chance had decreed that on this would centre the meaningfulness of his life. But not for his friends, not for anybody else who might be prepared to decide, by the bright light of a dialogue or the generosity of a party, which of all his days were the most fit to martyr the calendar, little suspecting that for Palinuro they were perhaps the most wretched or indifferent, those which buried his heart most deeply beneath a mound of neutral laces. At other times he had run away to the circus, the circus tinged with the magic of a zodiacal light and which sooner or later turned up in all the stories he knew, lending them their colouring and their acrobatics and which once, finally, appeared in his life. On yet other occasions, he would go with his friends to the stream in the woods, a rivulet carpeted with fresh green weeds and fringed with trees which intertwined their highest branches to form a tunnel of greenery and he and his friends scrambled to and fro, climbing up a tree as thick and strong and deeply rooted as their own childhoods, and they reached the weaker branches – which could no longer be distinguished from those of the tree on the opposite bank down which they would have to climb to the ground – they reached that highest point when Palinuro and his friends were thirteen years old and when the danger was greatest of plunging into the stream and breaking their necks or their souls and smearing their faces with duckweed which grew several yards below and many years above them. But Palinuro was that kind of child and adolescent and there was nothing to be done about it: he had chosen a purity polluted by improvisations and twisting turns and a disdain for easy treasures, for those not hidden on the very edge of the world and, by the same token, just as he liked to lengthen the paths to the river and the woods, he preferred to delay words and safeguard the infinite variations floating like marine phosphorescence almost within arm's reach. Meanwhile, until that moment came, Palinuro knew that a knight's device, an ancient device filtering away between his lady's colours, obliged the knight to search for himself, to ask after himself in the taverns and the inns, in the far reaches of the woods and at the gates of the city and to learn and to appropriate all the versions of his legend, to preserve them as he did his rags and his curls, and bound him to sing them only in solitude, when there were none to hear him but the birds and the honeysuckle, mid-way between a castle and a hovel, or between the ice-cream parlour and the streets where the children of the neighbourhood played hopscotch. Palinuro accepted and believed he had chosen this path, because he could not know what kind of man or child he had been in the eyes of those who were familiar with the triggering springs of his spirit, or in the eyes of those who had seen him only once, out of the corner of their eye in passing, a packet of fireworks and cards under his arm and nibbling a tamarind ice-lolly. This road was neither long nor easy, short nor difficult, and neither did it necessarily take him to many places or to none. It might take him, through a pallid winter devoid of floral games, to a kingdom without redemption because its continuity was foreseeable. It might also, this road, stop short in a dream which turned back upon itself to become a pillar of salt, a dream in which Palinuro

253

would be permitted to continue to invent himself in keeping with his subterranean wretchedness and of his contradictions and where all excesses were permitted. But the same path could combine with everyday life and cease to inhabit his eyes and everything, like God, and enter a more obvious area of fantasy and mimic itself to the extent of fusing with the most straightforward objects and truths. In the latter case, when convoluted awareness had taken charge of putting things in their proper place, he would be granted a crystallized deferment which would place him again in his grandparents' house, the house where he was born, the very same house which, years later, when it no longer existed and Palinuro was overwhelmed by a swarm of unfaithful memories and felt the need to cling to the first object with a beating heart that his imagination and his memory caught in flight and thus, winged as he was, transformed into a hunter of reflections, never again to seal his lips each time they parted to spew his demons and his angels and, before the fear of repeating gestures or even the shame of doing something well could start to dissolve in the pane duplicating the bell towers of other cities and the pages of other books, Palinuro vowed to inventory and relate, on his own account and at his own risk, to enumerate and describe all the rooms and every marvel contained in the house and thus trap all those slippery memories in a net of immutable words: his words and nothing but his words, perverted by an opaque sentimentality perhaps, and by the self-esteem which pluralized his life: but still, when all was said and done, his words and perhaps even his gestures, which might appear to be the most insignificant and yet signify everything, from a child-in-arms or a boat to an imitation, almost a plea, to share the dance, improvise the miracle. Sworn to secrecy, it little mattered that this net of words was limited to framing and masking irrecoverable gaps and that the only thing left for Palinuro to do was to form a terribly sad collection of forgotten memories, of empty boxes full of absences which would fail to remind him of who knows what places or what moments frozen in an irretrievable neighbourhood and an album of blank black pages bare of photographs of each of the dawns, the afternoons, the walks and breakfasts which Palinuro had forgotten for ever.

Because, once he had made the discovery and pledged and shared the secret, Palinuro's life changed into another being almost like himself, the other *I*, to be witness to his creation and to the loving patience which Palinuro lavished day by day on these metamorphoses and on the contrivances of sand and glass sketched by his eyes and his desires; which would see him tracing rose stilettos and their scent-enveloped corolla in the air and feel him transform the print of his foot into dry ice or into a torment drawing down the corners of his mouth. And it – this other *I* – would be grateful, grateful as a dog – or as a bitch, his bitch of a life – because, with each new word spoken by Palinuro, be it the most useless or ambiguous, would grow and dilate like a beach reaching for the horizon, while each word less would cause it to retreat and crouch in the foam, promising itself a few more years of waiting. But, from then onwards, his memories would be untouchable because they would be written down: written on his heart and written on his indelible memory; written on his tongue and written on the wind. The price he had to pay for this was not that high: it sufficed merely to halt time, say a prayer backwards, sing aloud at midnight and, particularly, become accustomed to the profusion of newcomers and sensations in the garden and new spaces and signs and orbits in the house: the house and its long, shadowed corridors and its carved furniture and its beams and its pantries and its lemon trees; the house and its sideboards, its mahogany pixies, its porcelain water jugs and its ruined balustrades; the house and Grandfather Francisco's beloved objects: his Stanley Tibbet record album, his Ernesto Icaza *charro* pictures and his Santiago Rebull bacchantes and his old La Salle automobile, its mudguards and doors and windows held on only by cobwebs, which had at one time had a lacquered folding roof and tyres with spats of English talc and which now, and since the twenties, slept a rust-free siesta in the garage behind the green and orange striped canvas curtains.

And it was also necessary to become accustomed to the new names of the inhabitants of his house and of his life:

His mother, who was pretty as a picture, he called Clementina and he gave her a special look, a chink hinting at dolls leaking sawdust and the silver slippers of her wedding day.

His father he called Eduardo and to him he gave some half-moon glasses, a wide tie red as a heart stuck through with a tie-pin and some accounting books over which, from Monday to Saturday, the tie's blood frayed.

His cousin, who was even then as beautiful and conceited as if she were of the illustrious realms of alabaster or the floating spirit of mercury, he called Estefania.

To his maternal grandmother he gave a phial of laudanum which received her mystical kiss each night and contained a few dreams less each morning and he called her the same name as his grandfather did each day when they met at breakfast: 'Altagracia'.

And his grandfather, to whom he gave a hundred and thirty kilos which came down in the world to seventy and a leg which was fatter than the other, he called by the name his Grandmother Altagracia used: 'Francisco'.

For it was thus, like twin powder flashes, merely pronouncing each other's names without adding the corresponding good morning (although for Grandmother it was always bad rather than good) that Francisco and Altagracia acknowledged each other when they met over the dining-room table and where on occasions, as on that morning, figs emasculated by the downpour dawned in the fruit bowl and, next to the fruit bowl and in the centre of the table and beneath the light cast at night by the chandelier, as though sent especially by Our Lord, resided the bread-basket.

Besides administrator of the bread-basket and queen of the kitchen, Palinuro named his Grandmother Altagracia administrator of her own illusions and impulses: illusions, for Grandmother, were fragments of stars sunk without trace in the sewers; her impulses – for example when a little bird whispered in her ear that her son Felipe would never study medicine – consisted of a slight fluttering of the left ventricle and the subsequent expulsion of a heart murmur which rose to her lips in an unchanging formula:

'May the Lord have mercy on me.'

And Grandfather Francisco:

'May the Lord, rather, fill your mouth with lilies.'

And he named his grandfather, not only because he was born in Baghdad and not only because he dressed up as Haroun al-Raschid for the carnivals in New Orleans but particularly because the first book that Palinuro read was *A Thousand and One Nights* and from that time onwards and for several years he dreamt that he would one day own a palace of oriental emeralds and topaz where he would eat pheasants stuffed with pistachios beside ponds fringed with Aleppo jasmine, for all these reasons he named his grandfather Commander of the Faithful. But so often, at school, in the streets, in bed, awake and asleep and between waking and sleeping, so often did Palinuro speak of the palace, so often did he say 'There in the palace this' and 'There in the palace that and the other' that Papa Eduardo folded the newspaper, laid it aside, and in the same tone in which many years earlier Palinuro's other grandfather, his paternal grandfather whom he never knew had said to Papa Eduardo: 'You are forbidden to talk about the war at this table', Papa Eduardo said: 'You are forbidden to talk about the palace in this house', and he got up and walked away, closing behind him the doors of the palace wine cellar, of the palace antechamber and of the palace steward's office and, turning to Mamma Clementina, asked: 'Would you like to go and see *Gone with the Wind* with Olivia de Havilland?' again in the same tone of voice as twenty years earlier the other grandfather had asked his wife Lisandra: 'Would Madame like to go and see the *Count of Luxemburg*? Emilia Leovolli is singing.' And then Papa added: 'The invasion of Sicily began yesterday,' and, in saying this, he was in fact completing that other sentence, about the Verdun offensive, which he had reluctantly been obliged to cut short when his father got fed up with the discussions between Eduardo and his brothers at table and which began in Haute Alsace, as the clams *nature* were served and ended in Mesopotamia when the remains of the carrot and tarragon were removed, shortly prior to the truce heralded by the maraschino-flavoured alpine dessert which, thank goodness – said Lisandra – quieted not only their tongues but also their martial instincts. But you – said his other more grandfather-like, truly grandfather-like grandfather Francisco, sitting Palinuro on his lap and letting him scratch his bald pate in the manner of his Circassian slaves – you will one day have children too and you will tell them that there in your palace, yes, in your palace, they served you earthenware jugs of rosewater while the night, as the poet said, lovingly sheltered Damascus beneath its wings.

And afterwards Papa and Mamma came into the dining room, said good morning to our grandparents and sat down on either side of the table. In the middle was the bread-basket, equidistant from Grandmother Altagracia and Grandfather Francisco. And at the same distance also from their male child (to whom Palinuro gave the name Felipe) despite the fact that Felipe never, or rather on only one occasion which Palinuro would always remember, appeared in the dining room early enough to have breakfast with everyone else. Because Felipe was young and a student, according to Grandmother, and because he sat up at night studying his medical books – yet another member of the family who had wanted to be a doctor – and because he went to bed late after a party which was but (according to Grandmother) a well-deserved break, and not only had breakfast in bed at eleven in the morning Mexican time, but also had the privilege enjoyed only by Grandmother (because she was the one who doled out the bread) and Grandfather (for the simple reason that he was Grandfather) which was that of choosing, the night before, the bun he would feel like eating for breakfast. And woe betide Flavia if she forgot to buy it in the morning and set it aside for young Master Felipe.

Consequently, the bread-basket lay at an infinite distance beyond Papa Eduardo's reach.

Because, to be a child was to have a Papa Eduardo who worked with his hands in the accounting department of a house of business in the centre of Mexico City, handcuffed to his books and figures with chains of paper and with sticking plaster over his mouth, secretly smoking an Elegante cigarette while his fingers, his fingers which had been born to draw mother-of-pearl-hearted quavers from the piano, hopped from one number to the next on the adding machine and the tendons of his flexor muscles danced like blue snakes on the back of his hands, playful and tame as those water eels which wrapped themselves about his legs when the child Eduardo escaped from the British College and its sung masses and *Tantum Ergo* to play truant in the waters of the Consulado River, filling his flask with tadpoles and staining his hands and knees with yellow clay; and this was the same Papa Eduardo who removed the sticking plaster to have breakfast, though he remained wordless as in his coffee and hot milk he dunked the bun which destiny and Grandmother had allocated to him on

257

that sunny morning which sketched a special smile on the happy side of don Prospero's face. And it was the same Papa Eduardo who sealed his lips after breakfast because he knew very well that the sum which he contributed to the household expenses, in part as a lodger and in part as son-in-law, the sum which had been stipulated by Grandmother Altagracia within whose centre of gravity all forces were counteracted by a vertical directed at the heart, was not so high as to entitle son-in-law Eduardo to insist on his right to selection as far as the bread-basket was concerned, nor so low as to prevent lodger Eduardo from dreaming of one day rebelling. For the same reasons and until that day came, when Papa Eduardo went to his place of business, Mamma Clementina had to continue helping Grandmother Altagracia with the housework, making beds with the care of one dressing a great gentleman who is indisposed, sweeping, dusting the goldleaf furniture of the Louis XV bedroom suite rented by the Japanese spy, emptying the chamber pot containing the stormy defecations of the Naval Under-Secretary's mother and taking Uncle Felipe his breakfast in bed.

As a child, Papa Eduardo had not been very different: son of the other grandfather, the Customs Inspector grandfather Palinuro had never known, who used every holiday to return to the city that had been that also of his birth, Veracruz, to hunt wild boar and roast them on Mocambo Beach, the child Eduardo was the Papa Eduardo who in his childhood had had (but not had) a piano in his house and had had (and again not had) a Beyer Method and, hidden in the attic of his house from where he had seen the mortars of the Tragic Ten Days go by, he buried himself in unexpected fermatas, drowning in seas of hemidemisemiquavers and wandering, lost but enthralled, in endless forests of notes until he fell asleep on the pages of wordless song, a song with strange and magical words and dreamt that he was a great pianist and that his mother Lisandra had not finished making the Christmas Eve lace tablecloth until exactly twelve o'clock and that the Rosenthal Victoria plates with chunks of roast turkey and the Baccarat glasses filled with Burgundy wine were already placed on the tablecloth but she continued to work on it saying just one more row, just one more row and between the trees ran rivers which rose in black forests and ended in black seas and there, in the distance, Lisandra was making a lace tablecloth which floated on the waves towards Terceira and San Miguel and just one more row, just one more row and Eduardo played Chopin's *Berceuse* on the piano in the manner of angels, just one more row and another and another. Where could that child have got to? And the shout awoke Papa Eduardo and awoke him for good because that same afternoon – when his sister Adelaide was at her wits' end looking for the Beyer Method – Grandfather said to Eduardo the child that he had better forget about piano playing if he wanted to grow up to be Eduardo the man, and that,

258

like embroidery and lace, music was for women and that if he insisted on learning to play the piano he would also have to learn to crochet and wear a skirt and grow his hair and, guessing the words that the child Eduardo had on the tip of tongue – because the child knew that his father went to the opera and enjoyed operettas – told him that it was quite another matter, as an adult, to enjoy music as you enjoy women themselves. And well, it was the Eduardo of a few years later, Eduardo the young man wearing a boater and carrying a cane, frustrated pianist with sticking plaster over his mouth and a smile embroidered on it by Grandmother Lisandra, who met Mamma Clementina, and it was Mamma, after rinsing her hair in beer and coaxing it into ringlets with hot pincers and, open-mouthed, pencilling her eyebrows into an arch and giving Grandfather Francisco a kiss on the uncombed sideburn on the side of his head on which he most often dreamed while asleep what he never imagined while awake, who put on her wedding dress and married Papa Eduardo.

Papa and Mamma had been living in our grandparents' house for several years when the morning came on which Uncle Felipe turned up at the breakfast table at seven on the dot, not exactly because he had got up early but rather perhaps because he had not yet gone to bed and Flavia served him his choosen bun. Then Papa Eduardo stretched out his hand towards the bread-basket and when Grandmother Altagracia told him that he had already eaten his share, Papa Eduardo replied that he would eat more because he felt like it and that was why he paid his rent and contributed to the household expenses and Uncle Felipe said show my mother more respect and Papa Eduardo replied that you are not entitled to voice an opinion, you are an idler kept by others.

Just like that, no beating about the bush, he told Felipe straight. Yes, Felipe, the male child of Altagracia, the very same who forced Grandfather to lie to himself and to others whenever they played poker and one of his friends asked him: Do you have an ace, Mr Senator? and he replied that no, he didn't, that he didn't have a single ace, but knowing that he did, that hidden up his sleeve he had an ace on which he bet his whole life and that ace was Uncle Felipe: an ace of diamonds faceted and polished by Altagracia's rough pampering until it shone with indecision and in whom Grandfather saw above all the son through whom he would have to channel his political talent which, according to him, had been curtailed not so much by the accident which incapacitated him in a shower of gold and silver but by the fact that his two closest ancestors on the genealogical tree, his parents, were perched on branches stemming from beyond the law delineated by the eighty-sixth and one-hundred-and-seventeenth meridians of longitude west of Greenwich and corresponding to the territory of the Mexican Republic and so, having been born to Spanish parents (said Grandfather, faithful to the ash of his cigar) I could not become president

259

because, had it been otherwise, as President Portes Gil said to me: Mr Governor, I myself would name you head of the government but the Constitution, you know . . .

And when Grandfather said this, his friends and children-in-law and grandchildren believed him absolutely because, among other things, Grandfather always looked like a national hero on the point of defrosting. Thus, when Uncle Felipe lost interest in medicine and ceased to join in the conversations on the subject which Uncle Esteban took it upon himself to initiate on Saturday afternoons (to the horror of Aunt Luisa whose attention fell into dumb absorption of a calla lily so as not to hear) and started saying that he wasn't interested in knowing whether James Bigger had been the first to transplant a cornea in 1835 and that he didn't give a damn whether Samuel Pepys had paid twenty shillings for a transfusion of sheep's blood and particularly when Felipe started to make fun of Uncle Esteban who proudly related the tale of Albert Liston and James Syme who as friends, enemies and friends again, sent each other organs and members of the human body between London and Scotland and Felipe demanded to know how anybody could possibly believe such humbug, how ridiculous the surgeon Liston must have looked in dressing-gown and slippers waiting for the postman at eight in the morning to see what his friend Syme had sent him, whether three fingers by ordinary mail or a registered stomach and when he added that what interested him in life now was no longer medicine but economics (which was the science of the future) Grandfather was not concerned, on the contrary: he thought that, as an economist, the doors of politics would be more readily open to Uncle Felipe without then suspecting (Grandfather) that in no time at all his Felipe, the apple of his eye, would be defeated by monopolies, oligopolies and other semi-bastards of economic science which already loomed threateningly, sailing downstream through the whirlpools of supply and demand and that this same Felipe would not delay in betraying economics and discovering chemistry which would, for some weeks – months, with luck – so he claimed, be his true and definitive vocation in life; by the time Grandmother Altagracia said to him on the next New Year's Eve, it's your turn for the drops of happiness, and serve him the last thirteen drops of the last bottle of cider of the year, the blue flame of Bunsen burners would already be blazing in Uncle Felipe's glass. In other words, Grandfather had no inkling that the most important card he was to play in his life and which he hoped one day to produce to the surprise and admiration of all, was but a diamond of ice which would melt in his hands.

Not that the others didn't suspect. The others, including Papa Eduardo, knew, not because a little bird had told them but by the parties Felipe attended, by the cars driven by his friends, by the hours he kept, by the girlfriends he perched on his knee:

'What do you mean, Felipe is an idler kept by others!' exclaimed Grandmother Altagracia, bursting with indignation.

'I studied medicine two years and now I'm going to study economics. What do you know about anything?'

'What I know is that you have never even set foot in the School of Medicine,' shouted Papa Eduardo, flinging his napkin into the middle of the table.

Then Felipe grabbed the napkin like one snatching up a gauntlet thrown down in challenge, his Adam's apple turned into an ostrich egg, he stood and walked to where Papa Eduardo was sitting and punched him in the face with a well-placed fist with his whole weight behind it and the leather dining chair went sprawling on to the roses of the carpet and with it went Papa Eduardo and beetle-like his shattered glasses landed on the same roses and Papa got up, he got up twice to hit Uncle Felipe and twice Uncle Felipe knocked him down and finally Papa Eduardo's legs turned to jelly and a macabre iodine flooded his eyes and he didn't get up again.

Apart from the fact that Palinuro swore one day to avenge his father against Uncle Felipe, apart from the fact that he felt like throwing his spinach soup in his uncle's face to see him emerge, vertically, like a corpse from the sea, pale and dripping weed, apart from swearing one day to empty a bottle of India ink on Uncle Felipe's white shirts when they were left to their fate in the wash tub and when Flavia came back to finish rinsing them she would think that the tap had regurgitated a mass of black butterflies which had settled permanently on Master Felipe's shirts, not only did Palinuro see the three times that Uncle Felipe punched Papa Eduardo, but for many years he would see the same scene replayed before his eyes, running forwards and backwards like a delirious film: the napkin flung down by his father returned alone like a tame bird to his hand and suddenly everything was how it had been a few seconds previously when Palinuro would have wanted life to stand still and for a few instants he made believe that nothing had happened; but then he remembered himself picking up the shattered lenses of Papa Eduardo's spectacles, scattered over the roses of the carpet like drops of frozen green dew and then he remembered Papa Eduardo with his swollen mouth and black eye and his piece of raw steak and his broken spectacles and his sticking plaster over his mouth; and it was for this reason and because Papa never again raised his hand to the bread-basket, just as when he was a child he never again dared to touch the piano keys; it was for this reason and because Papa Eduardo had not dared to leave our grandparents' house since the only way that he could keep a little money over to go to the cinema and to play poker on Sunday afternoons with the senator and the senator's other sons-in-law and drink the brandy brought by the general with the glass eye and Uncle Austin's whisky, was to continue living in our grandparents' house and endeavour to endure petty humiliations as best he might: it was for all these reasons that Papa Eduardo continued always to fall, always to be standing at the instant he was punched and always to fall and to get to his feet and fall again like a weakling, in syncopated movements intersecting each other, revealing an absurd and irritating harmony of stained-glass windows, chandeliers, delft-blue porcelain plates hanging on the walls, wallpaper and byzantine flowers and cabriole chair legs, the differing configurations depending on whether Papa Eduardo was falling or rising to his feet, always on the point of collapsing, always on the point of once more setting his bones one above the other and getting up yet again, while Grandmother Altagracia and Aunt Luisa and Mamma Clementina shouted: Felipe, an idler? Felipe, a brute? Felipe, a kept man? Felipe, a savage?

14

Further confessions: Molkas's Milkrun

The first time Palinuro opened his eyes, he saw Molkas in the dock once more. Which meant that Palinuro was entitled to a breather. But it was no more than that: just a breather. The questioning which had begun in the Imaginary Islands, together with the questions asked him by Walter – as though the voice of his conscience – the question he asked himself – as though the voice of Walter – were infinite. But he had to make the most of the opportunity, before his turn came round again, to torture Molkas and make him spit out the rest of the truth. If necessary, until blood flowed: 'Or until milk flowed,' said Fabricio.

Who was Molkas? Who was this odd, unreal character who was afraid of dying of Parkinson's disease for wanking and in whose honour the following ditty had been composed:

> *He had no hesitation*
> *In prescribing masturbation*
> *As the surest embrocation*
> *For his woe.*

Who was this poker-faced lad invariably dressed in his mustard-coloured university pullover, who was able to eat ten spam sandwiches in El Panuco, calling as witnesses to this feat the caricatures of rectors wilting on the Coca-Cola-stained walls and the puma of the university crest and the American football team complete with the cheers of plump adolescent girls, and who could, in one go, belch as many other dynasties? He was not, obviously, a second version of Cousin Walter's dazzling idleness. However hard he might will it, Molkas would never have the same patchwork waistcoat and the same dark glasses in which drowned the palaces of Venice and the Deux Magots café and not even by recourse to all chromatic possibilities could Molkas be compared to Fabricio who at that time already carried a medieval world on his shoulders and sported the talisman he had inherited from his mother: that is, a tongue long as a wriggling goldfish, on contact with which lilies were burnt to a cinder and the heart slid away along the left rib. So . . . who was Molkas?

'I am Molkas,' he said.

And, as though by magic and thanks to Fabricio – it should be remembered that Fabricio was a magician – the lad in the room turned into the Molkas that Palinuro had met a few weeks previously: a lad who claimed that, though he was not a magician – because he was in fact a fortune-teller – he had the power to bestow a medal on a sneeze, laugh at a guffaw in his own face or send a fart to hell because he, contrary to everything Palinuro and Cousin Walter told him, was lord and master of his whole body and all his functions, including not only his well-oiled cerebral convolutions which spun around at over a hundred thoughts a minute but also all his organs, however important and sacred they might be considered. At the same time, he was prone to sudden and brilliant and almost poetic turns of phrase and he was capable of abruptly turning his face to the skies and saying, for example: 'The sky is starry and blue, the stars shiver in the distance . . .' and then change the word 'stars' for some vulgarity to show his friends that he, Molkas, had no idols in his life other, of course, than himself. Although he sometimes invented phrases that were his own and nobody else's: 'When the horizon becomes compressed,' he said, completely drunk, 'and sheep run after their number plates, I can paralyse the dawn.'

'I am a man of great experience in such matters,' he had sworn to Palinuro when they met and started to discuss girlfriends, women and lovers without further ado. And then, also without further ado, he asked Palinuro: 'Have you ever slept with your girlfriend?'

Palinuro's testicles hurt at the mere mention of his girlfriends. He mentally reviewed all those he had had or could have had, including, of course, his cousin Estefania, the chemist's daughter, the little Sunday maid to whom he had made more than one sickly demonstration, the third-year primary school teacher's daughter who had the name of an Arabian princess and the face of a cherub bathed in mineral water. In other words, all those he had caressed with such delicacy that they were never even aware of it.

'Of course, that is not what women like,' Molkas assured him. 'On the contrary, they like you to cover them with your digital and genital prints, as a friend of mine whom you will meet if it ever stops raining, said . . .'

And that same morning, in the pouring rain and after repeating that he was a man of great experience in such matters and saying: 'Beware that Baudelaire's black flowers do not turn into the white flowers of leukorrhea,' which warning Palinuro never did understand, firstly because it was so cryptic and secondly because he was certain that Molkas had no idea who Baudelaire was, or Neruda, or any of the other poets whom he frequently quoted parrot-fashion, the two friends walked by the statue of St Luke. 'According to legend, he was a painter,' explained Molkas. 'And, according to the Epistle to the Colossians, he practised the art of Galen. He is, therefore, considered the patron of medicine among Catholics.' Molkas then went on to observe Palinuro's fingers and assured him that he would become a great surgeon if he exercised them, the best method being to relate them daily to the five senses. 'You suck your thumb with the single-mindedness of the ruminant,' he explained, 'starting the moment you discover that it is possible to transcend destiny. The index finger is, of course, for picking your nose in search of green mysteries, although this activity is only permitted on Saturdays and today, it so happens, is Saturday: and St Luke will forgive us for smearing his wisdom with snot. It says here that this venerable monument to the man who was scholar and physician was moved from the School of San Carlos to this spot in 1858. The ring finger is for rubbing the sleep from your eyes and excuse my not singing the praises of this congealed dry humour which cakes the eyelids and causes us to see coloured horses all over the place. You ask what IATPIK means? I have no idea,' Molkas answered Palinuro when he wanted to know the meaning of the inscription engraved on the scrolls of marble. 'Lastly, the little finger, as its name indicates, is the auricular or ear finger, specially designed to remove wax. Now I invite you to go to the portals of Holy Sunday Square to meet the Evangelists of the blue public clerks' desks. You will have noticed, of course, that I missed out one finger: the middle finger which is also the most friendly and which goes straight to the heart of things. I have left it till last because it is the finger reserved for pleasure. May I state the obvious? Clitoris, as Fabricius relates, was a young Greek girl, daughter of a Mirmillon gladiator. She was so tiny that Jupiter, who was in love with her, had to change himself into an ant to love her. Just revel in the glory of it and fear not the easy way. Clitorate the girls until you make them appreciate their incredible luck. I am a man of great experience in such matters.'

Moreover, as is apparent, you could become Molkas's bosom pal from one day to the next and treat him as if you had known him always and been living and drinking with him for years and playing dominoes in the same café where the hours pass and bottomless briefcases full of unreadable documents are left behind on two conditions: first, to take his vulgarity – or 'vulvarity' as he himself said – philosophically and, second, to be as Palinuro was in those days: a lad who believed that anybody who studied medicine was beyond the pale. And, as it happened, of the three friends, the exception in this respect was none other than Molkas, whose motive in studying the lively science, the adulterine science as St Victor called it, was not to march about the hospital dressed in white, medical bag at the ready to diagnose trembling cataracts of the crystalline lens and polymorphous eruptions appearing on the buttocks of suckling babes. In other words, he did not study medicine for the ideals that led Claude Bernard and Brown-Sequard to renounce literature and devote themselves to science. ('Thank

265

god,' Walter had commented, 'otherwise, just imagine the horrors they would have written.') And any interest in brain tumours was to be attributed solely to the fact that he had read somewhere that the operation to remove them – at the time, anyway – was the most expensive that the surgeon could perform. For the same reason, he scorned the setting of fractured forearms, which yielded but a few pesos profit. His greatest ambition was to become an abortionist in a country where, as in Mexico, it was illegal . . . for this reason and for this reason only was he an outstanding student, devouring books and magazines on gynaecology, though not necessarily because he wished to specialize – Molkas's idea of a specialist was a person who studied ever more about ever less until he came to know almost everything about almost nothing, which was very sad – no, what he was going to be was a humble general abortionist.

'The fewer women wanting to stay pregnant,' he said, 'the more pregnant my wallet.'

'But that in itself is a species of specialization, if you will excuse the repetition,' Fabricio said to him. 'And, while we are on the subject, it is my considered opinion that if you're looking for a quiet life and lots of money, you should concentrate on cancer research. As an illustrious contemporary researcher said, there are many more people living from cancer than dying from it.'

'I think a better idea,' said Palinuro, 'would be to devote yourself to plastic surgery which Harold Gillies so accurately called "the Cinderella of Surgery". Rich old matrons pay fortunes to have fat removed from their stomachs.'

'To have the bags removed from under their eyes,' added Fabricio.

'For a *ridectomie*, as the French say, a face lift. In other words, hide their wrinkles under their hair or behind their ears, so that they can never smile again. But neither can they frown when you present them with the bill!'

'How revolting! Just imagine opening up the belly of a fifty-year old bag and with your own hands removing three kilos of spongy fat!' exclaimed Molkas.

'True enough: it's like opening up a fish to take out its innards. Your hands get covered in grease that never comes off,' proffered Palinuro.

'To remove the hernias of fat which form bags under the eyes is equally awe-inspiring,' added Fabricio, with a learned air, 'when you inject the novocain into the lower lid, it comes away from the eye and swells up like a balloon . . .'

'How revolting!' repeated Molkas.

'And then,' continued Fabricio, 'the hernias come out, all in one go, like a cluster of coffee beans.'

'Ugh!' grunted Molkas.

'But, when all is said and done, you make a lot of money. Like fixing breasts. Flaccid breasts which have almost disappeared. Huge breasts containing tons of surplus fat.'

'Fixing breasts? Mmmmm,' said Molkas, 'that sounds more promising . . .'

'I don't see why. It's just as revolting. There are breasts that have an excess, no exaggeration, of up to a kilo of fat apiece,' Palinuro warned him.

'And breast fat is just as repulsive as any other: yellow and squishy.'

'Yes, yes, but the idea definitely has potential,' said Molkas, dreaming of a sign in his surgery saying, in golden letters: *Molkas, mammo-plastic surgeon.*

Moreover, Molkas was a useful friend to have. He knew all the ins and outs of the School of Medicine and, to both Palinuro and Fabricio, Molkas was their Baloo the bear who taught them the law of the jungle. This, apart from the fact that there was no mediocre book on the history of medicine or on infectious diseases or biographies of surgeons and discoverers of cabalistic drugs that Molkas had not read and he shared with his friends that absolute despair, that anguish of opening at random the dictionary of medical terms and finding that, of fifty words, they did not know the meaning of forty-nine and sometimes forty-nine and a half and, like themselves, he was convinced that such terms materialized from outer space for the sole purpose of complicating the life of medical students: Hyperpyrexia, sternocleidomastoid, phenyldimethylpyrazolonemythyaminosulphonic acid, in other words epsom salts, not to speak – among other reasons, because it was unspeakable – of the name of another substance appearing in the *Guinness Book of Records* which has 1,913 letters: that is, 1,813 more than Finnegan's thunderclap.

'Do you think these words are of human origin? Do you think there is a man with the balls to invent them?' asked Molkas with snorts of rage. Palinuro agreed, striding across Holy Sunday Square. 'Rokitansky's disease, the Babinski-Nageotte syndrome. Can you imagine more complicated names? Why couldn't it be Martinez' disease or the Perez and Perez syndrome? Could it be that in Spain and in Latin America there have not been men of science as available and with the pluck of other nationalities?' and Palinuro laughed cheerfully, wholeheartedly.

But Molkas's friends soon began to suspect that there was something odd in his preference for breast operations . . . *Oh los senos, bayas jugosas* . . . Breasts, juicy berries – wrote Gomez de la Serna – *Los senos bajo las blusas de lunares, tienen veinte mil pezones* . . . Breasts beneath blouses of beauty spots, have twenty thousand nipples . . . And Molkas shuddered convulsively whenever he repeated the lines aloud to himself and felt sorry for poor St Agatha, the one who had her breasts cut off. And the fact is that he had never told his friends that he liked women with large and generous breasts, breasts that overflow their own shadow; Ivory Alps as Marino called them, breasts which seek the navel and point to the Dioscuri; breasts graceful as two gazelle fauns as they are called in the Song of Songs; acrobatic breasts balanced by a whole sinful bibliography; breasts which the Valkyries' plaits could not cover; breasts perfumed by screens; breasts, finally, threatened by malignant tumours and first milk teeth . . .

'If Molkas can be compared to anyone at all,' Fabricio said one day to Palinuro (in confidence) thinking of the almost perfect way in which Molkas played the accordion, 'it would be with Brighella, the cynical and brutal Brighella.'

That was indeed the key to Molkas's personality: a youth who had several talents such as a magnificent ear for music, or drawing like a king, etc., but was quite unable to appreciate music or painting. 'It's not that he finds plastic surgery revolting,' said Fabricio, 'his revulsion, in fact, is for anything which reminds him of art.' 'The plastic arts for example,' said Palinuro. 'That's exactly it,' said Fabricio. 'But then . . . what about all this breasts business . . .?' 'That is something we shall very soon find out.'

In this *commedia dell'arte* Fabricio was not, as one would suppose, an Isabelle disguised, but rather a Scaramouch who, on the rare occasions he opened his mouth, fascinated his audience with accounts of his adventures. More than once he climbed up on to a bench in Holy Sunday Square to tell the postmen, the balloon vendors and the housewives out shopping, a story about the most famous surgeons and painters of antiquity, but making believe that their exploits were his own. And Palinuro, who could Palinuro be but Harlequin, not only because Cousin Walter gave him the famous patchwork waistcoat, but also because of the way he always appeared and disappeared in and out of other people's lives suddenly and unexpectedly (his friends managed to count up to forty-five occasions), and other tricks of his, such as lengthening and shortening his body to make himself look taller or shorter?

And, sure enough, the two friends soon discovered the reason behind the fiendish Brighella's obsession with breasts. And, incidentally, they learned that he had been very unhappy during a prolonged period of his adolescence and that this had a lot to do with his obsession with breasts and his early infancy passed in the arms of Mamma Molkas. And the fact is that Mamma Molkas – whose real name Molkas refused to divulge – had no nipples and could never suckle him.

'Scientifically speaking, she suffered *amastia*,' said Palinuro.

'How stupid can you be!' exclaimed Fabricio. '*Amastia* means absence of breasts. What Mamma Molkas had, or rather didn't have, was nipples, which is nothing but a run-of-the-mill case of *atelia*. The difference is the same as between a woman who has *polymastia* which is several mammae, and one who has *polytelia*, which is several nipples.'

268

'Anyway, mammastia or mammatelia, whichever, my mamma could never feed me at the breast.'

'In other words, more scientifically put, poor Molkas was an agalactous child who never had the opportunity to suck Mamma's Morgani's tubercles,' said Fabricio, taking advantage of the defencelessness to which Molkas was prone when he was dead drunk. But Molkas wasn't listening:

'So, my mamma brought me up on tinned Carnation milk . . .'

'The milk of happy cows, served in South Pacific pullman coaches,' pointed out Fabricio.

Palinuro remembered a ditty from his advertising days:

Carnation milk is the best in the land, in the land,
Here I sit with a can in my hand,
No tits to pull, no hay to pitch,
Just punch a hole in the son-of-a-bitch.

'Anyway, what happened to Mamma Molkas and her galactophorous ducts?' asked Fabricio.

Meanwhile, Palinuro groaned inwardly: 'Lord preserve us, this sounds like a clinical history made up by Freud.'

'The ducts dried up. Anyway, Mamma Molkas died many years ago and there is no point in talking about her,' said Molkas junior.

'Then be so good as to explain why you started talking about Mamma Molkas if she is irrelevant,' demanded Fabricio, who was more innocent than Palinuro in some ways, or perhaps more forgetful.

And Molkas told them his story.

He told them how, for many years, his greatest pleasure, and the only way he was able to get an erection, was to imagine himself touching and kissing the breasts of a woman, but that he very seldom dared to do it with his girlfriends, and when he did try it, either they didn't let him or, if they did, things went no further than that and he ended up with a damp patch in his trousers. And on the day that he decided to begin his inter-sexual life – a sad monogamic afternoon with ink-black stars that looked like melancholic asterisks – and made his way towards Las Vizcaínas Street, walking slowly with one hand in his pocket to raise his spirits and jerk up his inferiority complex, a great tragedy occurred. He already had a more or less photographic (or perhaps photogenic) idea of what his first prostitute would be like: she would be beautiful, like certain of the foam-rubber girls appearing in *Playboy*, and admirable in the most-accepted senses: her skin would be an alabaster of contradictions where blossomed honey-coloured beauty spots and jugs filled with waning moon juice. And, of course, not only would she want him with all her heart but she would defend her most intimate recesses like a butterfly turned on its back, to give Molkas the

269

sensation of raping a virgin in the most hard-fought way. In other words, according to Molkas's description and hallucinations, that admirable woman would be something very close to a pirate edition of Estefania. Thus, his disappointment was immense when that first prostitute of his tender years refused to remove her bra. 'They pay to fuck me, not to fondle and drool over my breasts,' she told him and flopped down on the bed, raised her skirts and was transformed totally into a hairy flower half-naked all day long and, as though that were not enough, with a smell, good lord! with a putrid smell that bore no relation to the bitter-sweet springs that Molkas had imagined.

'I suppose you couldn't do a thing,' said Fabricio.

'Nothing, nothing, nothing,' Molkas thrice confessed.

'I would almost venture to say that the terminal ejaculation did not occur,' Palinuro ventured, without the *almost*, to say.

'Idiot,' said Molkas, 'I couldn't even get it up.'

'That is psychosexual impotence,' asserted Fabricio. 'Between that and sexual aberrations there is but a step . . . peeping Toms and voyeurs . . .' he added, squinting through an imaginary keyhole formed by his index finger and thumb.

'Flashers,' Palinuro contributed, showing Molkas his cock.

'Fetishists,' added Fabricio, showing Molkas Estefania's bra.

'Masochists,' ended Palinuro, fetching Molkas a clout which would have landed him on the floor if he hadn't already been there.

'Leave him be, don't take advantage of his being drunk. We must take into account that his libido has remained in the parallactic stage.'

Palinuro again turned on the desk lamp and for the second time shone it into Molkas's face.

'You must confess,' he said softly. 'You must tell us everything, from beginning to end, omitting not a single detail.'

Molkas wept and his tears diluted his strength which had been sufficient to lift Testut's *Anatomy* single-handed. But they were crocodile tears: immediately afterwards he threatened to commit suicide. And, effectively, he took from the pocket of his raincoat a plastic pistol, got to his feet and raised the barrel to his right temple. Then he pulled the trigger. As was to be expected, no shot was heard. Neither did the pistol produce a bullet of iron, a bullet of steel or even a bullet of talcum powder . . .

He pulled the trigger again.

Another failure.

He pulled it a third time.

The same result.

In view of this circumstance, Molkas showed the revolver to an imaginary public and said: 'Ladies and gentlemen: this revolver is poisoned.'

He placed the barrel in his mouth and gulped the poison noisily: he fell flat on his face.

Molkas sought once more to make love to a prostitute but this time the problem wasn't that she wouldn't allow her breasts to be kissed but, simply, that she had no breasts.

'Scientifically speaking, she suffered *amastia*,' said Palinuro. This, with admirable confidence.

And again Molkas was incapable of doing anything. He then believed that he was impotent and would never again be able to sleep with a woman. 'One blessed afternoon . . . an afternoon on which I went with another prostitute – my fifth or sixth attempt, I don't remember . . .' That afternoon, when Molkas was alone with the woman, he sat bare-arsed on the bed, knees together, very sad, and the woman said to him: 'Come on, I'm in a hurry.' And he answered her: 'No, no I can't. I mean, I don't want to.' 'You're nothing but a child,' the woman said to him. 'No. I am a man. The fact is that I don't want to. But I'll pay you anyway, don't worry.' 'Yes, yes, you're still a child. I can tell by your face, the light in your eyes. Here, try this,' the woman said to him. 'She offered me her breast.' 'Her breast?' Fabricio and Palinuro chorused incredulously. 'And that's not all: the breast contained milk!' 'Milk?' 'Yes, because she had a child!' 'A child?' 'Yes, a child at the breast, a baby, yes, like you, go on, suck, my child,' the woman said to him. Molkas sucked and gazed at the erect nipple. Then he sucked harder and the milk dribbled from his mouth and down his neck leaving a trail as of ancient foam. And then he clung like a limpet and his reputation started to rise like a funicular on account of the beauty's shouts of pleasure which the other two friends would almost swear they could hear behind Molkas's words: 'We thought for a moment that you were murdering her.' 'We debated whether to call the police.' 'We voted on whether or not we should break down the door and burst into the room to save her.' 'We would have found him hanging from her breasts,' like a baby, drinking the silken luxury of those dark teats, while the beautiful, the admirable woman fondled his penis and, as always happens, suddenly, after a first gleaming drop had appeared on the tip of the pommel of his sword, the sperm shot out like a geyser and Molkas felt what no holiday had ever given him and the woman took his pulse until he had gulped his last and Molkas almost fell asleep in her arms. When he got up, the sperm and two threads of milk flowed together into the woman's navel, as into the centre of Eden.

'But you didn't fuck her?' 'Yes, afterwards, afterwards I was able to, for the first time in my life and many times after that.' 'How? Did you see the whore again?' 'Yes, she said to me: come back, come back next week, and I went back because I fell madly in love with her.' And, like an idiot, Molkas returned again and again to the same room submerged in a floral

271

obscurantism and where a smooth-necked stuffed dog, curtains awaiting chaste death and the hanger on which Molkas hung his hat and she her bras were witnesses to his visits, which he made without friends, every Monday, every Tuesday, Everyday, when the sun shone and the helicopters folded their blades, to love the woman and preside over the confluence of the milky sap of his body and hers on her new and admirable belly. And it was only after each such exchange that he was able to enter her and reach a second orgasm. Molkas realized that, while he could not repay these delights with devotion or tenderness, with fans and silks hanging to dry, he could at least feign them heart and soul. So he disguised himself as a good student, the kind that go to school armed with a ruler to calculate the diametre of an idea. He disguised himself as Prince Blue of Prussia. He disguised himself as an adult, allowing his wisdom tooth to grow, together with a moustache which was so shy that it hardly dared to appear in public. The woman embraced him, wept buckets over his head, told him of the old days of furious frigidity and the poverty of her parents, her sisterhood with the streets of the neighbourhood, her garters flung into the gods of the theatres. And nothing remained in the room to remind her of all this, of days past, even unintentionally. Her only company was the voice of a broadcaster on an anonymous radio, the wallpaper destroyed by courtly weeds, pictures of somebody or other with a little girl of the sea who was herself many years previously, together with the nuptial egg used to darn Molkas's socks. A silent train crossed the calendars, washerwomen chatted beneath the fruit-laden arches and a distant apothecary announced his ointments. 'But that is not love,' said Fabricio. 'Ah, but I started to fall in love when I began to tell her about my life.' And, effectively, Molkas in happy abandon told the woman of a fantastic past. He spoke of an endless succession of jobs, of auctions and of raincoats and old vests, of his being obliged to work miracles to fix pipes before the meridian. At first, he went at a snail's pace, sensing the spongy texture of his voice, but his fear of emptiness and the spasms of that admirable woman tempered his remorse: 'I have no mother,' he told her, 'I have no father, I grew up in an orphanage.' 'Stinking liar,' said Palinuro. 'I was very unhappy, they flogged me with quince switches and stole my pillows, they forbade me to cry and ordered me to have golden dreams.' 'Poor Molkas, my love, how you suffered! But suckle, my love, then tell me all about it,' said the beauty and the springs of the mattress leapt with pleasure. 'Then I had a girlfriend. I used to write her many letters of every colour and every perfume, I told her that I was very lonely among the orphans, that the school was grey, that the food was revolting and she wrote back the same: you say that you were very lonely among the orphans, the school is grey, the food is revolting and that every time that I reply I write the same as you have written to me . . .' 'Poor Molkas, my poor love, could anybody be

272

more miserable . . .' 'Of course, woman,' Molkas said to her. 'If the dogs and the wardens betray you and you yourself go back on your word and you live in a chaos of nights whose worth depends on their brightness, just imagine, and next day go to work in a bank, ten hours at a stretch. And you come back and bury yourself in this rabbit-hutch and listen to the murmuring of your sphincter muscles. Operating those machines, entering ten thousand cheques a day until you can't take any more, woman, and your friends and the telephones invade you, then existence turns to toffee. All for the sake of studying medicine, of going to the School in my white uniform and, standing, recite the prismatic epithelia and the adipose lumps of the mammary glands.' 'Do you know what I then became?' the woman asked him. 'A whore,' Palinuro said to him. 'What do you eat to make you guess?' asked Molkas, to which Palinuro very seriously replied: 'Every morning I breakfast on a dictionary *nature*.' 'That's right,' said the woman, 'just as you see me now, from then onwards I was a whore. I think I always was. I think I was born with my legs spread.' But Molkas wasn't listening to her. 'Then, when pay-day came around, I went out with my friends from the bank to get drunk, and my girlfriend was left waiting for me forever, beneath an ash tree, pecked by the pigeons.' But the woman was not listening to him: 'I took the tram home from school and an old man nibbled my thighs.' 'He tickled?' 'He nibbled. And the worst of it all was that the old man was my father.' Molkas got up, made a pass with his cape and told her, point blank: 'You shouldn't talk like that, woman. You cannot exhibit your family as though they were monkeys in the circus. That which is called dirty laundry, and in your case is putrid, should be machine-washed at home.' 'Molkas, my love, my child, I have never seen you like this.' 'And you will never see me again, you should be ashamed of yourself.' 'Yes, my love, of course, forgive me,' said the admirable woman, embracing his knees. 'Get up and go to hell.' 'Forgive me, baby, my dear heart, do!' and she kissed his scraped knees, his visits to the skating rink and his baseball matches. 'Your father, your father! If you say that of your father, what would you not say of me?' 'Jesus: what a drama!' gasped Fabricio, undecided as to whether he should believe a word of what Molkas was saying, but . . . 'children, drunkards and fooles, cannot lye' pointed out Palinuro, adding that, in this very particular case, Molkas was both drunk and a child. 'Once again she offered me her breasts,' said Molkas. He scorned them, took a grimy note from his wallet, scrunched it into a ball and flicked it at the picture of the recently appearing Virgin of Fatima. The woman called down to him from the window and again showed him the milky way. A few white drops succeeded in splashing Molkas who was soon lost among the unusual collection of phosphorescent skulls walking the street.

'And you never went back?'

273

Yes, he went back once, because he needed the woman's breasts, but she had lost her milk from fright and so lost Molkas forever.

'What a tragedy.'

'How awful.'

'And what did she do? Did she return to the straight and narrow?'

'You better tell us the real reason why you left her Molkas . . .'

'It was because of the child which squawked like the devil.'

'Ah, first you drink all its milk and then you complain when it screams with hunger! You're a disgrace!'

'You're despicable!'

'You're detestable!'

'You're morally destitute!'

'What did you do then?'

Molkas, unlike Palinuro, was not interested in stealing an itinerary where bloomed tins of oil and advertising alienations. Not for nothing had he grown up among scientific references to sex and gonococci and among homespun prayers for atmospheric occlusions that the alfalfa might grow greener. 'Was it very hard to leave the beauty?' Not a bit: the empty fruits barred the way to any shilly-shallying. 'You hit the bottle, to forget her?' He hit the bottle, he made some cleverer friends and frequented an infinite variety of whorehouses and strip joints. Then, mustering all the assiduity of which he was capable, he set about seeking a girlfriend who subscribed to his heresies. He haunted the parks at the hour when gardeners flog the grass with nickle-plated whips and bought candy apples to offer a blonde nursemaid. He waited at the gates of the Benito Juarez primary school and the Secondaria 18 for the schoolgirls to come out of class and he called suggestive remarks after them, making them blush from their ankle socks upwards. He visited the squalid quarters of the city and was jostled by drunks suffering from alcoholic insufficiency, hairdressers determined to peroxide their victims to death and blind men who pestered him with hats and flying zippers. He bought all the daily newspapers, including the red evening rags, and devoted himself to searching for lost adolescents: 'Martha, age thirteen, left home last Sunday and has not returned. She was wearing a blouse white as snow, a pink skirt, yellow ankle socks.' He winked at the concierge. He chatted up a widow who had long austral fingernails and was always laden with oracular gems and indulged himself in spanking the little cook in the Chinese café. The nursemaid allowed herself to be invited to one of those neighbourhood cinemas where, between cartoons, ships full of ice-cream sail by and where old ladies go armed with umbrellas to trip up the young men, and the young girls go armed with long nails to dig into the old men's legs and the old men go armed with their pipes, and etc. And the nursemaid let him fondle and kiss her breasts before a crowd of bedouins from Arabia Felix galloping

274

across Arabia Petraea. A young girl, lost one night in a filthy alley, let herself be taken to a garden and, beneath a lamp post from which hung five crystal balls for telling the future, she allowed herself to be masturbated on condition that Molkas do it without mussing up her pubic hair. The widow, gushing birthdays, allowed herself to be taken to a hotel room, removed her black weeds to show her ultra-violet knickers and then performed a belly dance for Molkas. Then she crashed out on the bed and started to snore like a rhinoceros. But Molkas had tasted milk and could make love no more.

'Never?' asked Fabricio. 'Never more?' Palinuro asked in turn, in biblical accents. 'Never, for a few months,' said Molkas, because in the end, almost by a chance, he met a washerwoman with eyes black as capulin cherries and chestnut plaits of copper sheen, who invited him to visit her. She lived alone in a room built on the flat roof of an apartment building from where you could contemplate the zodiac in its entirety. And how great was Molkas's surprise when, that same afternoon, he saw two dry, yellowish milk stains on the washerwoman's blouse. And she removed her blouse to show him her milk-swollen breasts. She told him how, for many years, large round tumours had grown in her womb, transparent tumours full of unmentionable things of all colours which overflowed from the operating table into sweetie jars filled with phenol in the pathology laboratories. But they were benign tumours, the doctor told her, which could only be eradicated by having a child. 'I didn't want to have a child,' the washerwoman told him. 'But my body did. So finally I made up my mind and had one.' 'Where is it?' Molkas asked. 'It's not here. I gave it away a few days ago. It will have a better life and they will love it more.' 'And you still have milk?'

'Still.'

'And does she still have milk?' asked Fabricio.

'Still,' replied Palinuro, on behalf of Molkas, because Molkas had fallen asleep.

From then onwards, the two friends began to understand Molkas a little better and nurtured his obsession (so to speak), assuring him that it was most unlikely that he would ever suffer from tapeworm and its attendant discomforts (anal expulsion of tapeworm fragments), since Savonarola no less had exalted the anthelmintic properties of mother's milk; reminding him that St Peter likened his teachings to the Corinthians to the milk given to children; urging him to save money that he might travel and one day see the fountains of Villa d'Este where there are sculptures of women – or one, at least – with incredibly large breasts; giving him photographs of Jayne Mansfield and a copy of the *Bizarre* magazine showing Rosalie Fournier, the woman whose thighs atrophied and turned into breasts and recommending that if he were asked to choose which animal he would like to be reincarnated as, he opt to be either a baby chimp because they suckle for years on end or else one of those ants specialized in caring for the plant lice which produce sweet milk or, failing that, a leech of the kind still employed in medicine, on pericarditis patients for instance, because it is often necessary to anoint the patients' skin with sweetened milk when it refuses to take hold. Cousin Walter who, of course, had to have his say (and, incidentally, christened the affair: *Molkas's Milkrun*) didn't agree with the choice and told him it would be better to have Mamma Molkas reincarnated as a monotreme mammal since the milk of such animals oozes from their pores, runs down their hide and has to be lapped up by their young while he, Molkas, should be reincarnated as a fish of the teleost type whose taste buds are situated all over the body. In addition, Walter obviously recommended reading Hindu mythology that Molkas might take heart from the legend of Lakshmi, the goddess who was born in a milky ocean which was very likely the same one in which Kama-dhenu, the winged cow with three tails, was also born and went on to relate to him the legend of Jupiter and the goat Amalthea and of Asclepius and his respective goat and read him the part from *Ulysses* where Leopold Bloom imagines that he is milking Molly's breasts straight into his cup of tea. Molkas tirelessly searched every shop in Mexico City selling antiques (beware of their antics! recommended Palinuro) when Fabricio told him that he remembered having seen a little marble statue of Diana of Ephesus in her guise as Polymastus, she of the multiple breasts. Later, Molkas copied from an encyclopaedia a drawing of Ceres Mammosa, wet nurse of the world, who was likewise depicted with a fair number of breasts. From textbooks he learned that it is the protein which gives human milk its bluish tinge, that the act of suckling is closely linked to uterine contractions and that cow's milk can be maternized by a centrifugal process which separates the casein from the fat. And when Fabricio told him that Orthodox Jews do not use the same knife for cutting meat as for cutting dairy products, he wondered what a Jewish surgeon would do if required to perform an operation on the breasts of a nursing mother and whether there was such a thing as Kosher surgery, so to speak. From a book on home remedies he found out that a mother's milk may be improved by giving her shrimp heads and ground silkworms dissolved in wine. Walter also acquainted him with the legend of the magician who had alternately changed from a man into a woman and translated for him whole sections from *Les Mamelles de Tirésias*. 'Do you suppose that when Tiresias stopped being a woman and went back to being a man, he still had milk in his breasts?' he asked Fabricio. 'I have no idea. The only thing I do know is what Papirius de Ebers says to the effect that a man's milk, in view of its incalculable rarity, is full of virtues.' Molkas shuddered because, for the first time, ever, it dawned on him that he might well, why not? be a homosexual. 'But is one a homosexual when one falls in love with a hermaphrodite like Zeus Stratius, the one with the big tits?' 'What's more,' said Fabricio quite irrelevantly, 'Tiresias admitted that the woman gets nine times more pleasure from the sexual act than the man. But beware: these extraordinary phenomena are not to be confused with other more common ones, such as what is known as witch's milk.' And, one afternoon, Molkas came home happy as rarely before because he had just discovered the story of Moses: 'The archangel Gabriel, when he left him in the cave, caused milk to flow from one of his fingers, so that he would not die of hunger. Just imagine how fantastic, to have a lactating finger and spend your life sucking it?' Molkas said in a transport of bliss. Because, deep down, Molkas was but a child. 'A child still tied to its mother's bra straps,' as Palinuro said.

Anyway, there was one thing that was quite clear and, when Molkas was through sleeping off his monumental hangover, he took it upon himself to remind his friends: he had been born a virgin, but not a Virgo and, even if he had been, he was a virgin no longer. Therefore he would not only have to initiate them in the mysteries of sex but also, why not? in the joys of necrophilia. For that very purpose, they would go to oft-quoted La Vizcaínas Street, where the pith of removal men was aroused and postmen left their bags in the middle of the street or in the stairway to go and deliver letters of love at first sight to the tarts. Each week, or each fortnight, doctors from the Health Ministry came to the street and parted the legs of the whores to prescribe antibiotics and emergency coituses. Students, as a rule, had their own visiting hours. Those launching out for the first time on the night-club circuit to the bitter and frenzied rhythm of beer and the *Poet and Peasant* overture, chose midnight, walking arm-in-arm and drawn on by the whiffs of fresh fish, appearing *en masse* with their hands full of promises. These were the Trojan students who were always ready to present arms. Other lads, from the secondary schools, who still cocked their own hand-guns by way of allegory, came in punctual ranks at the postman and broom vendor's hour, parading their beardless heat along the opposite pavement, from where they stared at the row of doors and windows. Some of the tarts flashed them a glimpse of recently talced holy grail and others an empress's bosom or a pair of thighs where a priest had lost his soul and his dentures. The women called out to them by the colour of their hair or their pullovers and they pretended not to hear. When school broke up they were rescued by the schoolgirls in heraldic uniform and went off with them, whispering love words, the tips of their desires barely touching. At midday came the drunks who urinated mercilessly in the streets and the pest control lorries to collect the rats killed by the blow of a

277

silver heel. Towards four or five o'clock, it was the turn of the small farmers who had sold their crops that day in the markets of La Merced or Jamaica. At nine or ten at night came the travelling salesmen who gave the girls miniature domino sets, plastic chocolates or hourglasses which took advantage of their admiration to impose a minute of silence. Every 29th of the month appeared the employees of the Banco de Comercio, the Banco Nacional and the Banco del Atlántico, after balancing the chequing accounts and their conjugal fidelity and, if not often, then at least once, an ambulance came to Las Vizcaínas to carry a dead prostitute off to the morgue: an unknown Ripper had slashed her stomach with a broken piece of mirror in search, perhaps, of a new image. They themselves had something along the same lines in mind but it was necessary, first, to decide whether to take the prostitute to the room in Holy Sunday Square and make love to her when she was awake and alive and then anaesthetize her and kill her when she was asleep or to carry out the autopsy when she was asleep and then afterwards kill her when she was still alive, in order to make love to her when she was dead. The other possibility was to take her to the room when she was already dead, in which case she did not necessarily have to be a prostitute. But she did have to be a young and beautiful woman who died in a downtown street of lifelong cardiac arrest; she should, if possible, be more of a stranger than the girls in their class and should live alone with her feline bodyguards and her Australian budgerigars clad in parsley and green dusks and should carry with her no identification card or love letter stating her name or the colour of her eyes in life. She would fall in the middle of the street among the pigskin shoes and be dragged past the indifference of pedestrians who would fall back like vanquished adversaries, for the woman, dead, would traverse a space illuminated by fear and presentiments. A slight crepitation of flowers would precede the heart attack. After ascertaining that her nostrils were decarburized, the police would give the corpse to the School of Medicine and the friends would take care of stealing it. Fabricio would arrive in a Green Cross ambulance while Palinuro and Molkas got Charon drunk. They would enter the Cave, picking their way among shadows of rushes, cold mosses and fermented spasms of the dead and bear her off on their shoulders. The big-bellied Buddhas eating marble grapes on the School stairs and the serpents entwined around worlds of onyx would shudder at the scream of the siren and the ambulance would speed through the streets of Guatemala, Brazil and Palma Norte and its echo would rebound against the wings protruding from the lintels and against legends created by colonial design and would, in passing, alarm the townsfolk who were at that hour exchanging kisses and abuse. And they would arrive, at about eleven at night, when the bells snatched the tongues from canephora. They would open the doors of the ambulance and lower their motionless

278

beloved and if any neighbour in pyjamas or evening dress were to ask what had happened, they would simply tell them that she was a convalescent recovering from a wound caused by an unlikely collision between aristocrats and chick-pea vendors and would show them her calm face and her eyes of an incognito lady. And, once in the room, they would reveal the full length of her Egyptian beauty, from the tip of her fibula to her hair in disarray on the pillow by way of salmon-coloured valleys and hills, pillars, tame, bare-nippled pines and concentrations of soft down. Then, they would make love to her as she seemingly slept. Another condition was, of course, that the body be fresh. And fresh, under these circumstances, did not mean warm, said Molkas, since it was inevitable that it would be cold and nor could it be expected to be hot though they did have to make sure that at least it wasn't frozen, just as it couldn't be soft and, moreover, could not be other than stiff, ideally it would be less rigid than necessary, no tougher than was probable. Then, all that remained would be to make love to her and to perform the autopsy, whether one before the other or one after the other or both at the same time, whether Palinuro first and Molkas afterwards and Fabricio last or all three at the same time or else two before and one afterwards or else the first two last and the last one first, as luck would have it or in alphabetical order (or the other way around) or according to height so that the tallest would perform the autopsy first and the shortest make love last (or the other way around) or according to the length of penises, added Molkas, either before erection or afterwards (or instead) and depending not only on whether the erection occurred in response to the prospect of making love first and performing the autopsy afterwards (or the other way around) but depending also on the degree, as in the case of the corpse, of each penis's hardness, softness, coldness, toughness, stiffness, warmth and flexibility.

Later their acquisition was right there in the centre of the bed.
And the bed was in the centre of the room.
And the room, in the centre of the universe.
Fabricio, Royal College of Surgeons, raised his hands as though awaiting applause. But, in fact, as his assistants understood, what he was really doing was waiting for them to put his gloves on.
'Know then that I have had the pleasure of draining the glass of a beggar without dismounting from my bicycle. What's more, a faithful copy of this original has been sent to Caesar, together with a bunch of grapes wrapped in Frutidor skin. What is the clinical history of our patient?'
'There is evidence of fever with hiccups which means, doctor, that the mercury in the thermometer is caught up in an obstacle race.'
'Epidemic encephalitis,' diagnosed Fabricio and with a gesture

279

instructed them to put on his mask.

'What else?'

'There is evidence of an acute persecution complex: wherever she goes she is pursued by her memories, her bad thoughts and a youth of twenty.'

'That's me,' said Palinuro.

'And what are we going to operate on her for?' asked Fabricio.

'Everything, doctor; fatty cysts, appendix, brain tumours, wisdom tooth . . .'

'Diphtheria, malaria . . .'

'We have to do a hysterectomy on her, doctor, a phlebotomy, a rhinoplasty, an ablation . . .'

'We have to bleed, intubate and cauterize her, doctor.'

'We have to operate on her for the measles which she has contracted in the knees, doctor, and for swallows which have appeared in her armpits.'

'For the grapes that have grown in her anus, for the oranges that have ripened in her lung,' insisted Molkas.

'For the crows' beaks obstructing her oesophagus, doctor,' said Palinuro. 'For the tropical flowers coming out of her nose. For the flies buzzing in her breath . . .'

'Hey, hey!' exclaimed Fabricio, waving his gloved hands. 'Get those flies off the corpse: their feet are vectors of microbes.'

'We have to operate on her for lanterns in the kidneys,' said Molkas. 'For poison-pen letters in the ovaries, for tickling in the pancreas . . .'

'For a cold, doctor. For the scarecrows hiding in her heart.'

Fabricio took the scalpel held out to him by Molkas, parted the woman's legs and pushed the scalpel into the vagina, cleanly, as far as it would go.

'What the hell are you doing!' shrieked Palinuro in horror.

Fabricio, who was a magician, took the scalpel from the sleeve of his shirt and with it, three different coloured handkerchiefs tied together.

That gave them another brilliant idea.

PART TWO

15

Love's labours lost

Everything started when, soon after Mamma Clementina's death – and sooner after her burial – Molkas and Walter tried to console me and started talking about the transmigration of souls, reincarnation and metempsychosis, Nietzsche's theory of eternal return, the Gnostics and of the birth of a butterfly every time somebody dies. What kind of butterfly would you like Mamma Clementina to be? asked Cousin Walter who, however, hated butterflies and remembered with glee the night he had been driving with friends along the coast road of Acapulco and the car engine over-heated and when they went to open the bonnet, he told Palinuro, they found that the radiator was plastered with black butterflies. They decided to cool the engine with iced beer and while they listened to the sound of the mantarays attacked by their enemies the goldfish and the poor mantarays tried to fly, raising themselves almost a metre above the surface of the water to fall with fins spread like open wings: splash, splat, splash, splat, we cooled the engine with iced beer and the foam washed away the black butterflies. There are butterflies, Walter told me, like the *Vanessa antiopa* which is the kind that returns to life when the winds die down and the sun comes out again; there are silver Hesperidae which wage incredible aerial combats with their winged confrères; there are butterflies with cocoons which break at the merest touch of the fingers; there are others which, rising from their nymphalid slough and spreading their wings, eject from their anus a red liquid like a shower of blood. There are diurnal butterflies which, he added, are said to die with their wings raised and joined. There are others which are nocturnal and die with their wings spread and drooping, like the mantarays. But I told Walter that I didn't want Mamma Clementina to be reincarnated as anything other than herself.

'As herself? Her self-same self, with all her wrinkles?'

'Every one of them,' I told him.

'One for every day she lived?' he asked me.

'One for every day she did not live,' I answered him.

'And all her grey hairs?'

'Every one of them.'

'And her unfulfilled desires?'

'And her shattered dreams.'
'And her fake suicides?'
'And her Papa Francisco.'
'And her milkless breasts?'
'And her narrow womb.'
'Mamma Witch?'
'Mamma Death.'
'Mamma Melon?'
'Mamma Fox.'
'Mamma Frog?'

'Mamma herself, Mamma herself and nobody else,' I insisted, 'no animal, no fruit, no other person, because then she would no longer be the same.' And Walter said to me: 'Quite impossible: Aunt Clementina could not be reincarnated as herself at the age she has reached; or rather, that she had reached, or rather, that she would have reached if she had lived another day; impossible, she could not have died yesterday, and if a person doesn't die there's no way they can be reincarnated.' And I answered him: 'You know what I mean: that she be reincarnated as herself being reborn, reliving her life.' And Walter stated that such reincarnation was not only possible but exists and has always existed and will always exist and when I said to him that if that was so then we would remember our former lives Walter said no, that memories of that kind are also impossible for the simple reason that those previous lives were the same. Imagine for example, said Walter, Mamma Clementina in her rocking chair is startled because she suddenly remembers that in her other life she was sitting in her rocking chair and was startled because she suddenly remembered that in her other life she was sitting in her rocking chair and she was startled because suddenly, and so on infinitely, like on packets of Quaker Oats where a Quaker holds up a packet of Quaker Oats on which a Quaker holds up a packet of Quaker Oats on which a Quaker and so on. And, moreover, you should place yourself not only in the position of the first of the Quakers but also in that of all the intermediate Quakers and think of how all the other, also intermediate, Mamma Clementinas would then remember that in a future life, or rather, in a thousand future lives, they would be remembering a thousand past lives in which they would be remembering a thousand future lives and so on, I repeat, to infinity. And, since remembering an infinite number of memories would similarly take infinite time, while at the same time a memory is confined to an instant, so Mamma in her rocking chair would turn into a living and breathing memory, without beginning or end, out of time; in other words, she would be like the long-memoried Funes, but the other way round, because her sole memory would be of a single, instantaneous and eternal present. And what about memories of childhood, the memories of childhood of another life,

284

were they not possible? I asked Walter and he told me that no, no way, neither could Mamma in her rocking chair remember that in another life she fell off her tricycle when she was three years old, she would simply be remembering what happened during her present life, which was exactly the same. So you see that this kind of reincarnation is a fact and we are living it and if you say that it is not possible to prove this is true, I will answer that neither is it possible to prove it is false, and I said to Walter: What of memories of the future? What if Mamma in her rocking chair five years before she died suddenly remembered everything that happened during those five years in her other life? And Walter told me that neither was that possible because to remember five whole years, with all their details, would take five years and would be equivalent to living them and if she only remembered some things, death itself, for example, that would simply mean that Aunt Clementina in her rocking chair . . . Here Walter interrupted himself and suggested that they endow Mamma Clementina with a few more decorative elements because otherwise it would seem that she was there in her rocking chair, alone and floating in intersidereal spaces like the old lady of the Sabritas crisps, unable to decide which planet to land on. 'Let us place beneath her,' he said, 'a carpet with a border of roses. Above, a lamp. On her lap, a ball of wool. Around her, the white house she never had and, around the house, trees and countryside, and in the countryside and among the wheat beneath the trees, blue wolves waiting for the fall of the old man's beard and flight of the chickens. And then, if Mamma Clementina suddenly has a presentiment of her death, it only means that in her other life, when she was the same age and was sitting in her blue rocking chair on her carpet of old man's beard, on top of a tree, with a wolf on her lap, her chickens around her, around her chickens the house which she never had and the roses of wool which awaited the flight of the countryside and the fall of the lamps, at that moment, I repeat, she had a presentiment also of her death. But no more than that, because we cannot remember what we have not lived, nor what we lived in our previous life, even if we had a thousand former incarnations, because one must have been the first: their number could not be infinite, Walter maintained, since, if that were the case, we would be able to remember the future. Moreover, each incarnation repeats all the details of that first life without previous incarnation, situated not in physical but in metaphysical time because, he stated, we are dealing here with a logical and not a temporal precedence, for which reason rebirth must occur in the same place on the same day of the same year, so that all incarnations occupy the same physical space as well as the same time. Therefore, during the first life when Mamma was sitting in her rocking chair, she had no other life to remember and, since each reincarnation repeats the previous one to the last detail so, from her second reincarnation onwards, Mamma would be the same lady sitting in her white house, above the countryside and the wheat, at her feet rocking chairs of wool, on her lap a chicken, her lamps round about her and around the lamps the blue rocking chairs awaiting the flight of the trees and the fall of the wolves, and she will have no business remembering her non-existent past nor her infinite future.

'So, in a way, there is only one life,' I said to Walter.

'Only one,' he answered.

'With its joys,' I stated.

'With its sadness,' he guaranteed.

'With its pleasures.'

'With its laryngitis.'

'And only one death,' I stated.

'Only one?' he asked me.

'Implacable death,' I answered him.

'Grim Death?'

'Death in Black,' I assured him.

'La Mort en Rose?' he asked me.

Estefania came to the conclusion that Walter was quite wrong and that the best way to console me was quite simply for her to become Mamma Clementina. For this to come to pass, for me to see my mother in my cousin, Estefania would have to have a child.

And so we put aside our collection of sheaths and contraceptive pills, sponges soaked in wine, douches of boric acid and all the intrauterine devices ever invented, from Mensinga's diaphragm to Marguilies' coil and including the little balls of gold used by Casanova and we abandoned also our vibrating dildos and all the other manner of things with which I was wont to penetrate Estefania. Because, just for fun, just for the sake of it, in total innocence and without remorse, during afternoons of leisure and of greatness, sometimes because I so desired and sometimes because she wished it, I used to penetrate my cousin with the most varied and legitimate objects my imagination could muster. The puritanical and the perverted may imagine any extravagance or fantasy they care to: curtain rails, broom handles, hairy carrots and rifle barrels. And they would not be wrong, with all these I penetrated her. But if the imagination ranges no further, ignorant of the gyrating combat waged by lovers under the auspices of the god Tantra, fortresses yielding to the beat of the conch or the ashen adventure in which love traces its eschatological landings, the imagination – your imagination – will remain kneeling at the mercy of its own ribs, failing to touch even the hem of our sheets. Because, in our room in Holy Sunday Square, and before and afterwards, on Mocambo beach and in the hospitals and in the ad agencies, I penetrated Estefania a thousand times with knives of butterfly wings, with battering rams of flour, with pixie hearts and almond hats, with fountains of fans and fangs growing from the backs of clouds in miniature on nights when the moon is full.

And why not tell you of my fingers for which, ever since we were children, Estefania's sex was like a glove of fire. I did not always penetrate her with loving intent for, without fail, when she returned to our room in the early hours, drunk, with mouse prints on her neck and a hint of red mint on her lips, I penetrated her with my index finger to berate her infidelity and point out to her the origin of her perdition; and also without fail, finally overcome short hours later by her adventitious nakedness lying beside me like an immobile omen and made fearful by the transatlantic blue flooding her eyes as her thoughts moved away from me and from our room towards her childhood beneath the coal temples of Pittsburgh, I would move closer to her in affectionate conciliation and penetrate her with my thumb to show I believed once more in her innocence.

All this besides the times that Estefania penetrated herself with myriad objects, not because she was partial to solitary pleasures, but simply on account of her natural coquettishness which followed her throughout her life, faithful as a velvet footman. The fact is that Estefania was not only coquettish with all living beings, regardless of the age, size or colour of their sex, but also towards inanimate objects crazed with love for her, and so it was not unusual that she sometimes allowed her breasts to be sucked by an old man whose toothless gums bore witness to the golden blows of time and wind or that, at other times, she sensed the infinite longing of a candle to penetrate her and with utmost docility permitted it to enter her and ignite itself by her uterine radiance.

But not thus are children born; my cousin was no Mary who conceived by the act and grace of the Holy Spirit, nor was she like the Badu women who, Pausanias relates, become pregnant when they look at their menfolk, nor was she Hoa-sse who was impregnated by the rainbow which descended on her. Hence, I devoted myself to penetrating Estefania with nothing more and nothing less than my penis, over and over and over again.

And the months passed and Estefania did not become pregnant.

I penetrated her with a syringe which I had filled with my semen, thinking that perhaps my spermatozoa were unable to reach her ovaries, but still she did not become pregnant.

I suggested then that we should obtain the semen of a donor, perhaps our friends Molkas or Fabricio or Walter. But she refused.

I suggested that we go to a sperm bank where she could be injected with the sperm of an anonymous donor.

But she again refused and not because women refuse on the grounds that

287

their child will be the product of an act of masturbation but because she got the idea that the anonymous donor might no longer exist and she did not wish her child to be conceived after the death of its father.

And most of all because she wanted to bear my child.

'Perhaps I'm sterile,' I said.

'No, I'm the one that's sterile,' she declared.

'There's another solution: we can get the ovule from another woman, fertilize it with my sperm in a test tube and then implant the embryo in your womb.'

Again she refused: 'How,' she asked, 'how am I going to tell my child that I carried it in my womb for almost nine months and gave birth to it, and yet am merely its incubator, not its mother?'

And her objection was not just on moral grounds, but because she wanted to bear her own child.

She would not hear of a clone child either, those strange beings created by modern genetics, the offspring of a single progenitor, and not because she considered the idea of an identical child to be aberrant but, most of all, because she wanted to bear our child.

So, for several days, we didn't make love.

And then we made love once more.

And Estefania became pregnant.

We never really knew at which precise moment Estefania's menstrual ovule finally came into contact with one of my spermatozoa. What happened was that one day I penetrated my cousin with a wand of hazelnut wood with a star at its tip and by magic a child appeared in her womb and I discovered it that same night when I penetrated her with a silver telescope in search of the constellation of Sagittarius; our child was to be born at the end of November, ninth month of the year by the ancient Roman calendar and the eleventh of the Gregorian calendar, the month heralding the beginning of autumn and crystallized promises. Therefore, it would be a child with all the attributes of its sign, destined to be the offspring of fire and mutations, its symbols would be the star and the bow and it would drink of the same milk as the goddesses of allegory who sang at the funeral of Ulysses.

Our happiness on finding that Estefania was pregnant knew no bounds, but for a few moments only, because my cousin at once started getting a lot of very strange ideas.

'Dear God! What will happen to my child if I suffer an embolism and can never again wake up?'

'You will have a child who is born asleep,' I answered, 'and instead of giving its first yells it will give its first snores. And, of course, instead of closing its eyes when it dies they will have to open them.'

Afterwards I was sorry for what I had said.

'My poor child – it will spend its life dreaming.'

'Yes, but its dreams will be like the dreams of those who are born blind . . .'

'And how are they?' Estefania asked me.

'The blind dream smells, touch, shapes, weights. They can't imagine or dream what a dog looks like in the distance, because dogs in the distance look much smaller, as does everything else. But, for those born blind things are always the same size. For us, as Berkeley said, visible objects are in our minds and tangible objects outside them. For the blind, only the second category of objects exists.'

'And your love,' my cousin asked me, 'is your love for me always the same size, even when I'm far away?'

'I don't see what connection one thing has with the other.'

'If you don't see it, you must be blind. And tell me – what will happen to my child if they think I'm dead and they bury me alive?'

'I should think you'd have an anaerobic child which lives without oxygen like the micro-organisms of the intestines,' I answered her, and again regretted it.

'But I would die for sure and my child would have nothing to live on, no milk or anything.'

'That's the least of it,' I said to her, and I regretted it for the third time. 'Your child could feed on the products of the various fermentations of your body: butyric fermentation produced by the fat of the corpse; casiac; ammoniacal. And, by the stage of black deliquescent decay preferred by the carrion beetle and other coleopteran insects, your child will be a healthy, chubby infant . . .'

'Wonderful!' exclaimed my cousin.

'Not really, because your child will be but another grub, poor thing, a mole which will never emerge from the tomb for fear of falling into the air and drowning. Its lungs, then, will be black as coal and as hard and difficult to cut as the lungs of Welsh miners.'

'Oh, no! Promise me that if I die you will freeze me so that my child can be born in a brighter millennium . . .'

'I promise,' I said to her and no longer felt regret. 'Your child, then, will be tremendously old, as though coming from far away, from the times when the glaciers started to recede; as though it had travelled through curved space, at the speed of light enveloped in an amniotic parabola. But nobody will know, because its lungs will be clean, new, soft, as easy to cut as those of an Eskimo . . . or even,' I added, 'being the child of both of us, since we are its bio-parents, we could put it in with a shipment of frozen embryos going to colonize other planets . . .'

'That is a brilliant possibility!' exclaimed my cousin. 'On which planet could our child live?'

'Which one would you like it to live on?' I asked her, making a mental note to buy *The Little Prince, Cosmicomics* and *Habitable Planets* by S.H. Dole so that I could talk to Estefania about the thousand and one planets that our child could colonize. Estefania smiled and I thought that we had got over the worst and from then onwards all would be happiness. But it was not to be: during her time as a nurse in the hospital – times which never really ended, because she always returned again and again to her patients like the nightingale of Florence – Estefania saw so many children born with congenital deformities that she was obsessed with the terror of having a monstrous child. She thought that, like Lilith of Talmudic tradition, she was destined to give birth to demons, and she got the idea into her head that it would be the most unfortunate infant in the universe, suffering from all possible imperfections.

'What,' she said, 'if we have an hermaphrodite child with its heart on the right-hand side and spina bifida and two heads, one mongoloid and the other hydrocephalous, one mentally retarded and the other blind, one deaf and the other mute and both with a hare-lip and cleft palate, what then?' wept Estefania, commending herself to the Roman goddesses Carna and Ossilago.

Her pessimism obliged me to turn once again to my old medical books which were stowed away in a trunk gathering dust. There, beside Kimber's manual of physiology, Testut and Jacob-Billet's *Atlas of Dissections* and Baker's *Technique of Necropsy*, I found Langman's *Embryology* and, after studying it for a few hours, I spoke with Estefania. I told her that the possibility of her giving birth to a monster was very remote; that neither she nor I were syphilitic; that we would take all possible precautions to ensure that she didn't get german measles; that I wouldn't let her take thalidomide; that it had never been proved that LSD modified the genes; that she had never been to Hiroshima and that I would never allow her to be injected with cortisone while she was pregnant.

I almost convinced her, almost.

She almost became her old self, dancing airily, with the dish towel she used to flick the multi-coloured flies and her arms like elongated jellies colliding with the air and whipping it into a spiral.

Almost.

But I committed the grave mistake of reminding her that we were related. What I actually did was point out that there was no family precedent. Because, although it was true that Grandmother Altagracia stopped talking to Grandfather Francisco when they argued and pretended not to hear when he spoke to her, she could not be said to be a deaf mute. Moreover, while everybody always said that Grandfather Francisco was big-headed, these same everybodies agreed that he was never macro-cephalous. Finally, although it was said without malice (or sometimes not without) that Mamma Clementina and Aunt Lucrecia were inseparable sisters, they were never Siamese twins.

'Anyway,' I told her, 'we're not closely related: Hypermnestra and Lynceus were first cousins and, none the less, procreated a normal child, Abas, who was none other than the grandfather of Perseus . . .'

'But Perseus didn't really exist, that's just mythology . . .'

'Ah, but someone who did exist, and was the son of two noble twins who committed incest at the instigation of the devil, was Pope Gregory the Great.'

'It would be amazing to have a child that became Pope,' she commented but then the brightness again went from her eyes.

There was no point in pursuing the subject further. I realized that it was useless to overwhelm her with my erudition – recently gleaned from books – and recite from memory that in a marriage between first cousins there is only a 15 to 17% chance of having a child with retinitis pigmentosa, 14 to 15% with amaurotic idiocy, 9 to 23% with hereditary deaf-mutism and 3 to 18% with mental retardation. It wouldn't have been any use, I repeat, because I already knew what her reply would be.

'What good is it for me to know that Jean Rostand says that in a marriage between first cousins the probability of having an albino child is only one in four hundred? Can you guarantee that our child will not be that probability?'

Estefania had inherited this contempt for statistics from Uncle Esteban. 'The only true and demonstrable statistic in the whole history of mankind,' said Uncle Esteban, 'is that of all people who exist, one hundred per cent were born and one hundred per cent will die.'

As always when Estefania was sad, I tried once more to flatter her vanity and told her that though I was a writer without books, a painter without pictures and a medical student without learning, I was nevertheless the only man in the world able to sail her from memory without wounding her eyes with reflections from my helmet and the only person capable of identifying the physiognomy of her shoes among a million plane-crash victims. And the only one who could catch a floating ambition in the air and, without clipping its wings, pin it to my throat to sing, as a microscopic bird flying across a globe, her innumerable beauties; I spoke of her hands, her ankles, her eyelashes, the copper unleashed in her braids and the debilitating saltpetre of her lips which gave her the appearance of a figurehead, of plaster about to detach from the skin and set out on a long journey to surprise the angels.

Estefania thanked me for the flood of metaphors, but her mood did not lift.

And so the days passed and our child started to grow in my cousin's womb and I, to further console her, said that I was almost certain that she would have a perfect pregnancy. That her legs would not swell like those of other women, that she would not suffer from albumin problems, that she would not get stretch marks on her breasts, that she would not develop varicose veins or piles. And that I was there to satisfy her least desires: pistachios, unripe quinces, fried chicken. That I hoped that her fancies would not be too bizarre like some women who suddenly feel an unpostponable need to eat strange things, but if such were her pleasure I would oblige and have made sweets of soap and chocolates full of toothpaste and cakes of earth and coal ice-lollies.

But it was useless.

In a renewed effort to calm her, it occurred to me to apply a little homoeopathic magic to exorcize the demons. I remembered Leonardo's famous *animalucci*, those monsters created with parts of different animals – similar perhaps to Dr Moreau's experiments – and, on the basis of this idea, I intended to create the most beautiful monsters on earth so that our child, when it was six months or a year old, could play with them: they were huge stuffed animals each of which combined the characteristics of at least two different species. Of the many I made, there were three which Estefania particularly liked: the Donkopotamus which, with a single ear-shattering bray, caused all the coconuts in the island to fall from the palms; the Tigerphant, which whetted hunters' appetites because its beautiful skin was equivalent to that of seventeen and a half Bengal tigers, and the Catodile which was greatly feared because, according to popular lore, on nights when the moon was full it stole into camps and drank the milk of the white missionaries.

By this time, our child was already into its sixth week and its nostrils were deepening.

'It's a pity we can't see it,' said Estefania.

But Momus had already railed against Vulcan for not giving man a window in his breast to display his secret thoughts and perhaps Shen Nung, the celestial emperor with the glass stomach had, like Perseus, never existed. And anyway, I explained to her, an ultra-sonic hologram had not yet been invented. So, that night, after reading to Estefania from the *Marriage of Heaven and Hell* and fixing all the domestic appliances which were broken (and assuring her that our child, like all modern children, would be born with a certain amount of strontium 90 in its bones) I gave my cousin a new gardenia perfume. When we went to bed, I dipped my middle finger in the perfume and inserted it into Estefania's vagina so that our child might marvel at the continuity of the parks. But she, who often interpreted things the wrong way round, did not understand – or did not wish to understand – the exorcizing intention of my animals:

'You are quite right,' she said. 'If our child is condemned to be a monster, the best thing to do is to surround it from the start with similar creatures so that it will think that its deformities are the most normal thing in the world.'

Estefania bought two identical dolls, whom she named Rosa and Josefa, and sewed them back to back, to turn them into Siamese dolls. She cut the arms off another doll and sewed on the arms of a smaller one to turn it into a thalidomide doll. She snipped Snow White's lip to create a hare-lip. And so she proceeded, not forgetting a bearded Little Red Riding Hood – like Mademoiselle Lemort who was exhibited in Spring Gardens – and Cinderellas as hugely fat as curiosities from the Atayde Circus, as well as a spastic Frankenstein's monster, a hydrocephalous Humpty Dumpty, a deaf and dumb ventriloquist's dummy and a cute Shirley Temple doll containing an ingenious mechanism producing artificial dribble which ran constantly down her chin and which never learned to walk or even to say 'mamma'.

Towards the end of the seventh week, when our child's tongue had already descended and we knew by the development of the gonads that it was a male child, we bought a bottle of champagne, drank his health and afterwards dipped the cork in the champagne and inserted it into Estefania's vagina so that our son would become accustomed to the taste of New Year.

By that time, I had been infected by my cousin's obsession and often dreamt that we would have a dwarf son. I comforted myself thinking – and so I told her – that many dwarfs were immortalized by famous painters such as Tiepolo, Ghirlandaio and Veronese. Or Velazquez, I told her, and many other famous people, kings and emperors surrounded themselves with dwarfs, like Suetonius. Sulla had a harem of dwarf women. Prognathous Philip II was also famous for his dwarfs who can still be seen on the façade of the Prado Museum, I told her, not to mention Rudolf II of Prague who collected monsters and mazes. And, throughout history, there have also been dwarfs with tremendous luck: Khnoumhopton, the famous Egyptian dwarf, Estefania, came to be the chief of perfumes of the Pharaoh's court and upon the marriage of Tom Thumb, the no-less-famous dwarf of the Barnum Circus, the Vanderbilts and the Rockefellers showered him in diamonds and President Lincoln gave him a suite of lacquered Chinese furniture inlaid with gold, I told her.

And so our son reached eight intrauterine weeks of age and though he was but a little squirt exactly the size of a thumb, he already had a human face and his eyes, as yet without eyelids, were completely open. I was so happy that I took Estefania to the cinema to see *Mayerling*, bought her the Dr Spock book, promised her that when our son was born I would cut the umbilical cord with my own teeth as mammals do and

293

treated her to a taxi home and we inserted the end of a periscope into her vagina to allow our son to cast an eye over the world outside. Estefania and I made faces at him, blew kisses and winked, showed him photographs of his posthumous grandparents and waved him goodbye, until next week.

I then decided to devote my life to the study of monsters, with a passion exceeding the best efforts of Pliny, Aldrovandi, Olaus Magnus and Ambrose Paré, comparable only to the single-mindedness of authors such as Charcot and Richter, Guinard and Chauvin, Dubreuil and Geoffrey Saint-Hilaire. I also set myself the task of compiling a list of monsters more extensive than Buffon's. I remember that I acquired, among other things, fourteen Regnault illustrations of Monsters of Nature, L. Martin's *History of Monsters from Antiquity to the Present Day* and F.E. Guérin's *Illustrated Dictionary of Phenomena of Nature*. I also wrote to Cousin Walter, who was in London, asking him to get hold of Lancereaux's *Atlas of Pathological Anatomy*. Our son continued to grow and grow in Estefania's belly. Fingers and toes appeared at the tips of his extremities; his viscera started to produce blood and his glands to secrete sweet liquids; his head became rounded and the size of his body increased pro-portionately; down appeared above his eyes and on his upper lip and Mamma Estefania started to endow him with her antibodies and gamma globulin which would protect him in life and, finally, when his testicles descended to the pelvis as his kidneys rose to the lumbar region, his whole body became covered in a whitish caseous substance with which he would be born. Shortly thereafter, Cousin Walter wrote to us from London, saying that he hadn't tracked down the *Atlas* but that instead he would send us photographs – as in fact he did – of certain extraordinary specimens he found in the Hunterian Museum of the Royal College of Surgeons: frogs with supernumerary limbs, which according to Walter, must leap in several different directions at once; a lizard with two tails, no doubt allowing it to escape death twice simultaneously, and a nightingale with two heads which (Cousin Walter pointed out) must have sung some beautiful duets. He also sent us, to Palinuro's immense satisfaction, photographs of a dove with supplementary wings and, to everybody's great amusement, a *Palinurus penicillatus* with an antenna in one eye, in accordance with Milne-Edwards' description.

And, meanwhile, no public holiday or weekend passed without our doing something to put our room, and the world, to rights; without thinking of making a mobile inspired by Miró's *Maternity* to hang over the crib or Estefania taking part in a demonstration against the Vietnam War or our both endeavouring to give our son a foretaste of the satisfaction of knowing something of the mysteries and miseries of life and showing him, through the peephole of Estefania's vagina, a tin soldier, a stick of rock, a battery torch with which we momentarily illuminated his intrauterine life.

294

And so, that our son might know from whence he had come, I often inserted my own paternal member into Estefania's vagina, disguised sometimes as a clown, sometimes as a one-eyed pirate and, at others, as a villainous hand-puppet threatening to kick him out into the world if he didn't pay the rent.

At that time I little suspected that the last objects I would insert into Estefania's vagina were the instruments with which I was to chop our son's body to pieces.

This happened during the eighth month, the month of pregnancy presided over by Saturn, devourer of his own offspring.

I will never forget that day. On my cousin's naked belly I had painted a hemisphere with the map of America and we were trying to guess which regions and countries corresponded at that particular moment to the different parts of his body. We reached the fairly elementary conclusion that his mouth must in Tierra del Fuego and his feet in Greenland.

'And his heart?' Estefania asked me.

'I think it must be about here, in Turtle Island,' I told her and, since she didn't agree, I went to fetch my stethoscope to listen to his heart as I did every morning and, on that day, I will never forget it, I heard nothing.

'How strange,' I said to Estefania, 'complete silence.'

'You don't hear him laughing?' she asked me.

'No.'

'Sighing?'

'No.'

'Perhaps he's crying.'

'No.'

'Perhaps he's asleep and dreaming that he has already been born.'

'No, and anyway foetuses don't laugh or sigh or cry.'

'You're wrong,' she told me, 'I heard him singing. Tell me: do you think he's dead?'

'Yes,' I answered her.

And it occurred to me that our poor son was one of the exceptions to Uncle Esteban's perfect statistics: one child who, never having lived, never died but, none the less, having died, never lived. We remained silent. I don't know why, but at those moments I remembered our mirror's death: perhaps because our son would also take with him, for ever, something of us both. I went down to the garden and came back with a bunch of daffodils. We remained thus for several hours: I, kneeling with my head bowed on Estefania's lap and she, lying face up on the bed, her eyes wide and her belly covered in flowers.

Estefania and I knew perfectly well what has to be done when an infant dies in the mother's belly and the womb refuses to expel it even with the aid of stimulants, so I returned to the trunk and, beneath the books, found the instruments I needed. Estefania refused to allow me to use an embryulcus covered with hooks, because she was terrified at the idea of our son's body being torn. Neither did she want me to use the cephalotribe to crush his skull. We finally opted for the Ribemond-Dessaignes embryotome with which, and with great difficulty, I managed to detach the head. That is how our first child came into the world, born in the manner in which kings and saints die: beheaded. And so it came to pass also, when I started to cut the rest of the body with Dubois' scissors in order to extract it, that Estefania's belly came to contain a series of monstrous creatures: the first lacked a head; the second lacked a head and arm; another was but a trunk with two legs and finally, a child without a head, arms, legs or trunk.

It was only when I had extracted the whole foetus that Estefania, still a little dopey from the anaesthetic which had even put the flowers on the pillow to sleep, dared to ask me the question hovering on the tip of her tongue.

'I think it was for the best,' I said to her. 'He would have suffered so much. Do you want to see him?'

'I only want you to answer a question . . . tell me: would he have been a monster?'

I bent my head and pressed it to the spot on my son's chest where I would have listened to his heart, if he had lived, and said to Estefania: 'Our son had, in his chest, a hollow muscle covered with fatty tissue and filled with blood.'

'How ghastly,' groaned Estefania, 'it was better that he didn't live.'

I kissed our son's ears and took his hands in mine.

'What's more, on each side of his face he had a cartilaginous convolution and on his fingers growths of hard, dry scales.'

'Poor innocent creature.'

'And there's more you don't know,' I said to her, thinking of our son's lungs, his eyes and so many other things. 'I've looked at his body and you can't begin to imagine what I discovered. His lungs never changed colour because they never filled with air and his eyes never lit up with fireworks because they never opened. His brain was an ungraspable world containing not a single good thought, nor an army, nor a barrel of oil in which to drown the sun. By which I mean that our son had no memories and no loyalties, no tears. Never have I seen a bronchial tree so full of naked birds which died of cold before they learned to sing. He was, moreover, a child without forgotten memories and without hopes, his glands hanging like dead weights from his least noble viscera and his organs like red sponges hiding their shame in rank bays and his cartilages lacking calcareous beliefs. He was a child without reflexes, without urine, without friends. In his entrails I found only nebulae governed by a viscous equation; foam washing his pancreas and the humps of the islets; whitest phlegms unapprised of prudence, reverberations and raw bones. He was a child devoid of acts of heroism and of feelings and who did not deserve to live. And, as though this were not enough, as though this whole whirl of chords of vinegar never purified by lymph and this whole sham of fruits, dark rooms, contrivances and marrow were not enough and, if you think it is little matter that, besides being a child without illusions and without an olive branch, who never in his life brought down a fairy and never knew the luxuriance of the orb, the air expelled by cherries, the slippers of the three kings and never dared to do battle with an angel, in the manner of Jacob, he afterwards went from school to school boasting of his winged fists. If you believe all this to be of little account,' I told her, 'you should also know that I have never seen a child with so many aberrations betraying his humble animal origins. I have never seen kidneys so similar to the kidneys of a pig, a bladder so similar to that of a rabbit, a heart so little different from the heart of a lamb and hands so reminiscent of those of a monkey. And, if you look closely, you will see that his eyes were going to be green like those of a tiger with reflections of a condor; and his blood was dark, like the blood of a dove and his skin was soft, like that of an antelope. And, if you look more closely still, you will find in his body reticular tissue as fine and transparent as the wings of a dragonfly, arteries like processions of blue serpents licking the wounds of the ancient Greeks and ganglia as round and white as fish eyes looking at you from all sides . . .'

'So, he would have been a normal child, wouldn't he?' said Estefania. 'Yes,' I answered her. 'He would have been a normal child.'

Estefania wept. My God, she wept so much that afternoon that, when I shut my eyes to forget our son and conjure up other things and other people, I suddenly found before me Aunt Luisa, who liked to dust fan tassels with blue frost. Aunt Luisa, the only person of all those I'd met who knew that things may simultaneously be one and legion and hence she lost her fear of words. I thought of her by association of ideas or, perhaps I should say, by association of tears, because when Estefania and I were little and we cried, Aunt Luisa sat us on her lap and took away our sorrow by repeating whatever nonsense came into her head, without fear of saying the wrong thing and making a huge blunder; there might appear the prince disguised as a juggler who with the arc of his sword cut off the head of the dragon who, because he had been so greedy, vomited up all the scaffolds that he had eaten in his better days, the live tail-wagging seagulls, the caravans of verses from the Bible, the domed ceilings and the grapeshot of oranges. Hurray for the prince! Woe to the dragon! Alas for the children who still have tears in their eyes! They don't know, they don't know what is cooked in their tears. In tears there are acid caterpillars which polish the streets, and vapourizers in every one of the city's trees. Tears don't know

297

the time of day and suddenly die in a blue funk. Woe to the witches, who are after the poor dragon! Tears can disappear, though they might not want to, in a whirlpool of amethysts. And, speaking of precious stones and dances of long sherbet ices, I will tell you that seahorses wet their tails in tears and then sprinkle liquid turquoises. My children, beware of sprinkled tears! Tears rise like round colds up the backs of divers: your Uncle Esteban will tell you, because he nearly died of pneumonia when the *Lusitania* sank. Olives grow in your tears and asparagus in your ears and tears make poets faint from fire sickness. Hurrah for my children, woe to my tears! I know some tears who promised to behave well since last year, and lemons, when they are thirsty, get inside a mother-of-pearl and drink the tears of the artistes: ask your grandfather, who knew all the ships docking in New Orleans. And, if you don't stop crying, just remember that in tears birds eat cobwebs and there are tears which are hunted by correspondence like white whales. Woe to the white whales, which are coming to an end, which are coming to an end! If you still don't believe it, let your Uncle Austin tell you that electric bulbs without mosquitoes are caught in tears like fish and let him dry those tears, under oath, with the hem born of the tablecloth as though salvaged from the wine. Hurrah for my children! Woe to the cobwebs! Oh for the divers! Ah for the wine! And anyway, why cry, children? if everything gets put right and tears melt when the music touches them with its thorns of water and when this doesn't happen, when things just won't go right, they get hung up on the wall, they get put in a frame of azaleas and in another of tears, what am I saying, tears! in any case, tears disguised with laughter and on to another matter, farewell, Hail Caesar! Hurrah to Aunt Luisa! Oh for tears! Alas for my children! Woe to the witches with their camphor-scented privileges!

16

A Technicolor mass

Where did you find her? What did you do with her? What is her name? Violeta, Beatriz? What is a differential diagnosis? Have you paid your income tax? Do you know the Our Father by heart? Why did you bring her here? What are you going to do now? Where did she live? In Holy Sunday Square? Las Vizcaínas Street? In Dos de Abril Street? Did you know that RH means Rhesus Macaca? That the word *malaria* means bad air? How did you kill her? At what time, for what purpose, with which hand, with what guts did you kill her? And, if it is said that we have 206 bones in our skeleton, why do babies have 350? Answer! Quickly! Did the rat get your tongue? Did it eat your bones? What does ICTUS mean? Did you know that certain rat poisons make fantastic anticoagulants? Why didn't you use them? Why did you let her blood clot? How old was she? What did she say to you as she was dying? What were her last words?

Fabricio, quite unabashed, untied the three handkerchiefs. With the green handkerchief he blew his nose. With the yellow one he mopped the sweat from his brow. With the blue one he wiped away a fictitious tear. Then he said: 'You ain't seen nothing yet! I can also produce white rabbits from Mrs Toft's womb, lobsters from Mamma Clementina's belly and, when I am grown up and a surgeon, I will produce real children, who will be future engineers, future policemen, founders of indelible empires, athletes who will participate in Underwater Olympics in Venice and even future great physicians like myself.'

Then he held out his hands: 'The instruments,' he ordered. 'I want to check them.'

'There's nothing missing, doctor. We have the arterial clamp, forceps for ligatures, Stryker saw, hammer . . .'

'Thermocautery, doctor, tooth-peeler . . .'

'Monkey wrenches, doctor, corkscrew . . .'

'Tumour squeezer.'

'Arterial screwdriver.'

'Did anybody think of bringing a scalpel or, in other words, a lancet, a surgical knife, even a penknife, an ordinary kitchen knife?'

'Ah, I knew there was something I was forgetting!' said Molkas, tapping himself on the forehead.

Palinuro took the liberty of reminding Fabricio that he himself had the scalpel and, moreover, in his hand.

Reader of *The Key of Solomon;* memorizer of cabalistic sentences and words such as *Elohim Essaim*! *Nekim Adonai*! *Abracadabra*! Holder of the knowledge that Greek fire can only be quenched with urine; expert in the cooling powers of amethyst and the antihaemorrhoidal virtues of topaz; holder, finally, of the knowledge that to quench another kind of fire, that of concupiscence, it suffices merely to carry against your breast the heart of a turtle dove in a bag made of wolf-hide – Fabricio the Magician was embarrassed by his already proverbial absent-mindedness which caused so many upsets in his life and so many physical discomforts that he decided to give a demonstration of his ultra-worldly powers: he went over to the window, opened it and, with the scalpel he held in his hand, he sketched a circle, thus cutting out a piece of reality the size of a mirror and, handling it with utmost care, placed it on the carpet so that the woman, when she woke up, could breakfast on smoking chimneys, a couple of clouds, a clothes line and, almost, a bird which evaded capture only to be drowned in Persian sands.

Molkas leaned over to look at the piece of sky.

'Extremely dangerous. A fence and a warning notice should be put up.'

'Beware of the sky,' said Fabricio.

Now it was Molkas who parted the woman's legs and decided to insert his finger, but this time the friends were sure the finger would not afterwards appear hidden in the sleeve of his shirt, because Molkas was not a magician: he was a fortune-teller and told the future.

'What are you going to do?' asked Palinuro.

Molkas approached the window and, his eyes fixed on the round black sun of melancholy hidden behind reality, foretold: 'The police will come at seven in the morning, looking for heroic drugs and Communist cells. They will find the corpse and they will arrest you. But we, your friends, will keep you supplied in prison with cigarettes and cigars, sweets and a manual for building aerostats.'

Molkas went on to foretell: 'Then will follow the time of plenty: an earthquake will raze the walls of the prison, enabling you to escape and lose yourself in the crowds.'

'Can't we change the future?' asked Palinuro.

'You, Fabricio, you're the magician, you change it,' said Molkas and continued to foretell the various future possibilities: if the police didn't come at seven in the morning, he said, then the green flies will. The chamois will proliferate in the woman's flesh, the miasmata will break their confines, the lice will abandon the body and a luckless odour will spread through the school. The police will come, anyway, and will find us inside an iceberg. Then, Palinuro, we will denounce you, pointing a finger at the region of your heart and you will feel an imprisoned shudder bursting in your breast and you will know that never more, oh yes, never more, my friend, will you be a student.

'You will leave me alone?'

'As you came into the world.'

'And then what will the police do?'

'They will ask you what the woman is called, why you killed her, if you believe in the Virgin, where you planned to hide the corpse, what is two and two, what is one hundred thousand nine hundred and ninty-nine plus two, what do you want to be when you grow up, what is the capital of Belgrade, whether she was single or married, if it is true that the biopsy is more important than the autopsy and whether you made love to her before bringing her to the room.'

Then Molkas returned to the present: 'This poor woman died in the middle of her period with a Tampax still inside her.'

'Idiot, that's not a Tampax, it's a vaginal tampon. When someone dies you have to tampon all the body's orifices.'

Molkas, nevertheless, managed to insert his finger again, and said: '*Introit*,' and then he sucked it.

'There are two things you must learn if you wish to be doctors, gentlemen: the first, to overcome revulsion. The second, to be observant. As you *doubtless* observed, I inserted this finger, the middle finger and, although it may not have been apparent, I sucked this other finger, the index finger.'

'I could never do it,' maintained Fabricio. 'I'm very absent-minded: every time I flick through a book I lick my middle finger and try to turn the pages with my index finger and, of course, it just doesn't work.'

But, just as Molkas forgave everything in the name of science, so he forgave Fabricio even more, in the name of magic.

In the name of magic, Fabricio produced a green scarf from a top hat, put it round his neck and said: 'This is the stole of the colour green which means hope, the green used from the octave of Pentecost to Advent.' In the name of the same joke, Palinuro took from the wardrobe the red belt of his dressing gown and stated that it was the cingulum, of the colour symbolizing the blood of the martyrs and which is used for the feasts of the Holy Cross and the Beheading of St John the Baptist. In the name of the same sacrilege, Molkas took from the cupboard a broom and said, 'This is your staff,' and from a drawer he took one of Estefania's shawls and said, 'This is your amice,' of the colour pink used on Laetare Sunday. In the name of all three, they rented a cassock from a fancy dress shop in Mesones Street which looked like, and was, a real cassock.

'White, white as the Pope,' said Fabricio.

And in the name of Christ, Molkas and Palinuro kissed the feet of their

Vicar on Earth, who sported purple socks which is the colour of mortification and sadness, of Lent and of the Four Ember Days, according to the statement of Fabricio who, besides being a magician, had been educated in a Jesuit school *ad majorem dei gloriam*.

What was supposed to come next was virtually an act of terrorism: to cut open the womb to reveal the place where Nero was conceived and, from between the ovaries and the jelly condoms, extract the emerald which must have fallen from the surprised eye of the emperor. They blushed at the mere idea and Fabricio, thinking better of it, placed the scalpel on the bed and turned the woman's body over, so that she rested in supine decubitus, with her buttocks in resolution.

'Gentlemen . . .' he said, placing his index finger on the Galliot point. 'This is the gluteus maximus . . . the upper surface of the gluteus maximus is covered by the aponeurosis, which sends . . .'

'Get out of the way, you haven't a clue how to do that,' Molkas said to him. Fabricio retired to a corner. Molkas placed his left hand on the woman's right buttock, straightened his tie, and, in stomachtic tones, began the lesson: 'Of the muscles of the buttock, gentlemen, this is the closest to the surface and the largest in volume. It generally expands with sadness in the bathtub and decapitates stoic dreams before mirrors. Its upper surface is covered by the aponeurosis and frustrated kisses, which aponeurosis sends numerous interfascicular septa, bad thoughts and phenomenal disappointments to the interior of the muscle . . .'

Molkas pinched a sizeable chunk of the woman's right buttock and continued: 'A thick layer of adipose tissue, gentlemen, increases the volume of this region, egocentric *par excellence*, moulding its shape until our mouths gape in shame. The lower limit is marked by the gluteal fold,' he added, tracing its curve at an unlikely distance, 'which, in women, descends to the curly splendour in which all the world's knowledge is periodically steeped . . . this fold is defined by the fibrous septa which attach the skin: first, to the gluteal aponeurosis and, second, to the obverse of history . . .'

Fabricio applauded. Palinuro half-died laughing. But Molkas guessed their intentions: 'You wouldn't dare!'

Palinuro didn't dare.

Beneath the woman were three sheets covering the bed and beneath the bed were the remains of the martyrs to science; not only photographs of Koch and Semmelweis and biographies of Hunter and Galen and Michael Servetus and articles on Dr Liceaga, but also a small skull which, according to Palinuro, was Pasteur's real skull and had been sold to Cousin Walter in Paris. 'But this is a child's skull!' said Molkas. 'But of course,' answered Palinuro, 'it is the skull of Pasteur when he was three years of age.' And both (or rather, all three) of them gazed at the acquisition in the middle of the bed, sleeping like a sleeping beauty on her laurels and defoliated roses, her hair wet from the slime of the gutter, naked, still warm, her closed eyes filled with the last windows of glass and aluminium through which could be divined an almost incidental disappearance and a comet which furrowed the sky leaving a trail of memories. On her lips, of the sea, a silken pride announced the advent of subterranean colours. Her head on the pillow, her breasts pointing to Scorpio, her neck in the position of the Swan and blue, blue as Shiva's, as though she had choked on life or on her own death. And so quiet that she seemed to sleep; it seemed that but a few hours previously the woman had been walking the cabarets with her shaved legs beneath a mink coat which made a silvery sound as it brushed against generals' boots.

'I will approach the altar of God, the God who is the joy of my youth,' said Fabricio and, after making a sign of the cross, backwards and with his left hand, he approached the ghastly, blood-covered image of a Christ by the Divine Morales hanging on the wall, which they had bought in the Polar stationery shop.

'Why are you so sad, my dear heart?' Molkas asked Fabricio, who turned abruptly:

'I'm going! I'm going! Do you hear? You don't believe in God. I do.'

Do you know the *I am a Sinner*? Do you know what *Credo quia absurdum* means? Where did you first see her? How long have you known her? Why are corpses which travel from one side of the world to the other placed in copper coffins?

'Listen, pal: if I believed in God, he'd be the loser.'

'And you, Molkas?'

'I don't believe in Him because I am made in the image and likeness of his pride.'

'Anyway, I'm going.'

'But how can you, doctor: aren't you going to operate on our little patient?'

Palinuro brought out a bottle of rum:

'What you need is a stiff drink.'

Fabricio snatched the bottle from him, raised it to his lips and started to drink.

'*Evohé!*'

'What incredible throat action.'

'*Testiculos habet e bene pendentes.*'

'That's enough, remember the poor!'

'You're not the only thirsty one around here,' protested Palinuro.

'As for me, I'm thirstier than sulphuric acid,' Molkas assured them.

Fabricio wiped his mouth with the back of his hand, adjusted his mitre of newspaper and asked: 'The condition of the tongue?'

'Saburral, doctor.'

'And this garland on her forehead?'

'Venus crowned her with pigmentary syphilids, doctor, because, like the Magdalene, she has loved much.'

Molkas took Fabricio's hand and pushed it towards the woman's body. The tip of the scalpel pointed towards her belly button.

'Someone once said that life gleams on the tip of a surgeon's knife. I read it in a book written by an Italian physician who was a fascist pig,' remembered Palinuro.

And, with the tip of his scalpel, on which life gleamed, he traced an imaginary circle on the woman's stomach, there where Yang and Yin and light and darkness and heaven and earth complement each other.

Are you interested in acupuncture? What are the burning spaces? Did you ever wish for your mother's death?

'Of course I'm interested!' said Molkas, as though answering the voice of his conscience. 'Much more fun than sticking pins in photographs of my enemies is to stick needles into the living bodies of my loved ones.'

But such skin-deep dissimulation did not deceive Palinuro, who hurried to point out: 'She's almost alive.'

'That's what you wish,' said Molkas.

'Perhaps she's just as alive as you and me,' insisted Palinuro.

'We'll soon find out,' said Fabricio, grasping the scalpel and cutting her jugular vein.

'If a stream of colourless blood which doesn't leave a stain on sheets comes out it means that she's dead.'

They stood silently, looking at the woman. Whole galaxies of thoughts possessed their minds, multiplied, betrayed their promises and their ciphers, drowned in the midst of a glorious host of possibilities: it was a vacuum filled with the things of this world that they most desired at those moments: photographs of a girlfriend, diplomas from the School of Medicine, sculptural groups of illusions. All terminated in a murky and purulent armistice. Suddenly, a fervent cheer resounded in the streets. From the wound flowed an endless and invisible clot which exactly reproduced the shape of each vein, of each artery, of each vessel which the woman harboured, jealously, within her bed.

'What was all the fuss about?' asked Palinuro and sat down on the edge of the bed, very sad, almost ready to set fire to the universe. Perhaps Estefania appeared to him at that moment, asleep among the passion flowers and plumbago. The afternoon sun cleansed her skin with silver maple leaves.

'Can we bring her back to life?' asked Palinuro.

'We're liable to land ourselves in real trouble,' said Fabricio. 'I think we'd better take her back to the dissecting room.'

'And lose this fabulous opportunity to rape death?' countered Molkas. But Fabricio ignored him: 'After all that, is she still alive?' 'Is she breathing?' asked Palinuro. 'Did you study her body by the rules of anatomy: first, comparative; second, descriptive; third, topographical?' asked Molkas. What day is it today: Monday, Wednesday? asked Papa Eduardo. Tell us: erysipelas, can it be cured with penicillin? asked the teacher. How many months since your last confession? asked the priest. Are you allergic to antibiotics? asked the nurse. Is *morbus* the Latin name for disease and *hallus* the name for the big toe? asked the master of etymology. Answer YES or NO. What does IHS mean? Time's up! You haven't told us yet how old the woman was. Twenty? Thirty? Forty in life and fifteen as a prostitute? Was she a widow? Divorced? Metchnikoff's most important contribution to science was: *a*) the phagocytic theory; *b*) the discovery of the properties of yoghurt. Ninety years old? One hundred and twenty? Answer! Quickly! Wrong!

'Why are you asking so many questions?' shouted Palinuro. 'No, she isn't alive, she never was! When I met her, she was already dead! When I brought her here, she was already dead!'

When Palinuro decided to weigh anchor and push off from the pages of the book revealing the nacreous blue of an intestinal wing and set off to wander the streets of the neighbourhood, the woman was already dead. When he walked in the rain and the hail which decapitated the chysanthemums and struck down the birds in San Ildefonso Street and laid at his feet a booty of feathers and roast chestnuts, the woman was already dead. And when he saw her beside the Gran Sedería shop, before a window framing her with morning luxuries and splendours and knew that she was a woman like any other that was like her: small, white, with her benzedrine sighs, her cloak of bad luck and hat pummelled by hail and fireworks, the woman was already dead. Palinuro went up to her, bowed, offered her a cigarette, seduced her by showing her a hundred times the Angel of Independence and the tourist posters in the travel agencies and they walked off towards Holy Sunday Square, he dreaming aloud of transformations in sexual intercourse and she dreaming of trips aboard a universal camel. She dawdled because they weren't holding hands and many times Palinuro had to tell her to come on, to hurry up, while she greeted Admiral Nelson, went down the Volga and up in the glass lift of the Eiffel Tower. She was quite small, in a green dress stained by eruptions and a bag of pigskin fattened on lottery tickets. Palinuro waited for her at the top of the stairs. Then, naked, he waited for her in bed. She, beneath the light, removed her clothes: she removed her stockings in the middle of the Gran Via, her green dress and her flowery panties on the slopes of Vesuvius and, finally, she removed her bra which she flung from the Bridge of Sighs and revealed her

305

chest, flat as a boy's: 'I don't believe a word of it,' said Molkas.

Have you read too much psychology? Have you read too little? Who do you think you are? Why do you try to supplant Molkas? Do you know the difference between repression and suppression in psychological terms? What does INRI mean? Is it true that we learn from the abnormal? That physiology derives from pathology? What is the difference between paranoid and neurotic? Between hebephrenic and psychotic? Between oligophrenic and schizoid? Do you believe in the split personality? In what way would you like to be like Fabricio? Are you Pali? Are you Uro? Are you Pali 'n Uro? Caught up in the spirit of the thing, Molkas asked himself other questions: 'When the hell did I stain my hands with iodine? And now what am I going to clean them with?'

'Iodine stains can be removed with thiosulphate,' Fabricio volunteered.

'That's true,' admitted Molkas and remembered Professor Fierro who said: 'And stains of Turnbull Blue can be removed with soda.'

And you Palinuro, companion, friend, how are you going to remove the stains of her breath from your hands? Do you know her family? Did she say she loved you? How are you going to remove the stains of her saliva from your chest, of her tears from the pillow? What does *Ecclesia abhorret a Sanguine* mean? Did you know that Prontosil was the first sulfonamide? That Purkinje discovered the distinctiveness of fingerprints in 1823? Postassium permanganate stains can be removed with hyposulphite: with what will you remove the stains of her fingers on your lips, the stains of her voice on your conscience, the stains of her screams on your heart?

Although Fabricio was not feeling well, so unwell that he had to go to the bathroom to spew up all his successive incarnations: as removal man, wolf, maiden who died at the stake and, finally, all the red wine that he had drunk and of which there was so much that for a few moments he thought it was blood and that he was dying, he none the less noticed Palinuro was so sad and alone in a corner of the room, so repentant and full of fear, of nostalgia and polar nights, that he felt sorry for him and suggested (not before shouting to Molkas: 'Yes, I know, the list of geniuses interested in necrophilia is very respectable, but I don't want to know! I'm sick of everything, of Leonardo, of Pontormo, of Freud, of every-fucking-thing!') he suggested, as we were saying, for the sake of gladdening Palinuro's heart and despite a feeling of involuntary and rhythmic trembling in all his striated muscles, despite the fact that through the framework of his conscience still shone a little light emitting signals of solidarity, he ordered that the Gregorian water be bought and the obligatory six candles lit and gave his blessing *urbi et orbi*.

'*Pax vobiscum,*' said Pope Falopius I.

Molkas, simultaneous interpreter, clarified: 'Peace be with you.'

Since Falopius was the name chosen by Fabricio when he was nominated (to use his own words) visible head of the Mexican Chaotic Apostatic Church, along with his additional titles such as Holy Father, Bishop of Tlatelolco, Successor of St Peter Pérez and Patriarch of the Autobuses De Occidente Bus Company. His traditional enemy, cardinal and future pope Eustace, raised his hands to his mouth and blew Falopius I a resonant raspberry.

> *Mariguana, called the Glorious,*
> *Had a son named St Fartorious.*

Which reminded Fabricio of laughing gas: 'Speaking of which: is there any chloroform? Do we have any novocaine? Chloretone suppositories?'

'There is no drug, either prohibited or legally restricted, that we do not stock in this theatre, doctor,' stated Molkas proudly and started to produce all kinds of bottles and boxes from Palinuro's trunk: 'Morphine! Nembutal! Cortisone! Isoniazid! We even have,' continued Molkas, brandishing a small tablet, 'a specimen of the first, factory-produced, contraceptive pill of 1952 . . .'

'An *incunabulum*!' exclaimed Fabricio.

Which reminded the three friends of the fun they had had when they walked the streets, filled with enthusiasm by the ideas that came into their heads every five minutes or every three lamp posts: when they went past the Capelo Francés shop, they thought of buying a glass bell: 'Better two,' said Molkas, 'to put the woman's brain beneath one and her warm heart with a basalt beetle beneath the other.' As they passed the Tagore Bookshop, they discussed the desirability of buying books on occultism and, effectively, they bought several volumes on the science of Hermes Trismegistus, *Isis Un-veiled* by Madame Blavatsky, all the satanic books that had ever appeared in the *Index Librorum Prohibitorum*, the writings of Margery Kempe and Annie Besant, the treatises on spiritualism by Allan Kardec and Austin Osman Spare's *Book of Pleasure*, although Fabricio – secretly – also bought Thomas à Kempis' *Imitation of Christ* and Bunyan's *Pilgrim's Progress*. When they walked by the Casa Prina in Catedral Passage and in the shop window they saw an electric host-manufacturing machine, they almost decided to break the glass, steal the machine and run through the streets flinging hosts to shopkeepers and employees, priests and policemen, in short, all the passers-by and pedestrians and doctors in Palma Street and the shoemakers and the professional men in Tacuba Street and the public clerks in the square and the booksellers in Argentina Street and the beggars in Equador Street and the vegetable vendors in La Merced market who pursued them, outraged, as the three shouted: 'Hosts, brother, glorious hosts, like hunks of meat for hungry dogs, like sacred seed on the wind and in furrows that from each host may grow a bloody Christ complete with

Crux Immissa; hosts, friends, hosts, wholesale, hosts by the gross, a rain of hosts, a hail of hosts like hunks of human flesh to vultures, manna to the unfaithful, pearls before swine!'

'Yes, but coloured hosts,' Palinuro had insisted.

They had laughed so much, the three of them, as they went from the Black Mass to the White Mass, to the Green Mass, to the Red Mass, to the Technicolor Mass! Their enthusiasm knew no bounds as they ranged from Black Magic to White Magic, to Green Magic, to Red Magic, to Technicolor Magic! They had had such fun buying masks of reptiles, of mythological birds, of demons and Michoacan devils; asking Charon to get them fat from corpses to make candles; buying artificial dyes to paint the hosts; cutting off the dome of the child Pasteur's skull to use as a chalice. 'Cheers!' said Molkas. 'Skol!' replied Fabricio. 'This wine is pasteurized!' exclaimed Molkas. And stealing sulphur from the laboratory to mix with the candle wax, and hydrochloric acid and ferrous sulphide to produce the rotten-egg smell of sulphohydric incense!

But Palinuro was inconsolable.

In a renewed attempt to cheer him up, Fabricio assured him that, contrary to what he thought, they had not left their innocence in the middle of some planet nor at the end of a parabola. Not even, he said, at the terminus of the rainbow. That Aldebaran and Mirfak were there, safe and sound, in the sky, along with all the other stars that had won a place in the firmament for the simple reason that they had preordained them. That in the world in which they lived everything was possible, because it was a world in which to be a doctor was to be in love with life and death in equal parts, where to have eighteen years under your belt was in reality to have another thousand which descended by the thread of a cloud to place at their feet the whiteness of the Halls of Fame, a world where the meteor carrying them to conquer their wondrous destiny had room for every dream, for the crystallized saga of the House of Troy and the unforgettable adventures of Eugene Gant and the girls serving little birds stuffed with bees in the eating houses of República de Cuba Street and the whole neighbourhood with its churches and its Robredo Bookshop and its public baths with stairs descending to the steamy depths. A world, in short, in which it was possible to give passion, by whatever name, a free rein: Gustavo Adolfo Becquer's swallows, the Tree of Knowledge, the suture of a living heart by Professor Luis Rehn de Francfort or excursions to the firing line of Las Vizcaínas, and drag it in the old-fashioned way across a bed of purple and wake it in the mornings to bathe it in kisses and whip lashes of saliva.

Standing before the woman who lay on the bed, dead, blind, Molkas raised his arms to heaven and cried aloud in melodramatic tones: 'Oh, if it were but possible to fill her full of birds!'

Fabricio placed a hand on his shoulder and continued: 'If it were but possible to cover her with the faintest smile of afternoon, rock her with murmurs and calumnies!'

Molkas knelt down, covered his face with the sheet, languished in liquid sighs and then yelled: 'If we could but sing her a trio every afternoon suspended from a telephone wire!'

Fabricio forgave Molkas for wetting the sheet, walked over to the window, drew back the curtains and shouted to the public: 'If it were but possible to sneeze in her face to show her the violence of our feelings!'

And Fabricio sneezed, laying a germ trap for the passers-by.

Molkas shook his fist in the air, threatening Fabricio: 'If it were but possible to lift statues from their pedestals to reveal the wasps' nests which nourish them!' he shouted, flushing in his rage.

And Palinuro was astonished by the beauty of the things his friends said and thanked them, but he became sadder still.

Fabricio the Magician who, even as a child hiding in the grey pergolas of the parks, had liked to change ducks into swans, caterpillars into butterflies and the climate of Mexico City into eternal spring, now knelt down, picked up the piece of reality on the floor and put it back in its place so that the room and his friend's heart were flooded with light.

But Fabricio was an absent-minded magician: 'It's the wrong way round! We're going to fall upwards!' shouted Molkas, pointing to the little Christmas lights of Park Avenue which had gathered in the nebula of Andromeda to celebrate the New Year.

'How embarrassing,' exclaimed Palinuro, 'the skirts of grandmother's photograph will fall down, I mean up, to show her pink bloomers.'

'What a disaster; the monocle of Uncle's photograph will fall out and remain hanging, immobile, like the pendulum of a hypnotized clock,' said Fabricio.

'Fortunately, however,' said Molkas, 'his neck will grow longer, as though Modigliani had taken his photograph, until eye and monocle meet in the midst of delirium.'

Then he added: 'What a calamity! What will happen to the pictures on our calendar now that the world is upside down?'

'In March, the snow will fall from the Swiss Alps and they will become covered in semi-tropical vegetation,' prophesied Fabricio.

'In May, the Tower of Pisa will straighten and start to show its square roots,' foretold Molkas.

'In August, the birds will fall from the trees of the Bois de Bologne.'

'In October, the canals of Venice will empty and the gondoliers will end up on the dole.'

'In November, the fog will fall from London and the English will discover that they are white as a fish's belly.'

309

'In December, the room will be turned upside down as if a bomb had hit it and the downstairs (or rather, upstairs) neighbour will complain to the administration of drips from the floor.'

'In January of next year, at zero hours and one second of the first day, we will tear the calendar into 365 pieces and we will telephone the travel agencies to plan our holidays before the earth becomes uninhabitable or falls on the moon and produces a crater of unimagined dimensions which will remain unnamed for lack of famous men,' said Fabricio and, stealing a march on events, he grabbed the calendar and ripped it to shreds. Then he put reality the right way up.

Molkas, relieved, put his feet back on the ground.

'And what happened next?' he asked Palinuro, as the blood returned to his feet and he turned transparent from the waist upwards.

In the face of his friend Molkas, Palinuro saw himself in bed next to the woman with a chest as flat as a boy's, saw himself drink until he recovered the beast lost in the scars of the Compass Rose and saw himself drink yet more in the hope of achieving a supreme spermatorrhoea. And the woman fell asleep, tiny and with her green eyes brimming with humiliations, tiny and with her silken skin shocked by its own tenderness. And the woman gave a sharp scream, a mighty scream, a scream which plunged like a waterfall down the length of her body and stayed the killer impulse in Palinuro's hands. Forgive me, Palinuro said to her and with his tongue cleaned the trickle of blood issuing from the woman's lips. Forgive me, he said again and with his hands, with those hands which he had inherited from Papa Eduardo, those large, veined hands designed to make love with gloves of fire, squeezed life from the woman to the last drop of lymph and dust and hair and saliva and tapered her voice and her soul and left on her neck the fingerprint of a joy reserved for the gods. 'Today I killed a girl. It was agreeable and stimulating,' wrote Alton, the English clerk and murderer, in his diary. Not a single leaf would tremble ever again in the woman's dreams to distil her summers, and the rotting blinds of hotel rooms rented by the hour would never again trace their zebra hide on her flat chest devoid of obstacles and galaxies.

Molkas covered the woman's face and sat down beside her. Did anybody hear the screams? What did you do then? Describe the catheterization of the heart. Are you familiar with the studies of the criminologist Bertillon? Beat your breast and repeat: by my fault, by my own fault, by my own most grievous fault. Describe the third cervical vertebra. Have you read *Crime and Punishment? Questionnaire des Chirurgiens* by Guy de Chauliac, written in the form of questions and answers? Did anybody see you when you left the room? Are you going to call the police? Do you have an alibi? Does your death urge prevail over your erotic urges or your erotic urges over your death urge? Did you know that, according to Plutarch, the Egyptians had a corpse present at their banquets so as not to lose sight of death while they were at their pleasures? How are you going to get rid of the body? Are you going to send it back to where it came from? To its birthplace? To Never-Never Land? To Timbuktu? Are you planning to eat it with Worcestershire Sauce as Lord Dunsany did? Immure it with a cat on its head as Edgar Allan Poe would? Chop it up and send it piece by piece through the mail, as Ambrose Bierce would? Answer! Have you read too much literature? Have you digested it? Or are you planning to dismember and boil it? What is the boiling temperature of Shakespeare? Is it true that steam from boiling water kills organisms by causing the cellular protein to coagulate? At what temperature does Persephone resuscitate? Oh, my friend, soul mate, companion!: Why did you kill her? What are you going to do now? What are we going to do? Bloody mess, damn it, bloody mess you've got us into. Answer, answer, you bastard! What are we going to do?

'Pray,' said Fabricio.

'*Labia majora*,' said Molkas. '*Ora pro nobis*,' said Fabricio. '*Struma ovarii*': '*Ora pro nobis*.' '*Pruritus vulvae*': '*Ora pro nobis*.' '*Uterus bicornis*': '*Ora pro nobis*.' '*Uterus planiformis*': '*Ora pro nobis*.' '*Uterus subseptus*': '*Ora pro nobis*.' '*Condyloma acuminatum*': '*Ora pro nobis*.' '*Vulvitis senile*,' said Molkas. '*Ora pro nobis*,' said Fabricio.

And Palinuro ran down the stairs two at a time and rushed demented into the street.

'Do you remember?'

'No.'

'What do you remember then?'

'Nothing.'

'But what did you do next?'

'You're the fortune-teller, ask your crystal ball.'

Molkas didn't know how to see the past, only the future. He couldn't, for example, see the dreams that he had dreamt the night before nor could he see Mary Stuart, Buffalo Bill, Pico della Mirandola.

'You're a magician, Fabricio, couldn't you take us back in time? Couldn't you take us back to a day when the today's past was yesterday's future?'

Nothing easier for Fabricio. On previous occasions, he had taken a newspaper, ripped it into shreds, put the pieces in his top hat, spoken an arithmetic stream of mysterious phrases in lunar language (*Wondelis Idusalin na Perixola Metartos*, for example) and drawn a paper aeroplane from his hat. Then he sent it flying across the room and it changed into Juan Ignacio Pombo's craft flying from Cape Town to England; the huge Pan American clipper for the first time in history crossing the transatlantic sky; the silver aeroplane of King Carol of Rumania and the light aircraft which crashed into the Empire State at everybody's time. Then he tore the aeroplane to bits, put them in his hat and drew out a paper boat. He launched it in the bath and the boat changed into the huge German cruiser, the *Karlsruhe*, reaching the coast of Acupulco one 1 April, how many years ago: twenty? forty? and into the *Siboney* sailing for New York and surprise, surprise! on board was Grandfather Francisco drinking a *nanche* cocktail. Then he tore the boat to pieces, put them in his hat and produced from it a row of little paper men holding hands which he set to walking around the room and they changed into themselves, into the three friends, and Fabricio led them by the hand along the streets of the neighbourhood to reveal to them the mysteries and magic of the National Press Library, of which he was as proud as if he himself had with his own hands placed the first stone or created each of the intricate patterns of the stained-glass windows or edited each *Excelsior* newspaper of 1935 or each *Revista Azul* of 1908. 'A Press Library,' he told Palinuro, 'is the place where you can go and read the newspapers of the day you were born or, if you live long enough, of the day you die.' And so it was, to Palinuro's surprise, reading newspapers from before he was born and learning what Captain Anthony Eden was doing at the moment when Mamma was rounding out her fertility, as well as what Mamma was doing when Anthony Eden was made Lord Privy Seal and he read newspapers of the day he himself was born and of the day he turned three and Papa gave him a silver destroyer to bring Nazi submarines to the surface. And then of course, predictably, they decided to play at pretending that these newspapers corresponded to the day they were living or that the day they were living corresponded to the newspapers they were reading and they went out into the streets discussing the obituary notice of a student who died in the mêlée of 1929 and, while they decided whether to go to the Opera cantina and have a Moravia beer or to go to the Politeama and see the *Hello America* musical revue or to the Balmori cinema to see *The Lives of a Bengal Lancer*, starring Franchot Tone, or to the bullring to watch Armillita fighting bulls from La Laguna, Fabricio grabbed a newspaper and made a paper hat which turned into a stetson of beaver skin, then grabbed another newspaper which he tore to pieces, put the pieces in the hat and drew out of it a paper car which, as it started to drive down Plateros Street, changed into a shining black Bentley and they loaded it up with baseballs from the Pinedo sports shop and climbed in and Fabricio put on a pair of white gloves and they said goodbye to the tourists coming out of the Ansco shop to take photographs of them and they said goodbye to Tarzan who slicked back his hair with Golba Petroleum and had just kidnapped Cuquita the Typist and then, when they reached the Benito Juarez roundabout, the steering wheel went mad and made the car drive round and round the fountains several times,

312

under the protection of the stone angels standing on tiptoe on the tree tops and who were startled by none other than the Captain and the kids who were having a picnic and couples of lovers who shivered with cold and Mamma herself who was there waiting for Papa Eduardo, Mamma Clementina with her rabbit-skin coat and her hat of artificial gardenias and her laddered Van Raalte stockings who was whistling *Ariadne auf Naxos* to the green envy of the birds.

But, this time, Fabricio refused. He refused to have the Virgin of Aviation, whose eyes were as clear as the water of the Potomac in which the *Sarabia* sank, appear in the room. Which reminded the boys of their visit to the Virgin of the Ascension in St Sebastian Church, dressed as a bride in her catafalque of glass and gold leaf and surrounded by silver and copper coins. Which reminded them of the Virgin of Copper before whom the three friends had knelt, in front of the altar in her chapel, beside the bronze candlesticks. Which reminded them of the bronze Corregidor's Wife presiding over Holy Sunday Square with her hair and hairstyle of bronze and the doves which perched on her shoulders and covered her in shit which the patina of years likewise turned to bronze. Which didn't remind them of anything in particular but from there, from the window overlooking the Square, there were many things to be seen: the printing and stationery shops beneath the arches; the blue desks of the public clerks out in the open, the House of la Malinche and her husband Juan Xaramillo and the Juan de Dios Peza building and Torres Quintero Square and the Aztec warriors armed with tridents and the golden lions with rings through their noses and they saw themselves, the three friends, walking the streets, happy, arguing, discussing the student demonstrations, the riot squads and the police; the refractive index of the tear gland; the trick with the ball of mercury; gastropods which copulate in a line, each acting simultaneously as male and female; the next football match between the University and the Polytechnic; Vintras who persuaded Alexandre Geoffroi to perform the Rite of Onan at the altars; the Chagas' disease transmitted by a big-mouthed bed bug and that to the Romans everything was a presage: a sneeze, the hooting of an owl, the whistling of a traffic policeman. And, of course, what they couldn't see from there, they could always conjure up with a little magic and goodwill. But Fabricio refused. He refused to have the National Library appear, or the Rio de Janeiro prostitutes' hotel, the herb sellers of El Carmen (who sold petiveria for kidney stones and germander for diabetes), Loreto Square, the Alianza Monte Sinai Beneficent Society, the Otomano Clock with its guitar-playing frogs and the blue spire of the Latin American Tower. He refused to have the barrows selling tulips and roses in the flower market appear. Likewise, the great bell of the cathedral: the Santa Maria de Guadalupe, weighing twelve tons. He even refused to have the Press Library appear, the cross of skulls and the Las Casas fountain with its workmen in search of contrasts and, to cap it all, he refused to countenance the appearance, there in the neighbourhood, there in the streets and before their eyes, of the schoolgirls of Las Viscaínas Street, the sweet, fresh schoolgirls who bled every twenty-eight days from the original wound.

It would have been easy for Fabricio: he had only to gather up the pieces of the calendar, put them in his hat and draw out, for example, a new and shining Friday, a luminous and virgin first Friday of the month which would have allowed Molkas to foretell:

I will be sleeping the sleep of the just. Fabricio will be wandering the streets, transformed into an imaginary football player. You, Palinuro, will run madly down the stairs and you will meet Fabricio and together you will come to wake me. I will dress. We will go out into the street, we will walk arm-in-arm towards Holy Sunday Square and you will tell us what happened. But Fabricio and I will not believe a single word of what you say. Fabricio will kick various things: a stone, a rubbish bin, a beer can. I pick up a discarded newspaper and prophesy that next day the news will appear on a front page spread over eight doric columns. Fabricio will kick an emerald green bottle which will shatter against a faun's afternoon nap. Finally, he will kick the air and the whole supporting structure of the wind will fall down and, with it, the walls of the room, the square, the trees and our underpants, leaving us unharmed but defenceless, before the eyes of the world . . .

Do you dream that you evacuate in public after masturbating? All lies: the process of defecation in the manufacture of saccharose has nothing to do with excrement. Were there any witnesses? Do you know the difference between the criminal psychopath and the ecological criminal? Did any bakers see you, public accountants, engineers? Where are you going to hide? Beneath the bridges? Beneath the clouds? Repeat: Credo in unum Deum. False: a hernia which loses the right of abode is not a hernia which sleeps on park benches. Do you like women, Palinuro? Apocrypha: invert sugar is not homosexual sugar. Did some chiropractor lend you his hands? Did an insurance salesman sell you a policy? Did a lawyer press charges? Who else was a witness, apart from the room and the window? The sky was a witness? God, your conscience, the birds were witnesses? Human saliva contains: a) amylase; b) maltase. Put a cross, two crosses, a star, two stars, a moon, ten angels.

Then we will reach the room of the crime, continued Molkas, and we will see her stretched on the bed, in all her length and nakedness . . . we will then think that she is alive and sleeping and that you deceived us, thank God. But, when we look at her face, we see that her tongue is hanging out. We will then think that she is alive and awake and making fun of us. But, when we examine her tongue closely, we will see that it is covered in mud

314

and mushrooms. We will then think that she is asleep and sick. But, when we look at her eyes, more closely, we will notice that they are protruding. We will then think that she is alive and mad. But when we look at her eyes we will see they are lifeless. We will then think that she is asleep and blind. But, when we touch her skin, which is cold, and take her pulse, which is still, we will then think that she is dead and died of love in your arms. When we look at her more closely, we will see that she has a purple mark on her lip. Then we will think that she is dead and that you killed her with love because she was blind and mad. Then we will ask you: why did you do it? Who was she? What is her name? Where did she live? When, for whom did she live? And in vain will you swear to us that she is dead, that she is alive, that she is awake, that she is blind, that she is mad, that she is asleep, that you didn't want to kill her, that you wanted her alive, that you took her there awake, that you drove her mad and that you killed her blind, because we won't believe a word of it.

Instead, as though nothing had happened, Fabricio put on his rubber boots to minimize static electricity, requested that the operating area be sterilized, put on his muslin mask, asked that her lipstick be removed and her nail varnish, because they might disguise cyanosis under anaesthesia and, apropos, asked:

'Well, what anaesthetic are we going to use?'

Palinuro, remembering his trip to the nether regions, suggested:

'Footassium soxate.'

'I have a better idea,' said Molkas, producing an amber-coloured jar, 'this is the only true drug of dreams: LSD.'

'How do you take it? Do you suck it?'

'You swallow it with milk or water or saliva. But it's better not to drink alcohol because it may produce undesirable side effects.'

'And when do the hallucinations start?'

'It depends on the pill. Some have more acid, some less.'

'And the hallucinations . . . do you have them with your eyes open or closed?' asked Palinuro.

Once upon a time there was a boy who was very fond of colours. Once upon a time, in a very old newspaper which Fabricio showed him when they were in the Press Library, there was an advertisement for mercerized thread of the La Cadena brand. 'Oh what naughty children!' said Aunt Luisa, quite violet with pleasure, since it was she who usually painted their tonsils with gentian violet. 'Oh what impossible children!' said Grandmother Altagracia, yellow with rage, because she was the one who used Orleans yellow to ice her cakes. 'Oh what mischievous children,' said Mamma Clementina, red with love, because she was the one who looked at Palinuro from a red photograph which turned darker every time it was

315

taken out of its envelope of black paper lined with silver and because she was the one who put a red bulb in Palinuro's room and red curtains at the window and squares of red cellophane over the panes when Palinuro had measles. He had been playing all afternoon, he and his cousin, in the garden of his grandparents' house, with the son of the Polish lodgers who later had to go because they couldn't pay the rent. I was born in Ostroleka, said the little Polish boy, who always went about with his socks sagging around his ankles and a faded cap on his head, and Palinuro and his cousin said to him: 'Ostro what?' 'Ostrolecture?' and he persisted with Ostroleka and they with Ostrolecture and so on until they made him cry and curse them in a language which was like talking with your mouth full of chocolates. But then they cheered him up and played hide-and-seek with him and he stood in a corner with his eyes closed as Palinuro and Estefania ran into Mamma Clementina and Papa Eduardo's room, which the little Polish boy was forbidden to enter and, when he had counted fifty, aloud and in Spanish, he looked for them in the garden, in the dining room, in the garage behind the green and orange striped canvas curtain, in the abandoned car, in the corridor and between the pots of geraniums, in the kitchen pantry full of saucepans and Talavera china, on the spiral stairs which led up to the flat roof and from there the little Polish boy peered down into the street and gazed at Rio de Janeiro park, at its fountains and its lawn scattered with dandelions, forgetting all about Palinuro and Estefania. 'Oh what naughty children!: would you believe that they took all the thread out of the sewing basket?' said Aunt Lucrecia who had gone to the city centre in a hat of organdie swirls. 'Would you believe that a vermilion-coloured thread stretched from my portrait in my wedding dress to the picture of Genevieve of Brabant that I have hanging on the opposite wall?' asked Mamma Clementina, who had put on her naphthalene-scented gloves to go to the city centre with Aunt Lucrecia. 'Would you believe that when we came back the whole room was full of threads of all colours draped from one side to the other?' Aunt Lucrecia asked again, returning from the city centre with a dress of fairy skin and a brooch of aquamarines. 'Would you believe that a pink thread stretched all the way from the engraving of the Plaza Mayor to a field of tulips and windmills embroidered in cross stitch?' asked Mamma Clementina who had returned from the city centre with a jar of Lydia E. Pinkham Vegetable Compound. 'Would you believe that an orange thread stretched from the cabriole leg of a chair to the elephant's trunk of an incense burner?' said Uncle Esteban to Grandfather Francisco. 'Would you believe that another grey thread stretched from Estefania's hands to the handle of the bevelled-glass door through which, perplexed, the little Polish boy watched them?' Grandfather asked don Prospero. 'Would you believe they're playing at getting under the red

316

bridge without touching it or jumping the green bridge, without touching it?'

'No, I don't believe it: you're a stinking liar,' said Molkas. 'I've never met anybody with such a wild and delirious imagination.'

'Do you know the legend of Theseus?' asked Fabricio.

'And would you believe that there was a blue thread which stretched from Estefania's eyes to the blue stained-glass window of the Santa Expiración Church to the Methylene Blue of chemistry sets?' 'And would you believe that there was a red thread which stretched from the African tulip flowering in June in Cousin Walter's house in Cuernavaca to the Starking apples that Aunt Lucrecia bought during the month of August in the Parian store, to the red room of the measles, to the photograph of Mamma Clementina bending over Palinuro's chest, red with love?' 'And would you believe that there was another white thread which stretched from Estefania's first communion dress to the white of Uncle Felipe's wedding cake, to the white of the salt which Palinuro and the little Polish boy (oh, what bad boys!) threw at the slugs which crawled out of the taps and at the snails in the garden to watch them die a squirming death? And would you believe that this same white thread stretched to the mouth of Mamma Clementina who, from the depths of her sacred siesta and her open grave said to Palinuro: "My son, if you're not thinking of going to sleep then don't think of anything, my son, think of white nothingness"?'

Palinuro closed his eyes and saw the woman sailing, whitely, over an ocean of foam and white vomit in a lofty catafalque of ice followed by flocks of white sea birds and he saw how his childhood, his childhood which was a magic window of colours and transparencies, was shattered when the white sea birds, the blind white sea birds, crashed against the glass.

And he dreamt that the woman was Mamma Clementina and that he, Palinuro, had killed her.

'But then again, listen, I have an even better idea . . . or rather, several ideas,' said Molkas who held a huge syringe in his hands.

Or rather, several syringes.

Palinuro opened his eyes.

And the woman's skin was whiter than the white of the flesh of the dead. Molkas had taken it upon himself to paint her with plaster-of-Paris water from head to foot. Her face, her closed eyelids, her secret smile: all white as milk. And her hair was white and white the down of her armpits and her pubis. And her nails and her moles, her teeth and her dreams were white. And the bed where she slept was decked in white sheets, on a white

317

floor, in a room with white walls from which hung calendars with white-blank months and pictures of landscapes with white skies and trees and summers, a room where a white-curtained window shivered with white ripples, opening on to an immense white city buried in soot as white as snow.

Molkas, Fabricio and Palinuro were also painted and dressed in white from head to foot; white their faces and their intentions and their hopes and white their fingers and their shoes and their sighs.

'The first syringe, gentlemen, contains a solution of Methyl Violet, a dye used in cultures of tuberculosis bacillus.'

The golden needle pierced the woman's tear glands.

'The second contains a dye which is normally used to colour the negative tissue of bacteria . . .'

Rose Bengal inundated the galactophorous ducts of the right mamma. For the left mamma, Molkas had chosen Prussian Blue.

'The fourth syringe contains a solution of saffron which is recommended, among other things, for colouring lesions of the liver produced by yellow fever. I have kept it for the salivary glands.'

The fifth contained Naphthol Green for the sweat glands of the woman's armpits. The sixth, Magdala Red for Molkas' sperm sacs.

Palinuro did not have to rub his eyes to see what he saw: the woman's white breasts started to flow with coloured sap: like milk of roses and strawberries in her right breast; like sky-blue cream in her left. From her lips and down her white chin and neck and on to the white blanket ran a trickle of saliva yellow as amber. Then, in her white armpits started to appear little drops of green sweat like liquid emeralds. Finally, her eyes brimmed over with violet tears which ran down her white cheeks and on to the white lace of the white pillow slip. Molkas undid the white fly of his white trousers and took out his huge cock, golden as the needle of a syringe, entered the woman and flooded her with sperm as red as blood. Palinuro closed his eyes. When he opened them again, he saw that from between the woman's legs ran a stream of blood, blood as red as the sperm was purple running down her white legs on to the white sheet and the white floor and draining away between the white cracks and through the white eyes of the keyholes and red, in all its redness, purple and crimson as red sperm, it splattered the white Sundays with red and stained purple the white voices and the white processions and crimson and scarlet the white mornings, the white shirts and white surprises. Thus, in all its redness, red and purple it trickled from the white sheets and down the white stairs and the white avenues, red, it slipped, purple, it slid, crimson, over the white alarm and the white shouts and the surprise, the pain, the panic, all white. In all its red and whiteness, white and pink and blue and snowy and milky and opalescent, spattering with violet the wings of the white crows, the blonde

318

mouth of the red wines, the green forgetfulness of the grey maidens, the blue perfume of the black roses.

'*Hymen imperforate*,' pronounced Molkas.

'*Ora pro nobis.*'

17

Oh my darling Clementine!

And *mamma* was such a gooey word, so worn out by time and epidemics. Because to say *mamma* was to acquiesce in the poverty of an innocent idiom, it was to try to surround her with zoos and birthday parties and endow her with a white head and immemorial wrinkles, things which Mamma never had or which Palinuro certainly didn't remember her ever having had. Although, on the other hand, Mamma was a little lady who was born a bit old and, thinking about it, examining it under a magnifying glass, looking at her dry skin, her unsatisfied desires, looking at the photographs of the debutante that she swore she had once been when she was Papa Eduardo's girlfriend and read *Bruges the Dead City* and he was afraid of the cathedral's gargoyles which frightened off the devil and marvelled at the angels which had violin strings for hair and wings in the shape of harps; thinking about it, Mamma was adorable, beautiful as algebra, with a dense and almost undeserved goodness and a perversion which fenced in her vertebrae . . . Mamma, who always begged him: never leave me! And now she had left him without blessing and without goodbyes, without return address and with no bitch to be called the son of.

Mamma (and I could repeat this word to infinity, until it loses its original meaning and comes to mean anything at all: kidney, tortoise, water melon). Mamma, damn it, who sank as a cathedral sinks into the sea, coughing green foam. Poor Mamma, Mamma Witch, Mamma Death, who was left with only her blue nightdress, her silver shoes and her feather hat, so poor, so rigid, so full of whistles and mazes and old snowflakes, so full of mushrooms and jellies, so porous, so green, so swollen, so poor, so rotten. Dirty Mamma, who peed in Palinuro's arms when he took her to the hospital. Dirty Mamma, who turned to dust in the tomb, who turned to marshmallow, poor thing. And then Mamma and her strokes, Mamma and her clots, Mamma and her funeral, Mamma and the tears, Mamma and the unforgivable delay, of years perhaps, between the idea Palinuro had of her death and that reality as it unfolded, naked as a country without blow-holes.

The first time was when Mamma was sleeping lightly and Palinuro was six years old and, like any lad who respects the delirium of his ghosts, he also wished to see her dead, to see her in her black box and see himself beside her, standing with downcast soul, weeping for the queen of the rabbits. Every afternoon after lunch, while he digested the inconclusive whims dancing in his stomach, Mamma Clementina took a siesta and while she slept and brayed in dreams, not a leaf moved, not a fly buzzed, not a flower reproduced, not a passenger liner anchored in the Indian Ocean, not a worm burrowed underground and time hardly dared to pass for fear of making a sound and waking her. Because Mamma's siesta was sacred, sacred as a belfry or as the leftovers of a litany and Palinuro tried to think of nothing because Mamma had told him – don't make a noise, sleep with me and if you're not sleepy think of white nothingness.

Thinking of all the things he shouldn't think about: about Papa Eduardo, about his tin soldiers, about the Sunday comics and about what he would do when he was grown up and a doctor, took up many afternoons lying beside Mamma, attentive to her breathing and her whistles, hoping that one day they would stop for ever and the room fill with the clamour of the universe.

One afternoon he tried to speak to her very quietly, in her ear, so as not to wake her. Mamma opened her eyes.

Another afternoon, when his first milk tooth came loose, Palinuro discovered that by just touching it with his tongue he felt pain and that this pain disappeared when he stopped touching it. And thus he learned to enjoy pain just for the pleasure of exorcizing it at will.

Then he would make a sudden noise so that Mamma Clementina would open her eyes and tell him off and he could then revel in his tears and Mamma Clementina's smiles of contrition. Mamma, Mamma who had been the gentlest, the most perfidious and foolish, but also the most beautiful, of all Grandfather Francisco's daughters and the one condemned to daily banishment for not living within her own life, in punishment for spending her time spying on her own life through a keyhole invented by camphor. Mamma, however, was much more important and dearly loved than a milk tooth and when Palinuro's Mamma Clementina was hurting, there was nothing in the world greater, more imperfect, more naked than that pain.

Until one afternoon, from so much thinking about everything, Palinuro's mind started to descend into white nothingness and he was with his Cousin Walter and then Mamma was dead in the garden and his cousin went to look at her. Palinuro was going to tell Cousin Walter not to speak so loudly, but he remembered that Mamma was dead and that from then onwards he could shout and sing and fire the cannon of his tin army. But when he saw that Mamma was dead on the grass, still as a mummy of moss, threatened by the climbing plants and the armoured beetles, Palinuro felt sorry and awoke with his heart beating wildly and Mamma Clementina was beside him, as always, and a cold sweat silvered her siesta.

'I had a nightmare, Mamma,' he said to her in a voice as gentle as holding snow between your fingers. Mamma didn't answer him. 'I had a nightmare and I dreamt that my heart was Cousin Walter.' Mamma's eyelids barely twitched. 'I dreamt that you died, Mamma, but I wanted you to die with my whole Cousin Walter.' A sadness, the size of a swallow, flew over Mamma and the shadow of a wing tip brushed her forehead. 'Sometimes when I'm awake I want you to die. Then I'm sorry when I'm asleep.' A grey pelican plunged from the sky, spearing Mamma's breast with the length of its beak, its feet in the air. 'Forgive me, Mamma, but sometimes I hate you and I don't want to be your son.' From the sea came a black gull which perched on Mamma's heart and pummelled it with its wings. Mamma started to make suspicious sounds. 'Do you forgive me, Mamma? Do you forgive me?' and Mamma, who already had little green bubbles in her mouth, forgave him a thousand times, but first made Palinuro swear as many times, by herself, by Papa Eduardo and by himself, on the honour of his toys and the realms of God, that never again would he wish for her death. Palinuro swore. He swore by his soldiers and the irrational battles sketched on the firing line: he swore by the sons of Captain Grant and he swore by Uncle Francisco's car and he swore by his colouring crayons and his trigonometry set and he swore by the fridge and by its ice cubes which contained crystallized fish. This made Mamma so happy that she started to whistle a song to dispel her sorrows. Mamma liked to whistle famous arias such as *Orpheus's Lament* and she did it with the window open, so that the whole neighbourhood learned of Eurydice's death. Then the tune that Mamma was whistling overflowed from the balconies and walked in the shadow of the red walls of the Palace of the Inquisition, between the fruit stalls and the pawn shops, and people stopped and asked where the song came from, who was whistling it: the butcher stood with hand raised to chop up an ox tail, the acrobat hung in the air halfway through an immortal leap; the factory sirens stopped hooting and the street organs and ambulances fell silent as the tune continued on its way and crossed the avenues, wound down the alleys, startled unsuspecting pedestrians and punted across the lake in the park, while people stopped and wondered and marvelled. Then Mamma stopped whistling and the windows closed, the curtains of copper paper hung motionless, Mamma's soul escaped in a trickle of saliva and Palinuro knelt by her side and mourned the Christmases when Mamma lit the candles on the tree and Papa came home with a bottle of brandy and Uncle Esteban with bags of Esmirma figs and Corinthian raisins, and he mourned his first pair of skates and the crystal anniversaries, the New Year parties and the Chinese lanterns lighting the corridor of his grandparents' house and he mourned his school and he mourned Mamma Clementina's siestas and false suicides.

Half an hour later Aunt Lucrecia arrived, muffled in silver foxes whose tails dragged through multitudes of dust and cotton wool soaked in Merthiolate and blue pus. She leaned against the door frame, took her spectacles from her bag and looked at Mamma: 'It's happened, I found out an hour ago. I felt a stab in the yolk of my heart and I said to myself: Clementina has died. Is that your mother, child? You won't believe it, but that's the end of her. We hadn't seen each other for five years. You know, Palinuro, child, the family has grown so much that some of us don't see each other except at weddings and funerals. Isn't that right, Clementina? Yes, yes, it is five years since we last exchanged gossip. Your mother had a mind of her own, you know, she was stubborn, headstrong. Isn't that right, Clementina?'

But it wasn't as though Mamma Clementina was always like that: like Aunt Lucrecia said she was. There were two things, among others, for which Palinuro was grateful to her:

First, for her obsessions. For example, Mamma's permanent obsession with Palinuro's willy which started the first time she bathed him and realized that baby Palinuro had a fleshy extension between his legs. Until then, Mamma's idea of a baby had always been closer to that of a roly-poly angel, like the ones that have a habit of escaping from the stained-glass windows of cathedrals and therefore, besides smelling of a decadent mixture of Johnson's talc and milk-shake, the baby belonged to a kind of eternal present, without possibility of change. Nevertheless, despite the fact that she herself, elusive as a sigh, was always sunk in a region of chiaroscuro composed of a murky past which never got around to passing and a luminous future which never really got started, she suddenly realized that inside baby Palinuro were testicles, hair and lascivious thoughts, which from then onward struggled to rise to the surface and would one day succeed, that Palinuro would not miss the great adventure of life, the ambiguity of the sexes and the origin of species. Papageno, Tsar Sultan, Princess Turandot: every single opera character could have come down to earth to console Mamma and their efforts would have been drowned in the dining-room carpet.

'We are going to put our little boy in the bath,' said Mamma, as his little willy raised its head for the first time and answered Mamma with a squirt. 'That's very rude,' said Mamma, drying her half-urine and half-real tears, and putting all the possible Palinuros in the bath.

And as soon as the bath water – though not holy water as Catholic rites demand nor bull's blood or honey as required by Tibetan liturgy – came into contact with Palinuro's body, with his tiny pink buttocks, with his feet and his nails and his back and his fat little miniature hands, it began to baptize him. In less than ten seconds, every part of Palinuro's body, every natural orifice, every fold and every protuberance, including his willy, were called Palinuro, for ever.

'He can't be called that,' said Grandmother Lisandra, from the depths of a waltz.

'I don't feel well,' said Aunt Luisa, not that her feeling unwell, at least that morning, had anything to do with Palinuro's christening.

'The best thing for haemorrhoids is toothpaste,' Grandfather insisted.

'Good heavens, Francisco, what things you do say.'

'In particular, because it gives you sweet breath if the rear guard decides to play a symphony.'

'I really must insist,' said Grandmother Altagracia and, meanwhile, a providential lack of attention on Mamma's part allowed the water for an instant to cover Palinuro's face, so that the irises and the pupils of his eyes, his nostrils and the cartilage of his nose, were called Palinuro, as were each of the musical parts of his ear, including the hammer, the anvil and the drum. And Palinuro took a good gulp, most of which flowed down and baptized his entire urinary system, including the double filter of his kidneys, reached the meatus and was ejected in the form of a warm yellow liquid, a repetitive phenomenon which, as any doctor can explain, is a straightforward case of Palinurinitis.

'That's also very rude,' said Mamma Clementina, who had a splendid, although not necessarily tragic, memory: she knew by heart her multiplication tables, the main steps of the Charleston, the eye-colour of her dearest friends in primary school, and the prettiest names of ingredients – like maraschino and cream of tartar – in the confectionery recipes which she collected with all the love and perseverance with which other people collect silver spoons, postage stamps or venereal diseases. But if she had only known, if only, as Cousin Walter insisted, Mamma Clementina had indeed been able also to recall the future when Palinuro returned home in a drunken stupor which denuded the walls, spewed up his guts over the embroidered screens and slept his siestas on the window sill that he might there pluck the plumage of his self-love. If for a moment she had imagined Palinuro and Estefania's quarrels, or worse, seen him lying in the square like a wilted helicopter, wounded and bleeding through the rips in his suit, Mamma Clementina would have collapsed into a chair in fright and surprise because, as Grandfather said: 'It's better to be sitting than standing.' Or she would have gone to bed on the brink of a migraine because, as Grandfather added: 'It's better to be lying than sitting.' Or she would have died, several years and several strokes ahead of time because, as Grandfather concluded: 'It's better to be dead than lying.' Or, without exaggerating, the least she would have done was to get up halfway through the meal, trembling like a bunch of newly cut violets; she spilt water over the tablecloth, she tripped over her chair and over the carpet, bruised herself on the door handle and the lampshade, her legs and eyelashes gave way, she hit her head on the pillow, she collapsed on the blankets, she became entangled on the bed and we had to run to her room and scratch her all over to stop her from trembling. Because Mamma Clementina always got an itch when there was a crisis. And so it had always been, since she was Papa Eduardo's girlfriend and the two walked in La Piedad park which had been a cemetery many years previously and where you might still come across a skull peeping from the ground. Mamma was perched up on a fallen trunk covered in moss and Papa stood before her with his thumbs stuck into the pockets of his waistcoat and his remaining fingers splayed as though he were about to play a famous romanza on the piano. Then Mamma slipped on purpose and Papa could but close his eyes and open his arms. And so, clasped in each other's arms and kissing the while, they walked towards a bench and sat down and continued to kiss, heedless of the red ants climbing into her shoes and stockings and of the bluebottles buzzing around the carbon lamps. Then the horse flies came. Papa felt an itch on his knee and scratched it. Then Mamma felt an itch on her ankle and started to scratch it, which was when Papa felt an itch on Mamma's right thigh and scratched it just above the flowered garter but, by then, Mamma had felt an itch on Papa's spine and with both hands scratched the entire length of his poplin back. Then Papa felt an itch in her Myrurgia perfume, just behind Mamma's right ear, Mamma in the hair of Papa's chest, Papa on Mamma's stomach, south of her belly button and the waist elastic of her sateen panties, and things would have gone a lot further: at least as far as an hotel of ill repute with rusted blinds and fluorescent condoms, if the time had not come for the park to close. Mamma remembered it all as though it were yesterday.

Mamma rinsed Palinuro as only a mamma can, lifted him out of the bath and placed him on a blue towel.

'Good boys don't touch that,' she said. 'Good manners forbid it.'

Palinuro didn't stop touching his willy, because he hadn't been touching it in the first place. However, he obeyed Mamma.

And, when all is said and done, one has so many bones to carry through life, so many muscles prone to mawkishness and injections and so many hollows and glands in which the lace of our childhood rots, that we would never get through naming them all. Suffice it to say that the water managed to christen the whole of Palinuro's anatomy and that, in some cases, it rechristened common places which have always, for generations of wise men and readers, had the same name and thus causing a series of reforms in the realms of geography and the mythological melting pots. In its passage through the corporeal landscapes, beyond the silvan valleys and olfactory deserts, the water reached the shore of the Islets of Langerhans, which everybody knows are in the pancreas, and baptized those crystal beaches with the name of Islets of Palinuro. From that time, also, the Atlas

325

vertebra and the Achilles tendon came to be called the vertebra of Palinuro, he who supports the world on his shoulders, and the tendon of Palinuro, the Greek hero, who as an adolescent fed on the marrow of a lion. The other thing for which Palinuro was, or should have been, grateful to Mamma Clementina was the plain fact not so much of having brought him into the world, but all the trouble (far more than that taken by Estefania) and all the sacrifices (far more than those made by my cousin) and all the pain she suffered to prepare her belly to bring him into the world.

Mama Clementina imagined that she suffered from complete sterility.

The doctor imagined relative sterility which could perhaps be attributed to tubular spasms caused by emotional upsets and tension.

Palinuro, after Mamma had without embarrassment told him how she had suffered from narrowness of the uterus and how she decided not to tell anybody and to cure it in secret and how one of Papa Eduardo's sisters called for her and the two said they were going to the cinema when they were really going to the doctor's surgery and how the treatment to widen the neck of her uterus caused her terrible pain and how she hid this from everybody and even found joy in the pain because it was as though Palinuro were already growing inside her, in a way, and martyring her unintentionally, Palinuro imagined – he couldn't help it – Mamma in the kitchen, Mamma eating breakfast, Mamma going to the park with Papa, with a laminaria in her uterus, a laminaria which expanded moment by moment to open up the way for him, Palinuro, for you, my son, to be conceived.

Mamma told him no more. But in Uncle Esteban's *History of Medicine* and in dictionaries and articles on obstetrics, Palinuro later learned that Albucasis had described the treatment of a woman's fractured pubis whereby a balloon was introduced into her vagina and afterwards inflated by the doctor and that this could be considered to be the first appearance of a colpeurynter. And that this device resembled an empty rubber bag placed in the uterus and then filled with water to correct the narrowness. And that other objects could be used as dilators to correct narrowness of the uterus – a sponge, a laminaria. And that laminaria was the name given to a type of seaweed, the *Laminaria digitata*, the peduncle of which served to correct relative sterility due to narrowness of the neck of the uterus in that, when inserted in dried form, it had the property of swelling with the humidity of organic liquids to a considerable volume.

And Palinuro imagined that Mamma Clementina, at night when Papa Eduardo was asleep, tiptoed to the wardrobe – where she kept her secret laminaria, in a jar with iodiform ether, together with her mementoes and her eyelash curlers and her underwear perfumed with sprigs of thyme – and put it to dry in the dew of the garden and then, when Papa Eduardo went off to his place of business, Mamma took down the dilator from its hiding place among the leaves of the orange tree, shook off the bees and the dew, locked the bathroom door and inserted it herself in her vagina and afterwards, as though she had not a care in the world, as though she felt no pain, as though her vagina and her heart did not harbour an ever greater and more humid hope of having a child, Mamma, who was always so resigned, Mamma who was always able to embroider legends on the robes of the holy statues and count her poverty in decimals, Mamma, as she dusted and swept the bedrooms of Altagracia's lodgers, started blithely to whistle a tune.

And I did this that you might be born, my son, repeated Mamma Clementina from all those uncomfortable places where she was dead. (But it was a lie.)

Until the day on which the gynaecologist, in whose spectacles danced two oracular stars, said to Mamma Clementina: 'You are ready, madam, that'll be two hundred pesos.'

Mamma left the surgery with her eyes full of resplendent landscapes, her belly corroded by enthusiasm and her heart wrapped in a shell of dreams and walked slowly through the streets and felt that she was undressing, that her clothes got tangled up in the trees and in the barbed wire and the birds carried them off and hung them from the flagstaffs and the electricity cables and thus, naked, she arrived home ready to give herself to Papa Eduardo and offer him the most varied of positions, as well as the total inversion of her flesh.

And the miracle came to pass, the miracle for which Mamma had so often beseeched the Virgin and for which she promised to take to her sanctuary a bunch of flowers wet with her synchronic tears and a miraculous gown on which she would embroider plumes and cosmoramas.

The miracle, in thanks for which she also covered the distance from the door of the church to the high altar on her knees. And it was there that Palinuro I came into the world, immersed in purple drops, in a full moon which scarcely moistened Mamma's thighs. 'This haemorrhage, madam,' the doctor explained to her, 'was an effluvium; in other words, you expelled the fertilized egg which had not yet adhered to the uterus. In further words, it was an abortion. But, if I'm not mistaken, you are quite capable of becoming pregnant again.'

But that was a lie: all that patience, that whole ultra-solar reserve of energies which Mamma demonstrated, that ability to transform pain into a sweet cataplasma were, in reality, dedicated to Palinuro the First who never progressed beyond the stage of being an ovule cut off from the family and relegated to a rubbish bin so that, in fact, Palinuro had already been conceived once before his conception and, though he inaugurated his mother's womb, he was not the first child in her breast, and so, when he was born, with the name Palinuro the Second, he was in effect his own younger brother. The only thing that Mamma Clementina did actually do for Palinuro II following that flooding pause and with lucid heart, was to agree with Papa Eduardo on the guidelines of a new sexual act, treacherous and almost simple, almost typewritten, whereby she finally succeeded in lodging Palinuro II in her belly, which he forsook nine months later in order to come into the world or in order for the world to come to him and open his eyes to its foolishness and nonsense.

Mamma had no reason to tell Palinuro this. Neither did she have any reason to say to him as she once did: 'Your father doesn't satisfy me', because Palinuro was not yet of an age to imagine that 'your father doesn't satisfy me' meant that Papa Eduardo didn't give her chocolates with topaz centres, that Papa Eduardo didn't take her to see Charles Boyer films, didn't fill her soul with hallelujahs and tamarinds or take her skating in Luna Park. It meant, simply . . .

Mamma, in other words, shouldn't have told him, ever, that she was a vulva with two legs and that Papa was a phallus with two hands. And that when Papa Phallus arrived home at night, Mamma Vulva opened her entire body and showed Papa Phallus the cosmic hole, the bottomless pit and, deeper, the ovaries hanging by their hooks like Christmas tree decorations and, deeper still, the egg-tomb which she gave to him when he was conceived and, deeper yet, the gelatine of her bones. And that Papa Phallus squeezed his head with his two white and bony little hands and on the top of his bald pate shone the pearl that he would deposit in Mamma Vulva, in Mamma Valve. But then Mamma Valve's labia majora started to grow and the more they grew the thinner they got and when they reached the size of a butterfly's wings, Mamma Valve escaped from Papa Phallus and flew over a landscape where baby Phalluses grew like poisonous mushrooms and a retinue of vulvas with black wings like the wings of bats followed her in her soft and graceful flight while the night decked the earth with its silver and malignant stars and its comets and coal and Palinuro floated in the yellow waters with his sea snail body stuck to a shell of sebaceous glands and dreamed of a huge red lobster which threatened him with its metal pincers. Then Mamma Valve looked at herself full-vulva in the mirror, attended by her retinue of butterflies, and combed her long straight pubic hairs which reached the tip of her toes, shouted for her favourite page to be brought to her and Palinuro awoke and changed into a page and Mamma sheltered him beneath her wings and Palinuro fell back to sleep inside her, floating again down a plastic river, beneath broken gargoyles towards castles of ash. Then Mamma Valve entered the sea and a school of dolphins sported around her and a black dolphin with scales of silver and leprosy balanced an enormous testicle on his nose, all pink and covered with blue veins, then tossed it to another dolphin but the testicle fell in the sea and a boiling jet spouted from the waters. And Mamma

Valve parted the lips of her sex and her wings burst into flame and the dolphins leapt one after the other through the ring of black fire.

And that meant that Papa didn't satisfy her and that Mamma began to get an itching in all the scabby orifices of her skin which distilled wasps' honey and then she would go out on to the balcony at midnight to weep and almost, almost, cry out to heaven.

No, Mamma should never have told Palinuro such things during those long afternoons when Palinuro was five years old and his liver too small to withstand the tangle of theorems which he bottled up in his heart and, Mamma Clementina holding him by the hand, he went to consult a homoeopath who knew very well how to reap benefits from her plea. And Palinuro had to pocket his golden illusions and his tin soldiers, his favourite captain who had been wounded, treacherously, and who was a past-master at giving a sound thrashing to those of his enemies who, by coincidence, bore a vague resemblance to the bullies at his school before whose very eyes he tore the enemy flag to shreds and gave each a different coloured piece. During those long, almost monastic hours that Palinuro waited in the surgery, he not only wrote his first poems harking back to that infancy of condensed almond milk which we have all lost once in life and which Palinuro lost twice, but he also came across a picture depicting death and a physician struggling to wrest a naked woman from its grasp and he regretted having wished for his mother's death and he vowed that when he became a doctor he would hang the same picture on the wall of his surgery and that every minute of his life would be devoted to fighting death and he swore that he would never let Mamma Clementina die, that he would put all her possible deaths in a sack and throw them into the sea and that any others he would shoot unsuspecting in the back and cause others to skid on the butter of the highways and others he would place before a sharp wind of mirrors so they would die of old age and he would paint black death white and feed pox to the chickens and change cancer's sign of the zodiac.

But this was yet another of his promises to Mamma Clementina which he could not fulfil. The invisible clot that Mamma had harboured within her since she was a child (just as she had always carried the little egg from which Palinuro was to be born) and which started secretly to circulate in her veins and her communicating vessels, feeding on dead cells and pale phagocytes and with the wish, firm as a rock and oft-repeated: 'I don't want to live long, I don't want to reach fifty and enter heaven as an old woman,' that clot, that little aerial bubble which grew with the years like a dirty snowball, finally became lodged in Mamma Clementina's heart. And there she was, burning up with sweat and serums, deserted by venoclysises, covered in clinical histories and silent electrocardiograms, dead in a hospital bed. Aunt Lucrecia was there too, swallowing her tiredness in yawns and repeating over and over: 'When I felt the stab, I tell you, I noticed that it was 2.47. Tell me, child – what time did your mother die?'

It happened between the salad and the fish, or perhaps between the fish and the meat, who knows, who will ever know? Memory – thought Palinuro – is a delirious ventriloquist who on our lips plants burning words and white, bewitched lies which burst forth disguised as adventures and cause us to confuse the fish with the salad, the first clot with the last. Or perhaps it was an innocent urge to sacralize those days which were lost anyway. The fact was that Palinuro came home from school and sat down to lunch with Mamma Clementina, just the two of them because Papa ate at work, stooped over his failures and his fried eggs, and the afternoon promised a pale folklore for dessert and the usual gossip and jokes which made Mamma forget what she called Palinuro's gross ingratitude. To understand this, to understand why anything that Palinuro did would always seem to Mamma to show ingratitude, you would have to live with her for a few years to learn that her heart, fragile as a god and vehemently refusing any pleasure in life, was, none the less, quite equal to practising blackmail and distilling the law of survival of the weakest. And so it was, that second time and the many other times, that Palinuro had an approximate idea of Mamma's death. What was to follow were the shouts, the medicines, the doctors, the house in chaos and Mamma Clementina rising from her ashes ten days later, ready to live a few more months – or a few more years – in that hazy sea in which the waves breathe, here and there, a sigh mingled with digitalin and smelling salts. If Palinuro gave up his medical studies to try his hand at painting, Palinuro was ungrateful. If Palinuro gave up painting for advertising, Palinuro was ungrateful. If Palinuro didn't side with Mamma when she and Papa started flinging insults at each other and ended up flinging plates, lamps, the house and the world, Palinuro was ungrateful. And Palinuro was ungrateful if he didn't remember her birthday, if he didn't respect her siesta, if this, if that, if the other. And when Mamma, in all seriousness, her voice laden with salamanders and white frogs which lived happily in her filth, told him that her next stroke would be her last, that it would carry her to a purgatory where Papa made love to her every hour of every day like a male waking anew at every instant, and Palinuro was not moved to tears by the tale, Palinuro was ungrateful.

Mamma wished to hear no more of Palinuro's promises that afternoon, between the salad and the soup, or between the meat and the dessert, who will ever know? – my leg hurts, she said, and her fork clattered on to her plate with a special gleam. 'It's a cramp.' 'No,' Mamma said, 'it's a stroke, my last!' Mamma tried to walk but she collapsed like a rag doll and so Palinuro lifted her in his arms to carry her to her bed and continued to carry her for ever, from that afternoon onwards, along with her hospital bed and

330

her iron box, her future incarnations and the earth flooded with flowers. But Mamma was so tiny, so light, that Palinuro felt like someone carrying in their arms a machine-gunned companion and hearing how the air whistles through the neck wounds and feeling how the blood soaks his hands. But no, it wasn't blood, son, my son, so embarrassed, I urinated, Mamma told him. It was only a sphincter which finally got tired from so much playing at opening and closing. And it was also another of Mamma's belated revenges. Then, in the blink of an eye, a grey dew planted Lent on the sweet mask she had for a face, on a tame ankle, in a corner of the brain where verbal fantasies are forged and it was Mamma can't speak any more, Mamma can't move her left leg, Mamma is wept in lotions and snowed in talc, Mamma and the hospital, Mamma and ten hours of peaceful sleep, Mamma and her death agony which started at 1.25 in the morning.

That was the moment when Mamma grasped the bars of the bedhead with those hands that embroidered the history of Genevieve of Brabant in wood, and a cluster of green bubbles rose in her mouth. At 1.26 Mamma let go of the bars and tried to say something, no one ever knew what, whether a beautiful sentence that might be hung ingeniously on the soft air or yet another curse against Papa or do you want more fish, child, because her face wrinkled as though twenty centuries had fallen on top of it and she lay quiet as a crumpled poppy with her eyes clouded. At 1.27 she started to wink at the nurses. At 1.28 her pancreas burst. At 1.30 her nightdress and the sheets started to throb above her heart. At 1.36 Mamma started to dance and the nurses had to tie her down at the wrists and ankles. At 1.42 her kidneys burst. At 1.47 Mamma urinated for the second time. At 1.48 the green bubbles turned into black vomit. At 1.49 long hairs sprouted from her heart. At 1.52 Mamma no longer wished to dance in her bed. At 1.55 Mamma started to spew up little bits of lung and snake skin. At 2.03 Mamma stopped winking at the nurses and closed her eyes. At 2.07 she opened them again. At 2.10 her ears burst and her anal sphincter gave way. At 2.12 the nurses washed and perfumed her with lavender. At 2.15 she lay still, wept a little blood and clawed the sheets. At 2.16 her hair fell out. At 2.18 Mamma started to breathe like a bellows. At 2.20 all the memories in her brain burst, her walks in La Piedad Park, her trip to New York, Lake Michigan which froze over in winter, Grandfather Francisco's fat leg. At 2.21 Mamma showed her tongue to the nurse and expelled a stream of mucus from her nose. At 2.24 she got pneumonia. At 2.25 she got typhoid. At 2.26 she got measles. At 2.29 she developed a complication of the right eyelid, of her eustachian tube and her semilunar ganglion. At 2.30 her right eye, her spleen, her left nostril and her sternon collapsed successively. At 2.33 all the photographs of her as a good child sitting on Aunt Luisa's lap and as a young girl of thirteen who took communion every first Friday of the month in Rosario Church and as a respectable married woman who went weekly to Dr Latorre's surgery, started to tear and fell to pieces. At 2.34 her pulse started its ascent from her wrists and her toes. At 2.35 her pulse was situated in her tibia and shoulders. At 2.37 it rounded the armpit and descended the crosier of the aorta. At 2.39 her pulse drowned howling in her heart and her heart started to clot and the long hairs fell out of it, together with her milk teeth. At 2.40 Mamma was technically dead. At 2.41 the nurses removed all the catheters connecting her with the outside world and inter-planetary spaces, with ashtrays and telegrams. At 2.43 the director of the clinic arrived, removed his raincoat and his jacket, rolled up his shirtsleeves, examined Mamma and, at 2.46, declared her dead. At 2.47 Palinuro realized. At 2.49 he left the waiting room, lit a cigarette and became aware that not only was Mamma dead there, in her bed, but also throughout the hospital, the walls and ceilings, the corridors and the urinals. Palinuro went over to the window where Mamma was also dead among the panes and the dead flies and saw that in the cars, in the people walking in the streets, on the rooftops and in the tanks of green water, Mamma was dead. Beyond the city and the ministries and the advertising agencies, Mamma was dead in the mountains, in the trees, in the stones. Beyond her illusions, Mamma was dead in all the counts and countesses of Flanders and dead in the *béguinage* and dead in Bruges the Dead City. Palinuro thought of their house and of the white house that Mamma was going to have some day. Mamma was dead in the sitting-room carpet, in the liquidizer, in the clothes lines, in the flowered kitchen curtains. He wanted to imagine her sitting in her spatial rocking chair, smiling, embroidering a posy of wild flowers on a pillowslip but he saw that she was dead in the rocking chair, in the needles, in the red threads, in her wolves and in her lamps. He remembered her letters in which she asked him to write to her every Sunday and he knew that Mamma was dead in the lilac scent, in the drawer of the writing desk, in the following Sunday. He returned to the room to look at her once more, dead in the bed, and he saw that Mamma was dead beneath the bed, on the right-hand edge of the bed, in the bedhead. He kissed her on the brow and knew that she was dead in her bones, dead in her hair and in her skin. Later, when Aunt Enriqueta arrived, when their friends arrived, he would learn that Mamma was also dead in Papa Eduardo's sticking plaster and dead in Aunt Lucrecia's bead bag and in Cousin Walter's patchwork waistcoat. And he understood that, for evermore, although things did not know it, although roadsweepers and grapefruits for sale in the Parian and policemen remained intact throughout Mamma's death, none the less Mamma would be dead everywhere, above the bed, beneath the sand and in the crabs' nests, above the waves and beneath the waltzes, dead in the cinema foyers, in fallen wages, in concentration camps and in botany studies; dead in the newsreels of Vietnam, in the Popocatepetl volcano and in Forty-second Street, and dead in letters to the agony column, dead in the repentant tiles of urinals, in St Ursula's eleven thousand virgins and in correspondence courses. There, in bars and in population explosions and in Memling's angels, Mamma was dead. And she was dead, also, in his words.

Aunt Lucrecia gave herself over to the yellow pages of the telephone directory to organize a fitting funeral for Mamma, complete with a coffin of ornate metalwork, mourners of various flavours and wreaths sprinkled with clichés. Then she gave herself over to the white pages to inform any relatives, friends or acquaintances within a fifty-kilometre radius of the hospital. 'I am sorry about your mamma's death,' said Uncle Austin, with a breath that caused the orchids on Aunt Enriqueta's chest to blush. In her turn, Aunt Enriqueta, who had lost twenty kilos and gained twenty years, hugged Palinuro and, between hiccups and sobs, exclaimed: 'Your poor mamma, who did not live to see her grandchildren.' Palinuro couldn't complain. Other aunts and uncles and cousins came. Grandmother Lisandra came, Uncle Felipe came. Molkas came and Fabricio came. They told a few jokes and stole a few ashtrays and they all gave him something: their condolences, a hug, a bunch of white gardenias or gladioli and they tried to take Palinuro's mind off his loss, speaking of the Nazi occupation, the devaluation of the peso, the floods in Mexico City which, as Uncle Felipe said, brought to the surface a fair amount of shit but also the ineptitude of the city authorities. Later they talked (apropos of what Aunt Enriqueta had said) of all that which Mamma would never know, besides her grandchildren. 'The trip to the moon,' said Cousin Walter. 'The Third World War,' said the manager of the funeral parlour. 'Colour television,' said Aunt Laura. And nearly everyone stayed a good while. Some for four hours. Others for two cigarettes and three cups of coffee. There was discussion also of the different kinds of agonies and deaths people can suffer. With morphine injections day and night. With frosty flatulence. With piercing spasms. Of cancer. In the bath. In the office when leaning over to drink water from the dispenser. On the wheel of fortune when a car comes loose and falls on the shooting gallery. The drunk who peed on a lamp post and electrocuted himself urinally. A short-sighted little man who had got the wrong funeral parlour approached Palinuro and said to him: 'I share your grief,' glanced at the floral explosions crowning the coffin and added: 'There is no doubt that he was a great man.' Then everyone started to say goodbye and promised Palinuro that they would come back in the afternoon to go with him to the cemetery. Palinuro was left alone. He sat in a chair and dreamt that Mamma was dead above her coffin and that their old friends, who were also dead, came to see her. The general with the glass eye, who leaned over Mamma and offered her a single tear and the tear ran down Mamma's face as though she herself had wept it. Ex-congressman Fournier, who placed his hearing trumpet against

Mamma's heart in search of a posthumous hope. And Grandfather, Uncle Enrique, Aunt Luisa who arrived at ten o'clock in the morning Paris time and don Prospero who, for the first time in ages, was sad on the left side of his face and sad on the right side. And Flavia the maid and Uncle Esteban eaten up by tuberculosis and the Polish family and Uncle Alejandro who lived for years between the living and the dead.

Mamma Clementina presided over her own burial. She travelled in a grey hearse with violet windows which awoke admiration and forgetfulness and behind her followed a line of cars of all colours and makes. As they passed the flower market, the vendors crossed themselves with marguerites and roses of Castile. As they drove through the park, the ash trees scattered some of their leaves. As they approached the fountain of Diana the Huntress, the wind spread a curtain of water illuminated by a triumphal rainbow. Three blocks further on, a hat vendor removed his ten hats simultaneously and a policeman crucified himself to stop the traffic and allow Mamma Clementina to pass. But, by then, the funeral cortège had been cut by traffic lights and defections. Three cars containing some of Palinuro's fellow students, dressed in white and with their anatomies on their laps, lost the scent at the corner of Paseo de la Reforma and Avenida de los Insurgentes and returned to the School of Medicine. Another five cars, including a brand-new red Volkswagen, took a wrong right turn and were borne away on the delirious litany of the great city. At the junction of Observatorio and Tacubaya, a black Packard raised its bonnet, shot a fountain towards the clouds and lay like a stranded whale while, at the corner of Revolucion and Siete, a beige Plymouth and a yellow Pontiac decided to desert to a cantina there to celebrate the decline of whisky. Mamma Clementina forged ahead, reflecting alleyways and telephone booths and beggars and barbers' signs in her windows and, in Mixcoac, half the cortège had to halt at the level crossing to allow thirty train carriages to pass, full of poor passengers eating tuna-fish sandwiches who crossed themselves and waved while their children vomited out of the windows. When the train had gone by and it became apparent that the street ahead ended in a sharp bend, a further fourteen cars desisted and another three went around asking bystanders and the petrol pump attendants if they had seen a funeral procession go by. But there were loyal cars in which travelled old friends, childhood cousins, Aunts Lucrecia and Enriqueta, as Mamma continued on her way towards the Jardín cemetery which awaited her with open graves. At the third milestone, Mamma caught up with a group of cyclists in orange shirts labouring up a hill in slow motion who served as her escort, then drew ahead into the distance on the down-run to accompany her again on the next hill, then descend swifter than melting snow towards the valleys and again escort her up the hill where the pine trees started to shade the road. Mamma Clementina came in nineteenth, crossing the finishing line with headlights blazing and the judges took their leave of her, flags in hand. When Mamma entered the cemetery, she was greeted with bells and doves, and then a shower of rain enlivened the proceedings and supplied the mourners with tears. Everyone wept from head to toe, everyone, including Palinuro who stood firm as a satin-clad page while the clods of earth buried the disciplines and hells of Mamma Melon, Poor Mamma.

When he was left alone after taking his leave with a handshake and a hug of all the relatives and friends, and when Mamma was lying three metres underground or, to put it another way, standing at the threshold of eternity, Palinuro remembered that he was virtually a child and from his pockets he took, to give to Mamma, the eight and a half wonders he kept there: a frog, nuts and bolts, an old coin, the story of grandfather and the captain with a bullet in his leg and the old gringo; a cricket in a cage of cork and pins, his boy-scout scarf, two almost-precious gems and three apricot stones. Then he frightened off the birds which threatened to carry away the wreaths in their beaks, sat down in the dust and, softly, so as not to wake her, he started talking to his darling Clementine.

18

The last of the Imaginary Islands:
this house of the sick

1

Good-day, Dr Palinuro. And when I say 'Good-day', you may rest assured that I mean exactly that. There are days, doctor, like cider factories, which sail on the clouds and scatter bubbles and the scent of apples: those are the days on which we get drunk enough to kill the idea. In my capacity as deputy medical director of the hospital, I have come to wish you welcome in the name of all the doctors, nurses, office staff and porters. There are other days when one feels like sending the whole world off on a toboggan with all its news correspondents, doctor, its cars, its romantic statistics and the frozen gaudiness of wedding cakes: those are the days like motionless lizards which move at the speed of the earth and you stay in bed reading, tracing a dawn between the ruins, sleeping. We have prepared a tour of all the wards so you can see how we have implemented the projects which you prepared during your exile in the ministry, Dr Palinuro, and it will be my pleasure to be your guide on this tour. There are other days – perhaps the majority – which are grey, doctor: they lend solidity to disorganized architecture, the city sprouts thorns of belfries, a murky liquor in which float thousands of green, sad pullovers, there are floods in the streets, steamrollers scatter dog turds and a pectroscopic mishap causes the rainbow to fall into puddles of petrol: those are days without remedy, the mediocre hours storing up trivialities, inoffensive and forgotten inventories. On our tour of the wards we will be accompanied by the most prominent surgeons and specialists on our staff, including a number of pathologists who have taken courses in karate to control the insane, as well as physiologists bound to the theories of Santiago Ramón y Cajal. I almost forgot to mention, doctor, that there are also days, like this one, that are good for visiting hospitals in order to understand that, though there are microscopes bathed in dribble and scalpels turning grey in jars of alcohol, there are also stars which are extinguished in the bathtub and pheasants which cross the sky carrying in their beaks the grapes with which they will be cooked beneath platters of syrupy silver. It seems almost unnecessary for me to mention, doctor, that your ideas have been the target of determined and open attack by many hygienists and sociologists, some of whom are undeniably distinguished. Envy can arise anywhere, doctor: in waistcoat gills and in the depths of solar batteries. Just look, for example, at these new patent-leather shoes which I bought last week. But allow me to hang your stethoscope around your neck and put on the rubber gloves which William Stewart invented for love of Caroline's hands. I was saying, dear colleague, that the strongest objections have, predictably, centred on asepsis, isolation of infected individuals and patients' morale. What is happening, in other words, is that humanity, while waiting for enlightenment by alms, has done an about-turn to go back to the period in history when it was most unhappy: look, doctor, at this photograph of me when I was twenty years old. The results achieved have, obviously, undermined such arguments: cases of contagion have been few; the majority of patients have the opportunity to savour the diseases of their neighbours in the next bed and it is edifying, moreover, in cases of fatal denouements, to see that fellow patients die of diseases other than that from which they themselves are suffering. But let us commence our visit, doctor; allow me to take your arm and we will walk down this corridor which regurgitates the grey bustle of nurses and practitioners talking and singing, kissing on the threshold of the operating theatres and pushing treatment convoys containing bunches of carnations, golden syringes and shining jars and who make way for our group and greet you, doctor, dazzled by your charismatic authority. You will know that Torquato Tasso relates how wizards travel through the clouds in carriages drawn by white unicorns. The point being that our trip will be no less marvellous: neither the sponges moistening delirium, doctor, nor the razor blades which pursue me in my dreams will spoil my pleasure in accompanying you. Return their greetings and wave your stethoscope in the air if you like. As we approach the Acoustic Ward I should add that the other attacks directed against us have proved to be ill-founded and we may therefore dismiss them, as we dismiss the quantum theory or Octavio Paz's instants which explode to become stars. We have responded to our enemies with more arguments than those used by Albertus Magnus against the Averroists. Hence, it is not worth even mentioning that they condemn this system of classification as grotesque, baroque and inhuman. These critics should bear in mind that the grotesque and the inhuman – for example, delitescent tumours, blood poured into outer space and worms which, soft as they are, shake the earth – occur autonomously in many ailments, quite independently of our taxological efforts which merely dramatize them. And they should also remember that there is nothing more inhuman than diseases themselves: invasions of microbes, loss of thought processes and leukaemias which change our children into cherubs of the Boucher and Vanloo school; in short, doctor, anything threatening this wondrous mechanism which is the human body. Forgive me for speaking in clichés but, when you say: 'the sky is sapphire blue', you are doing nothing more and nothing less than witnessing the meeting of the pennants. Finally, doctor, there are days which, though they do not cease to be blue and luminous, become simultaneously sad to match our own sadness. If it has not been your lot, doctor, on account of your youth, to witness such a day, you must imagine it as a day without alarms, without tragic bonuses, very different from those days which fall under the weight of clouds and linoleums, of inconsolable rains and yellow trams, or from those which are so sad that the sadness becomes something that can be spread on the face, on the trees and on the dogs, and then the face drops, the trees lose their leaves and the dogs fall ill with spotted sickness. No, doctor, you would have to imagine it the other way round, as a day on which sadness is not seen to arrive from anywhere, because it has always been within things themselves: if we put on a red hat with ostrich feathers, we are putting on sadness. If we mount a little horse on a roundabout, we are mounting sadness. Sadness is in the balloons and in the darts, in the helter-skelters, in the dumb storks who make their nests on the periscopes of submarines. Or, doctor, to use a happier turn of phrase, you would have to picture it as one of those sad days which travel incognito through the middle of the world falsifying the natural happiness of dragonflies and geysers. As though on earth there were nothing but little girls taking their first communion scattered among the angels! As though there were no daily dead – your dead, doctor – and there were not sick patients – our patients, colleague – and there were no old people falling in the bathtub and breaking their wishbone. This explanation, which has no basis in scientific fact, may at least give you a notion of sadness.

2

Regarding our patients and turning to the matter which most interests us, perhaps the first thing you will notice in the Acoustic Ward and which you will confirm later as we visit the rest of the wards, is their singular architecture. Ah, doctor, beside our wards, the domes and towers and constructions of Michelangelo, Le Corbusier and Frank Lloyd Wright pale with envy! There is no point in describing what you will see, dear friend, with your own eyes, so I will just point out occasionally the most notable details, like the shell design of this first room, which will no doubt remind you of your visits to a famous museum and, consequently, of the green and sonorous chords of Kandinsky sweeping New York's Central Park on St Patrick's Day. In this first room, in accordance with a concept which will make our hospital the most original on earth, we have grouped all the patients who for some reason or other emit particular noises. Anyone who has ever heard, doctor, the bombastic wind of a concert which kneeling begs that we go to the sea, and the voluntary sound of rivers peeping through the windows, will know what I'm talking about. Besides the classical trio of patients with asthma, bronchitis and emphysema, we have a great variety of shrillnesses from children with whooping cough, and of tracheal whistling from our patients with diphtherial laryngitis. Diphtheria is no longer the serious illness which carried two of my sisters, twins, to the grave when they were four years of age. All I remember of them is the image of a golden torso sinking into the snow. Now come this way. Say hello to Dr Palinuro, children, he's the director of the hospital and he is very kind to you all. Look, doctor, here we have a woman who has acquired the habit of ejecting certain gases from the vagina and so producing a noise similar to burps. We do not know the cause but we can state that, in this case, it is not merely a matter of the stomach's gratitude. Speaking of which, tympanites is characterized by swelling and excessive distension of the abdomen which becomes tight as a drum. See this poor old man who farts formidably as his only means of expression, since it is some time since he lost his voice. Perhaps, doctor, you would like to drum your fingers on the patient's stomach to confirm our diagnosis: like that rat-a-tat, rat-a-tat, rat-a-tat-tat. Are you cold, doctor? That's strange – the skirts of winter don't reach us here. Isn't that right, friends? Friends, that's what I call this group of patients with croup in whom you may observe the noise produced by the displacement of accumulations of mucus in respiration. As you know, in medical terms this is called *flag noise*. And now, if you will allow me to continue, I will explain that the hollow whistling that you hear is the resonant respiration of patients whose lungs, needless to say, are peppered with cavities in which viruses have formed veritable stalactites. Allow me to offer you my silk handkerchief to prevent you from contracting premature contagion. Yes, effectively, doctor, you will find in this ward many provisional patients who really belong in other wards. There are many whose classification has not yet been resolved and that is one of our most serious problems, to the extent that I have asked myself a thousand times where I left my soul, doctor, in which calcinated manger it drowned or whether I lost it among the New Year greeting cards or perhaps what happened was that I put it away in a capsule of cobalt 60, how should I know, doctor, in this day and age? What did you say? Yes, of course, patients who are normally in the Dejecta Ward or in the Optical Ward are brought here when their pain causes them to cry out. Those screams, for example, are from a patient in the latter stages of cancer. Anyone who has had a father, an uncle or a soldier who died of malignant growths, is familiar with it. In addition, we normally transfer to this ward patients suffering from different kinds of rales, including those omitting the death rattle. For instance, this youth of twenty-two, a law student, has a hoarse rale caused by the passage of air through the bronchials which have been constricted by spasms. Law, I would have liked to study law, doctor, and perhaps I will one day before death offers me its rude greeting and leads me, by bus, towards the flora of the cities . . . Come this way, if you would be so kind, and listen to this particular rale caused by the explosion of tiny bubbles, similar to the sound of hair rubbed between the fingers. Allow me to pull out a grey hair, Dr Palinuro. You have a lot of grey hairs for such a young man. Do you hear it? It is, of course, a crepitant rale. Careful of that bedpan, colleague! That's it, there we go, very good, you're very agile, Dr Palinuro. I'm sorry about the lack of space. Look, bend over this patient and tell me what you think of his major subcrepitant rale . . . Doesn't it remind you of blowing bubbles from a pipe and then going to roller-skate in the park and eat candy floss? We have it in various stages: fine, medium and thick, and it is caused by the air passing through the mucus and pus accumulated in the bronchials. One of these is a serious case of pulmonary tuberculosis. To save time, I will tell you that I graduated *magna cum laude* at twenty-one years of age, doctor, with the highest grades and then I went to fish for a whole summer in the rivers of Canada; I've always been able to adapt myself to the circumstances with a tamed temperature. So, as I was saying, we have whistling and trachial rales which produce the sound of the piccolo, the flageolet and the fife: some strident, others melodious and sweet, other monotonous, others muffled and hoarse. In short, all those that have been and will ever be. I remember that my mother at that time – when I graduated, that is – was mortally opposed to consanguineous monograms and refused to embroider the diplomas. Now, come with me, Dr Palinuro. I would like you to speak with some of the patients to observe their voices. Of course, we must be careful not to let those suffering from such problems realize the gravity of their condition. Good-morning, good-morning, how does our little patient feel this morning? So, tomorrow is your birthday, is it? How old will you be? Fifty-three? The management will send you a box with fifty-three chocolates, what do you think of that? You will have noticed, doctor, that the patient speaks with two completely different voices. When she returned my greeting and said 'Good-morning, doctor' her voice was as deep as the voice of those women who wear tartan ties to suggest that they're looking for lady trouble, doctor, and when she said 'Tomorrow is my birthday' her voice was thin and crystalline as though falling from the sky. 'Fifty-three,' replied the deep voice and it was the crystalline voice which said 'Thank you, doctor'. There is no need, of course, to tell you that these patients amuse themselves for hours at a time by talking to themselves until they reach the point, which is the most dangerous, where the voices fall in love with each other. This is, of course, a condition of bi-tonal voice caused by paralysis of the recurrent nerve

340

which is caused, in turn, by aneurysm of the aorta. By the way: have you
ever heard the sound, like that of a red-hot poker submerged in water, of an
arteriovenous aneurysm? Let us proceed, doctor; we have the whole
morning ahead of us, the whole afternoon and, in a way, our whole lives.
This is another gentleman, let's see how he is feeling, very good, the
temperature chart shows a marked drop, congratulations: very soon you
will be able to go after the girls in honey-coloured stockings which attract
drones. And now, say something to us, whatever you like, so that Dr
Palinuro can hear you. The *Commedia dell'Arte*, doctor! Actors who
urinate on the audience, Harlequin, servant of two masters . . . and the
unforgettable Pulcinella: yes, we call it the Pulcinella voice, for obvious
reasons . . . and take a guess at his diagnosis: exudative pleurisy no less . . .
ah, and here, in this pretty little bed, we have a cherub of twelve years of
age who has a little silver bell in his chest. How is our pneumothorax
coming along, my young friend? He is very proud of the name of his illness,
like patients with, for example, Auenbrugger's sign, Strümpell-Marie
disease or Wallenberg's syndrome relating to the posterior inferior
cerebellar artery. Fortunately, in this case, the complaint is not serious,
doctor: one of these days our little friend will rise from his bed and go out
into the garden and confirm that the chrysanthemums have a soft and
fragrant chimney in their waists. Do you like poetry? I am the tenebrist,
doctor – I am the widower, the disconsolate. I make up poems when I am
in the bathroom, on my way home from the hospital, contemplating the
inclination of the dawns or when I go to the cinema with my girlfriend and
I realize that her breasts trace their behaviour in the bottom of washing-up
bowls. But excuse my rambling, doctor, the only purpose of which was to
spare your feelings. There is no need to be moved by the screams of these
children between three and seven years of age, just imagine, the poor
things. Please, don't listen to them. Well, if you insist, that's all right by
me. In effect, Dr Palinuro, this brief and penetrating shout is the
hydroencephalic shout characteristic of children with tubercular meningitis, as you so rightly say. When I hear this humid, sticky and miserable
scream, I think of the high tribute demanded of such tender flesh: these
children, unlike our cherub, may perhaps very soon come to know the
silhouette of death. In other words, they will never grow beyond childhood
and the minute hand of fame will never dub them electronic engineers or
public accountants. Now may I ask you, doctor, like myself to make use of
the walkie-talkie, because we are now going to visit a special division of
other, also provisional, patients who are accommodated here while they
wait their turn to be operated on or transferred to other wards. I would
have liked, doctor, to spare you the crematoriums. I would have like to
spare you Hiroshima and give you the world ready-made so that you had
only to close your eyes to forget it, or open them to dream it, doctor, but it

was beyond me; so many people are daily flattened by cars on the viaducts of Los Angeles and of our own city, so many stabbed in the middle of a revolutionary night, so many suffer intestinal occlusions and hernias . . . but, do you read me, doctor? Over. So many others, I was saying, with strangulated hernias or suffering the jelly crimes of the Marines. What? What did you say, Dr Palinuro? Over. Or a renal or biliary colic suffices, or a comminuted fracture. Did you say you can't hear me? Over. Not to speak of trigeminal neuralgia. Ah, you can hear me. Over. What? Over. Of course, doctor, pregnant women are brought to this ward when the labour pains start and we only take them away again when the baby is about to be born. We are also accompanied here by patients subject to hysterics who suddenly shout or scream. I hope that, in honour of this room, you will forgive all the noise which is pretty well unbearable although but a humble sample of the wails, sneezes, laments, screams, howls and spasmodic hiccups which are daily to be found beneath the stairs and which, like Villaurrutia's shout, doctor, becomes an echo, a wall, a mirror, a murdered statue dying of sleep. Then, doctor, as Hamlet would say: The rest is silence. I had a music teacher in secondary school, with long white Porfirian whiskers sprinkled with B flat gold who sometimes, in despair, shouted: I want to hear silence! One day, finally, we fell silent when he dropped dead in the classroom and that was when I learned that silence can be heard. This will no doubt happen to you when I take you to the sub-divison of the Acoustic Ward of which we are particularly proud. As you may appreciate, the walls and doors are of cork, the carpets are thick and the whole design, in general, is equivalent to that of a radio studio. The difference here is that you do not hear the *andante cantabile* of *Symphony Number Four for Organ* by Charles-Marie Widor, or a news broadcast telling of the triumphal dynamite destroying the stores and public houses of Belfast: here, doctor, you will hear only a series of the most delicate sounds, soft as snow falling on a miniature city enclosed in a childhood paperweight; tenuous and slender as realms of silk are the sounds produced by this type of patient and which, thanks to the acoustic structure of the room, are audible to the naked eye or, if you will permit the expression Dr Palinuro, to the naked ear. Look more closely at that young patient whose long white arms are as a continuation of my adolescent desires and you will notice the snowy crepitation of sub-cutaneous emphysema. As its name indicates, the sound we are hearing is identical to the sound of snow as it is compressed. Do you remember the winters in Milwaukee, doctor, and how life flowed like snow between the hands and the girls had yellow scarfs around their necks which whirled to the dances of the Paper Doll? The proverb says it all: opportunities are few and return not from anger. We also have a case of dry arthritis: our patient has merely to clench and unclench his hand for us to hear the starched

342

crepitation which is its hallmark. And you will also distinguish, without recourse to your stethoscope, the panting breath of diabetics in coma and the whistling breath of unconscious uraemia patients as well as every existing and future pulmonary and cardiovascular variation of puffing and every conceivable type of diastolic and presystolic whirlpool. We have a few adolescent patients suffering from chlorosis who heave intense sighs: a misguided poet would easily confuse them with sighs at the disposal of altars. And, to save time, I will tell you that we have a worker suffering from the disorder of the cardiac muscle which produces a sound classified as musical in medical terminology, as occurs also in the case of chronic aortitis, and we also have several pleuritic puffs and some pericardial noises and lastly, a fine case of singing of the arteries . . . exhalations of the blood and which, as you well know, we also call Duroziez' double murmur.

Yes, Dr Palinuro, I can guess your criticism. Naturally, Dr Palinuro. Of course, dear colleague: we have not been able to prevent this constant roar of horned bellows, war drums and monstrous bowel movements which serve, among other things, to remind us that we are of flesh and blood, air and gases and that, wheresoever the ski-lifts or our intellectual aspirations take us, we are destined to carry with us the burden of the din, the crackling and the purring of our viscera and cartilages. There is nothing, even as we read aloud Tristan Tzara's *Approximate Man* or silently contemplate Desiderio Monsu's *Exploding Cathedral*, that wonderful combination of classical and Gothic ruins, romanic arcades and Indian filigree containing the light of so many centuries, there is nobody, I was saying, who can prevent the bolus from sliding through the cardia, duly impregnated and slippery with saliva, or prevent the pressure of liquid contained in the bladder from inducing urination. Similarly, as we passed through this last room, nothing could be done to spare us from hearing the vesicular and inscrutable murmurings caused by the entry and exit of air into and from the lungs, together with the odd gastric gurgling commonly denominated tummy-rumbling. Yes, doctor. No, doctor. Perhaps, doctor. But I will remind you that, for once at least, our game is obvious and it is for this reason that I have different names. I will give you a collection of cards so that you may choose the one you like best, depending on the day of the week, the length of your humour and the aggressiveness which you may at any given moment feel towards a humble servant. Everything is taken care of, even the mortal boredom which causes us to fall back upon child choirs.

3

Let us now proceed, dear colleague, to the next ward which lies at the end of this corridor and where you will find some nuns who have given up flagellation and come here to add variety to their methods of repentance.

We will pass close by the acid realms of the operating theatres and you will catch a whiff of disinfectants. By the way, let me give you a light-hearted run-down of one of our greatest frustrations. But first let me tell you that I will not waste time showing you the offices of the hospital. Suffice it to say that we have experts familiar with the ins and outs of administration and that we practise an altruistic form of accountancy which lends dignity to our business: to this end we merely apply the economic liberalism of *laissez-faire* as established by Adam Smith and the French physiocrats. I beg you to pay no attention to certain people who pass us in the corridors with averted eyes: they are asexual emissaries paid by other clinics and who bear us an orthodox grudge and try to inoculate us with spy viruses. From time to time, we give them a seductive dose of camphor to bring them over to our side. As you know: curiosity entails inner revolutions. But when one has a well-balanced, rational spirit, doctor, and one knows how to apply the fumigatory principles, the problem disappears. Neither is the prostration of those gesticulating drudges, responsible for reviewing soap dishes and counting sheets, of the least importance: they have forced us to deal with their aseptic blackmail in demanding a wage increase and threatening to form a union. But, fortunately, no sooner do we glimpse the bark of a second term than we change the system. You will notice that in this hospital there is no racial discrimination and that we have melanodermic and leukodermic doctors in equal proportions. I was going, dear colleague, to tell you that, for qualitative reasons, we were unable to create the so-called Olfactory Ward in which, as its name indicates, we would have grouped patients emitting strange odours including, of course, those in Zwaardemaker classification, ranging from the ethereal to the nauseous, by way of the empyreumatic and ambrosial. While this proved impossible, you will none the less be assaulted during our tour by certain aromas which you will easily be able to identify. I do not refer to those that are as common as the fragrance of Armenia paper incense, or the alcohol fumes inundating with wisdom any hospital worthy of the name. Neither do I speak of the scent of carbon paper emanating from our offices which will remind you of the smell of the electric train of your childhood. But, if luck would have it that you catch the smell of newly mown hay you will think, quite rightly, that it comes from patients whose urine has a high acetone content. And, with greater luck still, you will detect the scent of baked chocolate given off by the body of a patient with carbon oxychloride poisoning and the classic detectivesque odour of bitter almonds from victims of cyanide poisoning. I will refrain from mentioning the foetid sputum of gangrene of the lung which we usually counter by burning crystals of tartaric acid which produces a smell of toffee. Afternoons in the cinema, doctor! *Lost Weekend* with Ray Milland! Do you remember? Walking past the hospital bakery you will no doubt catch the sweet smell of our cakes and desserts, the fragrance and flavours of which have been accentuated with artificial ethers: iris tincture for raspberry tarts and nitrate essence for apple jelly. You will find that our staff smell sweetly of lavender and you may also detect the sporting aroma of vaseline with which they sculpt their hairstyles. I can safely state that the only bad odour we tolerate from them is that of their feet, considering it to be a mark of natural rebelliousness. After all, doctor, hygiene, as Chesterton said, is not a virtue.

4

Come in, doctor. No, no, after you. Thank you, doctor, but I insist: after you. Courtesy, dear friend, is not an obligation: it is a privilege, particularly in the main building in which there are so many revolving doors that if you don't pay attention you enter the same ward ten times. But that will not happen to us, don't worry. It is readily apparent, moreover, that this ward, or pavilion as we like to call them, is the result of the good taste of specialized architects who know the etymological origin of the word *pavilion* which, as you know, comes from *papilio*, butterfly. The ceiling, which is very high, is reminiscent of a huge lepidopteron, not only on account of the slopes which echo the angle of wings, but also the arrangement and irregular shapes of the panes of which it is composed. Our interior designers suggested that we hang these graphs on the walls of our pavilion. What looks like a multi-coloured silhouette of New York with red, blue, green and yellow skyscrapers, is in fact an allergic reaction graph. These are thermographs of the chest and brain in which cancer is revealed by the red which stands out among the other colours. Both the thermographs and the plates illustrating radioactive iodine absorbed by the thyroid gland are formed, as you will see, by thousands of little dots of all colours which look like mutinous rainbows. Speaking of which, the innumerable tiny rainbows spanning our white pavilion are projected by prisms set in the windows. After you, Dr Palinuro. I must ask you again to respond to the patients' greetings. I mentioned previously that, like anything human, our system is imperfect and that we have had to apply qualitative criteria. I am the most vocal critic of our methods, colleague, the *Advocatus Diaboli*. Thus, as we pass through the different wards, you will notice that many of our patients are provisional, just as you will notice the absence of others; an absence, I must tell you, that is not really as significant as it might at first appear if you take other symptoms into consideration. For example, in this ward we forgo patients suffering from yellow fever and black plague since we consider that their hallmark of vomiting and diarrhoea is a more important symptom than skin colour or the name of the disease. Forgive me for not dwelling at greater length on this question, but I want to keep some surprises for later. Come, Dr Palinuro, allow me to introduce our first patient. How do you feel today? You still haven't gone to the bathroom? Tut, tut. That won't do at all. Let me see: stick our your tongue so that Dr Palinuro can have a look at it. We have here, as you see, a yellowish tongue: who has not been constipated at some time or other? One has only to go on holiday, doctor, to the blue memoranda of the Bahamas, to lose all notion of where to leave one's waste. This run-of-the-mill case of constipation is alleviated with a laxative. And this next case is also very straightforward. Cuchi-cuchi-coo. A beautiful newborn baby with white patches on its gums, cuchi-cuchi-coo, which produce a fever which will very soon break, isn't that right, little one? One of my greatest ambitions was to be a broadcaster, dear colleague. Do you remember? This is the BBC in London, this is a panoramic view of the nylon factories of New Jersey, huh, little one? Allow me to take your arm again, doctor, perhaps you will even allow us to walk with our arms around each other's necks like two secondary-school friends who share the same *Roman History* by A. Malet, the same Motts and Calderon *Botany* and the same girlfriend. What times those were, doctor! But the young, as Minot said, grow old more quickly than the old themselves. I was saying that it is most important that patients realize that splendid friendships exist among the staff regardless of hierarchies, though these are respected. Unfortunately, I am not of the generation taught by the wise Isaac Ochoterena, but I once did a portrait of him, in India ink, which won me an honours grade; the professor was more interested in the spelling than in Lamarck's *Philosophie Zoologique* and more interested in the original meaning of words than in the dynastic mysteries of flowers. It is a genuine shame that not all our cases are curable, doctor, but that is something every physician has to face with *sang froid*. We have already seen a yellow tongue and white patches. This case, Dr Palinuro, is green: the lumps of greenish tissue on this boy's face, principally around the eyes and nostrils, are the result of a lymphatic chloroma no less, also known as Aran's cancer and which frequently accompanies leukaemia. How are you, my boy, how is that crossword puzzle coming along? Let's have a look. Thirteen down, starts with C and has nine letters. Mmmmmm. Childeric, son of the founder of the Merovingian dynasty. Uh? What did I tell you? As for this next case, Dr Palinuro, chance now bears us along a purple path. This man, black and blue from the tip of his eyelashes to the tip of his toes, is suffocating on account of pulmonary oedema. There is nothing we can do: every second that passes reduces his respiratory capacity and so also his ability to become fond of the mail, the sparrows and petrol. And of course this baby, which is completely yellow, is also dying before our eyes, in this case from jaundice. As is to be expected, there is no lack here of patients with what

346

we call invisible symptoms, like this anaemic little girl whose red corpuscles obstinately refuse to become coloured without the aid of tolidine blue. What of this blue blood, my dear little girl? Or this other young man who is suffering from aplastic anaemia and whose marrow has therefore turned the yellow of elder-tree wood. But I didn't study law, dear colleague. Neither did I become a broadcaster. Finally, I dreamed of becoming a famous surgeon, Great Knight of the Small Sword: the bistoury, doctor, which somebody said had the name of a blue bird. Unfortunately, here I am, a humble hospital doctor. I can shorten your tour of this ward, doctor, by listing some of the cases which, of course, you will already have anticipated. Thank you, doctor, for reminding me; here we have patients with all kinds of eruptions, intradermal extravasations, exanthemata, boils, lichens and vitiligos, blue ulcers which advance like snakes, carbuncles resulting from the action of the golden staphylococcus, hydatids, pink sarcoid nodules of tubercular origin, leprosy and any other type of illness of the skin causing a special colouring which may range from lobster red to flag green, by way of the black crust haloed with pus of grooms, doctor, and the nacreous stomatitis of smokers. Thus we have the yellowish chloasma on this woman's face revealing a disorder of the womb; and this electrician whose body is covered in images and adages caused by a lightning stroke; red tongues with tastebuds as large as raspberries revealing the beginnings of scarlet fever and black, hairy tongues attacked by mushrooms of the oospore genus; aqueous, lemon-yellow pemphygoid blisters and numerous patients displaying the diverse range of reds, blues, violets and yellows of spotted sickness. Am I over-doing it, Dr Palinuro? Perhaps we should pass this ward by and proceed to another. Well, all right, as you wish. I respect your professionalism, your spirit of sacrifice. In fact, it is only thus that one comes to occupy a position of such responsibility as your own. The feet of this thirty-seven-year-old woman display symmetrical gangrene of the extremities, hence the black and purple tissues, surrounded by whitish patches and barbarous rosy dawns. What did you say, doctor? That you feel you know that patient? You must be mistaken. Let us pass on to the next bed if you would be so kind. Let's see, let's see, open your mouth and say: Aaaaah! That thick black layer covering the gums is due to a serious infection: yes, yes, they're just bringing your tablets now. I have spared you the well-known glaucoma, doctor, also the black sweats of cutaneous cyanopathy and the starry marks caused by yellow atrophy of the pupil. But I do so with great regret and only because we have no such cases. But there are things you just cannot achieve and you can but resign yourself. I would love, for example, to have a purple fever of the Rocky Mountains, but the breeding ground is so far away. Instead, I cannot resist the temptation of showing you our collection of pus and urine from different patients which will transport you to a world of coloured memories of your first microscopy class. Ah, Dr Sanpietro tells me that the collection was moved a few days ago to another pavilion which we will visit later. So, that's that. For the time being, you will not be able to view a fine sample of blue pus coloured by the pyocyaneus bacillus and a pulmonary tuberculosis test whereby a one-to-one-thousand solution of permanganate is added to urine . . . as you know, a pale and luminous halo forms, like that of a saint fallen into disgrace. But this pavilion contains many surprises. Some of our colleagues still believe in chromotherapy: restoring health through the use of luminous rays of different colours. Let me invite you to pass through the blue room, the green room, the ultra-violet room. May I invite you also to observe the syphilitic boils of this man who, in another age, the age of obscurantism when there was no neon gas abruptly to sketch the gurgling of a Pepsi-Cola against the sky, would have been taken for a stigmatic on the tomb of Diacre Pâris. See the rough, red pimples on the palms of his hands and the soles of his feet which would have been the envy of Therese Neumann. We have a case of Addison's bronze-like disease and two patients with the pale yellow skin-colour produced by cachexia. You will note this classic case of the blue disease, doctor. Yes, as you say: its cause is congenital narrowness of the pulmonary artery. Last week we had a case of purpura fulminans. It is a shame you weren't here with us then. Such patients don't last long, as the name of the disease indicates. Now, doctor, are you ready? Come with me, come with us, lads. We will first greet this man whose hair and beard are green on account of chronic copper poisoning and then, Dr Palinuro, I would ask you to bend and closely observe the eyes of this old lady. Do you see that infinity of minute particles of brightness forming a floating constellation? Do you see that wonderful gold dust which is displaced by every movement of the eye? This miracle is due to softening of the vitreous body. The particles are crystals of cholesterol and tyrosine and the dust is formed by phosphates. I must immediately admit to you, doctor, my satisfaction when I realized that your visit coincides with a serious case presenting enviable characteristics. Come with me, we will go into the dark room. This man struggling on the stretcher and covered in diarrhoea and vomit is suffering from phosphorous poisoning. Would you be so kind as to turn out the light? That's it. Do you see those wonderful phosphorescent cascades, doctor, that green effluvia resembling swarms of fireflies? As you will have guessed, they are but the poor man's vomit and diarrhoea rendered luminous by the phosphorous. Very well, lads, turn on the light. Dose the patient with a solution of blue vitriol.

5

And now, doctor, I would suggest that we take a break to get a bite to eat in the hospital cafeteria and smoke a cigarette. But let us first have a look at our shop selling curios and souvenirs. Here we have postcards of our foetuses and monsters . . . Ah yes, doctor, I'll tell you all about this in a minute! If you like, you can buy life-size reproductions of legs in plaster and brain tumours. We also have hospital pennants and dishtowels reproducing illustrations from ancient medical books which we have coloured – apropos of our recent visit to the Optical Pavilion – with dyes obtained from our own patients. From our scarlet-fever patients we obtained several shades ranging from fiery red to frantic pink. From jaundice patients, a beautiful shade of jasmine yellow. Can you drink wine from a wine-skin, doctor! Take this wine-skin which, as you will see, has the shape and appearance of a kidney! Just a joke, doctor, like the helium-inflated balloons which are just like lungs! We have all sorts of things, including skulls which are absolutely full of surprises; this one, for instance, contains a luminous clock which can only be seen by peeping through one of the eye sockets . . . which means, doctor, that Time may be read only through the eyes of Death. For your children, doctor, for your nephews and nieces, there is a wide selection of books for colouring by numbers, showing children what should be coloured gangrene black and what leprous green; skeleton kits and miniature reproductions of crutches, stretchers and clockwork wheelchairs, as well as toy surgical instruments to amputate dolls' legs and perform circumcisions on stuffed bears. For you, doctor, we have reserved this musical box containing miniature doctors and nurses in white, an anaesthetist and a patient on the operating table. Every time you wind it up, dear colleague, the little figures dance and operate on the patient's heart to the rhythm of a Boccherini quartet. But, doctor, there is no souvenir more appreciated than the jewellery created in the hospital workshops from the different lithiatic conditions suffered by our patients. See these handcuffs of silver and broncholiths carved by our craftsmen and tell me what you think of this marvellous necklace of bladder stones mounted in gold, doctor. Ah, dear colleague! Fit for a queen, this diadem of pancreatic gems! Take for your girlfriend this engagement ring in which glitter twelve tiny lachrymal calculuses and allow me to offer you this tie-pin set with a salivary stone we recently removed from the mouth of a scholar! It is pointless to dig in the depths of the earth or in the strong boxes of Cartier in search of diamonds and sapphires, doctor, when it is inside our own bodies that we find the most expensive and noble stones: the opals of the kidney, the tourmalines of the large intestine, the lapis lazulis of the liver! And here we are at the doors of our canteen which, as you know, is a self-service, so we will have to queue just like any of our friends and employees, to show that we are quite capable of democratizing the bacon. Take your tray, doctor. Gentlemen, this is Dr Palinuro, director of the hospital. Thank them for their

349

applause, my friend, don't be afraid that your stethoscope will touch the floor and that you will hear the heart beat of our planet. Now then, let's see, what have we on the menu today. Aha! You've hit an international day, doctor, *haute-cuisine* you might say. Whenever you are tired, doctor, and hungry, you may here enjoy a filling lunch. You are vegetarian, you say? Have a wheat muffin with soya cream. Have you read Walton? I recommend these fish, pink as colchicum flowers. You will notice, of course, the ambiguity of the tablecloths, but pay no attention. How are you, osteopath Rodriguez? We have a meeting at five to discuss your rise, obstetrician Valencia. How's the sinusitis? Oh, I'm very well, thank you. During the war, doctor, things were different: you got nothing but machine-gunned artichokes. Well, as I was saying, you will have supposed, naturally, that we allocated a pavilion to monstrosities and you are correct. I warn you that you will see incredible oddities unknown to Gog in the Bottega di Ben-Chusai nor imagined by yourself and Estefania in your room in Holy Sunday Square. But look now, what a beautiful steak! Slice it through the isthmus, dear doctor: you won't regret it. I'm sorry to have to tell you, however, that we have not yet opened the pavilion . . . What, you say you are not hungry? What a shame. You will at least have a coffee? . . . We haven't opened it, as I was saying . . . a little cream? . . . because we considered that we don't yet have enough interesting exhibits. Sugar, doctor? Good-afternoon, Nurse Martinez. When we had rationing, my great aunts used to say that roast turkey had taken wing and that cows drank their own milk by means of extendable devices. Now, however, and not only in our humble canteen, the golds of flavour waft interminably. For the time being, we have a private collection of preserved foetuses. But here we also have war bread with oats and buckwheat for those suffering from nostalgia for the trenches . . . Ah! Here are the desserts, doctor. I particularly recommend the blackberry cake. Don't expect to find Ganivet pudding, doctor, Reims pastries or feather-light crullers with Lyonnese cream: do you remember, dear colleague, those wonderful desserts, such as Sarah Bernhardt tart or Boudoir Champagne, displayed in the dining-room alcoves of Porfirian homes, on tables covered with cloths embroidered in Palestrine stitch with a decorative border? It makes me feel almost feminine to think about it. But the blackberry cake is good. Excuse us, otorhinolaryngologist Navarro. As you see, or rather, as you hear, words rise in the heat of talk, gather above and suddenly rain down on the competing witty remarks, astounding jokes and discussions which may be reaped without fear of getting your hands dirty. But if you prefer a more intimate atmosphere and music, each table has individual headphones and you may choose the channel of your preference, like in aeroplanes: Vinteuil's sonata, doctor, the Boston Pops Orchestra, Ebony Concerto, Mexican country music or Elvis Presley's latest hit! Anything else, Dr

Palinuro? I'm terribly sorry, I think I stepped on your toe. I didn't? I'm so glad! Some, as might be expected, have no face. Who, you ask? I refer to the monsters, doctor, our monsters and I do not include among them the nurses suffering from Turner's syndrome and several porters suffering from Klinefelter's syndrome who are all running loose around the hospital. No, I refer to the newborn monsters which the Spartans threw into the river of the Taygetus and which we preserve in jars because we know – who was it that said so, doctor? – that the aesthete requires ugliness as a contrast and only the moralist tries to eradicate it. Others have no tongue and therefore, although they do have teeth, they cannot enjoy as I do the pleasure of saying aloud: *Personne ne connaît l'origine dramatique des dents!* But excuse me, I was saying that other monstrous babies are born with four buttocks and four legs. Others, in contrast, with two heads, two thoraxes and a single pelvis. This is the till. You can pay with pesos, dollars, pounds sterling or German marks, as you please. And, of course, as this is a hospital restaurant, you can order your food in more scientific language, so to speak: would you like two tablets of sugar? A fillet of sole weighing two hundred and fifty scruples? Forty centilitres of milk? On the subject of teeth, I must tell you that there are diodoncephalous children who are born, like sharks, with two rows of teeth. Or others, with legs joined like mermaids: Parthenope, Ligeia and Leucosia who sing on the rock of Scylla. We need napkins, doctor, and cutlery. Notice the design of these knives: extraordinary, don't you agree? I would say that in them we are seeing the nickle-plated foundations of the surgical instruments of the future. The surgeon, doctor, just as Arcimboldo's hunter and his cook are but the sum of their prey or utensils, the surgeon, I was saying, is merely the sum of his instruments: probes, pincers, scissors . . . those jewels, terrifying as a bouquet of steel of the kind mentioned in Iwan Gilkin's poem about the virgin of the bistoury! Forgive me for talking about so many poems . . . but didn't Novalis say that poetry is the art of constructing transcendental health? And was it not Baudelaire who spoke of the urge which drives certain poets to morgues and clinics? Good-afternoon, neurologist Samuels. As you see, we have a policy here of giving everyone their title. Others have arms growing from their heads, like octopuses. How are you, drudge Garcia? There's no shortage of dwarfs, of course. We will share a table with ophthalmologists Henriquez and Davalos. Whoops, excuse me, I've spilt half the coffee. Do sit. Good-afternoon. And where's urologist Núñez today? Ah, of course, he's on holiday! And the children with the various stigmata of congenital syphilis: dental anomalies, concave or saddle-shaped noses, hare lips, lupine throats and Olympian foreheads, in short, beautiful day, wouldn't you agree, Doctor Davalos? all known types of monsters including three of which we are particularly proud, but I will tell you about them when we have finished our snack.

351

Wouldn't you like to try the strawberries and cream after your cake? Strawberries and cream, in the opinion of a friend of mine, a Jew, who was imprisoned in Buchenwald, are the symbol of abundance. To return to the monsters of the pavilion, how are you paediatrician Arredondo? I was saying that, of course, in that ward we have at least one case of acromegaly, also called, as you know, adult giantism. You reach the age of thirty-five and you are a happy and normal man. And suddenly, from one day to the next, the bones of your feet start to grow, or of your hands, or of your jaws, doctor. In our canteen we also have variety shows and entertainment. We once hired a magician who performed his disappearing trick so well that we never realized that he was here until we noted a certain light scent of salamander clinging to the napkins. But he was a sad magician and one day, with a swift flourish of his fingers and the blade of a knife, he made his own life disappear. More coffee, doctor? Hot Spanish chocolate? In fact, we already have several patients of different ages with tumours, tubercles, furuncles, supernumerary testicles and neoplasms of all imaginable shapes and sizes. Pleased to see you, pathologist Steiner. Say a number, doctor, any number. Twenty kilos? We do, effectively, have tumours weighing twenty kilos. One thousand two hundred? There are also tumours, doctor, which weigh one thousand two hundred grams. How are you doing policeman Matsumoto? I remember, when I was at secondary school, I used to catch a tram every day bound for the spring and the driver had large lumps on his neck, as though he had swallowed several Adam's apples: Hodgkin's disease. You have, of course, seen testicles with elephantiasis which reach the floor and breasts the size of watermelons. On the subject of which, we have a woman who injected paraffin into her breasts. In time, the paraffin migrated and the poor girl became covered in breasts. That is, in malignant paraffinomas. Of course, what irony, these strawberries have been imported from Israel, doctor. Inexpert young men whose glands are covered in rough vegetation resembling cocks' combs and a few respectable examples of gentlemen with seafood in their anus – in other words, old, dried haemorrhoids – aren't even worth mentioning because, as you know, they are more common than might be believed and occur in the best of families. Take Dr Fellini, for instance, who has to sit on a bag of crushed ice. How are your strawberries, Dr Palinuro? The poet Robert Herrick very aptly compared a woman's nipples to strawberries and cream. On the other hand, we have several women who, like *Juliette*'s Volmar, have clitorises several inches long, including an old woman who looks more like an old man because hers is so over-sized. I imagine that you, as a doctor, don't mind talking about such things at table, doctor, so eat up your strawberries. Why hark back to mythology to find the Cerberus whom Orpheus sent to sleep with his lyre or the Leviathan residing over a quarter of the world: in our jars, preserved in carbolic acid, we have monsters surpassing any product of the imagination. By the way, doctor, in our canteen we also have an aphrodisiac menu including an abundance of cocoa and powdered Spanish fly and rhinoceros horn. See you later, accountant Paunescu. And now, the best possible way to round off the meal: the three cases I promised to tell you about. One of the foetuses is aedoeocephalous: its nose is like a penis and its ears, situated on the nose, are scrotum-shaped. No comment. Fine tie-pin, colleague Carvalho, where did you buy it? The second is merely a foetus which managed to achieve immortality before birth which is why it is covered in calcareous growths turning it into a terracotta worthy of Ambrose Paré. This coffee is a little cold, don't you think? The third, which would have been a joy to Geoffroy Saint-Hilaire, the great authority on Siamese twins and undoubted admirer of Rosso Fiorentino's entwined angels, is a double monster joined from the mouth to thè belly button, symbolizing incestuous love between twins, male and female, within the mother's very womb and the consequent punishment in perpetuity. We didn't perform an autopsy on the little female, doctor, but I like to think that if we had done so we would have found another miniature couple in her belly and so on until we reached the origin of species. What is love, dear colleague, but the prolongation of a single image through floods, tattoos and luckless nations? Mmmm. Aha. Mmmmmm. Excuse me. Ah, do give the group of patients at that table, the ones who eat convulsively all day long on account of a problem with the hypothalamus, as I was saying, do give them the shadow of a smile. We don't have any patients with tumours the size of an egg in their armpits like those formerly described by Boccaccio in the *Decameron*, though we do have a ward of women as monstrously fat as Aurignacian statues . . . and we have a case which is unique in these latitudes: a black Hottentot woman with incredibly elongated labia minora hanging from the vulva like an apron. Do eat something, doctor, or you'll end up under-nourished. I should remind you that if you wish to swim in the hospital swimming pool, you will need no less than 550 calories per hour; if you decide to write down your impressions of the hospital, you will need 30 and if you merely reflect on them, you won't need any: thinking costs nothing! Do you have any cigarettes? No, thank you, I don't smoke. I only asked out of curiosity. You will of course have noticed, doctor, my sadness in speaking of our foetuses conserved in carbolic acid. It is, in effect, tragic that almost all monsters are stillborn or die at the moment of birth and are wasted for the rest of eternity in Malthusian limbos. I would love to be able to keep them alive as a demonstration of what may be, perhaps, not so much a sign of regression as the dawn of evolution towards the infinitely varied. Would you care for a licorice lozenge, doctor? A chlorophyll marshmallow? A stick of fluoride chewing gum? If all human beings have different faces and voices, different handwriting, doctor, and a different way of interpreting acrostics and bothering elephants, why not a human race in which each individual has an original, unique and marvellous form? Good-afternoon, doctors, *bon appetit*. I would venture to suggest that genetics, that demiurgic science bequeathed to us by Mendel, the very same which allowed Hugo De Vries in Amsterdam almost a hundred years ago to perform miracles with hybrids . . . excuse me, gentlemen, I have matches here, doctor, by crossing different types of stramonium, opium poppy, celedonia and clover . . . don't thank me, doctor, couldn't genetics one day, good-afternoon all, yes, of course, produce an offspring, after you, doctor, beautiful as a manatee, goodbye, which we could put in a tank, thank you for your company, and feed, doctor, with living and burning lotuses, this way, to the right, to the envy of our friends, good-afternoon, the green cyclops, the yellow cockatoo, the basilisk centipede, the multicoloured makara and the bird-headed garuda?

6

Mucus, pus, urine, excrement, gastric juices, vomit, exudate: such is our daily bread, doctor. And, above all, blood, colleague, blood which Faust's Mephistopheles found so peculiar, groaning blood no swallow would drink. Let us leave *ex tempore* gatherings on scaffolds to widows and to astronomers who ponder on the filling of the atmosphere and Mars' deceptiveness, let us leave to them the seismological clamour. To us, doctors who follow the path of Fabriz de Hilde and the illustrious Dr Sydenham, the glory of working to the limit of our nerves and our humours and the privilege of amazement at the reactions of the cephalorrachidian liquid when confronted with colloidal gold. We are now of course in the Pavilion of Secretions, Discharges or Dejecta, whatever you prefer to call it. Some people become depressed when they visit this pavilion and others suffer an attack of vomiting which provisionally sets them among the ranks of the patients. Do you remember how we remarked on it in the canteen, saying that you and I, as men of science, are above such reactions and associations of ideas. You will have noticed the absence of patients suffering complaints typical of other latitudes but, as you will see, even some such alien ailments are represented in this pavilion. You ask how, doctor? A little patience and you will see. Vomiting, for example. There are violent cases where vomit shoots out like a missile. The patient is unconscious but quiet and beside him is a nurse reading a comic strip in the Sunday paper when suddenly an uncontainable fountain spatters the curtains, the carpet, the lamps, Nurse Perez's cap and Prince Valiant's armour. There is also vomit of regurgitation: it wells slowly in gushes full of lumps and bubbles which slide

354

down the chin or cheeks and soak the pillow or flood the windpipe and kill the consul. It would only occur to a narrow and morbid mind, doctor, to associate such manifestations with the fruits of the earth around us. Vomit is merely an interruption of the wondrous process by which a calf's flesh becomes our own. It is chyme, doctor, liquid bread and vegetables bathed in hydrochloric acid, pepsines, secretagogues; it is a step – I'm not exaggerating, doctor – towards the entelechy of the carrot and of rock salt. The green vomit of this spinster is simply bilious vomit. Moreover, it is corrosive poisons, stomach ulcers and the rupture of oesophageal veins which cause vomit containing blood. Here is also dark brown vomit: containing faecal matter. Perhaps our most notable case in this hospital, as far as types of vomit are concerned, is this old man with intestinal cancer. But I mis-state, doctor, it is not really vomit but rather a reversal of physiological processes. If we wait a minute or two, doctor, you will see how the patient expels his excremental matter through the mouth, as solid and perfectly formed as through the anus. It started two days ago and it seems that the patient is resigned: the only real anguish that he suffers is when the excrement rises through the oesophagus and chokes him. But once it has reached the mouth, it comes out gently, almost naturally, I would say. Then the nurses clean his lips, which are afflicted with bleeding ulcers which are, in a strange way, reminiscent of haemorrhoids. To complete this masterly irony played by destiny on this man, doctor, we are administering food through the rectum. Now tell me, doctor, when you examine semi-solid excrement, does it ever make you think of the filling of pumpkin pie? Good Lord! When you look at a well-formed stool, like this man's, do not sausages float through your mind? How ghastly! When you look at yellowish runny excrement, do you not think of the orange juice that you drink in the mornings? How revolting! These comparisons are in extremely bad taste! Oh, but I could give you examples *ad nauseam*. Another very different case is that of impetigo which reminds one of drops of honey on the face, and impetigo circinata of strawberry jam. Another is cardiac cirrhosis when the sample of the liver looks like a nutmeg. Moreover, there is no relationship whatsoever between melted cheese and the greyish substance issuing from this young man's nose. Neither has flour, doctor, to which we owe the saintly scent of bakeries as our poet said, anything to do with the millions of tiny white crystals covering the skin of these patients. In patients in the final stages of uraemia, crystals similar to the transparent dust covering the leaves of belladonna appear after an attack when the sweat, sticky and yellow as rancid butter all over their bodies, has dried. But I shouldn't make such a comparison, although I confess that I'm fascinated by the relationship between excrement and food. Dung, as everybody knows, is a magnificent fertilizer. When I was a child, doctor, I remember that the best water melons grew wild in the waste plots where the boys went to relieve themselves after eating water melons, and the seeds came out whole, undigested. Oh what water melons they were, doctor, which we cut into thick slices, like red shouts of laughter to mock the summer heat! I will show you a case which only looks serious. How are your physiological functions behaving, madam? A little upset? Don't worry: Dr Palinuro is going to examine you. Come along, that's right, you see, doctor? One often has the opportunity to observe different uterine discharges: some are whitish like diluted sour cream. Others are amber coloured and transparent like bees' honey. And others, finally, are sticky and colourless like egg-white: as in the case of this patient. Take a look at the labia majora and the rest of the external genital organs which seem to have been recently soaped – the waxy discharge shows us that there is cancer of the uterus. A hysterectomy might save her. But let us return to the first little patient we passed three beds back. You would say that this woman's complaint is very serious. Well, you wouldn't because you're a doctor, but a layman would. Yes, yes, I already told you, madam, that what we have here is a fistula connecting the rectum with the vagina and on which we will operate tomorrow. Of course, madam, I would also be extremely worried if I suddenly started to expel excrement from my vagina. For anatomical reasons, I would be even more frightened than you are. I don't wish to tire you, doctor. My father always used to say that there is nothing better for raising morale than a little abuse. On the other hand, I inherited my grandfather's fastidiousness: thanks to him, I daily wash my eyes, lips and every crease of my ears and my feet; my teeth, one by one: each incisor, each eye-tooth, each molar requires specialized cleaning. I will spare you the sight of a patient subject to trembling and jerking who expels from his nose torrents of all kinds of green and greyish oysters and, instead, we will say hello to this young man who, as you see, is shrinking to skin and bone, so much that his clavicles look like budding spears and all because of a prodigious loss of semen mixed with blood. Another uncontrollable and equally interesting trait is presented by this next patient. You will ask me why this man weeps, what we have done to him, what happened to him, and I will answer that he is simply suffering from a lachrymal fistula which causes him to weep constantly, quite independently of his state of mind which, though you might not guess it, is generally optimistic. Could I ask you to tell him a joke. Tell him, for instance, that when one dies the stomach digests itself and then just watch how he bursts into tears. But that would be contrary to hospital policy, as you know, Dr Palinuro, of course, only natural, obviously, quite right too; I admire your perspicacity, colleague. In effect, these two cases are the first illustration of one of the theories we apply in this hospital in accordance with your generous suggestions, doctor, consisting of what I might call the eradication of the conceptualist possibilities of illness.

356

However, this sacrifice is compensated for by the opportunity to profit from its metaphorical possibilities. For example, when we became aware of the enormous wastage of this patient's tears, we decided to regularly tell him heart-rending stories. Crimes, injustices, fratricides, explorers lost at the North Pole and turned into icebergs floating through dreams of death. Cases of cannibalism, rape of minors, orphan children searching for their parents from the early chapters of Dickens' novels and every other imaginable tragedy. I need not tell you, doctor, because you have seen with your own eyes that the room of the young man suffering from excessive seminal discharge is papered with current *Playboy* pin-ups and on Sundays we give him matinées of pornographic films. St Augustine perverted human thought for over a thousand years, colleague: we wish to free it of original sin. Flies buzz in vicious circles, doctor: they personify jealousy. And there, far away, houses with roofs red with fear: I have nothing against morals, colleague, on the contrary. Open the doors, lads, open them wide. This immense hall, doctor, full of glorious potions, will remind you of the ice-cream parlours of your youth with jars full of syrups and fruit essences, glass biscuit jars from our grandmothers' kitchens. Draw back the curtains, raise the blinds, turn on the fluorescent lights. Here, on these shelves, doctor, suitably illuminated, we have the world's most comprehensive collection of its kind: a permanent exhibition of secretions, exudates, discharges, extravasations, etc., etc., which is open to the public from Sunday to Friday for four hours a day and we spend all day Saturday polishing the jars and dusting the shelves. Unsolicited contributions are accepted: a litre of pink blood from a child with leukaemia, samples of laudable pus and false membranes of bronchitis sufferers. But take a closer look and note the sputum of bronchial asthma sufferers containing spiral filaments, tiny pearls and Charcot-Leyden crystals composed of amines very similar to cadaverine and putrescine. Speaking of which, this thick slime of necrotic tissues formed during the course of gangrene is a sample of putrilage no less. And the contents of this balloon-shaped bottle, reminding one of the black wine of Corinth, is a sample of the digested blood expelled from the mouths of syphilitic children. And, of course, this here is a humble, common and garden sample of the pusy mucus of the bronchials containing Dietrich's plugs: do you see them? Those little whitish pinheads . . . who would guess that they are composed of white corpuscles, the remains of red corpuscles, crystals of fatty acid and leptothrix pulmonarius. Shall we proceed? Now let's see, what's this then? The label of this jar has fallen off, but Dr Solís tells us that these grubs that you see are the famous vermicules: in other words, doctor, the threads of corrupt matter which emerge when you squeeze carcinomatous ulcerations of the face. This other sweety jar contains a collection of Trélat stools which have the mucous-like appearance of sputum and are streaked with blood. Look doctor, this is an impressive sample of the black faeces of patients treated with bismuth: I would say that that is very possibly what the devil's excrement looks like. And, on account of their whiteness and purity, I would say that angels' excrement looks like the pale faeces of those suffering from hepatic insufficiency. Since childhood, doctor, I have been obsessed with curiosity about what the natural waste, or rather, the supernatural waste of fantastic beings might look like: for example, a Unicorn's vomit, the Phoenix's excrement, Pegasus's urine. But step this way and admire this endless row of coloured jars, upon the absence of which I remarked in the Optical Pavilion, which demonstrate the different and widely varying colours that human urine can assume on account of various illnesses or when submitted to chemical reactions determining its similarity to Irish beer, the white wines of Alsace, the reds of Bordeaux and the sparkling rosés of Coimbra. Ah, what if Dr Myersbach, who was so often mocked, had not revived the art of the urinoscopy! But there is also a jar of urine with a blue stripe revealing the presence of blood while the violet colour reveals the presence of acetone and the green stripe the presence of bile. This is a fine example of milky urine with albumin and this of the coffee-black urine of alkaptonuria. On the subject of precipitates and reactions, colleague, this jar contains a putrid exudate of the pleurae with a fine pink clot produced by tannin; this is the serum of a syphilis sufferer which turned bright yellow in response to the Landau colour test; this magic phial contains peritoneal liquid submitted to the Rivalta reaction: hence the bluish precipitate which sinks slowly to the bottom like cigarette smoke. In conclusion to this brief visit to our exhibition and as I mentioned before, sicknesses foreign to our hemisphere are also represented here: this jar contains a sample of the black vomit of yellow fever and this next jar was given to us by our foreign colleagues, those martyrs to science who work *in partibus infidelium*, in pagan lands, and contains almost two litres of diarrhoea characteristic of cholera: as you see, it is a colourless liquid containing innumerable white flakes the size of grains of rice. If you shake the jar, doctor, they form a swirl of snow just like in *Citizen Kane* and then slowly settle at the bottom of the jar. Ah! But let us sit for a moment, doctor, tiredness fills my brain. Ah, how my legs hurt! However, I am happy. What Buddha considered the wretchedness of our body, what he viewed (because, let me tell you, he so described it in one of his *Gāthās*) as a body damned by tears, sweat, moisture, urine; full of drops of blood and filth of the stomach, of marrow, cerebral blood and liquids . . . I for my part believe to be the greatest wealth, doctor: *Inter urinas et faeces nascimur*. I will say no more. Here we have an illustrated catalogue, with sixteen colour plates and seventy black and white ones, which we sell for twenty-five pesos per copy. For you, doctor, it is free on one condition: in a few moments a nurse will come to take a sample of your blood and a throat smear, ah, doctor, what a relief to sit down and stretch my legs, and make a sternal puncture of the manubrium to take a sample of your bone marrow and another puncture, in the lumbar region, so that we can check the state of your cephalorrachidian liquid and I will give you an injection but, ah, doctor, allow me to take off my shoes to stretch my toes for a moment, that's it, there we go, and also an intravenous injection of Secretin, as I was saying, to stimulate the secretion of your pancreas and examine your duodenal juices and an enema of barium sulphate so we can take an X-ray of your colon. Ah, I should tell you that the nurse is as beautiful as that death disguised in the fair skin of a twenty-year-old woman who escaped some time ago from my arms and my testicles, doctor, but who I will find some day sitting in a white car, the bitch. Ah, doctor, what a relief to stretch my eyes! But I'll give her such a fright, I'll be so unfaithful to her! While we wait for our nurse and I treat myself to a brief siesta, doctor, I beg you to enter that room at the end of the corridor. You will find a jar in which to deposit your excrement. You can use a little wooden spoon to make it easier. You will find a test tube in which to put your urine. And another jar for your sputa and yet another for your nasal secretions. You will also find a laboratory container for your sperm, but perhaps you would like our beautiful nurse to help you obtain that sample. And, unless you suffer from erythrophobia, a rosy uproar will descend to your feet when she, with her fingers long and fine as panic, undoes the buttons of your fly. Ah, doctor, what a relief to stretch my teeth. Would you be so kind, colleague, as to allow us to make a plaster cast of your face, *in vivo*? I hate death masks. As you may suppose, what we want to do, doctor, is to ascertain that your urine confirms your kidneys' well-being by its normal content of urates which form a red precipitate; that your excrement is not mixed with the green mucus characteristic of dysentery; that your sputa do not display the rust colour caused by pneumonia; that your blood has at least five million erythrocytes and that each of your ejaculations contains the average number of three hundred and fifty million healthy spermatozoa. Ah, doctor, what bliss to stretch my nails! In other words, we want to see you in the *hygies* state of the ancients, doctor, we wish to see that your organism or, not just your organism, your *Gestalt* – if the term is correctly used – attain *eucrasia*, the correct and harmonious mixture of your forces and your four cardinal humours and ascertain that your allopsychic condition leaves nothing to be desired. But, of course, if any of these liquids presents some abnormality, we will take great pleasure in adding it to our collection and, should we discover a tumour, we will keep it to illustrate the colour cover of our next catalogue. And, if it is something less serious, let it not be said, doctor, that in this hospital we do not apply to perfection the technique of physical and moral care known as *hypurgia* . . .

and, if it were something very serious, God forbid! we will bring in the best specialists in the world who, by coincidence, are all in this hospital. We will beseech the Roman goddess Salus and, if necessary, we will invoke the spirits of the greatest physicians in history: Galen, doctor, Macareon, the scholars of the Salerno School, Avicenna the prince of medicine or Erasistratus who will count the beats of your heart with the aid of a clepsydra. I'm sure that the law of Karma, the homeostasis of your organism, doctor, its propensity to regain its undermined balance, is very powerful. In all events, colleague, any illness or symptom or bacteria from which you might suffer will bear your name since, as you well know, our hospital library contains only the latest editions of encyclopaedias and textbooks incorporating all neologisms such as Palinuroscope, Palinuritis, Palinurrea, Palinurophilia and Palinurophobia. I was forgetting to tell you, Dr Palinuro, ah, how I would love to stretch my liver! that you will also find there a jar containing propanol, the smell of which brings tears to the eyes. Be so kind as to smell it and deposit your tears on this slide. Later we will examine it under the microscope to find out what sort of infusoria or Palinurococci cohabit with the pupils of your eyes. Ah, doctor, how sleepy I am! But I don't need to tell you that every night when I turn off the light I sleep the sleep of the just with a clear conscience. But, beforehand, I read Schwob's *Imaginary Lives*, the *Autobiography of José Bálsamo* or the *Prophecies of Nostradamus*. Sometimes I yet again leaf through De Quincey's *Murder Considered as One of the Fine Arts*, Fénelon's *Dialogues with the Dead* or Chateaubriand's *Mémoires D'Outre-Tombe* and, if I have time, I look at a few prints by Beccafumi, Bronzino or José Luis Cuevas. Then, I sink into orthodox sleep, free of ghosts . . . or, as Eluard would say – Eluard again – I descend into my mirror like a corpse into its open tomb. Goodnight, doctor.

7

I had a very strange dream, doctor. Or perhaps it was two dreams. What time do you make it? You say they've stolen your American Waltham watch, a memento of your Uncle Esteban? I was in hospital, doctor, in this hospital if I remember rightly, and you were coming to see me. It seems to me, by the colour of the birds, that it must be half-past eight. How could I have slept for so long? Why didn't you wake me, Dr Palinuro? And we were walking arm-in-arm along these corridors when suddenly we were confronted by the pipe-smokers. Some were fat, some were thin. Some smoked Prince Albert tobacco and others, those allergic to nicotine, smoked pretend pipes. The room was full of clouds of maple smoke. But let us continue on our round as I relate my dream. I wanted to explain to you, doctor, that they were hemiplaegic patients, nicknamed pipe-smokers because of the way their paralysed cheek inflates every time they breathe, but when I opened my mouth to say this to you, instead of words, little clouds of smoke came out of it . . . just imagine, doctor, how funny! Little clouds of smoke! And you said to me: Are you crazy? And I answered: Doctor, our hospital would not be the most famous in the world and in its vicinity if we did not have wards allocated to the insane, aphasiacs, the delirious and the mad. So, next, we will visit the Kinetic Pavilion. No, I'm not mad, doctor, our modern criteria allow us to believe that all these people are not demented in the biblical sense of the word . . . in my dream I was an old man, old in years and martyrdoms, and you were a young man and I knew that one day I would have to bid you farewell with a handkerchief wet with goodbyes. We, on the contrary and like Friedrich Nietzsche, believe that they live in other dimensions of which we do not know the rules of play. Moreover, the patients have become attached to their pipes and clouds of smoke and the pretend clouds swirl in the air, doctor, swirl. If you look closely at this young girl's eyes, you will see that they have a recticular tremor which is more easily noticeable if you get her to follow an object with her eyes . . . see, my dear, look how this cloud is flying, flying . . . and the cloud, doctor, fell right into the hand of a patient with a myurous pulse reminding one of a mouse's tail, as its name indicates. Do you feel it, doctor? I ask you. This is a climbing pulse, which doubtless indicates a thrombosis of the myocardium. Do you feel how it rises in jolts? And, finally, we have a very slow Monneret pulse which arrived by air mail last week and which, of course, indicates some sort of congestion of the liver. What a strange dream, doctor. I was telling you that here, in this room, we have grouped all patients suffering from agoraphobia or, in other words, doctor, all those who are terrified of open and infinite spaces, town squares, the countryside and books on interplanetary voyages. To the right, doctor, Trafalgar Square. To the left, the Ponte Vècchio. Not even the Fortunio palace of Gautier's novel, with its dioramic windows daily depicting different cities, can be compared to this ward on the walls of which we project the ever-changing images of the most beautiful cities on earth, making it the ideal place to enjoy the infinite freedom offered to us by the universe. You, doctor, caught the cloud of smoke between your thumb and forefinger and showed it to them saying: this is the proof you are mad, what on earth possessed you to put all these patients together? What do the insane do in the Kinetic Pavilion? Strange dream. I said to you: calm down, colleague, your watch will turn up. In the first place, the definition *par excellence* of scholastic logic: man is a rational animal, lagging behind the superman, who is beyond all rationality. In the second place, when I was a boy scarcely as high as my knee now, doctor, I dreamed of visiting the Black Forest in Germany: here it is, to the left. To the right, at the end, the Sequoia National Park in

California with the only skyscraper trees in the world. Now, allow me to digress, if you will. But you've dropped the cloud, doctor, and it's hopping away. Quick, we must catch it! I said to you in my dream. Well, is there any difference, doctor, between this patient in the Kinetic Pavilion whose hand is in the swan's-neck position and this other patient suffering from nosophobia? But allow me to continue: when I was an adolescent and my head reached where it is now, I dreamt of visiting Paris. Here is Paris, doctor, the Eiffel Tower. Although I should tell you that as an adolescent, though I had the physical stature I have now, the same cannot be said of my intellectual stature. My aspirations today are more far-reaching: now I dream of visiting the stars. Then, doctor, you took a cloud of smoke from behind my ear. I said to you: wonderful trick, Dr Palinuro, and you, highly gratified, opened your hand and this cloud also escaped and this time rose to the sky and we watched it multiply into thousands of clouds. But let us return to reality, doctor, which surpasses all dreams: raise your eyes and see how the roof of this pavilion is in the shape of a planetarium and at night, against the black and velvety background, we reproduce the constellations with an exactitude dreamt of only by Hipparchus and a beauty which the Farnese Globe quite failed to show. This man, for example, suffers from a reflex ailment paralysing his hand in the swan's-neck position. How's the hand today? The same as yesterday? The same as tomorrow? Now see his companions. Some of them are suffering from that serious disease of the marrow called syringomyelia. As a result, one has preacher's hand with the wrist bent back at a right angle towards the forearm; another has succulent hands with the fingers stuck together and a third has scorpion-stinger hands. Ah, dear colleague: on the point of the pencil hangs a word, I hold it to the end, I give it a tail, I draw it out with suspension marks and I repeat it a hundred times like school homework that I might never forget it: pain, pain, pain, pain. Do you see the Swan constellation up there? Do you see the Scorpio constellation in the planetarium sky? You and I, in our dream, walked arm-in-arm through the days of the week and I showed you the patients who, in trying to escape pain, fall into pain. Our nosophobia patients, for instance, those with an obsessive fear of illness. They begin as hypochondriacs. Then they slide down the pharmaceutical slope. On Monday, this patient was in the tubercular patients' ward. On Tuesday, he was diagnosed as having leukaemia. On Wednesday, diabetes. Next Sunday, he will be told that he has tuberculosis. And we, on earth, are a faithful reflection of what could happen on high. Every day these two men play Chinese shadows and act out that the swan pecks the scorpion and the scorpion stings the swan in the neck and the swan pecks the scorpion and the scorpion stings the swan in the neck, and so on infinitely: the incarnation of metaphor, doctor, my old obsession. Sometimes though, especially on Sundays, we move our

362

patients to a ward we call our glass menagerie. There they are joined by the patients who have crab hands or duck hands with webbed fingers and also by patients who have a barking cough, lepers with leontiasis, elephantiasis sufferers and patients with tapir mouth caused by atrophy of the orbicular oris muscle. Ah, colleague, life is more amusing than you might imagine! For example, through this window which appears from the other side to be a mirror, you see a huge white room with lofty walls like those of a prison little imagined by Piranesi and there, squatting in the furthermost corner, is a man. This patient was interned in the ward because he is suffering from an abandonment complex which, like all phobias, has no real basis in fact. This is the same criterion that we apply to claustrophobia sufferers; in other words, those who fear closed spaces, small rooms and pocket-book editions. No, doctor, we have not forgotten the lessons on kindness to the insane taught by Pinel and so many others: this is not cruelty, but an attempt at cure by immersion. We do this so that the attitude of our patient ceases to be a phobia in that, in effect, this poor man is forsaken alike by God and man, and those suffering from claustrophobia are enclosed in boxes in which they can hardly move: hence their phobias become pure and unadulterated truth. But we do have one patient to whom we have been able to offer no relief: a man who one day discovered that he was shut up inside his own body and since then he has spent his time devising means of getting out alive. In other words, we cannot say of our establishment what W. H. Auden said of the sanitoriums where patients laughed progressively less as they lose hope of ever being cured. Ah, doctor, necessity had a temple in Corinth. Piety, a chapel in Latium. Disease has a cathedral, here in this sanatorium. Or rather diseases, the hundreds of demoniacal diseases listed in the *Yajurveda* which were so cleverly classified by Emil Kraepelin. Never has there been a hospital in all the world, colleague: the Bethlehem, the Castañeda, the Maison Charenton or the Williamsburg Hospital, that can be compared with ours. Moreover, who is not alone and abandoned? Who is not imprisoned in their own anguish? I remember that in my dream you and I were walking along through the hospital and suddenly we entered a ward in which there were four patients. One was a man of about sixty years of age who raised his nightshirt, showed us his behind and asked us to stimulate the skin of his anus. Another was a beautiful young girl who sat on the bed, raised her skirts, crossed her legs and asked us to tap her on the knees. Another of the patients was an old woman who stuck her feet out of the end of her bed and asked us to tickle them. And the fourth was an old man who lowered his pyjama trousers and asked us to pinch the head of his penis. And you were complaining because you had lost your American Waltham watch, doctor, while these poor patients, I was saying, have lost something really very important: their reflexes, doctor. A reflex – as you learned when you

363

burned the midnight oil one day to prove to Sir William Osler that he was wrong – is a peripheral stimulation which is transmitted centripetally to the nerve centre and returns centrifugally to the periphery as movement. In vain will you stimulate the skin of this man's anus: the sphincter will never again contract. And the legs of this little lady will never know the reflex of the rotula. Or you can tickle the soles of this old lady's feet but you will see that the toes never curl up. Or, finally, you can pinch the head of our old man's penis but you will find that it is likewise in vain, because the member does not recede. But come with me, doctor, perhaps here we will be safe from beggars. Allow me to continue describing the pavilion. I mentioned the constellations to you. It is still night-time and you can observe the rest for yourself. With a little imagination, you will on boreal nights see the kneeling Hercules slaying the fifteen stars of the snake. And on austral nights you will see Orion, the heavenly hunter who regains his sight every time he exposes his eyes to the light of the sun; the Pleiades, changed into doves, flapping frightened around the giant; the Bear, as Homer relates, keeps watch from afar; but Scorpio comes – the scorpion again, doctor – and attacks him from behind; then the Bear and the Lion rise rampant in the sky, majestically. This, as I told you, is the pavilion for those suffering from agoraphobia. And let them try and tell us now that Siger de Brabant was not right in stating that all events on earth are determined by movements of the heavenly bodies. What a strange dream, doctor! You and I were sitting in the middle of a huge plain, but not safe from beggars, nor pests, nor thieves. I see myself in the dream and hardly recognize myself. It was me, certainly, but at the same time it was not me: the Sosie delusion, doctor. Come this way: before telling you more about the dream, I will introduce you to a patient suffering from what the scholar Capgras called the Sosie illusion and which is in fact a phobia of partial negation in which the subject fails to recognize people he knows perfectly well, but is prepared to admit their similarity to those persons and considers them to be sort of doubles. Then we walked across the plain and we picked some flowers. I gathered a bunch of daisies for my dear patient, how are you? Do you remember me? I'm the deputy director of the hospital. What? You say that I'm not the real medical deputy director, that I'm his double? Perhaps you're right. But you must admit, in any case, that I'm the same double as the one who yesterday brought you this same bunch of flowers. What? You say that I'm the double's double? Perhaps you're right. Never are we what we were yesterday, doctor, never will we be the same tomorrow as we are today . . . and life passes us by as we imitate ourselves and try, like Kafka, to resolve the enigma of our own identities. Allow me to introduce Dr Palinuro, director of the hospital. Enjoy this wonderful opportunity that chance has offered you to be, here and now, yourself: the real Dr Palinuro. Tomorrow or this afternoon, perhaps, or even ten minutes ago, in my dream, you will no longer be the same. Another case is that of patients suffering dissociation problems who believe they see their own double, the *Doppelganger*. To please these patients, we thought up the idea of putting on masks imitating their faces when we visit them. Sometimes it works. But at others, if they happen to be with their doubles at the time, they think that we are their triples. Later I will show you a ward of deaf-mutes who talk all day long through a couple of ventriloquists hidden behind the curtains. And when you feel like taking a bath, doctor, I will take you to a ward where we house our ablutomania patients, who suffer from nothing more than an obsession with incessant and compulsive washing of the body. But, on the subject of imitation, doctor, I remember that you and I, in my dream, reached the seashore and there were beaches of golden sand which counted the minutes of happy days and beaches of black sand which counted the minutes of days of mourning. And from the sea came the inhabitants of the mirrors, mentioned by Borges. And they were the very patients we have here who suffer from a type of mania very well known, which consists of imitating all the gestures and movements of another person. Choose your patient, doctor, sit down before him and play mirrors: shave, knot your tie, wash your face with sea foam, wink, grab a handful of sand and scatter it over the harbour jetties and your human mirror will faithfully repeat each and every one of your gestures. But not everything is so sad, doctor. Come with me, I want to tell you that afterwards the men and women gave us little shells and mermaid scales. Which reminds me that we are on the threshold of the pavilion of those suffering from a generosity mania and who, as you know, cannot live without giving things to everybody continually. For economic reasons, in the first place and, in the second, bearing in mind that this mania is satisfied by the simple fact of giving and bears little relation to the price or quality of the object offered, we set up a special department with the daily task of wrapping and decorating insignificant objects which we put out for them at night, when they are asleep. (You know that no Greek traveller dares quench his thirst in the river without first leaving a gift, however humble, for the water spirits, the naiads, in niches specially created for this purpose.) Next day our patients discover them beneath their beds or under their pillows or in the drawers of their cupboards and they rush around the hospital offering them to the doctors, the nurses and even to other patients. So, don't be surprised when you enter the ward and one of the patients approaches you with a velvet box containing a few poplar leaves. Good morning, lads, how are you this morning? Ah, I see already: you have some presents for us. What a wonderful surprise! Let me see: this says 'For Dr Palinuro'. And this one is for me, how exciting! Endocrinologist Navarro got a button. Where will you put it, doctor? On your red shirt or on your orange one? That is a difficult decision for you.

Dr Iglesias: you don't need to unwrap your present to know what it is, since it is obviously a cigarette wrapped in cellophane. I am most envious but I will be generous because, as you see, in the little box that I received today is a match which I will use to light your cigarette. Did you see the grape which nurse Salazar was given? Never, in all my travels through Burgundy and Maipú, have I seen such a perfect, sleek and shiny grape. I beg you, Dr Palinuro, open your gift carefully because that paper can be used again. How wonderful: Dr Palinuro got last Sunday's newspaper. Look, colleagues, what exquisite texture, such discreet inks and particularly what news: 'Flood in Pakistan', 'Miss Brazil elected Miss Universe'. Far from the sea, doctor, and now in a shaded valley, I told you that not everything is happy: the newspaper, the grape, poplar leaves and shells are destined to disappear, because all things are merely on loan to us. For this reason, I become depressed by the dispossession complex described by Lévi-Valensi: this woman thinks she no longer belongs to herself, that the ideas of others invade her thoughts, that her voice, her gaze and her sense of smell are those of another person. It is comparable in some ways to Cotard's syndrome which is a systematic negation complex: this man has taken it into his head to deny everything: the passing of time, death, life, rain, sun. I, on the other hand, do not deny my dream, doctor, I do not deny that we walked through the valley and that we were followed by a multitude of patients who bothered us with their complexes and their paralyses, their uncontrolled movements and their manias. Four patients subject to spasmodic laughter on account of an affection of parts of the mesodiencephalon, waylaid us at the door of an inn and we had to waste our best jokes. A man suffering from total loss of topographical memory asked us where the lunatics' ward was and we had to think up all sorts of false instructions. I remember that afterwards we went into the ward of winds and lightning, housing patients with a manic fear of storms; through the blindingly bright pavilion containing those suffering from a phobia of light where we had to put on dark glasses to protect our eyes; along corridors full of snakes, tarantulas and scorpions, for those suffering from delirium tremens; through the transvestites' ward where I dressed up as Madame de Bennes, and lady doctor Fuentes de Caballero dressed up as Eon de Beaumont and we also walked through the ward in eternal movement of patients suffering from balance disorders of labyrinthine origin; how amused I was, doctor, to see that you fell three times! But just as well you didn't fall from the top of the skyscrapers where we have the patients suffering from fear of heights: wow, what vertigo, doctor! Then we descended again to the countryside and we were overtaken as though by shooting stars, in fact dromomania patients who feel an uncontrollable impulse constantly to move from one place to another. You ask why we don't shut them up, doctor? You maintain that our treatments and systems are contradictory? But, colleague, what is there more contradictory than life? See, for example, the behaviour of these patients: lie down! get up! drink water! very good! Heteronegativism patients, doctor, who do exactly the opposite to what they are told. But at first, to make them obey, we told them to do the opposite to what we wanted. But they soon saw through the subterfuge. So now, when for example we want a patient to stick out his tongue, we simply say: stick out your tongue! so he thinks that we really want him to do the opposite and, to disobey, he sticks out his tongue. Wonderfully simple, don't you agree, colleague? Later in my dream and in the shade of a tree, we stopped for several months to converse with a woman who suffers from an obsession with staying in bed for ever. And our cortège was ever greater, doctor. By the light of the moon we were followed by syringomyelia patients. The man with preacher's hands pleading for world peace. The man with fakir's hands who insisted on walking the path of the sea urchins' tongues. The woman with hands cupped as a holy water font who repeatedly emerged from beneath the bridge to offer us her precious liquid. Afterwards, a man with a black beard approached us on a bicycle and pestered us with all types of propositions: that the nurses should cut their hair, that the neurologists should use blue ties, that the cleaning of the hospital should start at one fifteen Greenwich time: you know, the reformer's mania. And, as though that were not enough, throughout the journey, throughout the night, the trees and the last-minute news, we were followed by a woman suffering from prophesying mania who foresaw that we would be afflicted with all kinds of divine punishments: universal sounds which would hush the noises of our Acoustic Pavilion, earthquakes which would destroy our Kinetic Pavilion, black rains which would fall from the sky to flood our Optical Pavilion. On the river bank, later, we met a very amiable gentleman whom we had to greet a hundred times because he suffered from the Salaam tic, doctor, which is a series of paroxysmal movements of greeting. And afterwards I showed you all the epileptics we bring to the Kinetic Pavilion while they have their fits and then remove when the crepuscular phase sets in, so you may well appreciate our efficiency if you bear in mind that the attacks usually last no more than a minute. You will certainly wonder why, in this ward which we call Kinetic, we have included paralytics. And I will answer that it is for two reasons: one is that, in most cases of paralysis, the patients execute some kind of unusual movement as in the case we have already seen of the hemiplaegics or, for example, in certain cases of total paralysis in which the jaws move spontaneously due to contraction of the chewing muscles and which we call the mumbling tic because it looks as though the patients spend their days mumbling curses. Moreover, if you look at many of our cases of partial paralysis, you will see that the posture of the patients gives a feeling of eternalized movement. And I was trying to explain all this to you, doctor, when we suddenly entered a tunnel and witnessed how two of our guards, descendants of the inhabitants of Sodom who tried to seduce Lot's angels, dressed up as devils to rape the two youths suffering from genital hallucinations who swore that every night they were subjected to unnatural erotic practices. In the middle of the tunnel, doctor, and in the middle of the journey of our life – to quote Dante – we met a crowd of patients suffering from speech defects. Some merely repeated the last syllable of each of our words. Others, standing up on soap boxes, made interminable speeches; others conversed among themselves with non-existent words in the fourteen languages Panurge took to using since he met our friend. From time to time, like stars, a few real words glittered in their dialogue. There were patients suffering from all kinds of dyslexia and aphasia. There was verbal blindness caused by damage to the plica semilunaris. There were jargon-aphasia sufferers who drew senseless words from bottomless philological barrels . . . Why continue? you are familiar with every variation. You know this world of chattering, of patients talking to themselves, verbiverations and eloquence reminding us of the best days of the Acoustic Pavilion and making one feel like Ovid on the banks of the Black Sea: *barbarus bic ergo sum, quia non intelligor ulli*: unable to understand or make myself understood, I am the barbarian. Nothing so far removed from analects and homilies and so close to the senseless syllable systems dreamed up by Ebbinghaus and Muller. But come this way, doctor, we must flee from the graphomania sufferers who have an unprecedented need to scribble every day, every hour and every minute. One of them, doctor, has spent five years and twelve thousand five hundred pages writing the history of our dear hospital and has not yet progressed beyond the prologue in which the numbers and the electrocardiograms remain unburied. At the end of this hall, doctor, or at the end of the tunnel – in my dream – we sat down again and discovered that we were naked and surrounded by a group of coprophages who not only ate their own excrement but smeared it all over their bodies and, not satisfied with that, smeared the stones along the way, the roots of the oak trees, the feathers of the kinglets and the wings of the dragonflies. But I was saying that we were naked, like Adamites in their paradises, doctor, and the fact is that some time ago we had a ward for kleptomaniacs and at first we allowed them to steal from us on our daily visits. But they lost interest because it was too easy and it then became necessary to allow them to roam the whole hospital so that they could steal from the patients too. But it complicated our lives somewhat: the patients complained that their savings disappeared or their tablets and the nurses complained when their thermometers and clinical histories evaporated into thin air. But we have trained a series of sadistic maniacs who keep an eye on them, catch them red-handed and humiliate them. Nevertheless, we have not been able to prevent a black market of stolen objects which are bought at exorbitant prices by the oniomania sufferers whose illness manifests itself in the compulsive purchase of anything offered to them. Does this explain the mystery of your American Waltham watch, doctor? They've stolen everything from us, colleague, underpants and hat, shoes and pipe! But don't take offence: they didn't do it with *aminus injuriandi* and remember that Proudhon, no less, at one point accepted the definition of private property as theft. Now, I should tell you that the only restraint we have placed on our kleptomaniacs is that they respect the property of patients in coma with symptoms of carphology who, as you know, constantly pick at the sheets in a way that makes them appear to be looking for something that doesn't exist. But, in such cases, doctor, we have made such objects exist: agate marbles, almonds, tin soldiers which we place in their reach and which perhaps serve to console them in that unconscious hell through which they must be passing. But the time has come to end our visit to the Kinetic Pavilion. You will note right away that I and all our colleagues, even you yourself, will adopt a different attitude as we pass through this next ward. Can you imagine, doctor, what an absurd dream? You sat down in a wheelchair and I got ready to push you, while you winked your left and right eye alternately at our patients. Dr Dávalos placed his hand in the swan's-neck position and started to pinch the breasts of the invalid old ladies. Osteopath Martínez walked the length of the ward as though he were dragging his feet along a river bed carpeted with gold nuggets. Dr Hernández feigned an attack of Chorea Sancti Viti. And the other doctors made all kinds of spasmodic movements *ad libitum*. Ah, doctor, the Quaker shakers, the leaping Welshmen and the Pentecostal rollers couldn't have done better! Oh, but it was like a pilgrimage of St Médard convulsionists struck by tarantism, a horde of Aquisgranum dancers foaming at the mouth! And please, I must ask you not to try and interpret the symbolism of my dream. For such purposes we have several patients with an interpretation mania for whom the most trivial sentences are loaded with hidden meanings. Objects too: they discover messages in the mysterious colour of a table, in the secret shape of an apple, in the unknown smell of bad breath. I don't need to tell you that such patients receive letters written in invisible ink and telegrams in code from the hospital administration. Let me just tell you the end of my dream. Ours, as I told you, was a band of deformed, paralytic and crippled beings. We were preceded by three bulimia sufferers who, like locusts, went around eating everything they came across, to the extent that our path was stripped of plum skins and stones. I must emphasize that our patients enjoy themselves tremendously. But those who have been here a while have lost all notion of normality. They sincerely believe that everybody suffers, to a greater or lesser extent, from some kind of paralysis or uncontrollable movement and, naturally, they start to ask themselves, to ask us, why they are here. But I forgot to tell you that, by this time, we had emerged from the tunnel and that we were again in the open countryside and that we were being followed in a stretcher on wheels, by a young man of nineteen years of age in the final stages of tetanus, bent like a bow so that only the crown of his head and his heels touched the stretcher. Very similar to the torso curvature of the hysterics described by Charcot. Our guides were two people with trembling tongues: mine a moribund old man whose tongue was hanging out like a tired dog's: a case of cynanthropy, doctor, and yours a fifteen-year-old with the trembling tongue of exanthematic typhus. And we walked through a village where half the people danced all day and all night, doctor, to the music of Poulenc's *Mouvements Perpétuels:* they were the patients suffering from St Vitus' dance, while the other half watched them: those suffering from aortic insufficiency revealing Musset's sign, unable to control the rhythmic nodding of their heads. Then we passed through the town of people suffering from loss of memory. There, half the people suffered from anterograde amnesia, whereby events are wiped from memory as they occur, doctor, and the other half suffered from the illusion of *déjà vu, déjà vécu* as discussed by Dwelshauvers and in which all perceptions are assimilated by the memory at the very instant at which they occur, as events of the more distant past. For this reason, half these patients are always happy: for them, life begins at each instant. It is as though for you this visit to the hospital begins with each word that I speak. And in a way this is so, is it not, Dr Palinuro? And the other half are always sad because they have seen it all before: for them, there is nothing new in life. It is as though you, doctor, were to have the feeling, with each word I speak, that you had visited the hospital an infinite number of times. And this is also true, isn't it, doctor? Place this perfumed handkerchief over your nose, esteemed colleague, because we are going to visit the ward of those suffering from a delusion that their bodies smell bad: you will of course understand that the patients entering this ward are forbidden to take a bath for the rest of their lives and every day their feet are anointed with rotten cheese juice and the rest of the body with the fat of dead dogs and every other imaginable filth. Then we entered another village, on our way to the land of Oz, where a man with a glass head fled at our approach, fearing that it would be shattered by the sound of our voices. And a man with skin of straw begged us to protect him from fire. And a woman knelt to ask us not to steal her golden kidneys. These patients are suffering from metabolic obsessions, doctor. And others suffer from asomatognosia: loss of awareness of the body or a part of it. Therefore, in my dream, there was another village where kidneys, brains and genital organs floated through the air, forgotten by their owners. In this village, we met a man who beckoned to us, since he thought he had lost his tongue. We also saw a woman who groped her way through the world and through Stheno's Gorgon fields where the light of the sun and the moon never penetrate, because she thought she had lost her eyes. And, finally, we met a grieving man who was roaming around in search of his body, but he didn't realize that we saw him because he thought he was invisible. Here is your watch, Dr Palinuro. It's not yours, you say? Of course not. But we are going to visit the ward of those suffering from chronophobia, those who hate time and spend their lives destroying any clocks or watches they come across: give them this toy imitation, doctor, and perhaps they will be deceived. In my dream, doctor, I had the feeling that, as we progressed from village to village, we were approaching a great city. Now come this way, colleague, all we have to do now is look in on a group of patients suffering from touching phobia and then we will reach the garden that will lead us to the last of the hospital's pavilions: the largest and most original of all. In this last village, we met delirious multitudes: women who had stroked shop windows and screamed that their hands were full of glass; men who waved us goodbye and complained that their hands were full of wind; old and young who approached us to touch our clothes and our faces and drew back afterwards, horrified, shouting that their hands were full of velvet and of flesh: their obsession is that they become stained or contaminated by contact with objects, doctor, leading always to nausea. But finally we left the last of the villages behind us and there, in the distance, we saw a city with golden domes and amber skyscrapers; the city had high, transparent walls and was surrounded by a garden as beautiful as this one; doctor, after you: I wish to show you the garden which rings the hospital in clover, dancing a riotous waltz in the grass. See how marvellous, look at the fountains, hear how in their liquid language they murmur a song of protest against the heat, admire the laurels of autonomous foliage wreathed in their own glory. Here, our patients find solitude and rest, the sex maniacs find consolation imitating the evil-spirited calla lilies pointing fingers of yellow dust towards the vaginas of a non-existent sky and amnesiacs marvel when they discover that roses repeat the inner memory of poets. In my dream, doctor, dawn was breaking as we approached the great city and the sun tinged with orange the Alhambra's filigreed stonework imitated by the flowering peach trees. As I said, the great city was surrounded by a garden, beautiful and labyrinthine, designed by Hans Vredeman de Vries, and in this garden the children played musical statues. They cast spells on the trees, on the fountains, on the lottery-ticket vendors. They also cast a spell on us, doctor. I myself, when I wish to flee from wild agoras and the vulgar smell of latrines, I come at dusk to this garden and remain until the petals open in the panes of dawn, absorbed in contemplation of the Andromedas which ushered in

371

pre-civilised ages. And in the garden all was motionless, like a frozen Arcadia: the nursemaids with their prams and babies, the balloon sellers and the gardeners who confined in their hoses the opportunity to change their way of life. But I digress, doctor, forgive me. I have the impression that the very music, a vague and dreamy harmony by Debussy, was frozen. What I wanted to show you, before going on to our last and most original pavilion, are our catatonia patients, possessed by other, though in this case ecstatic, demons, in the manner of Beatrice of Ornacieu. You are well aware that cerebral syphilis, chronic tuberculosis and acute encephalitic processes often cause a psychic and psychomotor syndrome relating to voluntary motor activity which Kahlbaum named Spannungsirresein, and which is generally characterized by a waxy flexibility: in other words, for hours and hours and sometimes days at a time they maintain a particular posture until they collapse in exhaustion. This is not to be confused with myosis, which is the ossification of the muscles; poor Lord Byron, half of whose heart was as hard as ivory by the age of thirty-six! So, the reason why all the human beings in my dream became musical statues was simply that they somehow symbolized these patients. Do you see that ice-cream vendor there on the opposite pavement offering his multi-coloured wares to a pair of lovers? All three are suffering from catatonia. We would have liked to freeze the ice-creams too, doctor, it's a shame that they're running down their hands. Just as it's a shame also that a constant thread of distracted saliva dribbles from the lips of the loving couple – one of the few symptoms in catatonia revealing that the patient is alive, that the patient's soul is in movement. Allow me now, doctor, to take your face in my hands and turn it, slowly, that you may see the rest of the bystanders. Yes, those motionless policemen with their raised batons are also catatonics. As is the drunk tipping a bottle to his lips for all eternity. And the young baseball player who, bat in hand, waits for a ball that will never come. And that band of motionless musicians – they are all catatonic. Allow me to open your mouth, that all the world's astonishment may enter you through it. And, finally, permit me to show you another type of catatonic patient, those with so-called rigid hypertonia: once they have assumed a position, they will never change it and there is no human power that will make them move a millimetre. And we have painted this group of patients, doctor, in white or gold, to decorate our gardens. You see, for example, this beautiful youth representing Michelangelo's *David* for the rest of his days and this matron in the position of the *Victory of Samothrace* until defeated by the centuries. Over here is Praxiteles' *Aphrodite of Cnidus*; there Benvenuto Cellini's *Perseus*; over there, mounted on the stone swan, is an eternalized *Aurora*. Allow me now, doctor – I said to you in my dream – to raise your arm and stretch your hand and your fingers that you might touch and feel for yourself that these patients are not of gold, doctor, nor of marble, but

372

of flesh and blood, like you and me. Do you remember your drawings, doctor, your statues stuffed with viscera? No, perhaps you shouldn't touch them for you might shatter the millenary glaciers symbolizing the immobility of hope. I speak from personal experience, doctor: thus, with the heat of our bodies and the sound of our words, are dreams shattered. You and I had reached the outskirts of the city and we were about to pass through its glass walls. And I knew that we had only to touch them and they would fall soundlessly and then the spell would be broken: Daedalus would come; the baton would start to tremble in the band leader's hand; the lover, his hand cupped, would hasten to catch the saliva falling from the lips of his beloved and the baseball would, at last, reach the youth awaiting it. All our statues would stretch their limbs in the woods, ready to undertake the journey back to mythology. Then the dream would cease to be a dream and I would forget it. And it would be as though I had never dreamt it, as though I had lost my ability to dream. That is something I could not bear, doctor. I live for my dreams. And my dreams are true. Let me give you an example: a few days ago I dreamt that I was telling you a dream. And you see, it is true. Hence the immense compassion I feel for patients in a state of psychotic insomnia who have lost the ability to dream; and not only physiological dreaming, that most beautiful example of the joint resolution of the muscular tone of physical activity, as Antoine Porot described it but, more important, doctor, paradoxical dreaming. But, fortunately, I can say that we have found an almost perfect means of eliminating their problem. We studied all existing theories and treatises on dreams, from the writings of Synesius of Cyrene to Freud's *Traumdeutung*, and the results we have obtained are worthy of Clément Vautel's dream machine . . . worthy, doctor, even of Antiphon's dream as narrated by Lucian and the visions of those Greeks who became possessed when shut up in Trophonius's cave. Every night, when the ward lights are turned out, all kinds of phosphorescent wonders begin to descend from the roof: green giraffes with red spots, yellow zebras with violet stripes, Etruscan figureheads and Polynesian masks, elves which flutter down on parachutes made of half eggshells, pixies mounted on the backs of blue pigs and larvae of steam and blood, offspring of incubus and succubus. The world of Bosch, doctor. And the atmosphere, like the French sky during the reign of Pepin the Short, is rife with palaces and gardens and ships. Ah, doctor, Thesaurus already said that dreams are no more than ingenious metaphors! Moreover, these animals move, walk, speak, like the automated lion built by Leonardo for Louis XII and robots with positronic brains like Golem and Vaucanson's mechanical duck producing artificial excrement and the golden statues of Delphi. Ah, doctor, no demon or monster invented by man or emerging from the depths of Gehenna fails to appear in the dreams of our patients: the Muslim efrits? The Japanese omi? The Indian rakasas,

373

the Scottish kelpies and the Arabian djinns? They're all here, doctor: the bad Lemures and the good Lares, the goblins of Gaulle and the giants born of the blood of Uranus, the capricious and malign elves of Languedoc and all the igneous, aquatic or lucifugous demons classified by Bunyan. Why go to Paris, I mused, to shudder at the masks of the Pont Neuf and the gargoyles of Notre Dame? Suffice it to close your eyes – or rather, in this case, to open them – to see them. But the real monsters, doctor, those engendered by the sleep of reason, as Goya would say, are played by professional actors who take the part of individuals in real life: the patient's parents, the cousins who went to Europe, the close friend who died in an accident. And they all turn into one another, get mixed up until they become unrecognizable or two or three merge into a single character or mingle with other ghost-characters by means of three-dimensional projections; modifications and tricks one and all, which are frequently necessary to establish the co-ordinates of a nightmare or a fabulous dream. One night when you cannot get to sleep, doctor, come and take a turn around this ward. Although, unfortunately, we tend towards tragedy, you will not be disappointed: in a recent survey, most of our patients stated that the dreams we offer them are the same as they would dream if they were able to. And the other patients, just imagine our satisfaction, doctor! the others were so convinced that these were their own dreams that they took offence at our survey and accused us of plagiarism . . . it is dawn, doctor, and this is the end of my dream. But . . . is it really my dream, colleague? Good-morning, gardener Navarro. Beautiful day, policeman Sanjuán. Hellow, General López. How are you, vendor Ortiz? A little nippy this morning, wouldn't you agree, postman Gutiérrez? Good-day, sweeper Morales. So long, milkman Diosdado. Good-morning, electrician Domínguez. And now, Dr Palinuro, it remains for me but to thank you for your visit and to say goodbye. So, thank you, Dr Palinuro, and goodbye. We have finished. What? You say I promised to show you our hospital's largest and most original pavilion and that I haven't done so? Forgive me, dear colleague, but that is not quite true. For the last ten minutes at least we have been walking through it. In fact, we have been touring it for almost a whole day. I would go even further, doctor, and assure you that we have done nothing in life other than tirelessly visit this pavilion. Can you guess? Of course, doctor! That is why I told you that we should remove our white coats, put aside our stethoscopes and forget that we are doctors. Quite so, doctor. This ward, the size of a city and with no specific name, is the Pavilion of the Sane. In the early days it was far more exclusive. And the size, merely, of a greenhouse. And in it we had a selective sample of people of all ages and social classes whom we lured here with different tricks. The poor, we paid. The rich, we enticed in the name of science. The elderly and the orphaned gave us little problem because they came here to find company. As you can see, we have everything: a reverberation of raving scholars, accountants, veterinary surgeons, ballet dancers, prostitutes, theology students, *caudillos*. How are you, cook Antonia? Western poets devoting themselves to smuggling Nirvana. Cowardly plumbers. Painters. Inveterate pederasts. Aspirin manufacturers. How are you, broadcaster Alvarado? As you see, they are all healthy, or apparently healthy, doctor, and they are living here a sort of obligatory holiday: they eat, they sleep, they work, they watch television, they play Uruguayan canasta, they commit adultery, they abuse each other. Optimistic carpenters invent rosewood. May students turn paving stones into birds. Feuding lovers hurl Montaguesque and Capuletesque darts. Meteorologists devote themselves to the study of encyclopaedia clouds and musicians hunt arpeggios and draw up their polyphonic wills. Or else the people play golf, billiards, they swim, do calisthenic gymnastics and fill in the live questionnaires that come on cereal packets, solve crossword puzzles where the words contaminate each other with their meanings, or merely come here to immerse themselves in spleen or *taedium vitae*, doctor, or sometimes in that total *angst*, that true *angst* discussed by Heidegger, hovering like a silent mist in the abysms of *Dasein*. But time passed, doctor, and the pavilion grew ever-larger, despite the fact that most of the sick, excuse me doctor, the healthy, left after being here three weeks. I say the majority, because some (a small percentage) remain with us. I will tell you, confidentially, that among them were doctors of this hospital disguised as agricultural engineers or language teachers who were responsible for keeping an eye on several patients each and report the appearance of the merest suspicious symptom in anybody. When this occurred, we stepped up our supervision and, if necessary, the person was removed from the ward, during the night, to be given an examination. A touch of diarrhoea, a nagging cough, a pain in the liver: all these can be extremely significant. In most cases, the diarrhoea was only a symptom of minor food poisoning or some unimportant disorder. But it may, on occasion, indicate the beginning of a tumour. Frequently, a fever may be the result of nothing more than a touch of exhaustion. How are you, manufacturer Mendoza? Good-morning, Archdeacon Correa. But, alternatively, it is the first symptom of meningitis. However, the pavilion continued to grow uncontrollably, doctor, in spite of the bad example frequently given by the old people whose deaths interfered with our objectives: there were some who gave up the ghost without giving us time to remove them alive. Attracted by the enormous fame of this pavilion, our patients' visitors started to apply to be admitted for a few days. Well, yes, you can guess, the ironies of life are infinite: several visitors died unexpectedly and shortly afterwards their sick friends and relatives, whose cases seemed hopeless, were cured almost miraculously . . . and then it was

375

no longer just the visitors: hundreds of people started to knock on the doors of the pavilion asking to be admitted. And others resorted to base tricks, doctor: for the purpose of entering the hospital and having an opportunity to mix with the healthy, they studied medicine and took jobs in the hospital; they studied to become cooks and started working in the hospital kitchen; they studied to become plumbers, doctor, dishwashers, book keepers and lift attendants. At the beginning, we had assigned several researchers tirelessly to follow up on all the people who left this ward and returned home as healthy as when they arrived here, in order to catch some day that first trembling, that first headache which is the beginning of death. But there came a time when we no longer knew who was the doctor disguised as a road-sweeper and who was the road-sweeper disguised as a doctor and our old spying system collapsed and had to be replaced with a more universal one, we had to teach everybody to spy on everyone else and also to spy on themselves. Of course, only a doctor can detect the signs of Ebstein's disease or Rokitansky's disease, but almost anyone can detect those first drops of brilliant blood baptizing a cancer of the rectum, the first cavernous breath proclaiming a hollow in the lung or the first mistake in the simplest arithmetical calculation preceding a progressive and general paralysis. The results of this infinite expansion have been very discouraging, doctor: we have many deaths. It is not only the old who die but also the young and even children, and newlyweds and hospital staff: only three days ago in the canteen, Dr Taboada's heart, perhaps jealous because he was an eminent cardiologist who never looked after himself, played the classic custard-tart joke on him: our colleague – suffering a heart attack – collapsed on the table and, already dead, buried his face in his birthday cake. Moreover, Dr Palinuro, as our pavilion has grown and on account of our desire that everyone in it have an apparently normal life, the number of our installations has also increased: we built parks, fairs, bars and restaurants, houses, casinos, churches and schools, until we realized that it was ridiculous to build a city within another city and that it would be better to pull down the walls and limit ourselves to imagining another wall, ethereal and transparent and most importantly mobile, doctor, allowing the inner city to invade the outer city, until the two merged in a single great city. And so it was, doctor, and then the city invaded the countryside and the woods and reached the shore of the sea and then the shore of the world, from which it plunges interminably. Thus, my life's greatest ambition was realized, doctor, the *desideratum* of creating the world's largest and most beautiful hospital, beside which were as nothing the Medical Centre in Chicago, the Santo Spirito in Rome and the Hospital of the Innocents in Florence designed by Brunelleschi. I'm sorry to abandon you like this, doctor, alone, in such a great city, leaving you to your own devices. But perhaps this will help you. Here you have the keys to the city. Actually, doctor, these golden keys, in the shape of a golden bough, are no good for opening the doors in the wall, because the wall does not exist. On the other hand, with them you can open all the doors in the entire city. They are like the keys of Rome, the eternal city, doctor, and do remember that all roads lead to Rome. You have some surprises awaiting you. There are doors which open into houses of friends who are expecting you for dinner. Others, to a concert hall, a cinema, a trip through the Orient. Most of them open into your own house, your bedroom, doctor, your manuscripts and your dreams. But, sooner or later, you will open the door of the tiger, doctor, and we will see you again in this house of the sick. Meanwhile, enjoy yourself, doctor, as Santayana advised when he said there was no possible cure for birth and death, except to enjoy the interim. And now, Dr Palinuro, if you are going to tell me that with this experiment we are achieving only a symbolic and therefore wretched copy of what life is, I will first remind you that the idea was your own and, second, that our aim is precisely that. Such is life, Dr Palinuro. Or, perhaps I should say, such is death. And now it remains only for me to tell you that, though I hope to see you here again, I hope that it will be as far as possible into the future and I feel that this will indeed be so: you are very young and you seem to be in good health, although I should tell you, now that I shake your hand, that you have a somewhat rapid pulse and perhaps you should have another medical check-up. Finally, doctor, I must admit to you that I am also a patient. But don't withdraw your hand so quickly: my illness is not contagious. Wait, don't go. My illness is mental, doctor. Hey! doctor, I was telling you that my condition is mental and is characterized by the loss . . . but, doctor, come back, I'm talking to you . . . by the loss, I was saying, of social and sexual inhibitions . . . Doctor, don't force me to run after you: my legs are so old and weak! and by a morbid propensity for jokes and verbosity, which goes by the name of moria. Doctor, come back, you're almost out of sight, don't make me strain my eyes: they are so old and weak! Doctor! Where are you? I wanted to tell you that, fortunately, patients suffering from my complaint are left free in the world that we might brighten it up with the funfairs spluttering on our tongues. Doctor, come back! I can hardly hear your steps! Don't make me strain my ears! They're old and weak, doctor. And I also wanted to tell you that I'm thinking of writing a book about it. Do you hear me, doctor? And unleashing a flood of royalties which will drown me in wealth. Do you hear me, doctor? Don't make me shout: my voice is old and weak.

19

A *story,* other stories

One night, years before Mamma Clementina's death, in the hope of distracting Papa's mind from the fight with Felipe, Uncle Esteban invited them to go out on the town with him and Aunt Lucrecia to the Copacabana Club, to Ciro's and wherever else they felt like going, and the four got into Uncle Esteban's Oldsmobile and Mamma Clementina said that she was going to order prawns in garlic butter and Uncle said that he was going to order a fried chicken breast *à la Maryland* and they left the house behind them and with it the Russians crossing the Donets and the Japanese occupying the Moluccas and they left behind the vitamins baptized by Casimir Funk and the shadowy song by Mary Ghost and, although the night, particularly on account of the obligatory blackout, was ideal for singing: 'My arm, which lay in your arm / has been taken by Doctor Vyse / and both legs have gone a-walking / to the hospital of Guys . . .' because Papa Eduardo had promised not to talk about the war that night, just as Uncle Esteban had sworn not to mention medicine, since their sole object was to dance 'Night and Day' all night since Cole Porter was on tour in Mexico, as though there had never been wars or operations, as though the English had not bombed the Ruhr Valley or as though the Maginot Line were situated at an unimaginable distance from Mexico.

At five in the morning, back home again, Uncle Esteban broke the agreement and said to Papa Eduardo that he had to go on a trip to Puebla and Veracruz to visit doctors and pharmacists – his laboratory's clients – and that if Papa would like to, he and Palinuro could go too and, if so, Uncle Esteban would take his daughter. At five o'clock in the morning of the next Saturday, after a feverish night when his whole body ached and after Mamma diagnosed that excitement was responsible for his temperature while Uncle Esteban insisted that it was an accumulation of lactic acid in the muscles which caused the pain, and after Uncle himself prescribed two aspirins and a cinnamon tea and Mamma Clementina for her part prescribed hieroglyphics of iodine on the soles of his feet which she drew with a little brush and which augured for him a world of sargasso and marine phosphorescence, Palinuro started to scale surprises in the darkness enveloping the city's sleep and when the tulip-shaped light in the bathroom went on and he heard the running of water, he rose from his bed, dressed and ran to see Papa Eduardo and watch once again that strange process which seemed to him a double waste: of the beard and of the foam achieved with such calligraphic zeal and which were both diminished daily with the linear sweeps of a razor blade sharp as the gospel, to disappear down the drain of the washbasin like a whirlpool of dirty snow heading for the sewers. The arrival of Uncle Esteban and the rising of the sun were announced with horn blasts. When Palinuro reached the yard, a yellow halo slid over the shining coachwork of the Oldsmobile. Uncle Esteban unbuttoned his coat, took a large watch from the pocket of his jacket and said: 'We leave in half an hour. Today we will reach Zacatlán where we will stay one day, then we will drive down to Orizaba where you and Estefania can catch handfuls of fireflies without even leaving the main square around which the girls walk at night while their boyfriends walk the opposite way and give them bunches of violets like dark secrets. Then we will go and see Veracruz, though we are really going to see Aunt Luisa who is visiting Jean Paul's grave and the next morning, very early, we will go fishing . . .'

And the Oldsmobile started to climb and plunge along the white-stitched road, winding up through the mountains and whirling down like a toboggan, and Estefania's skirts inflated like a balloon and afterwards it rained and the shadows of the drops of water on the windows painted on her face more freckles than she ever had and Uncle Esteban started to whistle and as the windscreen misted over with his shady songs and Papa Eduardo lit a cigarette and the windscreen clouded over completely and Palinuro started to feel sleepy and they passed through tunnels where it had never ever rained and Palinuro prepared himself for his first meeting with the sea: the sea glimpsed in conversations with Grandfather Francisco; the sea seen in all its beating dimensions in Grandmother Lisandra's stereoscopic illustrations; the sea heard in murex shells and mother-of-pearl turbans which the kings of Scandinavia mounted in silver to pour their wines and Aunt Adelaida used to prop open the dining-room doors, and as the Oldsmobile shot like a yellow arrow across the plains and won a race against the fog and another against the train, the windscreen wipers, like an *andante* metronome, beat the rhythm of Uncle Esteban's tunes and modulated the salty wonder of a vision in which the sea, having cast its peaceful mane upon the shore, pursued my cousin's footprints upon the sand and filled them with spectres before withdrawing to its solitary haunts.

There were three things that Palinuro would most vividly remember about that trip to Veracruz: the Vigil dwarfs of Zacatlán de Las Manzanas, the miraculous fishing and the endless conversations between Uncle Esteban and Aunt Luisa about Germans and crabs.

After eating in Puebla, where fruit barrows fizzing with grapes came

379

forth to greet them on every corner, stands selling sweets and potions, tiled patios with fountains in their centre bathed in yellow light, they reached Zacatlán on that same day, along the road of apples left over from the recent harvest and which the farmers dumped along the roadside that motorists and passers-by might regale themselves. They got out of the car and collected apples and put them in Estefania's skirt and they entered the town as a fine rain splattered gaily on the decorations of the allegorical floats, over which the blue convolvulus was starting to creep. That night they stayed in the local pharmacist's house, a friend of Uncle Esteban's, and next day Palinuro and Estefania went to walk in the countryside and they met one of the Vigil dwarfs. The little man carried in his hand a bunch of green branches, his flagellant booty from his latest excursion to the pastures, as he told them, peeping out from between hawthorn branches which framed his wizened face as in a garland of white butterflies. He smiled at the cousins, showing gold-capped teeth, and Palinuro realized that the dwarf was the spitting image of Papa Eduardo, only that he was smaller and less wrinkled. And when Estefania touched him to see if he was real, Vigil the dwarf said: 'Don't touch me, little sprig, or the porcelain will fall from your face and your skin will turn to cauliflower,' and as they walked along the red path he told them that his parents, the Vigil dwarfs, were from the hill where they could at that moment see Indians climbing down with their loads of oak charcoal, and that they had made their fortune manufacturing clocks for belfries and castles of cork and that they had had three children, but his father and brother and sister had died of leprosy and he told them that his mother, poor lady, had never been quite in her right mind since his little sister Girasol left them. They would see, they would see, he assured them, but first I'm going to show you the luminous rocks in Devil's Cave; and Palinuro, Estefania and Vigil the dwarf made a lacteous about-turn and climbed down into the valley where the cows were chewing the cud and greeted them with their fly-swot tails and the dwarf also told them that his mother, the mad lady, made him buy her grown-up people's dresses and she put them on and they trailed behind her all over the house raising clouds of yellow dust, he told them, and as she went she swept her path with her broom of twigs and sweet-smelling herbs and Palinuro and his cousin entered the darkness and followed the tracks left by Vigil the dwarf on the stele of soapstone winding its way over the waves of darkness to reach the cavern of the precious stones. And Vigil the dwarf was already there waiting for them, naked and sitting on a luminous expanse beside the water and on the tips of the stalactites shone stars which dripped upwards in an instantaneous filament and the dwarf said sit down on the stones and you will leave here with blazing buttocks and while you're thinking about it, I'm going to bathe in the green water, he said, and jumped into the pool and sank through the ripples and a few minutes later

380

a little voice rescued them from the wavering doubt to which they had succumbed, fearing that Vigil the dwarf had died in the arms of the moving tyrant; but no, he was not dead: it was his voice saying: guess where I am? Vigil the dwarf was alive, alive and green, phosphorescent, and then he told them that he was going to squeeze out the water that had stayed inside him and he started to pee and his urine drew a luminous bridge in the air. On their way back, Vigil the dwarf talked to the flowers and the humming birds, threw stones at the cows and climbed a silkwood tree to look at the house in which he lived with his mother and in which everything was miniature: the furniture, the plates, the lamps and the bath, even the house itself, because they were rich, he reminded them, very rich, even though they were dwarfs and even though they had had leprosy. And inside the house Mamma Vigil, in a long dress of watered silk, rocked in a rocking chair, ever on the brink of shadowy fringes, to the rhythm of the belfry clocks all around her, and looked at Palinuro and Estefania hazily, as though it were their fault, yawned hugely several times in succession, stretched her arms and, in the posture of a long-memoried heron, pointed to the cork castles and landscapes she carved on her good days, a discreet frou-frou accompanying her flapping arms; through the window could be seen the walnut trees and the wheat sprouting in Byzantine shoots and Mamma Vigil finally spoke and said, looking at them with her trembling eyes: 'Bye for now, bye for now,' and took refuge in a dream. And Palinuro felt a shiver run down his spine because Mamma Vigil looked like Mamma Clementina, except that she was older and much more wrinkled.

From Zacatlán they went on to Orizaba, where they were shut indoors and bored for a whole morning and afternoon. Then the Oldsmobile finally carried them to Veracruz, where they stayed in the same hotel as Aunt Luisa and two days later they went fishing with Uncle Esteban and Papa Eduardo.

Do you remember, Estefania? The Parroquia Café with its coffee machines coifed with Roman helmets, the cemetery cut in two by the highway, the cedarwood canoes and the diving ducks sending ripples across the waters of Mandinga Lake fringed with rushes and white mangroves with exposed prop roots which seemed to have fallen from the sky and the iridescent jellyfish through which the sea breathed and the story of the buffaloes which had escaped from the Island of Sacrifices and swam until they reached Veracruz harbour, and Veracruz and its square and its municipal palace which looked as though it were made of coloured sugar lumps and the street lights adorned with silver dragons and the flowering flame trees and the shells from Verde Island and the coral figurines: do you remember? And even these and other marvels which you and I saw on our journey were nothing compared to that morning when we set out at dawn, when the seagulls exchanged circling cries and we climbed into the boat and the heaving of the salt entered our skin and we set sail, unfurling also all our maritime and trading imagination, do you remember? And the boats dimmed their reflections with a thick and downy mist and the little boats of grey fishermen awaited us at the turn of each reef and so we sailed as the pelicans, awed by their own silence, barely blinked with a flash of sequins and a cloud traced our itinerary between the liquid anemones which stretched peduncles of foam towards us. We sailed in a silence imperceptibly broken by the merest murmur of waves wrenched from the moisture of the night which lapped the sand and with utmost gentleness stirred the water's depths, and the darter fish, do you remember? which took the waves for personal obstacles and straddled them with silver arches, and not forgetting the dolphin which veered away from our boat with unexpected trills and when the amber flight of the first reflections of the sun appeared above the veiled colonnades of foam, followed by a fine cold drizzle which strewed illusive diamonds on the mirror of the sea and an approaching greenness indicated shallower waters, or some translucent sandbank, islands of pink coral alive with little fish forming voluntary clusters, the local boatman stopped his craft and its glass bottom became a mirror in which you and I could contemplate the mystery of a sky revealing the glories of all the dusks ever invented since the day of creation, do you remember, Estefania? And standing in the boat, you and I and Papa Eduardo and Uncle Esteban, jerking our lines like cowboys spinning flowers with their lassos, we floated throughout that morning which was like a nest of burning oranges and Uncle Esteban shouted to me take care that your hook doesn't get caught in Estefania's hair, in its threads of lightening gold, and at that moment you and I, both of us, felt the tug of a fish and we shouted: another one's biting! another one's biting! And another, and yet another, and that morning was incredible, do you remember? with the sea offering its fish up to us and I caught a catfish with whiskers and blunt snout causing us to make faces of disgust and then a lavender blue fish with oblique black stripes and you caught a gilthead with an ochre mark on its forehead and Papa Eduardo a pink squirrel fish with fluorescent eyes and Uncle Esteban a fork-tailed sargo and then – how we laughed – he caught an old wife fish and soon the bottom of the boat was a heaving mass of damp and palpitating shapes and colours and, do you remember? there were red mullets with blushing bellies and barbels like saffron brands and fish like silver cutlasses with angels' wings and others purple as the sublime dahlia and with luminous eyes and there were rhomboid rays splattered with stains of black lacquer and the darters we had seen leaping the waves added their dark blue and their royal-blooded borders to the multi-coloured swarm and showed us their many incisively shining teeth and Uncle Esteban, do you remember? caught several soles like blades of silver and plump groupers and Papa Eduardo caught two

382

porgies with scarlet fins and tail and several pompanos with flesh as white and dazzling as curdled milk, do you remember? Do you remember, Estefania, that we caught so many other fish that promised infinite mysteries with names that seemed to have been invented by Aunt Luisa: porgy *menunière*, pompano *à la papillot*, when they appeared on Grandmother Lisandra's dishes and porcelain platters, platters of deliciousness, there, in Mexico City, there when we returned and I told her, to the murmur of other seas, of our wondrous fishing expedition? And do you remember that nobody ever believed us, Estefania, not even Aunt Luisa, because we returned to the hotel empty-handed?

'What happened?' asked Aunt Luisa, 'fish don't fly as far as I know.' 'Bad luck, ma'am, terrible: when we reached the wharf the boatman got out first and I gave him the end of the line on which we had threaded the hundred fish by the mouth; what am I saying, a hundred: the five hundred fish we caught, and I held on to the other end and suddenly a big wave comes and the boat moves further than expected and I don't let go of the line and neither does the boatman and so the line, well, ping! snaps and all the fish fall into the sea.' 'And were they alive, Mr Esteban?' 'Some were alive, others unconscious. Others were dead and floated away and others half dead or half alive, I don't know which, swam off on their sides, as though resting. Anyway, we lost them all.' 'And you, young lady,' Aunt Luisa asked you. 'Tell me: how come you go fishing, if you love animals so much?' 'Ah, but it's different, ma'am, as I said to Estefania herself: they were fish to be eaten.' 'Don't come to me with those tales, Mr Esteban: who is going to eat thirty-six fish?' 'We didn't catch thirty-six, but about five hundred.' 'All the more reason: who is going to eat five hundred and thirty-six fish? Uh? Tell me that.' 'What I will tell you is that right now I could eat a whole giant grouper because I'm starving.' 'And why didn't you jump into the water to catch some of the fish?' 'Because we were afraid of the sharks.' 'That is exactly what I told Palinuro and this little girl yesterday when I took them to the beach: careful of the sharks who are watching from out at sea because, before you know it, they're watching you from close by.' 'Ah, yes, they tell me that last year the sharks ate a Spaniard's leg.' 'Yes, the right leg.' 'No, ma'am, it was the left leg.' 'The left or the right, it's all the same, it's a shame that the shark didn't eat him whole. He deserved it, for being Spanish.' 'How can you say that, ma'am, since your parents are Spanish?' 'Ah, but it was as though they were French, don't forget that my father was educated at the Sorbonne.' 'You're always on about French this, French that.' 'And you're always on about the Russians that, the Russians the other. Are you afraid of the French?' 'I couldn't care less. The ones I *am* afraid of are the Germans, because they might win the war.' 'That's right, now listen to me: yesterday I said to Estefania and this little boy that they shouldn't go in the sea. And did you take any notice of me? Just like them.' 'You feel very safe, ma'am, when you see the American war planes landing in Tejería to fill up with red fuel. But the Germans are more entrenched here than you might believe.' 'It's bad enough that the Americans land here, but worse is what this little girl Estefania and this little boy Palinuro did yesterday on the beach even though I told them that the sea isn't too well behaved. Will you listen to me and stop fiddling with your ring, it makes me nervous! Where did you get that ring, Mr Esteban?' 'I took it out of the sea: it was there, floating, among the foam and the reflections.' 'Don't give me that, rings don't float, they're not made of rubber.' 'This is a gold ring with a real stone. And if I say it was floating, it's because I found it when the *Lusitania* sank: a corpse which drifted by my submarine was wearing it and all I had to do was remove it from his finger.' 'On the subject of things which float: did you see how many seagulls there were yesterday at the beach floating in the air?' 'What I said about my submarine reminds me . . .' 'But did submarines exist in those days, Mr Esteban?' 'It reminds me, as I was saying, that the Germans are right now approaching the shores of Chiapas on one side and those of Tabasco on the other. And they have even landed, just imagine!' 'And there was a magpie which hopped along, pausing in each of Estefania's footprints.' 'It wasn't a magpie, ma'am, it must have been a gannet.' 'It was a magpie, Mr Esteban, and not because I say that it was, but because it knew it was. You just go and tell a magpie that it's not a magpie and see how it will laugh in your face.' 'Excuse me, Aunt Luisa, but magpies don't laugh.' 'And then, when we were on the beach, I wondered: should I take the children to the sand dunes? And, since I have been thinking aloud, the children heard me and I had to take them.' 'And when you stand on the beach, in the little coastal villages along the Pacific, near Guatemala, you can see the Germans arriving in their boats.' 'And then we went to the square to catch a bus to Antón Lizardo, and the hunchback lottery-ticket vendor came by and I bought a ticket. Perhaps I will be rich tomorrow. Then four men came past looking as though they were going to bury a marimba . . . but what were you saying about the Germans coming in boats from Germany?' 'No, ma'am: they arrive in submarines, which stay far out to sea and then they get in their boats and disembark with gifts for the local people.' 'Oh, how I would like to stroke a submarine. Jean Paul also used to bring me gifts when he came from France.' 'He brought, ma'am, because he only came once.' 'Between used to bring and brought I see no difference. I used to be young, every day of my youth, so it wasn't just once. Then, on our way to Antón Lizardo, you should have seen the orange crabs crossing the road and how we crushed the poor things. I don't know if they were the same crabs that we used to see in the mangrove swamps and which we called fiddler crabs, but the fact is that we squashed them all.' 'Then the Germans climb the mountain mounted on Chamulas.' 'Chamulas? Is that some kind of ass?' 'With all due respect, ma'am, you are the ass: I'm talking about the Chamula Indians. And, since you insist on talking about crabs, I will tell you that the Chamulas carry the Germans as hermit crabs carry sea anemones. And let somebody try and tell me that the Chamulas are a weak race, ma'am.' 'Then, with all respect also, Mr Esteban, you are the weak one, in the head.' 'And when they get to the high plains, there is a town like in Germany, with Gothic houses and sloping roofs.' 'Poor crabs, such optimists, when they saw the bus coming they threatened it with their pincers . . . but we just squashed them all: scrunch! scrunch!' 'So, like the crabs, we should crush the Germans: just go, go to those places and you will see how in the heart of the tropics, here in Mexico, there are old men with white beards smoking Tyrolese pipes.' 'Would you just stop talking about so many things at once and listen to what these children did yesterday, your daughter and your nephew, in the sand dunes, Mr Esteban? Nobody is in the least interested in hearing about violin-playing Germans and Tyrolese submarines.'

'Do you remember, Estefania? That was just how Uncle Esteban and Aunt Luisa used to talk to each other.'

Estefania certainly remembered. But she didn't remember with the same words as I did, nor with the excitement, happiness or nostalgia that I expected.

'Nothing can be the same again,' she said to me. 'For example, when Papa Esteban used to play with his ring on the tablecloth and make Aunt Luisa nervous, the ring seemed to me very big, huge . . . and now it doesn't.'

'But things change,' I explained to her. 'People change also. You know what Ovid tells about Philomena, who had no tongue, and was changed into a nightingale. Then Tagliacozzi learned to turn hooked noses into the kind of nose people wanted, like that of Queen Nefertiti. I myself was once as small and sparse as the catechism taught to me by none other than Aunt Luisa herself and I liked to play draughts with her after the Tower of Babel which, at that time, seemed to me to be a very amusing game. But no longer.'

'What else?' Estefania asked me.

'How do you mean, what else?'

'Give me another example.'

'It's very simple,' I told her. 'Forget all the histories of art produced during the last centuries. Look: in this book there is a picture by Monet: Rouen Cathedral. I always used to think it was a beautiful picture. But I have seen it so often, for so many hours of the day . . .'

'At four o'clock?'

385

'At four o'clock.'

'At six o'clock?'

'At twelve, at the ninth hour, at the noon hour, at the hour the elephants come down to drink and then, this morning, at seven on the dot more or less, it suddenly seemed to me that it was not beautiful and it had never – do you hear me? – *never* been so.'

'That everything should change so much seems to me to be very sad,' said Estefania pensively.

'It seemed sad to me too,' I answered her. 'But now that I think about it, I don't think it's either sad or happy. It simply is.'

Estefania went to make coffee and I continued reading my book. She came back a few minutes later but she was no longer pensive.

'Yesterday you complained to me that you didn't have money to pay all the overdue bills,' she said to me. 'What are we going to do?'

'Nothing: send our creditors to hell.'

'That's not what you thought yesterday.'

'Yesterday I was worried. Now I'm not.'

'Then, how are you?'

'I'm nothing – neither worried nor sad, nor happy nor cheerful, not anything. Why does one always have to *be something*?'

'Are you angry?'

'No, I'm not even angry,' I answered her.

A few minutes later Estefania said: 'Do you know? Something's happened . . .'

'What something?'

'I was going to say *something awful*. But no, it isn't awful. It is something . . . something . . . I don't know, I can't find the adjective.'

'Well, when you find it, let me know,' I suggested.

You will by now have guessed, Palinuro, what happened to us: a considerable time was to pass before Estefania found the adjective she sought because, during our last voyage through Niels Bohr's planetary systems (where, effectively, we heard the movement of hydrogen clouds, we greeted the cepheid stars and ascertained the sun's velocity of escape), the absence of gravity, as you will remember, caused all the things in our room to float from their places. But not only the things belonging to us, like the furniture, the paperweights, the books and the mirrors, but also the things that belonged to the things: all their virtues, defects, attributes. Hence, the things were left destitute. But no, not even destitute but rather, beyond – or before – Aristotelian *ousia* and Thomist substance, like the dead of many centuries of whom we have lost all memory and who are no longer fat, tall, evil, hard, cowardly or spongy and are not even, like others, historical or immortal dead. The difference, of course, is that our things weren't dead – although not for this reason were they alive – they simply

386

were, a reference unto themselves, like the words which call them by their name and you well know that there are no square words, nor words that are happy, nor words transparent as water. And they simply were because, of all the possible universes awaiting us at the end of our journeys, there was one . . . but no, it was not a possible universe and neither was it an impossible universe but a universe which simply was, and where adjectives, during a period lost in the night of time . . . or not even in a period lost or found, nor in a period past or future, undeserved or golden, but just a period . . . adjectives, I was saying, had rebelled and disappeared. And it is not that they were absent but simply that they *were* not.

We had fallen into that universe.

'Good God,' said Estefania. 'To think that we will never again drink a hot cup of coffee, read interesting books and buy cheap strawberries.'

'Well,' I countered, 'on the other hand, never again will we drink cold coffee, read bad books or buy expensive strawberries. Swings and roundabouts, you know!'

This didn't console Estefania. And, in truth, it didn't console me either, just thinking of all the things that would in practice cease to exist, never to be again. Never again would there be wide shoes, wild comets announcing the birth of princes and beggars, mourning flags adorning the dawn, warm and aged wines. Never to return imperial Christmases, long journeys, weathercocks surprised by the wind's force, never again would we learn of tangled jungles, unjust deaths, bald buds, rainy protectorates in the love of which wheat ripened. And an eternal end would come to red ties and cruel cities drowning in a tasselled hate of stars. Neither would Estefania and I ever be the same again: neither her blue eyes nor my warm hands; neither her silly expressions nor my immense love. Not even would the belfries, old, slender, luminous and sad, ever again be the same in time. Not even in a lost or recovered time but, simply, in time.

But I can't say that we were unhappy. Moreover, Estefania never again said: 'Good God!' because there was no point: in that universe, God was neither good, nor omnipotent, nor evil. Simply, God.

Several days went by.

But I don't know whether they were fast or slow, whether rainy or bright: I only know they went by and that Estefania walked street after street of the city asking everybody for the beautiful and the enormous, but nobody seemed to understand her. There were always those who pointed to the Monument of the Revolution, the ahuehuete trees of the Calzada de los Poetas in Chapultepec Park, to the volcanoes there in the distance presiding over the valley, to a poster of Salisbury Cathedral hanging in the window of a travel agency. Meanwhile, I devoted every minute of my life to searching my desk drawers for the lost and the unexpected. But there was not a single lead pencil, photograph of Grandfather Francisco arm-in-

387

arm in Orizaba Street with President Portes Gil or razor blade which had been lost and the finding of which, however hard I tried, was unexpected. We also placed advertisements in the newspapers offering rewards to those who found the unusual or mysterious. And then to our room in Holy Sunday Square came magicians who promised to produce the magical, the surprising and the abracadabradizing from the depths of their silk hats. Cousin Walter bought himself a 1940 Cadillac limousine, hired a chauffeur to take him from the Advertising Agency to Nicte-Há, and stowed in the boot of the car an infinite number of little boxes of all sizes and colours, full of marijuana. And the poor chap went to all this trouble just to show us the extravagant. As you may imagine, it was not long before we started receiving telephone calls from people who did not wish to give their names offering us the obscene and the anonymous. Moreover, when we went shopping in La Merced market, we used to empty the bags in which we had carried the vegetables to see if in the bottom we might find the green and the fresh. The final straw was when one afternoon we received a postcard telling us that if we went to number such-and-such in such-and-such a street at such-and-such a time, we would discover the false. But when we went we found that no such street existed. We were on the point of giving up all hope when one night Estefania said: 'All this is ridiculous.'

'I quite agree,' I answered her. 'It's ridiculous.'

Then I started in my bed. Neither a big start nor a little one, just a start. 'Do you realize what we've said?' I exclaimed. 'The word *ridiculous* is an adjective . . . that means . . . it means no less, Estefania, than that perhaps not all adjectives have disappeared from the world, that some have remained. Or it means that only one has remained. When I was in secondary school, I had a natural history teacher who said that everything was ridiculous.'

'That would be terrible,' I said to her.

'Frightful,' she said.

'Horrifying,' I said to her.

Estefania started in her turn.

'You're right. All is not lost. Besides ridiculous, we have another three adjectives. Isn't that marvellous!'

'Amazing,' I said to her.

'Fantastic,' she said.

'Incredible,' I said to her.

'Irreproachable,' concluded Estefania and, while I couldn't really see what the adjective *irreproachable* had to do with what was happening, she looked so happy, so calm and so naked, that I was loath to upset her.

A few minutes later, I said to her: 'Of course, nothing is lost. You know that after each of our journeys, when we put our feet back on the ground, all the things that floated away through lack of gravity also come back to earth. And the same goes for adjectives. It's just that adjectives take longer.'

'Why?'

'They take longer on account of a natural process,' I told her. 'When I was two years old, I knew what a house was: our grandparents' house. When I visited the houses of our cousins, I realized that it was a big house. When I learned the names of colours, I found that it was a grey house. And, many years later, I learned that our grandparents' house, besides being big and grey, was a very beautiful house.'

'How many years later?'

'Too many, perhaps twenty, when it no longer existed.'

'What a shame that there is no longer a house on which to place a plaque saying that you were born there,' said Estefania and, after a pause, added: 'although, really, it doesn't matter. There will always be a street in which to place a plaque saying "Palinuro was here". And we will place plaques in the cantinas, restaurants and hotels: "Palinuro ate here. Drank here, slept here, etc. here". And in the toilets, the cinemas, on the beaches and in the place where you die and where you are buried. And so, if you are not famous, you will at least be . . .'

'Just a minute,' I said to her, 'who told you that I'm Palinuro?'

'Whether or not you are Palinuro, nobody will be any the wiser when you are both dead,' she answered me.

But anyway, to return to the subject and as you may well imagine, we thought that from then onwards adjectives, winged and tame, would fall from the sky and repopulate the world as they appeared in the dirtiness of the streets, the white of the ambulances and the inattention of pedestrians.

'So things will, then, go back to how they always were,' said Estefania. 'Think how wonderful. The arches will again be triumphal when the adjectives parade beneath them.'

'Fountains will be fresh again when bathed by adjectives,' I told her.

'Beggars will be grateful once more when we give them adjectives,' said Estefania, who sometimes had an excessively bourgeois notion of justice. 'Ah, how I would like to have all adjectives in my hands and distribute them throughout the world. How just it would be to have poor rich people, intelligent idiots, giant dwarfs . . .'

'And you and I, Estefania, run the risk of becoming childish if we continue to mess around with adjectives, so let's go to sleep,' I said to her, thinking that, in fact, adjectives are like snow. First they are sensed in the air. Then they start to fall, very slowly. They are small and barely touch. Finally, you are buried in them and catch pneumonia. 'Tomorrow we will wake up buried under a mound of adjectives.'

And so it was, because that night we forgot to shut the window and through it entered first the cold and the rainy and then the desolate and the freezing and Estefania and I awoke numb, wet, tired, sleepy and sticky. But also optimistic, because we thought that we were to have a luminous morning and drink hot coffee, that the postman would bring us a very pretty postcard from friends who had gone on holiday to Greece to visit the Pírgos Islands and that on the radio we would hear ghastly news. And that we would be able to remember, this time certainly as though it had been something fantastic, the trip we made as children to Veracruz and the road to Antón Lizardo covered in orange crabs and the north wind which deposited the sand of the dunes in Aunt Luisa's cleavage, or I don't know what else from our childhood: on the one hand, Grandmother Altagracia who always combed her hair with an ivory comb and the teeth of the comb every day whitened a few more of her hairs, on the other hand, my other grandmother who sometimes spent whole afternoons looking at pieces of beechwood floating in the mother liquor of the vinegar. In other words, we thought that everything would return to how it had always been: lemons, sour; summer nights, white, and the orb of wines resplendent.

But life is not always as simple as one thinks it. And sometimes not even as one lives it. Even as children we had bad moments: every time I wanted to play pirates, Uncle Austin got scurvy, Papa Eduardo had a leg amputated and was given a wooden one and Mamma Clementina was hung in Haiti. And every time Estefania wanted to be a ballerina Uncle Felipe dressed up as a rich businessman to seduce her and Aunt Lucrecia aged ten years an hour and died with her lips eaten away by ether. So I gave up my dreams of becoming a pirate and Estefania hers of being a ballerina. Because things are not that simple, we were told, and only Aunt Luisa, Grandfather Francisco and sometimes Uncle Esteban gave us trunks full of applause and crowns of glory and crêpe paper.

I realized that things aren't that simple, next day, when I sat down to breakfast and started to remember the dreams I had had the night before.

'I don't understand,' I said to my cousin. 'Before, my dreams were always good or bad, pleasant or unpleasant. But last night everything was different – I had sharp dreams, red dreams, acid dreams. I don't understand . . .'

'Don't worry, it must have been over-excitement. Would you like toast and marmalade?'

Estefania went to the kitchen and a few minutes later uttered a shout: 'Come here! Come quickly!'

I ran to the kitchen.

'Look!' she said to me. 'The bread is green.'

'How can it be? Yesterday it was white,' I said, grabbing a slice and seeing that, in effect, the bread *was green*.

'And that's nothing: worse things have happened. Do you know what

390

this is?' Estefania asked me, showing me a silver metal sphere which I had never seen before.

'I have no idea,' I said to her. 'Where did that come from?'

'It's the carving knife.'

'Knife? Are you mad? Knives are long, thin, sharp . . .'

'Of course: that's how they are when they have the correct adjectives. But the wrong adjective landed on this knife – it's a spherical knife.'

We didn't need to discuss things any further to realize what awaited us. It is true that, every time we made a journey, objects eventually recovered their weight and returned again to our room. It is also true that never, or very rarely, did they fall in the places they had occupied previously. This, however, was not irreparable: you can always take a pair of stockings out of the soup, wash the stockings and boil the soup, or take a pearl necklace out of the toilet, boil the necklace and wash your hands. You can also nail down the carpet again, remove the dirty plates from under the bed and put things back in their places. What is more difficult, virtually impossible, is for things to become again what they had ceased to be and to cease to be what they had become. You will appreciate the extent of the tragedy: imagine that before a very long journey you have not only a name for everything but also an adjective for every name and that when you come back from your travels you find that nothing is in its place, that many adjectives have landed where they weren't supposed to and that other adjectives are roaming around out there lost in space and can fall or appear from one moment to the next and you have to spend your time, day after day, making an inventory of each and every one of the objects that you have in your room to find out which has the correct adjective, which the wrong adjective, which an extra adjective and which, finally, has no adjective at all.

At first we are loath to acknowledge the truth. But, just as one's eyes gradually adjust to shadows, so we assimilated the idea and discovered, then, that the house contained a frightful chaos of adjectives:

In the bath floated the dirty and the superfluous.

The unpopulated had crept into the pantry and the useless had invaded the bookshelves.

Beneath the carpets hid the oriental and the obvious.

And into my novel had fallen the hyperbolic and the hollow.

And we had the distinct impression that the overwhelming and the desperate hung in the air ready to pounce on the task we were undertaking.

But, fortunately, it was not so: both the good and the bad had settled on our luck, and therefore we sometimes had the good luck of being able to do it and, at others, the bad luck of not doing anything.

We decided first to round up the adjectives that were roaming loose and put them in their respective places:

391

The glorious we used for a spring day.

The aristocratic we threw in the rubbish bin along with the details of our genealogical forests.

The coquettish was attributed by Estefania to a bikini which she put on that same day.

The new – which was also on the loose because all the things in our room were very old – we stowed away in a new little box which we bought specially.

The casuistic, the allotropic and other very difficult adjectives which were virtually incomprehensible to Estefania, we shut up in the *Royal Academy Dictionary* with the intention of never using them.

The unfortunate, finally, we dealt with a blow of the broom to our resident mouse who had always terrified Estefania.

When we saw the state the poor thing ended up in, I allocated him the dead while the compassionate Estefania kept for herself.

We agreed to attribute the contradictory to the situation.

The second step was to draw up a detailed list of all our objects, with all their customary attributes and defects, in order to make everything as it should be: the heavy, heavy; the translucent, translucent and the fair, fair.

Within a few days, almost everything was in order. I say almost, because we had a few failures. Monet's picture, it is true, had lost the beautiful. On our next trip to Paris, however, we visited the Jeu de Paume and gazed at Rouen Cathedral throughout the hours of a morning and an afternoon and, after immersing ourselves in its spurious reflections and lengthening shadows, we had to admit that it was a beautiful picture.

It is also true that the game of draughts ceased to be amusing. But, on our return to Mexico, we played a game and meanwhile reminisced about funny incidents during our childhood, among them Estefania's terror of swallowing orange pips because she thought they would grow in her stomach and knotted roots eventually emerge from her anus and orange blossom from her mouth. We laughed so much, that we played another game of draughts because it seemed a highly amusing pastime.

We could do nothing with Uncle Esteban's ring: twiddle the circle of gold and multiply its amethyst digits as we would, it never again seemed to us a huge ring.

So, we were left with the huge on our hands, together with another two adjectives: the unknown and the blue, which hovered in the middle of the room not knowing where to fall. Nothing in our room was huge. Nothing was unknown. Finally, everything that had to be blue, including Estefania's nightdress and blue eyes, a blue bedspread, our blue dinner service and our blue-jacketed books, including the blue covers of Adan Buenosayres notebooks, were just that: blue.

Some sky, some navy, some light and others royal, depending on their humour and their aspirations, but all blue.

And so the days went by: Estefania made love with an unknown man, we had blue weeks, heaved huge sighs. At other times, I wrote a huge book, we ate unknown apples, we lived in a blue universe. And during yet another period we went to an unknown restaurant, we ate a blue dish, paid a huge bill.

And so on and so forth, until we got tired of it.

The story ends when we went over to the window – our problems were always resolved when we looked out of the window, from which we could see a small, grey and familiar sky. And so it was this time: we opened the window, the sun came out at that moment and we allowed all the final adjectives to fly towards the huge, blue and unknown sky.

No, the story doesn't end here, because I don't think it is a short story, unless of course, you think so. I don't think so, because others have thought it long, though not endless, despite the fact that, in a certain sense, it might never end. Of course, in another less certain sense, it never started because it was not a true story, as I know some friends of Estefania's have remarked. But neither is it untrue, of this I myself, who lived it, can assure you. These and many others were the conclusions Estefania and I reached some time later, when we realized that, once we had decided to relate our story, its adjectives were no longer dependent on us and, for the same reason, it would seem to some people to be an impossible story and to others a silly story and to others a boring story. Uncle Esteban, for example, thought it an ingenious and amusing story. Mamma Clementina said that it was pretty. Ricardo the gardener reacted as though we had told him an incomprehensible story. Aunt Luisa exclaimed that it was an obscure story and, in reward, presented us with an invisible rose. Cousin Walter thought it was a trite story and also thought it trite that Aunt Luisa gave us a rose. Grandfather Francisco, for his part, was of the opinion that it was an excessively subtle and involved story although he did promise, as a consolation prize, to take us to see the lions the next time the circus came to Mexico City. Estefania and I were happy – if it is possible to be happy in this world – to know that our story would, in all events, always be something to somebody and not simply a story without adjective in life.

20

The Priaprank

By the Floral clock, it was five in the morning. By the night watchmen's unions, the violet-sellers' stands and the midnight concerts, it was twelve midday of the next day. By Aunt Luisa's tear clock, it was twelve fifteen left bank of the Seine time. By the migrating flight of the Peking ships, it was three in the afternoon. By Big Ben and the fertile corridors of London, it was eleven in the morning. By the South Sea Islands, it was three thirty-three in the morning of the previous day. By Grandfather Francisco's bald pate, the spasms of the port of Singapore, the glassy atmosphere of Brussels and the ancient quietude of Venice, it was sixteen hours and thirty seconds. Finally, by the blue spire of the Latin American Tower in Mexico City, it was seven in the morning.

Fabricio said that, to change the future, he had not only to turn all the clocks of the world back ten thousand hours, but he also needed some martyred bat's wings, the blood of a swallow, three tail feathers of a Quaker chicken and a hundred grams of a powder made up from a magic formula. Since the chemists and herb-sellers in Carmen Street were not open at that hour, Fabricio started searching in the cupboard, in the bottomless trunk, in the manila-paper-coloured chiffonier standing in a mysterious corner of the room and behind the curtains. He found Palinuro's warm ties, his undarned socks, a Salamancan student's cape, old shirts stained with green salt, Grandfather Francisco's congressman's identification card, a box of exploding lemurs, a stapler, a paperweight with flowers stranded in its centre, a knife of beaten fire and a wormy apple. But, since he did not find what he wanted, he decided to change the socks into bats, the apple into an eagle's heart, the paperweight into a living solitude and then to transform himself into a magician of another era, of the type that knew the power of electuaries, the secrets of fluidic larvae, the seventy-two elements of the Shem ha-Meforash of the name of Jehovah and all existing and future *mancies*: in other words, into an Adalbert, into a Diodorus Siculus, into a Le Lover. But Fabricio knew – since he was not stupid – that, to undertake these transformations, he would require other ingredients: a snake's tongue wrapped in virgin wax, two ounces of thousand-flower water, an ace of diamonds, a spring Friday. In vain also did he seek them beneath the pillow and in the darkrooms where photographs and adulteries are developed. He therefore decided to create these ingredients out of others: an eclipse of the moon, a salamander, two maggots' teeth, a stab in the back with a dagger of water, a cascade of lions, a bottle's laughter and a necklace of witches' warts threaded on a violin string, which ingredients he could in turn obtain from two goose testicles, a second-hand dinner jacket and two blue velvet roses which he could produce, he reckoned, from a tin containing eucalyptus pastilles, two histology tomes, a sponge soaked in the bile of a Home Office minister and three silver candlesticks with angels' wings. All of which, of course, turned up in the room: the horses shitting in the bed, the snowy salamander dancing in blue velvet fire, Aunt Lucrecia moistening her tongue in a jar of melted wax given to her by Fabricio, and Palinuro's testicles dressed in a dinner jacket and goose-stepping through the Champs Elysées, on the condition, of course, of collecting in that room, small and sad as a sub-let paradise, all the ingredients of the world.

A few seconds later, Fabricio had found all he needed and thus satisfied Palinuro's desire.

The woman's body started to awaken in the most unexpected places. A small profusion of reflections marked the outer confines of her skin in those spots where it was whitest and most suffocating. The woman raised her arms and the shadows of the morning entwined around her nipples like innocent ivy. She slightly parted her legs and displayed the result of a long journey – dead butterflies, beetles with their wings covered in pollen, dragonflies destroyed at the speed of light. Her flesh, like dark waves, broke over her thighs. Finally, endless processions of white ants which carried away her milk, travelled up her belly like a shiver, reached the alpine and exquisite regions, reached her breasts which started to fill and change – how Molkas would have loved to see that miracle – into breasts perfumed by screens.

But Molkas wasn't there.

Neither was Fabricio there, to exclaim: 'She's alive! She's alive!'

The price Palinuro had to pay for changing the future was the loss of his friends; never again would he know them.

In their memory – in the memory he would never have of them – Palinuro caressed the woman's body with Fabricio's hands to assist the revelation of the flesh. First, he touched her on the forehead. Then, on the unblemished dip of her lip. Then he placed his hand on the woman's throat and gently smoothed the shape of her breast, of her belly, of her thighs, of the universe. A slight tingling in his fingertips told him that she had started to feel the red torture of the blood, its almost biblical ebb and flow, its passage through the nets and tubes which would return her to life and warmth to her hands, the tip of her ears, her big toes. It was the blood, the blood beating in her lips demanding citizenship and galloping towards providential abysms, blue forests and magic haemorrhoids. And he knew that the woman's skin was contagious, that as he caressed it with Fabricio's hands it crept over his fingers like gloves and travelled over his body and wrapped around his penis and held it erect and he knew that he would never be the same again.

The woman opened her eyes and Palinuro, with Molkas' eyes, gazed at them and gazed at himself in them. And he saw that the woman's eyes were no longer the shattered domes through which filtered frozen stars and luminous chrysanthemum bulbs quenched by the wind. A circular rainbow pierced her pupils, trembling like irises on the skin of a fable and in them was reflected the window overlooking the square and the kingdom, Palinuro's face with Molkas' eyes crossed by nocturnal threads and there, far away, in the centre of a mandala, imprisoned in a prism, she herself, the woman, could be seen.

With his own lips, Palinuro kissed her mouth. And he knew that her breath was fresh and burning as absinthe and that it filled his mouth and throat with oceans and beds of transparent lakes and with a blue and green honey, as blue as walking through a tale, as green as spending the afternoon beneath a bridge, and he felt how it flooded his lungs, almost drowning him, with its aquatic repertoire of melted cobalt, poplar leaves, heavenly automobiles . . .

He knew, then, that Mamma Clementina was well off where she was: dead and buried; and that history – not the history of the world, but just his own, Palinuro's – had been a nightmare from which he was finally awakening and the woman was clean and alive and magnificent and had always been so and was called Estefania and had always been called so.

The awakening was slow, like a day dawning, like a town lathering itself in soap and surprised at its triumphs, temples, its wild intestines, the rain which starts to murmur a tense hymn: a rain which was nothing, less than drizzle, but, nevertheless, it was known at what moment it exploded in warm contact with the plants and its drumming could be heard on the fusilages of aeroplanes in flight.

However, before forgetting his friends Molkas and Fabricio for good, before learning that he would never – or perhaps never – meet them, Palinuro had the opportunity to experience with them two further great adventures: the Priaprank and Charon's Cave.

While they were in their anatomy class, Molkas explained to Palinuro and Fabricio just what the prank involved:

'First take three fresh corpses and sever their proportional incarnation of much-vaunted prestige. In other words, the cock.'

'The what!' asked Palinuro.

'The thing, you know . . .' intervened Fabricio, 'or don't you know what a cock is? Have you never heard of the virile member or penis, also called in the eighteenth century the *Arbor Vitae*, the purpose of which is to perpetuate the species by penetration of the *Frutex Vulvaria*? Have you never heard of a phallus? Or the Cainites who in the shape of this organ worshipped death because their creation was an infinite onanism and their redemption an eternal abortion?'

'Have you never heard of bone number two hundred and seven?' asked Molkas in his turn. 'In other words, bone at the age of twenty, muscle at fifty and flaccid skin at seventy?'

'Yes, yes, I know,' answered Palinuro. 'But all hell will be let loose.'

Just then Professor Flores arrived, wiped the sweat from his brow and neck with a grey handkerchief and, without preamble, sat down and started the class.

'Temporomaxillary articulation,' he said. 'Let me see . . . Rodríguez, describe the articular capsule and other types of joints.'

'OK: so all hell will be let loose,' agreed Molkas. 'But the general public will never get to hear of it. Do you think that there is a newspaper in Mexico capable of publishing a headline like: "Three cocks disappear from the School of Medicine"? No way. Our theft will one day become as famous as that of Eurytus's foals or Amyntor's crown, or even the Great Train Robbery in England; not because it will be published by the mass media but because it will pass from mouth to mouth, in the best traditions of the epic poem of ancient times. And it will be called . . . it will be called . . .'

'. . . zygomatic process . . .' said Rodríguez.

'Very good,' said Professor Flores, lighting a cigarette.

'No, I don't believe that that would be a good name,' said Molkas.

'How about Priaprank, then?' suggested Fabricio.

'Full marks,' exclaimed Molkas.

'You, gentlemen, at the back: if you're not interested in the class, you may leave,' shouted the professor.

'We're interested, we're interested!'

'Be quiet, then. Pterygomaxillary ligament, Navarrete.'

Palinuro nudged Molkas and whispered: 'Have you seen how his hands shake? How can he be a surgeon with hands that shake like a parliamentary stenographer's? He looks as though he's slicing jelly in the air . . .'

'Shhhhh! He'll throw us out of the class,' warned Fabricio.

'On the contrary: he's shaking because he's *not* operating. He's a sadist who has sublimated his homicidal instincts by becoming a surgeon,' said Molkas. 'You should see him when he's in the operating theatre. The moment he sinks his knife into soft tissue he achieves a millimetric precision: he's capable of performing a vasectomy on a mosquito. Now listen: the second step is to take the cocks to the room. In fact, perhaps it would be better if we got hold of four or five. Men, like cars, need spare parts. Then . . .'

'Gentlemen! This is your last chance: either you pay attention, or . . .'
The three friends paid attention.

In the student canteen, Molkas told Palinuro of some of the myths circulating about Charon. 'But is that his real name?' 'Of course. The very same as the oarsman on Lake Styx, son of Erebus and Night. Except that in his case he's called Charon Pérez.' Some said that as a young man he was a fisherman back in his place of birth, the Turkmen Republic, and that he had sought to flee with a friend's wife and was making for the coast of Persia when his boat was shipwrecked but a few kilometres from land and he had swum ashore dragging his beloved, but she was already dead and Charon, like Dimetes of mythology, watched his woman rot on the beach. Much later, having enlisted in the Greek merchant navy, Charon arrived in Mexico. Others said that this was all a story and that in truth Charon had been born in San Rafael, a little village in Veracruz where lived descendants of the bastard children of some Frenchman, and that this was why Charon had blue eyes and white skin but that, for the rest, he was as Indian as anyone else and that his accent was due to a congenital malformation of the palate. Whatever the case, it was known for certain that Charon had worked for many years in the School of Medicine, first as porter and then as custodian of the dissecting room and that of course 'Charon' – regardless of what Molkas might say – was only a nickname, unlike his dog who really was called Cerberus, not only because he had been thus baptized by a whole generation of students but also because he had inherited the name of his father – or perhaps his grandfather – who had in turn been baptized by a previous generation of students. But then other rumours would have it that Charon had worked in a maternity ward before going to the School of Medicine and fed his first dog on placentas and foetuses. The first dog's descendants, among them the current Cerberus, had to be satisfied with the stomachs and hearts of corpses. Charon had been working in the School for four or five years when he asked permission to wash the bodies and attend dissections during his spare time. Later, he learned to embalm by injecting them with zinc chloride and alcohol. Later, he somehow managed to perform a hydrotomy and, to cap it all, he proved to be an expert dissector. There was none to match him in making anatomical preparations which Professor Flores qualified as 'beautiful' although many students – Fabricio and Palinuro anyway – could not see what beauty had to do with a severed hand placed on a block with a nail in each finger and a series of flaps of skin held apart by hooks, while other hooks or forceps elevated the tendons. 'In short, Charon is the man,' said Molkas, 'to supply us with the male members.' 'Mutilations of this kind,' added his friend, 'shouldn't surprise Palinuro, as far worse things have been done in the dissecting room. Or rather, much better things. He assured him that events related in books like *Bodies and Souls*, for example the exploits of medical students who dropped human ears among the chips sold outside the Odeón, were more than just ribald literature: 'Future men of science, when heart transplants are perfected,' he said, 'will have to admit that this humble but beloved School of Holy Sunday Square was decades ahead of its time. I will invite you one day to a multiple transplant. We choose four or five fresh and unknown corpses and transplant the famous muscle of the first to the second, the second to the third and so on successively. Although a woman's heart is smaller than a man's – you will learn that it weighs on average fifty grams less – we do not believe in sexual discrimination, so we transplant hearts regardless of sex. The result is a pastoral novel in itself: Mario has Olivetta's heart; Lucinda, Mario's heart; Orazio, Lucinda's; Smeraldina, Orazio's; Leondro, Smeraldina's and Florinda, Leandro's. So the circle is completed, but it is a vicious circle because Florinda is lesbian and Olivetta has her heart. But there are other transplants and mutilations which are much more amusing,' continued Molkas. 'Before Flores we had another dissection professor who we called Magoo because he was blinder than an art critic. You would never believe the jokes we played. Once we sewed a male member to the vulva of a young girl and the poor old guy thought that he was going to go down in medical history when, in the Academy, he related what for a moment he believed to be an extraordinary case of superprotandrous hermaphroditism. The day he found a corpse with three kidneys, he thought that he had been visited by the Ides of March. Then we decided to play more elaborate jokes and went shopping in San Juan Market, to give the old man the pleasure of finding a sea urchin in a young man's stomach. Need I say more?' Although, in fact, he did say more: he assured Palinuro that in fact nobody was going to learn of the disappearance of the penises since nobody counted the corpses entering the school. Well, only Charon did, but he kept two sets of records. Moreover, Charon was a wonderful supplier of bones. It was said that he was in league with the caretaker of the Dolores Graveyard and that they stole bones from the old communal graves to sell to the students. 'Shall we go to Charon's Cave one day?'

The afternoon was warm when the three friends gathered in the room in Holy Sunday Square.

Molkas arrived with a black medical bag. He opened it and placed the four penises on the bed.

'Here's the booty,' he said and he picked up the penises, held them in a bunch in his hand and paraded around the room with his hand aloft, like

399

the Ithyphallus of the Dionysian festivals or like a bullfighter who has just severed the bull's ear and tail, nose and balls. And the friends were struck by how the nacarine beauty of the flesh, the butterfly light and shade hiding the spongy urethras and the cavernous bodies of the penises filled with troglodytic desires, lent the penises a bird-like dignity. In effect, it seemed that at any moment the penises would turn into pigeons and take flight from the hands of Paolo Uccello. Some, flying towards the left, would bear sinister tidings for humanity, raining down on the heads of mankind every manner of derision and obligation. The others, bearing a sprig of melodious licorice in their beaks, would fly towards the right completing the Victory V and bringing the universe a message of peace and fertility; down the sloping roofs will innocently slide Halloween pumpkins; coachmen, in their drivers' seats, will blow trios in bladders full of orange-blossom water.

Molkas started the miraculous distribution of the penises: 'To you, Palinuro, I entrust this black and hairy penis which reminds me of the frankness with which Professor Santisteban spoke on sexual matters . . .'

He coughed axiomatically and continued: 'For you, Fabricio, this member long and pale, which must have belonged to an illegitimate descendant of Charles V who, as you know . . .'

'. . . wielded his cock with a deft flick of the wrist,' said Palinuro and Fabricio.

'. . . and therefore contains over seven hundred veins through which blue sperm flows. Finally, I have kept for myself the one that is most similar to my own, but minus the tattoo which I had done on a particular occasion when I tinged my experience with the colours of every sea. In a brothel on Yellow Sea Street, I picked up a golden staphylococcus. In another brothel in Red Sea Street, a wine-coloured gonococcus. And so on, in the shadow of blossoming maidens . . . Anyway . . . Here also you have a good supply of pins and a pair of scissors each. I have just sharpened them. They cannot fail. You can have a ball and chop it in two at three in the morning.'

Then he demonstrated the technique they should use.

'With both hands take hold of the loose skin underneath, like that, that's right, as though holding a condom. You position it against your fly, which has been previously unbuttoned. That's it. You hold it in place with one hand. OK. With the other, you take the first pin and fasten the skin to the inner seam of the cloth. Uh-huh. Then with the other hand, you take another pin and fasten the skin on the other side. Excellent. And so you continue, until it is firmly attached . . . well, in a manner of speaking. In fact, it is held on with pins, like the penises of syphilitics in the quaternary stage. You leave it hanging, outside the trousers. There, very good! Now do up the top and bottom buttons. Don't fondle it too much because fame might go to its head and it would turn into its own obelisk: we would be in danger then, of wetting the flowers on our hats. Perfect, lads.'

Molkas tiptoed over to Fabricio, clutched the dead man's hanging penis and exclaimed: 'It's complete madness!'

'*Noli me tangere*,' warned Fabricio.

'Swear to me that it's not your own? I think you're deceiving us.'

Modesty sealed Fabricio's lips. However, a few minutes later, he ventured to say: 'I swear on my mother, may she rest in peace from these and other pranks.'

'It's a masterpiece,' said Molkas, absorbed in contemplation of the dead man's penis. 'Its aggressiveness proves it.'

'Don't try any futurism,' warned Palinuro.

'Finally,' said Molkas, returning to normality, 'take one large raincoat, put it on and button it up.'

'But it's very hot,' complained Fabricio.

'Without a raincoat, you can't play the joke. Anyway, penises have to be hidden at all times. We're not living during the days when the maenads paraded through the streets with an enormous *Phallus* erected on the processional carriage. But let's stick to the point: you'll also need, as I told you, a pair of sharp scissors which should be placed in your right pocket. Or in your left pocket, of course, if either of you are left-handed as I am.'

Then, though the afternoon was warm, they were to be seen leaving the house in long, slate-coloured raincoats and striding along the streets of the city centre.

'Watch out for the police,' said Molkas.

'Here comes one now,' warned Palinuro.

'Make out you haven't seen him,' said Molkas.

The three young men formed a single file and walked each with a hand on the shoulder of the one in front of them.

'That's it, lads, like Brueghel's blind men. Let it not be said that we aren't cultured.'

'Where are we going?' asked Fabricio.

'There is a whiff of peaches from the Peloponnese,' said Palinuro.

'We must be near the fruit market.'

And they forged ahead, dodging metallic hazards of all kinds. By them rushed ambulances and fire engines, leaving a trail of resins and imperfect shouts. But naturally: 'I have no wish to die young and beautiful,' said Molkas, half-opening his eyes when they had to cross streets.

'I detect the faintest scent of ripening cunts and sprouting pubic hairs imbued with love and piniferous acids,' said Palinuro.

'We're about to reach the Secondary School,' predicted Fabricio.

'Where the boys follow the girls with a constancy of amber, eyes riveted to the backs of their knees, there where the skin peeps above their socks,' completed Molkas.

They made right turns and left turns and walked straight ahead. They walked, blindly, past the windows of the Centro Mercantil store, devoted to the revelation of Sèvres porcelain, Royal Worcester dinner services and Doulton Tyrolese boys in their short trousers singing with cold: *Ailiroli, ailiroluuuuù!* And suddenly Palinuro detected a series of smells which brought him myrurgic memories: 'I can smell Marlène de Luxe, Dandy Male, Tangee Lipstick,' he said.

'That's because we're in the perfume department of the Palacio de Hierro department store,' replied Molkas.

They opened their eyes and found this to be so. Molkas approached the counter and, with an impartial air, asked for: 'Lanvin Arpège, please. And Lentheric Miracle. I have a girlfriend,' he explained, 'who has secretory glands behind her ears. But first, I would like to smell them.'

Molkas took the atomizer, sprayed the back of his hand and raised it to his nose.

Then, the symptoms started to appear: the floating aura surrounding delirium: 'Something hurts,' said Molkas, 'but I don't know what.'

Then he looked at his friends with an expression of infinite astonishment and, while they tried to find out what ailed him, whether the second cervical vertebra, the throat or the seventh commandment, he again raised the back of his hand to his nose and exclaimed: 'Ah, ah!' and started to jump up and down. Palinuro and Fabricio each took one of his arms, determined to prevent him from ascending body and soul; he was in danger (they explained to the salesladies) of breaking the skylight, getting caught up in the blades of a helicopter, interrupting the pollination of the angels and, in some degree, upsetting the luxuriance of the orb.

'Ah, ah!' exclaimed Molkas yet again, then his eyes crossed and he turned as pale as a tower of vinegar about to ferment, uttered an inarticulate bellow and fell full length on the floor: his full, young, student's length.

'What's wrong with him? What's wrong with the young man?' asked the saleslady.

'At this particular moment, the voltage of the entire public lighting system is going through his head,' replied Palinuro, proof to panic.

'You must do something!' said the other lady.

'Of course,' exclaimed Palinuro. 'Why didn't I think of that? Quickly, alcohol, smelling salts, anything, but quickly!'

Fabricio, after checking for rubefaction, mydriasis, perspiration and other neuro-vegetative symptoms, pronounced his diagnosis: 'Don't panic, ladies, keep calm, this is merely the tonic phase . . .'

'It's a heart attack,' said the other lady.

'Of course it's an attack: but of the ailment suffered by the cuckoo once a month,' explained Palinuro.

'Call the doctor!' said the other lady.

'An attack of so-called Hercules' Curse, with which the Elatian devils punished men,' said Fabricio.

'Call an ambulance!'

'An attack of the disease for which Joseph de Chesne prescribed swallows' water,' added Palinuro.

'Call the manager!'

'This is followed by the clonic phase,' added Fabricio, 'characterized by rhythmic and synchronized contractions of all the muscles.'

And, in effect, Molkas was beset by convulsions and an unsightly foam issued from his mouth.

'He's foaming at the mouth,' shrieked the saleslady.

'Oh, oh, oh!' wailed the other ladies.

'And now comes the indecent exposure, look out!' predicted Fabricio, although he was no fortune-teller.

Molkas jumped up, hammered his chest three times with clenched fists like King Kong, said 'Ah!' three times, whipped open his raincoat three times and three times revealed the dead man's prick which, of course, appeared three times to be his own. The customers shrieked, the saleslady dropped a bottle containing eight liquid ounces of Jean Marie-Farina lotion and Fabricio and Palinuro, blushing scarlet with embarrassment, tried to subdue Molkas.

But, it was already too late: Molkas, rolling his eyes and grunting symphonically, took the scissors from his raincoat pocket and, with the courage and determination of Attis on his wedding day, snipped the penis in two.

The severed end fell into the pool of perfume and ladies fainted right, left and centre.

'Next follows the fugitive phase,' said Fabricio as the three friends made a dash for it and, running for all they were worth, shot out of the store, crossed Constitución Square (not without pausing to salute the flag: Molkas the invalid saluted the colour green, Fabricio the pale saluted the white and Palinuro the shy saluted the red stripe), past the Monte de Piedad pawnshop, down Tacuba, Donceles and San Ildefonso, so reaching Holy Sunday Square where they collapsed on the edge of an improvised fountain.

'That was hysterical!' panted Fabricio. 'Did you see the little fat lady's face?'

'Never, in all my debauched life, have I had such fun,' stated Palinuro. 'And you, Molkas, were fantastic. Molkas! Molkas, I'm talking to you, speak to me!'

'Shhhh! He's still in his role,' warned Fabricio. 'In a second, he will stop breathing: apnoea, dear colleague.'

'The poor thing is going to suffocate on us.'

'Don't worry, it only lasts a few seconds. It is followed by a phenomenal grunt . . .'

Molkas belched.

'You see? The belch smells of Cardiazol and Cambray onions. A period of amnesia will follow and when he wakes up he will say: Who am I? Where am I?'

'OK, Molkas, a joke's a joke,' said Palinuro, threatening to slap his face.

'Don't do that, you might traumatize him.'

'When a joke goes on too long, it's not funny any more.'

'Then perhaps it's not a joke,' suggested Fabricio. 'Perhaps our poor friend Molkas really is epileptic. Perhaps he's suffered a cranial traumatism or acute encephalitis or is in the habit of dabbing himself with strychnine in the cortical area . . .'

'It could be a syphiloma or a gaseous embolus caused by an off-course fart.'

'Do you think?'

'Everything is possible in this life. Just look at the symptoms. The world's best actor couldn't simulate them with such mastery.'

'So what are we going to do?'

'Just wait.'

'Do you think we could play our joke in the tram?'

'Never.'

'In a church?'

'Impossible.'

'Where then?'

'Nowhere, we were extremely lucky to get away with it this time.'

'But what are we going to use all those penises for?'

'Penises can always be put to good use.'

'Anyway, I'm famished. Let's carry this lad back to the room.'

'We don't have to carry him: he's in the somnambulistic stage. We'll just take his little hand in ours and lead him slowly, without waking him . . .'

When they reached the room in Holy Sunday Square, they laid him on the bed and unbuttoned his shirt, removed his shoes and socks and closed his eyes.

'What shall we do?' Palinuro asked again.

'Just wait,' Fabricio repeated.

'Are you sure he's epileptic?'

Fabricio resolutely flipped through the Vade-mecum.

'We can confirm another symptom: the Babinsky sign. Tickle his feet.'

'I'm doing it.'

'Is his big toe standing straight up?'

'Yes.'

'There's no doubt about it: our friend is epileptic.'

'What a tragedy. We will commend him to the Three Kings, writing their names on parchment, as Jean de Ardenne recommends.'

'One last thing, involuntary ejaculation is common during epileptic attacks . . . undo his fly.'

Palinuro sat down on the bed beside Molkas and started to unbutton his fly.

'Wait a minute, don't do it!' shouted Fabricio, distraught.

'Why not?'

'I've just had a ghastly idea: just imagine that, with all the confusion, our poor friend Molkas, instead of . . . instead of . . .'

'Instead of what?'

'No, no, I can't say it . . . it would be too grotesque! Just imagine, my God! that instead of cutting the dead man's prick in two, Molkas cut off his own!'

'It doesn't bear thinking about.'

'But it's possible!'

'In that case, our friend Molkas is bleeding to death!'

'We have to face life with courage and determination. Palinuro, take off his trousers.'

Palinuro took off Molkas' trousers.

Fabricio covered his eyes with his hands: 'I haven't the courage to look,' he said and asked: 'Is it or isn't it?'

'Well, there's certainly a bulge of some sort in his underpants.'

'That's not enough. Take them off.'

Palinuro removed Molkas' underpants.

'Is it intact or isn't it?' asked Fabricio, peeping between two fingers.

'It is! It is!' exclaimed Palinuro jubilantly.

'It is! It is!' chorused Fabricio and rushed to the bed to gaze on Molkas' virility.

'There's yet another ghastly possibility . . .' said Palinuro.

'I don't see what: this has every appearance of being a penis.'

'But, are you sure that it's his? What if it's the dead man's?'

'I don't know. But it's easy enough to find out!'

'You're quite right. Dead men's penises are cold.'

Fabricio put on his surgical gloves: 'In effect, it's frozen.'

'Mmmmm . . . bad, very bad. However, the test is not conclusive. Give it a tug to see if it comes off,' said Palinuro.

Fabricio stretched out his hand, preparing to give the penis a little tug. For a moment he was afraid of ending up with it in his hand, as Horus did with Set's member.

'Let's see . . . this is all in the name of science . . . first one little tug to the left, then another to the right, that's it, great, left – right, left – right, left – right, about turn, OK!'

'Did it come off?' asked Palinuro, whose turn it had been to shut his eyes.

'No,' said Fabricio. 'But something very strange is going on: it has fever and it's turning hard . . .'

'I knew it!' exclaimed Palinuro. 'It's the tonic stage . . .'

'And now . . . now . . . good God! Green foam is coming out of the . . .'

'It's the clonic stage,' said Palinuro.

'Queers, you goddamn queers!' shouted Molkas, leaping from the bed. 'Brutes, pederasts, degenerates! Taking advantage of a poor unconscious epileptic! Go fuck yourselves, you buggers, I'm going to beat the shit out of you!'

But the effort was too much for him. He collapsed back on the bed and gazed at his erect manhood.

'Now look at the state you've got him into, poor thing, naked and confused . . . what am I going to do?'

'If you like, we can have a competition,' Palinuro suggested.

'Yes, yes, I know: see who's got the longest one. See who can spit the furthest. I know them all: any modern novel about adolescence has two creeps doing exactly that. Well: this will be an exception to the rule.'

And, no sooner said than done, in the wink of a button, Molkas was dressed again.

And a few moments later, the three young men were inseparable friends once more.

'While you were in a coma,' Fabricio and Palinuro told him, 'we decided not to play the joke again: a second time would be bound to go wrong.'

'I don't agree,' said Molkas.

Indifferent to his friends' opinion and quite irrelevantly, Fabricio recited aloud a quatrain by José Asunción Silva: '*De los filósofos etereos/Huye la enseñanza teatral/y aplícate buenos cauterios/en el chancro sentimental* . . . Theatrical teaching flees from ethereal philosophers and be sure to apply good cauteries to your sentimental chancre.'

'Gentlemen, if you don't make up your minds,' warned Molkas, 'the cocks will go off.'

He opened the bag and examined them: 'OK, for the time being, they appear to have a pacific consistency.'

They decided that chance, the same chance which threatened Palinuro from the pavement in the guise of a king of spades, should decide for them.

'Do you see the spire of the church belfry?' asked Molkas, pointing through the eternally open window. Palinuro saw the tower, slim and bathed in sun like a sentinel of summer and, behind it, the clear blue sky, newly painted.

'Well,' continued Molkas, 'if a white dove comes along and commits suicide by impaling itself on the tip of the spire, it means that we will repeat the prank.'

'OK,' said Palinuro, wondering what rare bird might commit such disrespect to the colour white. Fabricio ventured to suggest that if Molkas was so determined, they could play the joke on the whores of Las Vizcaínas Street.

'There is not a single prostitute around there who hasn't known that joke since Quiroz failed anatomy three times,' pointed out Molkas.

Palinuro continued to gaze out of the window. At last a dove appeared, flying just above the ground and raising waltzes of dust and footprints of pedestrians which followed its ascent. Then four partridges flew by on their way to Icarus's funeral. And also the eagle and the goose seen by Aeneas flying towards the right, and the muses turned by Apollo into magpies. And Itys the goldfinch and Tereus the hoopoe and Procne the swallow. Then Ibis, the sacred bird of Egypt, flew by and later a white duck which fluttered in the golden porticos announcing that the Gauls were at the gates of Rome. The dove returned and perched momentarily on the rim of the Siloam, the fountain of silent waters, before taking wing yet again.

'All this is loaded with symbolism,' commented Fabricio, not without a certain tenderness. 'Some day a psychiatrist will discover that the male member is a phallic symbol.'

Ideas, like supplies, grew increasingly scarce.

'Let's make a list of all the black and bloody jokes we can think of,' suggested Molkas.

And this they did: to send three of the penises, by registered post, to ninety-year-old spinsters, and the other, by telephone, to the physiology professor with the aim of breaking his ear-drum. To cast three of them in a bottle upon the sea, with a message hinting at the pleasures of desert islands and the other . . . but they rejected these and other ideas that occurred to them, ranging through the twenty-two degrees of the baroque, from baroque *pristinus* to baroque *officinalis*, which would accurately describe, for example, the idea of placing a couple of the penises in the eye sockets of a skull after painting them white with mydriatic pupils and another protruding from the hollow of the nose, or cremating them and scattering their ashes to fertilize the Valley of Mexico, or give them Christian burial and take flowers to their graves . . .

'Do you think that they will go to heaven?' asked Palinuro.

'They'll go, oh yes, to the surprise and delight of the Eleven Thousand Virgins,' stated Molkas and went on to say that, if his friends would allow him to digress, he would explain to them an idea he had for a business that had occurred to him a few days previously and which would make them all millionaires . . .

'As you know, we are suffering a population explosion which fully corroborates Malthus' theories. Therefore, besides contraceptive pills, one of the industries with the greatest future is condoms. I suggest that we start manufacturing them. But, bearing in mind the extent of possible competition, which is pretty stiff I must admit, we will be forced to flood the market with novel ideas. No problem. I have loads of them. I wish to manufacture a line of pastel-colour inflatable condoms for use on birthdays. For the military we will have khaki condoms. For widowers, black ones. For newlyweds, white condoms that look like silk. What do you think? For art lovers, we will have condoms with optical and abstract designs. Some, with drawings like those by Bridget Riley which will, by optical illusion, make the penis appear much longer than it is. Others, with Vasarely drawings, which will make the glans penis seem a perfect sphere. But we will also have more traditional lines of condoms bearing landscapes by Whistler and Constable. These we can sell in London. To San Francisco we can export fluorescent condoms. What do you think? Just imagine a condom gold and luminous as a Klee fish! The fish will turn into the hook. In Disneyland, we can sell condoms bearing pictures of Donald Duck and Mickey Mouse. To New York we will export pop condoms, in other words, red ones saying drink Coca-Cola and guaranteeing refreshing fizziness. It will be recommended that they be used chilled. For bald men we will have condoms with wigs. For use with decent ladies who wish for a moment to feel that they are the most abject, forsaken, irresponsible, vulgar and miserable of whores, we will manufacture condoms which exactly reproduce the irregularities and marks of venereal diseases as ancient as humanity: from the boil which ruined the sweet little shepherd Syphilis, to the growths on the penis described by Don Francisco Díaz (Philip II's court physician) and the velvety influorescences of the granuloma *pudendi*. What do you think? Such condoms will be part of our line for those who wish to make love sadomasochistically. But the best one will be a green condom in the shape of a cactus covered in thorns (which will really be innocuous nylon fibres) which we will sell exclusively in Mexico and which will be recommended for use during the woman's period (even though it's not strictly necessary then) so that it ends up covered in blood . . . what do you think?'

Palinuro and Fabricio did not think.

'No, I tell a lie! Our star product will be an ultra-sensitive condom which, like the chameleon, will change colour according to the stage of coitus. At the beginning it will be a bright and smooth bluish-pink, veiny and polished as marble. At the moment of penetration, it will turn red.

Later, purple, with the exertion. At the moment of orgasm, our condom will turn every colour of the rainbow and afterwards become white as paper and finally pink again, but this time the pink of a wilted rose. What do you think?'

Silence.

Palinuro approached Molkas and told him a secret. Molkas almost had another attack: 'Do you believe in cordless telepathy? I swear to you that I was thinking exactly the same thing!'

'I give you my word of horror.'

Three gentlemen in wigs and long waistcoats, wrapped in their bird-of-prey-coloured capes which flapped around their blue-jeaned ankles sweeping away cigarette ends and tram tickets, solemn as Van Eyck, came simultaneously from two different places: one was the Primary School's Museum of Natural Sciences where insects were preserved in oil of mirbane and butterflies were stuck with pins soaked in nicotine and a daguerreotype of Réaumur presided over the nebulae of the vivarium (this was the world which deposited them on the threshold of Bagheera the panther and Shere Khan the tiger who, because he had eaten too much, was trampled to death by buffaloes): the other place was, quite simply, The House of Troy (Palinuro, at that time, knew it almost by heart: *Pombiña branca com'a neve e rexiña com'aquellas nubes que vanse por ali . . .!*). These three gentlemen, as we were saying, went into the cantina, La Española cantina with its tiled floors and shelves on which sparkled whiskies, liquors and Bacardi glasses decorated with black bats and del Mono anisette.

'Three tequilas,' said Molkas, thumping his fist on the counter. Then he said to Palinuro, challengingly: 'You're not the only one who knows medical ditties . . .'

'Ah, do you too then?' Palinuro asked him.

And, once they had drunk the good health to all present, primly: 'Well, what do you expect? I am studying medicine after all.'

'I challenge you to a competition,' Palinuro said to him, in his turn glancing at a small group of drunks in one corner.

'*Cuerpo, loada seas en tu carne y heuso*: Body, praised be your flesh and bone,' began Molkas.

'*Tus nervios y tu sangre, tu semen y tu seso*: Your nerves and your blood, your semen and your brain,' completed Palinuro.

'Luis F. Franco, from Argentina,' stated Fabricio.

'*En mi encéphalo está tu imagen fija*: In my encephalon is your image graven,' quoted Molkas.

'*Desde el frontal al puente de Varolio:* From my frontal to my pons

409

Varolii,' continued Palinuro and, across the room, toasted the drunks in the corner.

'*Desde la fosa Silvia y el salterio*: From my Silvia furrow and my psalterium,' continued Molkas, joining the multitudinous toast.

'*A los tálamos ópticos*: To my optic thalamus,' Fabricio ventured to round off, ordering another round of tequilas.

Then it was Fabricio himself, beautiful as Astur with his weapons of many colours, who started the move towards the group of drunks. For some reason they looked familiar: among them was a one-armed lottery-ticket vendor. Another was an organ grinder. Yet another was so like the general with the glass eye, that it had to be him.

Although it was Fabricio who had made the first move towards them, it was Molkas who opened the conversation. Bowing deep: 'Kind sirs, forgive the interruption: we are three gentlemen who thrive on exhibitionism . . .'

'On what . . .?' asked the lottery-ticked vendor.

'On exhibitionism,' repeated Molkas. 'Unfortunately we know that many people consider it to be an offence against public propriety . . .'

'And that it is condemned by law as indecent exposure,' added Palinuro.

'But they don't understand,' added Fabricio, pointing to Molkas, 'that it is often the result of a temporary confusional or crepuscular state in the same way as, for example, drunkenness or epilepsy . . .'

'In all events, you needn't worry,' Molkas assured them, 'we are exhibitionists in the primitive sense of Lasègue.'

'In other words, we restrict ourselves to showing our cocks,' clarified Palinuro.

'Without manipulations of any kind,' continued Molkas.

'Without obscene comment,' promised Fabricio.

'Without fondling in the manner studied by Magnan,' completed Palinuro.

'And may we ask why the hell you go around showing your pricks?' asked the general with an impatient eye.

'The fact is that it's how we make our living, gentlemen . . . we have the longest pricks in the world,' explained Molkas. 'Longer than the penis of Priapus in the Dresden Museum, longer than the enormous Phallus of Delos and longer (although in this case I should say taller) than the twelve sacred Lingams of India, which are bathed in milk during the feast of Shiva.'

'Not longer than mine,' said the general, who prepared to reminisce about the good old days when he took the servant girls to the wastelands of Chapultepec Heights and gave them Oriental Pills to make their breasts grow.

'Your adolescent memories don't interest us,' said Molkas.

The general was not in the least put out: 'And not only is it long, but I can even get it up.'

'Come on, general: you don't still believe in the resurrection of the flesh, surely?'

'Could it be that you're one of these optimists who, when they wake up with an erection, believe it to be a proof of their virility, ignorant of the fact that what has actually happened is that the bladder, full of urine, exerts pressure on the prostate and thereby causes a purely mechanical, practically asexual, erection?'

'I'm quite willing to prove it,' replied the general and started to unbutton his fly, emblazoned with the national escutcheon.

'Just a minute, general,' Palinuro interrupted. 'First, we must make a bet.'

'Agreed,' said the general, 'here are twenty pesos.'

'Here are ten,' said the organ grinder.

'Here are half a million pesos,' said the lottery-ticket vendor.

'Excellent, excellent!' exclaimed Molkas, and continued: 'I wish to inform you, gentlemen, that you are going to lose your bet, because my ancestors were Moors, lock, stock and cock.'

'That's nothing,' said Fabricio, the aristocrat. 'I am a direct descendant of the Duke of Roquelaure who, as you know, had a penis of exceptional dimensions . . .'

'Do you remember the Laocoön sculptural group, gentlemen?' asked Palinuro. 'Well, an ancestor of mine was the model; in other words, it was his member that acted as the model for the huge sea serpent which strangled Laocoön and his sons Antiphas and Thymbraeus.'

'If you have ever been to Paris,' said Molkas, 'and visited the Salpêtrière and its refectories, you will have seen the murals painted by the students, of men with penises stretching right around the room. One of my grandfathers was the model.'

'That's enough talk of ancestors.' said Palinuro. 'Let us now concentrate on our own members. Did you know that the sweet potato and other vegetables grow better and bigger to music? The same happened to my penis: it grew and developed to the introduction of Mozart's *Magic Flute*.'

'Metaphors apart, I beat my friend Palinuro by a nose,' said Fabricio. 'You will have noticed that I have a particularly prominent one. What better proof do you want? As the Latin proverb so rightly says: *Noscitur a labiis quantum sit virginis antrum: noscitur a naso quanta sit hasta viro . . .*'

'Pay no attention to him, gentlemen. He is a pedant who never passes up an opportunity to show off his erudition. What I can tell you is that my penis represents the degeneration of mannerism in the serpentinata style.'

'My penis is so long,' said Molkas, 'that, when I was born, the doctor took it for the umbilical chord and almost cut it in half.'

411

'That's nothing,' said Palinuro. 'Mine is so long that I have had tattooed on it a complete, unabridged text of the *Kama Sutra*. But, since it is written in braille, it has to be read with the fingers.'

'That's less than nothing,' claimed Fabricio. 'My cock is so long that I trip over it, passers-by step on it, dogs pee on it, it gets left in lifts when I get out and I have to go and get it back from the fifth floor.'

'For my part, gentlemen, my cock is so long that if I lose this bet I'll commit suicide by hanging myself with it from a beam!' said Molkas.

'If I may,' said Fabricio, though it was not his turn, 'I will tell you that my cock is as long as that of Inuvalyla'u which slithered along the ground at night like a snake and raped the neighbouring women. I've had them all, starting with the girl next door . . .'

'Well,' said Molkas, though it wasn't his turn either, 'I have such a long cock that when I become king and sleep in the right wing of the castle, I will make love to the queen, living in the left wing of the castle, without leaving my bed . . .'

'Please, gentlemen!' interjected Palinuro. 'I have such a long prick that once, when I went to India, a snake charmer played the flute and my cock started to climb towards the sky and there I went after it, climbing up it hand over hand which, of course, caused it to continue to grow until, at last, above the clouds, I found the fountain of eternal youth and a pair of golden balls identical to my own . . . I have since become an initiate of Voodoo which is actually the cult of the serpent.'

'Gentlemen, if you will allow me,' said Molkas, 'my cock is so long that, when I worked as an extra in Hollywood, I used it in rodeos to lasso bulls. And more than once I made a redskin chief bite the dust.'

'And mine is so long,' added Fabricio, 'that in the Orinoco Olympics I won a gold medal in pole vaulting.'

'To conclude,' said Palinuro, 'I will tell you that my penis is so long that for a while I worked in Acapulco as a life guard and, without moving from my lookout post, I threw my cock to the swimmers who were drowning. I saved hundreds of lives. But, as my fame spread, I was forced to resign on account of the number of gays and middle-aged American ladies who asked for my help. Then, when I had to earn my living as an acrobat, I strung my cock between two buildings like a rope stretched between man and superman and tight-cock walked across it.'

'To conclude,' concluded Molkas, who always liked to have the last word, 'my prick is so long, gentlemen, that I enjoy the privilege accorded to dogs, which is to suck it myself – but only the tip because I once swallowed it whole and it went down my oesophagus fiery as Odin's spear Gungnir or as Lancelot's sword Excalibur and travelled through my whole digestive system including my twelve metres of intestines and stuck its head out of my arse, most surprised to be exiting where it normally enters

412

and complaining of stomach ache because, obviously, my stomach had started to digest it. It was a disaster.'

'Poppycock!' said the general. 'Enough talk! Show these cocks then!'

'Quite so,' said Molkas, 'enough exaggerating; I can tell you truthfully that my cock is so long that it reaches my feet . . .'

'I said enough talk,' warned the general.

'General, you will behold with your own eye,' said Molkas and rolled up his right trouser leg as though he were going to cross a puddle.

'I don't see anything,' said the general.

'Neither do I,' said the organ grinder.

'Sorry. So sorry, I forgot that today I put it down the other leg,' said Molkas, rolling up his left trouser leg. Out peeped the dead man's penis.

'Incredible,' said the lottery-ticket vendor.

'Monstrous,' exclaimed the general.

'I'm next,' said Palinuro. 'But first, I must ask you to overlook the fact that I suffer from a painful condition of perpetual erection.'

Palinuro unbuttoned his shirt collar and out peeked the dead man's penis.

'Gentlemen, this is the most amazing thing I have ever seen in my life,' admitted the general.

'Worthy of the Ripley section,' remarked don Prospero.

'And that's nothing,' said Molkas. 'If the truth be told, of the three of us, it is our friend Fabricio who wins hands down in penis size. Take a good look, gentlemen, because you are about to see the world's longest cock. It is so long that it goes up his chest, he puts it down his shirt sleeve and it comes out at the wrist. Show them, Fabricio.'

Fabricio stretched out his right arm and, with his left hand, pulled the penis from his shirt sleeve. It was as long, pale and perfumed as a Louis XV handkerchief.

The general's surprise was such that his eye fell to the floor, shattered and released an artificial vision of the world.

413

21

A bullet very close to the heart
and reflections on incest

'Ah, so you want me to tell you one of the captain's favourite memories? Ah, I've saved one for you that you will find delightful, as did General Pancho Villa. But, first, let me tell you that the captain was once shot in the leg . . . but, since then, a lot of water, my son, torrents, have passed under the bridge!' 'The captain was shot in the leg, Grandfather?' asked Palinuro. 'Yes sir, just as I say.' 'And he didn't die?' 'He didn't die, no sir, but the bullet stayed in his leg.' 'In his leg, Grandfather?' 'At first, in his leg, but not for long because, as you must know, bullets move inside the body. Very slowly, certainly, but they move. When the captain was twenty-five and he was a major in the army, he got cramps in the liver: which meant that the bullet had perforated the Glisson's capsule and had buried itself near the vein of the navel. From there, the bullet took six years to pass along the common bile duct and enter the major's, by then colonel's, gall bladder and, just at the time the colonel failed to be elected mayor of San Angel, the bullet perforated his bladder and the colonel spilled his bile. For years and years the bullet left the colonel, by then congressman, in peace. And, for a further eight years, the bullet also left the congressman, by that time interim governor of Tamaulipas, in peace; it concentrated on slowly, slowly moving downwards, executing a serpentine dance and making itself felt from time to time as stomach cramps which bothered the governor at night when he ate one lobster too many or took too little bicarbonate of soda. I know not by what intestinal mischance, but the bullet lost its way and, when the governor was no longer a governor, it entered the Denonvilliers ligament, my child, and, from behind, traitorously, perforated his pink prostate and fouled him up for good.' 'And then, Grandfather?' 'Then, just a few days ago in fact, after many more calm and resigned years, I found out that the bullet had taken off again, along the blue road of the arteries and that it is heading, my child, straight down the left coronary artery towards the heart. Look, child, put your hand on my chest . . . that's it, that's it, you see? The poor thing knows and is afraid. It hadn't beaten like this, so loudly, since the senator fell in love with Patty O'Brien, the colonel with Francine and the captain with your grandmother Altagracia. But, at my age, my child, the

414

only thing to do is to fall in love with death. Now I am going to tell you the memory that I promised. Come, come here, my bundle of joy, child of my sins, but only venial sins which never went beyond love beneath the lemon trees when the captain wore fifteen green years. Who would have said that I was going to be your grandfather and you were going to be my grandson? Who? Let's see, you tell me? The beggar on the corner, with the brocade top hat? The ice-cream seller, who sells vanilla illusions and chocolate adventures? You don't know? Well, I'll tell you. Or rather, the captain will, the captain who had not slept for two days, or had been on horseback for forty-eight hours which is almost the same thing, because General Villa had entrusted me with an extra-special mission or, rather, he had entrusted it to the captain in the name of Providence and, among other things, he had to go to Huahuanoyahua to recruit people to fight against your General Orozco. And I say *your* general because in this war you and I are enemies, uh? Your general is Pascual Orozco and mine is Francisco Villa. Fine thing, to fight beside the man who really was the Centaur of the North – you don't know what you missed – and head towards the Sierra Azul and know that five thousand soldiers are approaching Parral. Fine thing to slay dragons, like St George. Anyway, first I'm going to show you a book that the captain won at poker and which has a lot to do and hear with his memories. Let's see, let's see; no, this isn't it because it says *Conclusions of the Theologians of Freiberg*. And this isn't it either because these are letters from a Polish lady to the Marquis of Caracciolo. Ah, yes, these are beautiful books published in the land of my fathers, yes sir, *Delicious Theft* and *Tales of Madmen* which you will read when you are a fully-fledged man. Here it is at last. Oh no, this is *The Great National Decade*, my child, about the illustrious liberals of Mexico. You will learn about them one day. Ah, of course, this is it, finally. This book, which you see before you, bound in the Spanish style for which the skin of an innocent lamb had to be sprinkled with copper sulphate, was given to me – or rather, to the captain – by a man who was going to die, as happens to so many. The captain had not slept for four days because he had been summoned by General Pancho Villa himself, who was hobnobbing with Garibaldi's grandson and who said to him: "Captain, dear fellow: I am going to put an old gringo before the firing squad." "Why, general?" "Who are you to ask my reasons?" "Captain Francisco Villareal, general." "Ah, all right," said the general, "since you are my namesake I will forgive you, but don't let it happen again." "No, general," replied the captain, who had not slept for almost five days and knew that to cross swords with Villa was to invite death. All that I am telling you, my child, occurred almost in never-never time, like in stories, and General Villa went on to say, as he raised a cup of hot coffee to his lips: "I'm going to have him shot because he is a spy, the gringo bastard." And General Villa started to

415

squint, as he always did when he raised a cup of very hot coffee to his lips. And, with his left eye, my son, he covered the right flank of the army and, with his right, the left. With his right he kept an eye on Huerta's troops in Tierra Blanca and with his left he realized that Carranza did not wish Zacatecas to be taken. And, in the distance, outside General Villa's tent, somebody was singing, or nobody was singing: "*Un gorrión entre claveles*, A sparrow among carnations, *me digo en cierta ocasión*, told me one time, *no te creas en las mujeres*, don't you believe in women, *porque les mujeres son*, because women are, *redomas de todas mieles*, flasks of all honeys, *y amantes de traición*, and lovers of betrayal."

'It started to snow inside the general's tent, would you believe, and the snowflakes cooled Pancho Villa's coffee and fell on a map which the general kept on the table and the general said: "This bloody snow, damn it," and brushed it away with his hands and with one eye he saw Paris and with the other Hong Kong. "Tomorrow we'll swallow up Madrid," he said. "Yes, general." "The day after, we'll finish off Moscow," he added. "This bloody snow." "Yes, general." "And the day after that, we'll feast on Cognac." "Yes, general," answered the captain for the third time and, ready to please, as always, he said: "If you like, general, I'll brush the snow off you." You won't believe it, I'm sure, but the captain had not slept for almost six days and was dreaming that snow was falling, like that time that it really fell in the Sierra de las Nieves, the Mountains of Snow, which is why they bear that name. "What the hell are you talking about, my dear captain? If you mock me again, I'll have you shot." "No, general, no. I fell asleep and I was dreaming." "A good soldier," answered the general, "never sleeps even when he's asleep." "Yes, general, I mean, no, general," answered the captain with his eyes open as wide as he could, so much so my child, that Pancho Villa entered them lock, stock and barrel, just as he was, before an oil lamp drinking his hot coffee with his right hand on the handle of his pistol, and the general said to him: "So, I hear you fancy your English, captain, go talk to that bloody gringo and see what you can get out of him." And the captain answered: "With your permission, general, I don't speak English." "Such a modest boy," said General Villa. "It's true, general." "How come? You're from a good family, captain." "But I never learned English," answered the captain and, as he had not slept for almost seven days, he fell asleep again, my child, just as I'm telling you. "Oh this snow, this snow," said Villa, "it stops me from seeing Madrid, it really does," and he was wrapped in bearskins and his whiskers were covered in frost, his fine whiskers, my child, one pointing to the right and the other to the left; one towards the reveille, the other towards General Fierro's armoured railway carriage, and then he said: "You speak English, captain: that's an order. Do you understand? An order . . . do you hear me?" "Yes, general," answered the captain, waking with a start. "So go and see that bastard gringo spy sent by Pascual Orozco and get the truth out of him before dawn which is when I'm going to have him shot." "Pardon him, general," said the captain, who had a very large heart between his breast and his back. "And what do I get out of letting him live?" asked Pancho Villa and the captain knew not what to reply.

'And off I went, mounted again on my horse and after so many days on horseback, without sleeping, almost nine, we seemed to belong together as surely as bones and blisters. And I headed – or rather, we headed, my horse and I, my captain and my horse and I – to the tent in which the gringo was being held, away to the north east, there where the mountain copies its colouring from the tiger. And there we went, on and on, and inside I was singing: "*Tirar compañeras, tirar con valor*, Shoot, brothers-in-arms, shoot bravely, *dos a la cabeza, tres al corazon*, twice at the head, thrice at the heart . . ."

'And the snow was falling and I was shouting: "Stand aside, stand aside, let me just get my hands on those bastards," and there, my child, on the Cerro de la Bufa, the enemy was splattered with fear among the trunks and the goats. A fine night that was when the cannon balls were exhausted and we pelted the enemy with frozen birds while my horse, reading my thoughts, continued alone but for his soul towards the gringo's tent. And I, with my ice skates and plumeless three-cornered hat, directed the battle against Pascual Orozco, skating on a frozen river: "Fire that cannon!" shouted the captain. "Fire it, by a thousand on horseback, let's finish off those bastards!" And so, between sleeping and waking, with one eye in the dream in which the birds were all gone and we had to throw oranges at the enemy and another on the scrub and the cacti, in case they had laid an ambush for us at that hour of the night: just imagine, the captain had not slept for almost a month; "Yes, general," he said in his dreams that night when he almost fell asleep beneath a willow which wept into the furrows. And, to cut a long story short, I will tell you that he finally reached the place where they were holding the gringo who was an old man, a fairly old man, but not too old. Let's say . . . as I am now, fifty years from those days when we used to drink water from the wells, not knowing that in the bottom were the corpses of soldiers who died during the first assault on Torreón. "General Villa says: what is your name," the captain told the old gringo and the old gringo answered him in Spanish. You won't believe his answer, which was as follows, and this I swear as my name is Francisco and I am a retired colonel: he closed the book that he was reading, and which you now have in your hands, and said: "Since I am going to lose my name tomorrow at sunrise anyway, there's no point in hiding it: it is So and So!" The captain sat down, took from his jacket the notebook in which he had roughed out the next letter that he was going to send to your grandmother Altagracia and he wrote down the gringo's name, the very name written in

417

the book that you have in your hands, and then he started to dream. When you sleep beneath a willow, so it is said, you dream dreams of love, you dream of maidens whose pubic hair is shaved in the shape of a heart, my child, and I started to dream of your grandmother, who is as she is today, so old, because she has devoted her life to growing older each day, but that's all; but at a certain age, her golden age, her age of emeralds and lapis lazuli, my child, your grandmother Altagracia was like a Merovingian apple. Your grandmother was sad but beautiful, cloaked in snow in the way of a scarecrow that has been left outside and, sword in hand, I swore to her my eternal love and then I mounted my horse; that is, the captain mounted his horse and headed back to General Pancho Villa's tent and when he arrived said: "The gringo says he is called Such-and-Such." "You came just to tell me what the gringo is called?" said General Villa who was in a rage, with one eye on the death of Fierro in the marshes, bathed in gold, and the other on Benton's corpse. Then the captain, his horse between his legs, had to return through the thick of the battle. The federal soldiers, in red frock-coats and helmets which looked like Russian coffee pots, were throwing snowballs large as pumpkins which inscribed elliptical fires in the night and fell in the region of discord. "We're in for tremendous snowfalls, like in 1812," said Pancho Villa, spitting out bullet cartridges. "You're very tired," the gringo said to the captain. The captain allowed his horse, step by step, to bear him back to the truth and when he arrived he dismounted from his horse Palfrey, patted his croup, entered the gringo's tent, sat down, opened his eyes and answered: "That's because I haven't slept for over fifty hours." And so it was, although the captain felt as though he had not slept for a year at least. "Would you like a cigarette?" the old gringo asked the captain. "Thank you." "Thank you yes or thank you no?" "Thank you no . . . and tell me: how do you know you are going to die tomorrow morning?" "Because they say I am a spy and tradition dictates that spies caught at night must be shot at dawn the next day." "Are you a spy?" the captain asked the old gringo who was holding the bridle of his horse Palfrey. "No, captain." "I will report that to General Villa," said the captain and dug in his spurs. There where the pumpkins fell, illuminated inside, the snow melted and formed taciturn emblems. "How can you face death so calmly? Death is very serious," the captain said to the old gringo who was riding beside him through the quiet foothills of the Cerro de la Pila and pointed out to him some bonfires that could be seen in the distance: "Do you see those bonfires? They are burning the corpses of the federal soldiers. The stench was no longer bearable." The old gringo answered him: "How do I know that death is so very serious? I've never been dead in my whole life." And that night my child, was a night as black and smooth as Genoese velvet and the stars shone like oil lamps with iridescent prisms. "The old gringo says, general, that he's not a spy." "I don't give a shit. Go back and find out what that bastard gringo came to spy on." "What did you come to spy on?" the captain asked the gringo. "I already told you I'm not a spy. I am a journalist and a writer." "Aha," said Pancho Villa, "so he's a journalist and writer? Bullshit," and he continued to manufacture banknotes, by the hundreds and thousands: General Villa who handed out money like hot cakes: notes as blue as a gringo's eyes, notes as red as a dragon's blood. "Captain: what you should do right now is go and have a sleep," said the old gringo, on his return to the tent. "Thank you. I'm only doing my duty. You're the one who should sleep, so you wake up rested. And tell me: what are you writing?" "Stories." "True stories?" "All my stories are true," replied the gringo.

'Pancho Villa couldn't believe it: "So he's a writer, huh, captain? Look: a hundred of these banknotes, captain, are for you if you can find out for me what that gringo writes." And, my child, the old gringo took from his military haversack this very book that you see before you – which I won from the captain with a tierce of queens dealt in the first hand – and he gave it to the captain, who had not slept for five years. "This is what I have spent my whole life writing." "And he will never write again," said General Pancho Villa. "General Pancho Villa says that you will never write again," the captain warned him. "Wrong," said the old gringo, "I still have several hours to live and I plan to write another story." "Give him *neither* pencil *nor* paper," General Pancho Villa said to the captain. "Give him *neither* pencil *nor* paper," the captain said to the lieutenant. "Give him *neither* pencil *nor* paper," said the lieutenant to the sergeant. "Give him *neither* pencil *nor* paper," said the sergeant to the private. "I don't need them," said the old gringo, "all I have to do tonight is rewrite the story I wrote many years ago and which appears in this book." This time the captain accepted the cigarette the gringo offered him. "Without pencil or paper?" asked the captain. "Stories may be written in many ways," answered the old gringo. The captain took out his notebook and, my child, beside some verses that he had written for your grandmother Altagracia, he wrote: "Stories may be written in many ways." Outside, it continued to snow; or rather, inside, in the dreams of the captain who had not slept for ten years and ten days and from that time onwards dreamed when he was awake of being a colonel, of being a general, of being president of the Republic directing the taking of Zacatecas, which was certainly one of the pitched battles which forged my valour, my child: the captain and the old gringo travelled by train through the fields of alfalfa and the captain-president ignited the cannon shot with pyrophoric gobs of spittle and the enemy, you should have seen them, beneath those great black clouds, scurrying like seals, and the gringo and I roared with laughter fit to wake all our vertical ancestors and then the captain caught a bullet in the leg, the bullet which was to be the cause of all the problems of my fat

419

leg, my child, my leg like the Scott Emulsion whale, which I have dragged behind me for so many years and which everywhere leaves a wake of gunpowder foam and which one day I will take to my grave, as General Santa Anna did his, to the applause of all the doctors who had predicted its decease. "What's the matter, captain?" the old gringo asked him, respectfully. "Nothing, a bullet in my leg, it happened a few months ago, but it is nothing. And tell me, which is the story that you are going to write over again?" "Here it is, in this book. You keep it and read it later." "I don't read English," said the captain, forgetting the order he had received from General Pancho Villa. "Then I'll tell it to you," said the old gringo, shaking some snow from his shoulders. The captain took a last puff from his vanilla-scented cigarette which reminded him of the defence of Papantla and, mounting his horse yet again, he set off for General Villa's tent. On the way, he met a drunk lieutenant. "Captain: the gringo says he doesn't need pencil or paper to write." "How do you know, lieutenant?" asked the captain. "The sergeant told me." "How did the sergeant know?" "The private told him." "How did the private know?" "The old man told him so." "Ah, in that case, I must go to General Pancho Villa right now and I will say to him: the old gringo says, general, that he doesn't need pencil or paper to write." And Pancho Villa said nothing. Because, my child, when General Villa didn't understand something, he preferred not to hear it. And outside somebody was singing, I don't remember what song, I only remember that somebody was singing.

'On the way back to the gringo's tent, the night was darker, full of petals of sleeping gunpowder, my child, and the gringo started to tell the captain the story of Parker Adderson, philosopher: "It takes place during the War of Secession," he told him, "and it concerns a soldier who disguised himself as a Confederate to spy on the enemy's movements." "And what happened then?" asked the captain, who had not slept for twenty years and three public holidays. "The Confederates capture him and are going to shoot him next day. But Adderson the soldier is brave and does not fear death." "Aha," said General Pancho Villa, "so he's brave, is he? He's not afraid of death, huh?" he said, and started to rise slowly from his chair and, if I haven't already told you, I should make it clear once and for all: General Villa, my son, was a giant: every battle, every sentence he spoke, every man he had shot, caused him to grow taller and taller, so when he started to rise it seemed that he would never finish and down his trouser leg began to drain the battles of Saltillo and San Pedro de las Colonias and the convoys loaded with half a million cartridges and down the sleeves of his shirt drained all the women who greeted him with bunches of roses in León and the aeroplanes which bombed Ebano station and he asked: "Why is he not afraid of death?" The old gringo was riding along on his horse, very slowly so as not to tread on the partridges which, when they feel they

420

are are being pursued, nestle down and grasp the undergrowth with their little claws and hide, and he answered: "Sergeant Adderson is not afraid of death because he knows that while he is alive he is alive and when he is dead he will be dead and it won't hurt and he won't feel anything. He knows that death is an illusion." "So, it's an illusion, is it?" said General Villa from the lofty heights of his name. "Well, this old gringo will soon see how I am going to give him his illusion, right now in fact." "And what happened then?" the captain asked the old gringo. "I don't really remember, because I wrote the story over twenty years ago. But I think the Confederate general who is interrogating the sergeant loses his temper and orders that he be shot immediately without waiting for the next day." "Just a moment," said the captain and got down off his horse to collect eucalyptus cups. In those days I used to paint them all the colours of pixie hats and send them as a gift to your grandmother Altagracia. The captain mounted his horse again and asked: "What happened next?" "Next . . ." answered the gringo, "next the general sent for the captain and said to him: 'Captain, this is a Yankee spy and we are going to shoot him . . . how's the weather . . .?' " And the captain replied: "The storm is over, sir." "And the moon is shining," said the old gringo gazing at the moon, my child, which was shining like an iceberg in the sea of the depths of memory.' 'And then?' 'Then, General Villa said to me: "Take this pistol, my good captain. Shoot the gringo yourself and then we'll see how brave he is." ' 'And then what happened?' 'The general said to the captain: "Good; take a file of men, conduct him at once to the parade ground, and shoot him." ' 'And did Parker Adderson face death bravely?' ' "Parker Adderson," answered the old gringo, "started to weep and scream like an old woman and beg the general for mercy. And then, with a dagger just like this one, he killed the captain," the old gringo told me and he gave me this very dagger, my child, which is of pure Toledo steel tempered in the snows of the Pyrenees,' said Grandfather Francisco. ' "I, for my part," I answered General Villa: "I can't do it, general." "Would you dare to disobey an order, captain?" said Pancho Villa. "Yes, general, I dare." "You are very brave, captain, but you will pay dearly for it," said General Pancho Villa and started to count on his fingers the battles that he had won in his life and General Felipe Angeles lent him his hand because Pancho Villa's fingers were not enough to count the battles that he had won. Then he raised his cup of coffee to his lips and, with one eye on my death and the other on my pardon, he said, "For the simple reason that you are identical to my son, captain, I won't have you shot. But what I will do is have you excommunicated on bread and water for twenty days." "With the general's pardon . . . which of your sons do I resemble?" asked the captain, who did not know that Pancho Villa had any sons at all. "The one I never had," answered Pancho Villa and collapsed into his chair because his glory had by then started to weigh

421

heavily on him, like a ship loaded with dynamite and also because, in some way, he also had one eye on his past, on his hacienda in Río Grande, on the Battle of the Brooms, on the ten-year-old bugler who saved the siege of Celaya and on the men of the North Division which was like a huge golden bird: and the other eye was on Columbus and on the city of Parral where he died riddled with bullets and on a gringo who desecrated his grave to steal his head and take it to the States.' 'And then, Grandfather?' 'What I remember then is General Pancho Villa standing up again: he was always standing up again and borrowing my horse Palfrey in order to go himself and, by his own hand, kill the gringo. And the captain was taken to his cell and he was sad because they were going to kill the gringo, but not very sad, because he had hardly slept in his life and now he was going to make up for it, for that whole life, or twenty days of it anyway. And so it was. No sooner did the captain lie down on the camp-bed than he fell sound asleep and started to dream. He dreamt that he was riding his horse, slowly, across the plains and by his side, also on horseback, rode the ghost of the old gringo. We were, as I told you, going slowly, so as not to break the spell of the night, the crystal moon, the celluloid stars. "It's stopped snowing," said the gringo. "It's stopped snowing," repeated the captain, like an echo. And they continued slowly onwards, my child, as the rifles of ice hanging from the trees wordlessly fell and swelled the ranks of the rivers flowing towards summer. We passed by Sacramento. We passed by Noé. We passed by La Polvorera. And I didn't dare to ask the ghost of the old gringo if he had had time to rewrite his story, whether Sergeant Parker Adderson had, in the end, acted bravely. We passed by Cerro Prieto. We passed by the death of Victor Elizondo who had slit his wrists so that Pancho Villa could not have him shot. We passed by Indé and El Presón, where the *dorados* chatted about love by campfires kindled with cattle dung and I didn't dare to ask the ghost of the old gringo if he had had the time, if he had had the courage, if he had had the balls to rewrite the story. Slowly, on our horses, we reached the end of the valley, my child, which came into being at the foot of the mountains, spread forth like green foam and lived out its maturity beside the river, its autumn in shady woods, to die interminably, on the plain far away. "The sun's come out," said the captain. "The sun's come out," repeated the old gringo, like an echo and, turning around, he rode away and I never saw him again. Then the captain thought: "Who knows, who will ever know, what goes on inside great men when they have a bullet very close to the heart." '

The fact that Grandfather Francisco knew so much about Mexican history, so many stories, so many legends of thrice-guaranteeing flags, embraces of Acatempan, and never-to-be-forgotten betrayals, was a delight to his sister, Aunt Luisa, even though Grandfather decided to forget everything that happened before and was to happen after the day he had the accident with the cash register because, as far as he was concerned, the demise of his political career signalled the end of the whole of history. But, fortunately, the Mexican Empire, including the tragedy of Maximilian and Carlota, belonged to a distant past and there was nothing more natural or easier for Grandfather than to discover, between the story of the Empire and that of Jean Paul and Aunt Luisa, a series of coincidences and parallels of the kind which, as he himself said, would never appear in novels if they did not happen in real life. It is true that Jean Paul was French whereas Maximilian was not, but the Mexican Empire arose under the auspices of Napoleon III and the troops which supported it were French. And, of course, the emperor's body was taken to Veracruz under the custody of three hundred dragoons and it was not until the ship *Novara* left Mexican territorial waters that the Austrians ordered the hundred and one cannon shots of protocol. The embalmed body of Jean Paul, on the other hand, was taken to the same port by rail with the intention of shipping him back to France and, for one reason or another, on account of this paper and that paper, the authorities decided out of the blue to bury him in the municipal graveyard of Veracruz. But both Maximilian of Hapsburg and Jean Paul were fair-haired and had died young in Mexico. Moreover, while Jean Paul did not leave among his effects a Cross of the Knights of the Order of the Eagle and of Guadalupe, nor a *History of Italy* by Cesare Cantù, his possessions did however contain several objects recalling those distributed among the relatives and friends of Ferdinand Maximilian. The rosary received by Archduke Charles ended up in Grandmother Altagracia's possession. Grandfather Francisco became the custodian of the watch and chain given to the Duke of Flanders. The locket containing a lock of the empress's hair which was left to Queen Victoria of England, in this case containing a lock of Aunt Luisa's hair, she herself kept to bequeath later to a niece equalling her in beauty and who was, of course, Estefania. Finally, just as the Grand Duchess Sophia was given Maximilian's bullet-pierced scapula, Aunt Luisa sent Jean Paul's blood-stained scapular cloak to his mother back in France.

'Everybody knows what happened afterwards – or they should, Luisa: Carlota – like you – went quite mad, from the tips of her chestnut curls to the tips of her imperial toes and so, mad and dying of hunger, mad and deserted, she dipped her fingers in the Pope's hot chocolate. If you should ever dare dip your fingers in my chocolate, woe betide you, Luisa,' said Grandfather, unaware that Aunt Luisa was disturbed not so much by his allusion to her madness as by the fact that her brother should think that she would ever confuse him with Pope Pius IX. How could he think such a thing? she wondered. Infallibility, answered don Prospero, who had then

423

reached the letter P in the encyclopaedia and knew that Giovanni Maria Mastai-Ferretti, archbishop of Spoleto, who went down in history under the name Pius IX, had proclaimed the dogma of Papal Infallibility in the Vatican Council of 1870.

Besides, by one of life's marvellous ironies, no reference to madness could affect Aunt Luisa for, while all around her believed that an incurable and progressive dementia had been unleashed in her soul, she had in fact for many years been travelling a long and painful path towards sanity.

Her experience at eighteen years of age in *La Tour de Merveilleux*, when she became increasingly aware of the great love she felt for Jean Paul and for Paris as she travelled ever further backwards through space, made such a deep impression on her that she did not become aware of the immense pain she felt at the death of one and the distance of the other until she started to travel a type of reverse journey through time. During the first weeks after Jean Paul's murder, she never even mentioned his name, which made people think that Aunt Luisa was either insensitive or, like Chrysostom, a past master of the art of dissimulation. During the following months and years, she spoke from time to time of Jean Paul or of Paris in the vague and absent-minded way of one remembering very distant things with a tendency to confuse names and dates. For example, she would say 'Jean Jacques' instead of 'Jean Paul', or 'thirty years ago' instead of 'three years ago'. And so, as Aunt Luisa and her brother, Grandfather Francisco, grew older and Mamma Clementina and her sisters were born, and later Estefania and I, the memory of Jean Paul and of Paris became increasingly clear and defined and Aunt Luisa started to talk about them more and more, with ever greater pain and longing.

Countless years had passed since Jean Paul's death when Aunt Luisa started to travel to Veracruz every three months to visit his grave and take him flowers. Later, she went every month. Then, every two weeks. And one day, or rather, one year before a day arbitrarily fixed in time by Aunt Luisa's imagination or perhaps by a conjugation of the stars invoked by Jean Paul a few minutes before he was murdered in a park in Guadalajara when he was dreaming of himself as an old man covered in all imaginable honours on his deathbed, Aunt Luisa dressed in mourning and went to live in Veracruz that she might mourn Jean Paul's absence every day of that year. Those who saw her during that period told that she grew increasingly sad and wept ever more copiously to the point that she got it into her head not to leave the hotel and then not to leave her room and suddenly she went almost twenty-four hours without sleep, fainting and weeping, until she uttered a kind of groan, between a death rattle and a scream, between a snore and a guffaw, and fell asleep. She rose next day as though nothing had happened, put on a red dress with white flowers, powdered her nose with her swansdown powder puff, strolled to the terraces under the arches to drink a mint julep, bought herself a shell necklace and earrings, went to the cinema to see a Charles Boyer film and finally packed her things, took a taxi to the railway station and returned to Mexico City. By the time she reached our grandparents' house, she knew that Paris and Jean Paul had been one and the same thing for her and would continue to be so throughout her life.

That something could be itself and yet something else at the same time, or many things simultaneously, was nothing new for Aunt Luisa. Moreover, her dreams had taught her that a person can also be other people and, at the same time, none of them. So, she once dreamt that Uncle Austin, in Scottish kilt, was not himself but his own wife Enriqueta and also the friend who came to visit them and gave them a bottle of whisky in a box with deer antlers. On another occasion, she realized that a person can be a person and, at the same time, a thing or several things and she dreamt that one of her sisters, who had died of diphtheria, was the roses on her pillow and that the roses sank through the glass face of a clock. Then, her sister was half-past three in the afternoon and the second hand a red arrow which speared her in the throat. She once learned that a person can be many things and people at the same time, minus other things plus other people. But this revelation she received with open eyes when she realized that Grandfather, not only because he was so old and so forgotten by his political friends but also on account of all his fatness and elegance, was his own abandoned La Salle motorcar, plus his garden and his leg, less Grandmother Altagracia's quirks, multiplied by all his parliamentary victories and divided by a thousand islands and the love of his daughters. When she was quite certain of this phenomenon, she told her brother: 'Do you know something, Francisco? Things are one thing and another, at the same time. They are and they are not.' Grandfather raised his gaze from the snails burnishing the flagstones in the garden, ceased remembering the dirty laundry that had been publicly washed in the Convention of Aguascalientes, and asked: 'What have you been reading, Luisa? Haven't I told you that it isn't good for you to read books that you don't understand?' 'I didn't read it in a book. I read it in a flower,' answered Aunt Luisa. 'You don't read flowers.' 'The one I'm talking about wasn't a flower, it was a knife.' 'What the hell are you talking about?' 'I'm not talking,' said Aunt Luisa, 'I'm crying.' 'Why are you crying?' 'For Paris.' 'Paris is a long way away, I've already told you.' 'Yes, but it's alive and I miss it. I want Paris to come, I want to see it again and kiss it.' 'Oh, Paris!' groaned Grandfather, remembering the end of Charpentier's opera which, by pure coincidence, bore Aunt Luisa's name and added: 'It's no wonder they say you're mad.' 'I am and I'm not,' replied Aunt Luisa, who had learned the lesson of her dreams and so won the round.

Because, since then, since she started living by French time and writing letters to Paris which people believed to be the confirmation of her madness, Aunt Luisa learned to play at sometimes being mad and sometimes being sane, sometimes she was both and sometimes neither and nobody dared not to listen to her when she was talking about Jean Paul and Paris, for the simple reason that when she appeared to be lucid, everybody was eager to discover some hint of insanity and, during her moments of seeming insanity, to detect a hint of sound-mindedness.

There was one person who even played along with her. That person was, of course, Grandfather Francisco. One morning he presented her with the story that he had read in the newspaper that Paris was going to visit Mexico City. The same night at twelve – six in the morning on Boulevard Raspail – Aunt Luisa, dressed in her long skirts, her silver buckled shoes and around her throat a black velvet ribbon with which she strangled the wrinkles that had alienated her from the age of her blossoming, said to herself: 'I must organize a huge reception for Paris,' and started to draw up a programme of fiestas, speeches and banquets. The project, as she described it to Grandfather and his friends on Easter Saturday, thus earning a round of applause and looks of terror, was more or less as follows: Orly airport would be greeted at Balbuena airport by a military band. The Arc de Triomphe would parade beneath the Monumento de la Revolución. The Bois de Bologne would be offered an open-air buffet in Chapultepec Park, to be attended by all the débutantes of Mexico and they would eat roast mutton and drink clamours of old wine. Notre Dame would attend a solemn sung mass in Mexico Cathedral. The Monument des Invalides would lay a wreath on the Columna de la Independencia. Finally, the Champs Elysées might stroll as often as desired in the Paseo de la Reforma, eat in an expensive restaurant or simply read in an open-air café in the lithographed shade of the ash trees. Aunt Luisa thought of everything. There was not an alleyway or *arrondissement* of Paris, *porte* or avenue, bridge or monument, for which she had not planned every last detail of a fiesta, party, *soirée* or academic colloquium: from the Porte de Versailles to the Porte de Lilas; from the Ponte de Tolbiac to the Ponte de Mirabeau; from the Jardins de Luxembourg to the Hôtel Dieu. Thus, for many days, at five o'clock in the morning – eleven by the clock of the Café de Cluny – Aunt Luisa was to be seen leaving home to go and inspect Mexico City house by house, stone by stone and policeman by policeman, to ensure that all was in readiness for when Paris arrived.

Persuaded, thus, of the plurality of the individual soul of people and things, Aunt Luisa believed that she found the confirmation of her theory at every instant, not only in her dreams and in daily life, but also (how better) in the pages of the encyclopaedia which don Prospero read aloud to her on Sunday afternoons in the shade of the bougainvillaea.

It was thus that she learned – she, who had once dreamt that her brother

Francisco and her fiancé Jean Paul were the same person and that she married him (them) and had a son who was the same Grandfather Francisco reborn (or the same Jean Paul, anyway); it was thus that she learned – with an amazement quite beyond the capacity of her eyes and mouth – that the Greek god Adonis, as the incestuous product of the union between King Theias and his daughter Myrrha, was not only his sister's son and his mother's brother, but also his grandfather's son, his father's nephew and, as though that were not enough, his own uncle and nephew. Aunt Luisa, incidentally, used this to create a whole imaginary history – to the glee of those who believed her to be mad and to the wonder of those who, like Estefania and myself, knew that she was the most intelligent aunt that we could ever have had – and which, according to her, proved that it was the fear of enormous family imbroglios – and not the potential monsters which so terrified my cousin – which had led the wise men of old to forbid marriage between parents and their children and between brothers and sisters.

'You're mad as a hatter,' Grandfather Francisco told her for the umpteenth time.

'And you, you are more mistaken . . .' at that moment a worm peeped out from the grass and Aunt Luisa, who continued to believe that worms heralded rain and don Prospero had not yet told her of the role played by worms in the aeration of the soil, stated: 'You, Francisco, you are more mistaken than a worm,' thinking that such a helpless and insignificant thing as a worm had without doubt made the worst mistake of its life in not being born a bird. Then, she picked up her thread: 'I'm going to prove it to you with examples that are very close to home.'

No sooner said than done, Aunt Luisa shut herself in her room and, a few days later, forced Grandfather Francisco to sit down on a bench in the garden and listen to the interminable list of incests and resulting relationships that she had drawn up.

'Imagine, Francisco, that you married your daughter Clementina.'

'I would never commit such a crime,' Grandfather Francisco assured her.

'I said: *imagine*. It's just a supposition.'

'Well, all right, I'll imagine . . .' answered Grandfather Francisco and, after a pause, added: 'but, even so, I would never commit such a crime.'

Aunt Luisa didn't heed Grandfather's second rejection of her hypothesis because she had already started to read out her list. And she read it so often afterwards to Estefania and me that she herself ended up believing that it was a true and consummated fact, which indeed it was, in more ways than one:

When Grandfather Francisco (who, in Aunt Luisa's story, was a combination of Jean Paul, Uncle Austin and himself) was left a widower

427

by Grandmother Altagracia (who died of diabetes: her last words had the scent of rotten apples) he had a meeting with his two daughters (the elder Mamma Clementina and the younger Aunt Lucrecia or, from Estefania's point of view, the elder Aunt Clementina and the younger Mamma Lucrecia) and in this meeting the three of them (Grandfather and his two daughters) decided that they would seek among their kin a male to continue the line, for the dual purpose of keeping the fortune within the family and of vindicating Grandmother Altagracia's constant haemophilic passion, not only for her daughters but for all her future descendants – so she maintained – down through four or five generations. And, since Grandfather was not only a botanist, but also a great drinker and claimed that each bottle of whisky contained a genie which granted all his wishes as soon as it entered his body, Mamma Clementina and Aunt Lucrecia had no need to resort to the wiles of Lot's daughters to seduce their father: that very weekend, sober and in temporary possession of all his senses, Grandfather lay with Mamma Clementina (who in Aunt Luisa's story was a combination of Papa Eduardo and herself) and, as a result of this incestuous union, exactly nine months later was born Uncle Felipe who, and not because he was an archetype of male beauty, but because he was his grandfather's (Papa Francisco's) son, his mother's (Aunt Clementina's) brother and his own uncle and nephew, became the second Adonis of history. No sooner did he come of age than Uncle Felipe (or, to put it another way, Nephew Felipe) married Mamma Lucrecia (who was his half-sister and aunt at the same time and was, incidentally, on the point of having a tuberculous lung removed), thus (Uncle Felipe) becoming his mother's (Aunt Clementina's) brother-in-law, his father's and his grandfather's (Papa Francisco's) son-in-law and his own brother-in-law by marriage. In turn, Aunt Lucrecia became her father's (Uncle Francisco's) grandaughter-in-law, and daughter-in-law of the person who was simultaneously her sister, mother-in-law and stepmother, in other words, Mamma Clementina, who thus became her son's (Uncle Felipe's) sister-in-law, her daughter-in-law's (step-daughter's) sister and the aunt of her son-in-law, who was none other than her son, Felipe. From this union (between Felipe and Lucrecia), was born Aunt Luisa no less who, although she had been, among many other things, her father's (Uncle Felipe's) cousin, her mother's (Aunt Lucrecia's) niece and her great-grandfather's (Papa Francisco's) granddaughter, never became more than a combination of herself. But certainly, so original and so pretty that, when she reached seventeen springs, Grandfather Francisco himself proposed to her, whereby Aunt Luisa became her husband's (Cousin Francisco's) great-grandaughter, her mother's (Aunt Lucrecia's) stepmother, her father's (Nephew Felipe's) step-grandmother, aunt and mother-in-law, her own (Aunt Luisa's) grandmother and Mamma Clementina's (her great-aunt's) sister. By then,

Grandmother Clementina and Papa Felipe had had an incestuous nephew who was me: my half-sister's (Cousin Clementina's) son and grandson, Papa's (Grandfather Felipe's) nephew and my great-grandfather's (Uncle Francisco's) grandson twice over. Almost at the same time, only days later, was born a daughter of the union between Uncle Francisco and Great-grandmother Luisa: Estefania who was, among other things, her grandfather's (Papa Felipe's) aunt, her great-grandmother's (Mamma Clementina's) half-sister and her mother's (Aunt Luisa's) great-granddaughter, her great-grandfather's (Cousin Francisco's) daughter and also half-sister to her great aunt (Mamma Lucrecia, who did, in the end, have her lung removed and the space filled with acrylic spheres like little Ping-Pong balls).

This enormous confusion of relationships gave rise to other problems: at Christmas and on birthdays and silver wedding anniversaries, things became very complicated: each member of the family felt obliged to give each of the others as many gifts as they had relationships with them. Thus, for example, it was not unusual to find beneath the Christmas tree a series of presents saying: 'For Papa Felipe from his adored daughter Luisa'. 'For my nephew Felipe from his dear Aunt Luisa'. 'For my grandson, Felipe, from his Grandmother Luisa who thinks of him always'. 'For my son-in-law, Felipe, from your respected mother-in-law Luisa'. And, if things were looking good, 'For my fiancé, Felipe, from your future wife Luisa'.

For these same reasons, divorces, separations and other conjugal upsets and family quarrels became virtually impossible: when Grandfather Francisco and Mamma Clementina decided to separate for reasons of incompatibility, Grandfather could not bring himself to leave his daughter, and Mamma Clementina, in turn, could not find it in herself to leave her father, so they continued to live together, although from then onwards they slept in separate beds. When Aunt Lucrecia fell out with her half-brother (Uncle Felipe) and decided never to speak to him again she did, however, continue to speak to her husband and nephew, who were none other than the same Uncle Felipe. And once, when Aunt Luisa, already married to Grandfather Francisco, caught him in the arms of another woman beneath a cloud of smoke (Grandfather Francisco, observing a Chinese adage, smoked when he made love in order to postpone the moment of climax) and shouted furiously: 'I'm going back to my mother this minute,' she didn't in fact have to go anywhere: first, because we all lived together and, second, because the woman in whose arms she caught Grandfather was not the priestess Io but Aunt Luisa's mother herself, in other words, Aunt Lucrecia.

Other problems aside (including abrupt changes in relationship which suddenly allowed us to order our own fathers to go and buy the milk, or obliged us to show the courtesy and deference due to a father-in-law to someone who had until then always been our great-nephew; problems which progessively undermined the principle of authority and mutual respect), interminable discussions on resemblance arose whenever a new member of the family was born: 'He has his grandfather's nose,' said someone. 'No, it's his uncle's,' insisted another. 'Not at all: it is his father-in-law's,' stated a third. And, of course, the three usually referred to the same person, although the possibility also existed that it might refer to two, three, or five different people, or to any other member of the family, whether or not the grandfather, uncle or father-in-law of the newborn infant, because a long, broad nose was a feature we all inherited. Or rather, it was the primary common feature because, as we continued to inbreed, new descendants looked more and more alike, to the extent that a child born with its grandfather's nose, its aunt's eyes, its father's ears and its grandson's mouth could very well, for example, pass as the twin cousin of one of its uncles.

All this however, according to Aunt Luisa, was merely an exploration of possibilities because, in fact, only two children were born. Aunt Luisa's list was limited to eight incests (two of Mamma Clementina's, two of Grandfather Francisco's, two of Uncle Felipe's, one of Aunt Luisa's and one of Aunt Lucrecia's) which, in fact, were only four, because it takes two to consummate incest. Apart, naturally, from the occasional incest between family members of the same sex, which never gave rise to further genealogical consequences. Now: these four incests occurred over a period of more than thirty years. At least fifteen years had to pass after the first, the time for Uncle Felipe to reach puberty and commit the second with Aunt Lucrecia. And, though the third (consummated by Mamma Clementina and Uncle Felipe) could occur at any time between the second and the fourth, a further seventeen years had to pass before the latter could be consummated, in other words, Aunt Luisa's age when she married Grandfather Francisco. So, Aunt Luisa left to our imagination what might have occurred if, instead of four incests, there had been ten or fifteen and, by the same token, as many other incestuous offspring which, upon reaching puberty, might have continued to intermix with their parents and among themselves, producing an average of one child a year.

Finally, there were other disappointing results because, despite the enormous number of close, distant, blood, in-law, direct, indirect, transversal and collateral relatives we each had, the family consisted of only seven members, with the result that when Grandfather Francisco died and although the obituary notice in the newspaper read: 'You are asked to share the immense grief of his sons, daughters, brothers and sisters, nephews and nieces, great-nephews and nieces, stepmother, parents-in-law, brothers and sisters-in-law, cousins-in-law, stepsons, grandsons, great-grandsons, sons-in-law, daughters-in-law, wives, grandchildren-in-law, parents-in-law by marriage and other relatives,' the wake and burial were attended by only seven people, that is, the only six who could attend, although, on the other hand, on Grandfather's grave were placed over fifty-five wreaths from his own gardens and greenhouses, sent by his relatives. A few days later occurred the most serious storm ever to beset our family, when we realized that Grandfather Francisco, who had over the years accumulated a large amount of money and property, had not had the delicacy to make a will.

And this was as far as Aunt Luisa's story went and, with that patience only she possessed (capable of teaching the minutes and the hours to read that they might tell eternity), she wrote it down in her own hand, that Estefania and I (who were in fact first cousins) might believe that we were each other's great-grandparents once removed and simultaneously second cousins and, this being so, we decided to reserve the former kinship for when we were old and renounce the second, before a lawyer, that we might deliver ourselves into each other's arms without having hanging over our heads, and those of our children and our children's children, the curse of incest.

22

The tragicomic sense of life

That's right, I've just returned from London. From London! Can you
imagine? 'London: thou art the flower of cities all.' I lived there for several
years, in that city which never becomes real at all, in that Rome of today
and the epitome of our times, as Emerson called it. Too many years
perhaps. The ineffable Dr Johnson once said that when a man is tired of
London, he is tired of life. Therefore, there is no hope for me, since I am
tired of London. But how can you take any notice of somebody who
despised books as magnificent as *Tom Jones* and *Tristram Shandy* and who
said that he preferred the view of Fleet Street to that of any rural
landscape? I brought Uncle Austin a King's College tie. Although, I must
admit, I am also a city animal. I am one of those people who think that
God created the world to put on a show for himself and therefore it is up to
him to applaud the multitudinous acting of the Niagara Falls or get bored
with the interminable monologue of the Sahara desert. I'll settle for what
man has made for man. What more can I say of London: it is a city that
spends its nights sleeping and dreaming of its past glories. By that I mean
that life stops at eleven past the meridian. I've never seen people who go to
bed as early as Englishmen! Except, perhaps, English women who go to bed
at seven because they have to be home by ten. Meanwhile, the glow of the
traffic lights dances in the rain. How it rains, man! The other day, I got so
fed up that I went outside and beat the rain with my umbrella. But it was
no good. The rain was implacable and diamantine. And with that same
rainwater, I filled this bottle for Grandmother Altagracia. I'll tell her it's
holy water from Lourdes. All water is the same anyway and in it you find
the same microscopic algae in the shape of half moons and emerald sweets,
heliozoans like hedgehogs of light and fleas of blue gelatine which you and
I discovered as children in Uncle Esteban's books. And for Uncle, by the
way, I've brought several plates for his laboratory's magazine, including
Taddeo di Bartolo's *Hospital Scenes* and Hogarth's *The Reward of Cruelty*
which shows a dog eating the heart of the corpse on which the autopsy is
being performed which reminded me, as you can well imagine, of old
Charon's dog. For Grandfather, I brought an extremely old edition of
Atlas and Charts of the Mexican Republic. And for me, for Walter, I
brought a huge reproduction of Millais' painting showing the dead

432

Ophelia in the river before which, when I finally got the opportunity to see the original and remembering my good old days as a student and the microscopy set which Uncle Esteban later gave to our cousin and which had left me astounded by the worlds teeming 'on the stage of the aureate microscope' – who was it that said that anyway? Machado? – I realized that with luck we may also discover in the eyes and lungs of drowned people those wonders of iridescent symmetry, those little creatures that look like hourglasses, tiny crabs, bead bracelets and green tears with long hairs. Moreover, old man, every morning the English straighten their hair-pieces, tie their vocal cords, sew on their tongues, button their eyes, starch their smiles and start with equal punctuality to descend from the sky upon The City, complete with bowler hat and umbrella, as though painted by Magritte. Well, not exactly; although the English are all equal, some are more equal than others. I thought of you often, cousin, as I walked through London arm-in-arm with Eliot. I am neither royalist, classicist nor Anglo-Catholic but I conversed with him, none the less, in Hampstead, in Putney, on Primrose and other shady Hills of London. I thought of you and your illusions, as I walked along the banks of the Thames, through the Embankment Gardens, as I felt sorry for the tramps who at dusk roll themselves in time beneath the poet going up in flames with whom I also conversed, in his native land and tongue. Such wonders I saw, you cannot imagine! I personally met Lister's stethoscope and Liston's forceps. I almost had them in my hands. I thought of you, cousin, and of those nights when we walked along the streets, along Mesones and along San Juan de Letrán and along Reforma and through the Juárez district and afterwards, as dawn broke, we reached Chapultepec Park which we crossed from one side to the other, from the Paseo de La Milla to Molino del Rey. I could write a book called *A Tale of Two Cities*. Better still, I could write a book with a thousand pages on nothing more than the feeling of infinite melancholy that Ophelia produced in me. Anyway, if only to see the originals of the paintings that you know from illustrations, it is worth going to Europe, by way, of course, of New York to pay your respects to *Guernica*; *The Anatomy Lesson of Dr Tulp*, Rembrandt's *Anatomy Lesson*, of course, seemed to me infinitely more beautiful than I had ever imagined. So many paintings have I seen! I have beheld so many *Triumphs of Death*, including the one by Lorenzetti in Pisa and so many pictures of decomposing corpses including, of course, those by Valdés Leal! And not only did I think of you, of your illusions and of General Obregon's hand, do you remember? but I often spoke aloud to you, without fear that they might think me mad. There are so many mad people in that city, man, so many people who talk to themselves! Nobody takes any notice of them of course, not even the police who sometimes speak with two different voices: if you ask them for directions, their truncheons blossom like St Joseph's lily stem and they answer you in a friendly voice. But beware: with the other voice, the one they keep close to their transistorized heart, they may at any moment accuse you of being a pederast or a Pakistani immigrant. I saw a pair of dentures tuned in C major; in the Hunterian Museum I saw the most incredible collection of select pieces of the human organism. There they all are, in their transparent prisms, like the vessel found by Baron Münchhausen which sailed along enclosed in an iceberg. For Mamma Clementina, if she were alive, I would have brought a little ivory hand to scratch her back with, which I saw in a shop in Portobello Road. And while you, cousin, walked along San Ildefonso and Justo Sierra, with your *Microscopy Manual* under your arm and dreaming as I used to myself of one day finding in a drop of sea water or in the poet Shelley's eyes the luminous and transparent protozoa and the diatoms of masked chlorophyll which form the slime on the bed of oceans and are shaped like trains, flutes, swarms of bees and radiate circles, while you dreamt and you laughed thinking of Horace Wells at the moment he discovered the laughing properties of chloroform and wept thinking of Horace Wells when he was humiliated in Boston and rushed out into the streets to fling vitriol into prostitutes' faces while you swore to yourself – as I swore to myself – to one day qualify as a doctor, to learn to describe the varnish of the skull and the tidal net surrounding life, to learn to dissect tame corpses and to detect the martial propagation of adrenalin, all the while, I, your cousin Walter, was walking along Charing Cross Road with my umbrella and my patchwork waistcoat, poking around in the second-hand bookshops and dying a thousand deaths because I couldn't buy all those wonderful books . . . never in my life have I bought fewer books, man! and I was saying to you – I said to you – that we may indeed accept that, although you do not know when your life actually begins and ceases to be your own, in all events it is yours and nobody else's. Of course, you should have seen the look of alarm that the bookshop assistant gave me but, I repeat, not because I was talking to myself but because I was doing it in Spanish. But life, I continued, is not a thing. Life, although it seems you may use it and enjoy it and abuse it, is not a suit of clothes; life, I said, pointing to a beautiful hand-tinted map of Kent, is not ten hectares of land and, finally, life, I shouted as I walked out into the street, is not a car. Such cars in London, man! Faced with a Rolls Royce, all you can do is take off your hat and hold it out for alms. But if you ask the English for money to buy bread, they won't give you a penny. If you ask them for money to buy a pint of beer they won't give you anything either, but at least they look at you a little more sympathetically. Life, I continued as I walked along the sweeter and more shady side of famous Pall Mall, is to know how to enjoy the present moment and its small pleasures and, by association of ideas, I lit a cigarette (my last) and blew a cloud of smoke towards the flowers in the window-boxes of the Nova Scotia Bank, another towards the Institute of Contemporary Arts, a third towards the Florence Nightingale Monument. In contrast to all those books which I did not buy are all those books which I did read. I became a reader at the British Museum, man, and a member of the London Library, just think of it: a million books within my grasp, in English, Spanish, French . . . in all living languages and all dead tongues! And there, in the library, in the presence of the works of Pliny the Elder and of Gaius Salustius Crispus, Attic tragedy and the works of Thucydides (I copied a magnificent description by Thucydides of the Plague of Athens for Uncle Esteban), I reflected that anatomists had torn up Greek and Latin roots and with them baptized the parts of our body, and that the thorax and the crista galli, the jejunum and the septum lucidum, the tuber cinereum and the calamus scriptorius are of this lineage. Life may well, indeed, be a belonging, I assured Florence Nightingale, but the reason for its being a belonging would not even be, as Hegel suggested, a necessary extension of individual freedom, for the simple reason that you, Florence Nightingale, and you, cousin, and I, Walter, did not choose to live and be free. Life, I repeated, is not a thing, I said to the librarian who, by coincidence, spoke a little Spanish and thought that I was giving him the title of a book. Life what, sir? he asked me. *The Tragic Sense of Life* by Miguel de Unamuno, I said to him and, while he went off to look for the book, I went to the gents to pee. Never in my life have I peed so much, man! And the fact is, I spent my mornings drinking tea to overcome sleepiness and make the most of the respite offered by each day and then I spent all afternoon and evening drinking beer to overcome insomnia. But I can say that, like any good boy scout who knows his story of Mowgli bite by bite, I never went to bed without having achieved something good: without, at least, having conquered imagination for that day. And as I held my beloved reproductive organ or, in other words, a dearly loved extension of my individual freedom, I said to myself: well, yes, life is, among other things, a little heap of things on which it depends. Life is your brain, I said to myself as I looked at my reflection in the mirror. Not only your brain, but your brain plus your eyes, plus your mouth, plus your circulatory system, plus your this, plus your that, I continued as I washed my hands and went out into the hall and, while I waited for the librarian to bring my book – the English take their time over everything except sex – I started leafing through the *Guinness Book of Records* and, besides learning of the woman who could identify colours through her fingers and that the world's fattest man weighed half a ton and a bit and other such inanities, I read that of course, predictably, Turgenev's brain – one of the largest known to date – weighed two kilos twelve grams and that of Anatole France – one of the smallest – only one kilo and seventeen grams. And I say *of course* because, literary considerations aside, this confirmed, yet again,

435

that the human brain is *a thing*. You must forgive me, but I am afraid that all I could bring for you, apart from a few souvenirs, was the bow tie you asked me for. Would you believe, they hardly exist in London? How badly the English dress, man! And that's the least of it: how badly English women undress! And well, all these things, I said as I signed the receipt slip, are your life. I thanked the librarian and, at random, opened the book at the part where Unamuno relates how Leopardi saw the close relationship existing between love and death. I jotted down the sentence in my little black book to add to my collection of similar sentences and ideas – love has the smell of death, said Bataille while Thomas Mann had to turn to French to have his character say: *le corps, l'amour, la mort, ces trois ne font qu'un* – and I took my leave of the London Library with its doors of bevelled panes and went out into St James Square, hoping that the sun might by then have come out. No chance. In England, the sun is a brilliant exception and in winter but a dazzling hypothesis. It was, however, summer. The longest day of the year! Faced with this dismal prospect, I put the book in my pocket and I told myself that, to experience the tragic sense of life, one has only to live in London dreaming ever of a tropical dawn. I blew a kiss to a poster of Acapulco gazing blue-eyed at me from the window of a Pan American agency and went into a tobacconist to buy cigarettes. How expensive they are in London, old man! But, even so, I always smoked like one condemned which is indeed exactly the word because smoking, in our age, is equivalent to a mortal sin. But what is the use – I asked an organ-grinder – what is the use of sacrificing so many pleasures, if there is no guarantee that we will live? Because, though life is not a car, death, on the other hand, might well be: beware, cousin, in London they drive on the left and there is nothing in the world more dangerous than, fresh off the plane, crossing Park Lane. And everything happens so quickly: a car kills you in a tenth of a second; cancer in a hundredth of a century. Life is free, I said to the three pence change they gave me with the cigarettes; death, on the other hand, costs an arm and a leg, a liver and a thorax, a rib and a heart and I retraced my steps to give these three pence, plus another two, to the organ-grinder: such was my pleasure in hearing, at that moment in the middle of London, Juventino Rosas' waltz *Sobre las Olas*. Oh, you have no idea how sentimental you become over there! You always start by swearing that you will never be moved by Mexican folk songs or by rereading *Suave Patria* and you end by screaming at the English, perhaps not that in Mexico Church and State have been separate for over a century or that in 1938 we nationalized the oilfields given us by the devil, but certainly throwing in their faces that if it weren't for us they would have neither potatoes, nor tobacco, nor tomatoes, nor chocolate. Nor, most important of all, marijuana. Sooner or later you end up actually feeling proud of these same banalities and of the jade knives in the British Museum and the Mexican masks in the Horniman Museum. At the corner of Charles II and the Haymarket, I left a gob of spit containing not only a few sparks of microscopic mint, but also two fragments of tobacco and who knows how many millions of little beasties because, as it was said, who said? more beings live in a man's mouth than men in the world. And I thought that, of course, those things – I refer to our members and our organs – constitute only a part of our lives in that some, though not all, we can do without. Not only did Obregón lose a hand and Captain Ahab a leg, but Uncle Esteban lived minus one lung and the general minus one eye. There are also people who lose both: you can't begin to imagine the number of blind people in London. I've never seen so many. Never did so many blind people fail to see me. You come across them all over the place: in King's Road, on the Strand, in Petticoat Lane, tapping their very long white sticks with which, in revenge, they almost gouge out children's eyes. I can tell you that the English love children more than fairy tales would have us believe, but less than you might think when you cease to believe in fairy tales. Ah, in London I always woke up with a bad daily taste in my mouth and breath of smouldering brass and old drains which caused me to lose my friends in the mornings and to get them back in the afternoons, when the scent of coffee wafted among the orange trees. I tell a lie: that was in Paris. In London, I never drank coffee because it tastes of a mixture of chickpeas and chicory. For Aunt Luisa, I brought a transparent map of the City of Light, printed on mica, so that she can put it on top of a map of Mexico City and see what streets and which boulevards and which clocks coincide. For you, so that you can indulge your passion for revealing innards, I brought several prints including that of Rembrandt's *La Baigneuse* (in whose respect Cabañes diagnosed a hernia) and others of Giotto's frescos: of that charity without charity, that jealousy – to use Proust's words – which looks like a plate from a medical treatise illustrating the compression of the glottis by a tumour on the tongue. I turned down Orange Street, then along Whitcomb Street towards Leicester Square, where I assured a road sweeper that, of course, nobody can live without a heart or without a liver. Or, at least, not yet. Without a brain, even less, I told a couple queueing outside the Leicester Square Odeon. How often I went to the cinema in London! I was never out of the National Film Theatre! Plays too: the best in the world. But to choose, as I had to at that time, between going to a Ben Jonson play or a Shakespeare production is like trying to choose between Virgil and Homer. I bought a couple of hot dogs and sat down on a bench. I also bought the *Evening Standard* to look for a new flat without any hope, of course, of finding a large, warm and solid place where I wouldn't hear the creaking of the next-door couple's bed. There's no such thing in London. For Estefania, I brought a postcard from the National Portrait Gallery of Florence Nightingale, looking so innocent beside her sister

Parthenope. Of course I look after my liver, I said to the sausage (although I don't usually talk with my mouth full). But I look after it, not because I love it, but because I fear it: I could not love my liver even if I believed, as Galen did, that in it all veins converge, even if I thought, like the Hebrews and the Armenians, that it is the seat of love. For Uncle Austin, I brought a bottle of malt whisky. But, one never knows, I said to a pigeon. One never knows when the liver is going to come up with an acute yellow atrophy or an adipose deterioration. Never. That's why I look after it. How many times, sick of my liver, have I sent it to the devil and drunk myself into a stupor! But the next day I wish I hadn't and treat it with velvet gloves and stop drinking and give it its necessary proteins. For similar reasons, I said, almost choking on my hot dog in the process, I sometimes worry about my stomach and my lungs, I added, breathing in the fresh smog and the smell of pizzarias. In true English fashion, I licked off the ketchup that had dribbled over my fingers. How the English lick their fingers! You might almost say that to qualify as a surgeon and earn the title of Mister, you have to learn to lick your fingers after performing a rectal examination. On the other hand, cousin, they forgo the pleasure of dunking their bread in their coffee. I started to eat the second hot dog, gave a few crumbs to the pigeons and drew their attention to the fact that, just because I look after my organs, it doesn't mean that I look after myself. Far from it: I look after them because I know I am in their hands. Or rather, I am in their lobules and in their mucous matter. I know they are holy tyrants (General Liver, King St Pancreas, the Holy Arachnoid Trinity) who deprive me of some of my greatest pleasures. And of course you will say that, in any case, I assured the pigeon with ruffled chest perching on William's bald head, they don't deprive me, they deprive my tongue and my palate. And so it is: I am at their mercy too. They dictate how much I want to eat and what. They, together with my ribs and my kidneys, are the real bosses. So much so, I said confidentially to a park bench, that I have even ended up liking their famous fish and chips which stink of cheap vinegar, their steak and kidney pie which stinks of urine and, of course, the hot dogs I was eating which stink of English mustard and taste like the footbaths Aunt Luisa gave us when we had a temperature. That's the trouble with being poor. True, I had money enough to go to Europe to study but, once I got there, I was always a poverty-stricken student who never ate in Claridges. Nor in Simpsons either, and it wasn't for lack of a tie. But, in honour of Voronoff, I met some macrobiotics and I ate jellied eels in the East End. I left the last crumbs of memory in Leicester Square, piled my bones one above the other and, walking behind my nose and followed by my back, I said to myself (in a voice that I did not recognize as my own) that they, all of them, my organs and my viscera, conspired against me every moment of their lives. Not a day goes by, damn it, I shouted at Marlon Brando, but I

438

wonder when my stomach is going to start to sabotage my digestion, when my lymphatic system is going to declare war, when my lungs are going to start boycotting my heart or when my brain is going to go on strike without warning and, worse still, without my even realizing! Our organism, I added, is subjugated to an industrial regime in which individuality has to be defended by the very society it eventually destroys! That is why, like on that first afternoon in London, cousin, I feel defeated already and take refuge in the last corner of myself, in the smallest and most distant of all corners and I get down on my knees, with my eyes closed, to await the arrival of the ghosts and wonder which will come first: whether bronchogenic carcinoma with its retinue of whistles, or diabetes mellitus in its tunics of sweet blood. Because I know that, sooner or later, the organs of my body will triumph and be the death of me. In London, I saw every horror film ever made. Never, however, can you be alone, in the total centre of yourself, I said to Dr Caligari. Fichte already stated that pure self-awareness, with the *Ego* completely transparent unto itself, is an unattainable ideal, I assured Dracula, and *Dasein* does not exist except in its essential reference to an exterior which is the world, I said to Boris Karloff. And I knew, as did Hume, cousin, that when you try to dig down into the very deepest part of yourself, you always find some intimation of warmth or cold, of light or shadow, of love or hate, of pain or pleasure. Never have I been myself without my hands, I said to Orlac! Never has my nose been itself without me, I thought, remembering a Gogol story and then I felt hot, cousin, and I felt cold also, even though it was summer. But what am I saying: summer? Summer spends four or five days a year in London and then moves on because it doesn't like the climate. And I felt self-love and self-hate. And I felt, especially, that I was so alone, there in the middle of Leicester Square, and so exposed to the elements and so defenceless, that I would have liked to stamp and scream, to immure the world's commotion and spew up perversions. However, since I couldn't get into my soul, I took refuge in a telephone booth, searched for a two-pence coin in my pocket and dialled the tourist information service in Spanish to hear a voice in my own language and, while the voice talked about the Changing of the Guard, the latest John Osborne play, the Duke of Clarence's tomb, the Rolling Stones' concert, the Chelsea Flower Show and the stores of Knightsbridge, I shouted down the telephone at my organs that, although I didn't have the power to rent out my liver, file a suit against my stomach, kick out my heart or divorce my brain, I would have the pleasure and consolation of carrying them all with me to the grave, do you hear me? because never, are you listening? never will I give you the pleasure of remaining alive, sitting before your shop and waiting for your enemy's corpse to pass. Oh no, I repeated, never will I give you the pleasure of leaving you alive and brimming with health while I rot! In the

London Library I rediscovered Hermann Broch and the dying Virgil thinking of the separate life of his hands and the districts and provinces of his body and of man as an indivisible creature who is none the less divided into an infinite number of individual parts to each of which pertains an idea, as Spinoza would have it. But never, in any of those parts, did I find the soul in which I wanted to take refuge, nor the iridescent cocoon from which the soul would one day emerge transformed into a butterfly with polished wings and resplendent in lace and foam. And desperately I searched, like Dr Lucio Negri, in Flourens' vital knot, in my medulla oblongata and in my pineal gland and throughout the length and breadth of my brain which, according to Cantor, is supposed to be infinite (but which is turned into nothing, zero, when a tank drives over your head). I too, cousin, like the colleagues of the Argentinian doctor, was more afraid of finding it than of not finding it. The same fear, the same terror, felt by anyone, even those most strongly believing in a supramundane life, that a ghost might appear before them. Yet none the less, none the less, cousin, I left many fragments of my soul in London. I left them in the gardens of the Embankment. I left them in Soho, in the Aldwych, on Forest Hill, on London Bridge. I left them on Westminster Bridge every time I crossed it at dawn: the chimes of Big Ben, old man, postpone their grandeur until six in the morning, when they soar over the city, they fly to caress the kin bronze of the statues: the Rodin group in Victoria Embankment Gardens, Moore's sculpture opposite Vauxhall. But, as you may imagine, my organs gave me no answer: the troubadouresque dialogue between the brain and the heart written by the Marquis de Santillana exists only in literature, by which time the voice had finished its lengthy recital of tourist information and then started to repeat itself: the Changing of the Guard, the latest Osborne play, Jack the Ripper's tomb, etc., etc., so I thanked it in Spanish and left the telephone booth, trying to remember if it was Henry Miller who said that living in a country where you hear a foreign language every day makes you more aware of certain shades of meaning in your own language which you had never before imagined. You have no idea of the shiver that once went down my spine when, walking across one of London's melancholy bridges, Blackfriars' Bridge – or Bridge of the Black Friars might sound more impressive – and hearing the cries of some birds, I suddenly remembered those lines by Gongora: *'infame turba de nocturnas aves, gimiendo tristes y volando graves'* – odious rabble of nocturnal birds, groaning sadly and flying gravely. There are, of course, no bridges more beautiful than those in Paris. But there is one in London, Waterloo Bridge, which has the most beautiful view in the world. I'm talking as always of urban landscapes, not natural scenes. It was from there that Monet painted Charing Cross and the Parliament buildings at all hours of the day. From there also, Turner not only discovered abstract painting but also invented

440

the yellow light of London's winter dusks, if only to justify what Wilde wrote years later, in his essay on the decay of lying, to the effect that London's fog did not exist until it was invented by writers and painters. I have never laughed so much as when somebody told me that Turner painted as he did because his eyesight wasn't too good! But I didn't laugh for long. I thought of Gongora's madness, of Parmigianino's madness, that of Nietzsche and Nerval and so many others and I reflected again – like that time when we were in La Española, do you remember – on the extent to which our mental attitudes depend on our physical state. I, for example, get into a foul mood when I am hungry. Estefania, when she has her period. And etc. Never again will I speak to you of electric-shock treatment and lobotomies, I vowed to myself, never again will I mention electronic nirvanas and electrosex which will one day be achieved by electrical stimulation of the pleasure centre; never again will I subject you to talk – I vowed to you from there, from Waterloo Bridge, cousin – of the effect of ataractics, tranquillizers, hallucinogens and uppers, or of Pentothal which makes us talk about things we would never talk about when awake; never again will I speak to you of drugs which revive the memory of old people and make the young forget and the anti-riot drugs that will be used against revolutionaries of the future. Never, never again will I speak to you of all this, cousin, unless I develop a protuberance in the area of repetitiveness. Never again! Though that does not mean that I won't continue to rebel with my whole soul and all my neurons against the fact that being worse or better, more intelligent or more stupid, braver or more cowardly, more talented or more inept, depends purely and simply on our body and its material interchanges with the world around it. It almost seemed amusing to me to admit the possibility that it was George III's porphyria that caused him prematurely to lose the British Colonies of America or that Robert Walpole changed his political ideas as the discomfort he suffered from the stones in his bladder increased or decreased. I find it even more amusing that the destiny of France should have depended merely on Napoleon Bonaparte's constipation and I thought that perhaps it was since then that the stuck-up nature of the French became more defined and for this reason, and in reaction, the heirs of liberty, equality and fraternity are so partial to blowing raspberries and to the word *Merde* (how well I remember Aunt Luisa studying French in the garden and Grandfather making fun of her without Aunt Luisa realizing! Do you remember? *Madame Legrand vient de voir sa mère*, she said, and Grandfather: *Merde!* and Aunt Luisa: *Madame Legrand vient de voir sa merde*) but the joke ends there: to accept the possibility that Turner discovered the yellow light of London because he suffered from an ailment of the pupil, that Constable owed his originality to partial colourblindness, El Greco to astigmatism or Monet to cataracts, I find not in the least amusing. Munch also had the shadow of a bird in his eyes. Speaking of which, I brought you a reproduction of Munch's *Three Stages of Woman*. But, in this particular case, the dead woman and the naked woman are in love with each other, it's an idyll: love and death are one and the same, as Mirbeau also said. Feeling more optimistic because, after all, I was not on Waterloo Bridge one yellow winter afternoon, but walking through Leicester Square one summer's day – sunless it's true but, after all, a long summer day – and, having ceased to worry so much about recovering the delights of a virile and translucent language which melted in my hands like flakes of snow, my brain decided that this whole body which, according to Edison, has the sole purpose of carrying it – the brain – from place to place, should head south down Irving Street. And I don't know whether Malebranche was right or not. I don't know whether our legs move us or we move our legs (or God, our will *and* our legs) but the fact is that the three of us walked towards Trafalgar Square and then I remembered that right there, in that very street, such a coincidence! some dumb student of the kind that specializes in Latin American literature and knows more about Manuel Payno than we will ever know about Alexander Pope, said to me: so you're living in exile and I replied no, I'm living in London at the moment, in Irving Street to be precise. Really? In this very street? But what number? he asked me. And I told him: At number seven, which is my shoe size. And I continued on my way. Or rather, we continued on our way, I and all my members and organs (which by then were quite a crowd) with our home and our homeland and our world on our backs, like the snail.

Where were you then, cousin? Where were you as I walked past the National Gallery in London? Were you walking past the School of Medicine and dreaming that you were Dandy in Baltimore, daring to penetrate the third ventricle of the cerebrum? Were you walking beneath the plaque dedicated to Rafael Lucia? Or past the monument to Dr Carmona y Valle, surrounded by his four wise owls? Or were you reading *The Testament of a Surgeon* and wishing you were Humanus, that you might triumph over Nimbus? Or were you gazing at the shop windows full of laboratory instruments and apparatus, fascinated not so much by what you could do with them as by the names designating them, by the magic of those words replete with mystery and exoticism? Ah, cousin, I also fell in love with words and my first laboratory classes in secondary school added to their spell the magic of form and colour: the spheres of Jenna glass, the crucibles of nickel and the coils, decanting tubes and retorts which looked like pipes for fat, transparent giants. I already mentioned Hans Castorp . . . I did mention him, didn't I? But I must remind Grandfather and his friends, in order to make their knowledge more Mexican (or their

Mexicanness more knowledgeable) that the ill-fated and silent and mournful figure at which he gazes on the first morning of his stay in the mountains, Madame *Tous-les-Deux* (who, if anything, symbolizes death prowling around the Berghof Sanatorium) was Mexican. And also that Mexico City was the setting in which unfolded Papini's tale of a man approaching Gog to offer him *morte ai morti* (death to the dead). Ah, dear Palinuro: I climbed to the top of the self-same west tower of Glasgow University and from there, with eyes drowned in other skies, from there, I. swear, as I gazed upon that black and gloomy city, I thought rather of the moist track of Cernuda than of Lister, and I took pity on the poet and on the dead who forget each other and I wept tears of soot which swelled the water of the Clyde, turned silver by the cold. There was a day, I mused, when the *Rattlesnake* aboard which the illustrious Dr Thomas Henry Huxley was ship's surgeon was to be launched from the shipyards of the Clyde. But I never was, nor will I ever be, any one of the Huxleys, although I did have the privilege, as I told you, of being a member of the library used by Lytton Strachey and famous individuals such as Sprandell or the frustrated writer Philip Quarles who offered the novelist the rare opportunity to meditate at leisure on every imaginable aspect of his plots and stories, including the physiological and the physicochemical. And, as I descended the dark, tortuous stairs of the Glasgow University tower, I thought of the chapters of *Ulysses*, each of which is dedicated to a different organ and I thought of Borges ('A history of a man's dreams is not inconceivable; another, of the organs of his body . . .') and I thought of Henry James who maintained that any novel should be like a living organism, unique and continuous, and I vowed that the book which I would write some day would be as sickly, fragile and defective as the human organism and also, if possible (which it isn't), equally intricate and magnificent, I said, as I and my hundred thousand kilometres of blood duct descended the tower's spiral stairs two at a time, but it will not, I said (I repeated to distraction), it will not be a book with Apollonian skin, with a skin smooth and white and soft as the skin of Ophelia drawing an aesthetic veil over reality. No: it will be a book without frills, I said as I emerged into the streets of Glasgow, a Dionysian book triumphantly attesting to life in all its darkness and its horror. If the truth be told, I was actually in London and not in Glasgow when I remembered that Breton said that surrealism is a secret society leading to death and that Mexico (this he said on another occasion) is the most surrealistic country on earth. The general will bestow on me a grateful eye when I tell him. Everyone in Europe knows Posada's skeletons! I shouted when I saw Daumier's death playing the trumpet and Della Bella's death on horseback with its feathered hat flowing in the wind and deaths doing battle with fat women and thin, like Hans Baldung's and that of Niklaus Deutsch and so many others that were nowhere to be seen,

Palinuro, in the homoeopathic surgery to which Aunt Clementina took you every fortnight. However, it would be redundant to give you a whole list of picture titles and so, although redundant is an apt way of describing the citizens of the kingdoms of death, I will change the subject, I said, leaving the National Gallery, leaving the Louvre, the Prado and any other of the museums and galleries I visited in the United States and Europe: man does not live on death alone. But it was for another reason that I did not that day visit the National Portrait Gallery which is just around the corner; however long you queue, I told myself, you'll never get inside. Joshua Reynolds will never paint your portrait as he painted Hunter's and King George IV will never make you a baronet for ridding him of a sebaceous cyst as he did Cooper. On the gallery stairs I noticed that I had split a thumbnail which I bit off and left there as a souvenir. Never have I seen people bite their nails as much as the English! I crossed St Martin's Place, saw that there were still forty minutes to go before the midday concert started, turned into William IV Street and then down Chandos Place and suddenly (I was deep in thought and do not remember where, whether in a side street or an alley, whether in Floral Street or Maiden Lane, I really don't know) there I was, standing before a shop window containing all the instruments and glass worms which had given birth to the angelic art of chemical changes and potions and philters in the service of which Theophrastus and Nicholas Flamel and all the alchemists of the *ruelle de l'or* wore out their brains and their ambitions; not to mention the nozzles and syphons, the Erlenmeyer tubes and so many other things that reminded me of hydrogen spirit enclosed like a genie in a Plucker tube and the little glass spheres containing phosphamine which, when heated (oh, what times they were!), gave off a white smoke which rose in the air in beautiful, expanding, magic rings which made us think – or made me think, anyway – of one day setting up a halo factory. I blew a smoke ring with my cigarette, a humble and imperfect echo and, seeing myself there, reflected in the glass, image of an image as Plotinus would say, Cratylus before Cratylus, knowing not which was the Walter of flesh and blood and which the Walter of flesh and glass, I not only confirmed for the umpteenth time that we are more than cousins, Palinuro, we are twins, the *Pileati Fratres* crowned with will o' the wisp, but I also realized that, ever since we were boys studying laboratory experiments, Venetian turpentine has held for both of us the prestige of Canaletto's frozen palaces and showers of light and shade, and that the mere fact of its name causes the various points of Paris to burst into brightness when submerged in a warm bottle of Beaujolais. For Cousin Walter (or rather, for myself) I brought several bottles of French wine. Cheap ones mind you, but still. It was not for lack of interest, I can tell you, that I didn't there and then buy a still to produce my own whisky which is also extremely expensive in London. I made do with breathing on the shop window and writing the W of my name in the misted patch. But, if I remember rightly, I did once tell you that, while you swallow your words, I spit them out, and this is because we are condemned to shine alternately, like Castor and Pollux. So, perhaps, I must die that you might live. I speak of a symbolic death. I don't wish to die so young, which is one reason why I left London. It is to that city, cousin, that everybody goes to die. Freud, Nijinsky, Simone Weil and so many more! But, don't expect that somebody who did not have money to buy a bottle of Mouton Rothschild in a Sotheby's auction, an icon in the Maria Andipa gallery or a Victorian divan in Prides of London, will bequeath you anything more than a waistcoat. But I brought you a charming Letraset Catalogue that I was given in Gerrard Street. By the way, I never did manage to get out that wretched stain from the La Española snails which almost changed the course of my life, or at least, my imitative and almost jesting pose, because I can't unbutton my jacket without raising my hand to my heart to hide the stain. Some might say that I should submit it to the Adler's test which produces a bright Prussian Blue colour indicating the presence of blood. But no, I have not yet put a bullet through my heart although I would like to choose the dimensions of my death and I found John Donne's *Biathanatos* most interesting and, as I walked the streets of London, I felt sorry for those poor souls who had committed suicide and been buried beneath its pavements. The English still consider suicide a crime. 'Beware: if you kill yourself we'll put you in prison!' Sylvia Plath also died in London and I imagine that she must be buried, gnawed ankles and all, beside a mouse and a shrew. Nor, in England, are you legal owner of your body when you're dead – which seems to be more logical – to the extent that, if you want to bequeath it to science, you have to write to HM Inspector of I Don't Know What, in Alexander Fleming House. If you want to leave only your heart, you have to send it – or rather, it has to be sent – to the National Heart Hospital. Anyway, deciding that it was time for a pint, I dispatched half my heart to Westmoreland Street, the other half to the Cardiology Institute in Mexico, took my leave of the coils and glass jars, made an about-turn and set off once more with the rolling energy of a beetle: like Sisyphus, cousin, I am daily saddled with a great burden of stone: but I carve it as I go so that each day it is different from the day before. But anyway, I told myself, while it is necessary to get up, to have breakfast is not; to become frightened is necessary, to write to your friends is not; it is sometimes necessary to wear a tie, to wear a mask of tragedy is not; it is necessary to speak, also to remain silent; death is hereditary, sterility is not. And, I thought, not being Julius Caesar who bequeathed his gardens and his cities to his subjects, I could instead bequeath to you the whole planet with all its oceans and natural landscapes – to you who love them so much – not

445

forgetting the luckless clover fields and the volcanos subordinated to legend and history. But, if you like, I can also leave you my memories of Europe and my walk through London and my weekly visit to Dobell's where I always managed to listen to ten records for free, to every one I had them set aside but hardly ever bought. But, if you are to shine in my absence, I will someday have to give you my waistcoat, the very same waistcoat that Aunt Luisa made from the leftovers of the patchwork quilt that covered you, Palinuro, when you caught the measles and when they took your tonsils out. But I don't want you to inherit my aspirations along with my waistcoat, I said to you as I walked along Shaftesbury Avenue on my way to have my beer and I remembered, nostalgically, those times we went to the clubs in the Guerrero quarter and we read poems by Manuel M. Flores and The Bohemian's Toast and we drank whole cartons of beer and ended up at the top of traffic-lights, conversing on the most intimate terms with the green light. What times those were! You were sure that some day you would give your name to an unknown disease, to a new operation, to an original symptom. All von Helmholtz had to do, I said to the little tart who was with me – that was years ago, cousin, centuries ago, in the Blue Beard Club – was to think up the ophthalmoscope which allowed him to observe the depths of the living eye, for fame to look kindly upon him for ever more. I took a long swig of beer, lit another Rothmans (Gauloises I smoked only in Paris, like Cortázar characters) and you said to your girl: Farabeuf, to give another example, had only to invent his 'place of choice' amputation to get where he wanted to be. And, as was to be expected, when I put my hand in my raincoat pocket to pay for my beer, I remembered that not only was I still carrying Unamuno's book but also, in a manner of speaking, General Obregón's hand, which was what I had originally started talking to you about. How I used to criticize Aunt Enriqueta for starting to talk about something and then getting side-tracked until everybody was completely lost, but she always managed to get back to the original subject, guided by her wonderful conversational instinct! Anyway, walking towards Trafalgar Square and thinking of the progressive mutilation perfected by the men of the small work, the *hsiao kuung de ren*, quoted not by Farabeuf, but in *Farabeuf*, and thinking of the tin man in the *Wizard of Oz*, of symmetrical gangrene of the extremities and of modern operations such as the ghastly hemicorporectomy and of all the future possibilities of the cyborg – the monster which is half man and half machine – I asked one of the lions sculpted by the worthy Landseer when he (the lion) thought that, physically speaking, one started to stop being oneself: when they cut off a leg or when they cut off your mane? When they remove one arm or when they remove your skin to use it as a rug in a Northumberland Street club? Or when they remove your second arm after amputating both legs and your tail? And, by association of ideas, I remembered a very amusing joke that I was told in the most inappropriate place in the world: in Surrey, when we had been walking all morning from the red castle of Farnham towards Moor Park (where Swift found his beloved morning star) and we had crossed damp fields and ancient woodlands where wild mint and anemones flowered and walked country lanes bordered by yellow columbine and out of the blue one of my friends, an Argentinian, told me that when Valle-Inclán was in Mexico, Obregón invited him to a bullfight, to a play, whatever, and at the end Valle-Inclán, who was also one-handed, said to Obregón: General, lend me your hand to applaud. It was all very surrealistic, as though the band of the Queen's Guards had suddenly materialized in Windsor Park playing the Zacatecas March. I also picked blackberries on the way to Langford Court, when the sun began to distil the wine in the dandelions. And the fact is that since I left Mexico and spent a winter in an American village, cousin, I had begun to live in picture postcards. For Uncle Austin I brought – don't ask me why I brought more things for him than for anybody else; after all, he is English and it's a long time since he left his country – I brought him, as I was saying, loads of picture postcards, including one of Trafalgar Square where I happened to be at the time and, what is more, beneath another famous one-handed man: Admiral Nelson; not by chance, but because I had directed my steps towards his monument with all premonition and perfidy. Just for fun (the admiral had never done anything to me but, none the less, ever since I saw the portrait of the beautiful Lady Hamilton painted by Romney, I felt a yearning to steal it and write a story on the subject) I raised my umbrella as though it were a rifle, aimed at his single remaining eye which gazed towards the coasts of Calais from the top of his column and, pum! No, he didn't spit plum stones at me but, instead, sent a pigeon with a most expressive message: a liquid dropping which clouded the right lens of my glasses, thereby press-ganging me into the ranks of the one-eyed. I washed my glasses in one of the fountains in the very same Trafalgar Square where, every 31 December, a few mad Englishmen bathe – and I say mad because the others never take a bath at all, even though it's the only country which has an Order of Bath – and I entered St Martin in the Fields to listen to the midday concert. Handel also died in London. This, then – I said to myself – is the source of the horror aroused by mutilated people, to which is added the awareness of our limitations and our divisibility and, of course, the crime against sacred symmetry, and not just the dualistic triangular symmetry spoken of by Thomas Mann: that composed of the two eyes and the mouth, and the downy symmetry composed of the two armpits and the pubis. No, one mustn't forget the two arms and the two legs. Particularly the two legs since, having arrived late at the concert, I had to stand and my legs soon started to ache. Because, if one does *not* cease to be oneself when one's legs are cut off, why then do we have legs? Just for walking and playing football? Or, in my case, just for walking because I've never played football or run a marathon? And, because I couldn't remain standing the whole time even if they were playing the Hallelujah (which they weren't), I went out on to the street again. It had stopped raining and I headed for a Chinese shop to buy pickled chillis and a tin of abalone (I could, from time to time, give myself some little treat and with all the more reason on that particular day because, if I haven't already mentioned it, it was my birthday) and, as usual, I got lost and found myself suddenly before a bookshop specializing in the occult. They're springing up all over the place, man! Magic used to be the preserve of the initiated few. Now, what have they left us? There was a time when, for me, the *aqua regia* contained in the laboratory dishes bore no relation whatever to the acids of which it is composed but only to the water of a palace fountain in which a tremendously old princess, with breasts as cancer-infested as those of Raymond Lully's lover, had washed the gold from her hair. There was a time when, as far as I was concerned, the red and poisonous fumes given off by copper shavings bathed in nitric acid belonged to the realms of Red Magic, where the Grand Grimoire used to invoke the spirits of hell, rather than to anything connected with a simple, straightforward chemical reaction. But Madame Blavatsky also died in London.

In London there are no open-air cafés; there aren't even any non-open-air ones: you either go to a pub or go to a pub. But they are nearly all amazing. That second one I went to had proud, wooden representations of classical animals like the Lion of England, the Plantagenet Falcon, the White Greyhound of Richmond, the Red Dragon of Wales and the Unicorn of Scotland, and that afternoon it was full, precisely, of Scotsmen who had come to London for a football match between the Queens Park Rangers and the Heart of Midlothian: I ordered a pint of brown ale (warm English beer is better than is commonly believed outside England but worse than you think when you get used to it) and took Unamuno's book from my raincoat pocket, but a drunken Scotsman with red nose started asking me where I was from and when I said Mexico he insisted on drinking the health of all Mexicans, although he wasn't sure whether Mexico was a province of the United States or an island but he had heard they were going to hold the Olympic Games there, or that they already had, whatever, cheers! and I, faithful to my obsessions, insisted that we didn't necessarily have to be as we are, since we could have been like inhabitants of the moon who, according to Boucher de Perthes, have only one arm, one leg and no nose, but the Scotsman thought I was talking about maimed war veterans and explained to me that he had taken part in the conquest of the western

Rhineland but that he didn't like Rhine wine, each to his own taste, and I asked the Scotsman, I asked the Black Bull of Clarence, why our sexes could not be geometrical like those of the inhabitants of the imaginary country invented by Diderot in *Les Bijoux Indiscrets* and mentioned that William Tenn insisted that on Venus there were not two sexes, but seven. Can you imagine, I said to him, how many combinations of Greek tragedies could be created with seven sexes? But I realized, by the look that the Scotsman gave me, that my remarks could be open to ambiguous sexual interpretation and it might be thought that I was the kind of person who'll sleep with anything in a skirt, so I let him carry on talking about Montgomery – I always thought I knew a bit about European history, man, but I realized then that I knew nothing at all. But what did I care? The history of the world goes back to our own earliest memory – the rest is pure hearsay. By the way, I brought Uncle Esteban a little book on World War I medicine and surgery which I think he'll really like and it will remind him of when he made love with the Polish nurse in the trenches full of mud and lice and between explosions of the Big Berthas, or are the Big Berthas from the Second World War? I asked the Scotsman, but he didn't answer and continued talking about Monty (as he affectionately called Montgomery) while I assured him yet again that I was not South American, that only the south part of the Americas is called South America and that the United States stole everything from us, including the name of the continent which, I insisted, is America from Alaska to Tierra del Fuego and that his mistake was like calling his whole island, including Wales and Scotland, England. This he did not forgive me until I bought him a pint of beer and gave him tenpence to bet on Hearts for me and a postage stamp to send me the receipt. Anyway, we said goodbye the best of friends and I also said goodbye to the White House of Hanover and it was not until I was out in the street once more, bloody Scotsman, that I could again flick through *The Tragic Sense of Life* and, when I learned that man is a corpse-hoarding animal, I almost caught the tube to Archway to take a bunch of red geraniums to the author of *Das Kapital*. Because, my friend, it was not only Karl Marx who died in London: so did the international revolution of the proletariat. I have no idea whether Engels died there or in Manchester but I do know that, in accordance with his wishes, his ashes were scattered on the beaches of Eastbourne, where he had stayed on several occasions with Marx. As though the English beaches weren't already desolate enough! But I remembered that I had to buy tickets for *Tosca*, and so I set off instead for Covent Garden. It continued to rain. It always rains, as I was saying, but it doesn't pour like in Mexico, it is an endless drizzle, never a torrential rain, which I suppose is why César Vallejo didn't go to London to die. And, of course, I started to feel the need to pee again and I couldn't go back to the pub because it was already shut. The city is full of public lavatories, one can't complain. This is attested even by Wellington's triumphant battle after which was named not only a bridge but also a railway station – Waterloo, Water-loo; that is what happens when you learn English: certain words begin to lose their magic as, for instance, in the case of Liver-pool and Beef-eaters. But, of course, I didn't find one (a loo, that is) when I needed it and I reflected on how you could relieve this physiological need anywhere and without offending public decency if you could, for example, urinate with your teeth. Hell! I shouted at an eater-of-beef who gazed at me from the label of a gin bottle, hell! you should be able to urinate with your teeth, see with your knees, digest with your lungs, breathe with your thumb, think with your nose, manufacture sugar with your testicles and laugh with your eustachian tube! You should be able to do everything with everything, to be one, whole and true! And I continued walking and staring at my hand, surprised at its existence and once again I wondered when General Obregón's hand began to be his: when he became aware of it and started to move it? Or when he had to earn his living with his hands working in a flour-mill? I raised my hand and pointed to the left: I walked down Chandos Street. And anyway, I asked myself: When did it cease to be his? When he lost it, in Celaya? Or did it continue to be his when he put it in a jar of phenol? I turned left down Southampton Row striving not to occupy too much interplanetary space, always following my hand which drew me, implacably, along the streets and alleyways of Soho. What a tangle of a city! The streets dance, like arabesques, in the middle of your forehead. Not for nothing did Unwin, in the story of Abenjacan the Bojari say to Dunraven that for anyone who really wishes to hide, London is a better maze than a watchtower to which all a building's corridors lead. And only a few days ago a friend commented that the English lost the opportunity to build a rational city after the Great Fire, by not heeding Wren. Notwithstanding my respect for this and other English, or part-English, architects like Inigo Jones, I said to myself as I reached Covent Garden and glimpsed St Paul's Church – not to be confused with the cathedral built by the other one, Sir Christopher – here is the perfect place to empty my bladder. My bladder? Strange how, when people go to see General Obregón's hand, they never talk about the hand which *was* his, but of the hand which *is*. How can anything belong to somebody who no longer exists? How, for example, can newspapers say 'The student's body was found in a ditch', if the student who is supposedly owner of this pile of flesh, bones and cartilage no longer exists and if he did exist he couldn't be owner of his body – alive or dead – anyway, as though his body were an object (and none the less *it is an object*, a pile of objects) to be held in somebody's arms if dead, or helped to return to life, to walk and dream, if alive? So, as I sidled up to a pillar and unzipped my fly, I refused (but this time very quietly, because I didn't want anybody to catch me) to declare

450

myself owner of all those slimy, carnal and osseous objects of which I am composed, which are beneath and within me, around me, around and outside, above and on the periphery, and my continuing to refer to them or to others by possessive pronouns is merely because communication would otherwise be impossible. So, when I say *my bladder*, it doesn't mean that I am talking about Walter's bladder but simply about the hollow muscular organ at which I am pointing (with a finger which is not mine either) and the only function of which appears to be that of storing urine to be disposed of later – and, if that is its only function, we could well have done without the bladder in a less imperfect world – and which now, incidentally (I mean that day when I was in London) contained over half a litre which I was preparing to expel through the penis, not without first promising myself that if a policeman caught me, I was going to deny that the resulting puddle was *my* urine and, therefore, that it had come out of *my* member. But don't think that I am as pessimistic as all that. Well, sometimes I am; sometimes, like Schopenhauer, I think that this is the worst of all possible worlds and, moreover, that it gets worse every day. But I started to pee, how I peed that afternoon, Palinuro, more than Gulliver when he quenched the Princess of Lilliput's burning palace with his urine, more than Gargantua when he baptized Paris with urine! And then, as my bladder emptied, I felt a little more inclined to believe, like the meliorists, that the world may, at least, improve; and when I finished peeing I felt so far relieved as to think that perhaps Leibniz was right and that this is, after all, the best of all possible worlds. What is more, two famous phrases came to mind: after us the deluge and where I pee the grass grows no more. Not even English grass. Such wonderful parks in London, old man! St James's, cousin; Hampstead Heath where Keats wrote the poems of his youth; Green Park where Mrs Dalloway walked. They are always green, even in winter when all the trees are bare. As though green snow falls. But no, in London it snows very little. Which means that they suffer all the disadvantages of cold without ever being able to enjoy a white Christmas. Although, to be fair, you have to admit that the winter is never as harsh as in Paris, which is another thing that the English have to thank the Mexicans for: the Gulf Stream which warms their winters and their cruel Aprils. In contrast to the parks however, there is no sadder sight on this earth than a box of English tomatoes. You don't need to have a practice in Harley Street to be able to diagnose, on sight, a case of pernicious anaemia. Do you remember that chemistry experiment where you send a whiff of sulphurous air through a glass bell containing a bunch of violets, stocks and geraniums and, confronted with that hellish and stinking air, the poor flowers discolour almost immediately? That's what English tomatoes are like and they're not even any good for throwing at poor crippled Porgy at the opera. But perhaps – I said to myself when I

451

reached Covent Garden and saw an incredible explosion of carnations, roses, chrysanthemums, pansies, jasmine, forget-me-nots and trumpeting daffodils – perhaps the comparison with flowers is not fair either, because in England even the humblest wild flowers are reborn each year like a blessing. Kew Gardens, for example, is paradise. With the added advantage that it has the most impressive collection of Mexican magueys and cacti that I have ever seen (but don't tell that to Aunt Luisa) as well as a fair number of *Tagetes erecta*, which is none other than the humble orange marigold with which we commemorate our Day of the Dead. And, at that moment, the sun came out. The sun actually came out, a veritable miracle in Covent Garden! And I was so delighted that from the flower seller (who was as pretty and cockney as a fair lady) I bought a little bunch of violets for the corsage of the lady selling laces and ribbons, from whom I bought half a yard of blue velvet for the plaits of the lady selling oranges who was not called Nell Gwyn but had an unpronounceable name and from whom I bought three oranges to make love to one of those prostitutes in Soho who have to disguise themselves as models, masseuses and dolls, because prostitution is illegal. Well, what is actually illegal is to solicit. England, cousin, continues to be a rabidly puritanical country. Of course, you can't expect a society which condemned Wilde and *Lady Chatterley's Lover* to become permissive from one day to the next. The difference is that now they don't admit it and even go so far as to have their sex shops patronized, fleetingly as a shudder and in direst terror, only by virgin adolescents, impotent old men and tourists – terror, not at the display of ointments to produce erections or delay orgasm and anal stimulators and dildoes, but at the size of the dildoes. Never have I felt so full of complexes. But one advantage of culture, of course, is that a few blocks from the sex shops of Soho and Tottenham Court Road is the British Museum where, after gazing at the heroes of the Parthenon, you can confirm that the man of Greek civilization, about which John Burnet tells us, is the measure of all things. The English are the same about racial discrimination: most of them don't admit that it exists because it is not 'nice' to do so (by the way, I don't remember ever having seen a black dildo). But the sun went in again and a cold breath blew through Covent Garden and for a moment I remembered, one last time, our cherished chemistry laboratory and the mixture derived from carbon dioxide snow whereby fruit, flowers and leaves freeze instantly and turn brittle and which for me represented nothing more, but nothing less, than a frozen concentration of transparent intuitions in which a memory could be abruptly immersed – that night we got so drunk in La Española, for example, or any other night – and it would be crystallized but would, at the same time, be so fragile that, at the least slip, the coming and going of time, a wrong word, a confusion of ideas, it would shatter. And then it is no good trying to situate in time or place, or attribute to Grandfather Francisco, to Aunt Luisa, or any other person, to you, cousin, words they never said or experiences they never lived. And you should see what beautiful prostitutes, some of them! There is no doubt Jonson was right (the other one, the Elizabethan poet) when he said that the London climate is ideal for cultivating prostitutes. But the fact is that there are more beautiful English women than there are beautiful women of any other nationality. It's a feast for the eyes, but you begin to feel bad turning around to look at them, because the English never turn round: for them, the back view doesn't exist. I think that what most frightened them about Lawrence's book was the gamekeeper's buttock stroking. Another asset of English women is that they all keep, hidden between their teeth, the contraceptive pills with which they commit their platonic suicides. When I reached the box office I found that all the tickets for *Tosca* were sold out. I had to make do with *La Bohème*. Never have I tried so hard to like opera but never have I made less effort to buy the tickets far enough in advance! Furious, I took it out on General Obregón's hand, though it was in no way responsible, and with it did what it could never have done itself. Because, indeed, it may one day be possible, during an operation and with the aid of mirrors, for a person to look at their own living brain and, in particular, the convolution generating their amazement at looking at it. And we may perhaps, some day, be able to take a look at other remote corners of our own organism – did not a doctor once remove his own appendix? – and admire all its tropical splendour of aromatic ganglia, nerves with prop roots and intestinal marshes. But never, I said to myself as I made my way in a north-easterly direction towards the High Holborn Eye Hospital, never will we be able to hold our eyes in our hands, like St Lucy, and see them with our own eyes. Neither, I murmured as I waved goodbye with Obregón's hand to the psychiatric ward of the Old Charing Cross Hospital, will we ever be able to put our brain on a table and think with it about our own brain. I retraced my steps. I turned right down Garrick Street and I wondered whether perhaps I was not also, like the English actor, suffering from an attack of spleen or, at least, blonde apathy. I turned left on Great Newport Street, right on Charing Cross Road and left again on Shaftesbury Avenue where, in the window of an off-licence I saw a bottle of Cuervo Tequila which I promised myself I would buy in memory of our good old days and debated whether there existed even a remote possibility of distilling tequila from the magueys of Kew Gardens but, no, I said, it would in any case be easier to sow marijuana in Belgrave Square opposite the Mexican Embassy and harvest it each 16 September to celebrate Mexican Independence. General Obregón, of course, I said to the dummy in another shop window, did have the opportunity to look at his hand and meditate upon it. I looked at my hand, followed it south and blew on the back of it to send a little cloud of dead cells in the direction of the Hospital of Skin Diseases in Lisle Street and continued to tell the dummy that, without a doubt, General Obregón would have been very proud of his respective hand and particularly of the index finger which appointed so many generals, governors and ministers. He may perhaps even have ventured to hold it with the other hand and caress its palm, where the gunpowder had wiped away the clinging flour and been surprised that that hand, which had traced the contours of his women's skin and carried arms in the battles of Naco and Cananea and shaken the hand of Pancho Villa, Zapata and Grandfather Francisco, was but an object that could be given to a girlfriend, as Van Gogh gave his ear, or thrown in the rubbish. Then I threw it over my shoulder, as far as I could, to serve as food for stray dogs and I said to the dummy: But what General Obregón could never do was to take his right hand in his right hand, just as Santa Anna could not, in a fit of rage, kick his left leg with his left leg, just as Aunt Luisa could never lick her tongue if it were cut off (I don't like the look of those ulcers that have come up on it) and I entered the shop determined not to come out again until I had obtained a bow tie like the dummy was wearing and here it is, cousin, blue with white spots, like a night with a hundred moons.

In London, of course, there are no stray dogs. For Estefania, I brought the address of the RSPCA, which was founded over a century ago and has still not protested against fox hunting. Suffice it to say that the eyes of the hounds (which are the ones to destroy the foxes) are moistened with granulated sugar. And I suppose the English consider them human because I never saw a stuffed dog in the Natural History Museum. What an incredible museum, that one in Kensington! When I looked at the enormous collection of whales and giant sponges, coral reefs and stuffed panda bears, snakes and butterflies and bats and meteorites and horneblendes, I remarked to myself that anatomists had also turned to the flora, fauna, minerals and landscapes of our planet to populate our bodies with bronchial trees, blood lacunae, valleys of the cerebellum, deltoid muscles, trunks, roots and bulbs. I also brought you a book on microscopy dyes. I invite you, cousin, to enter the blue world of gram-positive bacilli. Please recommend the Feulgen reaction to Molkas: this process, I said, crossing Wardour Street (a street in which pornographic bookshops and massage-parlours abound) stains the basic protein of life a brilliant purple and the spermatazoa turn into wriggling matches. Ah, my dear Palinuro: what amphibian wonders await you! The exorbitantly suggestive range of colours beside which the Munsell system and the Winsor and Newton catalogue pale! I also brought a whole collection of earths and acrylic paints. With Auramine, I said to Sir Laurence Olivier who was gazing gravely at me from a theatre hoarding, salamander larvae reveal their predilection for fire. With Nile Blue, I muttered between clenched teeth as I crossed Windmill Street towards Piccadilly Circus, hydras attest their Pharaonic lineage and with Janus Black flowers disclose to the world the mystery of pollen factories. I also brought loads of souvenirs: little flags, T-shirts, double-decker buses, a Big Ben ashtray for Aunt Luisa. So many people in London! I almost poked a hippy's eye out when I pointed north-east, in the direction of the shadowy Middlesex Hospital and said aloud: with Cresilus Violet, ladies and gentlemen, the fresh tissue of tumours admits to its malignant and mournful stratagems. And, since I was in the very heart of the United Kingdom and of the British Empire, in Piccadilly Circus itself, and before the aluminium statue that everybody calls Eros because it claims to be the angel of Christian charity, I pointed to the winged figure and reminded it that the Gram-Poppenheim colouring is recommended for the pus of gonorrhoea. And suddenly I felt so ridiculous, cousin, there alone among the multitude of hippies, homosexuals, drug addicts and policemen, my hand raised with index finger pointing, all alone, damn it, like a guide deserted by his tourists, among that mass of Americans, Spaniards, Germans, Mexicans with their Harrods' bags and Brompton Road tartans, Japanese with their Yashica cameras, Italians and Swedes (the fog which returns to London every summer, my friend, and then the English get mad because they can no longer find a seat in the pub where they have lunch every day): No, there aren't as many drug addicts in London as they say: that is pure fiction. Carnaby Street has never been Cannabis Street. Nor as many homosexuals: that's another myth; there are bisexuals, asexuals and transsexuals. Neither is there any fog: that's an invention of Conan Doyle's. I also brought brochures and an illustrated map which I purchased in the map shop in St James's Street, to save myself describing all the places that I saw and listing all the streets along which I walked: I walked down Jermyn Street again, crossed Babmaes Street, turned right in Duke of York Street and found myself again before the doors of the London Library. I came out, I don't know why, with a copy of the *Guinness Book of Records*, fully determined to read it from cover to cover. How I always despised stamp collectors and people who collect cigarette packets, cousin, but suddenly, that afternoon, I saw in Astleys the most beautiful collection ever of pipe bowls and I discovered that I had at that moment become an inveterate collector and that I had misspent the best years of my life collecting anecdotes from the history of medicine, roses, unique eyes, animals martyred to science, quotations on death and love, illnesses and symptoms and who knows what else! I felt like a walking collection. What am I saying, collection: ten collections! And I thought that if you are a philatelist you may at least enjoy the satisfaction of showing your friends your orange stamps from Mauritius. If you collect coins, you can dazzle a money lender with a single five-guinea coin from the reign of Charles II. And then, collectors of semi-precious stones or shells can always leave to their children their collection of apache tears dug up in the foothills of the Rockies, or their collection of virgin nerita collected on the beaches of Atlantic City (which reminds me, I also brought Uncle a modest collection of postage stamps issued by Austria in 1937, in honour of the doctors of the old school of Vienna and which includes stamps in tribute to Billroth and Von Hebra). My collections are purely of words, like the *Book of Hermes* in which the capital letters are temples and the sentences cities, or like Cervantes' vessel sailing to Parnassus, its stern consisting of sonnets and '*la gavia, toda de versos fabricada*' – the topsail, all, of verses constituted. My collections, in other words, are like Neruda's dogless barks or Lewis Carroll's catless grins. I can quote a verse by Mallarmé: *La chair est triste, hélas, et J'ai lu tous les livres!*, but I can't show you Mallarmé. I had him in my hands, that is, I had his complete works in my hands, in the London Library, and I realized that my flesh was sad for precisely the opposite reason: I have not read all the books. Did I tell you before that I have read a lot? It was a lie: I have never read as little as I did in London. Confronted by so many volumes, I was overcome by a desperate anguish. When I learned that the library of the British Medical Association has over 80,000 volumes and that of the Royal College of Surgeons over 140,000, it dawned on me that I knew nothing about medicine. But, at the same time, that I didn't need to know anything, I didn't want to, and that I would never want to again. The few books that I have read served to confirm something that, deep down, I had always known: that medicine is not – never has been – more than just another profession, a way of life, and that the number of doctors who are saints is very few or, to put it another way, very few saints are doctors. As early as the twelfth century, Arquimateus advised his disciples to make it known if a patient's condition was serious: thus, if the patient died, they wouldn't be blamed; if the patient recovered, all the credit would be theirs. Already John Gaddesden complained of certain disagreeable illnesses from which the physician rarely gained any benefit. Even in ancient Greece, physicians left dying patients in the woods so that their death would not tarnish the prestige of the temple of Asclepius. Jealousy is nothing new in that profession: didn't Paracelsus publicly burn the writings of Galen and Avicenna? And already the surgeons of Cnidus, like those of Vienna centuries and centuries later, paid more attention to the symptoms than to the patients. Never, of course, will I tell Uncle Esteban of the medical crimes related by Barnesby, nor of Louis Ferdinand Céline's diatribes against his colleagues. Neither, I told myself, will you ever be Claude Bernard, nor will you be buried in Saint Sulpice, nor will your tomb be surrounded by lamps burning with green flames. And even my beloved

456

collection of names or parts of the human body was toppled when in the library I found an eponymic dictionary containing over 800 different names, from Abernethy's fascia to Zukerkand's bodies! Do you really think it was enough that the water christened your Atlas vertebra and your Achilles tendon with your name? Oh, man, let me tell you – I told you then, as I entered the Wellcome Museum of the History of Medicine – how few are those that know that you, that I, that everybody: the man selling newspapers in Euston Road, the student who died in the Plaza de las Tres Culturas, the *clochard* who gave me a little white elephant on the banks of the Seine, everybody, in short, carries around the place a series of holes, nerves and jellies which don't even bear our name! I also went, often, to the Royal Observatory in Greenwich and saw Newton's telescope. And so, I said to one of the observatory guards, just as famous astronomers win a place in the sky by gazing into the night for two minutes or for fifty years until they discover a new star (though perhaps already dead for a thousand years) and give it their name; just as in the sky – I said to the porter of the London Planetarium which is next door to Madame Tussaud's, a truly magnificent museum! – just as in the sky, bathed by neutrinos and antiparticles and black holes and rustling hydrogen clouds, the stellar ranks were swollen by the appearance of Biela's Comet, the Tycho's Nova, Bode's constellation boundaries and Messier's nebulous objects; so in the organism – I said to the human body of transparent plastic in the Wellcome Museum – so in the organism, bathed in lymphocytes and red corpuscles and to the joy of all those who said that the human body was a copy of the universe, there appeared among the clouds of lymph and the murmuring of blood, Hesselbach's triangle, Wharton's jelly, Ruffin's corpuscles, Fontana's spaces, Rolando's fissure and Lieberkühn's crypts. But neither can I show you all the parts of the human body of which I speak or of which I have spoken. Well, with the exception of a few, of course I can show you my eyes, my legs. I can show you my external genital organs (I also saw striptease and drag: I found them supremely boring, as I do pornographic films) but I can't show you my suprarenal glands. I can't show you my palatine bone, I said to the transparent plastic man in the Wellcome Museum who (an exception to the rule) did indeed reveal the entire magic interior of the marvellous body of Man with a capital M, *Homo Sapiens* of subfamily *Hominae*, family *Hominidae*, super-family *Hominoidea*, suborder *Anthropoidea*, order *Primates*. I can't show you my cystic duct, I said to the political animal, to man-conscience-of-creation. I can't show you the parietal pleura of my left lung, I said to biped, omnivorous, trouser-wearing man, man-Son-of-God, Max Scheler's man-of-the-eternal and Huxley's multi-amphibian man. I can't show you the fundus of my stomach, I said to the man of Jean Rostand's human adventure, to Unamuno's man who lives and dies and doesn't want to die altogether and to thinking, upright man with emancipated arms and stereoscopic vision who came down from the trees and the clouds to raise himself up on his toes and in turn become a tree, a *Deus in terris*, the *Homo faber* who built the Great Wall of China and the Apollo 10, the *Homo sedentarius* who discovered the secret of the marriage of plants and the *Homo ludens* who learned to play with dragons of steam and abacuses of hydrogen! All this I said and I swear that I was left almost breathless. I breathed in the night dew – remember that I was not really in the Wellcome Museum but in the Planetarium – and then I went on to visit yet again Madame Tussaud's wax figures. Did I tell you a few months ago how much I had liked it? Quite untrue: it left me indifferent. I've become a mine of contradictions. Did I also tell you before that I didn't like my organs and members? That's not true either. I love my legs as much as Walt Whitman loved his. I love my feet and I'd love them just as well if they were pierced like those of Oedipus. And if I was King Midas in my other life, I told John Kennedy, I assure you that I doted on my ass's ears. And if in mythology I happened to be Hercules Melampygus, I assured Muhammad Ali, I wouldn't have changed my black bottom for anybody's. Yes, I shouted, pointing at Winston Churchill: I would love my stomach even if it were as big as that of the Hindu god Ganapati. I would love my bald pate (I told Landrú) even if it were like Silenus's. Why continue?: even if my teeth were as big as Manduco's or Macmillan's they would spend their lives smiling and if my eyes were crossed like Thersites' or Jean Paul Sartre's, they could spend their time gazing lovingly at each other. If, finally, for the purpose of this story, I am Walter, of course I would love all the parts of my body and I wouldn't change them for anybody else's. I said to Queen Elizabeth, to Henry VIII, to the Beatles, to Eisenhower, to Marilyn Monroe, to Harold Wilson, to Prince Albert, to Madame Tussaud herself and to one of the museum porters I took for a wax figure and who invited me to leave and very politely accompanied me to the door to return my raincoat and umbrella. The good thing is that in London it is not usual to give tips. Of course, Jean Paul Sartre is not in the wax museum. Nor Kafka, nor Dylan Thomas, nor Vivaldi, nor Kant. If you're lucky, you might find Picasso, Ché or anyone else that our society, as Marcuse says, has seen fit to take to the chemist or the supermarket. But Marcuse isn't here. Neither are the massacres in Lidice and Dachau represented in the chamber of horrors. The best and the worst of man is absent. This is another quotation I jotted down: The best of man, said Eluard (or the most beautiful?) is better than man. And the worst? I asked myself. The worst is always equal to man. But, as I walked out, as I walked out again into the daylight and saw that the sun had reappeared, a truth, a certainty, dazzled me like a flaming parachute. I saw myself there, in the middle of Marylebone Road, I alone: not I alone and my soul, not I alone and my trillions of cells, not I alone and my conscience, not I alone and my vital reason, but I *alone*, nothing more, I as a point of view of the universe, irreplaceable and necessary only to myself and to no one else (or more, anyway, infinitely more, to myself than to anybody else), I alone as a psychic act based on the representation of what I said and did and what I do and say now, cousin, yesterday in London and today in Mexico, I alone, as man, not as Man, but as man, with a small m, as individual, like the youth whose autopsy you watched and then I said: lies, all lies, the human heart and brain appearing on pages 37 and 367 of the second volume of the Quiroz *Anatomy* might be the heart and brain of Man but those you saw, Palinuro, were indeed the heart and brain of a youth, of a concrete individual who had been born, lived and died unrecognized and forgotten by poets and philosophers: a youth of some twenty years of age; a student perhaps, why not; a youth who had played football in secondary school and failed maths and whose existence was completely unknown to James, Adler, Ortega, Kierkegaard, Stirner or any other of the apostles of individuality but who was none the less there, his corpse of cold marble occupying the same space that his inner world occupied in the world outside, in the outer world which had been extinguished when his heart and his brain ceased to function and who could be confused neither with Man nor with all men and not even with all the twenty-year-old youths who have ever existed because, just as he has a weight, a coffin, a label and a number in death, he once had a name, a girlfriend and a height in life which had been his and nobody else's and the heart which the professor cut with scissors and from which he cleaned the clots before placing it in a tray and the brain which the professor carved into sixteen equal parts was his, the youth's, and nobody else's in the entire universe.

But I don't want to become too solemn. What were Adan Buenosayres' last words? Solemn as an Englishman's fart. My own physiological needs, however, went no further than a sneeze: I always sneeze in the sun. But, on that occasion, I did so in the direction of Gray's Inn Road, which is where the Ear, Nose and Throat Hospital is situated. The sun also (for the first time in my life) made me want to pee again and I headed for the nearest pub, deciding that it was a good excuse for having a few more pints. I attributed my thirst to the sun too. In the lost property office in Baker Street I bought a detective's cap and, in a giftshop, a small collection of posters. You should see the posters in London. Art Nouveau is back, surrealism is back. I bought Aunt Lucrecia a Beardsley poster. For Aunt Luisa, a Mucha. And for you, by the way, as I told you, one of Ché Guevara. He keeps getting cleaner and more handsome with each new poster. They should show him (I said to the salesgirl) shaved and with short hair which is, after all, the image they have created. But Ché, I said to the girl on the cash register, was no saint. He was a man who had killed, who had often grasped his rifle with both hands. With those very hands, Palinuro, which you, or perhaps I should say, the hands which you and the rest of our generation, need to change the world or, at least, change the hated and beloved, the harsh and tender land of our birth. Because the hand of General Obregón, cousin, and that of Valle-Inclán, are no longer any use, even for applauding the Mexican Revolution. Which is precisely what I was saying all the way to the pub, I, can you imagine? who the other day, to look no further, went into Fortnum and Mason with the intention of ordering them to kill a caviare which had already escaped from my pocket three times but it proved impossible and I had to make do with a tin of tortillas and a jar of Yucatán honey and with another sneeze (the colds I had in London: I produced so much snot that I got stalactites in my nose), with a sneeze, I was saying, infested with millions of bacteria and incognito viruses that landed on the Brie cheeses and the Strasbourg pâtés. I, just imagine, who get so much pleasure from books and expensive records, enjoy good clothes and have the sensual capacity to fall in love, like the Lord of Phocas and Des Esseintes, with winking opals and oriental amethysts, with golden tortoises, luxurious bookbindings and clockwork fish, with the most exquisite papers and the most delicate and rare perfumes, liquors and wines. I who, walking along Fifth Avenue, Rue de la Paix and Bond Street, have so admired Christian Dior gloves and Irish linens and Jacob Petit porcelain and Cartier bracelets and cashmere sweaters and Beauvais tapestries and Persian rugs, remarked to myself that it was of course to incredible man-made things such as these that anatomists had had recourse in describing the saddle, vessels and chalices of our body, not forgetting the canals, chains and drums. I, just imagine, who before the possibility that I might never come to own these things, always felt deep reactionary sadness, yet again, and for the last time, to quote our famous poet. But that's another good reason why it's worth living in Europe for a while: to re-evaluate writers like Lopez Velarde and painters like Clausell. And yes, I was in Baker Street. Or was I in Green Park? Well, you will have noticed, or imagined anyway, that my walks through London, those long strolls when I thought of saying to you all the things that I am saying to you now, were numerous. I don't even know whether I actually did these things and accurately remember them or whether it is more imagination than memory. But imagination and memory are the same thing said Hobbes and I agree. What else could we be but memory? Nobody ever learns what mamma or the colour green is until they learn the word *mamma* and the word *green*. Literature begins – at least the kind of literature in which I am interested – when we say *green mamma*. My dear Palinuro, I don't need to tell you what kind of state I was in over there, alone but accompanied by Laetitia and Tristitia, alone but with my eyes open, paranoid as Penfield's cats, cross-eyed as your

General Pancho Villa when he had one eye on the Revolution and Justice and the other eye on Glory and fifty-thousand peso back-handers; delirious as a don Prospero imagining the world with both hemispheres of his brain at the same time: the tragic hemisphere of Agathon and the happy hemisphere of Aristophanes; and schizophrenic as a man who is simultaneously in London and Mexico City and has to drive on the right and on the left at the same time; I don't need to tell you, cousin, that I was a walking contradiction, the perfect Oxymoron incarnate, beyond the dreams of Marino, master and lord and slave of heavenly hells. But do you think that you can drive along the middle of the road, the exact centre? No way. The centre is an optical illusion. Only a Latin American country would have a city like Bahía, where you can drive for a while on the right and for a while on the left. I almost became a demagogue in London for going to Hyde Park so often! I remembered then that it was Sunday. I remembered that the sun had gone in again (you won't believe it, but that's what the weather is like in London) and I remembered that yet again it was my birthday, so I bought myself a little cake to celebrate and, always following my legs which in turn followed the one after the other and the other after the one, I walked towards Speakers' Corner in Hyde Park. At that point I took my leave of Eliot who, in fact, I only needed in order to give one more quotation: 'you say I am repeating something I have said before. I shall say it again'; yes, cousin, not only do I today contradict what I said yesterday, but tomorrow (and by tomorrow I mean in ten minutes' time or in ten years' time) I will wink forty times at my nightmare with the other eye and, as I told you some time ago in La Española, I may deny and be ashamed of all I now think and say. The important thing is that the Walter of now, as I believe, is intelligent and sympathetic enough to understand that a possible Walter of the future might be stupid enough not to accept the way in which the Walter of the past thought but might also perhaps have the necessary pity to forgive the Walter of the past for his inability to think like the Walter of the future: if we can never bathe in the same waters of a river or in the same blue of Estefania's eyes, less still, cousin, may we bathe in the waters of a same thought. And that is how the story of the brain transplant, which I will one day write, came to me and I developed it in my mind as I walked with Unamuno's book in my raincoat pocket, the *Book of Records* under my right arm, my umbrella hanging from my left forearm and a white box held in both hands, with such care and tenderness that, rather than a cake, it seemed it must contain my own brain, or a bomb at the very least.

It's about two brothers, I said, as I crossed Sackville Street. One was an architect, I added, nodding to the Victorian and renaissance and

461

magnificent Royal Academy. But, like Swift's architects, his aim in life was to build temples with beautiful domes, starting not from the foundations but from above, from the domes, I said, blowing a kiss, in remembrance, over Admiralty Arch towards the proud dome of St Paul's Cathedral. What buildings there are in London, cousin: Westminster Cathedral, which is a neo-Byzantine aberration or something along those lines; Mansion House, which can only be described as Palladian. And I further reflected, as I walked down Burlington Arcade (fine example of Regency architecture) and sent a nostalgic greeting to Tepozotlán and to Mexico City cathedral and, without going further afield, to the neo-Venetian palace of the courts of justice built over Ruskin's tombstone, I reflected that man had also looked to his houses and his cities and his temples and his factories to baptize the pyloric antrum, the vestibulum of the mouth, the labyrinth of the ear, the vertebral column. But the architect of my story will leave his work unfinished: no sooner does he finish one dome than he continues with another and yet another, so that they are all left floating in the air, empty, gleaming only for the stars with oceanic circumspection, without colonnades or arches to support them, without ruined columns taking advantage of the whole of antiquity to grow and reach them, to make them the living symbol of life and of the architect's talent, I said, sending a sigh across Berkeley Square to Marble Arch; in other words, he will be a man who never had his feet on the ground and will die, at a ripe old age, with his head in the clouds. On the other hand, his brother, a surgeon who will become a member of the Royal College of Surgeons, I said, pointing towards Lincoln's Inn Fields, was a man who departed from the deepest roots of knowledge and from the most modest also: from anatomy, starting with the anatomy of the bones, until he came to master all the mysteries of the organ hidden beneath the most sacred of all domes, the human brain no less, I added, most gratified by the idea, as I crossed Brick Street. *Brick* Street, I repeated to myself, reflecting that in London and in many other cities of the world, in Mexico City, in Paris, we have named streets a thousand different ways: we have given them the names of flowers, of saints, of kings and presidents and heroes, of other cities, of animals, instruments, seas, battles, stones, countries and continents and stars, but never of the parts of our body. So our surgeon – or perhaps I should rather say, *my* surgeon – obsessed with the idea of how grandiose would have been his brother's definitive work if his brilliant and diffuse talent had had a second opportunity to manifest itself in the disciplined body of a young and healthy man and so, after many years of failures and experiments, he finally succeeded in executing the first brain transplant. I pulled a little tatter of skin from my finger and with a puff sent it in the direction of St James's Palace, where the Lepers' Hospital had previously stood and I begged the Queen Mother to cure me with her royal

462

hand if I were ever smitten by *le mal de la rose*. Where, then – I asked as I reached Down Street – where is Nietzsche now, that he might accuse Christianity, yet again, of despising the body? Where is Swedenborg who called man microcosmos of creation? Where is Nicholas of Cusa? Where is Rousseau who taught man to look at himself in the mirror and fall in love with the fascinating and complex animal that he is? Where is Robert Boyle, inviting the soul to get to know the exquisite structure of the divine mansion it inhabits? Where are they? I asked, crossing Piccadilly towards Green Park, that they have failed to baptize the streets, squares and avenues of our cities with the names of our organism? Because, cousin, I for one have never visited Liver Square, Big Toe Alley or Spinal Cord Avenue. Reaching Green Park, I made for my favourite bench and I said to the pigeons: And so it was that on this gracious island endowed with such a wealth of natural gifts (I'm talking about the Imaginary Island of my story, not England which, besides lawn, produces only coal and coal miners' strikes) a living person opened his eyes in a dead body for the first time in history. Or, to put it another way, I said to some Hare Krishnas who danced past shivering with cold, we could say that it was the first time that a dead person opened their eyes in a living body, and we are not talking about a transplant of eyes preserved in citrated blood in Lariboisière. Because I should add that in my story, cousin, the brain transplant gave rise to the most bitter controversy in memory, since many said that it was immoral that a dead person should receive the benefit of continuing to live in a live body. But those who defended the operation – I said to a family of Indians weighed down with turbans, children and moles – argued that, on the contrary, the transplant was only possible when the brain was still alive and therefore it was a live person who continued to live in the dead body, I said to a Ugandan and two Bengalis, and I reflected moreover that this island and this world (I'm talking about England and our planet) produce ever more foreigners. And then both sides, in support of their respective arguments, reviewed the whole history of contributions made by the dead to the living since the time of Paré when they used bits of mummy to stop haemorrhages and from the moss growing on the skulls of executed criminals like a mask of green velvet they made ointments to heal wounds poisoned by gunpowder, right through to modern times when we freeze bones and transplant kidneys and hearts, when a dead child's artery can save another whose life is threatened by Fallot's disease and the pituitary glands of nuns who died with cobwebs of virgin wool over their sexes are used to produce fertility drugs. But they never could agree, I said as I approached my bench and, for a minute, I felt I saw myself sitting on the bench and saw myself walking through the park towards the bench to sit down. But the vision lasted only a moment: I was, in fact, already sitting on the bench and I decided that the best thing would be to start eating my cake at once and share it with the pigeons although unfortunately, at that moment, I yet again started to feel the urge to pee. To transplant a brain, said the detractors, is to kill a living person. On the contrary, claimed the apologists: to transplant a brain is to resuscitate a dead person. It's worse than that: it is to kill a dead person, said other decriers who were in a state of considerable confusion. In all events, it is to resuscitate a living person, said other equally confused defenders. But controversy over the ethics of transplants goes back to legend: three hundred years before the Christian era, Pien Chiao was condemned for daring to drug two men and exchange their hearts and stomachs, while the Ashvini brothers were held in high esteem because, in order to outwit the god Indra, they exchanged the head of the wise Dadhyanchi for that of a horse. The debate, which shook and divided academies of science the world over, including the Academy of Vienna, the Mexican Academy, the Royal Academy of London and the Imperial Academy of Brazil, was abruptly terminated with the death of the great surgeon. But his pupils and followers decided to preserve his brain which was intact and transplant it to a dead body – or a living one – they never did decide which – and a few months later the great surgeon was back in action and, although he was physically changed – from one day to the next he had gone completely bald, measured seven centimetres less, weighed twenty-five kilos more and had developed a hint of a cockney accent – he eloquently defended the transplant and challenged the anti-transplantists to continue the debate in coming centuries. But they all refused to back down or to allow their brains to be transplanted and one by one they died. Anyway, though it wasn't actually sunny, it was enough that the rain had taken a breather, I thought, to come to the conclusion that it was a beautiful afternoon or, at least, amiable. And my sentiments were shared by thousands and thousands of people who suddenly appeared, strolling along Piccadilly, through Green Park, down Park Lane and, in short, all the streets of London. Never have I seen so many people! Other scientists, I continued, taking a sizeable bite of my cake, started to question the efficiency of the transplant when it became apparent that the surgeon, in his second life, was not the sweet and affable man that he had been during his first existence but, on the contrary, a man full of pride and arrogance. The geneticists explained that the chromosomes of the cells of the mathematics teacher into whose body his brain had been implanted during his third life must have contained the hereditary 47XYY complement, associated with impulsive and antisocial behaviour. Endocrinologists, I said to the ash trees, attributed the melancholy and bouts of depression the surgeon suffered during his fifth life to a malfunction of the suprarenal glands of the young poet who passed his body on to him. Christian Darwinists interpreted the surgeon's impassioned conversion to Catholicism during his eighth life to the evolution of the brain over the years and quoted Thomas Aquinas to the effect that, while a little science alienates the concept of divinity, a lot of science draws God closer, but atheist scientists maintained that it was a case of regressive development. Astrologists attributed the surgeon's tremendous capacity for work, his new combative determination and dynamism during his ninth life to the fact simply that he had opened his eyes in the operating room the instant the transplant was completed beneath the sign of Aries influenced by a Taurus ascendant, thus combining fire and earth in his personality. I stood up, brushed the dust from the seat of my trousers and the crumbs from my jacket, put a piece of left-over cake back in the box and, for a moment, considered leaving the *Guinness Book of Records* in the park but I didn't want to get on the wrong side of the London Library so I yet again tucked under my arm the world's tallest building, the individual who spent thirty years in an iron lung, the Norwegian with a six-metre-long beard and the most alcoholic alcoholic in the world who was of course an Englishman who drank over thirty-seven thousand bottles of port. On the subject of drinks and the *Book of Records*, Guinness is an excellent beer although, of course, it isn't English, just as the best whisky in England is from Scotland, the best wool in England is from Australia, the best tea in England is from Ceylon and the best writers in England are, like Guinness, from Ireland. But, before continuing my periplus, I again opened Unamuno's book (not quite so randomly this time) at the page where it says: 'Who is able to find the cubic root of this ash tree?' I tore it out, made it into a paper aeroplane and sent it, cousin, winging over the clouds, over the Hilton Hotel, over Saint Mary's Hospital, over Mayfair and particularly over the trees. Phreno-logists, for their part, stated that the scholar's propensity to believe in astrology, magic and ghosts during his thirteenth life was the product of a very simple fact: the skull of the political sciences student into which his brain was implanted had a large protuberance in the area corresponding to marvellousness and the scholar's brain, once inside, grew and filled that space with all kinds of fantasies. I reached Hyde Park Corner and greeted Wellington mounted on Copenhagen, his horse. Looking at his monument, looking at Aspley House, I wondered what had happened to English good taste, what had become of the genius of the architects who built Westminster Abbey where, before the plaques and busts and niches of Jane Austen, Coleridge and Newton and so many other artists and personalities, I so often asked myself why, if we learned to see light with Turner's eyes, is the macula lutea of our retina not called the Turner macula? If we learned to understand the world with Einstein's brain, why do we not have an interlobular furrow called the Einstein fissure? And then – while I simultaneously thought of submitting to each of the world's academies of medicine a long list including the Proust reflex, the Plato cavity and the

Bergson risorius muscle – I continued to develop my story: our scholar – I said, walking towards the public lavatories in the tunnel passing beneath the Wellington Monument – our scholar had, throughout each of his previous lives, become successively indignant and depressed by the various theories but had either forgiven his critics or remained aloof dedicated to his work. However, during his thirteenth life he became an enthusiastic disciple of phrenology – the science which so fascinated don Prospero – and, since he had always been an admirer of English wit which Gall calls *esprit de saillie* and Spurzheim labelled *mirthfulness*, he arranged that his brain be transplanted to a skull which, like that of Rabelais or Piron, had two spherical protuberances in the upper and lateral part of the forehead, indicating development of the organs which Cubí y Sole labelled the organs of *chistosividad*. It was a disaster, I said, as I washed my hands. The surgeon's disciples chose the skull of an adolescent in whom these protuberances were excessively developed, I said, re-emerging into the light of day, but failing to notice that it also had two depressions in the areas corresponding to ideality. It was for this reason that, during the surgeon's last life, he became totally indifferent to scientific advance and progress of all kinds, quite lost his sense of humour, became sarcastic and sharp, started to mock his friends and enemies alike and ended up laughing at himself, at all his theories and brain transplants, saying that it was a waste of time to transplant a brain from one generation to the next for almost a thousand years and fourteen lives, merely to prove what can be proved in the course of a single existence: that one man during his lifetime can often change his ideas, beliefs and opinions to such a degree that he denies and destroys himself. And so it was. The great surgeon, at barely twenty years of age, like the young Werther, nine hundred and sixty-nine like Methuselah, blew his head off during his final life, so forever destroying his brain. When I write the story, I said to an ice-cream vendor, the epitaph on his tomb will be the phrase 'I saw how the worm inherited the wonders of the eye and the brain,' taken from Mary Shelley's famous novel *Frankenstein or the Modern Prometheus*. And when I took out tenpence to pay for my ice lolly, I realized of course that, predictably, I had left the *Book of Records* in the lavatories. This time I decided to leave it to its deserved fate and had no qualms about doing so because, by then, it had started to weigh a ton which was only to be expected with that collection of fat men and giants and Russian mothers with forty children and that other madman who stood in the shower for 170-odd continuous hours. That can't have been in London because they don't have showers there. Neither, cousin, have they discovered warm water. The moral of my story is simple. I recommend that, so as not to remain up in the clouds with the architect of my story, you should begin more modestly, from the bottom. A good medical student knows that he should abide first by the holy

466

trinity: anatomy, physiology and biochemistry. Of these three subjects, anatomy is the first to be studied, and anatomy – barring a fleeting look at tegumentary structures – begins with the bones. Visit Charon's Cave, cousin, and set out in search of the bones of your ancestors that you might discover where you came from and where you are going. I, meanwhile, having finished my story but not my walk, was striding towards Speakers' Corner in Hyde Park, resolved that if a policeman were to stop me for looking suspicious and ask me if I was carrying a time bomb in the cake box, I would tell him that I had nothing against foreigners – for me the English are foreigners, of course – and that actually I can like them or hate them as much as they do me and then I would add one of my favourite cliché sayings: first – I would say to him – I am a terrorist, indeed, but of the soul and therefore my case is of interest only to psychiatrists who are the policemen of the soul; second, the only time bomb I carry is inside my skull. The day it explodes, the entire universe will explode, including yourself: so sorry, but I can't make any exceptions. I also brought you, cousin, a copy of *The Unquiet Grave* and a pamphlet from the Wellcome Museum.

The Wellcome Museum, which is in Euston Road and can be reached by Underground on the Metropolitan or Circle lines, or on the number 68 bus among others if you live (as I did) in Camden Town, is actually two museums. Upstairs is the museum of the History of Medicine itself, open to the general public. One or two floors down there is another museum. Just of medicine. Though actually it's more of a pathology museum which can only be visited by doctors and medical students. You can't imagine the trouble I had to get in! I almost disguised myself as an English doctor, I almost had to swear that my interest in visiting it had nothing to do with a morbid desire to look at photographs of external genital organs with ulcers and keratopapillomas. I don't really remember what I saw in that and other museums. But that is irrelevant to what I want to tell you; upstairs is William Cheselden, surgeon to Queen Caroline. And Lister is there, manipulating silk threads to drain an abscess which appeared in one of Queen Victoria's armpits. Downstairs are photographs of women and children with ghastly Kaposi sarcomata. Upstairs is the physican-poet Oliver Wendell Holmes, just as he is giving the name 'anaesthetic' to chloroform, and here also are Levret's forceps and Flemish medical cabinets. Downstairs are photographs of the buttocks of some poor Brazilian Indians showing the putrid gangrene of the rectum, endemic to swampy areas. Upstairs is Jenner discovering the vaccine against smallpox. Downstairs, children blinded by smallpox. Upstairs is Ronald Ross discovering the half moons appearing in the blood in the presence of malaria and Yersin discovering the bacillus of bubonic plague and Koch with his hands covered in dyes and Dr Schweitzer beside the Ogooue River haloed in glory and flies. Downstairs these same flies are present in gigantic wax reproductions: the anopheles, the simulium and African and Latin American children dying of malaria and Chagas's disease and the poor Columbian Indians attacked by horrible leishmanias. Upstairs, cousin, upstairs are Pasteur and Erlich and Bruce and other hunters of microbes, just as Paul de Kruif described them years ago, when I was yet unaware of the stupidity, servility and superficiality of everything written by de Kruif. Upstairs is the illustrious surgeon and biologist and physiologist and writer and Nobel Prize winner Alexis Carrel making cultures of chicken heart tissue and writing *Man, the Unknown*, before I learned that he had approved of measures taken in Germany against mental retards and delinquents. Downstairs there are no photographs of Nazi victims, though there should be. Upstairs is Santiago Ramón y Cajal demonstrating the individuality of the nerve cell and also the stories he wrote (before I realized how trite and naïve Cajal was; the man with microscopic vision is here and also the vengeful Dr Forschung), and all the optical instruments into which man peered to discover the marvellous icosahedral adenoviruses which change the colour of tulip leaves, and crystalline viruses of the intestines, and bacteria like golden canes, and vibrions with long flagella, and the round micro-organisms with snowy nuclei which cause spherical death, and those which are essential to life, and the protozoa, and the rickettsiae, and those which travel, under the auspices of a white prestige, through the civil history of bacteria. And downstairs there are photographs of youths' penises with papillomas, women's faces with pyodermas, Uruguayan and Argentinian children whose livers and lymphatic ganglia are hypertrophied by kala-azar and of sufferers of cholera morbus and dysenteries and onchocercosis. Upstairs is the surgeon Eparvier writing *The Miracles of Surgery* which I read before understanding what he meant when he talked of the people mutilated in what he called 'the horrible war of Ho Chi Minh'. Downstairs, though there should be, there are no photographs of all the Indo-Chinese murdered by the French and the Americans. Upstairs is Alexander Fleming discovering penicillin and Eijkman, the father of vitamin B, and Banting discovering insulin and Domagk discovering the therapeutic value of Prontosil and Minot and Evans and Wagner-Jauregg and Pasteur and the ancient pharmacopoeias and the book by Francisco Hernández and the life of Constantine the African and the history of *aqua vitae* and the history of quinine and of sarsaparilla and of organotherapy and of pharmacodynamics. Downstairs there should be photographs of the Philippine convicts infected with beriberi by Colonel Strong and of the Mississippi convicts infected by Dr Goldberger with pellagra and there should be photographs of all the

Ethiopians, Pakistanis, Biafrans, Guatemalans, Indians, Mexicans and Vietnamese who have died of starvation, and the same goes for the history of patented medicines and laboratories like Abbott, Squibb, Lederle, Lakeside, Parke Davis and all the others that have grown rich by brutally trafficking with life and with disease, with hunger and with death. In short, cousin, upstairs is everything that I would have liked to see when I dreamed of myself as a surgeon dressed in white, as in a picture painted by Barbara Hepworth, beneath the light of a scialytic lamp which eliminates all possible shadows; when I dreamed of myself as Spallanzani effecting the first artificial fertilization in history, as Landsteiner discovering the blood groups, as Dr Percival Pott in his apple green jacket and shower of lace at his wrists sleighing along the snow-covered roads of Kent. And downstairs, downstairs is what I have never wanted, or been able, or known how to see. I almost became a demagogue, so often did I go to Hyde Park! I repeat to you, as I repeated to myself yet again when I was about to land in Mexico and gazed upon this huge and horrible city from the only angle from which it can still look beautiful, like a cloth of black velvet studded with precious stones, like an infinite swarm of fire flies, like a sapphire field in which stars graze: from above and at night. Because, from below, by day, this city in which it was our lot to be born and to live (and, if this is our lot, then what are we to do, as Fuentes says) is a sick and monstrous and grey and wretched city: and its lightless, budless, irredeemable wretchedness pours down the valley and over the mountains and through the jungles and across the deserts in which our poor Mexican race lives, but it dies more than lives and it dies of amoebiasis and parasitosis and gastroenteritis and starvation. As to the moral of all this, my dear Palinuro, soul mate of mine, I'm not going to tell you. I remember that Aunt Luisa used to keep in a box the morals of fables which she wrote down on scraps of paper as she read them. When you, when Estefania or I did something bad or failed to do something good, she used to draw out a moral at random. Of course, the moral rarely coincided and it was all extremely funny. The fun ends, stated Aunt Luisa, when the moral fits. That responsibility I leave to you: I bequeath it to you, along with my waistcoat. Not let me finish telling you . . .

Off I went towards Hyde Park, that is, towards the famous Speakers' Corner of Hyde Park went your cousin Walter on the point of becoming a heap of physiological needs, but happy and, particularly, surprised; surprised to see so many people, so many tourists going to visit Cleopatra's Needle or the Tower of London, to see so many teenyboppers, so many punks, so many teddy boys, so many hippies, so many skinheads, so many judges in white wigs, so many gentlemen of the Order of the Garter, so many yogis, so many people going to the Proms or to the Royal Festival Hall, so many coming to Hyde Park to sunbathe, to talk or eat or sleep, so many English people going to visit their old folk in homes and their mad folk in Maudsley, so many Samaritans, good Lord! so many members of the Salvation Army, so many mini-heroes, so many vegetarians and computerniks, so many freaks and so many workers, so many readers of Gurdjieff and Yoko Ono and so many responsible citizens and beggars; so very surprised to see so many Jews, so many Spanish refugees, so many Catholic and Protestant Irish, so many poet laureates; so many people, in short, who could at a moment's notice beat the world record in nail-biting or failing to take a bath, in cooking the world's most tasteless Yorkshire pudding or carving the thinnest slice of roast beef in history, foretelling the end of the world, playing the bagpipes, not speaking Sanskrit or speaking bad English (none like the Engish for cold-blooded murder of the English tongue) or the record for peeling potatoes and choking on them, of loving dogs and chewing chewing-gum, that anyone would have thought that humanity was a walking book of records, that it was a gigantic circus, but I, your cousin Walter, said: No, you are wrong, and I climbed up on a soap-box and I told them: No, the real circus is each and every one of us, the real circus – I told an audience of Rastafarians, black Muslims, English Nazis, Turks and girls going for and coming from abortions – is our own body: the two hundred and six bones, I told them, that rise one above the other to form the tallest of human towers! The dwarf male member that becomes a giant! The bearded pubis! The heart capable of spitting out 300 litres of blood per hour! The vocal cords which talk and sing! The lungs which ventilate twelve thousand litres of blood per day! And, above them all, enclosed in a tower of bone and ivory, lost in its own labyrinths, the ghost which believes itself lord and master of the circus, tamer of its tongue and nerves, towncrier of its voice, administrator of its stomach and vesicles, juggler of its testicles, rider of its legs, the illustrated man who in each convolution of his skin carries a tattooed story, a theorem or an illusion: the brain! The naïve, tyrannical and solitary brain which works and loses sleep walking a tightrope across the abysm of madness, flinging itself into the well of dreams, performing immortal leaps from one thought to the next and all for love of itself and love of a bladder, a tear gland and a pancreas which don't belong to it and which none the less urinate, weep or transform sugar for it or for themselves, but blind, dumb, deaf, not knowing what they do or why, where, when, how they do it and without you, Palinuro, without you – I said to a moon child, I said to an Italian, I said to an angel of hell, I said to an anonymous alcoholic, I said to a lord and I said to a theosophist, without you or anybody being able to know them and without them being able to know each other, to thank each other for their mutual favours and services and celebrate their delirious, irrational and fantastic association: the heart which distributes the blood, the blood which feeds the cerebellum, the cerebellum which

470

balances the skeleton, the skeleton which supports the nerves, the nerves which hurt the brain, the brain which moves the fingers, the fingers which feed the mouth, the mouth which chews for the stomach, the stomach which digests for the muscles, the muscles which move the lungs, the lungs which ventilate the blood, the blood which fills the heart and the heart which distributes the blood through arteries and capillaries fine as hairs, thus completing the web in which the soul is trapped; thus completing the circle of life, the magic, insane, dark, magnificent and vicious circle of life!

My long tourist walk through London – never was I anything but a tourist – my long walk through the flower of cities, through the dirty and dusty London of Byron, through the city of masts, through the clearing house of the world, through the London, in short, which Swallow's servant wished to see at least once before he died, cousin, my long day's journey into the beginning of a night which seemed would never come, my long midsummer day's dream, ended on Waterloo Bridge – no, I didn't dare to pee from that height – and, facing the Thames, liquid history flowing beneath my feet, it ended at the moment when I was about to tear another page from Unamuno's book, where he speaks of ridiculousness and heroism, and, making it into a paper boat stuck together with saliva, bid it farewell in a strange accent and send it to you over the warm gulf stream, with greetings, kisses, hugs and regards for all relatives and friends. But I didn't do it. I stayed there until the sun set – which actually came out, though you won't believe it, just in time to set – and the street lights came on, first red and then, when they warm up, yellow as winter light. I remember that there, in the distance, on Westminster Bridge and before the black silhouettes of Big Ben and the Parliament buildings, one street lamp had a Christmas attack: it flashed on and flashed off, it flashed off and flashed on, until at last it fell asleep, calmly, in shadow. My illusions also died in London.

471

23

The Brotherhood of the Flaming Fart

From Molkas, Palinuro inherited the art of vulgarity.

One afternoon, I remember, after eating a couple of dozen oysters which we bought in San Juan Market, adorned with parsley and sparkling crushed ice, and a tin of pleated sardines which my friend had stowed away in his sock drawer with Finnish foresight and some cakes, we were drinking grape liquor which we ostentatiously called 'cognac' when Palinuro burped, raised his left leg, said, 'By your leave, mate,' and farted.

Not believing my ears, I asked in all naïveté: 'Did you fart?'

'No: only half,' he answered, unperturbed, 'the other half got stuck.'

'You're revolting, disgusting, obnoxious, obscene!' I informed him.

'We could breathe deeply to make the smell go away more quickly,' he suggested.

I could take no more and flung a napkin in his face for want of a gauntlet, as Papa Eduardo had done years before to Uncle Felipe.

'You will pay dearly for this insult,' he said from behind the napkin, white with rage, perhaps because the napkin was white.

'Choose your weapon,' I answered him.

Palinuro sat pensive and sad behind the napkin. At last he removed it from his face, breaking into a smile: 'The very same that caused the outrage.'

'I don't understand,' I said to him, and the fact is that I truly had not understood.

'Shhhhh! Don't talk so loudly. It's a secret.'

He stood up, drew the curtains and continued: 'I challenge you with farts.'

'For heaven's sake, Palinuro, you disappoint me. I never thought that you could be so vulgar,' I said to him, genuinely disappointed.

Palinuro hid his face behind the curtains.

'You're right,' he said, scarlet with shame, perhaps because the curtains were scarlet.

'I who, in days of yore, modulated my verses to the sound of light oats.'

'And you are incapable now, Palinuro, of telling day from night, ' I answered him.

'Ah, but this is something very different!' he said gaily, emerging from

472

behind the curtains. 'Something you'd never guess.'

'I doubt very much that you can invent anything else. If you wish to win the sympathy of my liver, give me another "cognac" and we'll call it quits.'

But Palinuro persisted: 'Though your putrid mind leads you to believe otherwise, our competition will not be a matter of sound, duration or smell.'

'What then?'

'Light and colour. Yes indeed, though you look surprised: light and colour, as I said. You who love colour, you who love the Indian yellow obtained from the urine of elephants fed on mango leaves, you who love baked Sienna earths, Academic blue and the muted hues of Van Dyck; you who, like André Derain, use twenty-five colours on the palette with which you face life, will love the inflammability of farts.'

'The inflammawhat?' I asked him, the *Commentaries on the Gallic War* falling forgotten from my hands.

'Don't make me repeat such a long word, man. What I mean is, quite simply, that farts are inflammable.'

'You're having me on,' I said to him in all seriousness and resumed my reading at the page where Julius Caesar relates how the Britons painted themselves dark green with weld juice before going into battle.

'It's true, I swear: they are inflammable; in other words, they light up, they burn, they are devoured by flames.'

Thoroughly fed up, I deposited Julius Caesar on the bed and took up the second volume of *A la Recherche* to savour the chrysanthemums of various shades gathered in Odette's winter salon. Palinuro peered over my shoulder.

'You see? You can't get away from colours. You have been caught in the rainbow's net. But don't worry: at its end (or beginning) you will find a pot of Acapulco gold. But anyway, as I was saying, tonight you will enter with me the Brotherhood of the Flaming Fart.'

'Why does it have to be tonight? Why not right now?'

'Because farts are not only inflammable, but luminous.'

'I don't believe you.'

'What can I do to make you believe me?'

'Go to hell,' I answered him, without raising my eyes from Odette who, on that page, was more beautiful than ever.

'I see that I shall have to give you an empirical demonstration when night falls, or perhaps I should say: an empyrotechnical demonstration.'

Afternoon was drawing to an end, Estefania, and we listened to *Eine Kleine Nachtmusik*. In the neighbourhood haberdasheries, ribbons and Brabant cloth dissolved in a sudden thaw. Away in the distance, in the Plaza Mayor, the jelly vendors went into quarantine and around the bronze droppings of Carlos IV's mount, journalists created the evening scandals with epigraphs and palpitations. And still I could not believe.

'It's half-past seven. Do you persist in your disbelief?' asked Palinuro, highly indignant.

'I persist: seeing is believing.'

'Blessed are those who have not seen, etc. . . . . in that case, I will limit myself to listing a series of indisputable facts.'

'I don't see the point,' I said to him. 'Just give me the demonstration you promised.'

'In matters as serious as this, it is necessary to depart from a basis of theological revelation, although some notion of philosophy and a degree of general knowledge do not come amiss. The French philosopher Roscelin stated, for example, that a *universal* is nothing more than a *flatus vocis* and d'Alembert wrote a treatise entitled 'Reflection on the General Cause of Winds'. The former, of course, has nothing to do with the matter in hand and it is very likely that the winds to which the second thinker referred were of another ilk, of the kind Aeolus gave to Odysseus enclosed in a leather bag. On the other hand, a little verse I recall from Graham's *History of Surgery*, going something like:

Grave harm will ensue and ills without number
By holding inside the least murmur of thunder,

and the decision reached by the Emperor Claudius who, according to Suetonius, wished to issue an edict legalizing the emission of farts in all places and under all circumstances, are indeed germane to our subject, although not necessarily to the matter of inflammibility; likewise, at least one of the books found by Pantagruel in Saint-Victor's library: *Ars honeste petandi in societate*, in other words: *The Art of Breaking Wind Decently in Public*. But you had practical chemistry classes . . .'

'Like any other child.'

'Of course, like any other child living in the posh districts of Roma, Narvarte or Polanco who can afford to buy the books and waste time studying the bas-relief of carbon dioxide, instead of getting a job and bringing home a few pennies. But this isn't the time to discuss such things . . .'

'What things then?'

Palinuro haughtily ignored the question: 'You will then have learned, from your experiments, that potassium and strontium salts produce a red flame . . .'

'No,' I answered.

'You dare to deny a scientific fact?'

474

'When I say *no* I mean, simply, that I don't want to listen to you, that's all.'

'And that barium salts produce a green flame . . .'

'No.'

'And that sodium salts produce yellow flames . . .'

'No.'

'And arsenic salts a dazzling white . . .'

'No,' I repeated with as straight a face as I could muster.

Night fell, Estefania, and the daily nomads returned to their homes . . .

'And what of the plumes of boric esters?'

'No.'

And the prelates, in their temples, started to drink their foaming hot chocolate with all the secrecy of the confessional . . .

'And what of the flights of the aurora borealis stretching from one of the earth's poles to the other, over the snow-capped volcanoes?'

'No.'

And in the National Library the mercury lamps triumphed over the fame of Baron von Humboldt, the last universal man . . .

'And what of the phosphorescent infusoria, the colonies of actinia or petrified anemones which illuminate the water?'

'No'.

'And what about Westclox alarm clocks?'

'Also no.'

'In that case, I will limit myself to a straightforward analysis of a fart. As you know, every fart contains an average of fifty-nine per cent nitrogen and twenty-one per cent hydrogen, together with other smaller percentages of carbon dioxide, methane and oxygen and, of course, sometimes a little hydrogen sulphide which is responsible for the rotten egg smell. Now, the hydrogen and the methane, which are combustible when combined in the right proportions with oxygen, become explosive. There have been cases of explosions in operating theatres when the thermocautery is applied with the intestines open. There have also been cases . . .'

And in Chapultepec zoo, Estefania, the great bears rest on their constellations . . . Then Palinuro, naked as he usually was when he came into the world, walked over to the cupboard, opened a drawer, took out a candle, set it in a candlestick, placed the candlestick on the floor, lit the candle, stuck on some false whiskers to look like Sir William Wyndham, crouched down so that his behind was a few centimetres from the flame and said to me: 'Perhaps, then, you will be convinced by historic facts.'

'Perhaps,' I said.

Through the room, through the building, through the neighbourhood, Estefania, through the universe, these resounded the blood-curdling war cry of the Gauls: 'Sluagh-ghaaaaaaaaaaairm!'

And from Palinuro's arse exploded a searing red flash.

'Yes!' I said.

'Battle of Lepanto!' he exclaimed, and launched a luminous green fart in the shape of a cork screw.

'Yes, yes, yes!' I cried and dropped my trousers, lit a match, held it close to my bum and shouted: 'Trafalgar!'

And a spout of yellow light shot into the air and fell on the shoulders of the tourists in a shower of sparks.

You can imagine, Estefania, the number of battles and skirmishes that Palinuro and I waged in the intimacy of the night, the frays, the tournaments and jousts. You can have no idea, either, of the infinite variety of colours, lights and shapes which issued from our bodies. There were farts iridescent and changing as zodiacal light, black and concave farts, sharp and rectilinear farts, aged farts, extravagant farts, incendiary farts that set off the alarms.

'Chasseurs ardennais,' shouted Palinuro.

'*No pasarán!*' I answered.

There were opalescent farts and marbled ones, magenta and reddish mauve, and there were succulent farts which echoed Gaudí's edible architecture and heavy artillery farts and breech-loaders, burning farts and purple, assault farts, riot farts, meteoric and sordid farts, oblong and fondant farts, sparkling farts, stereophonic and hackneyed farts, farts vehement and mystic: there was everything in that room where we could no longer sleep in peace, where in the middle of the night, when least expected, Palinuro's war cry resounded: 'RAF!'

'Luftwaffe!' I answered back.

'Genetrix!' retorted Palinuro.

'Santiago!' I shouted and launched a firework which exploded suddenly like a Milky Way and carpeted the covers of *Amadís of Gaul* and the *Exploits of Esplandián* with stars.

Palinuro replied with a bombardment of amber farts.

And the room, and with it the world anew, was filled with farts like flashes of lightning and sparks which singed the grass of the carpet, with flame-throwing farts, with dark farts and swarthy farts, with sky-blue farts and ruby-silver farts, with cacophonous farts, with farts of gelignite and farts of sulphur, with violated and voluptuous farts, with firedamp farts and farts of gunpowder, with mellifluous farts, with amphibian farts and relative farts in the intermediate stage between matter and energy which unleashed a volcanic reaction.

'Phantom!' shouted Palinuro, at the peak of his excitement.

'Spitfire!' I answered.

'Savoia!' he insisted.

'Panzerdivisionen!' I retorted.

'God wills it!' he exclaimed, imitating Peter the Hermit.

'Limburg for its conquerors!' I replied.

'*Ça ira!*' I replied.

'England and St George!'

But, just as there were dithyrambic farts, flagrant farts and ignipotent, sharp-shooter farts, Estefania, and livid and sizzling farts, Palinuro and I also waged more romantic battles, encounters recalling the Wars of the Roses, the War of the Cakes and the War of the Buffoons, because there were gleaming, artificial farts like castles and pinwheels of fire, farts rippling and billowing like swarms of fireflies fanning out through the infinite night of Gothic gardens, stelliform farts, bucolic farts, blonde quintessential farts, meridianal farts, innocent farts in the shape of wings enfolding our backsides, photogenic farts, placid and relaxed farts, fugitive farts and salty and laughing farts, syncopated farts, glaucous farts, echoing farts and slippery farts orange as eels which crawled along the floor and instinctively sought the electrical plugs.

'Do you surrender?' I asked Palinuro.

'Never!' he replied and launched a few retreating, almost crepuscular farts.

'*Numance! Liberté!*'

And, as time passed, when the least excuse became a *casus belli* and we gained insight into the secrets of logistics, Estefania, we learned to choose our foods to determine the calibre of our artillery. Because, just as we discovered that lentils produce fragmented farts like confetti and cauliflower produces green and lethal machine-gun fire and broad beans white mold shot so, also, we learned that when we ate rotten cheeses we produced fatuous and rancid farts of heraldic blue; when we drank beer, we launched foaming farts with ultra-violet tendencies and when we lunched on pheasant (the rottener the better) we produced super-active farts which, like the great de Chéseaux comet, had several multicoloured tails which followed them faithfully through *Norton's Star Atlas*.

I had the pride and satisfaction of defeating Palinuro with an orphaned and swooning fart, nubile you might say: one of those timid, milksop farts, under-nourished and almost transparent, under-developed, which evaporate into thin air like ghosts.

Palinuro had exhausted his ammunition. But he refused to admit defeat. He stood straight and tall, hummed the opening bars of *La Marseillaise* and replied: '*La France a perdu un Georges Bataille: elle n'a pas perdu la guerre.*'

And from Fabricio (but more so from Cousin Walter), Palinuro inherited the art of rhetoric. Because later – not a few minutes nor a few hours, but several days, perhaps weeks, later; or it might be better to say: several

Palinuros later – my friend, still standing (later I would see him dragging himself through the remainder of his days; or, perhaps it would be better to say, the remainder of his hours) and in the same voice (not in the same voice he had always had, but in the one he was to have from then onwards) he said to me, very seriously:

'Absolutely nothing so far. We're waiting for the reply. The real agitators were poverty, ignorance and hunger. We students are organizing ourselves to put an end to them. These statues, as is to be expected in emergencies, have been witnesses. Not the statues of London, man, but those of Mexico: now it's our turn. Our statues – so used to posters advertising shows and couples of lovers, to folkloric events and children with their streamers of shiny paper – they saw and, it might be said, they felt. Certain Hertzian waves in search of a continent washed over the best frock-coat and wig of Primo de Verdad BA, standing permanently at the junction of Paseo de la Reforma and Rio Neva: this was the reply, still hanging in the air, mingling with the floating decrees, while a few pettifogging lawyers, armed with tricolour pen-holders, stir up the dust of old constitutions and other huge necropoli and pick out the best-aired laws and arrange them in a posy to offer the judges engaged in suspending constitutional guarantees. That means they're afraid of us: the converted members of the ruling class, the mendicants begging for a little presidential palm grease, ashen writers drowning their thirst for martyrology in their inkpots and, with them, bankers expert in churrigueresque deals, tumid ministers, congressmen and senators forever standing to attention, like obedient pricks. On to one such constitution, eternally open in the hands of Migel Ramos Arizpe, member of the Cortes of Cadiz, and not far from the first tub of geraniums, the helicopters flying over the city like olive green bumblebees dropped multicoloured Olympic fliers, along with carbon-monoxide droppings, while Ramos Arizpe, with his robust heart of moss and the patina accumulated in the course of seventy-one years of immobility, stood watching the people go by watching the cars go by. The people were butchers, labourers, bureaucrats and ice-cream vendors and the cars were sleak and black, with shining chrome, fog lights and wailing sirens and inside them were the same congressmen since it appeared that Congress was in session throughout the day in the golden room with green seats reminiscent of the autumn of the Revolution. They're afraid of us, all of them, along with the rich who fear contamination of their inheritances and their swimming pools and those who boast plutocratic airs and the government-paid apostles and workers and peasant leaders and military veterans sleeping on the plush dogmas of the Revolution itself. During our most recent demonstration, they and all the other ball-less sycophants peered out from the main balcony of the Presidential Palace and other lower vantage points and were blinded by the reverberation of our civic

478

courage and later withdrew into the French interiors like bats defending their historic bastions and licked their fingers which still smelled of the lobster with which they had celebrated the students' defeat. But no, they haven't defeated us yet. We will hold another demonstration, we will pour the enthusiasm of five hundred thousand hearts into the Plaza Mayor. The president said: Peace reigns; and one student, after a muddy battle with a policeman, fell dead just outside the main square on top of a pile of oranges and slices of watermelon and his hair, together with a little of his violet-coloured brains, stroked the prosperous chrome of one of those cars heading towards the Chamber of Congress and, when a photographer sought to dramatize the sacrifice in Kodacolour in order to show foreign readers the exact shade of his mustard-coloured pullover and the red of his blood and the watermelon, his camera flew ten metres and shattered in its turn, reduced to a mass of springs, splinters and silver chloride. But they fear us, we have made the Government tremble from the tip of its big toes, through all its administrative cartilage, right up to the presidential snout and consternation is seeping already from the buttocks of every state. You should have seen, from a privileged position, with unsheathed sword and sand-covered knees and wrinkles of bronze, all those worthy gentlemen, who only yesterday galloped on horseback through the unpaid ravines to the cry of Land and Freedom and are today so pot-bellied, with the line of happiness fostered by their exclusive imported whiskies, descending from their black and oceanic and armoured automobiles in their admiral-blue Sunday suits and lead-coloured ties, saying goodbye to their golden mistresses and their wives whose flesh and perfume proliferate in the leather-upholstered interiors, the same women who on supernational holidays, wearing national dress and other loud and ridiculous get-ups, chill the presidential champagne with the garishness of their glassy make-up. But it would have been good to be Hermenegildo Galeana and have not only a big pistol but the desire to fight again naked with the cut and thrust of the machete and with his battalion of blacks to scatter the realists; just for the chance to see them, you should have been Guillén de Lampart who, with utmost seriousness, on the Column of Independence, was reminded by the heat of his lost empire of Citerior America and his declarations of smoke and chocolate written on the sheets of the Inquisition, just to see those congressmen climbing two by four up the stairs of the building with their sharkskin briefcases and one-eyed eagle tiepins, not forgetting the colonels with chests dripping medals and land-owning cowboys of primitive coarseness trying to ignore the heavy odour, part headcheese and part onion, part nickle and another part blood and bureaucratic payrolls, which parted the multitude along the streets and in the barbers' shops and the dry cleaners' and the hardware stores, while, outside the building, whether the congressmen were aware of it or not, were the motherkins who had recently emerged from a Tenth of May who, widowed of their children, begged to be given the corpse of Juanito, sixteen years of age, biological sciences student, or of Manuel, eighteen, short and dark, humanities student, and of others besides; or at least a keepsake: the watch he was given when he started university or the socks darned with such devotion between soap opera and advertisement, between Maximilian in the Borda Gardens and the tenderness of Waldorf toilet paper. But in vain: policemen with automatic cudgels and whips danced a terrible waltz, driving the women back with force enough to shake the washing lines and send the shirts flying through the afternoon sky. Shirts and other articles of clothing, leaving a bra hanging from the hand which Christopher Columbus holds eternally outstretched to see if it is raining. But the only thing to have rained down recently, apart from insults and anthropomorphic promises, was tear-gas grenades, a yellow weeping creeping along the streets of the city, but which wet neither the feet of Christopher Columbus nor the buttocks of Diana the Huntress who, alternately coy and immoral like the rest of our national heritage, amused herself by firing blue arrows at the Goodyear Oxo zeppelins. I myself have a friend – or rather, I did have – whose chest was torn open by a pink-nosed bullet and there he lies, on the pavement hot enough to fry students' testicles, waiting to turn purple in the dissecting room and have a label tied round his big toe bearing the first name of a soldier and the surname of one of the Child Heroes and an age which they guess from his broken teeth and heliocentric caries. But they are afraid of us, Querol's Pegasuses, the Danaïdes of the Alameda Park, the congresswomen who come to the Chamber and who say goodbye to their spaniels newly emerged from their pedigree and their children who go to school in almost British uniforms: they're afraid we'll fuck up their Olympics, they accuse the machinations of exotic forces of trying to strip Mexico of prestige before the attentive eyes and ears of the world and, meanwhile, I have seen them, I have seen how they brutally blindfolded and gagged the students and how the valiant soldiers spoke to them in the language of rifle butts in the ribs and stood them up against the walls of the schools and shouted the order to prepare, take aim, fire the salute to the Motherland, because anything is possible in peacetime. And the cars continued to arrive and there followed embraces and greetings at the junction of the stairs and the lobby and I saw more than one minister walk towards the president's office enveloped in the ample aura of his millions and his silence and I saw a seemingly inoffensive worker leader in dark glasses and congressmen bright and timid as imported tulips and congressmen with moustaches à la favourite son of any town council and congressmen dancing around as though they had a lottery ticket tangled in their spurs and, further up the stairs, I saw the pillars, velvet curtains and stained-glass windows of the Capitol, I saw that paradise was bursting with citizens preconditioned to twiddle their eustachian tubes and pick their teeth with Swedish matches and last out a whole interminable session while the parliamentarians, still burping the waffles and *chilaquiles* on which they had breakfasted at Sanborn's or the Hilton, prepared to turn into smart iguanas and sleep on their feet in accordance with the liturgy by which parliamentary sessions are conducted, occasionally pierced by the notes of a pretty insipid national anthem to be heard in ceremonies of particular patrioticity and on those occasions when we have been pushed to the very limits of our idiosyncrasy. And when a general, who did not have a glass eye, made a plea for law and order and asked for the Chamber's support for the President, that solitary man who bears on his shoulders the enormous responsibilities of a whole nation, he said, full of loyal compassion for his barefooted people, his valiant citizens and a misguided young generation which he seeks at advice-point to set on the straight and narrow, the motion was crowned with splendour and the rounds of applause were such that the plaster fell from the dome of the Chamber on to the venerable bald pates of the veterans of the Revolution. Volunteers immediately scuttled along the rows of seats requesting a donation of silence to allow the Speaker to read the agenda which had arrived, as always, by direct telephone link from the lofty heights of the Los Pinos residence where the President, holding the mane of the Republic in his hands, sorts the seeds of his misguided mandates and strings everyone along to the left or the right according to the whim of Washington or the numismatic hunches of party leaders. The frenzy is contained and the politicians get at each other with speeches of fifteen thousand long live Mexicos. But we will rally anew to put an end to hunger, ignorance and poverty and the student songs will be heard again, bringing joy to the palm trees on the roundabouts and to the Volkswagens and the green crocodiles crawling along Amazon River Street and along Euphrates River Street and along the Danube and the Seine, the songs ascending to the street lights and to the information offices of the US Embassy and the fifth floors of hotels from where tourists watch this novel happening before returning to the mezzanines and the roof-garden bars to discuss, to the accompaniment of the frozen acidity of Martinis, the events of the moment. Everything degenerated – or it did that day anyway – into a monstrous feast: inside the Chamber, the congressmen had a recess and devoured their lunches with flapping jaws, and outside the Chamber appeared the sandwich and taco vendors and all the rest: the motherkins, the vendors of little flags from a hundred-odd countries confirming the cosmopolitanness of our Homeland – the very same as those flying above the five times admirable Olympic installations – and the congressmen's Indian chauffeurs and aspiring congressmen who had reached the political bandwagon too late and the balloon sellers with their round metaphors and the vendors of rattles and football emblems: all of them, including the police and the riot squads and many, very many students, succumbed to the picnic. But those are the students who will have to hide from now on. Who will have to climb into the showcases of international shops and promise to be dummies for the rest of their lives or hide in the anonymous façades of foreign universities, in the debris of grammar and in civil servant jobs.'

'Palinuro,' I said to him, 'I didn't understand a word.'

'That's the problem: nobody understands,' he answered me, 'but come and see me after the demonstration and I will explain.'

And the thing is, Palinuro is like that, he always was: everything he said in earnest seemed to be joke and everything that he said as a joke seemed to be in earnest.

However, before his friends Molkas and Fabricio forgot Palinuro for ever, before realizing that never – or perhaps never – had they known the real Palinuro, they had the opportunity to live the last of two great adventures with him. Charon's Cave was reached by way of a tunnel, a sort of gallery of about ten metres in length and less than a metre in diameter linking an empty tomb with a section of the old communal grave of the Dolores Graveyard. There, at the end of the tunnel, the old man had dug a cavern which served as a store for all the bones they could find by simply digging a little here and a little there. But it was not easy to find a complete skeleton in that mine of bones. Nor to find specimens in good condition. The dryness of the earth ensured that the bones were clean but this lack of moisture also destroyed them. Sometimes bones which seemed to be whole: a femur, a tibia, turned to dust as soon as they came into contact with the air. But anyone who wished to try their luck in Charon's Cave could do so whenever they liked, subject to payment of the fee stipulated by the old man. The price of the bones was separate, depending on quality and weight: Charon sold them by the kilo. Moreover, no detail had been overlooked: since the tunnel was only wide enough for one person to drag themselves along the ten metres of its length, Charon had thought up the idea of constructing a pulley device to transport the bones in a small sack hooked on to a rope and which went backwards or forwards as you pulled the rope on one side or the other. The three friends let chance decide which of them would be the hero to crawl at midnight through the tunnel with the risk not only of being given away and caught by the police (although this risk was run by all three of them) but, what was worse, of the tunnel or the cave collapsing in on top of them and burying them alive (and this was a danger to which one of them was exposed however solemnly Charon swore that everything was perfectly shored up). They tossed coins in the air. 'Heads,' said Molkas. 'Heads,' said Fabricio. 'Tails,' said Palinuro. 'You lost: you have to go to Charon's Cave.' 'No, I won: I have to go to Charon's Cave,' said Palinuro who, ever since he was a child, had liked to play at being soldier during the First World War (but really believing that he was Uncle Esteban) and that, crawling on his belly, he was making his way from the Balkans and Hellas towards Salonika through the maze of the lawn, encrusting subterranean rhizomes in his knees and with his chest exposed to bullets and dragonflies. Come on, come on! shouted some friend of his whose name he no longer remembered from the other end of the garden and the world. But Molkas, jealously, predicted that they would have to make several trips to Charon's Cave if they were going to fulfil their objective of collecting the bones of an entire skeleton and, therefore, they would take turns. However, Palinuro's luck was such that once was enough. Molkas checked the list: 'Trowel and sledge hammer, what's that?' 'A miner's hammer.' 'Mmmm . . . trowel, sledge hammer and headlamp. What do you mean, headlamp?' 'The kind you put on your head, idiot.' 'Ah, headlamp, vertebrae, paper, pencil, ribs, marijuana . . .' 'Who put down marijuana?' 'I did,' admitted Palinuro. 'Not necessary. In the Dolores Graveyard it grows wild, like tiger lilies and marigolds . . . ribs, marijuana, one bottle of Bacardi . . . wouldn't two bottles be better?' 'One will do.' 'One bottle of Bacardi, ropes, femurs . . . why the hell did you put all the bones on the list? You should have made a list of all the things we have to take with us and another list of all the things we have to bring back, don't you think?' 'Well, each of us has to take all our respective bones and organs with us anyway.' 'In that case, what we most need, and in their right place, are balls.' Fabricio took the list from Molkas and wrote: 'Balls'.

Palinuro tied the neck of the sack, pulled the rope and sent it back to his friends, together with a message which read: 'Send you twelve ribs. Stop. Suspect Adam's rib to be one of them. Stop.' Three minutes later, the reply came back together with a bottle of Bacardi: 'Let us drink a toast right now to the health of Adam's rib, drink and return the bottle. Why do you write telegraphically?' Molkas and Fabricio, at the other end of the tunnel, the end opening on to the empty tomb, opened the neck of the sack in their turn and found a sacrum bone and the following message: 'Send you sacrum bone. Stop. Cable message very expensive: Colon: must save words.' The friends returned the empty sack without comment. Two minutes later, an iliac bone, three vertebrae and a pair of femurs: 'Suspect that femurs belonged to Emperor Cuauhtémoc. Stop. Inform Geographical and Historical Society.' The reply was prompt: 'Glory be to us. Stop. Must drink emperor's health. Stop. Where the hell is bottle? Question mark.' The bottle was returned minus two or three gulps and: 'Wonder of wonders,' cablegraphed Molkas, 'a whole skull. Exclamation mark.' 'Suspect,' said Palinuro in his next message (accompanied by a tibia and a humerus), 'suspect skull of Patriot Benito Juárez.' 'Idiot: colon: Benito Juárez buried in the San Fernando Graveyard. Stop.' A minute of silence. The two friends opened the returned sack and found a pair of iliacs in magnificent condition and a message from Palinuro: 'Suspect iliacs of Father of the Motherland Miguel Hidalgo.' Palinuro, alone, at the other end of the tunnel, accompanied by the bones of all his ancestors, opened the sack: 'Idiot: colon: suspect female iliacs.' 'Then,' replied Palinuro, 'they must be the iliacs of the Mother of the Fatherland,' and started to thread (pushing the rope through the respective holes) all the lumbar, dorsal and cervical vertebrae that he had found and which he didn't bother to put in the sack: they sped through the cavern, like the living skeleton of a rattlesnake. 'We need sacrum vertebra,' said the message. 'I need air,' replied Palinuro. The reply came back in another sack, together with a bottle: 'The top half of this bottle is full of air. The bottom half of Bacardi. Drink the top half.' 'I don't find your bloody jokes funny,' said Palinuro five minutes later as he emerged from the other end of the cavern. 'Phew! I never thought that you could feel such relief entering a tomb. What time is it?' 'Half-past two.' 'We have plenty of time.' 'If you like, I'll go now,' said Fabricio who had always wanted to escape from a concentration camp. 'No, *I* lost, *I* go,' answered Palinuro and, checking the rope around his waist, he lit the lamp and started to drag himself along the tunnel again. When he reached Charon's Cave, he continued digging. Next Fabricio and Molkas received two astragaluses, countless phalanxes, metacarpuses and metatarsals, two rotulae, a stone which Palinuro mistook for another rotula, a tibia which Palinuro thought must have belonged to Emiliano Zapata, 'Zapata is buried in Cuautla,' cablegraphed Molkas; a calcaneum which Palinuro thought must have belonged to Pancho Villa. 'Pancho Villa is buried in Parral,' pointed out Fabricio. 'What, he's not in the Rotunda of Illustrious Men?' asked Palinuro in a prepaid reply message. 'That's hardly surprising,' replied Molkas, 'not all illustrious men are there and not all men there are illustrious'; as well as two or three fibulas, two atlas vertebrae and another tibia which Palinuro thought must have belonged to Miramón. 'Miramón,' wrote Molkas, 'is not here but in the Rotunda of Illustrious Traitors,' as well as several humeri, a number of cuneiform and cuboid bones that might have belonged to Mamma Clementina, Hernán Cortez, the Corregidor Ortiz de Domínguez or to Grandfather Francisco, if – as Fabricio took it upon himself to remind Palinuro – Aunt Clementina were not in the Jardín Graveyard, Hernán Cortez in the Hospital de Jesús, the Corregidor in Querétaro and Grandfather Francisco in the French La Piedad Graveyard. 'Conclusion: colon: only important find, bones of Emperor Cuauhtémoc and Adam's rib,' cablegraphed Palinuro. 'Impossible to prove authenticity,' replied Molkas. 'Impossible to prove non-authenticity,' replied Palinuro in his turn. In response, the bottle arrived. 'Cheers,' cablegraphed Palinuro. 'Cheers,' read the message that arrived two minutes later.

Never had Molkas been so happy. 'We have at least one and a half skeletons!' he exclaimed as he started to arrange the bones on the floor of the room in Holy Sunday Square. And indeed, besides a few duplicates, they did have an almost complete skeleton, lacking only perhaps one or two vertebrae and the odd bone in the foot. 'The only trouble is,' complained Palinuro, 'it's made up of bones from different people of different ages. Doesn't it look a bit deformed to you?' 'Well,' said Fabricio philosophically: 'if life isn't perfect, we can't expect death to be.' 'What the hell is this?' asked Palinuro. 'A dog's jaw.' 'And what the fuck's it doing here?' 'Perhaps they buried it with its master,' said Molkas. 'Perhaps it's Charon's first Cerberus.' 'Perhaps,' added Fabricio, 'it is the dog that accompanied Quetzalcoátl on his first journey through Mictlán, the land of the dead.' And, remembering the bone libraries in the American universities which dye the bones lent to the students different colours so as to be able to identify them, he asked: 'What colour are we going to paint our dead man?' 'Mexican pink,' suggested Palinuro. 'Wouldn't it be better . . .?' 'Mexican pink, full stop.' 'OK,' said Fabricio, though less philosophically this time: 'If there's a *Vie en Rose*, why shouldn't there also be a *Mort en Rose*?'

24

Palinuro on the stairs or the art of comedy

(Play on four floors with a prologue on the ground floor, an epilogue in an attic and several unexpected interludes)

(Reality is way back, towards the rear of the stage. Reality is Palinuro, who started out dragging himself through Charon's Cave, never to rise again. Reality is Palinuro beaten up, on the dirty stairway. It is the bureaucrat, the concierge, the drunken doctor, the postman, the policeman, Estefania and me. This reality is played out centre stage. Dreams, memories, illusions, lies, ill-intentions and imaginings, together with the characters of La Commedia dell'Arte: Harlequin, Scaramouch, Pierrot, Colombine, Pantalone, etc.: these all pertain to fantasy. This fantasy, which freezes reality, re-creates it, occurs not in time, only in space. Its place is front stage.)

PROLOGUE

(A street. The façade of the building in Holy Sunday Square in Mexico City. It is night. One after another, the lights in the windows go out. Bells are heard tolling the hour of three in the morning. Enter Rag-and-Bone-Death wearing a large feathered hat and with blazing eyes and pink skeleton, pulling a cart full of skirts, stockings, hats, capes and other articles of clothing, limbs and unidentified parts of dummies, lamps and scrap iron . . .)

RAG-AND-BONE DEATH: Sweatshirts? Who wants T-shirts with the University 'U'? Who wants some green trousers? Ladies and gentlemen, secretaries and sergeants: who wants a writer's nose? I have football jerseys to sell! I have an airman's ears, a stipper's sternum! I'll buy a gunman's scarves! Ladies and gentlemen, jugglers and geologists, linguists and drudges: I have a psychiatrist's coat, I'll buy an acrobat's thighs, I have a conductor's buttocks, I'll buy a traitor's masks . . .! Ladies and gentlemen, congressmen and labourers, milkmen and marble blasters, architects and nurses, I sell everything, I buy everything! I buy second-hand

486

lives, I sell new deaths! I buy sad lives, failed lives, famous lives, and exchange them for coloured deaths, heroic deaths, unknown deaths! I sell them for cash, gentlemen; I sell them on hire purchase and with discount, ladies! I sell them to the highest bidder! Who gives more, ladies and gentlemen, congressmen and painters, vets and cyclists? Who gives more for a Death-in-the-Square? I have an industrialist's armpits and a riot policeman's boots! I buy office clerks' Sundays! Who bids more for a Surprise-Death? *(Removes the hat and puts on a wig of blonde curls)* Who bids more for a Little-Girl-Death? *(Removes the wig and puts on false eyelashes)* Who gives more for a Beautiful-Death? *(From Death's mouth emerge blue flies; from its eyes, silk-worm butterflies. It moves away, calling its age-old street vendor's cry. Enter from one side Scaramouch dressed up as a student, although his mask and long tail of black sequins give him away. From the other side enter Harlequin, also dressed up as a student, but his back Michoacan devil's mask gives him away.)*

SCARAMOUCH: Hey, you, Spiders: go fuck your mothers!

HARLEQUIN: Hey, you, Citadels: go fuck yours!

(They start to fight, flailing each other with tails and hats. Enter Pantalone, in riot helmet and white devil's mask.)

PANTALONE: Enter me, dressed as a member of the riot squad . . .

(Enter Captain Mean, in a riot helmet and green devil's mask.)

CAPTAIN MEAN: Enter me, also dressed as a member of the riot squad.

BOTH: And we two, between us, are letting the students have it, we'll stop their tongues flapping!

(From Harlequin's and Scaramouch's mouths they draw long tongues of red silk which they proceed to beat. At each blow, sparks and fireworks fly. Enter Colombine and Pierrot. Colombine is wearing a white dove dress made of feathers. Pierrot, a pink suit of crêpe paper.)

COLOMBINE: Just look how they're beating the students! See how sparks fly, tracing ferns in the sky!

PIERROT: See how they crack the burning crown of their hair, how they rearrange their profiles!

(Exeunt Colombine and Pierrot. Exeunt also Pantalone and Captain Mean, dragging Harlequin and Scaramouch.)

HARLEQUIN *(as he is dragged along)*: Yes, yes: take a good look, so that afterwards you may not say that you did not see!

(Enter Author-Death with cart and hornrimmed spectacles. Reaches the centre of the stage and bows to the audience.)

AUTHOR-DEATH: What you have just seen, my lords, ladies and gentlemen, grocers and seamstresses, engineers and nuns, is a trailer of the play *Palinuro on the Stairs*. This small episode is in turn entitled 'Fight Between Two Schools'. This fight sketched student conflict, character and

487

play . . . *(bows)*. And what you are seeing at this very moment, face to face, is DEATH. Because I, ladies and gentlemen, am Everybody's-Death *(points to the audience)*, I am Your-Death. A-Student's-Death. A-Colonel's-Death. Grand-Leveller. Pale-Mourner. Harlot-of-the-Icy-Blush. And, sooner or later, I am going to send you, ALL OF YOU, to the devil *(a blue shiver crosses the stage)*. But meanwhile, until that time comes, ladies and gentlemen, opticians and admirals, broadcasters and shopkeepers, until the time comes for you to go with me to the devil, I invite you to join the cast of this play, whenever you dare or please or have no alternative . . . Ah! don't worry about costumes; here in my cart, as you know, I have all you need to dress up. I have a philanthropist's tights, I have an optometrist's hats, a schizophrenic's moustache! *(dons Rag-and-Bone-Death's hat)* Who will buy a minister's jackets? I have a student's sweatshirts! *(starts to leave the stage)* Ribs for sale? A Secret Service agent's raincoat? *(pauses for a few seconds)* . . . And, of course, ladies and gentlemen, landowners and prostitutes: you need have even less worry about what you are to say! It's all made up! It's all improvised! The only thing you need to know, ladies and gentlemen, cartographers and translators, is the plot . . . *Palinuro on the Stairs* . . . Palinuro knocked down by a tank . . . That's all! Simple as that! *(continues to leave)* I buy second-hand lives! I sell new deaths! *(puts on a pair of gloves and inserts a monocle)* Who wants an Elegant-Death? *(places a furled 'mother-in-law's tongue' extending whistle in his mouth and blows)* Who wants a Joke-Death? *(exit)*.

(Pantalone and Captain Mean enter once more dressed as riot police, carrying a stepladder. Lying on it, face down with arms and legs dangling over the sides, is Harlequin, in his rhombus-patterned suit made of scraps from scarfs and blankets. Pantalone and Captain Mean deposit the ladder on the floor, with Harlequin still on it, and exit. Enter Colombine with her mask of dove feathers.)

COLOMBINE: Oh, poor you, Emperor of the Moon! Poor you, Harlequin, Server of Two Masters! What became of your cunning and your acrobatics?

(A half moon is lowered from the flies and hangs suspended above Harlequin. Sitting upon it is Pierrot in his mask of shiny violet paper and holding a lute.)

PIERROT: What became of your loyalty and your mercurial nature? Oh, poor you, Harlequin, King of the Lions, Transvestite Prince!

(Exit Colombine, the moon ascends and disappears, taking Pierrot with it.)

(Enter Tartaglia in his postman's cap and blue devil mask, riding a monocycle and carrying a white parcel.)

TARTAGLIA: A PAPA! A paparcel for HAHA! For Harlequin!

HARLEQUIN: Could you open it for me, please? I'm very weak . . .

TARTAGLIA *(flinging the parcel at him)*: DODO! Do it YOYO! Do it yourself, you lazy sod!

(Exit Tartaglia on his monocycle. Resigned, Harlequin rolls over and sits up on the ladder. He has a pair of enormous testicles of coloured rhombuses. He opens the parcel, which explodes. Black smoke fills the stage.)

FIRST FLOOR

(We find ourselves in reality. The stage is the interior of an old building in Holy Sunday Square in Mexico City. It is dark. Just visible in the half light is the first-floor landing and the stairs – with sixteen steps – going up to the second floor. At the back, the doors of apartments numbered from one to four. The date is Wednesday, 28 August. The year, bearing in mind that Palinuro lived simultaneously in several periods, might be any year belonging to a known past or an invisible future. Let us say – but just in a manner of speaking – that it is 1968, the year when Mexico City was visited with Olympic swimming pools and copper sports palaces . . . the year in which the gunpowder of the May Revolution in Paris surged through the world like a galvanoplastic river . . .)

ESTEFANIA'S VOICE: Oh, there's something here!

(The sound of people mounting the stairs is heard.)

MY VOICE: It's me, don't be silly!

ESTEFANIA'S VOICE: No, no: there's somebody lying here, on the stairs . . .

(I light a match. Palinuro becomes visible, sprawled on the last steps of the flight from the ground floor. He is wearing his patchwork waistcoat.)

ME: Oh hell, Palinuro's been at it again!

ESTEFANIA: My God, he's dead drunk! And he promised us so faithfully that he wouldn't do it again!

PALINURO *(raising his head)*: I'm not bloody drunk: I'm injured!

(Palinuro drags himself along the landing. Estefania and I sit down on the first steps leading to the next floor, waiting for him. The match goes out.)

MY VOICE: Yes Palinuro, I can see it all: you slipped on a tequila skin.

PALINURO'S VOICE: If you don't believe me, turn on the light and look at me.

MY VOICE: The bulb's blown. I've been telling the concierge for the last week but she hasn't changed it.

PALINURO'S VOICE: Idiot: it's the ground-floor bulb that's

blown. Just turn on the light will you!

(I walk a few steps and turn on the light.)

ESTEFANIA *(bending over Palinuro)*: Have you seen the state Palinuro's in? His face is covered in blood!

ME *(going over to Palinuro)*: And his eyes aren't a pretty sight either! Who was the scrap with, mate?

(Palinuro drags himself up three steps.)

PALINURO: You can draw what conclusions you like from this honorific mock-up. I was beaten up and then almost run over by a tank. I've dragged myself this far and I can't go any further. They've fucked up my legs and my ribs.

ME: Let me help you . . .

(A door is heard opening and closing.)

ESTEFANIA: Who's down there?

DOCTOR'S VOICE *(from the ground floor)*: The doctor from number fourteen, who's up there?

ESTEFANIA: Ah, is that you doctor? Could you come up here, please.

(Palinuro manages two more steps. The doctor's footsteps are heard, climbing the stairs from the ground floor!)

ME: Let me help you for God's sake, you might have broken something . . .

(Palinuro's only reply is to crawl up a further three steps. The doctor appears at the head of the stairs from the ground floor, obviously drunk.)

DOCTOR: A broken bone? Careful, it might be a clarinet bell fracture!

(The door of apartment 2 opens and the postman comes out, in striped flannel pyjamas.)

POSTMAN: What is it? You knocked? Is the young man drunk? You must give him a good strong black coffee and put ice . . .

FEMALE NEIGHBOUR'S VOICE *(in the distance)*: Who is it? Is that you, children?

ESTEFANIA: But how do you think you're going to get upstairs by yourself, Palinuro, if you can't even stand?

PALINURO: Leave me alone, leave me alone, get out of the way!

POSTMAN: If you like, young man, we can carry you between the five of us. Or rather, the four of us. But, if not, just forget I suggested it, don't take offence, I beg you . . . I'll tell my wife to make you a good strong cup of coffee. *(He goes back into his apartment.)*

(The doctor's footsteps are heard climbing the stairs once more. Palinuro, in turn, drags himself up to stair number twelve and everybody else takes a few steps up so as to remain at the same distance.)

PALINURO: I tell you, I dragged myself along endless streets, so I don't see why I can't drag myself up a few floors and, as for you, where the hell were you when I was being beaten up in the Zócalo Square? Where were you, huh?

(They remain frozen beneath a blue light. In the foreground, enter Colombine in her white feather dress. She is chased by Scaramouch, in a suit of black sequins with a long black cat's tail.)

SCARAMOUCH: Give us a kiss, Colombine!

COLOMBINE: Up with the students!

SCARAMOUCH: Give us a kiss, Colombine!

COLOMBINE: Down with the riot squads!

(Finally, Scaramouch catches Colombine and smacks her. Colombine slaps his face and he falls on his bottom. A black imprint of Scaramouch's hand is left on Colombine's bottom. On Scaramouch's cheek is left the imprint of Colombine's white hand. She bows to the audience.)

COLOMBINE: Where were we? What were we doing while Palinuro was in the Zócalo? We had a wild time! We organized a fancy dress ball in the San Carlos School! Of course they were simple costumes, all improvised . . . tell them, tell them Scaramouch, what a good time we had at the ball! If you tell it well, I'll reward you with a kiss! Everybody was there . . .

(A wooden box is pushed on to the stage with a long pole, Scaramouch climbs on to it.)

COLOMBINE: The President was there . . . well, a student dressed up as the President was there . . . Napoleon Bonaparte was there . . .

SCARAMOUCH: Ehem! Ehem!

(Colombine starts to dance to the measures of the waltz 'God never dies'.)

SCARAMOUCH: Ehem! Ehem! I will start by telling you how we got on yesterday: yesterday afternoon, 250,000 people, yes, you heard right! 350,000 people . . .

COLOMBINE: No, no, don't tell them about the demonstration, tell them about the ball! Cleopatra was there and Abraham Lincoln, students dressed up as riot police, there were riot police . . .

SCARAMOUCH: Yes, yes, you won't believe it, 450,000 people . . .

COLOMBINE *(still dancing)*: I was there, dressed up as Estefania, and Cousin Walter was there, dressed up as Pierrot . . . and how we danced, we danced all night! There were students dressed up as secret police agents . . .

SCARAMOUCH: Yes, gentlemen, a mighty demonstration against Poverty, Ignorance and Hunger: those are the real agitators,

491

gentlemen, not the students!

(Applause and hisses.)

COLOMBINE: . . . and secret agents dressed up as students. How we danced, we danced all night!

SCARAMOUCH: Just imagine! Just try for a minute to imagine 550,000 in a demonstration in which all sorts of people took part; not just students and lecturers . . .

COLOMBINE: Lecturers dressed up as CIA agents . . .

SCARAMOUCH: But songs and dances too . . . and workers and paterfamilias!

COLOMBINE: And CIA agents dressed up as workers, dressed up as ordinary men and women, as firemen, as priests and lecturers!

(Scaramouch, exhausted by the effort, sits down on the box, but it collapses with a loud bang and Scaramouch lands bottom-first on the floor. Colombine takes a muslin handkerchief from her cleavage and wipes the sweat from his forehead.)

COLOMBINE: Do you remember, Scaramouch, do you remember, who won the prize?

(Scaramouch gets to his feet and takes Colombine's arm. Exeunt.)

SCARAMOUCH: And so, singing in one voice, all arm-in-arm, 650,000 people marched as one towards the Main Square: the Zócalo . . .

(Dottore peeps out from the stairwell, wearing a biretta and yellow devil's mask and his long violet brocade cloak with ruffled collar.)

DOTTORE: The Zócalo? The Zócalo? *Ubi gentium est quadra Zocalliana?* In other words: where the devil is the Zócalo?

(The stage darkens. 'God never dies' continues to be heard for a few seconds.)

(Let us return to reality. Palinuro on the stairs. With him, Estefania and myself.)

ME: After that, we came straight home. We never expected to find you here. We thought that you would be in the Square, celebrating our triumph: because we will triumph, Palinuro, we are triumphing! Never has there been such a massive demonstration in Mexico. You'll see, Palinuro, we're going to get the government to make radical reforms! And now, please, let me help you: you're completely done in.

PALINURO *(still on the stair number twelve)*: How dare you say that? I've always managed for myself, though there are times when my soul weighs heavily on me because it's too like itself. But, at other times, like now, it reconquers other ages and turns to laugh at me . . . I hardly feel it, it's like angel hair . . .

(The doctor appears in the stairwell.)

DOCTOR: If you will allow me . . .

492

ESTEFANIA: All right, Palinuro, but if you have a broken bone it's going to hurt horribly.

DOCTOR *(climbing a few steps)*: If it's a matter of broken bones or accidents . . .

ME: And anyway, it's very dangerous.

DOCTOR: Of course it is. A broken rib can damage the lung tissue!

PALINURO: That's what I want, I want it to hurt, I want it to hurt like hell!

DOCTOR: If you will allow me, I will examine him. I am a doctor. I studied at the National University. I'm not a traumatology specialist, but I've done my stint at the Red Cross. Let me see, young man . . .

ESTEFANIA: I can help you, doctor, I'm a nurse . . .

ME: I didn't know you had this masochistic streak, Palinuro . . .

(The doctor opens his bag. Takes out a bottle of tequila. Takes a swig. Puts it on a step. Continues to search in the bag.)

DOCTOR: I could have sworn that my stethoscope was in here. Mmmm . . .

PALINURO: Me, a masochist? Me? It's just so as not to forget, that's all! I want to prolong the pain and humiliation for hours, for days if necessary, so as never to forget them . . . Ahhhh! *(He conquers step number thirteen.)*

ME: What are you talking about?

ESTEFANIA: Shall I help you look, doctor?

(The doctor accidentally knocks over the bottle, which goes rolling down the stairs.)

FEMALE NEIGHBOUR'S VOICE *(in the distance)*: Is that you Pepe? Is that you, Memo? Is that you, children?

CONCIERGE'S VOICE *(from the ground floor)*: What's all this noise? Have they brought women in here again?

BUREAUCRAT'S VOICE *(from the second floor)*: Thief, thief, police!

MALE VOICE *(in the distance)*: Did somebody call? I'm coming, I'm coming. Just putting my socks on!

POSTMAN *(coming out of his apartment and looking upwards)*: Eh? What's going on? Ah, yes, it's you. Your coffee is heating, young man *(goes inside)*.

(Estefania has found the stethoscope and gives it to the doctor. He crawls up the stairs to Palinuro's side and starts to examine him.)

DOCTOR: Let's see, don't move. Why do you students get into such scrapes?

PALINURO: It's been a foul night man! It was raining like the devil, but not water: it was blows that rained on us! If you don't believe me, just go and take a look in the Square and there in the mature puddles of cement

493

you will see the prone students. They turned the entire stock of the barracks on us, brother, soul mate of mine: thanks to the eloquence of the President's foot and mouth. What I'm saying, in other words, is that students were injured tonight in the Main Square. I'm talking about dead students! I'm talking about students who have disappeared, carrying in their hearts a miniature armistice.

ME: I think you're talking too much.

DOCTOR: And moving more than you should. Keep still so I can examine you. Anyway, I've yet to see a dead student.

ME: You're not going to solve anything like this, Palinuro, let us carry you . . .

PALINURO: There's no solution for anything any more. It can only get worse. Trying to set things right or believing that they can be, is playing right into the hands of those bastards.

DOCTOR: Here's the key of my apartment, nurse. It's number fourteen, on the fourth floor. Bring me some rolls of orthopaedic bandage . . .

ESTEFANIA: Is something broken, doctor?

(Palinuro starts to climb the last three steps to reach the second floor.)

(They all remain frozen beneath the blue light. In the foreground, an allegory takes shape. Enter Dottore, with a very long stethoscope, which gets tangled around his feet.)

DOTTORE: If it's a matter of bones . . . yes, of bones, I was saying, I'm no specialist in bones, but that doesn't matter because I'm a doctor . . . *Dixi.* In other words, I said. And I said this, *dixi,* because, besides being a doctor of medicine, I'm a doctor of Latin and I give classes in ortheopic gonorrhoea. So sorry: in syphilitic grammar! Sorry again! But you know what I mean . . . *pane lucrando,* in other words: to earn a crust; though it might be better to say *tequila lucrando* . . . and it's not just for the sake of it, but because from time to time I like to have a little tipple. Cheers, gentlemen, cheers! And why should I not have the occasional tipple? After all, *Ars longa vita brevis.* In other words: the task is long, life is short . . . cheers!

(Raises the bottle to his mouth and then bows to the audience. Drops his stethoscope. Bends to retrieve it, then drops his Vade Mecum. Bends to retrieve it and drops his spectacles. Bends to retrieve them and collapses flat on his face. Roll of drums. Starts to snore.)

VOICE OF DETECTIVE-DEATH: Anybody seen a dead student? Tell me: have any of you ever seen a dead student?

(He enters, carrying a huge magnifying glass with a white frame and pink lens. He carries a furled umbrella and check deer-stalker. Enter Tartaglia the postman on a scooter with a large black envelope.)

TARTAGLIA: A LELE. A leletter for DEDE. For Death!

DETECTIVE-DEATH: Could you read it to me, please?

TARTAGLIA (opening the envelope): It SASA! It sasays: MM! MMY! My dear DEDE! Dedeath. SOSO! Sorry that I STST! that I ststood you up. But the BLBL! the blblows didn't FIFI! didn't fifinish me off THTH! this time. And so, to SHSH! to shshow the BABA! the babastards that my COCO! my cocomrades and I are STST! ststill alive and K . . .

(Enter Scaramouch, running and kicking up his heels.)

SCARAMOUCH: Alive and kicking!

(Enter Colombine.)

COLOMBINE: Alive and K-K . . . and cooking! *(Raises her skirt and shows Scaramouch her dove feather knickers.)* Bet you can't catch me, Scaramouch! . . . Cuc-koo . . . Cuc-koo . . . *(sung)* Cuckooruckookoóoóo . . . *(Scaramouch chases her.)*

TARTAGLIA: With so many interruptions I CACA. I cacan't read!

DETECTIVE-DEATH *(beating Tartaglia with the umbrella)*: Enough, enough! I can't stand you a second longer, Tartaglia, I'm going to take you to the devil!

TARTAGLIA *(twisting out of the way of the blows)*: MEME! MEME! Mercy! PLPL! PLPL! Please!

(Exit Tartaglia with Detective-Death after him, while Scaramouch continues to chase Colombine.)

COLOMBINE: Tell them, Scaramouch, tell them what we're going to do!

SCARAMOUCH *(stopping short as he thinks it over)*: Eh? What we're going to do? Ah, yes, of course! What we students are going to do, to show these mother-fuckers that we're still alive, is to organize a general strike in every faculty! We'll take over the University! We'll change the names of the auditoriums and the laboratories!

COLOMBINE *(dancing)*: And we'll organize parties. Won't we, Scaramouch? And fireworks on the University esplanade! And another fancy dress competition! And a fair, Scaramouch!

SCARAMOUCH: We'll call them 'Ché Guevara Auditorium' and 'Camilo Torres Auditorium'! 'Camilo Cienfuegos Laboratory'! We'll create brigades to work in the cities and the countryside . . .! Colombine, give us a kiss! *(Exeunt. The stage darkens.)*

(We return to reality: Palinuro has reached the second floor.)

SECOND FLOOR

(Palinuro is sprawled on the stairs, about to start the climb to the third floor. Estefania is crying. The doctor is comforting her. I am trying to help Palinuro, but he refuses to let me. The stage is virtually unchanged but for a few details: the lampshade and colour of the walls might be different. Or they might not. The apartments are numbered from five to eight.)

DOCTOR: The fact is that it's very dangerous to tangle with the authorities. What you young people should do is study. Of course, you also have to study social inequalities and injustices. But, when all's said and done, you should forget demonstrations and strikes. Real revolutions take place in the classrooms! Academic autonomy is the pride of our university . . . hence its motto: 'Through my race, the spirit will speak.' Don't cry, nurse, everything will be all right.

ESTEFANIA: Does Palinuro have any broken bones?

DOCTOR: I don't have X-ray eyes, miss. There appears to be no fracture in the legs. Now, bring me what I asked for.

ESTEFANIA: Yes, doctor *(exit)*.

ME: But what happened, Palinuro?

PALINURO *(drags himself along the landing and up the first two steps)*: I don't know. I was minding my own business, eating candy floss and watching the students from every faculty filing past with their banners . . . there were thousands upon thousands of young people singing, marching through the aurora borealises and suddenly I was among them shouting: Death to bad government! Death to the rich holed up in excrement and to the police feeling their way through the world!

MALE VOICE *(in the distance)*: I'm coming, I'm coming . . . I'm just putting on my trousers!

(Steps are heard mounting the stairs.)

DOCTOR: Mmmm . . . blood from the nose. I hope it's just an epistaxis.

(Palinuro manages another two steps.)

ME: If we carry on talking so much, we're going to wake everybody up.

DOCTOR: Your friend's right. And they could tip off the authorities: these days you can't trust anybody.

(From the stairwell emerges the concierge in her flowered cotton dressing-gown.)

CONCIERGE: Well, you've woken me up anyway, that's for sure! One day they bring women. Another day then don't pay me the rent. Another day, or rather, another night, they come home drunk and wake the whole building.

PALINURO: Nobody's awake in this whole bloody country *(drags himself up another step).* Those who aren't fucking, lost in a flurry of iliacs and legs, are dreaming of Zátopek and the United Nations' flags . . .

CONCIERGE: Ah yes, the flags, so pretty! My favourite is the Turkish one, with its star and half moon. But you young men haven't answered my question.

ME: I think, Palinuro, that I'm getting fed up with all this carrying on . . .

CONCIERGE: Just look how drunk he is! Aren't you ashamed of yourself?

(The postman appears on the stairs from the first floor.)

POSTMAN: Here's your coffee, young man. Do you take sugar?

ME: Palinuro isn't drunk, sir. He was knocked down and beaten up tonight, in the Zócalo, after the demonstration.

DOCTOR: He might even have a bayonet point fracture.

CONCIERGE: What? You mean they stuck a bayonet in him?

ME: I tell you that he was knocked down and beaten up. About three thousand students stayed behind in the Zócalo when the demonstration ended and suddenly the tanks came out of the National Palace and charged them all . . .

POSTMAN: I'll be off then *(disappears down the stairs).*

CONCIERGE *(sitting down on a step)*: It's bad to drink so much. My dear departed Ambrosio used to see pink tanks too when he came home staggering drunk. Next day, I used to give him a hearty breakfast. He worked at the slaughterhouse so we always had good meat in the house: he taught me how to cut up a whole animal *(peers at Palinuro).* Good lord, but he's bleeding! What happened to you, Palinuro?

(The door of apartment six opens and the bureaucrat appears in his nightcap and terry-cloth bathrobe.)

BUREAUCRAT: What is going on in this house? What's more, I might say: what's going on in this street, in this district, in this city, in this country, that people can't sleep in peace? And, above all: what is going on right here? Are you drunk?

(Palinuro drags himself upwards, managing another three steps.)

ME: Palinuro was flung over three metres by a tank. Then, when he was on the ground, he was kicked and beaten with rifle butts!

(On the stairs up to the third floor, those Palinuro is trying to climb, appears Estefania. She drops the bandages which unwind as they roll down the stairs.)

ESTEFANIA: Oh, I'm sorry, doctor, I'll pick them up . . .

(Palinuro manages another step.)

BUREAUCRAT: What? What did you say? Who? Pick these things up, they're getting tangled round my feet!

ME: The police.

MALE VOICE *(in the distance)*: I'm coming, I'm coming, I'm just putting on my shirt . . .

BUREAUCRAT: I might have known you were delinquents.

DOCTOR: Let me see, young man, stick out your tongue . . .

PALINURO: No, no, it wasn't the police this time, it was the army.

BUREAUCRAT: The army? The army? Ah, so you're students, don't deny it!

DOCTOR: Come with me to my apartment, nurse: these aren't the bandages I need *(as they disappear up the stairs)*. Do you know how to make a tourniquet? Do you know how to make a Thomas knee-splint?

CONCIERGE *(nostalgically)*: I always used to go and see the Independence Day military parade with my dear departed Ambrosio. As I was saying, he was a slaughterer and he loved all weapons: conventional weapons, unconventional weapons, all kinds!

THE BUREAUCRAT: And quite right too, madam! I too always go and see our glorious army . . . the Mexican army! And I have a collection of plastic soldiers and I paint on the uniforms myself. Well done, let me congratulate you!

(In the foreground, a nostalgia takes shape: General-Death enters, wearing a huge red Mexican sombrero and followed by Four Colonels: a white colonel, a green colonel, a blue colonel and a yellow colonel, who are Pantalone, the Captain, Tartaglia and the Dottore. They goose-step in single file around the stage. To one side, Pierrot with his guitar, lit by a beam of amber-coloured light. Paper streamers and confetti fall.)

PIERROT: And the army was, indeed, parading through the streets. It was 16 September, Independence Day! Paper streamers were wound around the rifles and the cannons fired volleys of confetti. The multitude applauded and children ate sandwiches and peanuts . . . and candy apples!

(Exeunt General-Death and Four Colonels. Enter Scaramouch and Colombine. Scaramouch had changed his tactics: he has passed the tail of his costume between his legs and holds it in his hands, so it looks like a huge black cock. He hops backwards, while Colombine hops forwards, trying to catch it.)

SCARAMOUCH: Look, look, Colombine!

COLOMBINE: Oh, was there ever anything so beautiful?

PIERROT: Ah, I remember the bayonets which, like a cascade of swordfish, plunged into the blue of the sky, there, way up high . . .!

SCARAMOUCH *(waving his tail)*: Give us a kiss, Colombine, and it's yours, all yours!

(Colombine, with a last hop, catches Scaramouch's tail. He clasps her in his arms and they fall to the ground.)

PIERROT: There, way up high, where the aeroplanes play hide and seek among the clouds of spun sugar . . .

(Several silver aeroplanes hanging from strings descend from the flies and circle the stage, Colombine and Scaramouch kiss and caress each other.)

PIERROT: And meanwhile, everywhere, on the television antennae, on the black ash trees and on the heroes' shoulders . . .

(Enter Pantalone and the Dottore dressed up as horseless heroes, in tail coats and silver ties. Behind them, Tartaglia and the Captain, dressed up as a piebald horse and, mounted on them, Equestrian-Death in a brocade uniform with epaulettes of gold noodles and a tri-colour belt. All carry paper doves on their shoulders and their heads are covered in droppings of green plasticine.)

PIERROT: Meanwhile, we were saying, on the television antennae, on the black ash trees and on the heroes' shoulders, perched the doves of peace with a sprig of coriander in their beaks . . . It was the 16th September! It was Independence Day! It was the flag, it was the National Anthem!

(Exeunt Equestrian-Death and the horseless heroes, marching to the strains of the National Anthem.)

COLOMBINE *(wriggling out of Scaramouch's arms)*: It's the anthem, Scaramouch, the anthem, stand up!

(The three stand erect: Colombine, Scaramouch and Scaramouch's cock-tail.)

COLOMBINE: Oh, Scaramouch, you do embarrass me!

(Colombine takes from her dove feather purse two red circular stickers and sticks them on her cheeks.)

(We return to Palinuro on the stairs.)

BUREAUCRAT: The young people of today, on the other hand, grow their hair and spend their time listening to pop music full volume on the radio and they have no respect for anything any more. They don't respect investitures, they don't respect the language, the army, their country. They don't respect the Zócalo Square! They told me that, this very night, madam, they started ringing the bells of the cathedral – I heard it myself – and what's more . . .

CONCIERGE: What do you say to some fried eggs in chilli sauce?

(Palinuro manages steps number twenty-seven and twenty-eight.)

BUREAUCRAT: What are you talking about? What do scrambled eggs have to do with the present crisis?

CONCIERGE: I didn't say scrambled, I said fried.

ME: What exactly happened in the Zócalo, Palinuro?

PALINURO: My eyes are streaming, my feet clothed in clay! We deconsecrated the Zócalo, man, we deconsecrated it three times! We asked permission to light up the cathedral and we did it, they gave us permission to ring the bells of the main church and we sounded them, man, with all our hearts! It was two of our friends, two fellow students from the School of Medicine who climbed into the bell tower to call the people . . . to urge them to rise up and put an end to the corruption of the political youth leaders, to bribes, to thievery by civil servants . . .!

ME: And what did the people do, Palinuro?

PALINURO *(dragging himself up another step)*: The people, I tell you, are asleep. That's why we turned on the lights and sounded the bells! 'The people must unite, the people must unite,' we screamed at the tops of our voices . . .

(The postman appears on the stairs from the first floor.)

POSTMAN: I've brought you some biscuits, young man. I think you've gone too far. Excuse me but, being a postman, I always think in terms of distances.

PALINURO: Then, man, then the whole Square was lit up, and the whole of Mexico was lit up! And the clappers of the bells exploded into pealing sound and we almost forgot that we were there, in the Zócalo, because it seemed like a party and I imagine that all those who weren't there, at those moments, when the bells resounded throughout the Square, throughout Mexico, all who were not with us right there beneath the banners which read 'Always on to victory' and surrounded by the angry shouting, like you, brother, who weren't there, and Estefania, who wasn't there either, all of you must have felt a little old and your heart must have shrunk a square centimetre at least. But, of course . . . time passed, we sang songs, and ate sandwiches and tangerines, we sang 'La Adelita', the speeches came to an end, the angels of the cathedral fell asleep with their heads under their wings, the people went home and I and three thousand other students remained on permanent guard in the Square . . . but suddenly the doors of the National Palace on which we had painted the word 'Assassin!' opened and opinions were divided: some doors said 'Assa' and other 'ssin' . . . and the tanks came out and disembarked on our beach!

BUREAUCRAT: There! You see? They desecrated the cathedral. Over 95% of our people are Catholic. Nevertheless, I am an atheist. I am of liberal ancestry. My putative great-grandfather, you might say, was don Benito Juárez, the patriot. But that's a long way from failing to respect a church: as far as from the earth to the sky! After all, my mother was a Catholic and I loved her very much. Now, I'm going to call . . .

(At that moment, the light goes.)

CONCIERGE'S VOICE: Oh, the light!

THE BUREAUCRAT'S VOICE: Must be a fuse gone.

THE CONCIERGE'S VOICE: Just what I was thinking – cursed

500

confusion. Anyway I'd best go down and get some candles ... I can't hear properly when I can't see.

POSTMAN'S VOICE: This reminds me of one time during the war ...

(Steps are heard descending the stairs.)

FEMALE VOICE OF THE NEIGHBOUR FROM NUMBER FIFTEEN *(in the distance)*: Why are you so late, children? Where have you been? Why didn't you telephone me? Have you had supper? *(A pause.)* Is that you, Pepe? Is that you children? *(drawing closer)*: What happened? Was there a fight?

POSTMAN'S VOICE: I was saying that this reminds me of the blackouts during the war. I used to march in the National Stadium every Sunday, as a volunteer, when Mexico declared war on the Axis powers. So brave of Mexico, to face up to the Germans and the Japanese! But after they bombed our tanker *El Potrero del Llano*, what else could we do? And we trained every Sunday, in the stadium, with wooden rifles ...

PALINURO'S VOICE: The tanks that flattened us, ladies and gentlemen, were not wooden ...

VOICE OF THE NEIGHBOUR OF NUMBER FIFTEEN: Tanks? Good lord! Why don't you call the police?

BUREAUCRAT'S VOICE: That is exactly what I am going to do right now: call the police.

MALE VOICE *(in the distance)*: I'm coming, I'm coming, I'm just putting on ...

(Front stage, a fantasy materializes: enter Pantalone with a lighted candle, by the glow of which we see Captain Mean sitting on a bench, wearing his green devil mask. He's asleep and snoring. Beside him he has a huge king-of-clubs cudgel.)

CAPTAIN MEAN *(still sleeping)*: Did someone call? I'm coming, I'm coming.

PANTALONE *(furious)*: Yes, yes, I know: you're just putting on your whiskers and your name, you're just putting on your stomach, you're just putting on your grandmother! *(To the audience)*: This is our police force, ladies and gentlemen ...

(Harlequin descends from the flies on a rope, got up as a fat piñata wearing his suit of Chinese paper rhombuses. Enter Colombine with Scaramouch behind her, each carrying a lighted candle. Scaramouch carries his in both hands at the level of his groin, so it looks as though his penis is on fire, pointing at Colombine's behind. They sing hymns.)

PANTALONE: This is our police, ladies and gentlemen ... always asleep! *(confidentially)* And ... shall I tell you a secret? Well, our police ... besides never being on watch ... so they say ... although, of

501

course, I'm not certain, but there are rumours, I have been told, perhaps it's just slander or lies, one never knows . . . *(more confidentially still)* don't tell anybody, it's likely, though not impossible, perhaps, supposedly, who can say, I may be wrong, but it is said . . . they do say . . . *(as confidentially as possible)* that he has killed some students!

CAPTAIN MEAN *(without opening his eyes)*: Students? Students? Where are the students?

(Still asleep, he gets up, grabs the cudgel and starts hitting out to right and left. Everybody runs away shouting. Captain Mean finds the piñata *and starts beating it. The Dottore appears with a candle.)*

DOTTORE: Careful, careful, it could be a bomb!

HARLEQUIN: Oh, oh, oh! the beating they gave us sure wasn't with foam rubber!

(Finally, Harlequin cracks open and all the goodies come tumbling out: Molotov cocktails, slings, stones, sticks, rockets, more stones and more sticks. The rope snaps and Harlequin falls to the floor.)

DOTTORE: You see? I told you!

(Exit Dottore. The stage goes dark while Captain Mean, panting, picks up the booty. Enter Colombine, with her dove's tail alight. Behind her, Scaramouch wearing a fireman's helmet and a long hose which he has placed between his legs.)

COLOMBINE: Oh, oh! My tail's so hot, help, I'm burning!

SCARAMOUCH: Come here, Colombine, come here: I have the extinguisher to quench the fire that consumes you, come here! *(Exeunt. The stage goes dark.)*

(We return to reality which is also in darkness. Though nobody notices, Palinuro has only one step left to go to reach the third floor.)

VOICE OF THE NEIGHBOUR FROM NUMBER FIFTEEN: Why don't you call the doctor in number fourteen? I have two sons who are students from Monday to Friday. Yesterday they got back early and I gave them their tea. But today they haven't come home. Perhaps, oh! they never will . . . I'm learning the way from here to the Ruben Leñero Hospital blind-folded. And then I'll learn the way into the hospital . . . Oh, help me, help me! I'm going to forbid my sons to be students! I want them alive, oh! oh!

BUREAUCRAT'S VOICE: Don't get hysterical, madam, allow me to comfort you!

VOICE OF THE NEIGHBOUR FROM NUMBER FIFTEEN: Yes please, thank you . . . where are you? Ah, here you are. Yes, yes, hold me close, like that, comfort me. Yes, yes, lower, lower, oh yes, . . . more to the right . . . there, yes . . . oh yes . . . faster!

(Meanwhile, without anybody noticing, Palinuro reaches the third

floor. Suddenly, the light comes back on, catching the bureaucrat and the neighbour from number fifteen in their comforting antics. The neighbour points downstairs to distract attention.)

THE NEIGHBOUR FROM NUMBER FIFTEEN: They ran away, they ran away . . . they went that way!

BUREAUCRAT: Who ran away?

THE NEIGHBOUR FROM NUMBER FIFTEEN: They ran away after beating up these young men! I don't know why my sons are students: one of them studies logarithms and will one day build bridges. The other is studying to be a vet and will one day build cows . . . what am I saying? Oh . . . the injured young man has disappeared!

(I run up the stairs, alarmed.)

ME: Palinuro, Palinuro! Where are you?

ESTEFANIA'S VOICE *(from the third floor)*: He's here, he's reached the next floor . . .

DOCTOR'S VOICE *(also from the floor above)*: Don't worry, we'll patch him up right now . . .

(On the stairs leading up from the first floor appears the concierge, with some candles in her hands.)

CONCIERGE: It was so dark that I waited for the lights to be fixed to look for the candles . . .

BUREAUCRAT: Well, if the police won't come to me, I'll go to the police.

CONCIERGE: You're not thinking of going out like that, in your dressing gown, are you Dr Martínez?

BUREAUCRAT: No, I'm going to telephone.

NEIGHBOUR FROM NUMBER FIFTEEN *(wringing her hands)*: Please, use my telephone! I live on the fourth floor, really, use my telephone . . . *(as they climb the stairs)* my telephone is very easy to use, you know, you can put in as many fingers as you like at the same time to dial more quickly, come with me!

(Concierge climbs the stairs behind them.)

CONCIERGE: Then, mince and potatoes . . .

GREAT STUDENT FAIR

(Interlude to collect funds for the student movement. Colombine appears, wearing a tutu of transparent gauze and silver stars, sitting on a bench beneath a beam of pink light, pulling the petals from a huge paper daisy.)

COLOMBINE: We WILL win, we WON'T win, we WILL win,

503

we WON'T win, we WILL win . . . *(only one petal is left)* Oh, oh, we WON'T win!

(She buries her face in her hands and starts to cry. Between her fingers trickle tears of blue glass which fall to the ground and shatter. Enter Pantalone, ill-disguised as Scaramouch, with a green tail.)

PANTALONE: Why is the little girl crying?

COLOMBINE: Oh, because we're going to lose! Wouldn't you like to contribute to the student movement? However much you like . . . *(holds out her hand to him).*

(The Dottore appears and examines Pantalone's tail while the latter caresses Colombine.)

DOTTORE: Would you not agree that *non sunt communes caudae hominibus*, in other words: that tails are not common in men? . . . and, besides, this tail is . . . green! *(Exit.)*

PANTALONE: There, there, don't cry, little girl! Come with me to my room and I will put some coins in that money box that you have between your legs . . . *(He raises Colombine's skirt and reaches underneath.)*

COLOMBINE: Dirty old man! *(She hits him with her purse decorated with feathers which come loose and flutter around the stage. The lights go out. A moment later, a beam of light shines on Saleslady-Death pulling her cart.)*

SALESLADY-DEATH: It's party time, ladies and gentlemen! Contribute to the students! Buy my wares, sell me yours! I'll sell you lives, I'll buy your souls! Chewing-gum? Chocolates? Crisps?! I sell sugar skulls, I sell dead man's bread! Who wants a machine for giving electric shocks? Cold drinks, ladies and gentlemen, of tamarind and pineapple, of blood and lemon! I sell almond testicles, sugared clavicles, nutcrackers . . . cigarettes . . . beer? I sell ribs of nougat! I sell everything, I buy everything! I sell happiness sweets! Nipples of almond paste! Vanilla ice-creams? Marzipan tibiae! Who wants an electric shock in the back of the neck? Who wants their Adam's apple crushed? I sell peppermint dentures, chocolate elbows, arsenic and melon ice lollies! Anyone have any grenades to sell? Explosive watermelons? Tear gas bananas! I sell toffee clubs, crystallized sugar bayonets! Contribute, ladies and gentlemen, linotypists and housewives, washerwomen and cardiologists, chauffeurs and secretaries, contribute to the student movement! Doughnuts? Mint machine guns? Fritters? I rent wishbones! *(Exit.)*

(Enter Pierrot carrying fireworks. Behind him enter Colombine, Scaramouch, Harlequin, also carrying rockets, pinwheels and other pyrotechnical devices. Between dances, they will set up their stalls, on wheels, on the stage, in preparation for the Great Student Fair.)

PIERROT: Paris was a moveable feast!

COLOMBINE: Mexico will be another feast!

SCARAMOUCH: Long live the National Strike Council!

HARLEQUIN: I am a painter so I will design the banners!

COLOMBINE: Please, make me one with two doves which says: 'Freedom for Political Prisoners'! . . . Another demanding the repeal of Article 145, another demanding abolition of the Riot Squad, another . . .

PIERROT: You and I, Scaramouch, being poets, will take the job of composing the songs, battle cries, slogans . . . what do you think of 'You're-a-disgrace-daren't-show-your-face-you're-a-disgrace-daren't-show-your-face'.

COLOMBINE: Brilliant! Brilliant!

PIERROT: And we'll translate all the graffiti on the Speaking Walls of Nanterre: . . . 'Forbidding forbidden'. 'The more I make Revolution, the more I make Love . . . the more I make Love, the more I make Revolution!'

COLOMBINE *(from her kisses stall)*: I sell kisses, peso a kiss in support of the students!

SCARAMOUCH *(from his intellectual's stall)*: This is the first time that a movement of this kind makes demands of a democratic nature! Who will buy this slogan: 'Rape your Alma Mater'?

PIERROT *(from his judge's stall)*: Who wants to marry? Who wants to go to prison?

HARLEQUIN *(cartwheeling and making spectacular leaps from stall to stall)*: How much for an acrobatic feat? How much for a jump of death? For two pesos, ladies and gentlemen, I move my belly button, for three, I stretch my neck!

COLOMBINE: Peso a kiss, peso a kiss!

PIERROT: Who wants to get married? Who wants to pay a fine? Who wants to go to prison or be tortured?

HARLEQUIN: For two pesos I'll wiggle my ears! For another four I'll cross my eyes!

COLOMBINE: Peso a kiss, peso a kiss!

SCARAMOUCH: Contribute, ladies and gentlemen, to the students . . . follow my example! *(He gets down from his intellectual's stall and goes over to Colombine.)* Give us a kiss, Colombine! *(Colombine takes from her feather purse a sticker in the shape of a pair of red lips and slaps them on to Scaramouch's cheek.)*

COLOMBINE: You owe me a peso!

SCARAMOUCH: I don't have any money on me!

PIERROT *(jumps down from his judge's stall and drags Scaramouch to a cage)*: To prison, to prison, for being a cheat!

COLOMBINE: Contribute to the students, ladies and gentlemen, pater and mater familias!

PIERROT: Anybody else want to go to prison?

HARLEQUIN: Contribute, clerks and executives!

PIERROT: Anybody else want to lose their freedom?

COLOMBINE: Contribute your money, your outspoken opinions, teachers and drivers!

PIERROT: Anybody else want to be tortured?

COLOMBINE: Peso a kiss, peso a kiss!

(The wind starts to blow. Wind and dust. Everything goes grey and it starts to get dark. Enter Pantalone and Captain Mean, both armed with clubs.)

CAPTAIN MEAN: I'll give them kisses, the morons!

PANTALONE: I'll give them prison, the mother-fuckers!

CAPTAIN MEAN: I'll move their belly buttons . . . with my club, the bastards!

PANTALONE: I'll . . .

(They start hitting out with their clubs. Sparks fly.)

VOICES FROM THE AUDIENCE: We've seen this already! We've seen this already! It's always the same!

(Suddenly, a tremor begins.)

VOICES FROM THE PUBLIC *(very frightened)*: It's an earthquake! It's an earthquake!

(Pantalone and the Captain kneel down with their arms outstretched. Colombine, Scaramouch and Harlequin run off stage. Tellurian noises, creaking and groaning are heard.)

PANTALONE: Hail Mary, mother of God!

THE CAPTAIN: Conceived without sin!

(The audience start to push and shove their way out. Enter Pierrot disguised as a building.)

PIERROT: An earthquake, an earthquake, hear how the country is shaken! *(His disguise starts to crack.)*

Pantalone and the Captain rise and run out. Enter Colombine dressed as the Constitution, Harlequin dressed as the Mexican Revolution, Scaramouch as the Institutional Revolutionary Party.)

COLOMBINE: Hear how the Constitution crumbles!

SCARAMOUCH: Hear how the Institutional Revolutionary Party cracks!

HARLEQUIN: Hear how the Mexican Revolution collapses!

PIERROT: Yes, listen, listen, so that afterwards you may not say that you did not hear!

(Their disguises fall to the ground with great noise. Exeunt. The earthquake stops. Enter Pantalone, the Dottore and the Captain disguised as road sweepers, each carrying a broom. The audience begins to return to their seats. Enter next Witch-Death astride a broom,

506

flapping around the stage.)

ALL: Oh, what a mess, oh what a mess!

WITCH-DEATH: Start sweeping, start sweeping I said!

FIRST SWEEPER: We're always the suckers!

SECOND: We're always the ones that have to sweep up the mess!

THIRD: It's always us who have to clean up the mess after earthquakes, the bits of paper and confetti when presidents, emperors and prime ministers come to town!

FIRST AND SECOND: We're always the ones who have to clean up the fliers and the blood!

SECOND AND THIRD: Sweep up the dust! Sweep up the shit!

THIRD AND FIRST: Clear away the incorrigible remains of the students, the leftovers of their honour, their pullovers, their sports emblems!

ALL: Oh what a mess, oh what a mess!

WITCH-DEATH: Start sweeping, start sweeping I said, idle layabouts!

(A spider's web descends from the flies and, hanging from it, Tartaglia with several hands and feet.)

TARTAGLIA: A me-me-MESS! And urgent message from TH'G TH'G from the government for the cu-cu- CUNT! For the country's road sw-sw-WEEP! Sweepers!

(He throws hundreds of little bits of paper in their faces with his several hands.)

ALL: Oh, what a mess, oh what a mess!

(Exeunt, sweeping up the bits of paper followed by Witch-Death, harrying them. Enter Colombine with a pair of castanets.)

COLOMBINE: The authorities are always thinking of the poorest and most under-privileged members of our society! The authorities didn't forget the road-sweepers and they sent them a message saying: 'Culture is the magnificent fruit of liberty'! *(starts to play the castanets).*

MUTTERING AMONG THE AUDIENCE: Ah, ooh! It was the President who said that!

(Enter Scaramouch with a large tambourine.)

SCARAMOUCH: The authorities know that they are responsible for combating nihilistic theories which threaten our Mexican identity! The speech goes on: 'The authorities have acted in response to a deliberately organized campaign of agitation and subversion . . .' *(starts to play his tambourine).*

VOICES AMONG THE AUDIENCE: Ooh, ah! It was the Mayor of Mexico City who said that!

(Enter Pierrot with maracas.)

PIERROT: The authorities are open to dialogue with the students, but dialogue without exhibitionism. The statement specifies: 'Mexico is a country in which freedom exists. We will not impose martial law'! *(starts to play the maracas).*

VOICES AMONG THE AUDIENCE: Ah, ooh! It was the Minister of Defence who said that!

(Enter Harlequin with a violin.)

HARLEQUIN: It is Mexico's honour that is at stake, as was said by . . .

(President-Death erupts on the stage with a tricolour sash across its chest, dragging an extremely long velvet cloak.)

PRESIDENT-DEATH: What does it matter who said it? Of them all, I make one man: the President! I, I said it all, I the President!

(Enter Pantalone, the Dottore and Captain Mean who fall over themselves bowing.)

ALL THREE: Yes, Mr President. Yes, Mr President. Yes, Mr President.

PRESIDENT-DEATH: I, and I alone, am and will be solely responsible for the measures adopted by the authorities to save the honour and peace of Mexico! I alone will be responsible historically, politically, sociologically, anthropologically, economically . . .

PANTALONE AND DOTTORE: Bureaucratically, healthologically, philatelically . . .

CAPTAIN: Policologically, lachrymologically, stylographically . . .

PIERROT AND COLOMBINE: Hysterically, brutologically, torturologically . . .

HARLEQUIN AND SCARAMOUCH: Dentologically, bastardologically, and mother-fuckerologically!

PRESIDENT-DEATH: Yes, siree: I and I alone!

(Scaramouch climbs on to Harlequin's shoulders and Pierrot on to Scaramouch's shoulders. The others help President-Death to climb on to Pierrot's shoulders. Exeunt Pantalone, Captain Mean and the Dottore. Totem-Death wraps itself in its long cloak which covers the three underneath.)

TOTEM-DEATH: What time is it?

COLOMBINE *(trembling)*: Oh, didn't you hear that Mr President wants to know what time it is?

PIERROT *(poking his head out)*: Whatever time you wish, Mr President! *(his head disappears back beneath the cloak).*

ITS-ROYAL-HIGHNESS-DEATH: What day is it?

COLOMBINE: Oh, oh, Mr President wants to know what day it is . . .

SCARAMOUCH *(poking his head out)*: Whatever day you like, Mr President! *(withdraws his head).*

ITS-SERENITY-DEATH: Of what month?

COLOMBINE: Oh, oh, Mr President wants to know of what month . . .

HARLEQUIN *(poking his head out)*: Whatever month you want it to be, Mr President! *(withdraws his head)*.

ITS-SERENE-HIGHNESS-MR-PRESIDENT-DEATH: I order, because it so pleases, gratifies and suits me, that it be eight o'clock at night of Tuesday 30th July . . .

(Each hanging from a parachute of coloured stripes, Dottore, the Captain, Pantalone and Tartaglia descend from the flies. Between them they carry an extremely long bazooka. His Highness-Death throws back his cloak to draw out a sword and, surprise, surprise, Scaramouch, Pierrot and Harlequin are no longer beneath it.)

DEATH-ON-STILTS: Prepare!

(Harlequin, Pierrot and Scaramouch enter and run around the stage in terror, together with Colombine.)

HARLEQUIN: That was at eight o'clock at night!

DEATH-ON-STILTS: Take aim!

SCARAMOUCH: That was at eight o'clock at night on Tuesday 30th!

DEATH-ON-STILTS: Fire!

(From the bazooka issues a bullet the size and shape of an orange, lit up inside, which slowly travels through the air in a straight line.)

COLOMBINE AND PIERROT: That was at eight o'clock at night on Tuesday 30th July!

HARLEQUIN AND SCARAMOUCH *(with butterfly nets)*: Stop that bullet, stop that bullet!

(The stage goes dark. We see only the bullet, which inexorably continues on its course.)

THIRD FLOOR

(Palinuro, lying face down on the landing, drags himself towards the stairs which will take him up to the fourth floor. The concierge and I are sitting somewhere on the stairs. The doctor, crouching down next to Palinuro, holds a pink skull in his hands. Estefania, hands full of bandages, scissors and jars, is beside him. The apartments are numbered nine to twelve.)

DOCTOR: I brought this skull to show you where the fracture might be situated . . .

CONCIERGE: How awful! When we exhumed my dear departed Ambrosio, seven years after his death, he still had a lock of hair! How he would have suffered to see himself like that, nothing but bones, when he

509

was a specialist in animal flesh . . .

PALINURO: Tomorrow, anyway, the sun will rise to shine on other miseries. Children will get up early and they will not know what happened this night, they will never know . . . *(to me)* come here, give me a hand . . . just one, I'm not feeling too good . . .

(The postman appears, with a plate.)

POSTMAN: Come on, young man, eat something. I've brought you a bit of papaya. I think it'll do you good . . . *(exit)*.

PALINURO *(to the doctor)*: And you, please, take that skull away. I'm not interested in anybody's bones but my own . . .

CONCIERGE: A stew, perhaps . . . my dear departed Ambrosio used to come home with his hands covered in blood, but always with a nice fresh leg or sirloin . . . I think I had better see first what I have in the fridge *(exit)*.

ESTEFANIA: The doctor, Palinuro, is an orthopaedic specialist.

DOCTOR: Yes, of course. Well, that is . . . not exactly, although I do know quite a lot. The truth is that my speciality – and I'm not ashamed to admit it, believe me – is what you might call secret diseases. Miss, would you please take this skull to my apartment?

(Estefania exits. Palinuro drags himself up the first step of the flight leading to the fourth floor.)

PALINURO: My disease is also secret, doctor: all the students have been beaten up and killed in secret, taken in secret to the Military Camp Number One, stripped naked in secret, incinerated in secret!

DOCTOR: But I'm proud of my profession. You yourself said it: it was a couple of medical students who rang the cathedral bells. And if you go to the Juárez Hospital, or to the Isidro Espinoza de los Reyes Maternity Hospital, the interns will tell you how they are looking after the injured students. Just like in Paris, a few months ago. The newspapers said that the heroes of the May Revolution, of the Odeón and the Latin Quarter, of Gay Lussac Street, were medical students. And, you will remember, a few months ago, the National Health Service doctors held a white demonstration in the Zócalo . . . noble profession, Medicine!

(Enter the postman again.)

POSTMAN: Excuse me. I forgot the ice. Put it on your testicles.

DOCTOR: On his testicles? You mean on his forehead . . . we have to stop that nose bleed whatever happens.

POSTMAN *(looking at the stairs)*: Oh, these are drops of blood on the stairs! *(looks up at the ceiling)*.

PALINURO: What do you expect to see? A stalactite bleeding to death?

POSTMAN: No, no, so sorry . . . I didn't mean that. I hope you feel better soon, young man, see you later *(exit)*.

510

(Palinuro climbs another two steps.)

ME: Come on, Palinuro, it's time we helped you, don't you think?

(On the stairs from the fourth floor appear the bureaucrat and the neighbour from number fifteen.)

BUREAUCRAT: I don't understand! One minute it's engaged and the next nobody answers! Either way, I couldn't get in touch with the police . . .

PALINURO: The police, my esteemed friend, are a metaphor until they put on riot helmets and go out to beat up students . . .

(The door of apartment ten opens and a very fat old man comes out in a police-blue woolly dressing gown.)

POLICEMAN: OK, OK, here I am . . . *(yawns)*. Auugghh! . . . I'm so sleepy! What's going on here then?

BUREAUCRAT: You're not a policeman . . . you're not in uniform! And, what's more, you have no sense of emergency: I've been calling you for the last hour and you just say: I'm coming, I'm coming . . .

(The policeman sits down on the stairs and closes his eyes.)

BUREAUCRAT: Are you listening to me? Are you listening?

POLICEMAN: I'm coming, I'm coming . . . *(opening one eye)* I'm a retired policeman. I devote my time to chess and my grandchildren. I've had my share of hardship in life *(closes his eye.)* Excuse me for not putting on my slippers, but my feet are swollen . . .

BUREAUCRAT: You have to arrest these young men . . .

THE NEIGHBOUR FROM NUMBER FIFTEEN: No, please, don't arrest them! My children are students . . . *(to the policeman)* and you, stop winking at me, it makes me nervous!

DOCTOR: What this young man needs is medical attention.

BUREAUCRAT: They're anarchist agitators!

PALINURO *(dragging himself up another step)*: The real agitators, as I'm sick of repeating, are Poverty, Ignorance and Hunger!

POLICEMAN *(opening one eye)*: That phrase was invented by a grandchild of mine who's studying at the Polytechnic. I have another grandson who studied to become a member of the riot squad. So unpleasant to have arguments between members of the same family, don't you agree? *(closes his eye and falls asleep)*.

NEIGHBOUR FROM NUMBER FIFTEEN: What does anarchist mean?

BUREAUCRAT: They are spreading panic! Don't you appreciate the freedom that exists in Mexico?

CONCIERGE *(appearing in the stairwell)*: Yes, yesterday all the petrol in the whole city was sold out.

PALINURO: Of course we know that freedom exists! Freedom to create government-controlled trade unions! Freedom to exploit the people!

Freedom to set up monopolies!

BUREAUCRAT: They say that there won't be any milk tomorrow!

CONCIERGE: Next it'll be bread. If my dear departed Ambrosio were alive, at least we wouldn't want for meat.

ME: What the hell? Don't you see that Palinuro is injured? He was thrown over three metres by a tank . . .!

BUREAUCRAT: You want to put an end to everything! Don't you realize? You're going to put an end to the Olympics and the prestige of Mexico!

POLICEMAN *(opening his eyes)*: Never! When I was young I was marksmanship champion of the Metropolitan Police *(falls asleep)*.

BUREAUCRAT: And, what's more, you talk so much about culture: for the first time in history, there will be a Cultural Olympics . . . Beethoven, Rubens . . .

NEIGHBOUR FROM NUMBER FIFTEEN: And just imagine if all those blonde Swedish athletes had to go back to their own country!

PALINURO *(dragging himself up two more steps)*: That's right, that's right! When you look at the Olympic flame, make sure you put on your Polaroid sunglasses to blot out the glint of bayonets!

(They remain frozen beneath the blue light. In the foreground a possibility takes shape: enter Tourist-Guide-Death dressed in pink and white, pulling an allegorical float carrying Pantalone, the Dottore and the Captain dressed up as tourists, with Kodak cameras, checked jackets, red wigs and false freckles. Throughout the scene they take photographs with flashes. In the background, the sound of car engines and horns. A kind of black frost falls, covering them all in soot.)

TOURIST-GUIDE-DEATH: O! O! O! O! O! MEXICO '68! Ladies and gentlemen, tourists and compatriots, travellers and Frenchmen, friends and gringos: you are in the heart of the 19th Olympic Games. Mexico, '68! On your right, the Latin American Tower, the tallest building in Mexico! . . .

(Enter Scaramouch, unrolling a length of pink toilet paper from the feet of Tourist-Guide-Death to the exit.)

TOURIST-GUIDE-DEATH: The pink trail you see on the ground leads to the University Stadium!

(Enter Colombine, Harlequin and Pierrot, who lay lengths of different coloured toilet paper on the floor.)

TOURIST-GUIDE-DEATH: On your right the Independence Column . . . the green trail leads you to the Sports Palace . . . in front of you, the District Penitentiary! Behind, the National Anthropological Museum! The mauve trail leads to the Xochimilco rowing canals . . .

(Enter Tartaglia on a wooden horse.)

512

TARTAGLIA: A T-T-TURD . . .

TOURIST-GUIDE-DEATH: Ah, a registered letter for me?

TARTAGLIA: No, a TURD! *(at her feet he places a roll of white toilet paper, all of it soiled and crumpled, which he unrolls as he leaves the stage).*

TOURIST-GUIDE-DEATH: Ah, yes, I was forgetting: the trail of shit, ladies and gentlemen, leads you to the National Palace and all the Departments and Ministries of State! . . . On your right, the Revolution Monument. On your left, the Bell Tower of St Thomas . . . above you, the helicopters . . .

(Enter Harlequin, Scaramouch, Pierrot and Colombine who hand Pantalone, the Dottore and the Captain the ends of some red streamers, which they unwind as they leave the stage at different points.)

TOURIST-GUIDE-DEATH: And the streamers of blood, ladies and gentlemen, will take you to the Morgue, the Rubén Leñero Hospital and the General Hospital, the Women's Hospital and the Communications Ministry Hospital, to the Police Stations and Military Camp Number One . . . On your right, the Chamber of Congress . . . on your left, San Ildefonso College . . . ahead of you, the Plaza de los Tres Culturas . . . behind, the army . . . below, the common grave. MEXICO '68, ladies and gentlemen, the blue trail will take you to the Olympic swimming pools . . . the silver trail . . . *(exit, pulling float. Explosion of camera flashes.)*

(Enter Scaramouch, Pierrot, Colombine and Harlequin carrying banners and chanting.)

ALL: We don't want Olympics, we want Revolution! We don't want Olympics, we want Revolution!

(Enter Pantalone and the Captain, dragging a huge television set which they leave on the stage and exeunt. The television screen lights up and Announcer-Death appears.)

ANNOUNCER-DEATH: Ladies and gentlemen, be sure to attend the tear gas grenade throwing event!

(Enter Tartaglia, dressed up as an Olympic athlete, who throws a large grenade at the demonstrators. The grenade explodes, producing yellow smoke. After this and other exploits, the audience is to be heard exclaiming: O! O! O! O! O!, each 'O' corresponding to an Olympic hoop. Scaramouch, Pierrot and Colombine run off the stage crying. Harlequin is overcome by a fit of coughing, his knees give way and he remains crouched on the floor.)

ANNOUNCER-DEATH: Ladies and gentlemen, don't miss the bayonet vaulting event!

(Enter the Dottore, dressed up as an Olympic athlete, with a rifle and fixed bayonet which he plunges into Harlequin's back as he vaults

513

over him. Harlequin collapses spread-eagled on the floor. Exit Dottore.)
ANNOUNCER-DEATH: Mesdames and ladies, don't miss the two metre flat student heat.
(Enter Captain Mean dressed up as an athlete, who runs over Harlequin's prone body and exits on the other side. Harlequin tries to stand. From the television screen emerges the hand of Announcer-Death, who deals him the death blow with an extremely long femur.)
ANNOUNCER-DEATH: Messieurs and gentlemen, don't fail to see the corpse lifting contest!
(Enter Pantalone, dressed up as a weightlifter. He approaches Harlequin's body, bends and raises him above his head.)
THE AUDIENCE: O! O! O! O! O! *(All goes dark, except the television screen.)*
ANNOUNCER-DEATH: And now, before continuing our programme, a short advertisement break . . .

(We return to reality, Palinuro on stair number six of the flight between the third and fourth floors.)
BUREAUCRAT: And anyway, it's all an exaggeration! What did you expect? That there wouldn't be any deaths after such provocation! After the students smashed store windows and sacked gun shops? You just go and see all the buses you seized, all the buses you burned. And, there again, did you know that there were a million deaths during the Mexican Revolution? And how many people died in the two world wars and in the Spanish Civil war, huh? And now you're surprised when they kill – how many students – . . .? Five? six? Even ten, that's nothing!
ME: But in Paris . . .
BUREAUCRAT: You said it: in Paris. But we're not in Paris, we're in Mexico. Here, things are different. If you like Paris better, go and live there.
PALINURO: Ten students, did you say? I think I heard that you work in the Statistics Department, is that right?
BUREAUCRAT: Yes. And, what's more, I pay my taxes . . . and my taxes go to pay for your education, which is practically free!
PALINURO *(crawling up another step)*: Well now, you just listen: before I tell you how the tanks sharpened their bitter hooves in the arena of the Constitution . . . did you say ten students? Before I tell you that the loudspeakers gave us a few minutes to leave the square . . . before I tell you . . .
BUREAUCRAT: But you're telling me now!
PALINURO: I said, before I tell you . . . did you say ten students? I tell you, I want you to tell me if you, who work in statistics, know that foreign investors take half a million dollars a day out of Mexico and that,

in our country, fifty per cent of national income is concentrated in the hands of two per cent of the population.

BUREAUCRAT: Why are you so intent on those ten students? Far more young people die every week when they are run over by cars! And what about all those who die of natural causes?

CONCIERGE: Did you get the tank's number plate?

PALINURO (climbing another step): These also died of natural causes. If you want to put an end to social injustice and corruption, if you set yourself up against tycoons and politicians, it's only natural that they'll send a tank after you, it's only natural that they'll beat you to a pulp, it's natural that they'll club you to death with rifle butts. But what I'm getting at is this: you, who work with numbers and statistics perhaps also know the area covered by all the red corpuscles of the body . . . do you know?

DOCTOR: I can tell you: over 2,500 square metres.

PALINURO: There you are, over 2,500 square metres. Well, Mr Bureaucrat: with the blood of ten students, just ten, you can paint the whole of the National Palace.

BUREAUCRAT: It would be difficult. Blood dries very quickly. And it would be absurd.

CONCIERGE: Don't worry, young man, tomorrow I'll clean the blood from the stairs. Really, it doesn't bother me . . . after so many years of washing shirts and trousers covered in blood!

DOCTOR: It might be a good idea to take a sample and find your blood group, in case you should need a transfusion.

POLICEMAN (opening one eye): Mine is compatible with any other policeman's.

NEIGHBOUR FROM NUMBER FIFTEEN: I'm going to bed too. Where could my children be at this time of night? Did you know that I can plan my dreams? It always works. I'm going to dream of my children. I'm going to dream that they come home early . . . (descending the stairs). Oh, oh, how my head aches! Does anybody have an aspirin they could give me?

PALINURO: Well, as I was saying, they set the tanks on us and smashed our ribs with rifle butts! (conquers step number nine).

BUREAUCRAT: Each to his own hang up! Aren't you going to do anything, Mr Policeman?

POLICEMAN (opening the other eye): I'm coming, I'm coming . . .

BUREAUCRAT: Well, let's go then!

POLICEMAN: Where are you going?

BUREAUCRAT: To the police station.

POLICEMAN: To the police station? At this time of night and when I'm so sleepy?

CONCIERGE: I'm going to sleep too. I don't know how to plan my dreams and I don't even believe that it can be done. But I always like to plan my menu in advance. Tomorrow, for example, we are going to have . . . *(descending the stairs)* besides, it's incredible that they let tanks run around loose . . .

BUREAUCRAT: Well, as sure as I am called Justo Martínez, at your service, I promise you all that tomorrow I will do honour to my name, I will make a statement and accuse them all of disturbing the peace of the Nation and of this building, attacking public transport, promoting social unrest, etc., including you, Mr Policeman . . .

POLICEMAN *(opening one eye)*: Yes, yes, I'm coming . . . you don't play chess by any chance, Mr Martínez?

BUREAUCRAT: No, I don't play chess or draughts or poker or noughts and crosses or anything else. And, you might as well know, as a child I didn't play with marbles or tops or yoyos or hide-and-seek or musical statues . . . as far as I'm concerned, life is no game!

POLICEMAN: Didn't you ever play cops and robbers?

PALINURO: Nor students and riot police? Workers and strike breakers? Hawks and doves?

BUREAUCRAT: No, sir, I don't play chess! Good night! *(descending the stairs)*: just you remember, remember that the President has reached out his hand to you . . . are you going to leave that hand outstretched?

(In the foreground an allegory takes shape: a huge, three-dimensional cardboard hand hangs outstretched, palm upwards, from cables. Harlèquin, Pierrot, Scaramouch and Colombine jump in the air trying to reach it. They move like puppets. Each is attached by threads from above which move them: Harlequin's are yellow, Pierrot's red, Scaramouch's silver and Colombine's black.)

PIERROT: No, don't leave that hand outstretched!

COLOMBINE: Lower it! *(jumps)*. Don't leave it outstretched!

(Scaramouch grabs Colombine's buttocks.)

SCARAMOUCH: I'll lift you, Colombine, if you promise to kiss me! *(tries to lift her but the effort causes the seat of his trousers to split and a stream of yellow confetti pours out)*.

HARLEQUIN *(doubled up with laughter)*: We must get, ha, ha, ha, we must get, ha, ha, ha, a ladder, ha, ha!

(Enter Ladder-Seller-Death).

LADDER-SELLER-DEATH: Ladders? Who will buy ladders? I sell ladders to reach the President's index finger! I buy extension ladders, ladies and gentlemen, to ascend from youth oratory champion to silent Minister! Ladders, ladies and gentlemen, step ladders? Spiral ladders to ascend from aspiring-deputy-congressmen to assistant-of-the-chauffeur-of-the-aide-of-the-adviser-of-the-secretary-of-the-minister! Ladders, ladies and gentlemen? I rent ladders to descend from the National

Palace anteroom to the hell of Tlatelolco! Who wants ladders? Ladders to buy, ladders to sell! Ladders which take you down, ladders which take you up!

HARLEQUIN *(still doubled up with laughter)*: I, ha, ha, I want, I want a ladder, ha, ha, ha! Wait, wait, ha, ha, ha!

(Ladder-Seller-Death takes no notice of him and continues towards the exit. Enter the Dottore, drunk.)

LADDER-SELLER-DEATH: Good evening, doctor . . . *(exit)*.

DOTTORE *(absent-mindedly)*: Good evening! *(coming down to earth)* . . . I know you, I know you, I know your stink, bitch! *Quo modo est mater tua?* In other words: How is your mother, Son-of-a-Bitch-Death? *(suddenly notices the outstretched hand)*. The outstretched hand! Beware, beware of that hand! It's dangerous, very dangerous . . .

HARLEQUIN: So, are you with us or against us?

DOTTORE: Don't you have a little drop for me? *Nunc est bibendum*, in other words: Now's the time.

COLOMBINE: You haven't answered our question, Doctor . . .

DOTTORE *(nostalgically)*: I too was a student once . . . *Plus minusve*: in other words, that sometimes – like yourselves – I was more a student and sometimes less a student. I also dreamed of revolutions, I wrote ardent speeches *calamo currente*, in other words: with flying pen. Or, more accurately, *typewriter currente*. I also had friends who have risen to congressmen and ministers and now refuse to grant me audience: last time I spent ten hours in a waiting room eating sandwiches, and all for nothing! I, I . . . what was I saying? Ah, yes, but that was before I sank into *aurea mediocritas*: in other words, golden mediocrity. But, as I was saying, I too was once a student and twenty years old . . . *in illo tempore*, in other words: in those days . . .

(A commotion is heard and a little door opens in The Hand, a rope ladder is thrown out and Pantalone, the Captain and Tartaglia descend, dressed as soldiers and policemen!)

DOTTORE: You see? You see? I told you: beware of that hand . . . it is the Hand of Troy!

HARLEQUIN AND HIS MATES: The Hand of Troy! It is the Hand of Troy! Let's get out of here, it's the Hand of Troy!

(The soldiers and policemen bring out huge knives with which they cut the threads supporting Harlequin and his mates, who fall to the ground like rag dolls. The stage goes dark.)

(We return to reality. Palinuro has climbed another two steps and is now on number thirteen. With him are Estefania, the doctor and I. The policeman snores on step number eight.)

DOCTOR: Of course, I'm with you and I understand. But you have

517

made many mistakes. I saw part of the demonstration this afternoon. You insulted the authorities . . . you were vulgar. Is there any need for that? Didn't somebody say that silence speaks louder than words? And I remember Professor Urrutia, the great Spanish physician, used to say: 'Silence is aseptic'.

ESTEFANIA: Silence? That's a good idea!

DOCTOR: Anyway, everything is stacked against you and you won't achieve a thing until you convince the workers and the peasants.

ESTEFANIA: That's exactly what we're going to do . . . we're organized in brigades. We'll go out into the countryside, the factories, the workshops, the markets!

(The neighbour from number fifteen descends the stairs.)

NEIGHBOUR FROM NUMBER FIFTEEN: Have you seen Mr Martínez? Oh, I can't sleep . . . I haven't slept a wink in the last five minutes at least! First I thought I was dreaming that I was awake, that I couldn't sleep, until I was forced to face reality, as my children are always telling me I should . . .

DOCTOR: I think you're living in a dream . . . in my opinion, it's hopeless.

NEIGHBOUR FROM NUMBER FIFTEEN: What, you mean young Palinuro won't pull through?

PALINURO: Oh, I'll pull through all right: I'll live to suffer many a day yet!

NEIGHBOUR FROM NUMBER FIFTEEN: Do you know which is Mr Martínez' apartment? I want to ask him to give me an emergency massage . . . I've such a headache!

ME: Mr Martínez lives in apartment two.

NEIGHBOUR FROM NUMBER FIFTEEN: Ah, thank God. And thank you all, of course . . . if you see what I mean: and you, young man, take more care when you cross the street . . .

DOCTOR: It was in the Zócalo, madam, these young people have told us often enough!

NEIGHBOUR FROM NUMBER FIFTEEN: Well then, you should take more care when you cross the Zócalo, shouldn't you? Anyway, I think they should put up traffic lights for the tanks and then the students could cross safely. Ay, where are my children now? It's so painful to try and think where they are with this headache *(starts to descend the stairs)* . . . you won't believe it, but I have a headache in my whole body! *(pauses, cocks her head to one side and cups her hand to her ear)*: tell me: all those ambulances rushing around the city, couldn't we call one to come for this young man? Listen to them: they're all over the place . . .

(As she descends the stairs the ambulance sirens are heard going to and fro and they are like the wind beneath the triumphal arches, they muddy

518

the antimony of the avenues, relaying the alarm from one nebula to the next. Palinuro, with my help, climbs another three steps and thus reaches the fourth floor.)

THE SILENT DEMONSTRATION

(Second major interlude for the purpose of collecting a little compassion and moral support for the students, preceded by several miscellaneous episodes. Front stage, the Dottore, with an extremely long pink stethoscope, examines Harlequin, who is lying on the floor. To one side, Colombine, distraught.)

DOTTORE: Mmmm . . . Mmmm . . . No doubt about it: several of his illusions have comminuted fractures.

COLOMBINE: Oh, doctor! Everything is going wrong!

DOTTORE: *Errare humanum est* . . . Mmmmm . . . . he seems to have several dislocated hopes and a haemorrhage of cephalo-optimistic liquid . . . Mmmm.

COLOMBINE: Everything, everything has gone wrong! We wanted to talk to the peasants, to the workers, to the housewives . . .

(Enter Dumb-Death who sits in the centre of the stage. Enter Pierrot and Scaramouch. Dumb-Death puts on a peasant's hat and covers its mouth with its hands.)

PIERROT *(very politely)*: Tell me, Mr Peasant, what is your view of the Jaramillo murder. Tell me what you think of the Atoyac massacre, of the fact that fifty per cent of the Mexican population lives in the countryside, that we have a thirty-seven per cent illiteracy rate. Tell me, tell me what you think!

DUMB-DEATH *(uncovering his mouth)*: I can't, I'm dumb!

PIERROT: What do you mean you're dumb, if you're talking?

DEAF-DEATH: So sorry, I meant to say I was deaf *(puts on a worker's cap and covers its ears with its hands).*

SCARAMOUCH: So, Mr Worker, when I say that the Revolution in Mexico is the opium of the people; when I say that MURO is a fascist group financed by the CIA and linked with Opus Dei; when I shout that the unions have sold out to the government and ask what you know of Ché Guevara . . . Can't you hear me?

DEAF-DEATH: No, I can't hear you! And don't shout at me, I'm not deaf!

SCARAMOUCH: But you told me you were deaf . . .

BLIND-DEATH: Beg your pardon, what I meant was that I'm blind . . . *(puts on a housewife's hat and covers its eyes with its hands).*

PIERROT: So, Mrs Housewife, you don't see what's going on in

Mexico, a country where the average income per inhabitant is less than 500 dollars a year! So you haven't noticed that Mexico is imprisoning its youth, the country's future, no less! Haven't you read the *Children of Sánchez*? Mexico is starving to death, madam! Open your eyes!

BLIND-DEATH: But I can't see, I'm blind. And don't waste any more of my time, I want to go and watch my soap opera!

PIERROT: What do you mean watch, you said you were blind?

DEATH-WITHOUT-SENSE-OF-SMELL: So sorry, what I meant was that I can't smell *(puts on a petit-bourgeois hat and holds its nose)*.

SCARAMOUCH: So, Mr Petit Bourgeois . . . you mean to say you don't notice the smell of oppression and demagogy? Doesn't your conscience stink? You don't detect the reek of gunpowder, or tear-gas, of blood, of shit?

FLESHLESS-DEATH *(removing its hand from its face)*: Of course not, idiot! Don't you see that I don't have a nose?

(The stage goes dark. A new beam of light illuminates a group composed of the Dottore, Harlequin and Colombine.)

THE DOTTORE: Mmmmmm . . . on the subject of noses, *rubet nasum*, in other words: your nose is red. And, as though that were not enough, *candet genas*, in other words: your cheeks are pale. Yes, definitely a case of acture studentitis, complicated by intermittent paroxystic ideology.

COLOMBINE: Oh, is it contagious, doctor?

DOTTORE: Extremely! He must be put in quarantine.

COLOMBINE: At home?

DOTTORE: In prison . . . and later, interned.

COLOMBINE: In a hospital?

DOTTORE: In a military academy!

COLOMBINE: Oh, I didn't realize you were a fascist!

DOTTORE: I didn't either, but discipline is discipline. What will things come to if we carry on like this?

COLOMBINE: Complete disaster, doctor . . . do you remember the orange bullet?

THE DOTTORE: The one that looked like a bazooka bullet?

COLOMBINE: It *was* a bazooka bullet, doctor!

(Enter Scaramouch and Pierrot dressed up as newspaper vendors, hawking their papers.)

SCARAMOUCH: Extra, extra! Paratroopers launch concerted pumpkin!

PIERROT: Latest, latest! Paratroopers launch concerted pumpkin on ancient doors of San Ildefonso College!

SCARAMOUCH: News! News! Paratroopers launch concerted

520

pumpkin on ancient doors of San Ildefonso College!

(Enter Rich-Death: with solid gold dentures, pink skeleton encrusted with jade, iridescent silk top hat, cream spats, extremely long amber cigarette holder and emerald-studded whip.)

RICH-DEATH: I'll buy all your newspapers! *(Buys them. Pierrot and Scaramouch exeunt, happily, counting their money.)*

UNSUBTLE-DEATH *(to the audience, confidentially)*: Besides . . . their newspapers are all sold out to the government anyway! *(puts on a newspaper hat).*

NEWSPAPER-VENDOR-DEATH: Newspapers? Who wants newspapers? I sell good news, I buy crimes . . . Revolution for sale? Coups d'etat? *(exit).*

(A white egg flies from one side of the empty stage to the other. A great ovation is heard. It flies back again, the other way. Another ovation is heard. This is repeated several times until Pierrot and Colombine enter on one side dressed up as university football players and on the other Harlequin and Scaramouch, dressed up as polytechnic football players. They pass the egg between them. Ovations and jeers. Suddenly they drop the egg and it breaks. They all stand transfixed and sad.)

COLOMBINE: You see? I told you. It was Pierrot's fault.

PIERROT: No, it was Scaramouch.

SCARAMOUCH: No, it was Harlequin.

HARLEQUIN: No, it was Colombine.

(The Dottore appears.)

DOTTORE *(to the audience)*: It's all the fault of all of them: all the students *(disappears).*

COLOMBINE: I have an idea . . . come here, all of you! *(they go into a huddled consultation).*

THEIR BABBLING VOICES: What? Shhhh, quiet! What? Quiet, shhh! Ah, yes, of course! Quiet! Shhhh! Shhhhh!

(All exeunt, on tip-toe. Silence. Enter, also on tip-toe, Silent-Death, mouth covered with sticking plaster and bearing a banner which reads):

DEATH'S BANNER: 'And so was organized . . .'

(Enter Pierrot, Colombine, Scaramouch and Harlequin, dressed up as students, their mouths covered with sticking plaster. Each carries a banner with a different word and each a sack from which they will take other banners as the scene unfolds. Some of these banners will be in the shape of balloons, in the style of comic strips. Unless otherwise stated, their banners will have a white background and black letters and those of Silent-Death will be black with white letters. The whole demonstration takes place in absolute silence: not even the buzzing of a fly is heard.)

PIERROT'S BANNER: 'The'.

COLOMBINE'S BANNER: 'Demonstration'.

SCARAMOUCH'S BANNER: 'Of'.

HARLEQUIN'S BANNER: 'Silence'.

(Pierrot, Scaramouch, Colombine and Harlequin drop their banners and produce others from their sacks.)

SCARAMOUCH'S BANNER: 'We were 300,000 people.'

HARLEQUIN'S BANNER *(in different styles of lettering in various colours)*: 'In silence we marched to the Zócalo.'

PIERROT'S BANNER: 'I wasn't there, but they told me about it.'

DEATH TAKES OUT A BANNER *(bearing a printed hand pointing at Pierrot)*: 'He chickened out.'

COLOMBINE'S BANNER *(with beautiful lettering in pink)*: 'Death to snobs!'

A BANNER IN THE AUDIENCE: 'I watched them go by in silence.'

ANOTHER BANNER IN THE AUDIENCE *(in small, timid letters)*: 'I stayed at home.'

DEATH TAKES OUT ANOTHER BANNER: 'He stayed at home just to be on the safe side.'

(A big blue fly descends from the roof on a thread, and flies around the stage, with a tiny banner saying: 'Bzzzz . . . Bzzzz'. Exit.)

PIERROT TAKES OUT ANOTHER BANNER: 'The immediate enemy is the bourgeoisie.'

ANOTHER BANNER IN THE AUDIENCE: 'It's the communists!'

PIERROT TAKES OUT ANOTHER BANNER *(with 'Old English' style letters)*: 'Lies: I am an intellectual!'

COLOMBINE TAKES OUT ANOTHER BANNER *(in capital Futura Bold lettering)*: 'Down with the monolithic Institutional Revolutionary Party, down with pyramidal power!'

(Silent dogs howl in the distance. Long signs hanging from the flies pass across the stage reading: 'Howl . . . Hooowwl' . . .)

HARLEQUIN TAKES OUT ANOTHER BANNER: 'Today, any student who feels shame is a revolutionary.'

(Enter Tartaglia on a silent motorbike with government plates from the exhaust pipe of which protrudes a sign reading: 'Brum . . . Bruuum!' Takes out a banner.)

TARTAGLIA'S BANNER: 'The REVREV! The Revolution has GOGO! Got down FROMROM! From its HOHO! Horse and GOGO! Got on a motorBIBI! On a motorbike!'

(Exit Tartaglia on silent motorbike reading: 'Brum . . . bruuum!')

522

PIERROT TAKES OUT ANOTHER BANNER *(in Romantique No. 5 lettering)*: 'The artists are with us.'

DEATH TAKES OUT ANOTHER BANNER: 'But the army isn't!'

(Enter Captain Mean dressed as a soldier. He sounds a silent trumpet from the end of which appears a sign reading: 'Tú-tú-tú-tú-tú-tú-tú'. Behind him, enter Pantalone dressed also as a soldier, playing a silent drum. To each drumstick is attached a little sign, making them look like rigid little flags; the left one: 'Rat-a-' the right one: 'Tat-tat'. 'Rat-a-'. 'Tat-Tat'.)

PANTALONE TAKES OUT A BANNER: 'I am a soldier and in five days' time I will occupy the University . . .'

CAPTAIN MEAN TAKES OUT A BANNER *(with spelling mistakes)*: 'I am a kongresman an the rektor is a sun-ov-£⁸%§?=(.'

(The Dottore appears with a banner.)

DOTTORE'S BANNER *(in italic lettering)*: 'Delenda est Carthago!'

PANTALONE TAKES OUT ANOTHER BANNER: 'The rector must resign!'

PIERROT TAKES OUT ANOTHER BANNER *(in elegant copperplate lettering)*: 'I am the Rector and I resign!'

DOTTORE TAKES OUT ANOTHER BANNER *(with a black border)*: 'University autonomy is in mourning!'

(Pantalone, the Dottore and Captain Mean unroll a long banner with brightly coloured letters which reads):

BANNER: 'We are the Living Forces of the Nation.'

ANOTHER BANNER IN THE AUDIENCE: 'It is up to you to guard our Mexican identity.'

(Silent bells toll in the distance. Round signs hanging from the roof cross the stage reading 'Clang! . . . clang', 'Clang . . . clang'.)

PANTALONE TAKES OUT ANOTHER BANNER *(in Helvetic lettering)*: 'Death to new-fangled ideas!'

HARLEQUIN TAKES OUT ANOTHER BANNER: 'Yes, death to the leftists!'

COLOMBINE TAKES OUT ANOTHER BANNER: 'But what are you saying, Harlequin?'

(Harlequin peers at the banner he is holding up and throws it away. He searches desperately in his sack for another banner. Finally, he takes a pen from his pocket and writes on the back of the discarded banner):

HARLEQUIN'S BANNER *(in letters red with shame)*: 'Sorry, somebody gave me the wrong banner!'

JOKER-DEATH TAKES OUT ANOTHER BANNER: 'Ha, ha, it won't be the last time!'

523

(Pantalone points a rifle at Harlequin.)
HARLEQUIN TAKES OUT ANOTHER BANNER: 'Don't shoot, soldier, you too are of the People!'
(Nevertheless, a sign pops out of the barrel of Pantalone's rifle saying: 'Bang!' Harlequin takes out another banner.)
HARLEQUIN'S BANNER: 'Ouch!'
(Silence falls. Colombine goes over to Harlequin, strokes his hair and takes out another banner.)
COLOMBINE'S BANNER: 'Goodbye!'
DOTTORE TAKES OUT A BANNER: '*Sit tibi terra levis* . . . in other words, may the earth lie lightly on you.'
(Captain Mean and Pantalone lay into Colombine, Pierrot and Scaramouch with their rifles, drums, trumpets and fists. Banners of different shapes, sizes and colours fly through the air reading 'Bang!' 'Scrunch!' 'Wham!' 'Wallop!' 'Take that!' and others: 'Ooh!' 'Ah!' 'Ouch!' . . .)
DOTTORE TAKES OUT ANOTHER BANNER: '*Et cetera, et cetera* . . . in other words: etc., etc.'
HERE AND THERE IN THE AUDIENCE BANNERS APPEAR: 'Clap, clap!' 'Bravo!' 'Hurrah!' 'Clap-clap!'
(The actors suspend the action and bow to the audience. The Dottore's hand appears with a banner.)
DOTTORE'S BANNER: '*Exeunt* . . .'
(And, effectively, exeunt.)
GRATEFUL-DEATH TAKES OUT ANOTHER BANNER *(in different coloured letters decorated with flowers and hearts)*: 'Thank you, dear audience.'
DEATH TAKES OUT ANOTHER BANNER: 'So ends the Demonstration of Silence. Now, we ask you . . .'
(Enter Harlequin and his followers, each carrying a banner which together compose a single phrase. 'OF SILENCE' 'A MINUTE OF' 'THE DEATH' 'SILENCE FOR'.)
DEATH TAKES OUT ANOTHER BANNER: 'No, no, it's in the wrong order!'
(The characters change places several times until finally it reads: 'A Minute of Silence for the Death of Silence.')
DEATH-AUTHORITY TAKES OUT ANOTHER BANNER: 'That's it! There's nothing like Law and Order!'
(The curtain falls noisily.)

(And we return to reality; Palinuro has reached the fourth floor.)

THE FOURTH FLOOR

(Reality, however, will never be the same . . . reality and fantasy begin to get mixed up.)

PALINURO *(at the foot of the stairs leading to the attic)*: The tear-gas grenades exploded like new additions to the zodiac. Feel my face, brother, touch the unplanned protuberances sculpted by the soldiers' boots! And listen, listen to the hammering like sweet moons exploding in my chest! And what became of the hot blood? . . . The women brought us their stockings, poor things, to make ourselves slings and they poured boiling water on the soldiers . . .

ESTEFANIA: Palinuro is delirious, doctor!

DOCTOR: He must have a fever. I have a thermometer here.

PALINURO: Of course I have a fever, doctor: I'm over forty degrees in the shade but my delirium is of another type. And I want to stoke my fury. When we marched hand-in-hand like well-behaved children, when we lit up the churches and set the bells ringing, then we were delirious indeed, but the tarted-up vultures set public opinion against us! And you can stick that thermometer up your own arse!

DOCTOR: I wasn't going to put it there. Anyway, I'm tired. I wish you goodnight. Tomorrow, young man, I will be happy to check you over. Ah, and watch out for the postman. He might look as if he wouldn't say boo to a goose but he's a guy who would denounce his own mother . . . goodbye *(exit)*.

ESTEFANIA *(to the doctor)*: Thank you very much, doctor . . . *(to the policeman)*: Wake up, Mr Policeman. Wake up and go to bed . . . if you sleep on the stairs, you might catch cold!

POLICEMAN *(opening one eye)*: Ah, yes, of course, I'm going! I was saying that I enjoy playing. Not just chess. Cards too. I like betting. Want to make a bet?

PALINURO *(dragging himself up two more steps)*: On what? That we, the students, are going to lose? We know that already. When the tanks landed on our beaches . . . yes, the tanks, with their death-dealing protuberances . . . then they charged us and we, in true Spanish style, said: 'No pasarán', we will not be moved! . . . but move us they did, the bastards!

(The policeman starts to descend the stairs.)

POLICEMAN: I can't stay awake a moment longer. 'Night all. I would have won my bet, you know *(exit)*.

PALINURO *(climbing another step)*: The tanks came out but our rage saved us from dishonour: I myself, like many others, gave a golden example: I took off my patchwork waistcoat and defied the first tank: aha, tank, aha! You should have seen me, in the middle of the square as though I were in the middle of the naked Republic, a great bullfighter, man, my twenty years against five tons of red-hot iron!

(Enter Harlequin dressed as a bullfighter. He dedicates the bull to the audience.)

ME *(pointing at Harlequin from reality)*: There he is, look, there, ready to cover himself in glory!

ESTEFANIA: Who's there?

PALINURO: I made a pass . . . a fabulous pass which sent the terraces into a paroxysm of expectation!

(Enter Pantalone with horns and Harlequin makes a pass with his cape.)

THE AUDIENCE: Oléééé!

PALINURO: I hadn't yet regained my balance when, to make matters worse, another tank materialized but I saved the day with another masterly sweep of my waistcoat.

(Harlequin makes another pass before Pantalone. Renewed applause.)

ME: There's Palinuro, over there, covering himself in glory!

ESTEFANIA: Where? Where? I can't see him!

(Exeunt Harlequin and Pantalone.)

ME: Here, Estefania, Palinuro is here: on the stairs.

ESTEFANIA: Bravo, Palinuro! Bravo!

PALINURO: Then from the palace windows, the bureaucrats praised the dexterity of my hinges and waved their hankerchiefs, moist with the disgrace visited upon our land! I wasn't the only one . . . *(managing a few more steps)* other companions followed my example and the square became a night of steps and passes, you should have seen the twirling of pullovers and polytechnic and university sweatshirts, in the Arena of the Constitution!

(Scaramouch, Colombine and Pierrot walk across the stage flying kites in the shape of sweatshirts and pullovers. Exeunt.)

ESTEFANIA: Olé, Olé, Palinuro!

ME: There he is, look, look, there's Palinuro!

ESTEFANIA: Where?

(The doctor appears, carrying bandages.)

DOCTOR: Upon reflection and after checking in my *Merck Manual*, I think the best course might well be to assume that young Palinuro has at least a luxation and perhaps even a dislocated bone, I don't know . . . better safe than sorry. Nurse, we'll bandage him *(takes a small piece of paper from his pocket and gives it to Palinuro)*. That is my bill. I am with you, as I told you, but I have to earn my living somehow . . . *(starts to bandage Palinuro, with Estefania's help)*.

PALINURO *(ignoring them)*: You should have seen it, oh yes, Oléééé! shouted the overnight owners of agrarian reform, and the candidates who will be anointed with their own pus during the next presidential term. Oléééé Palinuro, Oléééé, lads, that's it! I remember one fellow student, tall as a vertical landscape . . .

(Scaramouch the bullfighter appears, tall and elegant, covered all over – including his tail – with silver sequins. The bulls appear – horned heads on wheeled platforms, with handlebars – driven by Captain Mean and Pantalone. Pantalone's bull is white with red eyes. Captain Mean's green with yellow eyes.)

ME *(pointing to them)*: There's the tall student, look at him!

(Scaramouch starts to fight the white bull with red eyes. Harlequin the bullfighter appears, in his suit of multicoloured sequins. Pierrot appears, in pink and silver. Two more bulls: one, yellow with blue eyes, driven by the Dottore; the other, driven by Tartaglia, blue with orange eyes. They all fight.)

ME: Do you see Palinuro?

VOICE OF NEIGHBOUR FROM NUMBER FIFTEEN: Oh, my children, my children . . .!

PALINURO: Yes, there I am, look at me all of you: I was almost run over by a tank with two long machine guns like horns, if it hadn't been for a friend of mine from the San Ildefonso College who made a timely intervention, kindling the hurrahs of my heart! But, at a given moment, my cape or, I should say, my patchwork waistcoat, flew into the air . . .! *(Colombine walks by with a kite the shape of Palinuro's patchwork waistcoat.)* You won't believe it. Then, I wrapped . . . I wrapped . . . *(drags himself up two more steps and faints).*

ESTEFANIA: Oh, what's the matter with him, doctor?

DOCTOR: I don't know, I don't know, be quiet . . . let me listen to his heart . . . *(bends his head over Palinuro's chest. Bulls and bullfighters stand motionless and silent. Then, exeunt.)*

ESTEFANIA: He's not dead, is he doctor?

(Palinuro comes back to life. With an enormous effort, he reaches step number eleven and faints again.)

DOCTOR: He's lost consciousness again. Help me to carry him . . .

ME: No way! That would be to betray him: Palinuro intended to drag himself up and so he will.

DOCTOR: But you can't leave him here all night! He's so weak that I doubt that he'll come to for a time. Something must be done . . .

ESTEFANIA: We can drag him up . . .

ME: That's a better idea.

DOCTOR: All right. But be careful . . .

(Palinuro slides down two or three steps.)

ME: Well, let's go or we'll have to start all over again if we let Palinuro slide right down to the ground floor.

DOCTOR: As for me, I'm going to study my bones to find out where there might be a fracture. I'll come back early tomorrow morning to examine young Palinuro. I'm going to have to learn all over again how to make plaster and splints. Nurse: do you remember Böhler splints? We might need a Sayre's apparatus for head traction . . . who knows! Anything can happen, anything might be necessary . . . you do realize? How ridiculous that he should have dragged himself all the way up the stairs! *(goes down stairs towards his apartment, number fourteen).* I'll never forgive myself for having allowed it. Just imagine: if he had a broken rib he could now be suffering from damaged lung tissue . . . if he had a fractured pelvis, he could have a torn bladder, or rectum, who knows! What a disaster! *(enters his apartment).*

DOTTORE'S VOICE *(in the distance)*: *Palinurus dignus erat meliore fato!*

(Door of the doctor's apartment opens and he peers out.)

DOCTOR: Yes, precisely, as someone said, your friend deserved a better fate! *(disappears and shuts the door. The stage goes dark and so the fourth floor ends.)*

EPILOGUE

VOICES IN THE DARKNESS: Cries were exploding with the clamour of cornered bellows! And wicked hypotheses were afoot . . .! There were people, on the streets, prepared to provide denunciations and betrayals for those who were short of them. Meanwhile, the effusive virginity of the dahlias meekly shed its petals . . .

SECOND VOICES IN THE DARKNESS: It was a night of black and glassy butterflies. It was a night of snores and death rattles, mischievous curses and the crackling of martial torches . . .

FIRST VOICES IN THE DARKNESS: It was an ideal night for the cruel learning of symmetry . . . it was a night on which could be heard the howling of hunters and, among the rockets and other vernacular reports, sounded the lash of conjunctions of blasphemies, confined weeping, the laboured breath of the asthmatic rabble and the rattle of panic . . .

SECOND VOICES IN THE DARKNESS: It was a night without possible repatriation, a night of nitrous paradoxes and rutting intuitions, it was a night of archaeological pomp, black as a tyrannical funnel and the atmosphere was treacherous and, more especially . . . hard to crack!

FIRST VOICES IN THE DARKNESS: It was the night of tanks, tanks grey and enormous as sailing scaffolds!

528

SECOND VOICES IN THE DARKNESS: It was the night of the students!

FIRST VOICES IN THE DARKNESS: If you go now at dawn to the Square, before the bulldozers and the sweeping machines clear away the remains of the calamity, there where they were smeared by the grey spatulas of Death, you will see them . . . you will see the students, flung down in the oil, abandoned to the wind and the solar eminences . . .

SECOND VOICES IN THE DARKNESS: Or perhaps you will now find only their shoes . . .

FIRST VOICES IN THE DARKNESS: Their empty shoes . . .

(A beam of very pale and dusty light illuminates Rag-And-Bone-Death, walking in the swirling mist with its cart.)

RAG-AND-BONE-DEATH: Shoes? Who will buy second-hand shoes? I've got a philosophy student's moccasins! An engineer's mules, an intern's lace-ups! Who wants a biology teacher's slippers? *(exit).*

(Only the beam of light remains. On the illuminated surface of the floor a drain opens and from it billows green smoke and I enter dragging Palinuro who is bandaged from head to foot. Behind me enters Estefania.)

ME: 75, 76, Wow! I'm exhausted! 77, 78, 79 . . . and 80! Phew. *(I wipe the sweat from my forehead.)* Who would have thought that Palinuro would be such a dead weight?

(A beam of light illuminates a very high, narrow bed in the middle of the stage. We drag Palinuro to the bed.)

ME: What we have come to! Who would have thought that it would all end like this . . . after we had such a good time at the masked ball . . .!

ESTEFANIA: You better believe it! How we danced! Didn't we? We danced all night! And everyone was there: Lenin, Gandhi, the Spanish Grandees. The Mayor of Mexico City, Madame Pompadour and the Chief of Police . . .

PALINURO *(opening one eye)*: And where did you go afterwards?

ME: We went to the dissecting room of the old School of Medicine, we gave Charon a bottle of tequila and asked him to dissect a corpse for us!

ESTEFANIA: It was so exciting, Palinuro! At first we were very sad, because the corpse that Charon brought out was that of a very young man, who looked like a student . . .

ME: But somebody had the idea of putting a riot helmet on his head and that solved the problem!

ESTEFANIA: And, to dispel any remaining uneasiness, we gave him a hawk's mask and a white glove of the Olympia Battalion . . .

PALINURO *(opening the other eye)*: Fantastic, fantastic! What else? Did you also dress him in CIA socks and an Opus Dei watch and MURO trousers and Interpol spectacles?

ESTEFANIA: Yes, yes, ha, ha, ha! . . . Goodness, I'm going to wet myself if I carry on laughing!

PALINURO: And who was the murderer?

ESTEFANIA: Whose murderer?

PALINURO: The student's . . .

ESTEFANIA: Ah, the one who looked like a student?

ME: We have an oral description; any day now we'll catch him *(taking an imaginary piece of paper from my pocket and reading it):* The murderer, according to witnesses, had politician's eyes, a rich man's nose, a reactionary's bald head, and a son-of-a-bitch's ears . . .

ESTEFANIA: I told you! I told you: I've wet myself laughing! And then, of course, we gave the student the prize for the best costume of the night: and the poor thing got so excited that he came back to life and fell off the dissecting slab and almost killed himself for real but, of course, it was all a joke and he was only a corpse disguised as a naked student . . . What am I saying: he was naked, that is, he was a student . . . Well, you know what I mean . . . He was just like that, like you Palinuro, exactly . . . oh, what fun we had!

PALINURO: Just a minute . . . I'm neither naked nor dead. I simply am. But I don't know where . . .

ME: In the realms of glory, Palinuro!

(Hundreds, thousands of stars light up. The effect is of a planetarium: the walls and ceiling of the room in Holy Sunday Square have turned into a heavenly vault, black and velvety, in which twinkle the boreal constellations and their main stars and, with intense and special brightness, the twin stars of Castor and Pollux. Beyond the stars hangs the Milky Way, while across the floor creeps a whitish mist, produced with dry ice. On a thread from the flies hangs a luminous half moon which casts a white light over the stage. A swing descends on which Pierrot is seated with his lyre.)

PIERROT: 'The bones of Palinuro pray to the Pole Star . . .'

(The swing rises, carrying Pierrot off.)

PALINURO *(rubbing his eyes):* Ah, yes, I remember now what I was telling you. Then, as I was saying *(sits up in the bed),* I wrapped myself in the national flag, which had just been lowered . . .

ALL OF US: In the national flag?

(A little square window opens in the sky and Pantalone peers out wearing an orange Phrygian cap.)

PANTALONE: Heresy! *(He disappears.)*

(Another diamond-shaped window opens and Captain Mean peeps out wearing a T-shirt with purple and white tassles.)

CAPTAIN MEAN: Sacrilege! *(He disappears.)*

(A small round window opens beside the Great Bear and Tartaglia peeps out wearing a long Pinocchio nose.)

TARTAGLIA: BLA-BLA! Blasphemy! *(disappears.)*

(Palinuro stands up on the bed. He raises his arm to point towards the Pole Star which is just above his head. A shower of snow falls from the star.)

PALINURO: I wrapped myself in the flag, yes, you're hearing right! And then you should have seen me: decked in young rattlesnakes, huge in my huge cape . . .!

(On one side, enter Harlequin with a silk cape of green, white and red rhombuses. Clapping is heard. On the other side, enter Bull-Death, with long and pointed horns of carved silver. Fanfares are heard and the bullfight recommences. The back of the stage goes dark.)

PALINURO'S VOICE: It was the most beautiful cape you could imagine: all of silk and aerial eagles, insurgent greens and Aztec cacti! It was all covered in snakes and white religions and spangled with guarantees, branches of oak and laurel and imperial crowns!

ALL OF US: Oléééé, oléééé, Palinuro!

PALINURO'S VOICE: Ah, my beautiful cape! All coloured in Spanish reds and embraces of Acatempan! In hymns and betrayals and Aguascalientes conventions! And there I was, shouting at the tanks: aha, bull, aha! And looking towards the heavenly houses determining my fate and suddenly the whole monolithic greatness of a tank rushed at me . . . and I made a masterly pass which caused the greens to billow out in a fan of emeralds, and I stood fearless, man, wrapped in the flag, like a child hero ready to leap into history!

(Harlequin stands, motionless, wrapped in his cape of tricolour rhombuses. Exit Bull-Death.)

VOICES: Sacrilege! Heresy! Blasphemy!

(Enter Government-Death, pulling a cart containing Pantalone, the Dottore, Captain Mean and Tartaglia, all four with sheepskins on their heads.)

ALL: BEEE, BEEE! We must avenge the flag, BEEE! We must avenge the flag, BOOO! We must go to the Zócalo, BEEE! That is, they're taking us, BUUU! We're not going because we want to, BAAAAAA! But because they're taking us, BEEEE! We're bureaucrats, BOOO! But we're sheep, BUUUUU, BEEEE, BOOOO, BAAAA! *(Exeunt.)*

(The back of the stage is lit up again. The moon starts to descend and, as it drops, the light dims.)

PALINURO *(sitting on the bed again, starts to remove his bandages)*: Ah, but you should have seen what happened next, man! Not for nothing, since early morning, did tears come to the eyes of every mother each time they mistook a mound of earth for an unmarked grave or the corners of the Square where they thought their children's valves burst and their lives dribbled away!

A VOICE: Oh, my children, my children!

ME: Do you hear? It's the neighbour from number fifteen!

PALINURO: No, brother, no, soul mate of mine! It's not the voice of the neighbour from number fifteen: it's the voice of the Motherland, of our poor, poor, Motherland!

(Motherland-Death appears like a ghost, covered in coloured rags, wearing a mad woman's shift from which hang vanilla scorpions.)

MOTHERLAND-DEATH: Oh, my children . . .! Oh, my children! *(Exit.)*

PALINURO: And then, last night, in Constitution Square, brother, Pamplona was re-created and the students who weren't defying the tanks climbed on top of them and attacked them with sticks and kicks, with banners and stones . . . and the audience threw hats and cushions and flowers and bottles into the arena in our honour!

(Flowers, bottles, cushions, hats and underwear fall on all sides, thrown by the audience and by the characters: Pantalone, Captain Mean, the Bureaucrat, the concierge, the postman, etc., etc., who appear at the windows in the sky, from the wings, the flies, the boxes and the stalls, shouting that the blame lies with the students, with Hunger, the Vatican agents, they threw blue trousers, vases, beer cans, shoes, with the Bolsheviks, they leave the stage, the lights go out, enter Death, the concierge, the Dottore and the doctor and they blame the Opposition, Ché, the life-long students, the Shrines; the lights go on, the windows in the sky close, they throw watches, empty Coca-Colas, green socks, pink keyrings and they blame the Reds of the Communist Party, the students, the Downtrodden, Cohn-Bendit, the Outstretched Hand, the Freemasons, the students, they turn on the lights, they open the windows, they lean out, they throw yellow slippers, iridescent gobs of spit, carnations and they blame the political prisoners, the students, the CIA, the anarchists, the Sandwich Generation, the ex-presidents, the Hawks, the PRI presidential candidates, the Hawks, Ignorance, Pierrot, Colombine and Tartaglia disappear, turn off the lights, appear at the windows in the sky, on the moon and in paradise, and they turn off the lights, they turn on the lights, they close the windows, they illuminate the stage, and they lay the blame for everything on the students, petty officialdom, Rudi Dutschke, Arrabal, The Super Machos, the Red Berets, the sinarchists, the Tupmaros, they throw golden G-strings, linen handkerchiefs, otter-skin hats, bunches of violets, bottles of whisky and they blame the Mencheviks, the Katangais, the students, the Pasionaria, the students, the students, the students, and they disappear, they close the windows in the sky, they leave the theatre: they turn out the lights, they blame the students, the students, the students and the moon continues to descend and the light continues to dim.)

PALINURO: And there you have us, man, picking up all that

provocative rubbish: broken bayonets, childhood photographs, military-service books, leaflets and the lyrics of anti-government and anti-imperialist songs, our banners saying 'People unit,' 'People, open your eyes,' 'The People are Happening!' . . .

(The moon finally sets behind Palinuro's bed. The stars go out and the stage goes dark, although from time to time a sprinkling of white and luminous snow falls from the Pole Star. The black light goes on. Two, three, four phosphorescent students with mime masks start to drag themselves along the ground.)

PALINURO'S VOICE: There we were, man, picking up our veins, a blue handkerchief, our geography and logarithm books, our test tubes and our illusions, while the oceanic voice of a megaphone regurgitated its perversion and demanded of us an ear, an armoured back, a tail, two machine guns, the other ear and the cock of the tank infantry . . .

(The phosphorescent students continue their serpentine dance on the floor.)

PALINURO'S VOICE: We were covered in glory, man! And they were up to their necks in shit! We lost, but we lost without fear, as the good lose. More than one tank, as I said a hundred times, disembowelled a youth wearing a bullfighter's costume on which glowed hundreds of famous sayings and a few inoffensive slogans embroidered by his mother: it was the resurrection of sacrifice: they tore out our hearts, man, and we will never be the same again!

(The black light goes out, all is left in total darkness.)

PALINURO'S VOICE: What I most regret, man, is the tricolour death of my flag, that my flag was ironed by the tanks. And a large photograph of Ché . . . you don't mind me talking about my flag and Ché at the same time, do you, man? I was saying: how it grieved me to see that the poster of Ché was left in the middle of the Square, with the marks of boots and tanks' caterpillars across his face, my poor Ché . . .

(The stars come back on and a very weak beam of zenithal light shines on an object on the floor which does not become distinguishable until the light gradually intensifies.)

PALINURO'S VOICE: My poor Ché, up to his eyes in shit like a suckling child, with his silver star sullied by the smog of the newspapers . . .

(On the floor, in the middle of the stage, are two amputated hands. Palinuro, having freed himself of his bandages, gets out of bed and kneels down before them, in the beam of light.)

PALINURO: I just had time, brother, before the final onslaught, to grab his hands and put them under my shirt . . . *(picks up the hands and places them against his heart).* That they might cool my breast, which was streaming with sacred sweat! That they might support my heart which was, at those moments, like a reactionary acrobat!

(Palinuro raises his own hands to heaven in a posture of supplication and remains motionless. Very slowly, the light dims until all is left in darkness again. The stars go out and the black light comes on. The wailing of ambulances is heard again, calling death. The phosphorescent Motherland goes by, in its dress of phosphorescent rags.)

PHOSPHORESCENT-MOTHERLAND: Oh, my children . . . ahhh, my chiiildren! *(Exit.)* Where have they taken them? Ohhhh, my chiiildren!

VOICES FROM THE AUDIENCE: Yes, where have they taken them? We want to know where!

PALINURO'S VOICE: If you want to know, you bastards, ask the Compass Rose!

(A huge Compass Rose descends from the roof, formed by eight flaming torches. Eight students will appear successively in white mime masks. Each will grab a flaming torch, speak his line, and run and dance around the stage.)

STUDENT: You want to know where? To the Campo Marte!

SECOND STUDENT: You want to know where? To Military Camp Number One!

THIRD STUDENT: You want to know what for? To burn them!

FOURTH STUDENT: You want to know why? To turn them to ashes!

FIFTH STUDENT: Each dead student is a living torch!

SIXTH STUDENT: Each living torch is a dead student!

SEVENTH STUDENT: Look, see how their ashes fly over the skyscrapers!

EIGHTH STUDENT: Look, see how their ashes smother the Olympic flame!

ALL *(throwing their torches to each other, like jugglers)*: Each dead student is a living torch! Each living torch is a dead student! Each dead student is a living torch! Each living torch is a dead student!

(Exeunt. Silence. From the floor behind the bed begins to rise a luminous and orange sun of Chinese paper: Palinuro lies on the ground, dead. A trickle of blood issues from between his lips. We are beside him. In the distance is heard the voice of the Poet, as the sun continues to rise. The higher it rises, the larger it becomes and the redder.)

THE POET'S VOICE: *Has muerto, camarada,/en el ardiente amanecer del mundo.* You died, comrade, in the burning dawn of the world. *Has muerto cuando apenas/tu mundo, nuestro mundo, amanecia . . .* You died when your world, our world, was barely dawning . . .

(Everything remains motionless and the silence is absolute for a few seconds which seem an eternity. Then, the sun goes out and all is darkness again.)

Enter Ending-Vendor-Death with a languid glass eye and pink skeleton, lit up by a searchlight.)

ENDING-VENDOR-DEATH: Who will buy endings? Beginnings for sale? I sell endings made-to-measure, I sell endings on hire purchase and for cash! Truculent endings, happy endings! Who will buy an ending? Artistic endings? Endless endings? I sell mediocre endings! . . . Who will buy an ending?

(Enter the Dottore, drunk.)

DOTTORE: Hic! *Aeternum Vale*, hic! In other words: goodbye for ever. *Consummatum est. Requiescat.* Would you by any chance have a Latin ending?

(Ending-Vendor-Death unrolls an ending which reads: 'FINIS'.)

DOTTORE: No, no, I want something . . . hic . . . something . . . more highfalutin!

(Ending-Vendor-Death takes out a banner and gives it to the Doctor. He approves it enthusiastically and shows it to audience and readers.)

THE BANNER READS:

(in red and gold letters)

'ACTA EST FABULA'

(the comedy has ended)

25

All the roses, all the animals,
all the squares, all the planets,
all the characters of the earth

I swore that I would find my cousin, even if I had to go to the ends of the earth. That as soon as I saw her and found on her belly the drops of blood that had fallen from the butcher's forehead and on her breasts the flour left by the baker's hands and beneath her tongue the Malaysian stamp with the beetle left there by the postman's tongue, I would – I swore – crush a duck's egg on her head, tell her that Novalis had never existed, speak ill to her of Pink Floyd, change the colour of her eyes and the dedications of my poems, whip her with petals to scent her wounds, insult her from the waist downwards, take two hours to undress her and take her to a restaurant to eat fly cocktails, frogs stuffed with vultures' eyes, tarantula soup, breaded rats' tails, bug juice, skunk pudding, bat's-wing salad and rattlesnake ice-cream. Then – I would say to her – from a joke shop I will buy you a cup full of holes so that the hemlock pours down your chest and Lautréamont's hanged men will poke their tongues out at you and stick pins in yours to cure it of sleepiness and I will take you to a fake cinema where they show fake films and if you look closely the Columbia Statue is of fake Carrara marble and Robert Taylor is not Robert Taylor, but I know you won't notice and if you think that you'll get out of it that way, well no siree (no ma'am), because I also have an invention to make you lose all notion of time, to confuse the minutes and the days so that you will take a second to write your entire life story and you will spend ten years writing the first sentence.

But, as soon as I saw her, as soon as I met her; centuries or days later, beside the river and saw her so old but, my God, so very beautiful, with her rag name back to front, so badly dressed yet so lovely, her raincoat covered in cigarette burns and pigeons' piss, her black woollen stockings caked with iodine, crowned with lobsters eating the blonde wheat growing in her hair, beside her a bag bursting with the days' vegetables and eager to kiss me from one whisker to the other but not admitting it, the bitch, as though unwillingly, and I knew that just looking at me she felt again that sudden heat, that sinking into orange reservoirs and spinning swirls of butterflies

536

that she felt once, the whore, when I introduced her in a Mexico City bar to a friend of mine and another time in Paris when she saw an unknown soldier passing in a 14 July parade and yet another in the Swiss Alps when she fell hopelessly in love, faithless that she is, with an Austrian skier with skin tanned by the sun glare on the snow and tall as a red-headed fountain, I rued my resolves and told her that I loved her. I told her I love you for the afternoon, I love you for the frogs that croak in the damp, I love your teeth and honey powder, I love you for love, just because, I love you in my arms, I love you between five and the weeks, I love you entwined in my words, I love you for a record and a piece of wine. I love you for the foam, I love you between the leaves of a fish, I love you vein and headings, I love you beneath a taxi and on top, I love you a stocking and a husband, I love you for your armpits, I love you light and stars, sea and phone, I love you too much for the time being, and we started to make love in the midst of that long absence profuse with rejections and mortal coil, and we loved among the lapels of the plants, in the accordions of the clouds, in the garb of beehives, in the lining of gloves, in the salt marshes of tobacco, in the hunger of mirrors, in the crows' moon, in the intentions of turf, in the oldness of rivers, in the balances of the afternoon, in the oceans of the offices and the corners of the sun and, with us, the whole world and all things started to make love too: neighbours with neighbours, dogs with bitches, stallions with mares, corks with bottles, chimney sweeps with chimneys, bows with violins and obelisks with shirt cuffs and all conceived napkins, provinces, sports and flagons and watches which were born of our love nine months after, two hundred clouds later, while several autumns pressed on without stopping off in the world because we continued to make love, prolonging summer at will, sweating tears of mud and embracing in the mercury which vegetated in our veins and went to our heads and rejuvenated them with new wine.

And afterwards I made my cousin a gift of all the roses of the world: the mystical roses of Rubén Darío, Yeats's most secret, and inviolate rose and Omar Khayyám's rose of yesterday and I kissed her in the middle of her forehead and told her, like Alberti, that a rose is more a rose when inhabited by caterpillars and I took her to the cinema to see *Days of Wine and Roses* and I took her to philosophy to show her Locke's rose and that of Condillac and St Augustine's seminal rations which St Bonaventure compared to a rose bud which is not yet a rose but will be one day and then I hijacked a taxi and ordered it to take us home and on the way I told Estefania that the Zahir is the shadow of the roses and recited to her from memory *An Ode with a Lament* to surround her with roses and on the radio we listened to part of *Der Rosenkavalier* and I promised to take her to see *Mefistofele* that she might watch Faust dying beneath a shower of roses and, from these roses, from these to those crowning the goddess of Lust and Death in *The Temptation of St Anthony,* from these and from the roses which sang in the trees in Perpetua's vision, I almost stole one, I almost stole two, I almost stole, for Estefania, the submerged labial rose of which Villaurrutia also speaks, the heavenly white rose of Dante's *Paradiso,* Ronsard's roses of life and the pure, burning rose emulating Francisco de Rioja's flame.

It was, of course, the fault of our friends.

It was when my cousin found out, from third parties, that some of our friends said that our life was false and superficial because we never did anything seriously and transcendental things never happened to us, that she started to write *The Blue Eyes of Holy Sunday Square.* They also maintained that our existence was monotonous, unfolding as it did in a series of almost inevitable stages: we made love; we fell out or made up with objects; we quarrelled; we had a dream; we made up a game; the game reached crisis point and from the crisis was born another game; we made it up afterwards, we dreamed and we made love again.

We could, of course, have told our friends to go jump in the lake and mind their own business. But it was our aspiration that our life and, with it, all that happened in our beloved room in Holy Sunday Square, should interest others. Not that we cared what people might think – at least, I didn't – though she did, but for reasons I will explain later. The fact was that I loved Estefania so much that I wanted the whole universe to be able to peep into her soul and gaze upon a miniature version of its own image. Or, anyway, that our four or five friends should do so, that they might see how comfortably they lived in Estefania's soul and how, in there, she always had a rocking chair, music and riddles for them to amuse themselves, along with a collection of letters she never wrote to them. Moreover, I liked to see Estefania in relation not only to myself, our room and our objects but also in relation to other people and other objects. In other words, I always yearned for her to turn heads at parties and delight people, have them hanging on her every word when she related stories of her life or childhood memories, when she told them of John of Gaddesden's *Angelic Rose* or of Eucharius Roesslin's *Rose Garden for Pregnant Women.*

Our friends received the first draft of *The Blue Squares of Holy Sunday Eyes* when they least expected it. We could think of no other way to lend meaning and grandeur to our life. The only other possibility was self-contradictory: it would have been useless to burn it – that is, condemn it to silence – because then it would not attain even the fame of having extinguished its own glory. The first of our friends returned the manuscript to us with a few notes in the margin referring to certain spelling mistakes we made in our sleep and a want of syntax when we made love. He also criticized the endless repetition of profanities in the manuscript and the multiple references to our genital organs and physiological needs. No comment was made, however, on the number of times that Estefania wrote words like 'world', 'God', 'universe', 'rainbow', 'angels' or 'blood', nor did he notice the infinite number of roses appearing in the manuscript, though he did say, concerning the word 'blue', that the emphasis on the colour of Estefania's eyes seemed to indicate a racial prejudice by implying – according to him – a certain superiority of blue eyes over all other eyes of alternative colours. But what our friend didn't realize was that by then the title of the story had changed and that blue had ceased to refer to eyes and had come to refer to the Square and that it could not be claimed that a square, however blue, could be more important than, for instance, Red Square in Moscow.

But we had to read between the lines to find our friend's most serious objections to our story: he reproached us – he later told us – for living most of the time in a sort of past imperfect in which many things seemed to happen more than once and nothing ever happened completely. You can't say: 'we were sitting beneath the blossoming apple tree and eating in the shade', and expect me to be interested in all you did if you don't give me more specific facts; for example: 21 April – or any other date – and say, for example, 'on 21 April we ate beneath a tree, etc.'

We found it odd that our friend had not mentioned the blossoming apple tree either, since that was a more specific fact than just any old tree, but we accepted that we had nothing to lose in humouring him so, after altering the manuscript and giving it a new title of *The Blue Sundays of the Eyes of Holy Square*, we went on 21 April – which, by coincidence, was approaching – to eat in the park and our friend came with us. Another amusing coincidence was that we didn't find a single blossoming apple tree. But we decided that we would make further corrections to the manuscript and that it was just a question of substituting the apple tree for another tree we didn't know the name of. So we chose a big tree, covered in thousands of green leaves, we ate in its shade, we listened to some Charles Mingus records and slept a siesta peopled with zephyrs. Our friend not only took a new interest in our manuscript but he also became interested in a dying butterfly which fell, with out-spread wings, on the middle of the page and he studied and observed it for hours, while Estefania and I played at covering each other in saliva.

That was a game we discovered when Estefania once kissed me and got saliva on my hand by mistake and suddenly said: 'How strange, your hand smells of celery.'

I didn't want to tell her that what smelled of celery was her own breath (we had taken a celery salad on the picnic) and I allowed her to carry on with the game. So, while our friend was gazing – gazed, I should say – at the dry leaf that had fallen on the open page of the manuscript, she continued to discover the strange smells on different parts of my body, depending on the predominant smell on her saliva of whatever she was eating at the time. She was amazed by the number of strong and extravagant smells which she associated with processes of fermentation and organic mysteries. But what most surprised her was, precisely, finding a relationship between parts of my body and things which were outside myself and foreign to my epidermis. She was so disturbed by the discovery that she asked me to tell her what her body smelled of. It seemed that I had the opportunity to be more polite and delicate than she had been with me, so first I finished the sandwiches and cheeses, reserving the pleasure of smelling her until we got to the fruit.

I ate a mandarin, trickled saliva on her hair, smelled it and told her: 'Your hair smells of mandarin.'

I ate strawberries and deposited saliva on her nipples. I smelled them and told her: 'Your nipples smell of strawberries.'

I ate an apple and spread saliva on her breasts. I smelled them and told her: 'Your breasts smell of apple.'

By that stage, it had started to rain and we returned home.

Our friend said goodbye to us, grateful to us for giving him yet another opportunity to appear in our lives and proud to know that for a time it would not be said that Estefania and I used to sing, sweep or write on particular days and at particular moments of our existence because he knew, on the contrary, that we sang, swept and wrote on very specific dates which I will never forget: one 20 August, we sang from nine in the morning to midday. One 13 December, at dawn, we swept our room and the stairs of the apartment block. On 18 January, we wrote down everything that had happened to us the day before, 17 January, right up to the first minutes of 18 January, which was when we started to write it. And, in particular, that afternoon of 21 April when, before going home, we went to the fruit market and I bought pears, pineapples, mangoes and apricots to cover Estefania with saliva from head to foot.

But things were not as simple as our friend imagined. The problems arose when Estefania started to correct the chapter of our lives in which the park was mentioned. Because, while it was written that we were going to eat with our friend on 21 April, there were many details – like the zephyrs and the Mingus records, not to mention the butterfly-cum-dried-leaf falling from the sky – which did not appear in the original manuscript projecting our day in the country, as was the case also of a Queen Elizabeth rose and a Persian rose that I cut for Estefania. I told my cousin that it wasn't important, that she should merely make the necessary changes and in future refrain from indulging in proses and roses that neither had happened nor were going to happen to us.

All this would have been of no consequence but for the unholy terror

Estefania had always had of lies. Hence, precisely, her preoccupation with 'what will people say'. People's malicious gossip terrified her, not only because it undermined her standing, but also because they were lies that hovered over the world, disguised as truth. Therefore, whenever she could, she attempted to neutralize these lies with absolute truths. When it came to her ears that some people had said that she was a lesbian, she set out into the night in search of the truth and found it in the arms of a mannish woman with the eyes of a panther who initiated her in the delights of *fricadelle* and tribadism. That night Estefania's sex smelt of the sex of another woman. Another time, when she learned that somebody had said that she was a woman without feelings who laughed at everything and everybody, she laughed at the accusation and laughed at the person who told her, then she laughed at me, at Uncle Esteban's memory, at the earthquakes in Peru and at the Jews in Auschwitz. I had to tell her that somebody had said that she was sentimental and hyper-sensitive so that she could weep bitterly over everything that had previously made her laugh. But she wept, above all, for her previous insensitiveness.

I had to tell her, also, of the perennial rose of Hindustan described by Qutaybah ibn Muslim. I had to promise that I would take her to see Nijinsky dancing in *The Spectre of the Rose*. I had to buy her *The Rose and the Ring* by Thackeray. I had to read her Faulkner's *A Rose for Emily*. I had to tell her the story of Apuleius's donkey who eats roses. I had to recite to her Laforgue's *Miracle des Roses*. I had to tell her the life story of Rosas the dictator and the death story of Rosa Luxemburg and the surrealist adventures of Rrose Sélavy.

I also had to go to the supermarket to buy her a box of Star soap powder with which they were giving away a towel with a rose pattern.

But I soon realized that we hadn't learned the lesson.

Yet again, as always, we had let ourselves get carried away by our ingenuity and obsession with taking everything to extremes where magic and the combinatorial arts no longer had a place. You cannot penetrate such rarefied realms without staking the indulgences of the future. You cannot set out to buy one apple or one rose and come back with a hundred. You cannot, as Estefania and I so often did, decide that we were going to go out and walk all morning and then walk and walk all that morning, plus the afternoon with its honest far horizons, plus the night caught unawares by the cold, plus the twin morning of the next day with its round glories and sweet heralds, until nights, mornings and afternoons die, all together, with the explosion of a distant midday; experience teaches us that you come home with blisters, exhausted and with splinters of light beneath your skin, with no possibility of restoring to undeserved memories something of their incalculable beauty. Tired out, fed up, you can only let the world run its course . . . to the right, left, right again and then straight ahead until coming up against the vestiges of the infinite.

Because, had we learned the lesson, we would from then onwards have had to buy only half an apple or half a rose, walk a third of the streets, catch a quarter of a cold, share a lump of sugar, gaze upon a thousandth part of a bird's wing, drink water in shards of glass and content ourselves with a drop of omniscience.

It is true that we would thus have recovered at least a part – however small – of our lost tranquillity, in that it would have been enough for us to read a few pages of a book to take it as read in its entirety, write a letter saying only 'Dear friend' to take it as written and fulfil a sixth of our illusions to consider them all fulfilled. But, on the other hand, we would never again have enjoyed a complete orgasm since we would feel only the first halves and have to keep the rest for some future night when we disavowed our promise and could love each other with more than half kisses and hundreth parts of caresses. Moreover, Estefania would never have finished writing *The Holy Blues of the Sundays of the Square of Eyes* and, no doubt, half our lives would have passed in searching for the secret of half death.

But our walk in the country with our friend served to remind us that it had been a long time – two or three days at least – since we had made love orally.

None like Estefania, with her sad calf's tongue, for recognizing her master's salt road and turning my penis into a pillar of honey.

None like myself, with my thirsty greyhound's tongue (knowing well how to modulate its rhythm and edge and size to the qualities of her sex and her mood) for making my chaste, lubricious, innocent and immaculate and diabolical cousin cry out in ecstasy.

I had to read to her Rémy de Gourmont's *Litanies de la Rose* and Herrick's *The Parliament of Roses*. I had to lead her by the hand to literature to make the acquaintance of Valle-Inclán's *Paper Rose* and de Lorris' *Roman de la Rose* and Benavente's rose of autumn and Montherlant's *Rose de Sable* and William Dunbar's *The Thrissil and the Rois*.

I had to tell her how the poet Marinetti was wont to recite beneath an avalanche of roses and how Coleridge had asked us to leave the rose alone on its stem and how Juan Ramón besought us never more to touch it and how in the olden days leprosy was called rose sickness.

But it was to no avail.

I suggested that to salve her conscience and get to sleep, her best course was to employ the time-honoured method of counting sheep jumping a fence. Estefania had her reservations about the idea because she disliked following traditional conventions and becoming yet another of those sheep. She decided it would be better to give her imagination free rein and

542

allow all the beasts of the earth who so desired to jump the fence. Not unexpectedly, she found it so difficult to keep count of the number of tigers, ostriches, sharks and widow spiders jumping the fence that she decided to take a notepad and pencil to bed to keep track. As a result, she started going to sleep later and later and often I had to turn out the light at five o'clock in the morning and from her hands remove the opened notepad which each night contained a different list from the day before: 22 swallows, 708 salmon, 9 worms, 2,604 elephants, 1 chimpanzee, 1 macaw, 14 frogs, 1 cormorant, 3 centipedes, 4 boa constrictors, 27 silkworms. 'This method is no good,' I said to her, but she didn't agree: 'It's infallible,' she answered me, 'not only do I fall asleep with the light on, as you keep reminding me, but also at the most unexpected times imaginable: the other day I fell asleep in the agency and, yesterday, in the hospital.' 'And you consider it fitting to fall asleep in a meeting on which depends the entire spring campaign of Richard Hudnut Shampoo?' I asked her. 'You think it is responsible to fall asleep during an operation, at the very moment when the surgeon asks you to pass him the Hamilton skull perforator?' I added but, of course, Estefania had fallen asleep. I took the fork from her hand, removed a half-chewed piece of meat from her mouth, braided her plaits, carried her in my arms to bed, removed her clothes and her make up, put on her nightdress and her night cream and went to sleep beside her.

Finally Estefania agreed to choose a single species of animal to jump the fence and for obvious reasons, she chose the blue dolphin. She thus discovered a way of falling asleep which was much more elegant and original than counting sheep and, in the process, discovered by chance a system for waking up. For example, if on a particular night she fell asleep twenty-three minutes after starting to count and exactly at dolphin number 1,380 then, next morning, twenty-three minutes before waking up, Estefania dreamed of dolphin number 1,380 suspended in the air and then suddenly jumping in reverse as though it were a film shown backwards of a blue dolphin jumping forwards. Then would follow dolphin number 1,379, 1,378, 1,377 and so on until dolphin 0. Estefania would awaken with eyes fresh, bright and free of sleep and animals.

However, while the system always worked for sending her to sleep, it sometimes failed to awaken her when she was sleeping very deeply and, on such occasions, she was unable to detain the backward procession of dolphins with the result that, after dolphin 0, which was always invisible and round, followed red dolphin minus 1, red dolphin minus 2, red dolphin minus 3 until Estefania finally woke up much agitated. When this occurred, she had to go back to sleep again for a while, so as to allow the dolphins to jump forward again, like a film run backwards of red dolphins jumping backwards. Otherwise, Estefania would go around all day with a feeling of living in a minus universe in which the only thing she could do was to be minus-bored or minus-amused, minus-go-to-work or minus-stay-at-home, minus-read-St-John-Perse or minus-not-read-him. Fortunately, algebraic laws prevailed in that world, so that when things were multiplied they became positive: the only solution, when Estefania could not get back to sleep again, was to repeat everything we minus-did to make it real.

This, in turn, taught us that we should alter the tense throughout our story so that nobody would ever know how many times we had done things: whether once, or a thousand. Possible repetitiveness detracted from the miracle, but fortified the only reality we possessed.

And, since love-making and the thousand names of our bodies were one of the easiest things to repeat, we stripped naked and made love naked.

Afterwards we dressed and made love dressed.

Then, we made love naked-dressed and dressed-naked.

The former occurred when, with my acrylic paints, she painted on to my naked body a shirt, tie, belt, trousers and socks and on to Estefania's naked body I painted a bra, transparent blouse, trousers and gloves. But, of course, we ended up in a nasty mess: our saliva and sweat caused our clothes to fade, tear and run and our bodies ended up covered in smudges and blots of grey and lifeless colour, as though we had got ourselves up as dirty and wounded soldiers in camouflage. Some of the stains on the sheets were all that had retained their original colours, pure and glowing, as though in a single afternoon Estefania had lost several virginities, each of a different colour.

We started to make dressed-naked love when Estefania finished what she called our 'Adam and Eve costumes'. The costumes covered us from chin to toe, including hands and feet, and were made of flesh-coloured silk. They fitted our bodies so snugly and reproduced our contours and defects so faithfully that the illusion of our being naked was complete. Not only did Estefania have the patience to embroider on to those costumes each of her birthmarks and my scars, but the parts corresponding to hands and feet were made like gloves, each with five fingers or toes and an inset of white felt on each extremity, imitating the nails. My costume, of course, had an outside pocket the exact shape and size of my genitals, made of elasticated fabric accommodating full erection. Estefania sewed on the hair of my chest and pubis with tufts of black wool and for herself used a triangle of soft and fuzzy light chestnut-coloured plush and a few strands of gold for her armpits. The aureolae of her breasts she created with two circles of rosy satin and her nipples with velvet-covered almonds. And, not content with that, she also wished to reproduce her own external genital organs on her costume so as not to feel at a disadvantage beside me. The labia majora she made with folds of the same silk as on the costume and the labia minora with two ruffles of pink and iridescent damask. Moreover, the costumes had holes where they should have them, so that we could make love without difficulty or, more prosaically, go to the bathroom. On the night that Estefania first wore the costume, she took the trouble to insert a scrap of organdie from her fifteenth birthday dress in the orifice corresponding to the vagina, which I penetrated without difficulty . . .

I could never decide which of the two was my favourite way of making love. Perhaps making it dressed-naked excited us more, not only because when we started to sweat our costumes became soaking wet and it was as though beneath the skin flowed unnameable and dangerous liquids: transparent bloods, secret lymphs, nuptial serums, but also because it was always highly pleasurable to start making love with an alien flesh and end up making it with your own. Once, however, the long zipper down the back of Estefania's costume got stuck and I, in desperation, cut off her nipples with two scissor snips, tore off the labia majora and clitoris with my teeth and slashed her skin all over with a razor blade. I did not pause until I had stripped her completely and savoured the real velvet of her nipples, the real damask of her sex, the real silk of her thighs.

In all events, my cousin and I had to admit that we played too much with words. She, in particular. Everybody – you, I, the plumber and the poets – have played with them at some time or other. But none like Estefania, because she really played, materially played, with words. She played chess with them, she ate them. She played cops and robbers with them and when she heard a suspect word she followed its tracks implacably, through encyclopaedias and dictionaries, as occurred with the word *saprophyte* which she finally caught unawares in the depths of a wood, feeding on the viscera of violets and the blood of recently decapitated orchids. She banished it to exile and never again spoke the word. Sometimes, too, she liked to play hide-and-seek with words: she remained silent for hours and hours and, of course, words didn't find her. Or she would suddenly start to empty the drawers of the wardrobe and, when everything was on the floor – bras, stockings, visiting cards, aphrodisiacs and eau de cologne – she would go into the kitchen to continue her search. When I asked her what she hoped to find, she would answer that she had no idea. 'That's not possible,' I told her. 'People always know what they're looking for.' 'Not always. I'm looking for a word and I don't know what it is, because it's hidden,' she answered me and, about ten minutes later, she turned triumphantly, a corkscrew in her hand: 'This is what I was looking for. As soon as I saw it, I knew that it was the word *corkscrew* that had escaped me. Do you understand me now?' 'Of course,' I told her and rushed into the kitchen to start emptying the pantry. 'What are you looking for?' she asked me. 'I don't know. But as soon as I find it I'll tell you.' I returned to the bedroom with a bottle of wine: 'This is what I was after.' Estefania looked at me in utmost sadness: 'No, you haven't understood. It's not like that at all.'

You can't imagine how much we drank that night. But that time it didn't send us into fits of laughter, or inspire us to show each other the spirals of our tummy buttons to demonstrate the boreal stock of our grandparents, nor did I even think of talking to my cousin about Rilke's rose which represents the union of opposites, or of Villaespesa's corpses of roses in coffins of foam . . . No, high spirits were lost that night in a nasal and short-sighted labyrinth. That night we spat our guts in the sand, thorns prowled around Estefania's breasts and I felt that my tongue was buried in the dry heat of cries. And what we were really looking for that night, though we didn't know it, was a fight. We found it, at last, and we found terrible words – the existence of which our friend had never even suspected – and which we spoke to each other without the least compassion for our love, which shrank in shame until we lost sight of it.

Next morning, our love, a little bigger and with a clean face, was sitting on the edge of our bed waiting for us to make up. I got up, drank a grapefruit juice which brightened the morning somewhat and said to Estefania: 'It's not good for us to say such ugly things to each other.' 'We didn't say ugly things to each other,' she answered me. 'It was they who said them to us: they took advantage of our being drunk. What we must do from now on is hide them and, if they come anywhere near us, punch them in the nose.' 'I promise that that is how it will be,' I said. 'You give me your word?' 'I give you my word.' Estefania sat silent for a moment or two and then said: 'Well, give it to me then.' 'What?' 'Your word.' 'I already gave it to you.' 'No. You said that you would give it to me, but you didn't give it.' I understood what Estefania meant by this and I took pains to show her that I had not just one word to give her, but hundreds of them and I started again to write fairy stories for her in which kingdoms became invisible and percussions shut themselves up in their provinces of moss and jelly; love letters perfumed with the exhalations of a temple faded by the patina of autumn; children's tales in which trams were yellow elephants hanging on threads of sunlight and poems in which her eyes acquired the prestige of seething asteroids and her plaits that of two subterfuges covering her body with whiplashes. But, as time passed and I became involved with thousands and thousands of words which had no meaning for Estefania, I began to glimpse the truth and understand what Walter had tried to tell me on his return from London: there was not a single word that I could call *mine*, that I could possess to such a point and with such totality that I could give it to my cousin. She guessed my thoughts: 'That will teach you,' she said to me, 'never again to offer me things that you can't produce.' 'That'll teach you not to ask me for things that I can't produce, stupid,' I answered her and, at that moment, my eyes were opened to the truth, naked and in its entirety: it was apparent that I had no word. Estefania chopped a little onion and put it in the gravy. She wiped her fingers on her apron and said: 'Do you admit that I was right?' 'You're always right,' I answered her. Estefania tasted the gravy. 'Needs salt,' she said. She added salt and, with moist eyes, she answered: 'You're right, about me always being right.'

Thus perfect was Estefania. So much so that I learned that words, however beautiful, could add not a jot to her complexion and, rather, it was she who embellished words. For that very reason, I told her in another poem (and without her being offended) that her skin was soft as pus and her mouth sweet as albatross excrement.

I was obliged – when she returned from that long absence of minutes or centuries during which in some part of my heart, in one of those rancid agorae reserved for ghosts and double meaning, resounded an almost academic resentment which sprang up like a black sunflower: for having left me alone and forsaken in my solitary bed, castaway of her love; alone and forsaken and clinging to the bars of the bedhead like a prisoner condemned to perpetual chastity clamouring aloud for a coitus *de grâce*; alone and forsaken like a knight spending his nights guarding his only weapon which awaited her, faithful and erect as the mast of a transparent circus – I was obliged, as I was saying, to take her to a botanical garden to experience Bernardin de Saint-Pierre's perfume of a thousand roses which gratifies for but an instant and the aromatic air of the rose inhaled by Victor Hugo.

I had to go to an off-licence and buy her – and drink with her – a bottle of Four Roses bourbon.

I had to take her to mythology and show her Aglaia's rose and the rose in which clots the blood of the gods and the roses of Syrinx.

I had to take her to history to encounter the three blue roses of the Freemasons, the red rose of St George, the medal of the Imperial Rose of Brazil, the War of the Roses, the bed of roses which, in Emperor Cuauhtémoc's case, he had not got, the *sub rosa* secrets of council chambers and the life of Fair Rosamund, the legendary mistress of King Henry II of England.

I had, also, to tell her of the eternal rose of the wind in love with Ricardo Molinari.

But happiness did not begin to dawn in my cousin's eyes until I went to the bookshop and, as I had promised, bought Calvino's *Cosmicomics* and *The Little Prince* by Saint-Exupéry and, instead of talking to her about the planets on which our son would have lived, I spoke of the planets on which he was going to live. I reminded her that, before returning to the B-612 asteroid, the Little Prince had to die on earth. On which planet would you like our son to live? I now asked her. There are planets which are so far from their only sun, I told her, that they are inhabited only by the snow spirits. Those planets are so cold, so very cold, that the least exercise causes you to break out in a sweat of hail and if you light a fire you can never put it out because it is frozen for all eternity, as though making a monument to fire by sculpting the flames in a block of blue ice. Other planets, however, are so close to their sun that they are inhabited only by the silent spirits with tongues of asbestos and there it is so hot, so very hot, that tears evaporate as soon as they well in the eyes and turn into twin wisps of white smoke. I am told that, of the hundred or so stars closest to our solar system, forty-odd could well have habitable planets within their ecosphere. Where would you like our son to live? There are enormous planets, very fat planets where the power of gravity is so strong and the molecular density of all materials so great that the sea is of rock crystal and soap bubbles are of glass. Where would you like our son to live? On a planet of Tau ceti? of 70 Ophiuchi A? of Sigma of Draco? There are planets on which all countries are floating islands in perpetual motion. There are planets on which two moons pursue each other across the sky for all eternity, but nobody knows which is the pursued and which the pursuer because it is not known which of the two moons first started to revolve around them. And there are also planets with two suns which obviously do not pursue each other across the sky because the planet, of course, revolves around them, not they around it. The phenomenon of the midnight sun occurs frequently on such planets, and even that of the midday sun has been known to occur on occasions. I imagine, however, that there must also be planets with two suns, revolving first around one sun and then around the other, in a figure of eight. This happens because, as they are about to complete their orbit around the first sun, they start to be attracted by the second until they fall within its gravitational field, revolve around it to the point where they are attracted again by the first as they approach completion of their orbit around the second, and so on infinitely. There are others which are thin planets, quite possibly as small as that of the Little Prince, where gravity is so weak that on them our son would be very tall, his neck would be designed by Brancusi and Sylvia Plath's lofty rose would grow until it is lost in the clouds. There, if you whistle, your whistle travels much further. There, our son would be an Olympic athlete because when you hurl a discus, a stone or a metaphor, it flies out of sight like a bird. But, on such planets, you must know your own strength because there are treacherous metaphors which, when you think they are barely reaching the horizon, then carry right on round the planet and stab you in the back. On which planet would you like our son to live? On the planets of the floating islands, where nations travel more than men, where rain doesn't go to the countries: it is the countries which go to the clouds and the rain and that is why it is so difficult to forecast the weather: sometimes, when the country is travelling towards the Equator, it meets a hurricane on the way and is knocked off course towards the Pole. There are other planets which, like Saturn, have rings where intergalactic Coca-Cola vendors mount revolving shows. There are also planets which have an orange sun or a green sun or a white sun. There are even planets which revolve first around a yellow sun and then around a blue sun, also in figures of eight, with the result that such planets have blue years and yellow years. In what year would you like your son to live? Although, of course, living on such a planet does have its disadvantages in that time-telling is very complicated: according to astronomers' calculations, the planet first made at least one complete turn around the blue sun before entering orbit around the yellow sun. Other astronomers, however, are of the opposite opinion: that, before entering orbit around the blue sun, the planet made at least one turn around the yellow sun. The former are the bluist astronomers and the latter the yellowist astronomers. On the subject of colours, I can tell you that the shortage of oxygen on the thin planets would cause our son to develop very large lungs, which wouldn't necessarily mean that they were very broad but, on the contrary, very long; but the air expelled from our son's lungs when he whistled would be so concentrated that his whistle would be blue and, due to the absence of gravity, it would travel very far and it would be a blue and diaphanous streamer that would get tangled up around Papa Eduardo's feet as he went down the street leaping in slow motion and singing in the rain and would cause him to fall on his knees before his darling Clementina. But, on other planets where different coloured gases are breathed, the streamers could very well be pink or yellow and then not only Paris but the whole world would be a feast. In what feast would you like your son to live? In a yellow feast or a blue feast? On the planet of the two suns, time started to be counted when a prophet said that the end of the world would occur when the planet completed an equal number of orbits around each sun and, since the idea of having a blue end of the world appeared to almost all to be better than the idea of having a yellow end of the world, it was finally decided that the planet's first orbit had been around the yellow sun, and so it would end its days on completing its final orbit around the blue sun, and then the blue year started, at the end of which yellow year one began and so on until the end of the world. On which side of the planet would you like our son to live? There are unfortunate planets which revolve around only one sun, but the planets themselves don't revolve and so on one side it is always daytime and on the other always night-time. On those planets you can't travel to Europe or to America: you travel to the eternal tropics, to the perennial snows; you travel towards night or you travel towards day. If you travel towards night, you pass through countries of crepuscular men. If you travel towards day you pass through countries of awakening men. What kind of stories would you like us to tell our son? In the kingdom of

Midday, children are read the stories of *A Thousand and One Nights*. In the kingdom of Midnight, they are told fables of *A Thousand and One Days*. But there are also other reasons why life is complicated on the planet of two suns; if, for example, you are in June of the yellow year of 1970 and make an appointment for two months later, that is for August, there is no problem because the year doesn't change and neither does the colour. But if you speak in June of the blue year 1970 of something that occurred in the blue year 1969, you are in fact talking about an event that occurred not one, but two years previously because, in such cases, although the colour didn't change, the year did. On the subject of colours, there is no reason to suppose that, among so many millions and millions of stars, there might not be planets like those of the streamers where synaesthesia is a reality and where smells may be heard and colours touched and, likewise, the illusions realized of Flaubert and Rimbaud and of Wagenseil who speaks of the red melody of the afternoon and of those who say that Beethoven's music is black and Mozart's blue and of Rimsky-Korsakov who maintained that A Major was pink and of Scriabin who said that it wasn't, that it was green while I, for my part, Estefania, would say that one of the two was colour-blind, but we will never know which. Finally, familiar is the sound when you strike the white key of a pink piano with a yellow hammer. On which planet would you like our son to live? On the fat planets, where the air is not breathed but chewed and oxygen is used to make jellies, his neck and shoulders would be broader, as would his heart, and he would be much shorter, on account of the huge pull of gravity. On the thin planets, in contrast, you have no shadows because the shadows fly away. And on the planet of two suns, when you are instead in let us say June of the yellow year 1970 and make an appointment for exactly a year later, you need to say: I'll see you in June of 1970, referring of course to the blue year, because then the colour changes, but not year. But if you are in June of the blue year 1970 and make an appointment for a year later, it is easier because that means June of the yellow year 1971 since, in this case, both change: the year and the colour. How many years would you like our son to live? On the thin planets, where the force of gravity is so weak that, instead of raining downwards, it rains upwards, and so on account of the reduced effort he would have to expend to carry out his activities, he would live many more years than he would on Earth: perhaps 300. On the fat planets, on the other hand, where the force of gravity is so great that water evaporates downwards for which reason the centre of the Earth (that is, his Earth) is always cloudy, our son would only live for a few years. With the added disadvantage that, because they take a long time to revolve, the years, on those planets, last only a few days. That is, they might last a hundred of our years and it is for that reason that people there don't celebrate the successive years of their birthdays but the successive weeks.

There, Fontenelle's roses lasting but a day do not in fact last more than a hundreth of a day. And on those planets which do not take so long to revolve, only ten terrestrial months for example, you can make an infinite number of identical appointments for the same day, like having lunch with a friend at 93 hours in the morning and lunch with another – or the same – at 325 hours in the afternoon, or at 1500 hours. On the thin planets, on the other hand, the years are of only ten terrestrial days. There, birthdays are not celebrated yearly but each century and you can have breakfast, lunch and dinner seven times at the same time. How old would you like our son to be – how many years of how many days? On the planet of the two suns, he would always be either double his apparent age plus one year or double that same apparent age less one year, depending on which sun he was born under. Because, if someone was born in the spring of the yellow year of 1930 for instance and is, at a particular moment, in the spring of the blue year of 1949, that does not mean that that person is nineteen years old; likewise, someone born in the winter of the blue year of 1930 and reaching the winter of the yellow year of 1949, is not nineteen years of age either. The first is, in fact, thirty-nine: nineteen blue plus nineteen yellow plus the blue year in which he was not born, while the second is thirty-seven: nineteen yellow plus nineteen blue minus the yellow year in which he was not born. On the islands of synaesthesia, roses exude poems by Malherbe about roses, while violets (which might well not be violet but orange) would, on account of their shyness, have a stutter. The advantage of the planet with two suns is that there you can celebrate your blue birthday and your yellow birthday, as well as twice celebrating or commemorating revolutions and combative philosophies arising during the yellow years and reconciliations and melancholy philosophies normally occurring during the blue years. Although, of course, there are also planets which have four, five, seven moons to conquer, all revolving at different distances on interlapping orbits, so that they not only eclipse each other in beauty but also in physical reality with the result that there might be nights of four full moons, two waning moons and one waxing moon, or nights of five moons, one full moon and one new moon and, hence, a thousand different possibilities. On the planet of floating islands, wars are almost impossible: sometimes the enemy country is a few kilometres away and sometimes the same enemy country is on the other side of the world. But there also comes a moment when the planet of the two suns is paralysed: each time that it is about to finish one of its orbits and starts to be attracted by the other sun, its rotational movement starts to diminish, nights and days become longer and longer, until the dawn of the feared day of two dusks (or that of two dawns, because this is also under discussion and there are dawnist astronomers and duskist astronomers), on which the planet is totally paralysed for a fraction of a second which seems to the inhabitants to be an eternity because they are never sure whether the planet will effectively yield to the attraction of the other sun and start rotating backwards and life continue its course or whether it will remain paralysed for ever between the two suns which, viewed from the capital of the empire, appear on the two opposite horizons, one yellow and one blue, while the rest of the sky is green. That is why this day, and the days before and after it, are called the green days. But not only on that planet is life difficult for poets in that they have to change the colour of their metaphors each year and where Martí's white rose would be yellow one year and blue another and green for a few days, but also on the planet of seven moons where there are nights on which they have to be six times more inspired, just as there are nights on which werewolves become four times more wolf-like and woman's menstruations are five times heavier and nights, like those of the sacred full moon on which seven fat white cows are sacrificed in honour of the seven full moons, when no sailor, however brave, dares to sail the ocean of seven simultaneous tides. Would you like our son to live on a green day? It would be very dangerous because, on any one of those days, the planet might shoot into the vacuum and split in half. And that is what the prophet was saying and nobody understood: the colour of the end of the world will be neither blue nor yellow: it will be green like the desolate skies of Giorgio de Chirico. Or would you like our son to die on the planet of floating islands? There you may travel to a very distant country and think that you are far from your home and then, one fine day, you wake up to find it before your eyes. Or would you like our son to die on one of those planets where, while I write a novel and you, Estefania, prepare a love elixir of carrots and kidneys in the kitchen, an appetizing sound climbs the stairs, crystalline and furtive as a tear? On one of those planets where paintings in an exhibition exhale their own music and you hear Debussy when you look at the sea? Fortunately, the planet has so far survived thousands of years of changing suns sending it spinning in the opposite direction and, were it not for the fact that people grow old and things wear out and get used up, you would think at the beginning of each year, whether blue or yellow, that the planet begins to go back through time and that it would be necessary to set the clocks running backwards. No, time does not stand still and, sooner or later, each person has their blue or yellow hour. Or – why not – their green hour of the end of the world. Or would you like our son to die on those thin planets where the force of gravity is so weak that not only are hens' eggs as long as sausages, but the sea floats many metres above the level of the land, so that dead sailors have to be tied to buoys to keep them in the water? Or would you like our son to die on one of those fat planets where gravitational force is so great that not only are bananas round as baseballs but trees grow down instead of up and the most valuable mines are not of gold or silver but of apples and flowers and the dead are buried in the tops of the trees? And the question of whether the last hour, everyone's hour, will be bluish green or greenish blue, watermelon green or lemon green, depends on the opinions and preferences of each individual. But you have to decide, Estefania.

And then I was so pleased to see Estefania happy that, after taking her to a restaurant to eat flying-fish consommé, flambéed seals' eyes, zebra testicles with mint purée, mink kidneys in champagne, tiger's tongue encrusted with rock salt, scrambled bird-of-paradise eggs, pink flamingo liver pâté, mandrill buttock in rainbow sauce, giraffe-milk cheese and ice-cream with bat-stuffed cherries, I gave her a dozen roses consisting of Mallarmé's sad rose which grows alone and knows no other excitement, Jean Genet's miraculous rose and William Blake's sick rose, Gertrude Stein's rose is a rose, William Shakespeare's lap of the crimson rose covered in frost, José María Pemán's rose that knows not what it is, Nerval's violet-hearted rose and his white rose which insults the gods, Vallejo's auditive rose, D'Annunzio's rose of perfumed snow and the bewitched house rose and Péret's cigarette-smoke rose with which I almost set alight her soul along with my kisses, one for each of the world's roses and then we made love in the frozen bosom of the dawn.

And that is what we were up to when they told us, Palinuro, that you were about to be born. Your grandmother Altagracia was told by Robin Hood.

Robin Hood was told by Lady Windermere.

Lady Windermere had been told by the Count of Monte Cristo.

The Count of Monte Cristo, by the two halves of the Viscount.

The two halves of the Viscount by the two halves of don Prospero.

And then Dr Latorre, who was a gentleman with a single wart on the shadier side of his nose, sat down on the edge of the bed, yawned like a Comanche, lit his pipe and started to send smoke signals to the Arkansas trappers.

And Loyal Heart told Eagle Head who told the stuffed crow on his staff who told Robinson Crusoe who told Man Friday who told the Man who was Thursday.

And, to witness your birth, came all the characters in *Los Pardallán* and *Les Rougon-Macquart*.

And on horseback, raising a great cloud of dust, came also the Lone Ranger, Doña Bárbara, the Bengal Lancers, Don Segundo Sombra, Artemio Cruz and the Bandidos of Rio Frio.

Phileas Fogg came by express train from Iowa City, losing five days but recovering four and thus, in effect, travelling around the world in eighty-one days.

And Christmas came and Lolita, D'Artagnan and the Man without Qualities.

Tyl Ulenspeigel was told by Lord Jim.

Lord Jim was told by Tirano Banderas.

Tirano Banderas was told by the tin drum midget.

The tin drum midget was told by the valorous Roland.

Then Sinbad the Sailor told Captain Poison who told Captain Blood who told Mr K who told Pancho and Ramona who told the Queen of Spades who telephoned Ivanhoe who sent a telegram to Tartarin on the Alps who sent a heliographic message to Fortunata and Jacinta who told Baron de Charlus who wrote to Scheherazade who told Bertoldo Bertoldino and Cacaseno who signalled by flag to Swiss Family Robinson who took a plane to inform Zazie who emerged from the metro to tell Anna Karenina who got into a troika to go and tell Spiderman who slid down a spider's web to tell Arthur Gordon Pym who took a taxi to advise Sherlock Holmes who boarded a double-decker bus to go and tell Dick Tracy who sent a message with a bunch of flowers to Madame Bovary who sniffed her favourite perfume and told Bilitis who composed a poem to Manasidika and told Hans Castorp who lit a cigar and told Mandrake the Magician who hypnotized Lothar and told Leopold Bloom who bought a pig's kidney and told Damian who told Bouvard and Pécuchet who told Mafarka, the futurist, who told the Hobbits' thinking trees who told Captain Pantoja and his Special Service who told Eugene Gant who told Peer Gynt who told the Mayor of Zalamea who told Tartuffe who told Phèdre who passed the news on to the sorceress who told the Daughter of Jorio who told Omegar, the last of men, who told the Last of the Mohicans who told Dr Sangrado who told José Cemí who told Blue Beard who told Big Brother who told Doc Savage who told Beremundo el Lelo who told the portrait of Dorian Gray who told the Phantom of the Opera who told *l'homme qui rit* who told Dr Jekyll who informed Mr Hyde who told José Trigo who told Paul and Virginia who told Romeo and Juliet who told Lucia and Renzo who told Chichikov who told Lord Greystoke who told the Mad Woman of Chaillot who told Silvestre Paradox who told Saturnin Farandoul who told Fu Manchu who told Mr Here Comes Everybody who told Harlequin the flying doctor who told Dr Zhivago who told Dr Pascal who told Eric of Melniboné.

Barbarella was told by her robot Aiktor.

Aiktor was told by Carl, the robot of the year 2001.

Carl was told by Adam Link.

Adam Link by Eva Futura.

And the future Eve had been told by the general who had a glass eye who had been told by ex-congressman Fournier who had been told by his wife after she pulled a red thread which led from her bed to the big toe of the right foot of the ex-congressman who slept in another bed with his sound ear down on the pillow, with the result that ex-congressman Fournier started to dream that he was pulling another thread that went from his bed to the big toes of Rip Van Winkle, Endymion, de Fosca and other famous sleepy-heads, including myself and your grandfather Francisco and we awoke for a while to come and see you being born and, in passing, we told the Lady of the Camellias who told Marcus Vinitius who told Raphael de Valentin who told Pedro Páramo who told Fantomas who told Tom Sawyer who told Victor-Hugues who told Veryluna the Elf who gave you a green hat that you might see the soul of all things.

And Mamma Clementina's soul was like egg-whites beaten to the consistency of snow.

And then your grandmother Altagracia got up and walked along the corridor of the house with a silver bell bearing the names of the four evangelists and she started to ring it as she strutted in semi-circles and, with each ring of the bell, a lamp blossomed:

The overhead lamp in the dining room.

The tulip-lamp in the bathroom.

The lamp on my table for writing letters against Vice-president Aaron Burr who wanted to proclaim himself Emperor of Mexico.

And Aladdin's lamp.

And then Aladdin told the Men of Good Will who told the Forsytes who told the Thibaults who told Père Goriot who told all the characters in *The Human Comedy*.

And Baron D'Ormesan came to watch your birth, as did the three-tentacled, three-eyed *txalqs* and the triffids and Maupassant's Le Horla and Madame Atomos and Solaris's living ocean and Daudet's *morticoles* and the twenty-fingered men living under Paris and Mr Dupont Jean and *Alice in Wonderland* illustrated by Tenniel and *Lysistrata* illustrated by Beardsley and *Don Quixote* illustrated by Doré and *Beauty and the Beast* illustrated by Walter Crane and *Gargantua and Pantagruel* illustrated by Róbida and *Oliver Twist* illustrated by Cruikshank.

And then came Griffin and Wilhelm Storitz, but nobody saw them because they were invisible men and we only realized they were there when Dr Latorre's forceps, resembling a silver lobster, started flying around the room.

And Monsieur Plume came.

And there arrived first Gulliver in the land of the dwarfs and then Gulliver in the land of the giants.

And the Viscount of Bragelonne arrived.

And I, your grandfather, your eminently grandfather Francisco, said to you: Come, come with me and we will rise up on the fountain issuing from a bottle of champagne that you might see, from the heights, that by then the house had changed into a ship, an enormous sailboat drawn by a flock of seabirds, and Dr Latorre was driving his Hispano Suiza around the deck

555

carpeted with specks of foam and Ricardo the gardener was pruning the seaweed growing in the cabins and round about sailed all the vessels of Jules Verne's books: the *Forward* and the *Great Eastern* and the *Dolphin* and the *Chancellor* and the *Pilgrim* and the *Cynthia* and on the way we met the shipwrecked sailors of the *Jonathan* and the pirates of the *Halifax* and the sons of Captain Grant travelling in the *Duncan* and beneath the house sailed the *Nautilus* and we almost, almost collided with Noah's Ark in which all the animals of Orwell's *Animal Farm* were coming to see you, together with all the lions and crows and foxes of *Aesop's Fables* and *Mother Goose* and Platero the donkey and I and Dumbo and Sir Oran Haut Ton and Mickey Mouse and Puss in Boots and Baloo the grey bear and Tracy's tiger and Sirius the dog and Professor Tornada's macrobes, and Rocinante and the houyhnhnms and Snoopy and the dinosaur from *The Skin of Our Teeth* and the blue mammoth of Great Euscaria and, behind it, sending up a great jet of water, the white whale Moby Dick.

But, before meeting them all, before encountering Bachiller Trapaza, Lazarillo de Tormes, Guzmán de Alfarache and the Itching Parrot in the corridor and on the stairs and balconies, before that, son, I licked my whiskers scorched by the years, I sternly shook myself awake, got out of bed with all the to-do of a retired sailor, put on my dressing gown and, looking at myself in the mirror, saw that I was more grandfatherly than ever.

Come, come with me and I will tell you. Climb on to my shoulders and walk over my bald head which is the wisest half of all the worlds to have existed and come, come and gaze from there upon the house where you were born. Come and see your cousin Estefania. Come and look at Uncle Austin in his knickerbockers. Come and see the cabaret artiste in her robe of liquid gardenias. Come and see the yellow sargasso blowing sleepless in the salt marshes and the opulent rains beating down on the jungles. Come and see how the general puts in his marvelling eye to watch your birth. Come and see how Grandmother Altagracia arms herself with teeth to smile. Come and see her hair which imitates the fall of winter. Come and see how Aunt Luisa tells the praying mantis and the grooved woodlouse in the orange tree of it. Come and see how you started to be born between your mother's pushing and the doctor's pulling. Come and see the couples of lovers kissing in the light of the lamp-post or in the shadow of the world, little knowing that we see them from a picture postcard. Come and see the pin-cushion in the shape of a red heart where your Aunt Lucrecia gives vent to her witch's instincts. Come and see how the sun bounces from window to window until it reaches paradise. Come and see and learn the hour of love on the dot. Come and see the horsemen mounted on their swords who drink beer in flakes of snow. Come and see how my Homeric breast is filled with love for you. Come and see how my whiskers point at the electric light in pure joy. Come and see the magic sinking of certain gardens. Come and see yourself being born. See how Aunt Enriqueta laughs like a cackling hen and lays a sock-darning egg each time she laughs. Come and see how your Aunt Lisandra plays the pianola which smells of mangoes and crocodiles. Come and see Aunt Adelaida dreaming of cockroaches rolled in apple flour. Come and see Flavia who is bringing you a bottle of recently rained water. Come and see yourself being born. Come and see the immortal petioles of the morning star. Come and see the sunburned snow. Come and see how the water recommences its translucent adventure through the pipes. Come and see the swallows leaving the satin-smooth jaws of the stone lions and swoop their circular death through the trembling squares. Come and see how the traffic lights come to life with peristaltic movements. Come and see the hard-hearted pious women who try not to step on the crosses formed by the intersection of each four paving stones. Come and see the sea sprinkled with whiteness. Come and see how the ochres dream on a mountain of blue cadmium splinters. Come and see the clouds sailing through the sky like drifting temples. Come and see how Aunt Luisa opens the balcony door and a ray of darkness falls on the pavement. Come and see how she says that not only Paris comes from Paris but that children also come from Paris. Come and see how your Uncle Esteban died in an oxygen tent from which he bade farewell to the walkers on their way to Vladivostok. Come and see yourself being born. Come and see how Dr Latorre's silver lobster finally gets a grip on a nostril or a frozen ear to draw you from the maternal winter.

And inform Sergeant Parker Adderson while he is alive.

Inform Grabinoulor, the traveller of all time and the whole universe.

Inform Flash Gordon. Tell Domingo Gonsales to come back from the moon.

Multipliandre to come back from the future.

Inform the time traveller H. G. Wells.

Tell Saint-Menoux and Hector Servadac.

Ask Remedios the Beautiful to descend enveloped in a moon beam.

Tell Lieutenant Gulliver Jones to come back from Mars on his magic carpet.

Tell Cyrano de Bergerac to bring a jar in which to keep Mamma's tears.

And tell the spirit of Faust riding through the sidereal spaces.

Mexico City–Iowa City–London

ABOUT THE AUTHOR

Fernando del Paso was born in Mexico City in 1935. He enrolled in medical school, but wound up studying chemistry and economics instead, and for a while worked as a publicity agent. His first novel, *José Trigo*, appeared in 1966 and was awarded the Xavier-Villaurrutia Prize. He began writing *Palinuro* in 1969, while attending the University of Iowa's Writing Program, and in 1970 earned a Guggenheim Fellowship. In the early seventies he moved to London where he worked for the BBC and contributed to various newspapers as he continued work on the novel.

Despite having earned the Premio Novela México, *Palinuro of Mexico* was not published in the author's native country until 1980, after it had already been published in Spain (1977). A French translation appeared in 1985, and Quartet published it in English in Great Britain in 1989. Since that time the novel has also appeared in German and Dutch translations.

From 1985 until recently del Paso was cultural attaché at the Mexican Embassy in Paris. His third novel, *Noticias del Imperio*, appeared in 1987. He is currently director of the Biblioteca Iberoamericana in Guadalajara, Mexico.

DALKEY ARCHIVE PRESS

"The program of the Dalkey Archive Press is a form of cultural heroism—to put books of authentic literary value into print and keep them in print."—JAMES LAUGHLIN

Our current and forthcoming authors include:

GILBERT SORRENTINO • DJUNA BARNES • ROBERT COOVER • WILLIAM H. GASS

YVES NAVARRE • COLEMAN DOWELL • HARRY MATHEWS • RENÉ CREVEL

LOUIS ZUKOFSKY • LUISA VALENZUELA • OLIVE MOORE • EDWARD DAHLBERG

JACQUES ROUBAUD • FELIPE ALFAU • RAYMOND QUENEAU • DAVID MARKSON

CLAUDE OLLIER • JOSEPH MCELROY • ALEXANDER THEROUX • MURIEL CERF

JUAN GOYTISOLO • TIMOTHY D'ARCH SMITH • PAUL METCALF • MAURICE ROCHE

CHRISTINE BROOKE-ROSE • MARGUERITE YOUNG • JULIÁN RÍOS • RIKKI DUCORNET

ALAN ANSEN • HUGO CHARTERIS • NICHOLAS MOSLEY • RALPH CUSACK

SEVERO SARDUY • KENNETH TINDALL • MICHEL BUTOR • VIKTOR SHKLOVSKY

THOMAS MCGONIGLE • CLAUDE SIMON • DOUGLAS WOOLF • MARC CHOLODENKO

OSMAN LINS • ESTHER TUSQUETS • MICHAEL STEPHENS • CHANDLER BROSSARD

PAUL WEST • RONALD FIRBANK • EWA KURYLUK • CHANTAL CHAWAF

STANLEY CRAWFORD • CAROLE MASO • FORD MADOX FORD • GERT JONKE

PIERRE ALBERT-BIROT • FLANN O'BRIEN • ALF MAC LOCHLAINN • PIOTR SWECZ

LOUIS-FERDINAND CÉLINE • PATRICK GRAINVILLE • W. M. SPACKMAN

JULIETA CAMPOS • GERTRUDE STEIN • ARNO SCHMIDT • JEROME CHARYN

JOHN BARTH • ANNIE ERNAUX • JANICE GALLOWAY • JAMES MERRILL

KAREN ELIZABETH GORDON • FERNANDO DEL PASO • SUSAN DAITCH

ALDOUS HUXLEY • WILLIAM EASTLAKE • PHILIP WYLIE • LAUREN FAIRBANKS

WILFRIDO D. NOLLEDO • EVELIN SULLIVAN • C. S. GISCOMBE

To receive our current catalog, write to:

Dalkey Archive Press, Campus Box 4241, Normal, IL 61790-4241
phone: (309) 438-7555; fax: (309) 438-7422